A NEW BEGINNING

By the morning after the pogrom, fifteen hundred shops and homes had been ransacked or destroyed. Estimates of the dead ranged from fifty to one hundred and fifty, with more than a thousand wounded.

Among the dead was Mendel Isakharov. Many came to pay their last respects. But after no more than a few words with well-wishers, Zalman walked away. Rachel clung to his arm, trying to pull him back.

"Zalman, Papa's friends want to arrange food for us while we mourn."

"There will be no week of mourning. No purpose will be served by it."

Rachel let go of his arm. "Did Papa mean nothing to you? What will he think if he is watching?"

"He meant everything to me. And if he is watching, he will agree that we can mourn him best while we travel."

"Travel where?"

"Out of Russia, away from this land of blood and tears. We will take the gold, the watches, the jewelry, whatever money we can find. We will leave immediately."

Rachel squeezed her brother's hand. This was exactly what their father would have wanted. His greatest dream—perhaps his last dream—had been to see his children enjoy a new beginning.

In death, there was also rebirth.

Lewis Orde

By Blood Divided

ZEBRA BOOKS
KENSINGTON PUBLISHING CORP.

ZEBRA BOOKS

are published by

Kensington Publishing Corp.
475 Park Avenue South
New York, NY 10016

First Zebra Books paperback edition: February, 1992

Printed in the United States of America

This is a work of fiction.
Any similarity to real people or events
is entirely coincidental.

This book required much research. Special thanks to the following for making that research a little easier: Ruth Ross; Paul and Elena Lankau; Manny Mitchell; Paul A. Fulford; John Beaver; Bob Whitaker; and last, but most certainly not least, Derek J. Knight of Stanmore Library in England, who filled in several blanks.

PROLOGUE

Kishinev, Russia—1903

Fresh blood stained the snow. A thin, early-morning sun picked out the naked body of a young boy, his skinny arms stretched wide as if in crucifixion. Two peasants, bulky and awkward in heavy winter clothing, stood motionless by the corpse. Breath froze in front of their faces. Horror filled their eyes. Never before had they seen such savagery. Deep lacerations crossed the boy's arms and legs. Stab wounds punctured his chest. His penis and testicles had been hacked off. Life had poured out through the wide gash that severed his throat. Minutes earlier, these two men had been on their way to work at the army stable on the outskirts of Kishinev, the provincial capital of Bessarabia. Now, the soldiers' horses would have to wait until the peasants informed the police of their gruesome find.

By the following afternoon, the case was solved. The boy's uncle, a notorious drunkard and bully, confessed under police questioning to the brutal murder. The chief of police felt particularly satisfied with the speedy solution of the crime. Kishinev, close to Russia's western border with Rumania, was a bustling city of one hundred thousand people, many of them squeezed together in squalid poverty. Such crowded areas were breeding grounds for discontent and revolutionary thought. The city had to be carefully controlled. With the political unrest sweeping across the country, the guardians of Holy Mother Russia had to remain doubly alert.

The uncle was charged with the boy's murder. The ma-

7

chinery of justice ground into sluggish motion. A trial date was set. Evidence was stored, lawyers appointed. Then, four weeks after the murder, the police chief received an evening visitor.

There was nothing unusual about this visitor. The editor of the *Bessarabatz,* the province's only newspaper, was a frequent guest of the police chief. The two men often played chess over a glass or two of wine. The newspaper editor won twice as many games as the police chief did. His analytical abilities were much sharper. He had the ability to gaze far into the future, and create his strategy from what he saw there. For that skill, the police chief respected him.

But on this night, there was no chess or wine. There was just advice, delivered in the tone of an order. "It is best that you release the boy's uncle at once. Release him, and explain that a mistake was made. The uncle, it turns out, is an innocent party to this horrible affair."

Stunned, the police chief could only ask, "What about his confession?"

"Everyone who knows the man agrees he is unbalanced, a slave to vodka. He was desperate for attention. Admitting to such a heinous crime was a means of achieving that recognition."

"If the uncle did not commit the murder, who did?"

The editor of the *Bessarabatz* answered obliquely. "Look around you. Russia's factories are plagued by strikes that occur on an almost daily basis. Socialist groups meet brazenly to call for the overthrow of the Czar. They win more converts among the intellectuals with every week that passes. My friends in the Ministry of the Interior believe something should be done to divert the working people's minds from such dissension, before it becomes an attraction for them. The death of this boy gives us the opportunity for such a diversion."

"Diversion?" The police chief understood that when the editor spoke of friends at the Ministry of the Interior, he referred to the minister himself, Count Plehve. The editor received a regular payoff for publishing whatever Plehve wanted published. In the province of Bessarabia, the *Bes-*

8

sarabatz was eyes, ears, and mouth for the Minister of the Interior. "What kind of a diversion?"

"A little Jewish sport."

"Are you suggesting that we accuse the Jews of killing that boy?"

"Their Passover occurs soon. The ignorant *muzhiks* will be happy to believe the *zhidi* used the child's blood to make their unleavened bread. A spontaneous uprising will occur. And the uprising that begins in Kishinev will soon spread. My friends will see to that. Mark my words, Russia's turmoil will lessen once its people experience the joy of pulling Jewish beards."

The police chief nodded his head at the cynical simplicity of the solution. Blame the Jews, a ploy as old as Russia herself. Give voice to the lie of ritual murder, and lure the *muzhiks*—Russia's illiterate, drunken peasants—away from their own misfortunes with the promise of good fun.

What would Russia do, the police chief wondered, when there were no Jews left? When they had all been driven out, converted, or killed? Who, then, would the government find to blame for the country's manifold ills?

The *Bessarabatz* wasted no time in publishing a lurid account of the boy's death, mixing fact with speculation and outright lies. The boy's uncle, released from prison, was quoted as saying he had seen his nephew enticed away by three bearded men in dark clothes. A bogus medical report claimed that all the blood had been drained from the boy's body. The editor's accompanying commentary blatantly accused the city's Jews of ritual murder.

As days, then weeks, passed, the *Bessarabatz*'s tone became more strident. "Why have we been so vilely cursed?" editorials demanded. "Why does God allow the vermin who spilled the blood of His only son to spill the blood of our sons, too? Is God unwilling to help us? Or does He want us to help ourselves?"

A week before Easter, as the Jews prepared to celebrate the feast of Passover, emissaries from the Ministry of the Interior arrived in Kishinev. A long meeting was held with provincial authorities. At its conclusion, the editor of the *Bessarabatz*

9

gave instructions to the men who operated the newspaper's presses. Thousands of handbills were printed and distributed across the city. The handbills exhorted the good Christian citizens of Kishinev to wreak a bloody vengeance upon the Jews for their murderous ways. Those who could read eagerly passed the information to those who could not.

The police chief had been right. There was nothing like a pogrom to take the peasants' mind off their own troubles.

Part
One

Chapter One

On holy days, the table in the Isakharov home was always crowded with guests. Zalman and Rachel could remember it no other way. Their father, Mendel Isakharov, was a warm and generous man who maintained that God had created Sabbath and the festivals not for His own glory, but to afford comfortable people the opportunity to share their blessings with those less fortunate.

"God bestows prosperity on people to test them," Mendel told his children whenever they encountered one of the many beggars crowded into the cities of the Pale of Settlement. "He wants to see how unselfishly they use their wealth to benefit others." Then, smiling at the uncomplicated beauty of such a philosophy, he would unobtrusively give the beggar enough money to buy food.

Zalman and Rachel had grown up to regard each holy day as an adventure, always wondering who would grace their table. Their mother, when she was alive, had never known how many to expect. Invitations were extended right up to the last moment, when Mendel might encounter a man or woman, or sometimes an entire family, with nowhere to go. He would bring them home, assuring the visitors that Sophie, his wife, would welcome them as if they were her own flesh and blood. And Sophie, during their twenty years of marriage, never disappointed him.

This Passover was no different, except that it was seventeen-year-old Rachel who prepared the food. Cooking for the family was a responsibility she had undertaken for the past

13

two years, ever since Sophie Isakharov died of pneumonia in the harsh winter of 1901.

On the first night of Passover, six people gathered around the table in the Isakharov home behind the family's tiny drapery shop. Mendel Isakharov, a barrel-chested man with bushy hair and beard, sat at the head of the table. Zalman, taller and thinner, sat on his father's right. Rachel, slight and slender as her mother had been, with the same vibrant auburn hair, sat on Mendel's left. The other three places at the table were occupied by guests. Sarah and Rivka Potack were widowed sisters-in-law, earning scarcely enough money from sewing work to exist in the single room they shared. Schmuel Laskar was an elderly carpenter, whose hands were now so crippled by arthritis that he could barely hold a saw.

After the meal, Rachel, helped by the two widows, cleared the dishes. The men remained at the table, talking. The subject of their conversation was the continuing editorial attacks in the *Bessarabatz*.

"Haven't the Russians done enough to us already?" Schmuel Laskar asked. "They have driven us out of our homes, stolen the little we owned, and deprived us of any basic rights. They have crowded us into cities where half of us are forced to live on charity provided by the other half. Now this hate-filled maniac at the *Bessarabatz* is saturating his newspaper with the filthiest lies about blood ritual. We are three years into the twentieth century. Why does such evil superstition continue to exist?"

Zalman laughed. "The rest of the world might be three years into the twentieth century, but Russia, as always, lags at least two centuries behind." Zalman's deep-set brown eyes, which often gave him a brooding, pensive appearance, took on a mischievous gleam. "I wonder if King Edward of England plays hide-and-seek with his friends, as our Czar does? Or if the Kaiser, like his cousin the Czar, spends hours each day filling his diary with delirious accounts of picnics and hunting parties?"

"Stop repeating the gossip you hear at your political meetings," Mendel admonished his son. Nonetheless, he pondered Zalman's derisory words. Did Nicholas the Second know what went on across the vast empire he had inherited from

14

his father, Alexander the Third? Did he care? Or did he simply leave the running of the empire to the bureaucrats?

Schmuel Laskar sided with Zalman. "Gossip is a useful tool, Reb Mendel. Look how that swine at the *Bessarabatz* uses it to incite the peasants." The elderly carpenter clenched his gnarled hands into fists. "I pray each night to God that I live long enough to take part in the revolution that must surely come."

"God will not help you," Zalman said. "In Russia, God's allegiance is with the Czar. He finds more to admire in Romanov riches than in Jewish piety and poverty."

"Listen how my son Zalman mocks God," Mendel said sadly. He stroked his heavy beard, once jet-black but now, like his hair, streaked with white. The sons of Mendel's friends had beards, but the face of his own son was clean-shaven in the modern style. The absence of facial hair had nothing to do with fashion. A beard was the sign of an observant Jew, and Zalman did not consider himself observant. Sometimes Mendel wondered whether his son even considered himself a Jew. He never went to the synagogue, nor did he ever participate in prayers at home. Like tonight, Mendel thought. While the other five people at the table had followed the ancient tale of the Israelites' escape from slavery in Egypt, Zalman the dreamer had stared into space, his mind occupied with other matters. With changing the world.

"We are very different people, my father and I," Zalman told the carpenter. "I doubt, while he believes. I find neither rhyme nor reason in religion, while my father finds everything he could ever want."

"Envy the believer who has no questions," Mendel responded. "And pity the poor nonbeliever who can find no answers."

Zalman sat back, frustrated and angry that his father placed such blind faith in God. All his life he had heard it. God would protect. God would provide. God would deliver His people from the hands of their enemies. It was the dogma of people content to go through life without ever thinking for themselves.

The evening ended with Mendel asking Schmuel Laskar to perform some carpentry work in the draper's shop. The counter was old; it needed replacing. Rachel made a similar proposition to Sarah and Rivka Potack. The covers of the *perenes,* the down-filled quilts, were falling apart; new covers would be needed for next winter. Later, after the details of this work had been agreed upon, Zalman escorted the guests home, the Potack widows to the room they shared, and Schmuel Laskar to his rented room.

Walking home along the narrow, dingy streets, Zalman wondered how it would be to rely on charity for survival; even if such charity was, like his father's donations, tactfully disguised. How would it be to exist as one of the *Luftmenschen,* the countless men of air who, without trades or skills, scavenged around for enough kopecks to feed their families? Zalman realized how fortunate he and his sister really were. With their modest drapery shop and home—a small room each for Rachel and her father, and a space by the brick stove in the room where they ate for Zalman to place his straw mattress every night—the Isakharovs were not well off by normal standards. In comparison to the vast majority of Russian Jews crowded into cities like Kishinev, though, they were wealthy beyond all measure.

The Isakharovs had not always owned a drapery shop, nor had they always lived in Kishinev. Twenty-two years earlier, when Mendel had married Sophie, he had been a skilled watchmaker in Moscow, having learned the trade from his father. But the year that saw Mendel's marriage to Sophie also witnessed the assassination of Alexander the Second, an event that was to have far-reaching effects on every Jew in Russia.

The assassination was followed by a series of pogroms throughout southern Russia and the Ukraine. Then, in May 1882, Alexander the Third enacted the May Laws, under which no Russian Jew could settle in a rural area. Jews were expelled from the villages they had occupied all their lives and forced into the larger cities of the Pale of Settlement. Simultaneously, many professionals living outside the Pale, in the Russian interior, were deprived of their right of domicile as quotas for Jewish doctors and lawyers were slashed.

Certain people were exempted, artisans whose contributions to Russian life were irreplaceable. As a watchmaker,

Mendel was included in this elite. He worked hard, enjoying life with the son and daughter Sophie bore him, but always knowing that such peace and prosperity could never endure. Not in Russia.

The serenity lasted for nine years. In 1891, the Grand Duke Sergei, brother of Alexander the Third, was appointed governor-general of Moscow. His first act was to banish the entire Jewish population of Moscow. Police swept through the city. Homes and possessions were confiscated. The great synagogue of Moscow was boarded up, its use forbidden. In one day, fifteen thousand people were uprooted. Zalman was seven, and Rachel only five, when the family was expelled from Moscow with little more than the clothes they stood in, and forced to move west to Kishinev.

Mendel had prepared for this event. He had secretly amassed a cache of gold and jewelry that could be smuggled in his clothing. Some of the gold was used to pay for the new start in Kishinev. The draper's shop had been Sophie's idea. Before marrying Mendel, she had worked for her parents in such a shop. She knew fabrics; she understood how to buy from the weavers, and how to sell. And, like her husband, she knew how to dispense help to those who needed it. In Kishinev, the Isakharovs lived simply. Earnings above their basic requirements were passed on to the most needy.

Mendel had also shown foresight where his children were concerned. As reports filtered through about the new life to be made in the West, he had pushed Zalman and Rachel into contact with people who spoke other languages. Now, Rachel spoke German as well as her native Russian and Yiddish, and Zalman had learned enough at the gymnasium to converse almost fluently in both German and English. Mendel's only regret was that while such secular exposure had helped to form Zalman's political interest, it had also created his bias against religion.

When Zalman returned home, he found his father and sister sitting at the table. In front of them, resting in a wooden box, was the remainder of the treasure Mendel had smuggled out of Moscow twelve years earlier.

"Sit down," Mendel said. Zalman took the chair on his father's right, opposite Rachel. "These baubles were being saved because your mother and I wanted to give you both a good start when you married." Mendel ran his fingers through a dozen gold chains, some rings and trinkets, and two elaborately formed gold-and-enamel watches. "Unfortunately, these must now be used for something else. Zalman, Rachel, thousands of years ago tonight, our ancestors fled from the land of Egypt. I want you to follow their example. I want you to take all this and use it to begin a new life for yourselves out of Russia."

"What about you, Papa?" Rachel's voice trembled. She reached out to rest a hand on her father's arm.

Mendel smiled fondly at his daughter. There was so much about her that reminded him of his wife. The blazing auburn hair, the wide-spaced hazel eyes, the petite and delicate frame. Rachel had even inherited her mother's superstitious nature—the snips of red ribbon she carried on her person to ward off the evil eye, the mock spitting on seeing a tragedy to keep such ill fortune from afflicting her own family. "I have already started one new life. I am too old to begin another. Perhaps when you and your brother are settled—"

"Too old?" Rachel asked hotly. She could no more imagine life without her father than she could envision a Russia without repression. "How can you talk so? You are not yet fifty."

"Here I am old." Mendel touched a hand to his heart. "And here is the only place that matters."

"What has caused this sudden decision?" Zalman asked.

Mendel pulled a crumpled piece of paper from his pocket, straightened it out, and showed it to his children. "These posters have started to appear all over Kishinev, encouraging the peasants to start a pogrom."

"Every Easter the priests incite the peasants," Zalman said. "We will board up the shop like we always do, and wait for Easter to be finished."

Mendel's eyes grew misty as he lifted up the two watches and admired them in the candlelight. The gold-and-turquoise enamel cases were shaped and detailed like large beetles, even to the heads and short, stubby antennae; the wings opened to reveal the faces. Each watch had its own tiny key. The watches were identical, except for the chains. One had a gold chain to be passed through the buttonhole of a man's jacket; the gold chain of the other was fashioned to be worn around a woman's throat. As Mendel slowly wound the springs, his mind slipped down the pathway to the past.

"Thirty years ago, my father made these watches. He copied them from a French design. He was offered much money for them, but he refused to sell. See . . . ?" Mendel indicated minute letters engraved on the inside of each case. "There is my father's name, Zalman ben Itzhak. You, Zalman, are named in his memory." For several seconds, Mendel sat staring at the letters before snapping the cases closed with an air of finality. "I want you to take all of this and use it to get away. But save the watches until the very last. Perhaps . . . perhaps you will be able to keep them."

"Put away the watches and the jewelry, Papa," Zalman said. "Rachel and I are staying here with you."

"Did you not hear what I said?"

"We heard," Rachel answered. "But if we leave, who will help you protect the shop? The *muzhiks* will steal everything, and then how will you perform your charity?"

Mendel looked from one child to the other. They stared back, unblinking. Did children no longer honor their father's wishes? Deep within him, sadness and pleasure mingled. Above all else, even above his love of God, he wanted his children to be safe. Yet he was touched by their refusal to desert him. Sighing, he replaced the treasure in the box from which he had taken it. He knelt down and slipped the box into a space behind the stove in the corner of the room.

"Should you change your mind, you know where it is."

Of the eight days of Passover, only the first and last two are considered holy. During the intermediate four days, a man is free to follow his normal routine. For Mendel Isakharov, that meant opening the small draper's shop. Business was poor. Only a couple of customers ventured through the front door, and they did not buy. Their minds, they explained apologetically, were too full of the frightening prospect of Easter Sunday, the traditional day of pogroms. What was the point of spending precious money on cloth that might well be stolen or destroyed by a mob? That sentiment was echoed by Schmuel Laskar, when he came to start work on the new counter in the draper's shop.

"Why spend your rubles on good wood that will only be wrecked next Sunday?" he asked Mendel.

"Build it well, Reb Schmuel, so it will withstand even the strongest blows."

The carpenter shrugged and went about his business.

Rachel encountered similar fears when she shopped for food. Many traders were absent from the market, while those who were there had even less stock than usual. Zalman was the only member of the family to hear positive news. He returned from a midweek political meeting to tell his father and sister of the discussion to organize a self-defense force.

"We talked of arming ourselves with clubs and appearing on the streets as a warning to those who would attack us."

"While you and your friends talk and dream," Mendel answered, "the mob will roar through our homes like a wind from hell."

Zalman refused to be daunted. "If we do not have time to prepare a defense against this attack, we will certainly be ready for when it occurs again."

"That will be small consolation for those who have lost their belongings or their lives." Mendel turned away, wishing that he had not been so hasty in rejecting his children's plea to leave. To save his son and daughter, he should have agreed to accompany them in an immediate flight from Russia. It was too late now. A drunken peasant rabble guarded each city exit; fishermen tightening the net to make sure that not even a minnow escaped.

"If knowledge of a pogrom is so widespread, will not the authorities do something?" Rachel asked. "Surely they will not look away when they know such disorder is to be perpetrated?"

Mendel gave his daughter a patient smile. "The *Bessarabatz* calls so loudly for our punishment, my naive child, only because the authorities condone it."

Despite such pessimism, when Mendel accompanied Rachel to the synagogue for Sabbath services on the day before Easter Sunday, his misgivings decreased. Police were everywhere, standing on street corners, patrolling on horseback.

Rachel, in her youthful innocence, might be wiser than her father, Mendel reflected. The authorities had been unable to ignore the possibility of mayhem. Perhaps the talk of self-defense by Zalman's Socialist group had also helped. Knowing their own blood might flow in the streets had quenched the anti-Semites' thirst.

Easter Sunday coincided with the last day of Passover. In the morning, Kishinev's churches and synagogues were full. Songs of praise lauded God's glory in both Russian and Hebrew. Walking to the synagogue with Rachel, Mendel noticed that the police were no longer in evidence. He understood. Policemen also worshipped God; they were as entitled as any other man to pray on such a holy day.

Following the service, Mendel invited Schmuel Laskar to eat with the family. Rachel ran on ahead to prepare the table. As the two men turned into the narrow street in which the Isakharovs lived, they heard yelling. Toward them raced a gang of one hundred teenage hooligans, brandishing lengths of wood. Leading the mob was a giant with shaggy blond hair and bright blue eyes that gleamed with holy fire. Above his head he swung a heavy wooden mallet, all the while screaming:

"Free Russia from the Jews! Free Russia from the Jews!"

Behind him, the teenage army of liberation paused only to smash the windows of the houses and shops they passed, to batter down doors and wreck whatever their eyes fell on.

Mendel grabbed Schmuel Laskar's arm and pulled the carpenter into a narrow alley. The mob swept past. Some of the youths carried loot that had been easily accessible. The shouting grew faint, the crash of broken glass indistinct. Mendel emerged onto the street, walking quickly. Laskar, hampered by his arthritic joints, lagged behind.

Broken glass cracked beneath Mendel's feet as he hurried toward his home. The shop meant nothing. Windows could be replaced. So could cloth. Only his family mattered. Mendel voiced a silent prayer that neither Rachel nor Zalman had been foolish enough to intervene.

The small window at the front of the shop was smashed. The door had been kicked in. The inside of the shop was a shambles. Laskar's half-constructed counter was in ruins.

21

Fabric that had not been taken lay ripped across the floor. Mendel ran through the shop, shouting his son's name.

The door at the rear of the shop opened. Zalman stood in the doorway, a long-handled axe clenched in hands that were white with tension. When he saw Mendel, his body sagged.

"Where is Rachel?" Mendel asked.

"In the back. When she told me you were following with Schmuel Laskar, I thought for certain . . ."

"They ran right past us. We stepped into an alley, and they did not even see us. All they wanted was to break, to smash, to destroy. And for that, I suppose, we should be grateful."

Rachel appeared. She ran toward her father, tears of relief streaming down her face at the sight of him unharmed. "The police!" she sobbed. "Where were the police!"

Mendel had asked himself the same question, and he had arrived at an answer that reeked of skillful deception. "Their presence yesterday was part of a greater scheme. The sight of so many uniforms assured us. We relaxed. Because of that, the mob met no resistance." He heard Schmuel Laskar's footsteps echoing behind him. Turning, he rested a hand on the carpenter's shoulder. "I grieve for your counter. After all the work you did, it now lies in ruin."

"I can build other counters, Reb Mendel. Be glad that the damage was only to wood."

The rioting continued throughout the afternoon. Roving gangs of teenagers wrecked hundreds of homes and shops. Only as the springlike afternoon turned to evening did the destruction halt. The gangs vanished. Like survivors of a storm, the Jewish residents of Kishinev ventured out to see for themselves the damage their adherence to an ancient faith had caused.

Schmuel Laskar returned to his single room. Mendel walked the neighborhood with Zalman and Rachel. No place had escaped. Boards covered broken windows. Brooms fought a carpet of shattered glass. The synagogue Mendel and Rachel had attended that morning lay in ruins. The Torahs, the holy Scrolls of the Law, had been trampled into the dirt of the street. The ark had been toppled and hacked to splinters. Despite the devastation, the Isakharovs considered themselves fortunate. Compared with the deadly pogroms that had swept Russia following the assassination of Alexander II in 1881, the so-called Storms in the South, Kishinev was nothing more than a light dusting.

Later that evening, the light dusting became carnage. The second wave struck. This time it was not teenage ruffians bent on destroying property. This mob comprised thousands of drunken peasants wielding whatever weapons they could lay their hands on. The earlier cry of "Free Russia from the Jews!" became "Kill the Jews and Save Russia!" While Kishinev's police continued to remain in their barracks, the rioters forced their way into homes and attacked the inhabitants. Babies were ripped from their mother's arms to be impaled on knives or smashed to death against walls; men were castrated, women raped.

The Isakharovs nailed closed the shop door. Then they barricaded themselves in their home, boarding up windows and piling furniture against the door that led to the shop. All night long, and into the next day, father, son, and daughter sat in darkness, nerves screaming in anticipation. Every so often, they heard shouts as groups of rioters ran through the street.

It was early Monday evening, more than a complete day after the pogrom's beginning, when the first blows sounded on the door of the draper's shop. The three members of the family stiffened, their fatigue of moments earlier chased away by terror. Zalman gripped the axe he had held the previous day. Rachel grasped a long, sharp knife. Mendel, his belief in God as strong as ever, clutched a prayer book to his chest.

The assault continued. The door crashed to the ground. Boots stomped through the shop. The onslaught began on the door leading to the living quarters. Clubs and mallets beat a thunderous tattoo. The wood gave. The stacked furniture swayed beneath the impact of muscular shoulders. The barricade yielded. Half a dozen peasants spilled through. One slack-jawed, drunken brute led the charge, huge hands clenched around an enormous club that he swung to clear the way. Zalman parried the club with his axe. The axe was almost torn from his hands. As he tried to regain his grip, the club swung again. Mendel's prayer book, his words to God,

23

offered no defense. The club smashed down on his head, cracking his skull like an egg.

Rachel's scream was eclipsed only by Zalman's roar of rage. He swung the axe with all his might. The blade sliced across the peasant's stomach, parting cloth and flesh. An expression of amazement crossed the man's loose face as he dropped the club and clutched his steaming intestines in his hands. A shocked whimper broke from his mouth. He turned around, as if to show his friends. They ran. Still clasping his intestines, the wounded peasant tried to follow. He got as far as the street before collapsing facedown.

The roar of fury erupted again from Zalman's lips as he leaped over the peasant, swinging the axe as he had seen the young blond giant swing the wooden mallet the previous day. He had fought back. He had tasted blood. It was addictive. He wanted more, much more, before he would be satisfied.

The peasants fled from the madman with the axe. Zalman raced after one man, axe held high for a mighty blow. At the very last moment, the peasant dodged. The axe sliced through air before biting into the earth. Zalman lost his balance and fell. The peasant, too terrified to take advantage, kept on running. When Zalman climbed to his feet, the man was fifty yards away, still moving at top speed.

A column of horsemen wheeled into the street. Axe in hand, Zalman watched the fully armed soldiers draw close. The leader towered above him.

"Get off the street. We have the situation under control."

"Why has it taken you a full day to appear?"

The officer touched the sword he wore at his waist. "If you know what is good for you, you will do as I say."

The blood-lust fled from Zalman's veins. In his excitement, he had forgotten all about Rachel and his father. He ran back to the house. Rachel knelt on the floor, white-faced and crying as she cradled her father's head in her hands. Blood leaked from Mendel's nose and ears. There was no breath, no pulse, no heartbeat. Zalman began to weep. If he had killed a thousand, it would not have been enough.

By the following morning, with heavily armed troops in control of the streets, the extent of the devastation became fully known. Fifteen hundred shops and homes had been ransacked or destroyed. Estimates of the dead ranged from fifty to one hundred and fifty. The wounded were placed at more than a thousand. The casualties would have been even greater had not troops appeared to disperse the mobs. The soldiers had acted after their commander had received a telegram from Count Plehve, the Minister of the Interior, instructing him to restore order. But word quickly spread that the minister had sent the telegram only after knowing of the pogrom for more than twenty-four hours.

Burials took place. Among them was Mendel Isakharov, who was interred next to his wife. Many of the people who had benefited from Mendel Isakharov's friendship and generosity came to pay their last respects. Zalman was brusque. After no more than a few words with well-wishers, he walked away. Rachel clung to his arm, trying to pull him back.

"Zalman, Papa's friends want to know how they can help. They want to arrange food for us while we mourn."

"There will be no week of mourning. No useful purpose will be served by it."

Rachel, shocked and angered by her brother's words, let go of his arm. "Did Papa mean nothing to you? What will he think if he is watching us now?"

"He meant everything to me. And if he is watching us, he will agree that we can mourn him best while we travel."

"Travel where?"

"Where do you think? Out of Russia, away from this land of blood and tears. We will take the gold, the watches, the jewelry, whatever money we find. We will take only what we can carry, and we will leave immediately."

Rachel squeezed her brother's hand. Now that she understood what he meant, she could only concur. This was exactly what their father would have wanted. His greatest dream—perhaps his last dream—had been to see his children enjoy a new beginning.

In death, there was also rebirth.

Chapter Two

Leaving everything but what they could comfortably carry, Zalman and Rachel left Kishinev the next day. With no governor's permit—the official consent required to emigrate—they dared not travel by train. They used other means of transport. When they were lucky, they rode in the cart of a friendly farmer; mostly, they walked. They slept wherever they could, occasionally in a convenient barn but more frequently in the open, using their clothes for blankets and the bags they carried for pillows. When they were hungry, they ate bread and cheese or herring they bought along their route. When they were dirty, they washed in clear streams. And whenever they saw men in uniform, they hid. They were never discovered, and Rachel ascribed that good fortune to the piece of red silk ribbon stitched to her shawl.

After three weeks of such furtive, arduous travel, they reached the border of Galicia and the Austro-Hungarian Empire. Two gold rings from Mendel Isakharov's treasure trove persuaded a border guard to help Zalman and Rachel across. They stayed overnight at an inn, where they bathed properly and slept for fifteen hours. Before moving on, they bought new clothes to replace the garments that had become grimy rags.

From there, the way led west, to Budapest and Bratislava. They sold jewelry to buy railroad tickets. Sometimes they covered two hundred miles in a day; at other times, they remained in a station for two days, waiting resignedly for the next train.

More than seven weeks after leaving Kishinev, Rachel and Zalman reached the Dutch port of Rotterdam. As evening fell, they found lodging at an inn close to Hoog Straat, the long, straight thoroughfare that ran along the dike dividing the old city from the new. The inn was owned by a middle-aged married couple, Willem and Anna Klaas. Zalman made himself understood by speaking German, which Willem Klaas translated for his wife.

The innkeeper showed them to a third-floor room that contained two short, wide beds with spotless white linen and huge feather pillows. Rachel sat on the edge of one bed, her shoulders bent with fatigue. Zalman flopped down onto the other, sinking his head into the pillow's embrace. He stretched out his arms, reveling in the softness of the mattress. Had he ever slept in such a comfortable bed before? Or had he always slept on a straw mattress by a stove? He was so tired he could not remember. Not that it mattered. From this day forth, he would always sleep in soft beds. Straw mattresses belonged in Russia.

"Now that we have reached Rotterdam, we can go no farther by land," Rachel said. "We have to decide where to go by sea."

"America," Zalman answered unhesitatingly.

"Why not England?"

"England? That country is controlled by the same family of tyrants that rides roughshod over Russia. They are all cousins, the King, the Kaiser, the Czar. The evil that afflicts one land afflicts them all. Only America is different."

A note of petulance crept into Rachel's voice. "England is closer. I feel like I have spent my entire life traveling. Now I want to rest, to put down some roots."

Zalman rolled over to look at his younger sister. "I am responsible—"

Rachel laughed. "You? Your idea of responsibility was to attend your stupid political meetings and stare into space while you planned the revolution that will never happen. I am the one who worked. I ran the home after Mama died, and I helped Papa in the shop. If either of us understands responsibility, it is me. It is certainly not Zalman the dreamer."

Zalman grew angry at having the nickname thrown into his face. He had stopped dreaming when the *muzhik*'s club had shattered his father's skull. He had become a man of action when he had swung the axe. "I am the oldest. I am the man, the head of the family. Therefore, *I* will decide the course we will take. And my choice is America, because the farther we get away from Russia, the better it will be for us."

"We have to cross a huge ocean to reach America. To reach England, all we have to cross is a small sea."

"After what we have crossed already, a huge ocean will present no greater obstacle than a puddle." Without another word, he fell asleep.

Rachel could not sleep so easily. For ten minutes she listened to Zalman's even breathing. Then, drawing her shawl around her shoulders, she left the room and went downstairs. She walked along Hoog Straat, marveling at the nighttime bustle. Shops in the ground floors of houses enjoyed brisk trade. Patrons spilled out from the cafes and taverns. Despite being among so many people, Rachel felt completely alone. The short, dumpy women and the serious-looking men all seemed to have blue eyes and blond or reddish hair, just like the innkeeper and his wife. Rachel was acutely aware of how out of place her own features were. Her clothes, also, were so distinct, and why shouldn't they be? She was a refugee from Russia suddenly set down in a Dutch seaport. Yet the people of Rotterdam—men in somber colors, women in long skirts and white caps, sailors on leave from their ships, even soldiers in uniform—passed right by as if she did not exist. No one made any comment. No one, she thought with a sudden thrill, even seemed to notice her.

Gaining poise, she took more interest in her surroundings. Everything was so unique. Accustomed to the dark and dirty streets of Kishinev, she was amazed by Rotterdam's brightness. Lamps gleamed from the bridges that crossed canals, from the masts of boats, from the corners of every house. And the houses, both brick and wood, sparkled with cleanliness. Every house had flower boxes and white curtains in its windows. Rachel had never seen such color and gaiety. What a joyful city this must be!

Then she noticed something that caused her to blink in

shock. She ran back to the inn and up to the third-floor room. Zalman slept. Rachel grabbed his shoulder and shook him.

"What is it? What is the matter?"

"Come look and you will see!" She dragged him by the arm toward the window.

Zalman pushed back the white curtain and peered out. The moon cast odd shadows across the street, giving the buildings a new, angular dimension. "What am I supposed to be looking at?"

"The houses! All the houses are falling over in different directions."

"It is the way the moonlight strikes them."

"No. Every house leans. Some lean forward, some lean backward. Some to the right, some to the left. Some lean together like an arch."

Zalman stared through the window again. Rachel was right. The tall, narrow buildings leaned all over the place like a bunch of vodka-soaked peasants. He pushed open the window and gazed down. The inn's base sloped inward, like the side of a cliff. "Do you think"—Zalman began to laugh—"that whoever designed Rotterdam was drunk at the time?"

Rachel threw her arms around her brother. They stood by the window, their bodies shaking with laughter. Simultaneously, they realized this was the first time in eight weeks that they had found anything to laugh about.

Early the next morning, Zalman asked the innkeeper for directions to the docks. Klaas sketched a rough map. Using it, Zalman led Rachel to the Boompjes, the dike that protected the city from the Nieuwe Maas, the tributary of the Rhine linking Rotterdam with the North Sea eighteen miles away.

The sight that greeted them ripped their breath away. Who in Kishinev had ever seen a real boat? Here, hundreds of vessels were tied up at the docks: sailboats plying local trade; brightly painted steamboats that connected with the neighboring ports of Dordrecht, Arnhem, Gouda, Schiedam, Briel, and Zealand; and larger, stately ships bound for the great ports of Europe and beyond. They walked around the docks for hours, totally fascinated by the unceasing activity.

They crossed drawbridges, turning bridges, and bridges made of stone. At last, Zalman guided Rachel onto a very high bridge. Less than a hundred yards away sat an enormous ship with two masts and one funnel. Dockworkers loaded cargo. Sailors shined brass fittings and touched up paintwork. Zalman squinted in the bright midday sun to make out the ship's name. *Potsdam.* Next to it was the name of the company: Holland-America.

A man in uniform crossed the bridge. Rachel beckoned to him and pointed to the *Potsdam.*

"England?"

The man shook his head. "America. New York."

Zalman turned to Rachel, his face solemn. "The first boat we ask about is bound not for England but for America. Surely you must agree that this is not a trifling coincidence, but an omen. A sign that we, too, must go to America."

Rachel considered her brother's words. At last, she nodded. "All right, America."

Zalman's face glowed with triumph. He had counted on his sister's superstitious nature being the key to making her agree with him. That was why, when receiving directions from Willem Klaas, he had specifically asked the innkeeper where they would be able to see boats bound for the United States.

Zalman and Rachel visited the Holland-America office that afternoon. After waiting in line for twenty minutes, they approached the ticket agent's desk.

"*Kun ik oo helpen?*"

Zalman ran through the languages he might have in common with the agent. "*Sprechen Sie Deutsch?* Do you speak English?"

"English," the agent answered. "Can I help you?" Glancing at their clothes, he identified them as Russian Jews. Western newspapers had carried horrifying accounts of the Kishinev pogrom. More such atrocities would no doubt soon follow. The shipping lines that connected Europe to America were gearing up for the increase in passengers.

"My sister and I wish to go to America. When does your boat, the *Potsdam,* leave for New York?"

"At midday tomorrow. But we have no space on a ship to New York until the middle of June, when the *Rijndam* sails."

Zalman turned to Rachel, who had understood nothing of the conversation. When he relayed the information, she frowned.

"Can we afford to stay here two more weeks?" she asked.

"Of course." To allay Rachel's fears, Zalman yielded to exaggeration. "We could stay a month, pay our fares, and still never have to part with those watches."

Rachel knew that her brother would rather beg on the street than sell the beetle-shaped watches. Her frown lessened, but only by a fraction; after years of living among wretched poverty, even a hint of abundance was difficult to accept.

"Try other shipping companies," the ticket agent whispered. "Perhaps you will be able to sail earlier with another line. But if you do not have good fortune elsewhere, come back within four or five days to book passage on the *Rijndam.*" He leafed through the pages of a ledger. "The first- and second-class berths are already fully booked, and our eighteen hundred third-class berths are filling quickly."

"Thank you very much for your help." Zalman shook the man's hand before holding open the door for Rachel. A thin, elegantly dressed man who had been studying a timetable followed them out.

"Excuse me," the man said in faintly accented English, "but I could not help overhearing your conversation. I think I might be able to help you."

"How?"

The man offered his hand. "I am Leopold Metgot. You are . . . ?"

"Zalman Isakharov." He took Metgot's hand; it was firm and dry. "This is my sister, Rachel."

Metgot doffed his black derby to Rachel. "My wife and I are booked to sail tomorrow on the *Potsdam.* Sadly, my wife has been taken ill. I tried to return the tickets, but the company would not accept them because it is too near sailing time to make a cancellation. Would you and your sister care to purchase them?"

Zalman translated the offer for Rachel. "We would be able

to leave tomorrow," she said excitedly. "We would be in America . . . When would we be in America?"

"When does the *Potsdam* reach New York?" Zalman asked Metgot.

"On June the sixteenth."

Zalman translated the answer. Rachel looked at Metgot's dark suit, the heavy gold chain across the front, his manicured hands. The only incongruous part of his appearance was a narrow scar that ran from below his right eye to the corner of his ear. "How much does he want for the tickets? He does not look the kind of man who would travel third class."

Zalman switched to English. "What kind of tickets are they?"

"Second class. But I am willing to ask of you only what you would pay for third-class tickets. That way"—Metgot shrugged expressively—"we would both be in pocket. You would pay less than the going price. I would recoup some of my expenses. And you and your sister would not be separated in third class."

"Separated?"

"Of course. Third-class cabins are airless, windowless compartments with beds that stretch from floor to ceiling. Sexes cannot be mixed there."

The prospect terrified Zalman. "Agreed!" he said, and grasped Metgot's hand to seal the bargain before it could disappear.

"The tickets are at my home. Let us meet this evening and close our deal." Metgot wrote down directions to a tavern owned by a man named Landheer. "Meet me there at six o'clock." He doffed his hat again to Rachel and walked away.

Zalman and Rachel returned to the inn of Willem Klaas and told the innkeeper and his wife that they would be sailing to America the very next day. Klaas celebrated their good fortune by pouring four glasses of clear, fiery liquid. "May your voyage be calm, and may your new life be all that you want it to be."

At six that evening, they found Landheer's tavern. Metgot waited at a table. "I have the tickets. Do you have the money?"

Zalman pulled out money. While he counted, Metgot motioned for Zalman to check the tickets. Zalman showed them to Rachel, pointing out the name of the ship, the date, and the class.

"How can we travel in such luxury dressed like this?" Rachel whispered. "We will look out of place."

"When we leave here we will go shopping. A dress for you, a suit for me. We have worn rags long enough."

Metgot finished counting. Zalman, clutching the tickets, guided Rachel to the door. They bought clothes for the journey. Zalman bit back a smile as he watched his sister ask the shop owner to sew a scrap of red ribbon to her new dress.

That night they were too excited to sleep. Rachel tried on her dress, while Zalman clapped his hands in admiration. When she grew tired of admiring herself, she sat down on the bed and gazed at her brother. "We have been so fortunate. Reaching Rotterdam, and then being offered a second-class cabin on tomorrow's boat for the price of a third-class ticket. Do you think Papa is watching over us? Do you think he is guiding us?"

Two months earlier, before Kishinev, Zalman would have dismissed such a question as an example of Rachel's superstitious nature. He would have taken some perverse pleasure in telling her that there was no afterlife; that the dead had no effect on the fortunes of the living. Now, he could not disappoint her so coldly. "Perhaps," he answered after a few seconds.

Rachel closed her eyes and clasped her hands together. "I know he is. We will be safe, Zalman, as long as he keeps watching over us."

Zalman smiled. His sister's faith was so powerful that he could feel himself almost believing her.

The next morning, Willem Klaas drove his guests in a horse-drawn cart to the Holland-America dock. Passengers waited to board the *Potsdam*. Rachel indicated the longest line of all, for the cramped and airless third-class berths. "That would be us in two weeks time if Papa were not watching over us," she said.

They approached the gate. A man in uniform held out his

hand for tickets. Zalman presented the second-class tickets he had bought from Leopold Metgot. The man looked at them before snapping his fingers. A policeman appeared. A flurry of Dutch ensued. The policeman took the tickets and motioned for Zalman and Rachel to step out of the line. Confused and anxious, they followed him to a small office.

The policeman spoke German. "These tickets are forgeries. Where did you get them?"

"I bought them from a man who approached me outside the Holland-America offices. He said his wife had been taken ill—"

"And it was too late to cancel the reservations?"

"Do you know the man?" Zalman asked hopefully.

The policeman shook his head. "I know of many just like him. Confidence tricksters. They flock here to prey on the refugees who seek passage to America. The German ports of Hamburg and Antwerp will be the same. So will the English ports of Liverpool and Southampton."

Zalman saw the horrified expression on Rachel's face and wondered if she still believed that their father was watching over them. After giving all the information to the policeman, they made their way back to the inn. Willem Klaas was beside himself with anger when Zalman related what had happened.

"To steal from people who have lost so much already!" the innkeeper declared. "If the dog is ever caught, he should be given to the army for target practice."

Anna Klaas was more practical. "Will you be able to afford more tickets?" she asked.

"To do so we would have to sell two watches that are family heirlooms," Zalman answered. How he regretted spending the money to buy the clothes that he and Rachel would have worn in second class.

"You may stay here as long as you wish," Klaas said. "We want nothing in return."

"Thank you. We can get passage on the *Rijndam,* which leaves the middle of the month. That gives me a chance, at least, to find this man who calls himself Leopold Metgot."

"My two sons and I will help you to look. We will find a thousand of Metgot's kind in the taverns."

Zalman smiled tightly. "That is where I intend looking."

While Rachel remained at the inn, Willem Klaas and his two teenage sons accompanied Zalman on a tour of Rotterdam's taverns. For two days, they sought the thin, elegant figure of Leopold Metgot. They scanned the faces of five thousand drinkers, seeking the narrow scar that Rachel had deemed out of place on such a debonair man. On the morning of the third day, Zalman visited the Holland-America offices. The same ticket clerk was on duty.

"Do you still have third-class passage on the *Rijndam?*"

"Perhaps two hundred berths. They go quickly now. More of your compatriots arrive daily."

"I hope they have better luck than I did."

"I heard about your trouble. I am sorry."

Zalman dug into his pocket and produced the two watches. "I need two third-class berths on the *Rijndam*. I look everywhere for the thief who swindled me. If I cannot get back my money, I am prepared to sell these watches to pay for passage for my sister and myself. Will you hold us two places, please?"

"I will hold them until three days before sailing."

"Thank you," Zalman said, and left the steamship office to return to searching the taverns.

On the seventh night, the search ended. Zalman was with Klaas when he spotted Leopold Metgot entering a cafe on Hoog Straat. He nudged the innkeeper. "I just saw him go in there. Wearing a dark suit and a hat, and carrying a cane."

Klaas entered the cafe, squinting in the dim, smoky light. A minute later he returned to Zalman. "He sits with a group of men, pimps and pickpockets most likely."

Zalman and the innkeeper waited for an hour until Metgot emerged alone. They followed at a distance, through a maze of streets, across a large square, and down a narrow alley on the other side. He stopped in front of a house. As he fumbled with a key, Zalman and Klaas broke into a run. Metgot swung around. His shout of alarm died as Klaas locked an arm around his throat.

"I want my money! All of it! Now!" In his excitement, Zalman spoke in Russian. He calmed down enough to trans-

late the demand into English, the language in which Metgot
had concocted his crooked deal.

Metgot pointed up to a second-floor window. Klaas eased
his grip. "In my room. I have money in my room."

"Release him," Zalman told the innkeeper. Metgot opened
the door. Zalman and Klaas followed him up a flight of stairs
to a door which Metgot opened with another key.

"Your money is over there." Metgot strode across the
room to a highly polished bureau. Zalman followed, but he
was not quick enough. Metgot jerked open the top drawer.
Instead of money, he pulled out a revolver. "Threaten me,
would you? Who the damned hell do you think you are?"

Once more, Zalman saw the *muzhik,* club raised to smash
his father's skull like an egg. He leaped forward. Metgot
squeezed the trigger. Thunder filled the room. The bullet
smashed into the wall as Zalman wrestled Metgot to the
floor. The swindler screamed in pain as Willem Klaas's heavy
boot slammed down across the wrist of the gun hand. Bones
cracked. Metgot's fingers opened, the revolver came free.
Klaas kicked it away.

"Let him go," the innkeeper told Zalman. "Dutch justice
is best left to the Dutch."

Zalman stood up. Klaas bent over, grabbed hold of Metgot's broken wrist, and pulled the man to his feet. Metgot's
scream of pain was more piercing than the gunshot. Zalman
understood none of the guttural Dutch that spewed from
Klaas's mouth, but its meaning was more than evident.

"Scum! Is this Dutch hospitality? Who gave you permis-
sion to steal from those who have already lost everything?"
Ringing slaps that threatened to tear off Metgot's head punctuated the questions. "Pig, where is the money you stole from
this man?"

Metgot's eyes, glazed from the beating, swung slowly toward a wardrobe. Zalman opened it. Hanging inside were
expensive suits and coats, the elegant swindler's stock in
trade. He pulled each garment from its hanger, checking the
pockets before throwing it unceremoniously onto the floor.
In the pocket of the last coat he found a wallet, full of money.

"Take it all," urged Klaas.

"I only want what is mine," Zalman answered as he

36

counted out the exact amount he had paid Metgot for the counterfeit tickets. "The remainder belongs to other people he has cheated. Let us hope that they come looking for him, too."

Shoving Metgot away, Klaas followed Zalman from the room. Two elderly women, drawn by the commotion, stood outside the door. Klaas spoke to the women, then he and Zalman walked down the stairs to the narrow alley.

Once outside, Zalman began running. Klaas called him back. "The police," Zalman said. "The two women will summon them—"

"Those women are sisters who own the house. They will not call the police. They will do nothing to help Metgot. He terrorizes them. What we did tonight they have waited a long time to see."

They returned to the inn and showed the money to Rachel. "I told you that Papa was watching over us," she said. "He must have blinked to allow that man to trick us, but he would not allow us to be cheated permanently."

Rachel and Zalman returned the next morning to the office of the Holland-America Line, where they booked two third-class passages on the *Rijndam* to New York.

On the evening before the ship sailed, Willem and Anna Klaas presented their guests with a farewell gift. Rachel unwrapped the gift—a framed studio portrait of the Klaases.

"We wanted you to remember us," Anna explained.

"We would have remembered you always," Rachel replied after Zalman translated. "You and your wife have been wonderful friends. We will treasure this picture forever."

Zalman and Rachel went to their room. "We have kept our promise, Rachel. We are going to America, and we still have the watches." He pulled them from his jacket pocket. The man's watch he wound and replaced. The woman's watch he handed to Rachel. "Papa meant this for you. Wear it."

Rachel fastened the chain around her neck. The watch rested like a pendant against her bosom. "That gift was very kind of the Klaases. We should get them something in return."

"I thought the same. We will find a clock for them. That way, whenever the hour strikes, they will remember us."

"You go," Rachel told Zalman. "I will stay here."

"Are you all right?"

"All the excitement has made my head hurt."

"Lie down and rest so that you may be well for tomorrow."

Zalman kissed his sister on the cheek and gently closed the door. He walked along Hoog Straat. His pace was slow, and he entered any shop that interested him, browsing at leisure. The shops remained open late. He was in no hurry. After all, who knew when he would ever be in Rotterdam again?

Rachel lay on the bed for forty-five minutes, eyes closed, a cold, damp flannel pressed to her forehead. At last, she sat up. She was too excited to sleep. She could think only of boarding the ship the next day, watching the ropes being cast off, feeling the deck move beneath her feet. She had never been on a ship before. In the last two months, she had experienced so many new things.

She stood up and looked out of the window. Had Zalman found a clock? Or was he, also, too full of anticipation to concentrate on a single mission? She opened the window and breathed deeply of the cool evening air. She could smell the sea . . . ! The ache in her head lessened. Instead of lying down, she should have gone out with Zalman. She would go out! Not shopping along Hoog Straat, she decided as she picked up her shawl, but to the docks. To check that the *Rijndam* was where it should be.

As she left the room, she lifted the watch from her bosom and opened the beetle's wings. It was past nine. Zalman might return soon. He would worry. She turned around and scribbled a note to say that she had gone for a walk. Leaving the inn, she looked over her shoulder. Every window was dark. Willem and Anna Klaas, their sons, and their guests must be asleep already. And why shouldn't they be? They had nothing as thrilling as a transatlantic voyage to contemplate.

Rachel's head cleared quickly. She walked fast and breathed in deeply. At the docks, she climbed the high bridge on which she had stood with Zalman. Moonlight bathed the river in brightness. In the same spot that the *Potsdam* had been moored two weeks earlier floated the *Rijndam,* an enormous ship with a single funnel standing proudly between two masts. Rachel clenched her fists and chewed her bottom lip. The decks were large enough to hold an entire town.

She knew she should return to the inn, but she could not tear herself away from the glorious sight. If she had her ticket, she would board now. Another few minutes, she promised herself. Just another four or five. Then she would return to the inn and tell Zalman that there was nothing for him to worry about.

The *Rijndam* was exactly where it was supposed to be!

It was fifteen minutes before ten when Zalman found a clock for the Klaases. He began to retrace his steps, eager now to return.

He caught the smell of burning wood when he was still a quarter of a mile from the inn. Apprehension tickled his spine. He walked faster. The smell became sharper. Ahead, he saw a glow in the sky. He joined the men and women running toward it.

A mass of people blocked the street on which the inn was located. At the very front, a bucket chain worked with a frantic rhythm. Faces glowed with sweat and heat. Water splashed and sizzled onto the flames that engulfed the entire building. The crowd parted to make way for a horse-drawn water tender, but it had arrived too late. The fire's grip would not be loosened until the wooden building was nothing more than ashes.

Zalman shoved his way through the crowd, following the water tender. He gazed around wildly. "Rachel! Where are you?" he screamed in Russian.

A man's voice answered in the same language. "Who do you look for?"

Zalman saw a man with a dark beard and old-country clothes. A refugee like himself, who had floated with the stream to this Dutch port. "I seek my sister! We were staying at the inn."

The man pointed to another house. "I stay there. We saw

the fire begin. So sudden. An explosion, and then the house stood in flames."

Dropping the clock, Zalman grabbed the man by the shoulders and shook him. "My sister! The Klaases! Their sons! The other people who stayed at the inn! Where are they all?"

The man's face twisted itself into a tortured grimace. "Inside. No one got out."

Zalman ran toward the house. Two men tackled him. As they pulled him to the ground, the inn's roof collapsed. Huge flames roared up to the sky. The crowd shrank back from the searing heat. Tears scalded Zalman's eyes and spilled unchecked down his cheeks. Why had Rachel not gone with him? Why had she needed to rest? Now she could rest forever.

He lay on the ground, eyes screwed shut, head bursting. The bearded refugee's words echoed in his brain. So sudden! An explosion, and then the house stood in flames! Was this what Rachel had meant by their father watching over them? And if he were watching, what would he expect Zalman to do?

With tears still streaming down his face, he stood up. Men watched him warily, prepared to stop another desperate plunge into the fiery building. Instead, Zalman backed away, retreating through the crowd, his eyes never leaving the blazing inn.

He had a debt to pay.

Rachel hurried back to the inn, all the time glancing at the hands of the watch that hung from her throat. Eleven-fifteen, eleven-twenty, eleven-thirty. Even with the note she had left, Zalman would be worried sick about her. She should never have stayed out so late.

She turned into the street to see the crowd in front of the inn. Pushing through, she saw firemen and volunteers wetting down the smoldering remains. She looked around for Zalman, the Klaases, the other guests. Where were they? A shocked gasp erupted from the crowd as two firemen pulled something from the wreckage of the inn. Rachel turned to look. Her heart filled her throat. Like a sack of coal, the two

40

men dragged a body from the ruined building. A human body so badly burned that it was impossible to tell whether it was man or woman, fair or dark, young or old. As Rachel watched in shock, two more firemen lugged out another corpse and set it down beside the first.

Rachel thrust a hand into her mouth. Now she understood why there was no Zalman. No Willem and Anna Klaas. No one at all. Unable to escape, they had been burned alive, their bodies transformed into unrecognizable lumps of charred meat.

Screaming in horror, she pushed through the crowd, shoving people out of the way in her haste to get clear. She ran as fast as she could, not knowing where she was going. Not caring. Her vision filled with Zalman's face, his brown eyes sympathetic as he had told her to lie down and rest so that she would be well for tomorrow. Never had she dreamed that they would be the last words she would ever hear him speak.

Her knee buckled. Thrusting out her hands to stop herself from falling, she felt the cold touch of stone. Her eyes focused. She stood in the center of a bridge that spanned a wide canal. She heard the clatter of hooves, the rumble of wheels. Glancing left, she saw a carriage drawn by a single horse. She watched it pass. Behind the driver a man and woman sat talking, oblivious to everything in the world but each other. Comfortable in their little cocoon, Rachel thought bitterly, they could never imagine the tragedies she had suffered these past months.

Zalman was gone. Dead. Like her father. Like everyone else. She was all alone, a seventeen-year-old girl marooned in a country whose language she did not understand. The nightmare journey from eastern Europe—the sacrifices, the privation—had all been for naught.

She climbed the wall of the bridge, balanced for an instant, then flung herself toward the water's soothing embrace.

Zalman had no difficulty remembering the way to the house where Leopold Metgot lived. He banged on the door. A woman opened it. Zalman recognized her as one of the two women who owned the house; the sisters who had, in fact, waited a long time to see Metgot receive his just desserts.

41

He pushed past the woman and ran up the stairs to Metgot's room. The door was locked. Zalman's heavy shoe smashed against wood. The door shook, but held. Before he could kick the door again, the woman produced a key. Zalman opened the door and went inside. The room was empty. He checked the bureau. The revolver lay in the top drawer. Zalman removed the revolver and held a finger to his lips. The woman nodded and backed out of the room. Zalman followed her along the corridor to her own room which she entered and locked from the inside. Satisfied that his meeting with Metgot would be undisturbed, Zalman returned to the swindler's room. Locking the door, he settled into a chair.

Zalman waited all night long. When the sun rose the following morning, he still occupied the chair. He pulled the gold-and-enamel watch from his pocket and checked the time. How much longer could he stay? At what time did he have to leave to board the *Rijndam?* There was no doubt in Zalman's mind that he would sail today. To do otherwise would be a total betrayal of his father and sister.

Just before eight o'clock, he heard the downstairs door open. Footsteps ascended the stairs and crossed the landing. They stopped outside the door. A key turned in the lock. Zalman stood behind the door. It swung back in his face and Leopold Metgot entered the room. Zalman raised the revolver so that it pointed directly at Metgot's head.

"Turn around."

Metgot turned. His right arm and broken wrist were supported by a sling. His left hand held a silver-topped cane. "You!"

Had Zalman needed proof of guilt, the shock contained in that single word would have provided it. "Alive, no thanks to you."

Metgot advanced, the cane held in front of him. He slashed the air. The end of the cane flew off. In its place, protruding two feet from the cane's handle, was a thin steel blade. Metgot leaped forward, flicking the blade at face height. Fire burned Zalman's left cheek. His hand reached up, felt blood. Metgot's pale eyes gleamed in triumph as he lunged for the death blow.

Zalman squeezed the trigger. The bullet smashed into the

center of Metgot's chest, slamming him back against the bureau. The swordstick dropped from his hand. He coughed up a mouthful of blood before sliding slowly to the floor. Zalman dropped the revolver on the floor, turned around, and left the room. He ran down the stairs and along the street, slowing only when he reached the corner.

He touched his cheek. He had been lucky. The cut was long but shallow. Already, the blood was congealing. He halted at a fountain long enough to wash the drying blood from his face. By the time he reached the Holland-America dock and took his place in the line for third-class passengers, the bleeding had ceased.

Rachel's eyes opened to stare at a high, unfamiliar ceiling. Light flooded through a window above her head. She lay on a bed. Her chest felt sore, her limbs leaden. Most of all, her head throbbed excruciatingly.

The headache jolted her memory. She had been suffering from a headache when Zalman had left to buy a gift for Anna and Willem Klaas. That had been night. Now—she looked up at the window—it was day. What day? She closed her eyes again as the memories came flooding back, recollections more painful even than the ache in her head. Her brother, her last blood relative, was dead, and God had even denied her the privilege of taking her own life.

Footsteps echoed on the hard floor. Rachel twisted her head to look. Past a row of beds occupied by other women walked three people. Leading the way was a gray-haired nurse. A step behind came a short and portly man with a Franz Josef mustache, and a slim woman who wore a long blue coat and a wide blue hat with feathers coming from it.

The nurse led the couple to the side of Rachel's bed. "What could be so terrible," asked the woman in the feathered hat, "that you would want to kill yourself?"

Rachel's eyes opened in amazement. The woman had spoken not in Dutch, but in Yiddish. "Why do you address me in Yiddish?"

"That was what you were speaking when our driver pulled you from the canal. You were very fortunate. Had we not

43

been passing by, you would surely have drowned. We brought you here, to this infirmary."

Rachel remembered the horse-drawn carriage that had crossed the bridge just as she jumped. "When was this?"

"Last night."

Rachel's hand touched her throat. Her fingers came in contact with the coarse fabric of a nightdress.

"Do you seek this?" The man held out the gold-and-enamel watch. "I fear the water did it little good."

Rachel took the watch and opened the wings. The hands stood at seven minutes after twelve. She listened for ticking, but heard only silence. She wound it with the tiny key, then shook it. Nothing helped. The intricate mechanism was ruined.

"What is your name?" the woman in the feathered hat asked.

"Rachel. Rachel Isakharov."

"I am Hannah Dekker. And this is my husband, Tobias. Now what was so terrible that you preferred death to life?"

Rachel slipped the watch chain around her neck. The weight was reassuring. In a low voice, she described everything that had happened since the beginning of April.

"You poor child," Hannah Dekker said when Rachel had finished describing the blaze at the inn. She sat on the edge of the bed, holding Rachel's hands in her own. "What will you do now?"

Rachel stared into the woman's compassionate brown eyes. "I do not know."

"Would you want to return home?"

"To Russia? God forbid that I should consider such a thing."

The woman smiled. The lines in her face softened. Rachel tried to guess her age, but it was difficult when she had only Russian women to use as a yardstick. Poverty and repression had aged those women before their time. She concentrated, instead, on Tobias Dekker. He was easier to place. His face was round and smooth, but there was ample gray in his flourishing mustache and light-brown hair. Nearer fifty than forty, Rachel decided.

Tobias bent down to whisper a few words to his wife. "My

husband is concerned that we are overtaxing you. Rest, Rachel, and recover your strength. We will return to see you tomorrow."

Tears formed in Rachel's eyes as she watched her visitors leave. After all the tragedy she had known, she was touched that someone cared enough to visit her. To have pulled her from the canal even!

The pounding in her head lessened as she found herself anticipating the Dekkers' visit the next day.

The *Rijndam* sailed that afternoon. Zalman stood on the crowded third-class deck with the rest of the steerage passengers, grateful for the salty breeze that whipped his face. That murdering swindler Leopold Metgot had told the truth about only one thing: the squalid condition of third-class accommodation. Zalman knew that he would be spending every possible moment on deck; if the weather obliged, he would even sleep up here.

When the *Rijndam* cleared the mouth of the Rhine and headed out into the North Sea, passengers gazed toward the continent of Europe which, for one reason or another, they were leaving. Italians, Germans, Poles, Austrians, Hungarians, Rumanians, Russians—they all looked back. Zalman, alone, faced forward, back rigid, arms folded resolutely across his chest. He refused to look back. Nothing was there to make him feel nostalgic. Behind was superstition and bloodshed. People who believed in one God slaughtering those who believed in another. They were all wrong. There was no God at all. God was simply a convenient excuse created by man when he could not or would not accept responsibility for his own actions.

Staring into the fifteen-knot wind, Zalman silently vowed that he would never use such excuses. Nor would he ever accept them from anyone else.

He opened the wings of the gold-and-enamel watch. The hands showed half-past eight. He was spending his first night away from Europe. Already he felt as if a great weight had been lifted from his shoulders. Around him was a mass of misery, people whose discomfort on the choppy sea was multiplied by doubts over their decision to seek a new life in

America. Zalman shared none of their misgivings, none of their misery. What lay ahead had to be better than what he had left behind.

Tobias and Hannah Dekker visited Rachel again the following afternoon. They remarked immediately how much better she looked. "You have color in your cheeks," Hannah said. "Can you see the difference, Tobias?"

"I see life in her eyes that was not there yesterday."

Rachel welcomed the compliments. She felt far better, and she was glad that someone other than herself recognized the improvement a day had made.

Hannah sat on the edge of the bed. "The nurse has told us that you are almost well enough to leave here. Have you thought what you will do?"

Rachel had lain awake the previous night wondering just that. The knowledge that people cared had opened her mind to the future. "I will try to find work. Perhaps I will be able to save enough money to go to America."

"What kind of work could you do?"

"I know about fabrics. I could even be a housekeeper. I kept house for my family in Kishinev."

Hannah glanced up at her husband, who nodded. "My husband is English, but I am Dutch. I moved from Amsterdam to London twenty-five years ago to marry Tobias. He is a merchant there, importing fancy foods from Europe. We remember how it was twenty-two years ago, after the assassination of the Czar. London was deluged with refugees from the pogroms. When English newspapers published the story of Kishinev, we knew there would be another exodus. My husband has frequent business in Rotterdam. I accompanied him this time, because we wanted to see how we could help."

"We crossed that bridge so late that night because we were on our way home from dinner at a friend's home," Tobias added. "But I believe the real reason is that God meant it to be that way."

"My husband's business here will be finished tomorrow. We will return to London the day after." Hannah gazed softly at Rachel. "We would like you to accompany us."

Rachel closed her eyes as tears welled up. How often had

46

she cried these past few months? How many tears had she shed in fear, in anger, and in grief? These tears were new. She was crying from happiness. From a renewed belief in the goodness of people. Two glistening beads rolled down her cheeks as she opened her eyes again. "I will work in your house. I will clean and dust and cook. I promise I will repay this kindness."

"If we sought a housekeeper," Tobias said in a pompous but kindly tone, "we would place an advertisement in the *Times*."

Rachel decided that she would allow Tobias to believe that God had meant for him and his wife to ride across the bridge at that precise moment. She knew better. Her father had been watching over her. It was he, not God, who had made Tobias and Hannah Dekker choose that exact moment and that exact route.

England . . . how would it be to live there? Anxiety surfaced as Rachel recalled Zalman's derision of the country's Royal Family. "Your king, what is he like?"

"Edward the Seventh?" Tobias drew a large copper coin from his pocket and passed it to Rachel. "That is he. He is a warm and worldly man who is not afraid to be touched by the fears and joys of his subjects."

Rachel looked at the King's image on the penny before turning over the coin. "Who is this on the other side?"

"That is Britannia," Tobias answered proudly.

"What does she do?"

"Do? She rules the waves."

Rachel's hand closed tightly around the penny. She would not release it, not until she set foot in her new country. Her most precious possessions were a copper penny and a ruined watch. She smiled. So soon after seeking death, she recognized a future.

Rachel was discharged from the infirmary late the following afternoon. Wearing new clothes bought for her by Hannah and Tobias Dekker, she rode in a carriage with her benefactors to their hotel. She ate dinner with them before retiring early.

The next morning, Rachel requested a favor from the Dekkers. "I need to see where my brother lies."

Tobias and Hannah accompanied Rachel to the burned-out inn. The smell of wet charred wood hung in the air. Rachel stepped down from the carriage and stood staring at the ruins for fully five minutes. She knew now that she had been spared from both the fire and her suicide attempt for a special reason. She was responsible for the continuity of the family.

Two soldiers from Rotterdam's small garrison walked along the street. Rachel, still wary of uniforms, stepped back to give the soldiers right of way. Hannah stopped them to ask where the victims of the fire had been taken. One soldier answered that a mass funeral had taken place the previous day; many of the bodies had been burned beyond identification. He pointed the way to a churchyard.

Leaving Hannah and Tobias at the churchyard gate, Rachel approached the freshly dug grave that held the victims of the fire. There, surrounded by cross-adorned tombstones, she whispered Kaddish, the Hebrew prayer for the dead. It was a supplication on behalf of her father as well as her brother.

That evening, clutching the copper penny and the broken watch, she boarded the ship that would take her to England and the new life she would dedicate to the memory of her brother Zalman.

Chapter Three

Rachel and the Dekkers occupied adjoining cabins during the overnight voyage from Rotterdam. Dreams plagued Rachel's sleep. She saw her father and brother, as each had been during her final moments with them—Mendel Isakharov seeking defense in prayer, and Zalman urging her to rest. Moments before awakening from her fretful slumber, she heard her father's voice stressing that her life now had an irrefutable purpose. "You must go on from here. It is your responsibility, Rachel, to leave a footprint on the pages of history, so that people, many years from now, will know the Isakharov family once lived."

Just after dawn, the boat docked at the English port of Harwich. Rachel and the Dekkers boarded the train to London. As the train pulled out of the station, Rachel began to learn more about her benefactors. "Tobias belongs to a well-established English family," Hannah said. "Although he speaks Yiddish, he is a descendant of the Sephardic Jews who were admitted to England by Oliver Cromwell in the middle of the seventeenth century."

Rachel glanced across the first-class compartment to Tobias, who sat half hidden from view by a copy of the *Times*. She had no idea who Oliver Cromwell was. She did not even know what was meant by Sephardic Jews. Did different classes exist? And didn't all Jews speak Yiddish as a matter of course? They did in Russia. She felt she had to say something. "You must be very proud of your heritage," she told Tobias.

"What I am most proud of is that my branch of the family has remained loyal to our faith. The other branches, to ensure acceptance and success in a Christian country, took baptism into the Church of England. My branch, despite the cost, did not." Tobias looked sternly at Rachel over the top of his reading glasses. "But do not think for one moment that being Jewish makes me less of an Englishman, or less proud of my country, than those of my family who long ago became Christian Englishmen."

"I do not," Rachel answered immediately.

The sternness gave way to a smile. "Good. One day, Rachel, you will love England and be as proud of her as Hannah and I are."

Rachel looked out over lush green fields. She liked the country already, even if she could not comprehend a word of its language. For her benefit, the Dekkers spoke Yiddish. The times they used English, she felt lost. "How is it," she asked Hannah, "that a man from one country can marry a woman from another?"

"We were introduced. Tobias visited Amsterdam regularly on business. One of his suppliers was a friend of my family. He asked if I would like to meet a charming young Englishman. We met, we fell in love, and four months later I moved to London as Tobias's wife." Hannah looked across the compartment at her husband, her brown eyes filled with fondness.

Rachel marveled at how an attraction could have blossomed between two such dissimilar people. She had fully warmed to Hannah, who was gracious and outgoing, but Tobias puzzled her. He seemed to be a very stuffy and somber man. "How do your children feel about belonging to two countries? Do they believe they are English or Dutch?"

Tobias folded his newspaper and set it down on the seat. "We were never fortunate enough to have children of our own."

"I see." Rachel dropped her gaze to her lap. In Russia, peasants spent more on drink than on their children. Here, two people who would have made loving parents had been denied the opportunity. Life was unfair not only under the Czar; it was unjust all over the world.

"But if we did have children," Hannah said quickly, "they

50

would most definitely feel English. Tobias would allow them to feel no other way. Is that not right, Tobias?"

When Tobias laughed at his wife's ribbing, Rachel began to understand better how they could have fallen in love in spite of their differences. Sometimes those very contrasts provided the attraction.

At London's Liverpool Street Station, a porter wheeled the baggage to a waiting carriage. The driver loaded the bags, then helped Hannah and Rachel to board. Tobias followed them inside. The driver cracked the whip, the horse broke into a trot, and Rachel pressed her face against the window.

"What is that?" She pointed through a crowd of horse-drawn transportation—carts, omnibuses, and hansom cabs—to a tall, ungainly vehicle that rocked along the street on steel rails.

"An electric tram," Tobias answered. "They have only just been placed in service. They take power from the line above."

"And that?" Rachel's finger indicated a smaller vehicle that moved without the aid of any animal.

"An autocar."

"Where does that take power from?"

Tobias laughed. "It provides its own power through something called an internal combustion engine."

Rachel shook her head in amazement. "One day soon there will be no need for horses."

"Thank God," Tobias answered. "When we can live without horses, we will be well on the way to unclogging our streets." He stroked his mustache. "For several months, I have been considering purchasing an autocar for my own use."

Hannah wagged a finger at her husband. "As long as you are married to me, considering is all you will do."

"If you do not move with the times, Hannah, you risk being left behind."

"Perhaps so, but I will be left behind in comfort, while you forge ahead in the greatest discomfort . . ."

"How many people live in London?" Rachel suddenly asked.

"Four and a half million."

So many . . . ! Rachel could not even begin to imagine such

a number. She kept her face to the window for the entire journey, watching in wonder as the densely packed buildings of the city's commercial center gave way to suburbs, and the suburbs themselves became grander, the houses larger and more graceful.

Hannah and Tobias lived in St. John's Wood, a bastion of dignified respectability on the northwestern edge of Regent's Park. Rachel's first glimpse of the Dekker home took her breath away. Tall, white, and elegant, the house sat in a garden full of blooming rosebushes and flowers of every color.

"Your home is like a palace," Rachel said.

"Thank you," Hannah responded. "We hope you will be very happy while you share our palace with us."

The carriage stopped. The front door of the house opened and a gray-haired man appeared, wearing a black tailcoat. Behind him walked a dumpy woman in a black dress with a white lace collar. Before the driver could open the carriage door, the butler swung it back.

"Welcome home, sir," he said to Tobias. "I trust that you and Mrs. Dekker had a pleasant trip."

"Excellent, thank you, Edwards."

"Madam . . ." The gray-haired man offered a hand to help Hannah descend, then Rachel.

"This young lady is our guest, Edwards," Tobias explained. In Yiddish, he added, "Rachel, this is Mr. Edwards, our head servant. In England, he is known by the title of butler. And that woman in the black dress is May, our housekeeper."

Rachel's eyes widened. "Two servants?"

Hannah put her arm around Rachel's shoulders and squeezed fondly. "Two servants would never be enough to run a house of this size. We have four."

Four servants! The lavishness of the house and grounds, the casual regard for so much wealth, made Rachel dizzy. She had exchanged reality for fantasy. Even as she followed Hannah and Tobias toward the front door of the house, she was convinced that at any moment she would wake up and find herself back in Russia. At the door, she stopped. There was her anchor to the truth. Fixed to the doorframe of this opulent house, exactly where God had declared it should be placed, was a *mezzuzah*. Rachel reached up to touch the sacred object, then kissed her fingers.

Tobias took her arm as she crossed into the entrance hall. "Welcome to your new home, Rachel. Your first task is to learn English, and there exists no better way to learn a language than to use it to the exclusion of everything else. From now on, we will speak only English. Do not forget your other languages. They will be valuable in the future. But from this moment, let English become your first language. After all, if any finer language existed, would Shakespeare not have written in it?"

Scared of showing ignorance, Rachel did not ask who Shakespeare was.

Rachel's life turned upside down. She had a complete wardrobe made by Hannah's dressmaker. She visited Tobias's business, a store in Regent Street that specialized in gourmet food and wine imported from Europe. She lived in greater comfort than she had ever dreamed possible. Yet while surrounded by all this luxury, she was beset by confusion and frustration, and the knowledge that she did not belong.

The Dekkers' servants spoke only English. When Rachel wanted something, she had to gesture; the servants, in turn, had to accompany their English responses with mime. Tobias spoke English exclusively when he returned home each evening from his business. Only Hannah exhibited a little sympathy, using Yiddish to explain the meaning of an English word.

The bewilderment accompanied Rachel even to the synagogue. Accustomed to Russian synagogues that were, by necessity, unpretentious, she was stunned by the splendor of the house of worship she attended with Hannah and Tobias. Stained-glass windows admitted light; marble pillars supported lofty ceilings. Rachel felt she was at a church.

After two weeks, Hannah entered Rachel's bedroom to find the young woman sitting at her mahogany dressing table, sobbing. "What is it? What is the matter?"

Rachel turned her tear-streaked face to Hannah. "I do not

53

belong here. You and your husband are more kind than anyone could ever be, but I am out of place. I cannot communicate with other people except by sign language. I can hear, I can speak, but I can make no one understand. Nor can I understand them."

"Be patient, Rachel. You will learn soon, believe me."

The next day, when Tobias returned from his store, he gave Rachel three books. One was a Russian-English dictionary; the others were textbooks of English for Russian students. Rachel examined them joyfully.

"Where did you find these?"

Tobias wagged a finger at her. "In English."

Rachel thumbed through the dictionary, writing down the words she sought. At last, and with no little pride, she asked, "Where you do find these books?"

Tobias beamed. English words coupled with Russian syntax was enough to make him cringe, but it was a noteworthy beginning.

Rachel spent hours each day studying. She deliberately sought conversations with Hannah. She talked with the servants, with deliverymen who came to the door, with anyone who would talk to her. At night, when Tobias returned from work, she showed off what she had learned during the day. And on the evenings when the Dekkers gave formal dinner parties, Rachel involved herself in every conversation, no matter what the subject. After four months of such furiously dedicated study, she could speak and write English passably.

Confident now, she broached a subject which had bothered her more and more as time had passed. "I owe you so much," she told Tobias and Hannah. "I must begin to repay you for the kindness you have shown. I could work for your business. Now that I speak English and other languages, I would be an . . ." She struggled for a moment before recalling the proper word. "An outstanding asset."

"An outstanding asset, eh?" Tobias smiled at her choice of words. "Indeed, there *is* an area in which you could be an outstanding asset, but it has nothing to do with my business."

"Then tell me, where?"

"The trickle of people fleeing from Russian tyranny has become a surging tide. Those who can afford to do so sail on to America. Thousands of others end their journey here. London's East End, already a teeming slum, is saturated with penniless refugees. It is the responsibility of established Jews to help these newcomers settle down and become responsible members of society."

Rachel felt a spontaneous warmth toward Tobias. She wanted to hug him. "Your words remind me of my father. He always said that God gave people wealth as a test, to learn whether they would use such riches to help those less fortunate."

"Much work is needed to assimilate these newcomers," Hannah said. "Many are illiterate in even their own language. Left to their own devices, they would speak Yiddish forever. They would never leave the ghetto. Instead, they would bring the ghetto way of life here, to England, and imprison their children in it."

"Unless we change the ghetto mentality, these newcomers will remain outcasts forever," Tobias said. "Then all Jews, including those who have lived here for many generations, will suffer."

"Do you offer help because of a genuine desire to assist less fortunate people or simply to protect yourself?"

Tobias gazed solemnly at Rachel for several seconds before answering. "The two reasons are inseparable."

"How could I help?"

"I am reasonably wealthy. Not in the same league as the Rothschilds, with their five-story mansion in Piccadilly and their liveried coachmen and servants, but I am very comfortable. It has long been a dream of mine, Rachel, to build a settlement in the East End, a club for boys that, while offering fellowship, will build character and patriotism. Two such organizations exist already. There is more than enough room and need for a third such club, which is the one I shall open."

"The boys and their parents will need models to look up to," said Hannah. "You will be such a model."

"Me?" Rachel could not keep the surprise out of her voice. "I am a girl. How could I be a model for boys?"

"Only a few months ago you went through hell in Kishinev. You lost far more than most. You will be a shining example of what can be achieved if one has the will to achieve it."

In bed that night, Rachel lay on her back and stared up at the ceiling. Was this the reason that she had been spared? To help other victims of oppression? To settle them before their strange ways, their starkly different culture, made them victims of yet another persecution? Was this the footprint her father wanted her to leave?

Somehow, it all made incredible sense.

Escorted by Tobias, Rachel toured London's East End. After four months of pampered life in St. John's Wood, the sudden immersion into the seething nucleus of eastern European immigration was a trip back in time, returning Rachel to the worst areas of the Pale. Dilapidated houses burst with people; women with scarves dragged around their heads argued loudly with bearded street traders; a torrent of Yiddish echoed along narrow streets and courts that reeked of cooking.

"Are the refugees who went to America better off?"

Tobias shook his head. "In New York, immigrants gather in an area called the Lower East Side, where they face the same struggle they face here. The same rack-renting landlords, and, God forgive me for saying it, the same abusive Jewish employers who live off the backs of their immigrant workers. And just like here, the virtuous Gentile store owners, while loudly criticizing such exploitation, are only too willing to enrich themselves by selling such produce for an exorbitant profit."

"However poor these people are here, their lot is still not as unfavorable as it was in Russia. Bloodthirsty mobs do not run riot, nor do sword-swinging soldiers ride through the streets."

Tobias chuckled at the manner in which Rachel defended her adopted country. "No, Rachel, such things do not occur. At least they have not occurred since All Saints Day in the year 1290."

In March 1904, Tobias bought a derelict warehouse in Whitechapel, in the very heart of the East End. An army of

56

plasterers, carpenters, and painters labored steadily to change the main storage area into an assembly hall, the offices into activity rooms. Tobias spent as much time as possible at the club site, overseeing the work. When he could no longer afford to be absent from his store, he asked Rachel to take his place.

"From now on, I will only be able to spend a few minutes here each day," he told Rachel. "It will be up to you to watch that the builders do their work properly."

"Why do you not ask Hannah to do this? The men would be more likely to respect a mature woman."

"She is busy with other matters, while you have the time to stay here. Don't worry, you will manage such authority well." Tobias had confidence in Rachel; anyone who had survived as she had done surely did not lack inner strength. Yet he knew that sometimes she doubted herself. By giving her such responsibility, Tobias intended to show Rachel just how strong she was.

At first, the builders paid little attention to the young auburn-haired woman who studied the plans and checked the work being done. Such indifference ceased when she took aside the foreman, a tall, black-haired Irishman, to complain about flooring work in an activity room. "If my slight weight can make the floorboards squeak and move, what will happen when heavier people walk on them every day? You have used poor wood."

"And what would a little girl like yourself be knowing about good and bad floorboards?" the foreman asked.

Rachel looked into the man's broad, florid face. He stood a foot taller than she, and he was grinning. The other men watched, enjoying the unexpected show. Her words came through clenched teeth. "I am not a little girl. I am eighteen—"

"Eighteen, are you? My, that is ancient." Amusement gave way to irritation. "Well, Miss Eighteen, I work for Mr. Tobias Dekker and that's the only person who tells me what to do. No man takes orders from a slip of a girl like you."

"And I speak for Mr. Dekker."

"Do you now?" The foreman turned his back on Rachel and walked away.

Quite calmly, Rachel left the building and traveled to Tobias's store in Regent Street. Tobias returned with her to the East End. He walked once across the floorboards and told the foreman to replace them. "I am a busy man, too busy to be called here to discuss every inconsequential detail. In the future, you will kindly heed instructions from Miss Isakharov."

"The men won't like it, sir."

"Really? Then we will have to find men who do."

There were no more problems.

As the weather improved, the work moved outside. Rotten gutters and drainpipes were replaced. Wooden trim was scraped and painted. Rachel supervised the delivery of furniture and equipment—tables and chairs for the reading and games rooms, desks, sporting equipment. Finally, in the first week of October, six months after the project's start, a blue-and-white painted sign was fixed into place over the building entrance. It read: The Dekker Boys' Club. Above the sign fluttered the Union Jack. Just inside the entrance was a smaller sign listing the club's officers. At the top, as founders, were Tobias and Hannah Dekker. Tobias's name appeared again on the line below, as chairman. Beneath it, and a size smaller, were the names of the club's dozen volunteer managers, enthusiastic young men from respected families who would help to shape the sons of England's newest immigrants into citizens who would be proud of their country, and of whom England would be proud.

Across the bottom of the sign was the title of Administrator. Next to it was Rachel's name.

The Dekker Boys' Club met with instant success. More than four hundred boys, ranging in age from ten to sixteen, joined during the first week. Despite a diminishing rate of enrollment during the following weeks, the club's volunteer staff was stretched to breaking point.

Early each weekday morning, Rachel traveled by omnibus from St. John's Wood to Whitechapel, arriving at the club just after nine-thirty. At that time of day, her only company was the caretaker. In her third-floor office, she read reports left by the managers who had supervised the club the previous evening. She noted what activities had been popular; also if there had been any trouble. Afterward, accompanied by the caretaker, she inspected the entire building to check whether maintenance was required. In the afternoons, she made herself available for anyone who had business with the club. She discussed noise complaints with local officials, and gave information on activities to the reporter from the *East London Observer,* the local newspaper. Mostly, though, she met with anxious parents of boys who attended the club.

These meetings almost always followed a pattern. The parents entered Rachel's office, uncomfortable in the presence of this self-assured young woman whom they assumed to be English.

"How can I help you?" she would ask.

The answer was delivered in painful, halting English. "We came to this country so our children would have a future, but now we find that our sons are becoming strangers to us. They learn things here and at school which separate them from us."

"Would you prefer to speak Yiddish?" Rachel asked.

Shocked, the parents stared at Rachel. "*You* speak Yiddish?"

"I am from Kishinev. I left there a year ago." Each time she made the admission, she could see the barriers being lowered. Despite her appearance, the parents knew they were speaking to one of their own. "At school and in this club, your sons absorb ideas. They learn about this country, about a different way of life. This should not make them strangers to you. You must try to keep up with them."

The parents left Rachel's office with information about adult evening classes where they could learn to read and write English, if necessary to add and subtract. Most important, they left with the knowledge that in coming to England they had made the right decision. Now it was up to them to capitalize on it.

Rachel left the club at six o'clock, as the managers for that evening's activities arrived. Her work was not finished. Three times a week she attended night school to study typing and Pitman shorthand. When she returned to St. John's Wood, she informed Tobias and Hannah of actions she had taken that day at the club. Tobias always approved. In a country where women were only just awakening to the knowledge that they did not even have the right to vote, Tobias was content to let a young woman, not quite nineteen, care for the day-to-day operation of his dream. His opinion of Rachel as a hard-working, conscientious young woman was reinforced with everything he saw her do.

Tobias and Hannah visited the club each Sunday afternoon, to watch activities and talk to members and managers. One evening a month, when the club was closed, the managers came to St. John's Wood for dinner. Afterward, in the drawing room, club matters were discussed. By January, after three months of studying shorthand and typing as tenaciously as she had studied English, Rachel was skillful enough to record the minutes of the meeting. Proudly, she read them back to start the February meeting.

"Montague DaCosta reported that the reading room is finally being used."

"Is that welcome trend continuing?" Tobias asked.

DaCosta, a dark-skinned young man who worked for his father's bank in the City, nodded. "I am happy to say that it is. I have also been asked if books could be taken home. I think we should entertain the possibility of operating a lending library."

Rachel noted the suggestion. "Max Goldschmidt"—she raised her head to look at Goldschmidt, who was serving articles with a law firm in which his father was a partner—"reported that the debating club was becoming very popular."

"The boys no longer shout at each other like common street traders," Goldschmidt said in a satisfied tone. "Now they put forth reasoned arguments."

Rachel returned to her notes. "Benjamin Beerbohm reported the only problem. An outbreak of gambling."

"Is that still happening, Benjamin?" Tobias asked.

Beerbohm, a twenty-year-old who intended to follow in the footsteps of his doctor father, nodded. "Among a group of older working boys, it is an epidemic. We told them gambling was forbidden, but it made no difference. In the games room, while others play chess or dominoes, these boys brazenly play cards."

Tobias's face wore a pained expression. "How do we deal with this awkward problem?"

A forest of arms shot into the air; voices called for the guilty boys to be barred from the club. Tobias shook his head. "Our mission is to bring boys into the club, not throw them out. We need something more original than the threat of expulsion." One hand remained aloft. "Jacob?"

Jacob Lesser lowered his hand. "Have you noticed, Benjamin, whether these boys play any particular game?"

"They favor one." Beerbohm's clipped voice echoed with distaste. "A game with three cards, where pretending to have a good hand seems to be as important as actually having one."

"Brag, an old English game." Jacob smiled. "I consider myself a skillful enough cardplayer to be able to teach these boys a lesson at Brag which they will never forget."

Rachel's pencil hung in midair. "You would play cards with them? We want to deter these boys, not encourage them."

"Winning every farthing they have will be a deterrent."

"And just supposing," Hannah said, "these boys win every farthing *you* have?"

"I can support my skill with legerdemain. Sleight of hand is a hobby of mine. If you have cards, I will demonstrate."

Hannah fetched a pack. While everyone watched closely, Jacob shuffled the cards with long, slim fingers, held them down in a fan, and offered them to Rachel. "Choose a card." She did. Jacob's bright blue eyes twinkled. "Why did you make it so easy for me by choosing the ace of diamonds?"

Flustered by Jacob's attention, Rachel started to protest. "I did not make it easy . . ." She lifted the card. It was the ace of diamonds. Jacob told her to take another, and guessed right again. He proceeded to amuse his audience by performing a couple of card tricks, ending with a demonstration of dealing from the bottom of the pack, and dealing the second card.

"You would cheat boys out of their money?" Hannah

61

asked. She looked at Tobias. "I am not certain we can allow this."

"Would you prefer the boys to lose a little money," Jacob asked, "which I will return to them later on? Or would you rather they were expelled from the club?"

"Swindle the little gamblers out of everything they have," Tobias said. "It will teach them a valuable lesson."

"Should I include this in the minutes?" Rachel asked.

"Certainly," Jacob answered. "I want it on record that I am a bad influence."

Rachel wrote down that Jacob Lesser had offered to solve the club's gambling problem by cheating at cards. His unorthodox solution came as no surprise. Tall and fit, with curly fair hair and an open face that inspired friendship, he was different from the other volunteer managers in nearly every possible way. While most had opted for careers in commerce or law, often in companies controlled by their fathers, Jacob, whose own father was a cabinetmaker, had selected the poorly paid profession of teaching. Twenty-four years old, he had taught for the past two years at the Jewish Free School in Bell Lane. In the operation of the club, his contributions were oddly diverse. DaCosta, Beerbohm, Goldschmidt, and the other managers stressed cultural and academic pursuits. Jacob's idea of a good time for the boys involved group activity and strenuous physical exercise. He gave boxing and wrestling instruction, conducted a club choir, and planned to lead country hikes once the weather turned decent.

"When will you work your deception on these innocent boys?" Rachel asked.

"Tomorrow night. Why do you ask?"

His eyes nearly hypnotized her. She saw laughter in them, as though he was willing her to smile back. She refused. She would not let him know how much he had affected her. "I want to be there. I want to see you lose."

The laughter spread from Jacob's eyes to his face. "If I can make an intelligent young woman like you choose the card I want you to choose, do you think I'll have trouble with foolish boys?"

* * *

Benjamin Beerbohm pointed out the gamblers. Four boys of fifteen and sixteen years—two and three years younger than Rachel herself—played cards at a table, while others in the games room moved dominoes or pushed chessmen around a board. The gamblers were boys who had left school at fourteen and worked in factories or shops. Rachel understood why managers like Beerbohm scorned such boys. With their own backgrounds, most of the managers could identify only with boys who had higher aspirations.

"Morris Bloom is the boy dealing," Beerbohm said. "The others are Nathan Rabinowitz, Ben Scheff, and Harry Myers."

"They play for matchsticks," Rachel said.

"Matchsticks must represent money," Jacob explained. He led the way over to the card game. "Who's winning?"

Harry Myers, a skinny youth with an expression of fierce concentration stamped on his face, pointed to the pile of matches in front of him.

"I've got some matches. How about letting me play?"

Morris Bloom put down the cards. A heavyset boy, his coarse accent was pure East End. "Why not? Your matches are as good as anyone else's, right?"

Jacob pulled up a fifth chair. Rachel and Beerbohm walked away, pretending to be interested in other games. Every minute or so, they looked over to the table where Jacob played.

"That's the third hand in a row that he's lost," Beerbohm whispered as Jacob threw down his cards. Myers reached out to pull in the pot of more than two dozen matches. "The only lesson they're going to learn from him is that gambling pays."

Rachel swore she heard satisfaction in Beerbohm's voice. With the other managers, he thought the gamblers should be thrown out. But when Jacob lost a fourth, fifth, and sixth hand, she began to wonder whether Beerbohm and the others were not right.

"See how flustered Jacob is," Beerbohm said. "He is being hoisted with his own petard."

Rachel looked. Jacob did seem nervous. He talked excitedly and pushed more matches into the center of the table. Rachel's eyes dropped to Jacob's hands, those long, slender fingers that had bewitched the cards at the Dekker home the previous evening. There was nothing reckless about their deft movement; nothing that paralleled the rest of his demeanor. While Jacob talked, his fingers cradled the cards, caressed them, then flicked them across the table. The boys picked them up. A smile flashed across Harry Myers' face, there one moment, gone the next, as he realized he was advertising his good fortune. Similar smiles appeared momentarily on the faces of the other boys. Jacob's face wore no expression at all.

"Look how they eagerly wager," Beerbohm whispered to Rachel. "This time they are going to bankrupt him."

A betting frenzy was taking place. Each boy pushed out a bigger pile of matches than the boy before him. And when it came to Jacob . . . stone-faced, he shoved out the biggest pile of all! Harry Myers looked from the mountain of matches in the center of the table to his own hand, to Jacob's face, then back to his own cards again. The bet increased. Rachel walked to the table. No one took any notice of her. Ben Scheff and Morris Bloom, with no matches left, dropped out. Nathan Rabinowitz pushed out his last matches. Jacob equaled the bet, and raised one more time.

"You bluff," Myers said harshly. He pushed out everything he had in front of him. Rabinowitz, with no money left, folded. Without looking at his cards, Jacob equaled the bet. "Three kings," Myers said smugly.

"Three aces," Jacob responded calmly. He looked up at Rachel and winked.

While Myers stared numbly at the winning hand, Rabinowitz muttered in disbelief, "I had three queens."

"Are you going into the match business, Jacob?" Rachel asked.

"No. I am going into the money business. Each of these matches is worth a penny. I would like"—he counted leisurely, letting tension build—"eight shillings and tenpence, please."

Myers dipped into his pocket. "I lost three shillings . . ."

"I lost half a crown," Morris Bloom grumbled.

Rachel drew in her breath. Such sums constituted a fortune for these boys. Jacob took the money, stood up, and walked away. Rachel followed him. "Are you not going to return the money?" she asked.

"I will, but first I'm going to let those little miscreants worry for a while. Why don't you and I go out for a walk?"

Rachel fetched her coat. Once they were two hundred yards from the club, Jacob slipped his arm through Rachel's. "I saw you watching and worrying," he said. "Was Benjamin Beerbohm claiming that I was making a fool of myself?"

"With every breath." Rachel impersonated Beerbohm's terse speech. "The only lesson they're going to learn is that gambling pays. See how Jacob is hoisting himself with his own petard."

Jacob roared with laughter and squeezed Rachel's arm. "I bet stupidly early on. I lost deliberately to show I was a poor player. Then I arranged the cards. They were so busy watching my face, eagerly anticipating how much they could win, they neglected to watch my fingers. I gave them very good cards, but I saved the best for myself."

"You are a very clever man, Jacob Lesser."

"And you are a very perceptive young lady."

They remained out for half an hour. When they returned to the club, they found the four gamblers in the reading room. "If I give you back your money, will you promise never to play cards here again?" Jacob asked.

The boys agreed. "I've got to know something," Harry Myers said. "That last hand—was it honest, or did you cheat?"

Jacob's face turned red. "You think because a man is a better card player than you, he is a cheat? How dare you?"

Myers dropped his gaze to the floor. "Sorry, Mr. Lesser."

"That's better." Jacob handed back the money he had won. "Remember, no more gambling in the club. Or outside, if you know what's good for you. You four are sheep among wolves."

The March meeting of club managers coincided with Rachel's nineteenth birthday. An elaborate cake finished off the dinner. In the drawing room afterward, Rachel read her report: " 'I am pleased to report that gambling is no longer a problem. Despite a general feeling that the boys in question be barred, Jacob Lesser's unconventional method proved most satisfactory. The boys have promised to refrain from gambling in the future. I propose that we record a vote of thanks for Jacob.' "

"And I second it," Tobias responded.

Rachel caught Jacob's gaze. His face was crimson again, just like when he had feigned indignation. Only this time he was blushing. Rachel liked that.

Eager to see more of Jacob, Rachel worked later at the club. Her daytime hours overlapped the hours worked by the managers. To her disappointment, Jacob did not return her interest. When he arrived at the club after teaching all day, he greeted her only with simple courtesy. Any warmth of feeling was reserved for the boys. Rachel could almost touch the bond that existed; the boys responded to him like youngsters with a favored older brother. Whatever activities he supervised—boxing and wrestling, choir practice, or giving a demonstration of his conjuring skills—he elicited adulation. Even, Rachel saw, from the four boys with whom he had played Brag!

They approached her after watching a magic show. "Mr. Lesser did cheat us that time, didn't he?" Harry Myers said.

Rachel kept a straight face. "No, he simply taught the four of you a well-deserved lesson."

Laughing, the boys walked away. Watching them, an astounding revelation struck Rachel. She was jealous! These boys lived one step above poverty—they barely knew that a world existed outside the squalor of London's East End— and she was jealous! She envied the closeness they shared with Jacob Lesser!

Rachel took her problem to the only person in whom she could confide. "Hannah, how do I make Jacob aware that I exist? The other managers pay attention to me, but Jacob . . . ?" Rachel snapped her fingers. "That is all I am to him."

"The other managers are not Jacob Lesser. Max and Montague and the rest do splendid work, but it is done as much for their own egos as for the boys' welfare. Jacob is different. He is selfless. He cares only for the boys. He works with them at school, and he continues his work at the club. Tobias wanted Jacob to be a manager because he saw much of himself in Jacob."

66

"I see no similarity."

"You have to look deeply. The club means everything to Tobias. If it were humanly possible, he would involve himself in every activity. He is a boy who never grew up. In Jacob, he sees the same youthfulness, the same determination. And in Jacob, Tobias sees the man who will eventually take over complete control of the Dekker Boys' Club and carry it into the future."

Rachel held up her hands. "That is wonderful, but it does not answer my question. How do I make Jacob interested in me?"

"Involve yourself directly with his work."

"It will be difficult."

"Nothing worthwhile," responded Hannah, "is ever easy."

At the beginning of April, Jacob announced he would lead a country hike in two weeks time, and asked who wanted to join him. Twenty boys immediately volunteered. So did Rachel.

"You?" Jacob asked.

"I have stout walking shoes."

"Yes, but you are a girl."

Rachel saw the same expression on Jacob's face that she had witnessed on the face of the Irish building foreman. The blend of amusement and disbelief infuriated her. "I walked halfway across Russia. Do not talk so disparagingly of my being a girl."

On the day of the hike, Rachel took her place with Jacob. Under a cloudy sky, they rode the train for an hour to a small village in the Essex countryside. There, they walked along narrow rural roads and across open fields. For many boys, it was their first glimpse of farm animals and open country. Rachel, heading the human crocodile with Jacob, overheard snatches of excited conversation. Suddenly, the subject changed.

"Mr. Lesser's brought his lady friend with him."

"Wonder if he's going to kiss her?"

Biting back a smile, Rachel looked sideways at Jacob. He strode along, head up, blue eyes wide and clear, fair hair lifting in the breeze. Hannah's description of Tobias echoed in Rachel's mind: the boy who had never grown up. She could see it now. A big boy happy only when in the company of other boys.

Without turning his head, Jacob said, "Is their gossip embarrassing you?"

"Not at all. I find it quite amusing."

After an hour, when they had covered more than two miles, Jacob held up his hand. "After all that exercise, you should have wonderful appetites. We'll stop for lunch."

The boys sat down on the grass to eat the sandwiches they had brought. Jacob, sitting off to the side with Rachel, offered her one of his cheese-and-cucumber sandwiches. In return, she gave him one of her own. He peeked inside and raised his eyebrows. "Smoked salmon. Thank you."

"When I live in the home of a man who owns a gourmet food store, what else would it be?"

Jacob chewed the sandwich, all the while gazing at Rachel. "What do you feel about Tobias and Hannah Dekker?"

"I love them both very dearly. Sometimes"—Rachel twisted a piece of grass between her fingers—"I feel that I could not love Hannah and Tobias more if they were my own mother and father."

Jacob was silent for a while. At last, he said, "When they found you alone in Rotterdam after you had lost your brother and brought you to England, they did everyone an enormous favor."

Only then did Rachel realize that Tobias and Hannah had never told anyone that she had tried to kill herself. Her love for them grew even deeper. Jacob leaned across and touched her hand. "Didn't you hear what I just said?" Rachel regarded him blankly, and shook her head. "I paid you a compliment. I showed that not only am I aware of your existence, I am also delighted by it."

Rachel recognized her own words. "Did Hannah speak to you?"

Jacob just laughed.

After the boys finished eating, Jacob gathered them in a semicircle for a singsong. Before they were halfway through the first song, rain started falling. Jacob pulled out a pocket watch. "A train leaves for London in forty-five minutes. I propose that we catch it."

The return to the station was made in a half-walk, half-run. Rachel was soaking wet and breathless when they arrived. Her hair clung to her head; water ran into her eyes. "How does this compare with walking halfway across Russia?" Jacob teased.

"This is nothing. We did ten times as much before we stopped for breakfast."

Jacob reached out, took her face in his hands, and kissed her. A chorus of wolf whistles erupted. Jacob turned around. "If you put as much energy into your singing as you put into your rude gestures, we would have a chorus of nightingales."

The train arrived ten minutes later. Twenty thoroughly soaked boys spent the entire journey singing at the top of their lungs. Twenty-one, Rachel thought, if you included the biggest boy of all, who conducted his makeshift choir with a twig. When they reached Liverpool Street Station, their faces were flushed with pleasure, and their eyes brimmed with excitement. Despite the rain, the hike in the country had been an enormous success. And for Rachel, clothes hanging soggily from her body, it had been the happiest day she could remember.

Next day at the club, Jacob took Rachel into her office and closed the door. "I am sorry that the weather was not better for our first rendezvous."

"I did not realize that yesterday was a rendezvous."

"We went out together, did we not?" He laughed, and Rachel joined in. "May we try again later this week? Thursday, perhaps? I could call for you at St. John's Wood; we could go out for a walk, or even see a show."

"But you live so far away, Jacob."

"Shoreditch? It is not so far." He shrugged his shoulders to dismiss the distance. Shoreditch, where Jacob shared his parents' home, was located two miles north of the club. "You make longer journeys each day to Whitechapel. I would gladly travel twice that distance to be with you."

Warmth coursed through Rachel's body. No man had ever spoken to her in this manner; nor had she ever felt for any man the way she felt for Jacob. From the moment he had used her to demonstrate his conjuring skill, she had been

69

under his spell. "Thank you," she told him. "I look forward to Thursday."

But when Jacob traveled to St. John's Wood three days later, it was not to take Rachel out. That morning she had woken with a streaming nose and a high temperature. Hannah had contacted Jacob at school to say that Rachel would be unable to keep their appointment. Rather than miss seeing her completely, he chose to visit her. Unexpected, he arrived at the Dekker home that evening. Edwards, the butler, led him through to the dining room, where Hannah and Tobias were just sitting down to eat.

"Jacob, what are you doing here?" Hannah asked.

"I came to see Rachel."

"She is in bed. She ate dinner in her room. You cannot go in there. She'll give you her cold, for heaven's sake."

"As I am responsible for her catching the cold in the first place, that would seem only fair. Besides"—he held up a box of chocolates—"I thought these might cheer her up."

Tobias turned to the butler. "Please ask May to see if Miss Rachel is up to receiving a visitor."

"A very special visitor," Hannah added.

The housekeeper entered the dining room a minute later to announce that Rachel would welcome her visitor. Jacob followed May to Rachel's bedroom. The smell of eucalyptus filled the air. Rachel sat up in a four-poster bed. Jacob thought she looked like a child, so tiny against the huge pillows that propped up her back. Her face was swollen, her eyes red. Despite her discomfort, she managed to smile at Jacob.

"Did our rendezvous in the country cause this?" Jacob asked.

Rachel shook her head. "I refuse to believe that anything so joyful could bring on something so miserable. This cold must be from a germ I picked up when we returned to London." She saw the chocolates. "Are those for me?"

"If it were later in the year, I would have brought you red roses instead."

A tear formed in the corner of Rachel's right eye. Instead of dabbing it with the lace handkerchief she held, she allowed it to run unchecked down her cheek. Jacob leaned forward and stopped the tear's path with his finger. "Rachel, our love has not enjoyed the most auspicious of beginnings, has it? Our first time together, we got soaked. And our second time is spent in your sickroom."

Rachel laughed. "If love can survive those hardships, it can survive anything."

Disregarding germs, Jacob leaned across the bed to kiss Rachel on the lips.

Chapter Four

The *Rijndam,* carrying Zalman Isakharov, reached New York on June 30, 1903. The voyage had altered Zalman. He had lost ten pounds. His nose seemed longer, thinner, the deep-set eyes more hollow. Beneath a two-week beard, his cheeks stood out sharply. Despite the weight loss, and the staleness of the clothes he had worn since leaving Europe, he felt exceptionally well. The sea air had cleared his head. Anticipation filled his brain.

The ship docked initially at the Holland-America pier. Watching first- and second-class passengers disembark, Zalman thought about Leopold Metgot, the Dutch swindler who had sold him the forged second-class tickets for the *Potsdam.* Had Metgot been an honest man, he would still be alive. And Zalman, with Rachel, would be among those passengers now disembarking.

From the Holland-America pier, the ship made its final stop: Ellis Island, for immigration processing. Zalman joined lines, answered questions, endured examinations. Because he was young, healthy, and spoke English, his progress was swift. Around him, families cried out as they were separated; entry into the United States, for one reason or another, was denied them. Zalman remained aloof from the turmoil. His only concern was to board a ferry carrying approved immigrants from Ellis Island to Manhattan.

An immigration officer stunned him with a totally unexpected question. "Do you wish to change your name?"

Zalman considered the proposal. A family name was a

treasure to be passed from generation to generation. It was not an old piece of clothing to be discarded when its usefulness was ended; to do so betrayed a heritage. "What could I change it to?"

"Whatever you like."

He left Ellis Island with a new name: Zalman Isaacson. He had coupled his own given name with an American version of the totally alien Isakharov. It was a compromise, not a betrayal.

The ferry berthed at the Battery. People crowded Battery Park, eager to meet newly arrived family members. Zalman paid no attention to the joyous reunions. He checked his gold-and-enamel watch. The hands showed fifteen minutes after three. He had to find a place to stay, and a shop to buy fresh clothes. He ran a hand across his beard. A razor also. He was starting life all over again, but he was not worried. In a country where you could change your name in the blink of an eyelid, an ambitious man who was willing to work hard could go very far.

Notwithstanding such positive qualities, Zalman made slow progress. He tried many jobs, among them waiter in a restaurant, clerk in a hardware store, hat salesman, and manager of a penny arcade. Although his soft-spoken manner and able performance won praise from superiors, he rarely stayed in one job more than three months. He learned whatever he could and moved on.

He spent his twenty-first birthday working in Paddy Mulligan's downtown saloon. Six days a week he poured drinks and talked to customers from early afternoon until late at night. Of all the jobs he had held, this was his favorite. Mulligan was a genial bald-headed man who treated his staff well. The pay, including living quarters above the saloon, was good; the customers were generous. The greatest appeal, however, was the diverse crowd Mulligan's attracted: City Hall employees, businessmen, lawyers, policemen. In two months behind the bar, Zalman learned far more about his adopted country than in two years since leaving Ellis Island.

Most interesting of all were the newspapermen from nearby Park Row. Mulligan's was a favorite hangout for employees of Hearst's New York *American.* Zalman's expe-

73

rience of newspapers was limited to the *Bessarabatz;* the lesson he had learned there was that the printed word represented power. The *American* men fascinated him. He reserved his best service for them, and when he was not busy, he hovered nearby, eavesdropping. No one paid attention to the uninvited listener until one September night, when conversation among four Hearst men centered on that morning's rush-hour crash of an elevated train at Ninth Avenue and Fifty-third Street.

"Twelve dead, bodies everywhere, and half the damned train hanging off the track into the street," declared a tall, burly man in a dark-gray suit. "What a godawful, glorious mess! The minute we got a good picture, we had an extra edition on the presses, and the newsboys all set to hawk it." He paused to take a deep swallow of his beer. "Now if there's a better way to sell papers than splashing blood and guts all over the front page, my name's Teddy Roosevelt!"

Zalman had seen the speaker often. Red-faced, with thick black hair, he patronized Mulligan's two or three evenings a week, drinking heavily and dominating whatever conversation he joined. The other men called him Jimmy. "How can you speak so callously about the misfortune of others?" Zalman asked.

The four men turned around. Jimmy answered. "Because in New York, newspaper publishing is a very callous business."

"It is the same all over the world. Where I come from—"

"And where would that be?"

"Russia."

"Russia, eh?" Jimmy's dark-brown eyes sparkled with mischief. "What do you call yourself then—Mulligan's Jew?"

As laughter burst from the Hearst men, Zalman vaulted over the bar. He swung his fist. The blow caught Jimmy on the shoulder, knocking him back. Before Zalman could strike again, two men grabbed his arms and held him helpless. Jimmy regained his balance and stepped forward. Zalman tensed in anticipation of the punch from the much larger man, against whom he was now unable to defend himself.

Instead, Jimmy raised his hands in a gesture of peace. "It

74

was a joke, my boy. A pun. Haven't you heard that us Irishmen are famous for our wit? There's a dish called Mulligan Stew, so in a play on words, you're Mulligan's Jew. No offense was intended." He signaled for the other men to release Zalman. "Jimmy Doyle's my name. What do you prefer to be called?"

"Zalman Isaacson."

"Well, Zalman Isaacson, shake my hand and tell me you accept my apology."

"I accept your apology," Zalman said, shaking Doyle's hand.

He returned to the other side of the bar. Jimmy Doyle and his friends left Mulligan's ten minutes later. When Zalman collected their glasses, he found a dollar tip and a note in wide, flourishing letters that read: "No offense . . . Jimmy!"

Whenever Doyle entered Mulligan's after that, he raised his hand to Zalman and called out, "No offense intended!" And Zalman always replied, "None taken!" If Doyle came in alone, he stood at the bar talking to Zalman. The Irishman loved to talk and Zalman, eager to assimilate information, loved to listen. Despite dissimilar backgrounds, the two men learned they had much in common. They quickly became friends.

"You Jews talk about the hardships of Russia," Doyle told Zalman one night. "Believe me, Ireland under the British was no bargain either. I was twelve when my father brought us here from County Cork back in '85, and the only times I can remember from Ireland are hard times. Never any food in the pot, never any fuel for the fire, and never any clothes for our backs."

Zalman nodded sympathetically. "What difference is there between any of us? We are all refugees seeking a better life."

"That's what the beautiful lady in the harbor's all about. She wasn't there when I came over, but she must have been a welcome sight for you." Doyle's eyes softened. "Let me see now:

'Your huddled masses yearning to breathe free,/
The wretched refuse of your teeming shore/

75

Send these, the homeless, tempest-tossed to me:/
I lift my lamp beside the golden door.'

"That's the last four lines of the poem inscribed upon the lady. It was written by Emma Lazarus, you know, one of your people."

Zalman laughed. "It might have been written by one of my people, but no one could have quoted it with such intensity and meaning as an Irishman like you."

Doyle bowed his head at the compliment. He picked up his hat and coat, ready to leave. "I like good poetry. All Irish do. At least, the handful of the Irish who can read like it."

Zalman automatically assumed that Doyle was a reporter. It was a misconception he labored under for a month, until he asked why he never saw a Jimmy Doyle byline on a story.

Doyle looked at him as though he were mad. "A reporter, you think I am? A writer? I scorn the bloody word!"

"If you're not a reporter, what do you do?"

"I'm in circulation! That's the most important department of all! Without us there would be no newspapers. Circulation's the paper's lifeblood. Increase it, and you can increase your advertising rates. That makes more money so you can open more newspapers. Reporters . . . ? You can train a blasted monkey to be a reporter! Their stories fill the space between advertisements. And let me tell you something else, advertising salesmen aren't any better than reporters . . ."

Once started, Doyle could not stop. Zalman knew the Irishman exaggerated his own importance, but he so enjoyed listening to him that he did not interrupt. "Advertising people sell space on the basis of circulation, which people like me build up. You think the *American* gets around town by accident, do you? You think it's magic that folk in the Bronx and Brooklyn can get it? The hell it is, boy! It goes on sale everywhere because of hard work by people like me. Hard and dangerous work."

"What danger exists in selling newspapers?"

"Plenty. The *Sun,* the *World,* the *American,* and all the rest of them are after the same readers. Sometimes a circulation man's got to make his point with his mouth. Other times he's got to use these!" Doyle lifted two large red fists into the

76

air. "These have sold more newspapers than all the reporters put together." He shook his head in disgust. "And I thought we were friends, Zalman. How could you possibly mistake me for a bloody useless reporter?"

Zalman had only one response. "No offense intended."

"My boy, you came within an inch of offense being taken." Doyle slapped Zalman on the shoulder and laughed loudly.

Two weeks later, Zalman witnessed the perils of a circulation man's job. Jimmy Doyle entered Mulligan's just after midday, standing alone at the bar. Zalman was in the kitchen when the commotion started. He heard a crash, a shout, and a roar of rage. He rushed out to find Doyle with his back against the bar. Blood poured from a gash in the side of his head. Fists up, he faced three men, one of whom held a two-foot length of wood. The three other bartenders on duty stood like statues, while Paddy Mulligan, in the far corner of the saloon, yelled for someone to fetch a policeman. Zalman was the only person to move. He grabbed beneath the bar for the baseball bat that rested there and launched himself across the top of the bar. One of Doyle's assailants yelled in pain as the bat smashed across his upper arm. The man holding the length of wood lunged at Zalman. A swing of the bat knocked it clean out of his hand. The three men turned to run. Zalman chased them down the street, yelling at them not to come back.

He returned to the bar to find Doyle sitting down. Paddy Mulligan held a wet towel to the cut on his head.

"It's lucky you've got a thick Irish skull, Doyle," the saloon owner said. "Anyone else would have been knocked cold with that wallop he gave you."

Doyle grabbed Zalman's arm. "Jimmy Doyle owes you, my boy. Whenever you need anything, you know where to come."

"Who were those men?"

"*Sun* thugs who didn't take kindly to having a few thousand copies of their yellow rag end up on a bonfire yesterday."

"You destroyed your opposition's newspapers?"

"Now I didn't say that, did I? I've no idea *how* those papers got burned, but those *Sun* plug-uglies think it was

77

me." Doyle shook his head in exasperation. "They should know better than to believe such a thing. William Randolph Hearst would never allow his men to engage in such chicanery."

Maybe not, Zalman thought. But what Mr. William Randolph Hearst did not know could not hurt him.

Jimmy Doyle was the first real friend Zalman made in America. Two weeks before Christmas, Doyle came into Mulligan's and asked Zalman what plans he had for the holiday season.

"None. Why would Mulligan's Jew make Christmas plans?"

"I'm not one for all this religious malarkey, but it's a great excuse to have a good time with friends. My wife and I would like you to spend Christmas Day with us. Kathryn, that's my wife, drags the kids to church and all that, but I promise that no one will try to convert you."

Zalman accepted. He had never been invited to a Christmas Day celebration. He wondered what gifts to take. Whiskey for Doyle, flowers for his wife. What about Doyle's three children? He decided to buy toys. Early one morning, before Mulligan's opened, Zalman walked along a stretch of Fifth Avenue in the Forties. A children's shop called Blue Stone, in the Windsor Arcade, attracted his attention. After studying the window display of rocking horses, dolls, and games, he went inside.

One sales clerk was on duty, a young woman with long black hair tucked into a bun. Her black skirt trailed the floor; a stark white blouse with puffed sleeves covered her upper body.

"May I help you, sir?"

He looked into her eyes. They were deep brown, with a luminous, liquid quality. "I want to buy toys for three children, but I don't know where to begin."

Her smile lit up her entire face, but it shone brightest in her eyes. "How old are your children, sir?"

"They are not mine. They belong to a friend. Boys of eleven and nine, and a girl of eight."

"Perhaps the boys would like some clockwork toys, sir. And no eight-year-old girl ever refuses a doll's house."

Her formality made him uncomfortable. "My name is Zalman Isaacson, not *sir*. And you . . . ?"

Crimson tinged the young woman's cheeks. "Julia Bluestone."

Zalman remembered the shop's name. "You own this place?"

"My father, Louis Bluestone, is the owner. I'll find some toys your friend's children will like."

She disappeared into the storeroom, returning with an ornate doll's house which she set on the counter. "This is from Germany. As you can see, no effort has been spared in the construction of this charming house. The wall swings back to reveal the interior. Look at the furniture in each room, how attention has been paid to the smallest detail."

"Very nice. How much is it?"

"Twenty dollars, Mr. Isaacson."

"I am afraid that such a sum is out of my range."

"I understand." Julia returned the doll's house to its place. She came back with a blond-haired doll and two clockwork tinplate toys—a trolley and a train. Zalman accepted them.

"I hope your friend's children like their gifts."

"I am certain they will." Now that his business was over, he was reluctant to leave. "If they do not, would it be possible to exchange them?"

"Of course." The door opened. Two women entered. Julia turned her attention to them, and Zalman left.

The following morning, carrying the blond-haired doll, he returned. Julia stood alone at the counter.

"I wonder if I could exchange the doll."

"Was there something wrong with it?"

"No. My friend's daughter wants a doll with hair like her own. Beautiful black hair. Just like yours, in fact."

Julia's face reddened. "I'm sure we have something that will satisfy her." She took the doll from Zalman, tearing her eyes away from his with difficulty. This man unsettled her. He was unlike other young men she knew. They were self-assured, comfortable, set in prosperous career paths.

Zalman's leanness reminded Julia of a tightly coiled spring; the sharp lines of his face emitted power and energy.

She brought back a doll with jet-black hair. Zalman examined it closely. "Perfect. It even has the same beautiful brown eyes that you have."

"I thought you were seeking a doll that resembled your friend's daughter."

Zalman just smiled.

The following morning, he repeated the trip to Windsor Arcade. This time he carried the clockwork trolley. He had his excuse all prepared: his friend's son wanted a stagecoach. He chuckled. Julia Bluestone would get a shock when he walked in again. Instead, the shock was Zalman's. Julia was not in the shop. Another woman stood at the counter, stern and middle-aged, with gray hair, a stout figure, and an enormous bust.

"May I help you, sir?" she asked.

"I . . . I wanted to exchange a toy I bought here two days ago. The young lady sold it to me."

The woman accepted the clockwork trolley. "What would you like to exchange it for?"

Zalman took back the toy. "I am not sure. I'll come back later, after I've thought about it."

He was turning to leave when the front door opened. Julia entered. Recognizing Zalman, she smiled. "Was there something else you wanted to exchange, Mr. Isaacson?"

"Perhaps later. Good morning." He touched the brim of his hat and walked past her. Before the door closed, he heard Julia call the other woman "Mother." He waited a hundred yards away. After half an hour, he saw the older woman leave. Within a minute, he pushed open the door.

Julia stared at him. "Mr. Isaacson, do your friend's children dislike something else you bought for them?"

Zalman ignored the question. "In America, how does a young man become friendly with a young woman?"

"How is it done where you come from?"

"Russia? Through introduction."

"The same applies here. They have to be introduced."

"We have been introduced already. I told you my name, you told me yours. Now let us become friends."

80

Julia shook her head. "I'm afraid that doesn't count as an introduction. I am a young woman from a good family. A young man from a similar background would be formally introduced. An approach would be made from a common party. Would I be interested in meeting this young man? If the answer were yes, arrangements would be taken a step further."

"Have you met any young men that way?"

"Two."

"And what happened?"

"Absolutely nothing." The bright smile that centered in her soft brown eyes shone on Zalman. "My mother and father approved of both young men, but I could tolerate neither of them. They were pompous, full of themselves, and thoroughly conceited."

"I am none of those things."

"I am certain of it. But the fact remains that we have not been properly introduced."

"Wait a minute." Zalman went outside and grabbed hold of the first person he saw, a policeman. "Will you come with me, please?" The surprised policeman allowed himself to be pulled into Blue Stone. "Please tell this young lady that I am Zalman Isaacson, a young man of clean habits and impeccable character." Laughing, the policeman made the introduction. "Thank you, sir." Zalman told him. Then, turning to Julia, he said, "How much more formal an introduction do you need?"

"But my parents have never met you."

"Your mother has."

Julia nibbled her lower lip. She did want to know this young man better. The fire in his deep-set eyes drew her like a magnet. "Would you like to have dinner with us?"

"I work every night but Sunday."

"What do you do?"

"I am in the entertainment business."

"Really? Next Sunday then, at seven-thirty." She wrote down an address. As Zalman opened the door, Julia called out, "Does your friend's daughter really have long black hair like mine?"

"I have no idea. I have never seen her."

81

Julia's gentle laughter stayed with Zalman all the way downtown. By the time he went to work at Mulligan's, he was convinced he was in love.

The Bluestone family lived in the Central Park Apartments at the southern edge of the park. Zalman arrived at seven-thirty exactly, carrying a bouquet which he presented to Julia. She took him through to a spacious drawing room filled with overstuffed mohair-covered chairs and dark mahogany tables.

"Mother, Father, I would like you to meet my friend, Zalman Isaacson."

"Friends of Julia are always welcome in our home," said Louis Bluestone. He stood up, a tall, portly man with stiff gray hair and piercing blue eyes.

Zalman shook his hand, then turned to Frieda Bluestone. "I believe we have already met, Mrs. Bluestone."

"Yes, I remember." Frieda smiled icily. "You're the young man who couldn't make up his mind."

Over dinner, Zalman underwent a relentless cross-examination. Louis and Frieda Bluestone asked where he came from, how long he had been in America, what family he had. Zalman looked across the table at Julia. She seemed embarrassed. For her sake, he tolerated the Bluestones' rudeness, until, at last, came the question he had been anticipating.

"Julia tells us that you are in the entertainment business, Mr. Isaacson," Louis Bluestone said. "What is it that you do?"

"I am a bartender in Mulligan's saloon downtown."

"A bartender?" No actor could have equaled the revulsion that Louis injected into the response. He looked at his wife. "Did you hear that, Frieda? Julia's friend is a bartender."

"If that occupation makes me unwelcome at your table, I regret it." Zalman stood up and bowed slightly in Julia's direction. "I am sorry, but quite obviously your parents would prefer my absence to my presence." Without another word, he left the apartment. He expected Julia to follow, to apologize for the way her parents had treated him. When she did not, he resolved never to think of her again. The resolution dissolved by the time he had walked one hundred yards.

Julia was not to blame for her parents' rudeness. He would find some other way to see her.

Mulligan's was busy the following evening as Christmas trade built up. Jimmy Doyle spent an hour drinking at the bar with *American* people. When he left, he shouted out for Zalman not to forget about Christmas Day. By eight o'clock, the level of noise was deafening. Suddenly, the din diminished. Young women alone were rare enough to cause such a reaction. Julia Bluestone stood just inside the entrance, looking around nervously. Paddy Mulligan, who would not want any of his four daughters seen in a saloon, picked his way between tables.

"Are you looking for someone in particular, miss?"

"Yes. I seek—" She broke off and pointed toward Zalman, whose mouth hung in shock. "That is the man I seek."

"Then you'd better speak to him." Mulligan escorted Julia to his office at the back of the saloon. Zalman joined her there.

"What are you doing here, Julia? Young women from good families do not patronize Irish bars."

"I came to apologize for my parents' behavior last night. They had no right to treat you that way, but you have to understand some things about them. They were both born here. Their own parents came from Germany before the American Civil War. My family is totally assimilated, and like many others in the same position, they fear that this new influx of immigrants will reflect badly on them. I tried to tell them you are different, that you speak English, that you are not mired down in centuries of superstition, but they would not listen."

"And on top of everything else, I pour beer in an Irish bar."

"I told them that the job was temporary, to support yourself while you studied."

Zalman laughed at Julia's inventiveness. "What am I supposed to be studying?"

"Medicine. I told my parents that you are taking courses at a preparatory school on East Broadway."

Mulligan's fist rocked the office door. "I'm as romantic as

83

the next man, but it's Christmas week and good Christians can't drink to the infant Jesus' health with empty glasses."

"I have to go." Zalman held Julia's hands in his own. "I will come to see you in the shop."

"Thank you. And thank you for the flowers as well. They are beautiful."

Zalman visited Blue Stone the next five mornings, right through to Saturday, the last business day before Christmas. Frieda Bluestone was with her daughter the first day. The next four days, Louis Bluestone was also there, tall and forbidding in a black suit and stiff white collar. Zalman made no purchases, nor did he bring anything to exchange. He had come courting.

Whenever the shop was empty, the Bluestones continued their cross-examination. "We understand from Julia that you are seeking a career in medicine," Louis said.

"I am also interested in banking. With the languages I speak fluently—German, English, and Russian—international banking seems natural."

"Whichever path you eventually decide to follow," Frieda said, "it seems obvious that you will be unable to support yourself in a proper manner for some considerable time."

"I am a patient man, especially where something I want very badly is concerned."

At the end of each visit, Julia walked him to the door. On Saturday, as he prepared to return downtown, he said, "Their impression of me is no better than it was a week ago."

"The only impression that matters is mine," Julia answered. Her index finger traced the sharp lines of his cheekbones. "We have never been out together, Zalman, not even for a walk, and I am in love with you already."

He kissed her lips softly. Behind her stood Louis and Frieda. He had never seen two less happy people in his life.

Christmas Day proved a welcome change for Zalman. The Doyles were as relaxed and fun-loving as Julia's parents were tense and bleak. Kathryn Doyle, a plump woman with lively blue eyes and short salt-and-pepper hair, welcomed Zalman into the West Side apartment with all the enthusiasm of a long-lost relative. Telling him he was too skinny for his own good, she forced food on him. Simultaneously she protected him from the three Doyle children, Brian and Patrick, dark and boisterous like their father, and Mary, a tiny girl with ringlets of golden hair. Thrilled with their presents, they wanted to know more about this stranger to their home.

In the evening, before the children went to bed, Jimmy Doyle told them how Zalman had come to America from Russia. Doyle's story bore no resemblance to the truth, but it made fascinating listening, especially for young ears. He painted a picture of Zalman fighting giant soldiers who rode fire-breathing horses, climbing snowcapped mountains, and crossing mighty seas in nothing more than a rowing boat. Zalman listened, as entranced as any of the children. Doyle was a wonderful storyteller. Watching the children's rapt expressions, Zalman made a silent promise that should he ever be blessed with a family, he would tell stories to his children every night. There was a closeness here that he had never seen before.

After the children were in bed, Doyle lit a pipe and relaxed. "Mulligan's is still seething with excitement over that young lady who visited you, Zalman. What's the story there?"

"Her name is Julia Bluestone, and I'm going to marry her."

"You are? God bless us all. This calls for a drink." He poured whiskey for himself and Zalman. "Your responsibilities will change once you get married, you know. You'll be wanting a proper, respectable job."

"Are you saying I should get out of Mulligan's?"

"Mulligan is a good friend of mine and I'd be the last to say a word against him, but you've got too many brains to be wasting your time there. Pouring beer in an Irish bar is a job any Mick fresh off the boat can handle. Mulligan's Jew can do better."

Zalman's relationship with Julia continued into the New Year. He traveled to the shop every weekday morning to be with her for an hour or so, and he spent most of Sunday in her company. In the afternoon, they enjoyed a walk or a carriage ride. It was the only time they could be alone. They held hands; in the privacy of the carriage, they kissed. Zalman spent the entire week longing for Sunday afternoon.

Sunday evening, and dinner with Julia's parents, slammed him back to earth. Louis and Frieda Bluestone treated him with icy reserve. They asked no questions about his work, as if blotting out the fact that he tended bar. Conversation centered around current events. Zalman yearned for evening's end, when Julia walked him to the street. There they shared a long embrace before Zalman made the journey back to his room above the saloon.

At the end of February, during a Sunday-afternoon carriage ride, Zalman asked Julia to marry him. She accepted even before the words were fully out of his mouth. When they returned to Central Park Apartments, Julia took him into the library where her father and mother sat reading.

"I would like to introduce you to my fiancé."

A glance passed between both parents. Louis inclined his head. "I want to talk to you, Zalman."

Zalman saw anxiety in Julia's eyes. He smiled to reassure her. Louis led the way into the dining room, where he sat at the head of the mahogany table. "Julia is our only child. We had her late in life, and she is precious to us. We want only what is best for her. Quite honestly, we never considered a Russian immigrant who works in an Irish saloon to be in that category."

"I do not intend to work in a saloon for all eternity."

"Please do not insult my intelligence by repeating the story Julia told us about studying medicine." Louis waved a hand to dismiss the fiction, and changed the subject. "At the beginning of November, Julia turned twenty-one. She is old enough to do whatever she wants. Nonetheless, her mother and I need to be certain that the man she marries will support her properly. Therefore, we will take you into the store. After we are gone, it will belong to Julia, so you may as well begin learning the business immediately." Louis ran his eyes over Zalman. "Do you have enough money to buy an adequate engagement ring?"

"Of course I do."

"Good. My wife and I would hate to see our daughter wearing a ring that was beneath her."

Zalman smiled thinly. He had no idea where he would find the money to buy an *adequate* engagement ring, but he'd be damned if he would admit that to Louis Bluestone.

Zalman studied rings in jewelry stores. The prices shocked him. He could never afford Louis Bluestone's *adequate*. Except . . . ! One course of action remained open. If he could not buy with cash, he could trade. He could exchange the gold-and-enamel watch. He was shocked. How could he think of parting with the sole memento of his family? He rationalized the act. Surely trading the watch to buy an engagement ring for the young woman who would help to continue the family was permissible.

He toured a dozen jewelry shops, explaining his predicament and asking how much trade value the watch had. The best offer came from a shop on Broadway. The owner carefully examined the gold-and-turquoise case. He fingered the short, stubby antennae, opened the wings to reveal the hands and face, wound the mechanism with the tiny key. "I will exchange it for a ring to the value of one hundred and seventy-five dollars."

"Thank you. I will return tomorrow with my fiancée."

Julia inspected a selection of rings equal to the value of the watch. She chose one priced at one hundred and sixty dollars, a single diamond surrounded by smaller stones on a gold band. Slipping it onto her finger, she kissed Zalman.

"Are you quite certain this is not too expensive?"

"Please don't worry about what I can or cannot afford."

From the jewelry shop, Zalman and Julia went to the Windsor Arcade. Frieda Bluestone lifted her daughter's hand. Zalman awaited the verdict. "Very nice." She passed her daughter's hand to her husband as though it were a piece of meat. "What do you think, Louis?"

"It does not shame us."

Zalman left to return downtown. Julia stood outside the door with him. "They like it, they really do."

"I know. They just have trouble admitting such feelings."

"They like you, too."

Zalman could not swallow that claim so easily. "It only matters how you feel about me."

"I love you." She kissed him. "I love you, and I cannot wait until we are married."

They broke the embrace. Coat over his arm, Zalman turned to leave. Julia called him back. She pointed to his vest, where the watch chain had always been displayed. "Your watch? Where is your beautiful watch?"

"I was in such a hurry to see you this morning, to put a ring upon your finger, that I left the watch in my room. I'm lucky that I remembered to wear socks." He blew a kiss to her and walked away quickly.

They saw each other every morning. Julia's eyes always dropped to Zalman's vest. She made no comment until their Sunday date, then she said, "Did you dress so hurriedly all week long that you forgot your watch each day?"

"I was too upset to tell you the truth. I lost it."

"Don't lie to me, Zalman. You sold your beautiful watch to buy my ring, didn't you? You had no business selling that watch. It was a family heirloom. I returned to the jeweler's the very next day, to buy it back. I was too late. He had already sold it. For a handsome profit, he was not shy to tell me."

Zalman was touched. "I sold the watch because I did not want you to be shamed."

"My parents would have been shamed, not me. I would have worn no ring at all. Remember that, Zalman. I love you for what you are, not for what you own. I would love you just the same whether you were wealthy or poor."

The wedding was set for August. Four months before, Zalman quit his job at Mulligan's and started work in Windsor Arcade. The change required him to find a new accommodation. He rented a room in a hotel ten minutes away from his new place of employment.

Normal business hours had unquestioned advantages. Not only was Zalman with Julia during the day, he was able to see her every evening. At last they could behave like any courting couple—going out for dinner, seeing a show, dancing. The disadvantage of working in the shop was the constant contact with Louis and Frieda Bluestone. They scrutinized his every action.

"You were far too familiar with that customer," Frieda told him tartly after he had sold a rocking horse to a woman with a young daughter. "Please remember that a better class of person patronizes Blue Stone. Include *Madam* or *Sir* in every sentence." As she walked away, Zalman heard her whisper to Louis, "Really, I cannot imagine what Julia must have been thinking when she agreed to marry that Russian peasant."

Another time, it took all of Zalman's willpower not to explode when Louis gave him a five-minute lecture on the correct way to greet a customer.

During slow periods, Louis educated Zalman about merchandise. He spoke about toys and games in the awed manner of a scientist describing the origin of the universe. Zalman listened, bored beyond belief. Most galling of all was the way in which Louis and Frieda did not allow him near the cash register. "Do your parents not trust me?" he asked Julia when they were alone.

"You have to remember that Papa built this business by himself. He is very proud of it, and very jealous."

"What's to be proud of? Playthings that captivate a child's interest for five minutes . . . What kind of work is that for a grown man? Serving beer in Mulligan's was a more worthwhile job."

"It did not pay as well, did it?"

Zalman had to agree. Despite his dislike of her parents, they were not cheap when it came to paying him. That was no surprise, though. It would reflect badly on the Bluestones if Julia was engaged to a man who earned a paltry wage.

"Once we are married, everything will change," Julia assured Zalman. "You'll see."

After Zalman had been at Windsor Arcade for six weeks, Jimmy Doyle came visiting. The Irishman gazed around in wonder. "A treasure chest," he breathed. "A veritable cornucopia of children's dreams."

Zalman asked Louis if he could be excused. He went with Doyle to a restaurant, where they ordered coffee. "Mulligan's isn't the same without you, Zalman, my boy."

"If it were not for Julia, I would go back there in a moment. This place bores me to tears. Adults being deadly serious about children's toys—it isn't natural." He stared into his friend's wide, red face. "What's happening in your line of work? Have you been assaulted lately because you misappropriated someone else's newspapers?"

Doyle chuckled. "Things could be heating up. You ever hear of a couple of gentlemen named Henry Bladen and Woodrow Holmes?" Zalman shook his head. "No, there's no reason you should have done. They're publishers. Bladen owns papers in the Midwest—Chicago, St. Louis, Ohio and the like. Woodrow Holmes does the same thing in San Francisco, Seattle, and Denver. Now they're both thinking about establishing themselves in New York."

"Buying an existing paper?"

"No. Hearst, Pulitzer, Ochs, and the rest of them aren't interested in selling. New York can support another daily, so Henry Bladen and Woodrow Holmes are going to have to battle it out with the established papers and each other. On the surface, Bladen's a classy character, but he's a rascal who'll cut every corner he can. Holmes is ten times worse. He's a pirate. He uses a thug called Wilf Hagerty to spearhead his circulation drives. Hagerty specializes in hiring the meanest plug-uglies in any town where he operates. It should all," Doyle said with lip-smacking satisfaction, "be very interesting."

"You sound as though you're looking forward to it."

"I am. What Irishman doesn't relish the prospect of a scrap? Challenge, my boy, that's what life's all about. Challenge! Without it, mankind would just wither away and die."

Zalman appreciated the sentiment. The thought of spending the rest of his working life in a toy shop—even if he and Julia did inherit it one day—was a living death.

The wedding was held at Temple Emmanu-el on Fifth Avenue and Forty-third Street. Zalman and Julia honeymooned for a week on the Jersey shore. It was the first break from work Zalman had taken in the three years since arriving in America. He had never walked on a beach, had never sat beneath the sun's warming rays, had never bathed in the sea.

Julia taught him to swim. He began with a struggling breast-stroke that barely kept him afloat and achieved little in forward momentum. He remained in the water for hours on end, until the skin of his fingers was white and wrinkled. By the end of the week, he was an accomplished swimmer, his lean body knifing through the water like a fish. At night, Julia held that hard, sinewy body close to her, a hand pressed to his chest so she could feel the beating of his heart.

The week passed far too quickly. As the final day dawned, they lay in bed awake, arms encircling each other. Zalman felt Julia break free of his embrace. She slipped out of bed and walked to the dresser. She took something from a drawer and returned to the bed. Zalman sat up.

"You gave me a ring. I want to give you this."

The sun, low in the east, blazed right through the window, shining directly onto the gold watch that Julia held out. Zalman took it. Inside the case, engraved in tiny script, was the date of their wedding and the words: "Zalman, I will love you for all eternity. Julia."

"This is very beautiful. Thank you."

"I'm afraid that it doesn't make up for the one you sold."

Zalman kissed her. "Believe me, it does."

Returning from their honeymoon, the newlyweds moved into an apartment on West Forty-eighth Street, full of dark, heavy furniture and ornate china given to them as wedding presents.

The first time Julia's parents visited the apartment for dinner, they came with a surprise. "I'm making you manager of the store," Louis told Zalman. "From now on, you will be responsible for buying merchandise, for stocktaking, for the overall well-being of the establishment. Julia's mother and I have earned a rest."

Zalman caught Julia's eye. The relationship with his in-laws was improving. "Thank you for showing such faith in me."

"You are our daughter's husband," Frieda responded. "How could we possibly feel otherwise?"

But Zalman soon found out that he was manager in name only. Louis and Frieda spent as much time as ever at the shop. Louis examined every order Zalman made. When he did stocktaking, he did it with Louis standing at his shoulder. When he tallied the daily receipts, Louis checked the figures. Each evening, Zalman returned home bursting with aggravation. He tried to hide his feelings, but Julia was too sensitive to be fooled. "Would you like me to talk to my parents about your unhappiness?" she asked.

Zalman shook his head. "What difference would it make? They know I am unhappy without you telling them." He slapped a hand against the wall and his temper exploded. "Children's toys! How can grown-up people be so serious about toys?"

"My parents have found it a very good way to earn a living."

"It is a meaningless way to earn a living. People who have no soul earn such livings. Your parents have no soul, do you know that? They have no inner being."

"What would you rather do?"

"Anything."

"Zalman, you must be more practical."

"Julia, from the moment I stepped off the boat, I wanted to run my own business. That has been my burning dream. Now I am in the most ironic of situations. I work in a business that one day will be our own, and I cannot tolerate it! I bow and scrape. I act like a servant to a king. I would not mind if these people to whom I bow and scrape were kings, but they are nothing! They buy toys, and to them I have to prostrate myself!"

Julia's eyes burned. Above everything else, she wanted Zalman to be happy. As happy as he had been in those early days of their relationship, when he had worked at Mulligan's and they had seen each other in the morning hours. "Zalman, find another job. It doesn't matter what you do, or how much you earn. You know I'll stand by you."

Chapter Five

In June 1905, after eight months of operation, the Dekker Boys' Club showed off its achievements with an open day. Special events were planned, local dignitaries invited. Rachel understood the importance of such invitations. Politicians courted popularity by playing on ignorance and fear. They sought votes by demanding an end to Britain's open-door immigration policy; they stoked prejudice by claiming the newcomers from eastern Europe formed a divisive force which would never be absorbed into British life. Open day provided a means to disprove those allegations.

Tobias became absorbed in the event. For two weeks, he spoke of nothing else. Each day, he visited the club to check on preparations. Each evening, when Rachel returned home, he pestered her for more news. Finally, during a dinner when Jacob Lesser was also present, Hannah scolded her husband.

"Tobias, you are worse than a man whose wife is having a baby! Leave Rachel alone! Can you not see that she has other, more important things to concern herself with?"

"I just want to know what is happening!" Tobias turned to Jacob for support. "Is that such a terrible thing, wanting to know what is happening in my own club?"

Before Jacob could think of an answer, Hannah said, "You make Rachel crazy with all your questions! Now you try to make Jacob crazy as well! Soon you will make everyone crazy, and there will be no one left to work in the club for open day."

"It is all right, I am not yet crazy," Rachel assured

Hannah. "Max Goldschmidt met with the members of the debating society to decide on the best subject for the open-day debate."

"Ah! And what topic did they choose?"

"Socialism—the only path to justice for all."

Tobias grimaced.

Open day dawned damp and cold. After dressing, Rachel pushed aside the plush, tasseled curtains and looked through her bedroom window. Raindrops slid down the glass. She sighed. What terrible weather! Such disapproval made her smile. How English she had become! Criticizing the weather was a national pastime of her adopted country.

Knuckles rapped on her bedroom door. Hannah's voice called out. "It's time we were going, Rachel."

Tobias added his voice to his wife's summons. "Please hurry, Rachel. It will be in poor taste for the founder and chairman of the Dekker Boys' Club to be late for such an important occasion."

Rachel's smile widened. Tobias's occasional lapses into stuffiness always amused her. Sometimes he took himself so seriously! She glanced around the room to see if she had forgotten anything. Her wide hat with its curling ostrich feathers lay on the dressing table. Next to it was a dark-green silk purse that matched the long coat she wore. She opened the purse and dropped in two items: her watch and the copper penny Tobias had given to her as she lay in the infirmary in Rotterdam. These were the talismans without which she never left the house. Red ribbon remained important; she continued to conceal a small piece on everything she wore. But the penny and the ruined watch were her most significant good-luck charms. Especially the watch. From the moment it had been broken during her plunge into the river, her fortunes had changed dramatically.

Hannah's urgent summons pierced the door once more. "Rachel, we really must be going."

Rachel closed the purse, set the feathered hat on her head, and left the room. Edwards held an enormous umbrella aloft to protect Hannah, Tobias, and Rachel as they boarded the carriage. Tobias was still considering the purchase of a motor car; he studied advertisements and talked at length with owners. But each time he brought up the subject, Hannah put her foot down, refusing to ride in a car until it provided the space and comfort that a carriage did.

The club was packed. When the guests of honor—the Mayor of Stepney, and the local Liberal Member of Parliament—arrived, Tobias escorted them inside.

"May I present our volunteer managers—all from the most impeccable backgrounds," Tobias assured the mayor and MP.

Faces set in a smile, the dignitaries shook the hand of each young man, complimenting him on the work he was doing. Only when they were introduced to Rachel, and informed of her background, did their expressions alter.

"I must congratulate you on the fine job you are doing here," the MP said. "It cannot be easy for a young Russian woman to work in an English boys' club. Do you miss your own country?"

"Russia was my country by accident of birth. This is my country by choice."

The mayor took over. "England's generosity in sheltering innocent people from persecution is well documented," he told Rachel. "It is gratifying to see a refugee set out to become an exemplary citizen, as you have done, displaying the kind of patriotism that is best in the British character."

Rachel's eyes were on the mayor, but on the edge of her vision she saw Tobias glowing with pleasure.

The two dignitaries toured the club. They watched boys play chess and bagatelle. They listened for ten minutes to Max Goldschmidt's spirited debate on Socialism. The last stop was the large assembly hall. Five hundred people filled the seats. On the stage stood Jacob's choir, eyes fixed on the baton he held. Tobias showed his guests to reserved seats in the front row. The baton dropped, and the choir broke into "Greensleeves." The mayor and MP sat absolutely entranced at this rendering of an English classic by immigrants and the children of immigrants.

When the song finished, the two dignitaries applauded louder than anyone. "Wonderful!" the mayor said to Tobias. "They sing as well as any English boys."

The concert continued with a selection of favorite English

folk songs. At the end, Jacob turned to the audience. "Please rise and join us in the singing of our national anthem."

Everyone stood. The choir began to sing "God Save The King." Rachel felt her heart swell with pride as she watched Jacob's baton rise and fall. Her hand slipped inside her purse to touch the broken watch and copper penny. Of all the luck they had brought her, nothing came close to Jacob.

The distance between St. John's Wood and Jacob's home in Shoreditch became less of an obstacle as Rachel spent two or three evenings a week and every Sunday in his company. They enjoyed open carriage rides and walks in Hyde Park. They attended music halls and theaters. Jacob took Rachel to meet his family—his parents and married sister and brother. His mother, a large, heavy woman, gave Rachel a hug that left her breathless.

"You're the first girl I've ever brought home," Jacob explained. "My mother is already seeing us married."

The regularity of their meetings was disturbed in the latter part of August, when fifty club members went on a week-long summer camp. A farmer in Essex, close to where they had taken the rain-interrupted hike, allowed the club to pitch tents on an unused meadow. Jacob and five other managers oversaw the camp. They organized activities, supervised hygiene, and operated a field kitchen.

Lonely for Jacob's company, Rachel stayed one night in a village inn close to the campsite. Jacob took her to the camp to participate in an evening singsong around a fire. The songs were followed by a ghost-story contest. Eerie tales, accompanied by shrieks and wails, sent shivers up Rachel's spine.

When Jacob returned her to the inn, she said, "I could have slept in a tent."

"After those stories, you would have jumped out of your skin at every sound. You are better off in a feather bed."

"I slept—"

Jacob placed a hand over her mouth. "I know, when you marched halfway across Russia, you slept on beds of rocks with nothing but leaves for blankets. But that was Russia. In England, you belong in a comfortable bed."

"You spoil me."

"How else should I treat the girl I'm going to marry?"

Two months later, at the end of October, Rachel married Jacob. The ceremony took place in the Great Synagogue in Duke's Place. Members of the Dekker Boys' Club packed the building. All had given presents, some alone, some as a group. The gift which most delighted the bride and groom came from the four gamblers; they had joined forces to buy a baize-covered card table.

Jacob stood under the traditional wedding canopy with his parents. Rachel stood with Tobias and Hannah, who substituted for her mother and father. When Jacob crushed the glass beneath his foot, Rachel stole a glance at the Dekkers. They could have looked no prouder, no happier had they been her own flesh and blood. Joy filled Rachel's heart at the knowledge that she was responsible for this moment of pleasure in their lives. It paid them back in part for the love and kindness they had given her.

Rachel and Jacob began married life in the top floor of a house in Hackney. Jacob's parents, who lived a mile to the south, had offered part of their own home, while Hannah and Tobias had proposed buying the newlyweds a house as a wedding gift. Both suggestions were refused. Jacob explained to his mother and father that the late hours he and Rachel worked at the club would create a disturbance. Rachel took on the more difficult task of turning down the Dekkers' generosity.

"You lived with us for two and a half years," Hannah said. "We regard you as our own daughter. The least we would do for a daughter is make certain that she and her husband have the best possible start to their marriage."

Tobias took over the argument. "Rachel, you are accustomed to a large, beautiful home, not a rented flat in someone else's house. You are used to having servants wait upon you."

"I was not always accustomed to such luxury. Besides, renting is only temporary, until Jacob and I have time to search for a house we truly like."

Tobias tried again. "When you do find such a house, will you allow us to help you then?"

Rachel sighed. It would be so easy to say yes. The Dekkers could afford the four- or five-hundred pounds a good-sized house would cost, but neither Rachel nor Jacob wanted to take advantage of their generosity. The home in which they raised their family would be a home they had scrimped and saved to pay for. How could they impress proper values upon their children if they themselves did not abide by such values? Still, there were occasions when compromises were necessary. "Jacob and I would be very grateful if you would help us to furnish our house."

On their first night in the flat, Rachel found it hard to sleep. Odd noises intruded. The building creaked. Trees rustled in the breeze. Light from the gas lamp in the street flickered across the ceiling. Rachel felt Jacob's arm beneath her neck. She turned and snuggled into him, burying her face in his chest. She was like a child in the embrace of a giant.

"What is wrong, Rachel?"

"Nothing."

"Are you uncomfortable here? I know that the rooms are smaller than the rooms in Tobias's home—"

She cut him off. "They are larger than the home I grew up in. Size is of no concern. Being with you is all that matters."

Jacob kissed the top of her head, caressing her hair with his lips. "I love you very much, Rachel."

"And I love you." His arms tightened around her. The noises stopped; the light from the gas lamp no longer bothered her. She closed her eyes. Her last thought before falling asleep was that she could live in this rented flat forever. Just as long as Jacob was with her.

Rachel found the daily journey from Hackney to the club far easier than the lengthy trip from St. John's Wood. Each morning, with Jacob, she traveled by tram to Whitechapel. When Jacob finished his day at the Jewish Free School, she rode back to Hackney with him. On those two or three evenings a week he worked as a club manager, she also stayed late. One night a week, they traveled to St. John's Wood for dinner with Hannah and Tobias. On Friday nights they walked the mile or so to Jacob's parents for Sabbath dinner.

And one night a week both older couples came to the flat in Hackney. Rachel prepared dishes she had learned from her mother: beet borscht and cabbage soup; gefilte fish, herring salad and herring balls; hearty stews; honey cake and mandelbrodt. After each meal, Jacob sat back, hands clasped across his stomach, a huge, satisfied grin imprinted on his face.

"Now I ask you—does my Rachel cook like an angel?"

Each time Rachel would stop whatever she was doing to lean over the table and kiss him. "And does my Jacob eat like a horse?"

"How can I do otherwise when my tiny wife creates such delicious meals?"

In the middle of all this activity, they found time to search for a house of their own. Their criterion was simple. Whenever they inspected a property, they asked one question: would children like to grow up in such a house?

Three months after their wedding, they found such a house. It was in Dalston, in a long, tramline-bisected street called Graham Road. Rachel fell in love with the three-story house the moment she entered its small front garden and climbed the concrete steps to the porticoed door. She walked with Jacob through the bedrooms on the middle and upper floors. Lastly they explored the parlor, dining room, and kitchen on the lower floor.

"Children could grow up happy here," Jacob said.

"A *lot* of children could grow up happy here."

"How many are we going to have?"

"As many as I think are necessary."

"Necessary to leave a footprint in history?" Jacob knew of Rachel's vow, the dream in which her father had appeared.

"To leave a very big footprint."

"Do you want to see more houses?"

Rachel shook her head. "None will be as perfect as this."

Jacob held out his arms. Rachel stepped into them. Nowhere could she be safer. Wrapped in her husband's arms, while standing in her own home, nothing in the world could harm her.

"You made your mind up very quickly. One look, and that's it. Are you quite sure, Rachel?"

"We do not have time to waste."

Jacob ran his hand between their bodies, letting it rest on Rachel's stomach. He swore he could already feel movement. "No, we don't have time to waste, do we?"

When they moved into the house eight weeks later, Rachel's pregnancy was halfway through its fifth month, and showing dramatically on her slight body. She sewed extra pieces of red ribbon into everything she wore, and frequently stopped whatever she was doing to fondle the broken gold-and-enamel watch and the copper penny. With all those talismans, her baby would be the luckiest, most perfect child in the world.

The advancing pregnancy necessitated changes. At six months, Rachel's work schedule became too arduous for her to continue. Over dinner at the new house in Graham Road, she told Tobias that she was resigning as club administrator. "I take the step very reluctantly, but I do not feel I can go on any longer."

Tobias set down his fork. "To tell you the truth, neither Hannah nor I thought you would last this long."

"I didn't, either," Jacob surprised Rachel by saying. "But none of us was about to suggest you stop working, because you would have undoubtedly told us that in Russia the women worked until the very moment they delivered."

"They do. Who will take over my work?"

Tobias indicated Jacob. "He will resign from the Jewish Free School to become general manager of the club. He will be the only manager receiving a salary, but no other manager will be doing so much work."

"What will happen when I return?"

Beneath the table, Jacob held her hand. "You have said often that you want lots of children. You'll be so busy looking after them all, you'll have no time to do anything else."

"Then you will have to give me a daily report on what happens at the club."

"I will," Jacob said. "I promise you I will."

Jacob kept his promise. Each night when he came home, he gave Rachel a detailed account of everything that had taken place that day. He told her of the camp being planned

100

for the coming summer; because of Rachel's condition, he would not be going. He even brought home the managers' reports for her to read. And when she made suggestions, he listened.

By the start of her eighth month, Rachel was so large that she could barely move. Her legs and ankles were grotesquely swollen. Walking, or standing for any length of time, was torture. Sitting was awkward. Only lying down was physically comfortable, but mentally it was the worst position of all. Wherever she looked, her view seemed to be blocked by the small mountain her belly had become.

Hannah, who traveled daily to the house in Graham Road, voiced the possibility of a multiple birth. "Were there any twins in your family?" she asked Rachel.

"None that I know of."

"Perhaps in Jacob's family?"

"He has never mentioned such an occurrence." Rachel ran her hands over her belly, as if feeling for two separate bodies. "Do you really think I could be carrying twins?"

"Would it not be wonderful if you were?"

Rachel was unsure how to answer. "I do not know whether I could manage."

"You, so uncertain? So doubtful of your ability?" Hannah shook her head in wonder. "Never did I think I would live to see such a thing."

Rachel was not carrying twins. She had only one child inside her, a boy who was born in the third week of July 1906, weighing just over eight pounds. He had blue eyes and a mane of fair hair, just like his father. Only Rachel and Jacob were unable to take pleasure from such similarity. Their fair-haired, blue-eyed son was stillborn, strangled by his own umbilical cord which, during the journey down the birth canal, had somehow become wrapped around his neck.

The tragedy shattered Rachel. The composure she prided herself upon disappeared. In its place was left turmoil and confusion. She walked around the house with her hair unbrushed. Household chores received little attention. Dust and dirt built up. She did not cook. The death of her son was the greatest catastrophe Rachel had ever known—more stunning even than the violent deaths of her father and brother.

She did not know how to cope. Hannah came every morning and stayed until the evening. Twice a week she brought May, her own housekeeper, to clean. Jacob remained at home, comforting Rachel when he himself so desperately needed solace. He held her, talked to her, tried to guide her out of the depression that had her so firmly in its grip. He spoke of the club, of current national news, of the weather. No matter what subject he chose, Rachel always brought it back to the dead baby.

"We were going to call him Mendel, in honor of my father," she said as they sat together on the edge of the bed. It was almost midday, and Rachel had only just gotten up.

"Emmanuel," Jacob whispered. "Not Mendel, but Emmanuel. We were going to honor your father, but we wanted our son to have a more English name. Remember?"

"Emmanuel, that's right."

"So we'll call our next son Emmanuel." He tried to make his voice light, when all he wanted to do was cry. Losing his son was bad enough; watching the tragedy's effect on Rachel was destroying him. "How does that sound to you?"

Rachel carried on talking, as though Jacob had asked no question. "Perhaps God does not mean us to have any sons. Or any children at all . . ." Her voice faded to a whisper at such a frightening prospect. How could she keep her promise to her father if God objected to its simple terms? All the red ribbon in the world was powerless against God's decisions.

"That child's death was not God's work. It just wasn't meant to be, that's all. Next time—"

Jacob's words finally registered. "Next time? *Next* time?" Her eyes opened in horror. Her voice turned sharp, fearful. "There will be no next time. Do you think I want to carry another dead child for nine months?"

Jacob lifted his eyes to Hannah, who stood in the bedroom doorway, watching and listening. She motioned for him to leave. When he was gone, she closed the door and sat beside Rachel.

"Was this why Tobias and I saved you from drowning in that Rotterdam canal? So you could drown here instead, in self-pity? I have watched you cry for yourself every day for

102

a month. Do you believe your grief is unique? Do you think no woman ever lost a child before?"

Rachel swung around to stare at Hannah. The sharp tone of the older woman's voice was like nothing she had heard during the past four weeks.

"You and Jacob can have more children. Tobias and I were never fortunate enough to be given another opportunity."

"What do you mean?"

"We, too, lost our first child—a boy, just like you and Jacob. Something went wrong. An emergency operation had to be performed. I nearly died. As well as saving my life, it made certain I would never be able to become pregnant again."

Rachel's insides twisted into a tight knot. "I'm sorry," she whispered. "I never knew . . . I never dreamed . . ."

"It was not something we made public. It was our grief, and we kept it to ourselves. But we would have given anything for a second chance. I would have happily risked"— scorn punctuated each word—"carrying another dead child for nine months just to have the chance of giving birth to a live one."

Rachel turned away, ashamed. Hannah was right. Her grief was not unique. Only her reaction to it. Women had lost children from the start of time, and they would go on losing them until the end of time. It would not stop the cycle, though. They would just try again, and keep on trying. Wasn't that what life was all about? Wasn't that why she had left Russia?

Hannah took Rachel's chin between her fingers and turned her face around. She saw something in the hazel eyes that had not been present moments earlier. Among the flecks of green and gray was the knowledge that life had to continue.

Another month passed before Jacob and Rachel made love. He was as gentle as he knew how, frightened that even the slightest haste, the merest suggestion of roughness, would throw Rachel back down that dark tunnel from which she had just emerged. Initially, Rachel held back, reluctant to commit herself totally. Jacob persevered, whispering encouragement, holding and touching her until he felt resistance begin to ebb. In the darkness, she could not see the happiness on his face when he felt her arms draw tight around him, her fingernails dig hard into his back.

Rachel lay in his arms afterward, head on his chest, listening to the rhythmic beating of his heart. Jacob angled his head to look down. Her hair was spread across his chest in a fan. When he asked if she were awake, he saw her head move.

"What are you thinking about?"

"I was wondering if the miracle is taking place."

"If not tonight, then the next time."

"I will give you many sons."

Jacob felt the wetness of Rachel's lips on his chest. "If you gave me a daughter, I would not throw you out of the house."

Rachel became pregnant again within a month. With memories of her earlier pregnancy etched indelibly in her mind, she followed a more careful routine. She traveled little, and did no strenuous physical activity. In the third week of July, a year to the day after the birth of her stillborn son, she gave birth to another fair-haired, blue-eyed boy. Another Emmanuel. This one kicked and screamed from the moment he was delivered. Rachel sat up in bed, cradling the baby in her arms, showing him off to visitors.

"See, Emmanuel, this is your Papa . . ."

Glowing with pleasure, Jacob leaned over the bed to kiss his son on the forehead.

"And these are your grandparents . . ."

Tobias became flustered, but Hannah took her honorary role of grandmother in stride. She lifted the baby from Rachel's arms and held him tenderly in her own, rocking him back and forth while she crooned a lullaby.

When the weather was fine, Rachel took her son outside. She talked nonstop, believing that he could understand every word. "Can you hear the beautiful singing of the birds, Emmanuel? Do you see the horse pulling the cart? Do you feel the sun on your face?" When the weather did not cooperate, Rachel held Emmanuel up to the window. "Can you hear the rain falling on the leaves, Emmanuel? Can you see the clouds?" Never was Rachel more happy than in those moments that she was alone with her son.

Early in 1908, Rachel became pregnant again. This time, she had no fear, no concern. Pregnancy was old hat. As her body blossomed once more, she carried on with her normal routine. She cleaned and cooked and cared for the two men in her life: her husband and her son. At six months, she even went on a club outing with Jacob when he took twenty-eight boys to the opening ceremonies of the Olympic Games in the new stadium at Shepherd's Bush, on London's western edge.

It rained during the opening ceremonies, of course, but by now Rachel was quite accustomed to the English weather doing its best to ruin everything. She huddled up to Jacob, her arm through his, hands clasped, fingers entwined. The enormous crowd gave off a visible energy that made the air shake and shimmer. Carrying the flags of their countries, more than two thousand athletes marched proudly around the vast stadium.

Rachel's greatest thrill had nothing to do with the athletes. Every few seconds, her eyes darted across the stadium to where the King sat. She was in the same place as King Edward the Seventh, the King of England! She had to pinch herself to realize she was not dreaming. She fished in her purse and withdrew the copper penny Tobias had given to her. It was him! She had never been so excited in her life.

"Look!" Jacob tugged her arm and pointed to a small group of athletes who marched without the benefit of any flag. "The Finns. Do you know why they march with no flag, Rachel?"

She shook her head. "Why?"

"They refuse to march under the flag of Czarist Russia."

Rachel clapped her hands and shouted at the top of her voice, "Three cheers for the Finns!"

A spate of booing erupted around the stadium. Rachel and Jacob looked to where King Edward sat. The American team was passing in front of him. Unlike the flags of other countries, which had been dipped in front of the British monarch, the Stars and Stripes remained upright. Rachel cupped her hands to her mouth and joined the tumult.

"Shame!" she cried. "Shame on you! God save the King!"

105

Turning to Jacob, she asked, "Who do these Americans think they are that they do not respect our King in our own country?"

"*Our* King? *Our own* country?" In the middle of all the excitement, he gave her a huge hug. "I love you, Rachel. In our own country, or in anyone's country!"

In November, a second child was born. Another fair-haired son, named Sidney. At Rachel's urging, he was given the middle name of Edward. Rachel would never forget the dreary summer's day when she had finally seen in the flesh the man whose profile in copper she had carried and treasured for five years. A year later, she and Jacob had a third son, Bernard. His wisps of dark hair and his dark-brown eyes made Rachel happy. At last, she had a child who looked like *her* family.

Hannah and Tobias visited, their arms weighed down with clothing and presents for the new baby. "You have three children under two and a half to care for," Hannah said. "Please allow us to hire a nurse to help you."

"A nurse?" Rachel was shocked by the idea. "Why would I need a nurse?"

"Because you will wear yourself out with all the work that is required to care for three small children." Hannah looked to Tobias for assistance.

"Stop being so proud and accept a little help once in a while," Tobias said.

"Looking after three children is no more work than looking after one. Besides, this is not work. This is pleasure. I love feeding them. I love bathing them. I love playing with them. I love them, whatever they are doing. Even when they are asleep, I love to just sit and watch them."

Hannah and Tobias stopped arguing. They remembered Rachel throwing herself into her duties at the boys' club. That hadn't been work, either. There existed a difference between mundane work and enjoyable responsibility. Rachel was a fortunate young woman because she understood the distinction.

* * *

In the first week of May 1910, King Edward died of pneumonia. Rachel, along with the rest of the country, grieved deeply. She felt as though she had known the King personally. His likeness on the penny she carried signified for her the freedom Britain represented. She had been offended on his behalf at the Olympic Games, when the American team had refused to lower their flag. A special bond had linked this popular monarch with his people, and Rachel had felt herself to be a part of that attachment.

Edward's son, George the Fifth, was crowned thirteen months later. Rachel was among the festive crowd which lined the streets from Westminster Abbey to Buckingham Palace. With her were Jacob, Emmanuel, and Sidney. Bernard, too young at twenty months, remained at home in the care of a neighbor. People made way for the couple with two young children. They sat Emmanuel and Sidney on the barricades at the front of the crowd, and gave them tiny Union Jacks to wave. The boys were fascinated by the spectacle. They gawked at soldiers in dress uniform, and were awestruck when a mounted policeman stopped to talk to them.

The clatter of horses' hooves announced the return of the coronation procession from Westminster Abbey. The Household Cavalry rode past, breastplates and helmets gleaming. Members of European royal houses, splendid in uniforms and jeweled gowns, waved to the cheering crowds. The noise increased as the newly crowned king approached. Feeling the crowd sway, Rachel and Jacob held the children tightly. The gilded carriage came into view. Seated in it were King George the Fifth and Queen Mary. Rachel gasped so loudly that Jacob turned in concern.

"What's wrong?"

"That face! It is the Czar!"

"The Czar?" Jacob swung around to look. The carriage was only ten yards away. "The King and the Czar are cousins; there must be some physical similarity, but that is all. Pull yourself together before people think you are mad."

"No." Rachel tried to control her suddenly rapid breathing. Inside her ribs, her heart pounded wildly. Her legs felt weak. Pictures she had seen of the new king were of poor quality. Now she was getting her first proper view—the face, the beard and mustache. He was the image of the man with whom she associated terror! As the carriage came abreast of her, she took a step backward, fearful that the man inside would see her and the children. Then they would all be in fear of their lives.

He did see her. King George the Fifth and Queen Mary looked right at the spot where Rachel stood. Emmanuel and Sidney brandished their flags wildly. Smiling happily, the royal couple waved back to the children. Then the carriage was past.

The trembling in Rachel's body subsided. This was not Russia. This was Britain. Her children had nothing to fear here. They were British. And so was she.

Russia, with its injustice and horrors, belonged to the past.

Chapter Six

Zalman remained at Blue Stone until the end of 1906. The reason he stayed so long was Louis Bluestone's ill health. Midway through September, Julia's father suffered a heart attack. He remained in the hospital for two weeks, followed by a long period of convalescence. Frieda Bluestone spent every hour of the day with her husband, leaving Zalman and Julia to manage the shop. Without his in-laws hovering over his shoulder, Zalman was far more comfortable. He was able to view the toys as items of merchandise, commodities to be exchanged for money; in that light, they were less objectionable. He even began to believe that his father-in-law would never return. Ill health would force him to hand over the business. Perhaps, Zalman mused, he could live with that.

Two weeks before Christmas, Louis returned to the shop, well rested and eager to participate in the busy season. With him came Frieda. Louis pored over the accounts. He questioned Zalman over minute details and criticized the Christmas orders he had made. At the end of Louis's first day back, Zalman told Julia that he would start seeking new employment immediately after the New Year.

"Your father will never retire. He flaunts the possibility like a carrot on a stick, but he's never going to do it. They'll have to carry him out of the shop."

On Christmas Eve, Jimmy Doyle visited the shop. Customers waited for service. Doyle, towering over them, indicated for Zalman to meet him outside. Zalman followed the

Irishman. He came back ten minutes later, face alight with excitement.

"Two men named Henry Bladen and Woodrow Holmes will soon be opening newspapers in New York," he announced. The Bluestones and their customers turned to listen. "My friend Jimmy Doyle is leaving Mr. Hearst's New York *American* to work for Mr. Bladen as circulation manager. He wants me to work with him."

"You know nothing about the newspaper business," Louis said.

"I knew nothing about this business, either. At least newspaper publishing is a business fit for a grown man."

Julia stared. She had not seen Zalman this happy since their marriage. If working on a newspaper was what it took to keep him happy, she was all for it.

Henry Bladen's paper was called the New York *Messenger.* It cost one cent, and was launched at the beginning of April. Zalman was a subscription solicitor. He banged on doors in the outlying districts and persuaded homeowners to subscribe.

Selling came easily to Zalman. He expounded on page make-up with the authority of a man who had spent a lifetime in the composing room. "Look at that design. Pastel-colored newsprint, red and blue ink for headlines. It's art as well as information. When you've finished with the *Messenger,* you can have it framed."

An avid reader, Zalman scanned every story in both the *Messenger* and its competition. He loved to find news that only Bladen's paper carried. "Pulitzer's *World* didn't get this," he told customers. "Nor did Hearst's *American.* Only the *Messenger* got it, just like we get a dozen exclusives every week."

Julia, who continued to work for her parents, had dinner waiting when Zalman returned home each night. She did not complain about the long hours he worked, nor did she mention that the money was less than he had earned at Blue Stone. None of those things mattered when compared with the happiness and excitement that shone in his eyes.

At home, Zalman talked of little else but the *Messenger.*

"Do you know what pride and pleasure I feel to see people reading *my* paper?" he asked Julia over dinner.

"*Your* paper?" She laughed at his enthusiasm. It was as evident in this job as it had been missing in the toy shop. "Are you sure you don't mean Mr. Bladen's paper?"

Zalman dismissed the question with a shrug. Henry Bladen spent most of his time in Chicago, where the nucleus of his publishing empire was located. When he visited the *Messenger* building near Union Square, he conferred only with department heads; he never met with the organization's rank and file. "The *Messenger* belongs more to me and Jimmy Doyle than to Henry Bladen," Zalman said, and Julia knew that he meant it.

At the end of May, two months after the *Messenger*'s launch, another new paper appeared on the streets. This was the New York *Dispatch* of Woodrow Holmes, the San Francisco publisher. Battle between the two newcomers commenced immediately. Holmes's operation lived up to all the invective Doyle had heaped on the Californian. The *Dispatch* copied the *Messenger*'s design; its advertising salesmen guaranteed editorial plugs for contracts; its circulation men bullied newsstand operators into promoting the *Dispatch* over the *Messenger*. When Zalman gave his sales pitch, he no longer knocked the established New York papers. He concentrated on the *Dispatch*. If a customer mentioned the similarity between the two new papers, Zalman answered, "Those Johnny-come-latelies have two reasons for copying our style. The first is that they know a good product when they see one. The second is that they have no design people of their own. What they don't know is that imitation is the sincerest form of flattery, and we're tickled pink that they think so much of us." Other customers noticed that the *Dispatch* carried many of the stories the *Messenger* claimed as exclusives. Zalman had an answer for that as well. "Their editions come out forty-five minutes after ours. That gives them time to steal our first copies, see what they've missed, and replate. When we get this much flattery, we know we're doing well!"

One day Zalman came home beaming. He had earned a twenty-dollar bonus. "Jimmy Doyle said that our subscription business is knocking the pants off the *Dispatch,*" he told Julia gleefully.

Another time, he marched in angry. When Julia questioned his mood, he told her that customers he had signed up in Throgs Neck were not receiving their copies. Bundles of papers left for distribution were being stolen and thrown into the East River.

"That's terrible," she said. "Can you do anything about such unfair tactics?"

Zalman maintained a straight face with difficulty. It was only unfair when it was done to you. When Jimmy Doyle's crews practiced similar tactics, it was strictly business. "We'll think of something," he answered.

Two days later, Zalman and Doyle took the papers up to Throgs Neck, relieving the regular driver. Also in the open Reliance truck were two brothers named Carlo and Franco Brunelli. Carlo was twenty, Franco two years younger. Doyle introduced the Brunelli brothers to Zalman as men with special talents. Zalman had little doubt what those talents were. Menace oozed like sweat from their beetle-black eyes and swarthy faces.

The drop-off point was an empty shed a hundred yards from the river. At four-thirty in the morning, they left papers and drove off. After a mile, they swung around and headed back the way they had come. They were just in time to see three men throwing the *Messenger* bundles into another truck.

"Will you just look at those thieving bastards!" Doyle yelled. He accelerated. The solid tires grabbed for traction. Doyle aimed the truck at the three men. They froze in horror. At the very last moment, Doyle braked hard. The two Brunelli brothers leaped from the truck before it stopped. Zalman flung himself after them. A face loomed in his vision, a thin white face with a thick ginger mustache and narrow eyes set close together. Zalman launched a punch. Teeth raked his knuckles, then a fist with a heavy ring smacked into his own mouth. He tasted blood and swung again. This time the man went down.

The fight was over in seconds. Carlo and Franco Brunelli each held one man. Zalman lifted Ginger Mustache to his feet. Doyle, who hadn't left the truck, yelled, "They throw our papers into the river! Show those bastards what cold water feels like!"

Zalman and the Brunelli brothers ran their victims to the river and threw them in. Zalman was so excited that he failed to notice the pain from his split lip and cut knuckles. When he reached home, he met Julia's look of horror with a wide smile. "Our papers won't be stolen anymore. We caught the men who were doing it and taught them a lesson they won't forget."

It was not necessary for Julia to ask who had been with Zalman. She knew that the first name out of his mouth would be Jimmy Doyle. A powerful bond existed between the two men. They were as close as brothers, and saw each other as much out of work as in it. Jimmy and Kathryn were frequent guests at the Isaacson home; just as often, Julia went with Zalman to the Doyle apartment. Each occasion developed into a contest between Doyle and Zalman to see who could tell the most outrageous circulation story. Such closeness was a revelation for Julia. Her own parents deemed aloofness the only proper way to deal with people; they treated family with the same cool courtesy they reserved for customers. The Bluestone home had been a bleak and lonely place for a young girl. Julia's friends had been chosen by her parents. She had endured a passionless life in cold surroundings. Zalman's outburst at her parents' dinner table had enthralled her. She had failed to run after him only because she had been too stricken to move. Visiting the noisy saloon the following night had been the most daring deed she had ever undertaken, but had she not done so she feared that she would never see Zalman again.

Confident that no more papers would be stolen, Zalman carried on with his subscription sales. A week later, in Unionport, a new Maxwell roadster drew up beside him. The driver stayed at the wheel. The passenger climbed out. It was Ginger Mustache. His left eye was still half closed. Zalman clenched his fists.

"Don't want to fight with you, boy," Ginger Mustache said. "Just want to talk to you is all. I'm Wilf Hagerty,

113

circulation manager of the *Dispatch*. Do you know that name?"

"I know it."

"I've seen the job you're doing in subscriptions. I've got some respect for the way you handle yourself as well. Whatever the *Messenger*'s paying you, I'll top it."

When Zalman hesitated, the Maxwell's driver whispered ominously, "Smart guys don't turn down Mr. Hagerty's offers."

"I'm not smart. I just sell subscriptions."

Hagerty resumed his seat in the car. He touched his swollen eye. On his third finger was a heavy gold ring with the initials W.H. "Don't think I've forgotten this, boy. See how well you sell subscriptions with your legs all busted up."

Zalman ceased work and returned to the *Messenger* building, where he learned that two other subscription solicitors had been approached by Hagerty. The next day, the subscription men went out with bodyguards. Carlo Brunelli accompanied Zalman.

Carlo was a talkative young man. Within twenty minutes, he told Zalman all about himself. "My brother Franco and me, we come over with our parents from Sicily four years ago. We don't live with them no more, though. Our old man cut us dead after we got six months in the reformatory."

"What for?"

"We robbed a store. When we got out, the old man had moved the family to a different damned city! Franco and me don't worry, though. We know how to look after ourselves. We've got our own gang. Doyle pays us more in one week than my stinking father ever sees in a stinking year. My old man, he lived in a shack—me and my brother, we live real fancy, in the Stuyvesant Hotel on Lexington Avenue." Carlo clapped his hands together. "Some place, this country, eh? You're a Hebe from Russia. I'm a Catholic from a stinking little town called Lercara Friddi, Jimmy Doyle's a Mick peasant, and the three of us represent a fine upstanding newspaper. Only in America!"

"Only in America." It was like a toast, Zalman thought. Where else could three men of such diverse backgrounds come together? Carlo's English was peppered with slang and

114

profanity, but he possessed a wry humor which Zalman enjoyed. For once, working the outlying districts was not a lonely job.

"You know why Jimmy Doyle put me with you?" Carlo asked. "I'll tell you. He's putting his best with his best. You're his best subscription man, and Carlo Brunelli"—he dug himself in the chest with a stubby index finger—"is his best muscle. 'Carlo' he said to me, 'I'm teaming you up with Zalman Isaacson. Protect him like he was your mother, because I've got big plans for him.' "

Zalman laughed. How would Doyle and this small-time Sicilian thug react if they knew that the man they wanted to safeguard had already killed twice? "How will you protect me, Carlo?"

"With this." Carlo pulled a pistol from his pocket and waved it in the air. "This is all anyone needs."

"Did Jimmy tell you to carry that?"

"He wears one, too. So should you."

Zalman fell silent. The sight of the pistol reminded him that newspapers could be a dangerous business. Sometimes in the excitement he forgot that.

Carlo had no need to use the pistol. The knowledge that the Brunelli gang protected the subscription solicitors was enough to forestall trouble. The Brunelli brothers were young, but their reputations were taken seriously.

After six months, Doyle made Zalman chief of the subscription solicitors. Twelve weeks later, he removed him from subscription sales completely. "Starting in the New Year, I want you to be my personal assistant," Doyle told him over a drink. "We've licked the *Dispatch* in the outlying areas, but they're holding us here, in town. Woodrow Holmes's thugs are putting on the pressure. Newsstand vendors have been pushed around, a couple of the stands have been burned. Wilf Hagerty's on a huge bonus to put us out of business by the end of Nineteen-oh-eight. That's a year from now. If we don't stop Hagerty, we're going to be eating a lot of newspapers. And Jimmy Doyle's business is selling newspapers. He doesn't eat them for anyone."

That evening, Zalman took Julia for a celebration dinner. They toasted his promotion, then Julia said, "Do you know what I like best about your new job? The fact that you won't come home with any more bloody lips."

"With bloody lips I could not kiss you."

"I like you kissing me." He held her hands, wondering whether he was doing right by shielding her from the truth. Doyle had talked of newsstand vendors being burned out. The Brunellis carried guns. Carlo boasted about the toughness of his gang. An all-out circulation war was brewing, and Doyle wanted Zalman with him because he wanted fighters. Did the wives of fighters have the right to know?

Zalman began his new job at the beginning of January 1908. No longer was he an isolated soldier in the field, obeying orders he received from headquarters. Now he was part of the *Messenger*'s central nervous system. He met the writers favored by Henry Bladen, men who were always on their way to cover the biggest story of the century, women who could wring a thousand tears from the simplest drama. He learned the mechanics of putting out a newspaper, soaking up the knowledge like a blotter absorbs ink. The first time Zalman watched newspapers spewing out from the press, heard the deafening rattle of the machinery, he knew they were sights and sounds of which he would never tire. Halfway around the world from the place of his birth, he had truly come home.

Jimmy Doyle gave Zalman a guided tour of the newsstands. He took him into shops where newspapers were sold, and introduced him to the newsboys who hawked each edition of the *Messenger* the instant it came off the press. He showed him the busiest street corners, the best locations. "We worked hard to build up our business here," Doyle explained. "If we lose it, we might as well close up shop and go home. Your responsibility is protecting these locations. Think you can handle that?"

"You bet I can."

Zalman set a simple plan into operation. Whenever the *Messenger* was on sale, from early morning through to the final edition, he had Brunelli gang members patroling the streets. More men accompanied delivery trucks. The *Messen-*

116

ger was making a clear statement that it did not intend to cede its position in the city's newspaper market.

Zalman's routine changed dramatically. He rose at two in the morning, leaving Julia asleep. The start of his day coincided with the distribution of the paper's first edition. He finished in the afternoon, when the final edition went on sale. Some days he rode delivery trucks. Other days he walked foot patrol. In the first two weeks, he witnessed seven fistfights between his men and Wilf Hagerty's *Dispatch* crews. Each time he mentioned a fight to Doyle, the Irishman wanted to know only one thing.

"Who won? Us or Hagerty's men?"

"We did."

"Good."

Zalman noticed that none of the incidents received a single line of publicity. Newspapers were notorious censors when it came to their own welfare.

Each weekday, Zalman went home to an empty apartment, to eat a meal that Julia had prepared before leaving for her parents' shop. By the time Julia arrived home, Zalman was ready to fall asleep. The strain of the new job was obvious to Julia. Never heavy to begin with, Zalman became even thinner. When she held him, it was hard to tell where wiry muscle ended and ribs began.

After two months of escalating violence, Doyle called Zalman into his basement office. Beaming, he held out a sheet of paper. "For the fourth week in succession, our circulation's up. The *Dispatch* is down for the fourth week in a row. We've proved to the vendors that we'll use our fists to keep what's ours."

Two weeks later, as dawn broke on a Saturday, fists became obsolete. Zalman rode in a delivery truck driven by Franco Brunelli. They rolled along a narrow, empty street. From the opposite direction, a car approached. A Maxwell roadster. In the gray light, Zalman saw a pale, familiar face and ginger mustache. Two gunshots rang out. Franco screamed and slumped over the steering wheel. A bottle with a flaming wick arced through the air to land on the truck's bed. Gasoline splashed across the newspapers. Gathering speed, the burning truck lurched left and mounted the sidewalk. Zalman flung himself from the vehicle. The last sound he heard was the shattering of glass as the truck slammed into a hardware store.

He regained consciousness to see Jimmy Doyle's red face staring anxiously into his own. "Are you all right, boy?"

Zalman tried to move. Thunder crashed inside his head. His face was grazed. His ribs ached like he had been kicked by a mule, but no bones were broken. "Who called you?"

"Police. Five minutes ago. Said one of our trucks had run amok. You've been out for twenty minutes."

Zalman looked past Doyle to the hardware store. Firemen struggled to contain the blaze fueled by hundreds of gallons of paint, turpentine, and kerosene. At the very center of it, plainly visible, stood the skeleton of the delivery truck. A charred figure lay slumped across the steering wheel. Doyle saw the direction of Zalman's gaze. "What the hell made Franco do something crazy like that? Was he drinking?"

Zalman shook his head. "He was dead before the flames got him. Someone shot him, then threw a firebomb to make sure."

"The hell you say! Did you see who it was?"

"Hagerty."

Doyle's face twisted itself into an ugly mask. "Not a word to the police, understand? You saw nothing, heard nothing. We take care of our own."

In Zalman's statement to the police, he omitted any mention of the Maxwell roadster. He said that the truck had accelerated inexplicably. While he had jumped clear, Franco Brunelli had tried to avert a disaster. The police were satisfied. Zalman returned with Doyle to the circulation manager's office in the basement of the *Messenger* Building.

They remained in the basement until ten-thirty, when Carlo Brunelli returned from street patrol. He came in grinning, teeth gleaming in his dark face. "We sent four stinking *Dispatch* men to the hospital. How's that for a good day's work?"

"Sit down, Carlo."

The grin faded. Suspicion filled Carlo's dark eyes. He looked from Doyle to Zalman. "Hey, who beat the hell out of you? Wait a minute, you were with my brother. Franco . . . what's the matter with Franco? Where is he?"

"Franco's dead," Zalman whispered. "Hagerty shot him."

Carlo grabbed Zalman's coat lapels, and pulled him from the chair. "Then how come you're alive? What did you do—hide while my brother got shot in the back?"

Doyle wrestled Carlo away from Zalman. "Leave him alone! There was nothing anyone could do! Franco was shot from a passing car, damn it!" He pushed Carlo into a chair. "Zalman, tell him what happened."

Zalman related the circumstances of Franco's death. Carlo sat perfectly still. His eyes blazed hatred. For the first time since the circulation war had started, Zalman pitied anyone who worked for the *Dispatch*.

"You'll get plenty of opportunity to pay off your brother's debt," Doyle told Carlo. "But right now I want you to take some time off. Attend to your brother."

"Vendetta." The word dripped like molten lava from Carlo's lips. "My brother is dead. His blood must be avenged."

Doyle stared him down. "Revenge is a dish best served cold."

Zalman watched Carlo leave the basement. "Will he listen?"

"He'd better. Now let me see about getting you home."

"I can manage on the train."

"Take off a few days. Get some rest. We're going to need everyone fresh."

On the way out, Zalman picked up the latest edition of the *Messenger,* still wet from the press. Across the front page, above a picture of the blazing hardware store, headlines screamed of a *Messenger* man's noble sacrifice. The accompanying story described the bravery of newspaper employee Franco Brunelli, who had seen two young children run directly in front of the truck. Rather than hit them, he had forfeited his own life by swerving the truck into the hardware store. Zalman was mentioned—as a survivor who had jumped clear—but the main story concerned Franco, his immigrant background, his hard work and desire to get on. Even a tearful quote from the girl he had planned to marry.

119

Barely a word of the story was true; nonetheless, it made both a marvelous epitaph and circulation-boosting headlines.

When Zalman opened the front door of the apartment, he called Julia's name and told her not to be frightened. Instantly concerned, she rushed into the hall. She saw his bloody face and shrieked. Zalman held her. When she wrapped her own arms around him, the pain in his ribs was excruciating.

"There was an accident this morning. One of our drivers died." He showed her the front page of the paper. "See?"

Shaking, she sat down to read the story. "This poor man. So young. But it could so easily have been you."

"Accidents can happen anywhere."

"Zalman, I want you to promise me that you'll be very careful in the future."

"I am always careful."

"I want you to be even more careful. There is a reason."

"A reason?" He squatted down beside her. "Tell me."

She touched a hand gently to his injured face. "I am going to have your baby."

The pain in his ribs disappeared. His face no longer hurt. His head stopped aching.

"I planned to tell you tonight, over a special dinner I was making. Will you promise to be more careful?"

Zalman, theatrically, held a hand to his heart. "I promise."

"Stop making fun of me, Zalman. I am serious. I want my child to have a whole, healthy father."

"So do I, Julia. So do I."

Zalman took the entire week off. He claimed he needed that long to recover. His real reason was to spend an uninterrupted period of time with Julia. Since he had started on the *Messenger* a year before, they had enjoyed no more than a couple of days together at a time. He had not even taken a vacation; forcing the *Messenger* into the public eye had precluded such luxury.

They remained in the city, eating out and attending shows. The day before Zalman returned to work, they had dinner at the home of Louis and Frieda Bluestone. There, Julia told her parents that she was pregnant. Zalman swore that Frieda's face almost broke into a smile at the news. Louis, though, remained as reserved as ever. He led Zalman into the dining room in a repetition of the night their engagement had been announced. Zalman wondered what wisdom Louis wished to share this time.

"Your news," Louis announced somberly, "is quite disturbing."

"Disturbing? How dare you! Instead of complaining, you should be leaping with joy. Do you know how valuable life is? Do you know what happiness it is to bring another generation into the world? To ensure the continuation of a family?"

Louis weathered the storm. "We would be happier if your work was less dangerous. Julia told us about the accident. It was a week ago and your face still bears the marks. My daughter is entitled to know that her husband will come home safe each day."

"Like I would if I still worked in Windsor Arcade?"

Louis nodded tersely. "It is a more suitable place for a young man in your position."

"Then my wife would quickly become a widow, because I would die of boredom." Zalman turned to leave. Louis called him back.

"I want you to understand that if I consider your behavior to be detrimental to my daughter's welfare—and to the welfare of my unborn grandchild—I will not hesitate to intercede."

"Interfere in my marriage, and you make a lifelong enemy."

Louis smiled icily as if accepting a challenge.

Zalman returned to the office the next day. Doyle took him into a storage room. Fixed to one brick wall was a target. The Irishman pulled out a revolver. "It's about time you learned to use one of these."

Zalman cocked the hammer, raised the weapon to eye level, and squeezed the trigger. A bullet smashed into the wall, high and to the left of the target. He adjusted. The next bullet hit the outer ring. Bullets three through six slammed into the center.

"You've used one of those before," Doyle said.

"Only once."

121

"Wear it."

"I don't feel comfortable walking around with a gun."

"Wear it," Doyle repeated. "I think too much of you and Julia to let you go out there without one."

Zalman compromised. He wore the revolver in a shoulder holster during working hours. Before leaving the *Messenger* each afternoon, he tucked the gun away in a desk.

A month passed before retaliation was taken for the death of Franco Brunelli. Midway through May, Doyle called Zalman into his office. "I'm giving Carlo his revenge. Tomorrow morning, he's going to wipe the *Dispatch* off the streets."

Zalman turned up for work at the normal time the next night. Carlo arrived as the early editions were loaded onto trucks. The Sicilian was accompanied by thirty men. Some of them boarded trucks; others left in cars. When Zalman prepared to leave, Doyle called him back. "You don't want to be out there. Mark my words, it won't be fit for man or beast."

Zalman remained in the office with Doyle until seven in the morning, when Carlo Brunelli returned. The Sicilian's dark face wore a grim, satisfied smile, and Zalman knew, even before Carlo spoke, that his brother's death had been avenged.

"We beat up a dozen of their newsboys, shot a couple of their bodyguards, ambushed their trucks and set fire to them. They reacted just the way we figured. They threw all their men onto the streets to stop us. That's when we went over there to turn their presses into scrap metal and drop a few matches around the place. That stinking paper don't print no more."

"What about Hagerty?"

The satisfaction left Carlo's voice. "We didn't see him. But if he's got any brains, he won't stick around this town."

Zalman unbuckled the shoulder holster and handed the revolver back to Doyle. He felt an instant of relief. Being armed made a mockery of his promise to Julia. "I don't need this anymore."

Doyle gazed speculatively at the revolver. "I don't know. Hagerty got away . . ."

"You heard Carlo. He won't be seen in New York again."

Doyle dropped the holstered revolver into his desk drawer. His hand came out holding a large paper bag which he pushed across the desk to Carlo. "Here's what we agreed on."

Carlo spilled the money across the desk. Zalman could not even guess how much the bag contained. All he saw was a fortune. A fortune to drive an opposing newspaper off the streets. To destroy property and spill blood.

"Pleasure doing business with you," Carlo told Doyle. "You need me again, you know where to reach me."

"The Stuyvesant Hotel," Doyle said.

Carlo snapped his fingers in farewell and left the office.

The *Dispatch* did not print the next day. Nor the next. On the third day of its absence, owner Woodrow Holmes announced the closure of the newspaper following a disastrous fire. In the future, Holmes said, he would concentrate his efforts in the West, where he was well established. The next edition of the *Messenger* carried a story on the demise of New York's newest paper. Included was a sorrowful quote from Henry Bladen. "Despite the fierce but wholesome rivalry which exists between newspapers, no publication ever takes pleasure in seeing a competitor go out of business . . ."

The death of the *Dispatch* brought about Zalman's first meeting with the *Messenger* owner. A week after the closure, Henry Bladen visited New York. Instead of seeing only department heads in the top-floor boardroom, he entered Doyle's basement kingdom. Zalman was impressed. Bladen looked exactly how a newspaper owner should look: a tall, gray-haired man in his fifties, who carried himself with the authority befitting someone of such importance and influence.

"The value of your contribution to the success of the New York *Messenger* can never be overstated," Bladen told the circulation staff in a rich baritone. "Your hard work and selfless attitude have been inspirational. Because of you, our reporters wrote stronger stories, our advertising people sold more space. You can be proud of yourselves."

Doyle introduced each member of the circulation department to Bladen. Zalman was last. "This young man did a fantastic job running subscription sales, Mr. Bladen. And during the recent troubles, as my personal assistant he organized the security of our best locations."

Bladen shook Zalman's hand firmly. The expression on his face was that of a father congratulating a favorite son. "You did excellent work and I'm proud of you."

It occurred to Zalman that Bladen was not aware of men like the Brunellis. Or if he were, he ignored them. He could not afford to be seen to sanction such savagery. He paid the bills such men cost, but he kept himself totally divorced from their activities. "Thank you, Mr. Bladen. I had good men to work with."

"Mr. Doyle thinks you have a big future. I hope he's right, because I always need good people." Then Bladen was gone, back to the top floor where he felt far more comfortable.

With the *Dispatch* off the streets, there was no longer any need for Zalman to put in such long, awkward shifts. His hours changed from night to day. With less time needed for street work, Jimmy Doyle assigned Zalman other responsibilities. Among them was accompanying Doyle to the daily meetings where planning and policy were made. Any questions about the presence of Doyle's assistant at high-level conferences were swept away within a couple of weeks, when Zalman orchestrated the solution to an advertising problem.

The problem concerned a Madison Avenue department store called Benchley's which, following an unfavorable story the previous week, had canceled its considerable advertising in the *Messenger*. Editor Jake Thomson and publisher Len Bennett blamed each other for the revenue loss. The meeting to discuss the cancellation quickly turned into a slanging match.

"How can we get firms to advertise if you print damaging stories about them?" demanded Bennett. He was a short, muscular man whose shirtsleeves were always rolled up, as though he were seeking a fight. "If you can't write something good about an advertiser, don't write about him at all, that's what I say!"

Jake Thomson remained as calm as Bennett was hot. "This newspaper carried stories that build readership. The story

124

about Benchley's selling inferior quality furs while charging for top quality was good material."

Bladen himself was present for this meeting. He had imported both editor and publisher from Chicago to start the *Messenger.* "Instead of squabbling, we should be asking ourselves how we get Benchley's to advertise again," the owner said.

A chorus of answers erupted. Thomson suggested that Bennett offer free ads to the store. Bennett, bristling with anger at the very idea of giving away precious advertising space, came back with the equally odious proposal that the *Messenger* should create a favorable story about Benchley's. When Bladen called for order, Zalman slowly raised his hand.

"I have an idea."

"Let's hear it, lad," Doyle said encouragingly.

Zalman addressed himself to the circulation manager, as though no one else existed in the room. "We've got dozens of delivery drivers, scores of newsboys—why don't we let them persuade Benchley's to resume advertising?" He continued speaking, and when he had finished, Doyle was smiling like a piano teacher who has just heard a star pupil perform Chopin's *Polonaise* faultlessly.

The following morning, when Benchley's opened for business, sixty delivery drivers and newsboys paraded outside the front doors. "Benchley's robs the public!" they shouted in unison. They carried placards that read: "Read all about it in your *Messenger!*" Customers shied away from the doors. Employees remained inside, too frightened to come out and face the demonstrators. Even the police who answered the summons from the store's management could do little. The army that Zalman had amassed at a few hours notice was too powerful to challenge. Within half an hour, publisher Len Bennett received a telephone call from the store's president. If the demonstration stopped, Benchley's would resume their advertising. After that, Zalman's presence at the daily meetings was never questioned again. He was seen as the man Jimmy Doyle was grooming to be his successor.

* * *

Life followed a comfortable pattern. At work, Zalman's star was in the ascendancy. At home, he was utterly contented. Julia's advancing pregnancy soothed him; a baby would fill any remaining gap in his life.

Frieda Bluestone visited her daughter each afternoon, remaining until Zalman returned from work. Zalman made no attempt to become closer with his in-laws. He felt comfortable with the courteous coolness that passed for a relationship.

In September, when Julia was midway through her eighth month, she was as slim as a woman two months earlier in her term. She cleaned and cooked, and shooed away Zalman's concern. Zalman was amazed. Jimmy Doyle had drawn horrendous pictures, describing how each of Kathryn's three pregnancies had bloated her to gargantuan proportions. "Sometimes we thought she must be having triplets, she got so bloody big. Put my arms around her? I couldn't get a rope around her! Couldn't do a thing for herself, either. Just lay there the whole time like a stuffed elephant." Then, seeing Zalman's anxious expression, he clapped him on the shoulder and said, "I'm teasing you, lad, that's all. Don't listen to me, I'm just having a little fun at your expense."

Doyle's eloquent images remained. When Julia underwent an examination at the beginning of her final month, Zalman waited anxiously. Only when the doctor spoke to him did he relax.

"There is no need for you to worry, Mr. Isaacson."

"But she is still so active. So slim."

The doctor laughed. "Don't complain—be grateful. I've no idea who's been filling your head with such nonsense, but let me assure you that your wife could not be in more robust health."

The following morning, Zalman proudly told Doyle of the examination results. "You and your stuffed elephants!"

"Ah, maybe it's just Irish girls who blow up like whales then. I'd say that Julia's examination result is a good excuse for a drink or two after work."

"We have guests tonight. Julia's parents, for dinner."

"Sounds like a damned good reason to be home late."

Zalman grinned in agreement. "All right, one drink."

They left the office at five o'clock. Instead of going to a saloon near the *Messenger,* they chose an old haunt. Mulligan's. More than two years had passed since Zalman had left the saloon, yet little had changed. Many of the same New York *American* faces crowded the bar. Questions popped like bullets about the circulation war with the *Dispatch.*

"We heard you hired Carlo Brunelli to sabotage the *Dispatch* plant," said one circulation man who had worked with Doyle. "How much did you have to pay him?"

Doyle roared with laughter. "Why do you want to know? To see if you can afford him?"

"Did Brunelli's brother really die like you told the police he did?" another man asked Zalman.

Before he could answer, a fresh drink was thrust into his hand. He swallowed it and said, "Would I lie to the police?"

When Zalman looked at the clock above the bar it was ten minutes before six. When he looked again, it was six-forty. "I have to go," he said, and backed away from the bar. His legs felt strange, his head light.

"One more drink," Doyle said, and was immediately supported in his plea by the *American* men. "You can't leave without just one more."

"All right. One more." He was late already. Julia's anger would be no worse if he arrived home ten minutes later. The ten minutes stretched into fifteen, then twenty as Doyle invented stories about the war with the *Dispatch.* Memories of other circulation fights surfaced among the Hearst men, and when Zalman looked at the clock again, it showed seven-thirty.

"I really have to go. My wife . . . my wife is pregnant, you see. Not pregnant and helpless like a stuffed elephant the way Jimmy's wife always was, but she still needs me." He bowed theatrically to the men at the bar and walked toward the door. Doyle followed him.

They walked toward the closest station. The evening was warm and muggy. The elevated track restricted the breeze. Zalman's clothes clung to him. He wondered what story he could tell Julia when he arrived home in this state. A train rumbled overhead, blocking out the little evening light that remained.

"Jimmy! Jimmy Doyle!"

Both Doyle and Zalman turned. A car had come up from behind, its engine noise deadened by the elevated train. Two men were in the car. One drove. The other, white-faced with a ginger mustache and small, close-set eyes, held a revolver.

Wilf Hagerty squeezed the trigger twice. The first bullet seared the air to the left of Doyle's head and smacked into a wall. The second, as he flung himself desperately to the side, smashed through his forehead, blowing away the back of his skull. Zalman, rooted to the ground in shock, saw the revolver swing toward him. Hagerty's eyes gleamed. His index finger, white against the trigger, exerted pressure once more. Zalman, trying to beat the bullet, flung himself forward. The hammer dropped. Hagerty cursed loudly as the gun misfired. Before he could advance the cylinder, Zalman was on him, gripping his jacket with both hands and smashing his head into Hagerty's face.

Blood gushed from Hagerty's shattered nose. He swung the gun like a club. Zalman lost his grip. The driver accelerated, and Zalman slid down into the road, watching as the car sped away. He heard a police whistle, then the sound of running feet. This time, when he gave a statement, he told the truth. He identified the gunman as Wilf Hagerty.

Zalman arrived home just after ten o'clock. Anxiety covered Julia's face. Guilt swept over Zalman. He should have contacted her, told her he would be late and prepared her for the news, but he had been too upset to think properly. The Bluestones were still in the apartment. Cold anger filled Louis's eyes that Zalman should have kept them waiting, and then come home reeking of drink. Before he could utter a word, Zalman said, "Julia, Jimmy's been shot. He's dead."

Julia covered her mouth with a hand.

"The police were sending someone to tell Kathryn. I begged them to let me do it, but they wouldn't listen."

"Who was it?"

"Hagerty, the old circulation manager from the *Dispatch*."

Louis Bluestone's face tightened. "So your work is as dangerous as it ever was."

Zalman, in no mood for recriminations from his father-in-

128

law, ignored the comment. "Julia, will you come with me to see Kathryn? She and the children need our support."

Before Julia could answer, Louis stepped between husband and wife. "What kind of man are you who would drag a young woman in Julia's condition out on an errand like this?"

"I told you what would happen if you interfered. Get out of my way!" He shoved his father-in-law aside. "Julia, will you come with me, please?"

Julia looked from Zalman to her parents. Zalman knew he was engaged in a tug-of-war for his wife's loyalty. In this crisis, he wanted one thing. The Bluestones, who had controlled Julia for most of her life, wanted another.

He lost. Frieda took her daughter by the arm and led her to a chair. "My husband and I will stay with Julia until you are finished with your business."

When Kathryn opened the door to Zalman, her eyes were rimmed with red. Dried tears stained her cheeks. In the doorway, he hugged her for fully a minute without saying a word.

"I knew you'd be coming," Kathryn said at last. "You were Jimmy's best pal. He never stopped talking about you."

"Julia would be here as well, but in her condition . . ."

"I understand." Kathryn led him through to the dining room. On the table, spread out like a poker hand, were family pictures. "I've been looking through these ever since the policeman left. Funny what you take for granted until you don't have it anymore."

Zalman sifted through the pictures. Doyle and Kathryn alone at Coney Island. Carefully posed shots of Doyle and Kathryn with one child, then two, and finally three. It had been a loving family group. Now it was just a memory contained in a collection of photographs that would one day fade. "Do the children know?"

Kathryn nodded. "Little Mary cried herself to sleep."

Zalman felt sick. Little girls with golden ringlets should be made to laugh, not cry. "And the boys?"

Kathryn pointed with her chin toward their bedroom. "Brian and Patrick were still awake when I looked in on them fifteen minutes ago. They were talking about how they were going to find the man who did it." She went to the bureau and opened a drawer. "I think I'd better hide this before they get any ideas."

Zalman took the revolver from Kathryn. "Jimmy always used to wear this. He made me wear one, too."

"He stopped wearing it when the trouble ended. Said there was no longer any need." While Zalman wondered if Doyle's decision had been caused by his own choice to disarm, Kathryn said, "You told police it was that bastard Hagerty, didn't you?"

"It was him, all right." He set the revolver down on the table. "Put it away carefully."

"I will. The boys won't find it." She looked around for a hiding place. "They thought you were a hero, my children did, after the story Jimmy told them that Christmas. Remember it?"

"Fire-breathing horses and snow-covered mountains? Of course I remember it. No one forgets a Jimmy Doyle story."

"He told good ones, didn't he? I always said he should be a writer for the papers, not a circulation man, but he just laughed at that idea." She took down a large china vase from the shelf that ran around the room and placed the revolver inside. "No one will ever look in there. Now you'd better be getting back to your Julia. She needs you more than I do."

"How are you fixed for money?"

Kathryn made a shooing gesture with her hands. "Jimmy always took good care of me. And Mr. Bladen himself telephoned me not ten minutes before you arrived to say the paper would continue to pay me Jimmy's money for a year. Wasn't that nice of him?"

Zalman left the apartment thinking it was the least the owner of the *Messenger* could do.

When Zalman arrived home, Louis and Frieda Bluestone left without a word. Julia went to bed soon after. Zalman stayed up, sitting in an armchair by the open window and reliving the events beneath the elevated railroad. He saw Doyle's head explode, saw the revolver swing toward himself, heard the click of the misfire. Because of a fluke he was still alive. A faulty round which had chosen that particular chamber in the revolver's cylinder. One chamber earlier, Doyle would still be alive. One chamber later, they would both be dead. His mind went back to Rotterdam. Had he not chosen to buy a farewell gift for the Klaases, he would have burned alive in the funeral pyre started by Leopold Metgot. And Kishinev, what fate had decreed that he should escape from that hellhole? Had he been religious like his father, he, too, might have died while seeking defense in a prayer book. Not lived while finding safety in an axe.

He fell asleep in the chair. Julia found him there the following morning. When she roused him, he asked if she believed in fate. She regarded him strangely, and he started to tell her of his lucky escape. She held up a hand.

"I don't want to hear about such things."

"A good friend died, and your husband escaped because of a miracle, and you don't want to hear about such things?"

"Mother told me not to get upset. It might harm the baby."

"Will visiting Kathryn and the children upset you?"

Julia said nothing. Zalman imagined the persuasive arguments her parents must have used while he was out the previous night. Later in the day, when Julia's mother came for her regular visit, he left the apartment and traveled to the *Messenger.* There, at least, people mourned for Jimmy Doyle as he did. Openly.

Jimmy Doyle was buried on Monday morning, five days after his murder. The crowd at the grave side was a who's who of the *Messenger.* Henry Bladen, tall and somber. On either side, like bodyguards, were the men who spoke for him in New York, editor Jake Thomson and publisher Len Bennett. Other employees fanned out in a semicircle, their importance to the paper dictating their closeness to its owner. Next to the grave stood Kathryn Doyle and the children. Brian and Patrick snapped to attention like sentries, eyes following the casket as it dropped into the gaping black hole. Mary stepped forward to toss a rose into the grave. Zalman studied Kathryn. She seemed detached from everything taking place around her. A slight smile flickered on her lips, as if she were reliving a happy moment. A lump clogged Zalman's throat; tears clouded his eyes.

131

After the service, he kissed Kathryn and held her tightly. "Julia wanted to come—"

Kathryn cut him off. "I wouldn't expect any woman in her condition to visit a place like this."

"Thank you," Zalman said, and walked away. He felt guilty at Kathryn's acceptance of his lie. He had not even spoken to Julia about the funeral. It seemed pointless. In the five days since Doyle's death, Julia had grown distant. Their marriage was experiencing its first serious tremors. Zalman knew much of the blame was his. Failing to find consolation over his friend's death at home, he had sought it at the newspaper, in the company of men who had known and respected Doyle. Zalman had little doubt that Julia's parents were doing their best to exploit the situation. They had never accepted him. In their eyes, he remained an ungrateful immigrant. Turning down their job, and telling them what he thought of their toy shop, was a slap in the face from which their self-esteem had never recovered.

The stocky figure of Len Bennett blocked Zalman's way as he left the cemetery. "Mr. Bladen would like you to accompany him back to the *Messenger.*"

Surprised at the summons, Zalman followed the publisher to Bladen's chauffeur-driven White Steamer. "When I was your age, Isaacson," the newspaper owner said as the car pulled away, "I was ready to conquer the world. I was an ambitious young devil, nothing could stop me. You're not lacking in ambition, either, eh? Let me see, you've been in this country what . . . five years? Working on newspapers for less than two, and Doyle thought you were good enough to be his personal assistant. I'd say that's ambition. Doyle spoke of you a lot. A natural, that's what he called you. A natural newspaperman. I agree with him. Young as you are, you're the obvious choice to take his place."

"Are you making me circulation manager, Mr. Bladen?"

Bladen laughed. "Hold your horses. So far, you've only earned consideration for the job. Now I'm giving you the chance to earn the job itself." Bladen lowered his voice to a whisper. "Doyle's been dead five days. Wilf Hagerty's arrest warrant is five days old, and it hasn't been cashed in yet. We all want to see Hagerty get what's coming to him. You arrange that, and I promise you that no one else will be considered for the position of circulation manager of the *Messenger*."

Zalman, unable to believe the bizarre terms of the offer, sat speechless. Bladen, mistaking silence for acceptance, said nothing until they reached the newspaper building. He patted Zalman on the shoulder and said, "Let me know how much you need."

Bladen's proposition dominated Zalman's thoughts for the rest of the day. By the time he arrived home, he knew he was going to accept it. He decided to tell Julia a small part of the story—just that he was in line for a major promotion. Such good news might heal the breach. But when he called her name, no answer came. He walked from empty room to empty room. On the dining table, he saw an envelope. He ripped it open. The note inside, signed by Julia, told him that she needed time alone to consider the future of their marriage. He sat staring at the sheet of paper for a minute, unable to believe she had left him. She had not done so alone, he was certain of that. She'd had help. He left the apartment and traveled to his in-laws' home.

The door opened on a chain. Louis Bluestone's sharp blue eyes glared through a six-inch gap. Behind him stood Frieda. "I'm here for Julia," Zalman said. "I want her to come home with me right now."

"She will not go with you."

"What do you mean, she will not? She is my wife. She belongs at home with me."

"As her parents, we do not think her interests are best served by being with you."

Zalman exploded. "What do you know about Julia's interests? You've choked her all her life. You've chosen her friends. You've told her what she could and could not do. Did you even tell her what to write on that note?"

Louis closed the door in Zalman's face. Zalman launched himself at it. His shoulder bounced off. He threw himself at the door again. It opened long enough for Louis to say, "My wife is summoning the police. If you persist in this behavior, we will not hesitate in pressing charges against you." The door closed once more. Zalman walked away. He couldn't cope with this right now. Not on top of everything else. The Bluestones had chosen their moment well. They had attacked when his mind was so full of other problems that he was unable to react.

He wandered aimlessly for an hour. He had nowhere to go, no wife to run home to. Only a mockingly empty apartment waited for him. He stepped out into the road. A man shouted. Zalman jumped back. A hansom cab clattered past, its driver gesturing angrily. Shaken, Zalman looked around, amazed to find how far he had walked. He was at Lexington Avenue and Twenty-ninth Street. A block farther south, he saw a five-story building; outside was a sign for the Stuyvesant Hotel. Wondering why the name seemed so familiar, he walked toward the hotel. As he reached the door, he remembered.

"Please inform Mr. Brunelli that Zalman Isaacson is calling," he told the desk clerk.

The clerk instructed a bellboy to ask if Brunelli would see Zalman. The bellboy returned two minutes later to lead Zalman to a suite on the top floor.

"Come in, come in!" Carlo shouted when he saw Zalman. He sat at a table with two other men. Playing cards lay scattered across the tabletop. "This a social call, or are you newspaper people needing help again?"

"Business," Zalman said, and looked at the two other men.

Carlo understood the glance. "You want to give me a few minutes in private with my friend here?" The two men got up and went into another room. "What brings you to the Stuyvesant?"

"Hagerty. The police haven't found him yet. Could you?"

"You think I haven't been looking? Only last week I heard he was holed up somewhere out west. Then he turns up here and kills Jimmy Doyle."

"I want him, Carlo. I want him dead."

Carlo's black eyes shone. "How bad do you want him dead?"

"One thousand dollars."

Carlo whistled. "You want him dead real bad."

"I do. He killed your brother. The man he killed last week was like a brother to me."

* * *

134

The knowledge that he had placed a price on a man's head weighed heavily on Zalman. No matter how deserving of death that man was, there was something cold and premeditated about negotiating a fee. The peasant in Kishinev and the Dutch swindler . . . Zalman had killed both men in anger. If he had killed Hagerty in the struggle that followed Doyle's shooting it would have been easy to accept, but doing it this way, through Carlo Brunelli, was different. The truth finally hit home. Henry Bladen was moving him around like a chess piece, and Zalman was allowing himself to be moved. No matter how he tried to rationalize it, he had ordered Hagerty's killing for his own ends. Certainly, his action involved squaring Doyle's account, but Zalman's ambition had played at least an equal role.

That night, he was grateful for Julia's absence. He could never have faced her. His own actions—the understanding of his motivation—shamed him. What little relief he found in the situation came from understanding that he could still be shamed.

The next morning, before he went to work, he visited Central Park Apartments. No one answered his knock. He traveled to Windsor Arcade. Louis Bluestone was alone in the shop. Zalman's tone was calm when he asked where Julia was.

"She is at home with her mother."

"I was just there. No one answered."

"No one will." Louis was surprised at the change in Zalman's attitude. There was no sign of the previous night's aggression. Zalman stood meekly, as if realizing that the reasoned discussion of civilized men achieved more than shouting ever could. Louis grew confident enough to lecture. "You must understand that my wife and I are deeply concerned about the life you lead. In her delicate state, Julia should not have to worry about your safety. She should be spared the anxiety that comes from marriage to a man in your dangerous vocation."

"Are you saying that you'll allow her to return to me only if I quit newspapers?"

"And come back here to work. Think it over carefully, Zalman, and decide what is more important—Julia and the

135

child she carries, or this unsavory business you find so exciting."

Zalman turned and walked from the shop. He was too tired to argue. Too unsure of himself. He no longer knew who was right. Did he, with the satisfaction he found in newspaper work, know best? Or did the Bluestones, with their toy shop? He was forced to admit they had one solid argument: success in the toy business did not require spilling blood.

He reached work just before eleven. As he entered the basement, the normal hectic rush ceased. An eerie silence descended. Men stood around looking at him; when he met their eyes, they turned away. Finally, one of the drivers approached.

"Mr. Bennett sent his secretary down looking for you. Said you're to go up to see him as soon as you get in."

Zalman climbed the stairs toward the publisher's office. Did Bennett want to talk to him about becoming circulation manager? Had Bladen, confident that Zalman would complete the assignment, already told the publisher that he had chosen Doyle's successor? If he expected to see a smile of congratulation on Bennett's face, he was disappointed. Bennett wore a somber expression. He nodded toward a chair, waiting for Zalman to sit before he spoke.

"Kathryn Doyle shot her three children and then turned the gun on herself."

Zalman fought to compose himself. "When did this happen?"

"Thirty minutes ago."

Zalman stood up and ran from the publisher's office.

Police were everywhere when he arrived at the West Side apartment. The neighbor who had heard the shots was being interviewed by a *Messenger* reporter. Zalman knew the man; he specialized in gut-wrenching stories about people's tragedies. The bodies lay where they had fallen, Brian and Patrick in one room, Mary in another, and Kathryn across the bed she had shared with Doyle. The children's eyes were open, faces peaceful. It was as if they had welcomed the bullets. Four more, Zalman thought. Wilf Hagerty was responsible for four more deaths. With one shot he had wiped out a family of five.

Zalman stood over Kathryn. She had shot herself through the heart. The blood that covered the front of her blue dress had spread to the beige eiderdown. Her right hand still held the gun. Zalman stared at it, remembering when Kathryn had sought a safe place to hide it. He should have taken the gun from her there and then. He should have shown some initiative, made the decision to do the proper thing. Then Hagerty would have been cheated of four lives.

The destruction of an entire family . . . Zalman understood the pain. Had he not lost his own family? He had been lucky, though. He had been given the opportunity in America to build another family. Another group that would one day encircle him with love. And even now, even as he looked at Kathryn's body, he knew he was in danger of losing that family.

The *Messenger* reporter cornered Zalman when he came out of Kathryn's bedroom. "You can answer some questions for me."

"I don't have the time. I've got an appointment to keep." When the reporter continued to block his way, Zalman pushed past him roughly. "You can find out all you want from anyone who worked with Jimmy Doyle. Don't bother me."

The reporter followed Zalman to the door. "You were friends with the family. I want to know about them. Kathryn . . . what was she like? How about the kids? What did they want to be when they grew up? That kind of sentimental hogwash sells papers."

"Go to hell, you ghoul."

"What kind of circulation man do you call yourself? You won't even help your own damned paper to sell a few more copies!"

Zalman ignored the gibe. He left the building and jumped on a passing trolley. At Fifty-seventh Street, he changed. He got off at Seventh Avenue and ran to Central Park Apartments, arriving hot and out of breath. He did not knock at the Bluestones' door. Something far more dramatic was necessary. He lifted his foot and kicked out as hard as he could. The door shuddered. He kicked again and again. The door

137

shook more each time. After the fourth kick, he heard the sound of a lock being turned.

The door opened six inches. The safety chain cut Frieda Bluestone off at the neck. "I am calling the police. They will put you where you belong, you madman."

Zalman gave his mother-in-law a sweaty grin. Frieda jumped back in fright as he lashed out one more time with his foot. Locks and bolts might withstand the assault, but the safety chain alone could not. The door flew back. Before Frieda could gather strength for a scream, Zalman was in the wide reception foyer.

"Julia! Where are you?"

He roared through rooms like a tornado. Frieda followed, shouting threats at his back. Julia appeared at the door to her bedroom. Zalman's eyes dropped from her face to her belly. The swelling of his child strengthened his resolve. He held Julia's wrists and pulled her close. She looked past him, to her mother.

"Don't look at her! Look at me!" Obediently, Julia gazed up into his eyes. "Tell me the truth . . . That note you wrote, is it you who needs time to consider our marriage, or is it your mother and your father?"

Julia's gaze wavered.

"Look at me!"

She looked up. "My parents. They told me that I would never be happy with a man who loved his work more than his wife."

"I promise you, Julia, I will never love anything in the world more than I love you and"—he stroked her swollen belly—"our children."

Her eyes filled with tears. "Will you carry my bags?"

Frieda stood by the door as Zalman walked past. He could not resist a smile of victory. They took a cab home. At one intersection, Zalman saw a *Messenger* newsboy. There would be a special edition on the presses right now. In death, the Doyle family would continue Doyle's work in life—selling newspapers. Zalman slipped his arm around Julia and told her what had happened that morning. Her face turned white with horror.

"Kathryn couldn't cope with Jimmy gone," Zalman said.

"And I wouldn't be able to cope without you."

Zalman squeezed her hand and made a silent vow never to cause Julia another moment of concern. She was the most important person in the world to him. Because of that, he would conceal trouble from her as skillfully as the *Messenger* had hidden the truth in its front-page story on Franco Brunelli's death.

Carlo Brunelli contacted Zalman early one morning the following week. The two men met in a restaurant. Brunelli passed Zalman a gold ring on which were inscribed the two letters W.H. Staring at the initials, Zalman found no joy in the death of this man. A Wilf Hagerty for a Jimmy Doyle and his family was a very poor exchange. "Where was he?"

"Denver."

"I'll get you your money."

Zalman took the ring to Henry Bladen. "That piece of jewelry is worth a thousand dollars."

"I'll have it for you in ten minutes. You can do whatever you have to do with it."

That afternoon, Zalman met once more with Brunelli and passed him one thousand dollars. "That pays our account in full."

"Pleasure doing business with you," Brunelli said. When he offered his hand, though, Zalman turned away. With Hagerty's death, the only bond that linked the two men was severed.

At the end of October, Julia gave birth to a girl. Zalman was captivated the first time he set eyes on his daughter. She had light brown eyes and wisps of red hair. Rachel's red hair. His sister's hair.

Zalman had only one regret about the birth of Helen, as the baby was called, but he kept it to himself. He had really wanted a boy. More than anything he longed for a son he could name after his friend Jimmy Doyle.

Chapter Seven

All through July 1914, Rachel read the newspapers with increasing apprehension. Nations exchanged threats with the reckless abandon of street traders offering bargains. Fortunes were spent on arms. Across borders, armies faced each other belligerently, waiting, it seemed, for some adjudicator to drop a handkerchief. Rachel wondered whether Europe had gone mad. Jacob tried to explain the complicated political treaties that both bound and divided the Continent, but such loyalties made little sense.

Most terrifying of all was Jacob's belief that England would be drawn into a war. Conflict would bring change, and Rachel did not want change of any kind. The last five years, since the birth of her youngest son, were the most serene and fulfilling she had ever known. Russia was a dim recollection, easily banished to the farthest recesses of memory by the pride and sense of belonging which England generated. Her husband was English. Her sons—Emmanuel and Sidney, both of whom attended school, and Bernard, who would start next year—were English. There were even people who mistakenly believed that Rachel herself had been born in England. How many times each day did she whisper a prayer of thanks that Tobias Dekker had insisted she speak nothing but the language of her adopted country? Her speech was now fluent. Only when she became upset and talked quickly was it noticeable that before learning English she had spoken another language.

On the last Sunday in July, Tobias and Hannah Dekker

spent the afternoon at the Dalston home of Rachel and Jacob. The invitation had been extended a week before, and all week Tobias had mysteriously hinted at a surprise he would spring. The surprise was a car, a Lanchester four-seater which Tobias proudly drove along Graham Road, roof folded back, with Hannah sitting stoically beside him.

"It took ten years," Tobias said, "but I finally got Hannah to agree that a car offers as much comfort as a carriage."

"I said *almost* as much comfort," Hannah argued, but Tobias did not hear. He was too busy showing off his new possession to neighbors who left their houses at the sight of the bright yellow vehicle. He lifted the bonnet and talked with authority about the six-cylinder engine producing thirty-eight horsepower.

"I never knew Tobias had such mechanical aptitude," Rachel whispered to Hannah.

"He doesn't. He memorized everything the Lanchester people told him. Doesn't comprehend a word of it, but he likes the impressed expressions on people's faces when he quotes figures and technical-sounding words."

"Ah, the little boy who never grew up."

Hannah smiled at Rachel's memory. "Precisely."

"Does he drive well?"

"You will find out for yourself. Tobias insists on giving the entire world a ride."

Tobias never got the chance to offer rides. Jacob pushed his way to the front of the admiring crowd. Behind him trailed Emmanuel and Sidney, fair-haired like their father, and Bernard, dark-haired with the deep-set soft brown eyes that reminded Rachel of her brother. "How about a ride, Tobias?" Jacob asked.

Tobias's face shone. "Of course." He swung open the rear door and ushered the children inside. Jacob climbed into the front passenger seat. "Rachel, are you coming?"

"One moment." She ran back into the house. When she emerged a minute later, a woolen shawl covered her shoulders. From her neck hung the ruined gold-and-enamel watch, and her right hand clasped the copper penny; years of serenity and fulfillment had not softened superstition. She climbed into the back with the boys. Tobias pulled away, sounding the horn with an enthusiasm that scattered birds from trees.

Emmanuel, the oldest and most precocious of the boys—he had turned seven just the previous week—stood up and called out, "Faster, faster!" Rachel told him to sit down. At twenty miles an hour, the car was going quite fast enough to suit her. The breeze lifted her auburn hair, and she had to hold onto her shawl to prevent it from being whipped away.

Tobias drove for ten minutes before returning to the house. While the boys played in the back garden, the four adults took tea in the parlor. Talk centered on the crisis facing Europe.

"Do you really think the Russians will come to Serbia's aid if Germany attacks?" Jacob asked Tobias.

"Germany wants to fight Russia now. The Kaiser's terrified that the Russians will attack in a couple of years, once they've finished rearming. If he can get them to fight before they're ready, he'll solve his problem." He looked up as Rachel poured tea from a heavily flowered pot. "Does that frown on your face mean you disapprove of our discussing the possibility of war?"

"I disapprove of everything that has to do with war. I have three sons. Such sons grow into young men, and it is young men who fight the wars, young men who die in them, young men who are sacrificed so that older men might bask in glory."

Tobias tried to soothe Rachel. "If war does break out, and even if it should involve England, it will be over long before we need worry about Emmanuel, Sidney, and Bernard."

"This war might be the forerunner of bigger, more destructive wars," Rachel argued. "The appetizer. From motor cars, men will learn that they can wage war more speedily and efficiently. Quite probably, they will be able to find some devastating use for aeroplanes, like dropping rocks on each other's heads."

Tobias clapped his hands. "With ideas like that, I think you should be given a cabinet post." He winked at Jacob. "Just wait until I learn to fly one of those machines."

Hannah's face whitened. "Never! I would divorce you first."

Having elicited exactly the reaction he knew he would get, Tobias roared with laughter. Jacob waited for a moment of silence before saying, "Feelings run high at the club over the possibility of England being drawn into a European conflict. On one side, members who were born here say they would rush to fight if we went to war with Germany. On the other side, boys who came from Eastern Europe argue that to fight for England against Germany is to fight for Russia. Germany and Austria-Hungary, in these boys' eyes, are not the enemy. Russia still is."

"I can understand that," Rachel said. "To people who suffered at Russian hands, Russia will always be the enemy. Which position do you take, Jacob?"

"One's feelings toward Russia are irrelevant. The only correct position is that those who elected to make their homes in England must fight for England. That is why, if this war should involve England, I will immediately volunteer my services."

Rachel gasped. "Are you in such a hurry to forget your responsibilities as a father?"

"I also have responsibilities as an Englishman. This country gave my family opportunity. If I did not repay that generosity, I would be an ingrate."

Rachel turned to Tobias, who nodded slowly in agreement. "Remember the role of model that you filled ten years ago, Rachel? Such a role still needs filling. Only now, Jacob will be the model. The boys whose family memories of Russian tyranny make them shudder at the thought of fighting Russia's enemy will follow his example."

The discussion was broken up by the return of Rachel's three sons, sweaty and shining from their exertions in the garden. Emmanuel held a pack of cards in his hands. He spread them into a fan which he offered to Hannah.

"Pick a card," he told her. Hannah did so. "Why did you make it so easy for me by picking the seven of clubs?"

Hannah looked at Rachel. "Jacob?"

"Need you ask?"

Jacob, who had taught Emmanuel the trick only that morning, indicated for Sidney to step forward. The middle brother shoved Emmanuel out of the way. "Watch closely," he said, holding out a bright new marble in his right hand. Hannah watched. He closed his hands into fists, passed one over the other so they just touched, then held them out to Hannah again. "Which hand?"

Hannah touched the right hand. Smirking, Sidney held open his left hand. The marble lay nestled in his palm. "One more time." He made both hands into fists, touched them together, then extended them again. Hannah touched the left hand. Sidney opened his right hand to show the marble. Hannah touched the left hand again. "I want to see what is inside that one."

Sidney's face tightened. His jaw stuck out defiantly. "Don't have to show you."

"I want to see."

"No." The boy shook his head vigorously. "A good magician doesn't show his secrets."

"You have a marble in each hand, don't you?" Hannah tried to hold Sidney. He broke away and ran from the room, left hand still clenched. Everyone laughed. Hannah gazed reproachfully at Jacob. "I'm not sure what kind of a model you really are, Jacob Lesser, teaching a boy not yet six to cheat. What chicanery does Bernard get up to?"

"Nothing yet. When his hands get bigger, he'll learn. Wait and see, by the time the boys are thirteen, I'll have them winning fortunes in card games on board the *Lusitania*."

Hannah and Tobias left shortly after six o'clock. The three boys went to bed and Rachel sat in the parlor with Jacob. "When did you decide that you would join the army?"

"The moment I realized that my country might be in danger."

"Why did you not approach me with your decision?"

"I thought you would understand without being consulted, Rachel. I believe wholeheartedly in patriotism. It is a noble emotion, without which no true Englishman is complete."

Rachel knew better than to argue. Jacob's love of country equaled his love of family. Tobias was the same. These assimilated English Jews were a different breed to the Jews of the Pale, who had no idea that such a word as patriotism existed.

144

Which was not surprising. Why would any man feel loyal to a country that hounds and persecutes him?

She reached out to take Jacob's hand. "If the worst does come to the worst, will you promise me one thing?"

A gentle smile lit Jacob's blue eyes. Rachel's face was too expressive for her to ever keep a secret. He leaned across to kiss her. "I promise to keep my head down."

She kissed him back. "Keep everything else down as well." Silently she prayed that war would never come. At least, not a war that embroiled England. She was not sure that she could care for three young children *and* worry about a husband away at war.

August and war commenced simultaneously. In the first three days of the month, Germany went to war with Russia, then with France. On the fourth day of August, the Kaiser's army invaded Belgium, and Rachel's worst fears were realized. Vowing not to stand by with its arms folded, Britain declared war on Germany.

The following day, the Royal Automobile Club ran an appeal in the *Times* saying it would be glad to receive the names of motorists willing to offer their vehicles and their own services to the war effort. Tobias, too old to serve in any capacity, immediately donated the Lanchester, and the car became the transport of a staff officer.

Anti-German frenzy gripped Britain in the war's early days. Invasion rumors surfaced every half hour; enemy spies hid behind every tree. Houses owned by people with German names had windows smashed. Shops were boycotted. Anything associated with Germany became a target for mob hysteria, even things that merely sounded as though they had a German connection. Late one night, a week after war was declared, someone tossed a firebomb through the window of Tobias Dekker's food store in Regent Street. By the time the fire brigade arrived, the interior of the building was ablaze.

Tobias inspected the burned-out store the following day. His heart sank as he saw the wreckage of everything he had worked for. Understanding failed him. "Is it because I sell a cake called Black Forest that I am suddenly an enemy?" he asked a police officer.

"The mob probably became confused by your name, sir. Dekker does have a German ring, doesn't it?"

Tobias regarded the policeman as though he were mad. "My God, man, don't you know that Dekkers have been English since the days of Cromwell?"

"Whoever started the fire obviously didn't."

At the beginning of September, Jacob, after appointing an interim general manager for the Dekker Boys' Club, joined the army. Midway through December, he returned home for a weekend—Saturday morning to Sunday evening—before leaving for the front. He looked lean and fit in his subaltern's uniform. His face glowed with health, his blue eyes shone with belief in the cause he espoused. Rachel, who could remember when a uniform created terror in her heart, fell in love with him all over again.

Jacob's sons clustered around him. "Have you killed any Germans?" Emmanuel demanded.

"Not yet."

"Will you kill some?"

"At least a dozen. And if I hear from your mother that you're behaving, I'll bring you back the Kaiser's helmet. With the Kaiser still inside it!"

"Don't talk so much of killing," Rachel told him when they were alone. "Even jokingly."

"It's what the boys want to hear. Between you and me, I doubt if I'll even see a German."

Rachel knew he was lying, but she said nothing.

"Why don't we go out for dinner, and then see the show at the Holborn Empire?" Jacob suggested. "We'll be extravagant and sit in the royal fauteuils—"

Rachel pressed a finger to his lips. "I would rather cook dinner for you here. We do not need to sit in the royal fauteuils at the Holborn Empire to enjoy ourselves. Once the boys are sound asleep . . ." She let the sentence trail away.

By seven-thirty, all three boys were in bed. By eight o'clock, they were asleep. Jacob led Rachel to their bedroom at the front of the house. After making love leisurely, they lay side by side, perfectly still, as if by their own immobility they could stop the passage of time and preserve this moment for all eternity; there would be no war, no killing, no reason for Jacob to leave the following day. But every fifteen minutes, the faint chiming of the drawing-room clock mocked their efforts.

Together, they watched dawn creep into the room. Footsteps echoed along the hall as the boys got up. Rachel felt Jacob move. "Why do you rise so early?" she asked.

"The army teaches you to rise early."

"This is one morning away from the army."

"Would you deny me the chance to spend time with my sons?"

"No." Rachel fell back, staring at the ceiling as Jacob hurriedly dressed. When the door closed behind him, tears she had been holding back streamed down her face. She understood the fear shared by every woman with a man in uniform.

That afternoon, Rachel accompanied Jacob to Whitechapel. On the stage of the assembly hall in the Dekker Boys' Club, where he had once conducted a choir in the singing of "Greensleeves," he lectured on the value of patriotism. Among the hundreds of people were young men of military age in civilian clothes. Jacob singled them out. "Why are you men not in uniform? In your country's moment of crisis, you should be only too willing to defend it." When some of his targets argued that the Central Powers were not their enemy, Jacob responded scathingly. "If England is good enough for you to live in, it is good enough for you to fight for." He stepped down from the stage to applause.

From the club Rachel accompanied Jacob to Liverpool Street Station, to catch the train that would return him to camp. On the platform, she held Jacob tightly, scared to release him. He tried to ease the pain of parting with humor.

"Don't spoil the boys while I'm away. I don't want to come home and find three unmanageable monsters."

The guard's whistle shrilled across the platform. Jacob saw tears streaming down Rachel's cheeks. A lump formed in his throat, his vision blurred. "Will you stop crying, for God's sake? You'll start me off, and what will that look like, I ask you, a soldier crying?"

"Perhaps if all soldiers cried, there would be no war."

Tears spilled unchecked from Jacob's eyes. The guard's

whistle pierced the station noise again. Steam burst from the engine. The train jolted into motion. Jacob gave Rachel a final kiss. Tears mingled. He slipped from her embrace and jumped into an open doorway. As the train gathered speed, Jacob stood there, waving back to the desolate figure on the platform.

During the first three months of Jacob's absence, Rachel had been consoled by knowing he was somewhere in England. Now, aware that he was in Europe, his absence terrified her. She worked hard to occupy every waking moment. When she was not busy with her sons, she spent time at the club, handling whatever tasks she could find. She knew that if she lessened her frenzied activity, she would only dwell on Jacob, and then, fearing all the terrible things that could happen to a soldier at war, she would go mad.

Each night, before she fell asleep, she whispered a silent prayer for Jacob's safety. Early each morning, she rushed downstairs to look for letters. Every ten days or so, she found an envelope addressed in Jacob's distinctive upright handwriting. She sat down on the bottom stair, reading and re-reading the letter until she knew it by heart. Just feeling the paper which Jacob had held brought her closer to him. He wrote of many things, but he never mentioned fighting. He even mentioned that he had bumped into a former volunteer manager of the Dekker Boys' Club, Benjamin Beerbohm, who was now an army doctor. "Still an insufferably pompous ass, but decent at heart" was how Jacob described the man who, ten years before, had mocked his attempts to stop gambling at the club. Jacob's failure to mention the hardships he faced worried Rachel more than the truth could have done. She read in the papers about the bloody battles, and she knew he had to be involved. Her imagination was more horrifying than any truth could be.

After each letter, Rachel's sons clamored for news. They wanted to know how many Germans their father had killed. Rachel found herself inventing heroic tales. The boys missed Jacob as much as she did. The only way they would be happy about his absence was to know that he was killing Germans left and right. "Dozens," she replied. "He's killing dozens of them."

One evening toward the end of February, after the boys were in bed, Rachel heard the door knocker rattle. She opened the door and for one wonderful moment thought Jacob had returned. A man in uniform stood outside. As Rachel saw that he was too short, too thin, to be Jacob, her joy turned to fear.

"Yes?" she asked in a quavering voice.

"Don't you know me, Mrs. Lesser?" She looked hard into the thin face and shook her head. "I still play cards, Mrs. Lesser, but I make sure I don't play with anyone who can make them stand up and talk like Mr. Lesser could."

"Harry . . . Harry Myers. I didn't know you were in the army."

"I joined in December. I was one of the people sitting in the club when Mr. Lesser gave that speech. I looked at what I was doing, working in a shop that sold tailors' trimming, and I knew that he was right."

Rachel, suddenly proud of the influence Jacob had exerted on this young man, felt her cheeks flush. "Thank you for coming to tell me that, Harry."

"I'm leaving for the front tomorrow. If I should see Mr. Lesser, is there anything you want me to tell him?"

Rachel remembered a photograph Tobias had taken of the boys only two weeks before. She handed it to Myers. "Would you give him this?"

"Of course I will." Myers shook Rachel's hand. "See you when I get back, Mrs. Lesser. And don't you worry, I'll keep an eye on Mr. Lesser for you."

"God bless you," Rachel called out.

Three weeks later, she received a letter in which Jacob thanked her for the photograph of his sons. Harry Myers had been assigned as a replacement to Jacob's company. In the same letter, Jacob mentioned that Benjamin Beerbohm had died. The news made Rachel physically sick.

Letters arrived regularly until the end of April 1915. Then they stopped. Rachel heard nothing through May, then June. She waited fearfully for news. Her only comfort was the knowledge that had Jacob been killed, she would have received a curt note from the War Office.

It was not until the first week of July that she received another letter. It was from Jacob, but the handwriting was misshapen, like that of a child learning the rudimentary skill of communicating with pen and paper. Rachel sat on the bottom stair and ripped open the envelope. " 'My darling Rachel,' " she read aloud. " 'You must forgive me for not having written for so long, but fortune deserted me momentarily. A vehicle in which I was riding turned over. Not to worry, though. I received nothing more serious than some cuts and bruises. Writing was a bit difficult, but I think I've overcome the problem now.' "

Rachel looked up as she heard footsteps. Emmanuel stood beside her. "Is that from Papa?"

"Yes."

"Did he say why he hasn't written for so long?"

Rachel smiled. "He was so busy killing Germans that he didn't have time to write."

Emmanuel nodded sagely. "That's all right then."

Another letter from Jacob arrived the following week. The handwriting was still awkward, the characters leaning backward at differing angles. It reminded Rachel of the times when, as a child, she had tried writing with her left hand instead of her right. Jacob's letter was cheerful. He described how much better he was feeling. At the very end, her heart lifted at the words: " 'All being well, I hope to be home by August. We will be able to take the boys away for a summer holiday.' "

Rachel counted the days. On the calendar, she circled the first day of August, crossing off each intervening day before she went to bed. She received another letter midway through July. In it—she shrieked with joy—Jacob said he would be home on July 24. He asked Rachel not to organize a party for him; all he wanted was to be alone with her and the children.

On the morning of July 24, Rachel hung a huge sign on the front door. "Welcome Home, Jacob!" At four in the afternoon, a taxi drew up. A man in uniform got out. Holding a single bag in his left hand, he climbed the stairs to the front

150

door. Rachel, who had been watching through the window, pulled open the door before he could knock. She flung her arms around Jacob and hugged him. They kissed and clung together. When at last she stepped back, she forced herself to stare only at Jacob's face. She dared not look elsewhere, especially at the empty right sleeve that was pinned so neatly to the jacket of his uniform.

"I judged it best not to tell you in a letter," Jacob said.

"I think I knew already."

The three boys appeared behind their mother. Jacob did not push himself onto them. He waited for them to choose their own time. Unlike Rachel, the boys' eyes never left their father's empty sleeve. Sidney and Bernard pushed Emmanuel forward. "Where's your arm?" the oldest son asked.

"I left it at a place called Ypres."

"The Germans used gas there, didn't they?"

Jacob was amazed at how adult Emmanuel sounded for a child who had just turned eight. "He read the newspapers every day since you went away," Rachel explained. "Every time he saw stories of Germans being killed, he would tell Sidney and Bernard that he knew exactly where you were."

Jacob ran the fingers of his left hand through Emmanuel's fair hair. He knelt down and kissed each boy in turn, holding them tightly with his left arm.

"Do you miss your right arm?" Sidney asked.

Rachel sucked in her breath at the frankness of the question. Before she could chide the middle boy, Jacob said, "One arm is enough for anyone, don't you think? Soon I'll be able to do everything with my left hand that I could ever do with my right."

"What about magic?" Sidney asked. "Can you still do tricks?"

Jacob reached out his left hand and withdrew a shilling from behind Sidney's ear. "Didn't know that was there, did you?" He turned to Bernard. "And I see sixpence behind your ear."

Bernard felt behind his right ear. "There's not."

Jacob reached behind the boy's left ear and produced the tiny silver coin. "Wrong ear."

"What about card tricks?" Sidney asked.

151

"Give your father a chance to sit down," Rachel pleaded.

Jacob overrode her objections. "Of course I can still do card tricks. I'll show you in the parlor." Emmanuel ran on ahead. When Jacob reached the parlor, he found a pack of cards waiting for him in the center of the table. "You'll have to shuffle them for me." Once the cards were mixed, Jacob cut them again and again with one hand. The boys watched his long, slender fingers. Rachel focused on his eyes. She saw rigid determination not to disappoint his sons. The tricks were simple deceptions which a skillful conjurer could master with one hand, yet they were sufficient to enthrall the boys.

After ten minutes, Jacob leaned back, the resolution in his eyes replaced by satisfaction; he had demonstrated to his sons that one arm was enough for anyone. On his chest were three medals. He unpinned them, giving one to each boy. "Show them to your friends. Tell them how heroically your father fought."

The boys ran off clutching their prizes. Jacob let out his breath in a long sigh. "I practiced ten hours a day to do those easy tricks."

Rachel watched his body shrink. He looked tired; his eyes were dull and empty. The display of carefree confidence had been for the benefit of his sons. With his wife, he no longer pretended. "Did a vehicle really overturn, Jacob?"

He shook his head. "My company was rushed in to reinforce our troops after the German gas attack at Ypres. We charged enemy positions. I was hit by machine-gun fire. Someone dragged me back toward our lines, screaming at me, 'Don't die, Mr. Lesser! Don't die! I promised your wife I'd look after you.' "

"Harry Myers," Rachel murmured.

"Yes. I found out later that it was Harry who'd saved me."

"Why did you lose your arm?"

"The doctors had no choice but to amputate." He looked down at the empty sleeve and shivered slightly. "The bullets almost ripped my right arm clean off."

Nervously, Rachel touched Jacob's right shoulder. He tried to shrink back, but the chair stopped him. She ran her fingers down the uniform sleeve. The arm ended in a three-inch stump. "Those last letters you wrote to me, they were from England, weren't they? From some hospital in England?"

Jacob nodded. "Near Southend, a rehabilitation center."

She touched his ruined arm once more. "Is patriotism still such a gleaming ideal?"

Some of Jacob's pride returned. He sat straighter in the chair, fire flickering in his eyes. "You should have seen the men at the rehabilitation center, Rachel. Far worse than me. Men missing both arms. Missing legs. Men with lungs seared by gas. And they still believed in the cause they fought for."

"Do the Germans believe just as fervently in their cause?"

"I would be surprised if they did not."

Jacob resumed his position as general manager of the Dekker Boys' Club. He had good days, when he was as cheerful as he had ever been, mixing with the boys and being genuinely interested in their welfare. On his bad days, he found fault with everything, criticizing everyone from the club janitor to the volunteer staff. Rachel soon learned how to judge his moods. The Jacob who wore a suit to work was an abrasive, dissatisfied man spoiling for an argument. Only when he wore the uniform—with medals gleaming on his chest, and the right sleeve pinned neatly to his jacket—was he civilized. Then some of the boys saluted him, and he remembered happier days when his body had been whole.

At the end of 1915, Harry Myers came home on leave. Rachel invited him to the house for dinner. The evening started with tales of gallantry as Myers assured Emmanuel, Sidney, and Bernard that their father was the biggest hero who had ever walked the earth. After dinner, when the boys had gone to bed, the mood changed dramatically. Sitting in front of the fire, Jacob invited Myers to talk to club members about the war. Myers greeted the request with cynicism.

"What do you want me to tell them? How we spend six days at a time in muddy trenches? How we eat in them and sleep in them? And how, each time our lords and masters decide to attack, it costs fifty thousand lives just to gain fifty yards of mud."

Jacob bristled. "Such talk is disloyalty."

"No, it's truth. After listening to you at the club, I rushed out to join the army. That day I came around here to see Mrs. Lesser, I was as full of patriotic pride as any man. What I've seen since that day has changed me. I thought that"—his eyes fixed themselves on Jacob's empty sleeve—"might have knocked some of the jingoism out of you as well."

Rachel saw the mood descending like a cloud. Jacob's eyes hardened in a suddenly pale face. "My injury served only to strengthen my faith in my country. And what I read in newspapers about our military successes strengthens it even more."

Myers laughed out loud. "You read what the government wants you to read. The stories are censored. I've been in disorderly retreats—total routs!—that were reported in the press as great triumphs. If the truth were printed, no young men would rush in like me to fill the hundred thousand gaps left by the dead."

Jacob's voice became an icy whisper. "Please leave. I will be forever grateful to you for saving my life, but I never want to see you in my house again."

Myers left. Rachel saw him to the door. When she returned, Jacob still sat by the fireplace. "Rachel, never mention the name of Harry Myers in my presence."

Rachel said nothing. Arguing with Jacob, trying to make him see any other point of view, was a futile exercise. She never mentioned Myers' name again, but each night, before falling asleep, she prayed for him as she had prayed for Jacob.

The war dragged on. A plaque was erected in the assembly hall of the Dekker Boys' Club. On it were listed the names of young men killed in action. Benjamin Beerbohm's name topped the list, the first man associated with the club to die. Slowly, the list grew longer until, in November 1918, when the armistice was signed, it included seventeen names. Harry Myers' name was not among them, and Rachel knew that God had answered her prayers.

Not all the losses occurred on the battlefield. After the armistice, a different war victim emerged. As the war's support industries halted, unemployment rose. Former soldiers—privates and officers alike—competed for menial jobs.

154

The promised nation fit for heroes became a drab and miserable place, and Britain would never be the same again.

Tobias Dekker was one of the postwar casualties. In September 1919, he and Hannah invited Rachel and Jacob to St. John's Wood for dinner. After the meal, Tobias poured cognac for himself and Jacob, and then calmly announced that he was financially ruined. Jacob and Rachel were stunned by the news. Only Hannah remained unfazed; she had lived with the knowledge of her husband's failure for a long time.

"That fire in the first days of the war devastated me," Tobias explained. "My insurance company never paid me for the damage. They claimed that the fire came under one of two exclusionary clauses—an act of war, or riot and insurrection. They refused to part with a farthing. I sued, of course, and lost. To rebuild the store, I used whatever money I could lay my hands on. Business remained terrible. Because of the war, many of the goods I stocked were no longer available. I fell deeper and deeper into debt. I mortgaged everything. Even . . ." He spread his hands in a helpless gesture. ". . . this house."

Jacob started to ask Tobias where he planned to go. Rachel interrupted before he could phrase the question. "We have plenty of room! You know you are welcome to stay with us for as long as you wish."

Hannah smiled fondly at the younger woman. "Thank you, but we have already rented a small flat in town. It is sufficient for our needs."

"When are you moving?"

Tobias exchanged a glance with his wife. Rachel saw secrecy and guilt. "Tomorrow," Hannah answered. "This is our last dinner in this house. We wanted you to share it with us."

"What about the staff?"

"Only May and Mr. Edwards remain with us," Tobias answered. "I have managed to make arrangements to safeguard them. They will both receive an adequate pension. I am afraid, however, that the news concerning the Dekker Boys' Club is not so good. The building will be attached by my creditors."

Voice breaking, he hid his misery in the glass of cognac.

Rachel searched deep within herself for some words of solace. She doubted that the failure of the business was as brutal a blow to Tobias as the loss of the club. That was the cruelest trick fate could have played. For the first time, Rachel noticed lines in Tobias's round face. The chubby cheeks had yielded to a gaunt tiredness, the once-flourishing white mustache drooped wearily. Had he really aged so suddenly? Or had he been growing visibly older all the time, and she had simply failed to notice it?

Hannah spoke. "Somewhere in London, Tobias, are hundreds of successful young men who achieved their starts because the Dekker Boys' Club cared. These young men will remember your name for as long as they live."

The comment triggered a bout of reminiscing. Rachel recalled the time she had stood up to the Irish foreman of the building crew. "I was absolutely terrified of the man, but I dared not let him see it," she related. Hannah talked of the club's open day, and then Rachel touched a note of sentimentality by summoning up a memory of the first summer camp when Jacob had proposed to her. She hoped the recollection would draw Jacob into the conversation. The news had shocked him into silence. He just sat there, though, sipping the cognac that Tobias continued to pour.

As the clock struck nine-thirty, Rachel stood up, saying it was time to leave. Tobias waved at her to sit down. "I will drive you and Jacob home. I may as well get some use out of my car before I lose that, too."

Rachel sat. She had wondered about the fate of the Vauxhall which Tobias had bought early in the year, when everyone had still been full of peacetime optimism. That would be taken by the creditors as well.

"Do you remember, Rachel," Hannah asked, "when you wanted to know how to make Jacob aware of your existence?"

Rachel's face brightened. "Apart from hundreds of successful young men who will recall the name of Tobias Dekker for the rest of their lives, Jacob and I have you to thank for our marriage."

"Are you thankful, Jacob?" asked Hannah.

Jacob raised his glass to Tobias. "I drink to your health, sir," he said loudly.

"And I drink to yours," Tobias responded.

When the clock struck ten, Rachel stood once more. "Our neighbor's fourteen-year-old daughter is staying in the house until we return. To leave any later would be unfair."

"Your chauffeur awaits, madam," Tobias responded.

Hannah also stood and gazed out of the window at the clear sky. "I will come with you. It's a nice evening for a ride."

Tobias drove with the roof folded down. Jacob sat next to him. Hannah and Rachel, a plaid rug stretched across their knees, shared the back. After a few hundred yards, Tobias broke into song. The piece he chose was Elgar's "Land of Hope and Glory," which had become such a rousing avowal of patriotism during the war. Beside him, Jacob used his left hand to conduct an imaginary orchestra. From the back of the Vauxhall, Hannah and Rachel added their voices. They sang for the entire journey, moving from one wartime song to another. Only when the car rumbled across the streetcar tracks in Graham Road did they stop.

Rachel stepped from the car. Hannah embraced her. "Tobias was dreading the thought of making his failure known to you. Thank you for helping to make the occasion less terrible."

"You both know you'll never be a failure in our eyes," Rachel kissed Hannah good-bye, then leaned into the car to kiss Tobias. Hannah climbed into the front passenger seat. The Vauxhall pulled away. High above the engine noise, Tobias's off-key bass launched once more into "Land of Hope and Glory." Laughing, Jacob slipped his left arm around Rachel's waist. She realized he was drunk, and then she reasoned that perhaps he had needed to get drunk to knock down the barriers he had erected.

In bed, Rachel thought about Tobias. How could he possibly regard himself as a failure when he had helped so many? She dearly wished there was some way she could help him now. She wondered about her own husband, who had fallen asleep within a minute of lying down beside her. How would the closing of the club affect him? He would go back to

157

teaching. How effective would he be, a one-armed teacher trying to control a class of children in this strange, new postwar era? Most important, how would he feel about returning to teaching after he had managed the Dekker Boys' Club? Perhaps—she forced a ray of optimism into the bleakness of reality—Tobias's creditors would have a stroke of human kindness in them. They would see, as Tobias had seen, the importance of the club, and they would allow it to continue. On that hopeful note, she finally fell asleep.

Footsteps racing along the hall disturbed her. She looked around in bewilderment. The alarm clock on the bedside table read five-forty. As Jacob awoke and sat up in bed, knuckles rapped on the bedroom door. Emmanuel's voice called out. "There's a policeman who wants to see you."

Jacob and Rachel jumped out of the bed together. Rachel was first out of the room, pulling a robe over her nightgown as she rushed past Emmanuel. Behind her ran Jacob, the empty right sleeve of his nightshirt flapping grotesquely. A police constable stood just inside the front door.

"Mr. Lesser? Mrs. Lesser? A Mr. Alan Edwards gave us your name and address."

Rachel remembered that Alan was the first name of Tobias's butler. Her heart leaped into her mouth.

"Last night, Mr. and Mrs. Tobias Dekker were involved in an accident. Their car overturned. I'm afraid both were killed."

Rachel left the cemetery with the knowledge that she was tragically unique. How many other people lost their parents twice? How many other women buried a mother and father two separate times, so many years and continents apart?

Tobias's will included a provision for a trust fund to administer the club, but the will had been drawn up before his financial troubles. The estate did not yield enough to pay off his creditors. Jacob held one final meeting at the club. Past and present members packed the assembly hall. He thanked them for their support in the past, and he hoped that they would always remember the part the club had played in their lives. Then he announced it was closing. Pledges of money—from pennies to pounds—came in from people who, in many

158

cases, could barely afford to feed their families. Jacob turned them down. It was too late to attempt a rescue. When he came home, he sat in the parlor for two hours without saying a word to anyone. Rachel left him alone with his thoughts and memories.

Jacob returned to teaching, not at the Jewish Free School, where he had taught before joining the Dekker Boys' Club, but at a state school. It was a job, nothing more. He left home in the morning and returned in the late afternoon with barely a word to say about his day. His love for working with young people had disappeared. The war had damaged his body; the closure of the club had wrecked his spirit. Each, by itself, he could have dealt with. Together—and never in her most pessimistic mood had Rachel imagined that such a thing could befall Jacob—they had destroyed him.

The teaching job paid less money than the club had. Rachel found it difficult to get by with the smaller sum Jacob gave her every week. She didn't tell him so; to do that would further wound him. She just dipped into the family's savings to pay the bills. By March 1920, six months after the death of Tobias and Hannah, Rachel could see bottom. She had no alternative but to tell Jacob. She tried to be tactful.

"Do you not think it amazing how much the world has changed since the war?" she asked as they lay in bed that night. "Look at all those women who went to work in the factories while the men were away. They worked because their country needed them to work, but then they found out that they liked it."

"Would you want to go out to work?"

"I think so."

"What work would you do? Surely not factory work?"

Rachel had her answer all ready. "I was happy when I was a typewriter doing the office work at the club."

"Such women are called secretaries now. They have their own identity; their position is no longer named after their machine."

"Then I could be a secretary."

Jacob considered Rachel's proposition. She was unable to tell whether or not he accepted her reasons for wanting to work. Finally he said, "All right, if that is what you want, become a secretary." And then he turned his back on Rachel, telling her everything she needed to know about the way he felt.

During the following week, she applied for half a dozen secretarial positions in banks and lawyers' offices. Each time she met rejection. In twelve years away from work, her skills had atrophied; younger women typed and took dictation twice as fast. The next week she lowered her sights to small businesses. More rejections followed. Just after lunchtime on Friday, she prepared to endure her final interview of the week. She entered a building in Charing Cross Road and climbed two flights of stairs to the office of Harold Parker, theatrical agent.

The agent's office contained a single desk and some chairs. Harold Parker, a short, stocky man with a red face and spiky gray hair, sat at the desk, talking on the telephone. The stubby fingers of his right hand gripped a cigar which he waved in the air as he spoke. When Rachel entered the office, he pointed with the cigar to a chair on the other side of the desk. She crossed the worn carpet and sat down. While Parker continued talking, Rachel's eyes swept over the variety-theater posters covering the walls. She recognized the names of several acts, and wondered which of them Parker represented.

Parker ended his telephone conversation. "Can I help you?"

"I'm Rachel Lesser."

"Where did you work before? What references do you have?"

"I haven't worked for almost thirteen years."

"Thirteen years? I need someone who can manage this office, take care of the clerical and bookkeeping work. I don't want someone I'll have to train." He got up from the desk and opened a cupboard. Inside, Rachel saw half a dozen tea chests that overflowed with papers. "My last secretary left a week ago. I haven't been able to find a thing since. I've spent more time trying to bring some semblance of order to this mess than booking clients, and that's not what I'm in business for."

"I am perfectly familiar with managing an office. Because

160

I have not worked for thirteen years, it does not mean that I have forgotten all I ever knew."

Parker sat down again. "Why are you seeking work after such a long time?"

"My husband lost an arm in the war. We have three sons and it's becoming harder to make ends meet."

"I see." Rachel spotted sympathy in the agent's eyes. After two weeks of searching, she was becoming desperate, but the last thing she wanted was pity. She need not have worried, though. "I'm sorry, Mrs. Lesser, but I'm really looking for someone who'll take a load off my shoulders. I hope you find something."

"I understand." Rachel stood up and straightened her skirt. As she turned toward the door, the telephone rang. Parker answered it. He mentioned train stations, timetables, and hotels. Voice doubling in volume, he repeated each piece of information. At last he yelled, "What do you mean, you don't understand? I'm talking in plain English, aren't I?" He saw Rachel looking at him, and he rolled his eyes. "The Kerenskys, a Russian dance troupe—they're supposed to be appearing at the Liverpool Olympia tomorrow night. They don't know how to get to Liverpool, they don't know where they're supposed to be staying, and they don't speak more than half a dozen words of English between them. Now who'd be an agent, I ask you!"

Rachel took the telephone from Parker's hand. *"Allo? Chem vam pomoch?"* While Parker looked on in amazement, she carried on a conversation in Russian. Holding a hand over the mouthpiece, she said to the agent, "Give me details about the trains and the hotel and I'll translate."

While Parker scribbled down train times and hotel names, he asked, "How is it that you speak Russian?"

"I was born there."

He passed her the information. Rachel interpreted it for the Kerensky dance troupe. When she finished, she set down the telephone and walked toward the door. "Wait a minute!" Parker called out. She turned around. "Is Monday morning soon enough for you to begin taking a load off my shoulders?"

* * *

Rachel began to work for Harold Parker. She learned that before becoming an agent, he had been a music hall comic. A fall had ended his career on the boards and he had turned to representing other artists as the free-and-easy fashion of Victorian music hall yielded to the more structured and formal style of variety theater. As an agent, he dealt with both the major theater circuits and small independents. The difference was that he arranged mostly minor acts for the circuits, while with provincial independent theaters, he sometimes put together an entire bill.

"Those are what we call combinations," Parker explained. "The circuits employ bookers to put together their bills. With the money they can pay, they have the cream of the crop. Smaller houses without the funds for such an organization are only too grateful if we can put together a combination for them, a good mixture of singers, dancers, magicians, acrobats, and comedians, with a couple of well-known names for feature and star acts."

Rachel dealt with Parker's clients. She learned which performers were easy to get along with, and which ones needed a velvet glove. Her typing and dictation speeds picked up; her bookkeeping competence created order out of Parker's chaos. Her ability with languages found frequent use. In one afternoon, she dealt with an Austrian team of acrobats and a Swiss high-wire act, whose native language was German.

"If you could learn French and Italian as well, we could corner the market in foreign talent," Parker told her.

"What did you do before I came?"

"You saw, with the Kerensky dance troupe."

"You just shouted at the poor people."

"That's right. I always thought that if you shouted English loud enough, everyone understood."

One of her many record-keeping responsibilities concerned updating the vacancy cards that listed the dates performers were unbooked. These were mailed to theater managers, to be stacked with countless other vacancy cards sent by other agents. Managers consulted these cards when organizing a bill.

"Are all vacancy cards the same size?" Rachel asked Parker after she had been working on them for several weeks.

"Regular postcard size."

"Why don't you invest some money in having special cards made up? Cards that are a fraction of an inch larger? They'll stand out from the others, so they'll be picked first."

"Where did you think up a trick like that?"

"My husband was a skillful conjurer before he lost his arm. The first trick he taught our sons was how to make a person take the card he wanted them to take."

Although Rachel worked five days a week, she did not neglect her family. Before leaving the house each morning, she made sandwiches for the boys to eat when they returned home at lunchtime. When she finished work in the late afternoon, she came home to cook dinner for the family and do household chores. On weekends, she prepared special meals to compensate for her absence during the week.

Money went back into savings. What was left over from Jacob's and her own salary, Rachel put away. Only half went into a bank. The remainder she concealed in a glass jar under a floorboard. For the first time since leaving Russia seventeen years ago, Rachel understood want. So she acted as her father had in Russia: she kept money within easy reach.

One Saturday evening during early summer, Rachel took the three boys to the Hackney Empire. Jacob had not wanted to accompany them; he showed no interest in Rachel's job, as though by ignoring it he could make himself believe she was not working. One of Parker's clients, a young man named Lenny Blount, was the second-spot comic on the bill. Blount's act centered around his impersonation of a drunk dressed in baggy clothes. He staggered around the stage, musing aloud on life, and finishing off with a witty song which drew loud applause. The three boys loved the act. After the show, Rachel took them to meet Blount. He gave the boys a tour of backstage, an experience they talked about for a week.

In August, Rachel used money from the jar to pay for a week's vacation with Jacob and the boys. Eagerly, she returned to Parker's office. To her surprise, she found herself liking the work more with each passing week. When she had first considered working, she had looked on it as a way to pay the bills. There would be professional pride in a job well done,

163

but that would be all. The possibility of enjoyment had never entered her mind. Just as she was always thankful that Tobias Dekker had forced her to speak English, she was grateful to the Kerensky dance troupe for telephoning Harold Parker at that particular moment so she could demonstrate her fluency with Russian!

One evening in September, she returned home to find Emmanuel nursing a split lip. Before she could ask him why he had been fighting, he fired a question at her: "Are we poor?"

She stared into her eldest son's blazing blue eyes. She saw accusation there, as though he had already decided that the family was indeed poor and he was blaming his mother for it. "Of course we're not. We live in a nice house. None of you want for anything. Does that sound like we're poor?"

"Then why do you go out to work? Boys at school say only in poor families do mothers have to find jobs. They say we're poor because you work. They laughed at me, so I fought them."

"You should be proud to have a mother who works. How many boys have mothers capable of doing something so important? Before you fight again, ask the other boys if their mothers take them backstage at the Hackney Empire?"

Rachel's response did not satisfy Emmanuel. He continued to be haunted by the notion that only poor families sent mothers out to work, and he quickly convinced his brothers that they should do something about it. Two weeks later, on a warm afternoon, Rachel came home early from work. She walked through the house to the dining room and stopped in surprise. Through the window she saw thirty neighborhood children sitting on the lawn of the small back garden. Boards raised on bricks formed a stage. A curtain—Rachel almost screamed; it was her best tablecloth—hung from a makeshift frame. As she watched, the curtain was pulled back by Bernard. Behind it, smiling broadly, stood Emmanuel. He wore the top hat in which Jacob had been married. Jacob's bow tie was fastened around his neck. On the table beside him rested some of the props Jacob had used during his conjuring days. Her shock turned to amusement as she watched Emmanuel flawlessly work his way through half a dozen tricks. Some were solo; others used members of the audience. When the curtain fell, Rachel found herself applauding in time with the garden audience.

Bernard stepped in front of the curtain. Rachel raised the window in time to hear her youngest son introduce Sidney. She wondered what she was going to see. The curtain rose once more. Wearing one of Jacob's suits, sleeves and trousers rolled up to fit, Sidney staggered around the stage like a drunk, singing and making silly jokes which convulsed the audience. Rachel smiled. Her middle son was impersonating Lenny Blount, the comic they had seen at the Hackney Empire.

After Sidney's performance, Emmanuel returned with more conjuring tricks, then Bernard announced the end of the show. "Thank you for coming to see the Lesser Brothers." The children filed through the scullery and dining room, past where Rachel stood, and into the long hall leading to the front door. Some seemed surprised to see her. Others greeted her with a cheerful "Hallo, Mrs. Lesser!" When the last ones had gone, she stepped out into the garden, where her three sons were busily dismantling the stage. Sidney, who was trying to fold the tablecloth back into its original creases, was the first to see her.

"Oh, oh," he said, and nudged Emmanuel.

"What was that all about?" Rachel asked.

"We put on a variety show," Emmanuel said.

"Did you ask if you could use my table and cloth for your show?" She took the cloth from Sidney. It needed washing, but she was grateful that it had not been torn. "Did you ask your father if you could wear his clothes and use his equipment?"

"We didn't do it for ourselves," Emmanuel answered.

"No, you did it for half the neighborhood."

Emmanuel dug into his pocket and pulled out a fistful of loose change, farthings, half-pennies, and pennies all mixed up together. Wordlessly, he handed them to his mother.

"What's this?" She counted it quickly; there was more than two shillings. "Where did you get all this money?"

"From the show," Emmanuel answered.

"You charged your friends to watch you?" Rachel did not

165

know whether to be angry or to laugh. "What do you need so much that makes you take money from your friends?"

"We don't need anything. We're doing it for you, so you won't have to go out to work."

Rachel looked away, blinking to force back the tears that suddenly burned her eyes. She turned back to her sons and held out the money. "I don't mind you entertaining your friends, but I don't want you to charge them. Return their admission money."

"We need it," Emmanuel stressed, "so you won't have to work."

"No matter what the boys at school say, I work because I like to work. If I didn't like it, I wouldn't do it." Her face, despite the wetness of her eyes, broke into a happy smile. "What you did just now was a very wonderful thing. You thought your family was in trouble, so you tried to help. I'll tell you what . . ." She looked from one boy to the next. Bernard's likeness to Zalman—the lean face, the deep, searching eyes—was becoming even more pronounced as he grew older; he looked as Zalman had done at the same age. "When you grow up and earn your own living, then your father and I will be only too happy to let you help us. How does that sound?"

Emmanuel took the money from his mother, promising to return it. Rachel kissed each boy in turn before taking the tablecloth and side table back into the house.

The Lesser Brothers! Who would have thought her sons were such showmen?

Chapter Eight

None of the war fever gripping England in August 1914 was apparent in the United States. Three thousand miles of ocean shielded America from the bloodshed in Europe. Pacifism became the second most popular word of the American people. Isolationism was the first.

At the New York *Messenger,* the editorial position was neutrality. Henry Bladen believed in that, and used the eight newspapers he owned to relay to America the message that the United States had no business being entangled in Europe's family squabbles.

During the past six years, as *Messenger* circulation—coupled with a flourishing Sunday edition—had risen to become the highest of any newspaper owned by Bladen, he had grown far more involved with his New York operation. Believing that the headquarters of a publishing company belonged in the city of its biggest seller, he had relocated his base of operations from America's second city to its first, turning the boardroom on the top floor of the *Messenger* building into his private office. From there, Bladen made his pronouncements on Europe.

The main voice of dissent to Bladen's policy came from the newspaper's circulation department. Zalman opposed neutrality, not from any emotional commitment, but because of dollars and cents. "In New York live hundreds of thousands of people with German ancestry," he told a morning meeting of department heads. "Add to that people of Austrian and Hungarian descent. Throw in the Irish as well. If we adopt an anti-British position, we'll gain them all as readers. Everyone dislikes the British, so let's capitalize on it."

Jake Thomson picked up the previous day's newspaper and read from the lead article which had been written by Bladen himself. " 'Let the Europeans slaughter each other if they wish, but no acre of European architecture, no priceless crown from some pampered royal European head, is worth a single drop of American blood.' I think that expresses our position admirably," the editor said, glancing at Bladen, who nodded acceptance of the implied praise.

Zalman shook his head sadly. "We're passing up the chance of extra sales. Poor Jimmy Doyle must be writhing in his grave."

Bladen rocked with laughter. Whenever Zalman could not get his own way he invoked the ghost of Jimmy Doyle, as if respect for the dead would overcome opposition to his own ideas. The Russian immigrant who had replaced Doyle as circulation manager needed no help from spirits. He had earned his own respect. Under his guidance, readership had soared. He had used a combination of sound marketing ideas—such as moving the paper's most popular section, the comics, to the back page so that the *Messenger* masthead faced out when people read the comics on the way to work—and promotional hoopla that would have looked at home in a circus. Bladen's favorite stunt had occurred three years before, when Zalman had gone aloft in a balloon to drop ten thousand tiny, numbered parachutes across the city. Every day for a month after that, the *Messenger* carried a different lucky number. Prizes increased daily from ten dollars to three hundred, and circulation rose by eight thousand.

The meeting ended with Zalman's request falling on deaf ears. He wasn't overly disappointed about the defeat. Even the most successful generals lost a battle now and again. He spent the rest of the day planning a promotion with two men named Frank Brennan and Bill Regan. They were childhood friends who had worked their way out of Hell's Kitchen, first with the *Evening Journal,* then the *Messenger.* Brennan, red-haired and rangy, was the same age as Zalman. Regan, dark, with gleaming brown eyes and a shock of black hair, was two years younger. They were both assistant circulation managers. Zalman had made the appointments two years ago, recognizing in the men the physical and mental toughness, the eagerness to succeed, that Jimmy Doyle had once seen in *him.* Around the newspaper, Brennan and Regan were known simply as Zalman's henchmen.

Zalman left for home shortly after six. For the past year, home had been an elegant apartment in the Essex House, on Central Park South. Zalman lived up to nearly every penny of the salary Bladen paid him. Julia had help to run the home. And Helen, who was two months short of her sixth birthday, had started to take riding lessons in Central Park.

Riding lessons for the daughter of Zalman Isaacson! Zalman had to pinch himself to realize it was not a dream. From a Kishinev hovel to New York luxury. If only his parents had lived to see such a thing, they would have been so surprised! Not Julia's parents, of course. Louis and Frieda Bluestone had always expected their granddaughter to go riding in Central Park. Louis, however, had not lived to see it. A heart attack had killed him three years earlier. Frieda had woken one morning to find him cold beside her. After his death, she had carried on the toy store alone for a year, until much of Windsor Arcade had been pulled down for redevelopment.

Only one empty area existed in Zalman's life. He did not have the son he so desperately wanted. Since Helen's birth, Julia had become pregnant three times, but each pregnancy had ended in a miscarriage. Was fate, he wondered, determined to deny him the son he would name after his friend?

Arriving home, Zalman gave Julia a kiss and a hug, then he turned his attention to Helen. She was in her nightclothes, ready for bed. Zalman lifted her up as though she weighed no more than a leaf. "And what did my little princess do today?"

"I rode a horse in the park."

"A big horse?"

Helen's auburn hair bounced on her shoulders as she shook her head. "I'm too small to ride a big horse. I rode a very small horse. Did you ever ride horses?"

"Of course. If you're still awake after dinner, I'll tell you all about it." He carried her into her bedroom, tucked her in, and kissed her good night.

169

Over dinner, Julia described her day. Her mother had visited during the afternoon. With little to do, Frieda Bluestone was a frequent guest at the Isaacson home. Zalman had no objections. He was not worried about Frieda pouring poison into Julia's ear when he was not there; he had won that battle long ago.

Later, Zalman looked into his daughter's room. Helen was sitting up in bed, willing herself to stay awake until her father came in. "Tell me about the horses you rode."

"I remember one horse in particular," Zalman said, sitting on the bed. "Donerail. I won the Kentucky Derby on him last year. There I was, a hundred yards to go, a dozen horses ahead of me, and not an inch of space to be seen. Somehow I had to get by."

Helen's eyed widened. "What did you do?"

"I pulled back on the reins, dug in my heels, and yelled at Donerail to jump. He leaped . . ." Zalman drew a sweeping curve with his hand. "You should have seen him leap, Helen. He leaped clean over all the horses and landed at the finish line. Of course, the other jockeys objected, but we still won."

Helen gazed levelly at her father. When she studied him that way, through light brown eyes that were flecked with green and gray, Zalman saw a young Rachel. Sometimes, despite the different languages, she even sounded like his sister. "You're too big to be a jockey," Helen said at last.

"It's in the *Messenger,*" Zalman protested. "I can bring you a picture." Zalman knew he could find the halftone of Donerail's victory the previous year and persuade a typesetter to make up a simple caption that would include his name.

"You're too big," Helen repeated in the flat, matter-of-fact tone that Zalman could remember Rachel using. He found the similarities between his sister and his daughter eerie. Eleven years had passed since Rachel's death, yet she lived again in her brother's only child.

Another voice added its contribution. "Maybe you can pull the wool over Henry Bladen's eyes, but your daughter's too smart to be fooled by such tall tales."

Zalman turned around. Julia stood in the doorway, smiling. She had listened, unnoticed, to the entire tale. Zalman

170

kissed his daughter good night and left the room. Julia followed him. "How was I?" he asked.

"As good as Jimmy," Julia answered.

Zalman hugged her. A storyteller could want no finer praise.

They went walking in the park, arm in arm like two young lovers. Zalman related his unsuccessful attempt to alter the *Messenger*'s platform of neutrality. Julia threw her support behind Bladen. "Avoiding bloodshed is far more important than selling newspapers, Zalman."

"Nothing is more important than selling newspapers."

Julia laughed and responded the way Zalman knew she would. "Now you really do sound like Jimmy."

He kissed her. But even as he tasted her lips, that first encounter with the Irishman flashed before his eyes—the New York *American* crew celebrating the extra sales they'd made because of the elevated train crash on Ninth Avenue, and Zalman accusing them of being callous. He was no different now. The constant battle for circulation was a wicked mistress.

The apartment was quiet when they returned just after ten. Zalman lifted Julia in his arms and carried her toward the bedroom. She looked into his face as he set her down on the bed. "You have the most unusual eyes I have ever seen. They can sparkle with fun, as they do when you weave your fantastic tales for Helen. Sometimes they brood, and then I can see your deepest thoughts reflected in them. But always they are gentle. Before you, I never knew a man with such gentle eyes."

"Too many people have mistaken gentleness for weakness."

Julia recalled the conflict with her parents six years before. No weak man fought so fiercely. No weak man succeeded as Zalman had done, rising from bartender to circulation manager of a daily newspaper. And before that, traveling across half the world to reach America. Julia might have married a man with gentle eyes, but he was the strongest man she had ever known.

She encircled his body with her arms and drew him close. He was as lean as the day they had married, all bone and

171

muscle and pulsing energy. She watched those gentle eyes draw nearer, felt his lips on hers. Tender at first. Then urgent. Bruising as his passion rose. Deep within her a spark ignited, glowed brighter, burst into surging life. She knew how badly he wanted another child. A son. She was determined to fulfill his wish.

She felt his fingers picking at her clothes. Her own hands responded, moving past cloth to caress skin. Her lips slid from his mouth to his neck, along his shoulder to his chest. "How do you say 'I love you' in Russian?"

"*Ya vas lyublu.*"

Julia repeated the words and Zalman laughed. "No, like this." He told her again, mouthing each syllable separately. At last, she pronounced it perfectly. Zalman congratulated her by saying, "*Ya vas obazahu.*"

"What does that mean?"

"I worship you."

Before they fell asleep, Julia rolled over on her side and whispered in Zalman's ear. "I think we made a son tonight."

Julia became pregnant again. Her doctor ordered her to remain in bed. A nurse kept constant watch, and Frieda Bluestone visited the apartment every day. Zalman was grateful to his mother-in-law. For the first time, possibly, they shared a single hope. Julia's welfare and a healthy baby. A healthy baby boy.

After four months, when the doctor was certain that the fetus was properly attached to the wall of the womb, Julia was allowed limited activity. During the fifth month, when she felt movement for the first time, she pressed Zalman's hand against her belly. "Does that feel like a boy or a girl?"

Zalman snatched his hand away theatrically. "No girl punches like that." He called Helen into the bedroom and held her hand against Julia. "Say hello to your brother."

"What's his name?"

"Jimmy," Zalman answered immediately.

"Jimmy Louis Isaacson," Julia said. She looked at Zalman as if expecting him to challenge her choice of a middle name. He just smiled, too overjoyed to care. Julia wondered how she would ever console him if the baby failed to be a boy.

The doctor took no chances. Despite the apparent normality of the pregnancy, the three earlier miscarriages portended possible trouble. Toward the end of April, more than two weeks before her due date, he checked Julia into the Sloane Hospital for Women on West Fifty-ninth Street.

When not visiting the hospital, Zalman made certain he stayed occupied. He spent hours with Helen each night, keeping the young girl up long past her bedtime. He taught her to play rummy. Her hand was too small to hold all the cards, so she laid them on the table, hiding them with a book while she decided what to keep or throw. Zalman teased her by peeking over the top. When she complained, he threw a card she needed. Nothing delighted him so much as the expression of pleasure on his daughter's face as she recognized a card that made a set or run.

During the day, he threw himself just as fervently into the work of increasing *Messenger* sales. When he was not busy in the office, he visited newsstands and shops that sold the *Messenger,* maintaining the contacts he had created eight years earlier. Such ceaseless activity took his mind off what could go wrong.

Two weeks after Julia's admission to the hospital, the war in Europe provided Zalman with all the activity he could want. A German submarine torpedoed the *Lusitania,* a British passenger liner, off the Irish coast. Of the eleven hundred civilians who died, more than one hundred and twenty were American.

Zalman moved into high gear. Nine months earlier, when the war had started, he had sought to increase circulation by fanning anti-British sentiment. Now he would make sales by capitalizing on a British tragedy. He told Bill Regan to collect the liner's passenger list from the Cunard offices. When Regan returned, Zalman poured over the list, seeking New Yorkers. Anyone foolish enough to interrupt him was yelled at. He wanted to be left alone to do what he loved: figuring out ways to sell more papers.

He conferred with Jake Thomson and publisher Len Bennett. Headline writers penned different front-page heads. A special edition for the north Bronx was headlined: "Riverdale

Doctor Perishes in *Lusitania* Piracy." For a Manhattan edition, a headline read: "Murray Hill Family Dies in *Lusitania* Piracy." Other headlines pinpointed different neighborhoods in the *Messenger*'s catchment area. Zalman stood watching newspapers roll off the press, as excited as any small child with a new toy.

Someone touched his arm. He swung around, still not wanting to be disturbed. Frank Brennan stood there. "What is it?"

"Your wife."

Zalman grabbed Brennan by the shoulders. "What about her?"

"She had a baby."

"When?"

"Couple of hours ago."

Pushing Brennan away, Zalman began running toward the door, the special *Lusitania* editions suddenly forgotten. "Why the hell didn't anyone tell me?"

"We tried to!" Brennan yelled after his fleeing boss. "You kept yelling at us to leave you the hell alone!"

At the door, Zalman skidded to a stop and swung around. "What was it?"

Brennan gave a wide, lopsided grin. "What you wanted, of course! A boy!"

Zalman screamed with joy, jumped into the air, and clicked his heels. No man on earth could be happier than he was at that moment.

Having a son fueled Zalman's ambition. Until now, his enthusiasm had served Henry Bladen. It was time to benefit *himself* as well. For weeks, he spent every spare minute considering moneymaking schemes, but the ease with which he invented strategies to sell papers did not extend to his personal finances. It occurred to him that the only area where he truly succeeded was newspapers. Away from the rattle of the press, he was just another mortal.

"Is that right, Jimmy?" Zalman murmured as he stood over his son's bassinet. "Is your old man no better than anyone else once he leaves the newspaper?" The baby slept, tiny lips pursed in a chubby pink face, a button of a nose, and thin black hair; he was the most gorgeous child Zalman had ever seen. The family name would endure. Americanized perhaps. But it would endure.

The harder Zalman concentrated, the weaker his imagination became. At work, he continued to create sales promotions. At home, success eluded him. But after four months, as summer began to fade, he received help from an unexpected quarter. Frieda Bluestone visited for Sunday lunch. The maid had the day off, so Frieda helped Julia set the table. Zalman, reading a book with Helen in the dining room, paid little attention to the two women until Frieda said, "I can't find any teaspoons."

"Look in the cabinet," Julia answered from the kitchen.

"That's where I am looking. They're not here."

Zalman's attention picked up. He left the book with Helen, walked to where Frieda stood, and gave her a kiss on the cheek.

Frieda jumped back, her enormous bust quivering with surprise. "What was that for?"

"You've just made us very wealthy."

"I have?" Frieda looked at Zalman as though he were mad.

Zalman went into the kitchen and kissed Julia. He rushed back to Helen and kissed her, then he leaned over his son and kissed him, too. To all, he repeated the assertion that Frieda Bluestone had just made them rich.

After lunch, Zalman locked himself away in his study. He stayed there the entire afternoon, scribbling notes and figures on sheets of paper. He wouldn't tell Julia what he was doing, but when he came out his eyes shone with excitement. Julia knew that he had found the wealth-producing idea he'd sought since the day of Jimmy's birth.

Carrying his sheets of paper, Zalman met with Henry Bladen the next morning. "What do households never have enough of?"

"I haven't the slightest idea. I leave the running of my household to a perfectly adequate staff."

"Teaspoons," Zalman said. "Only yesterday, at my home, we couldn't find any. The maid had misplaced them. We had to stir our tea with forks, can you believe that?"

Bladen, recognizing the excitement in Zalman's eyes, felt anticipation tug at his stomach. "Go on."

"I want to use silver teaspoons as a promotion. Not just for the *Messenger,* but for all your papers. This will work as well in Chicago, St. Louis, Cleveland, Cincinnati, Indianapolis, Milwaukee, and Minneapolis, as it will in New York. The papers will carry coupons enabling readers to buy a silver teaspoon at a better price than they could from a shop. You'll get increased circulation right across the whole chain. People will buy your newspapers just for the coupons."

Bladen's expectation dimmed. The idea possessed the ingenuity he associated with Zalman, but it lacked reality. "I can't see people buying our papers just to save a few cents on a spoon. It sounds like a lot of effort and investment for something that will fizzle out in a week."

"Who said anything about a week? I'm not talking about a single pattern. I'm talking about silver teaspoons with official state seals on them. Collectors' pieces. How many states are there, Mr. Bladen?"

"Forty-eight." Bladen's eyes began to widen as the enormity of Zalman's idea became clear.

"We run this promotion for forty-eight weeks. A different state each week. People will want the whole set, and we'll increase sales for almost an entire year."

Bladen considered the idea for a full two minutes. Zalman, certain he had baited the hook perfectly, waited confidently on the other side of the desk. "Where will you get the spoons?"

"I'll look into it immediately." Zalman got up to leave, but Bladen called him back.

"My business is publishing. I don't know the first thing about silver teaspoons. You might want to think about setting up a company of your own to handle the supply."

"That's precisely what I'm going to do," Zalman answered.

Bladen laughed. He never objected to the men who worked for him turning a profit, as long as they did not forget that their first loyalty was to Henry Bladen.

* * *

176

Zalman ordered samples. A silver manufacturer created two dozen delicate silver spoons, each embossed with the seal of a state in which Henry Bladen published a newspaper. Zalman showed them to his henchmen. Frank Brennan and Bill Regan took the samples and traveled across Bladen's publishing empire to gauge the reaction. They returned a week later to report that circulation men at the group's other papers were ecstatic about the promotion.

Zalman created a company to handle ordering and shipping. He named it the American Memento Company. With the thousand dollars that represented all his savings, he leased offices at the bottom of Sixth Avenue and hired staff. If the promotion worked as planned, he would recoup his investment a hundredfold.

The promotion began in January 1916, with coupons appearing Monday through Friday in all of Bladen's newspapers. Twenty cents and all five coupons purchased one silver spoon from the American Memento Company. Readers who bought the complete set of forty-eight spoons received a complimentary pine display stand.

The success of the promotion astounded even Zalman. The American Memento Company added staff to cope with the rush of orders. The silver manufacturer hired extra shifts. In one week, when the state seal was that of New York, *Messenger* readers alone mailed in more than one hundred and forty thousand sets of coupons. Bladen was thrilled. In his eyes Zalman could do no wrong. *Messenger* circulation during the promotion soared by almost seventy thousand. Bladen was pragmatic enough to know that many subscribers would drop off once the promotion ended, but he fully expected to keep thirty percent of them. Across the chain, newspapers reported similar surges in readership.

In the forty-seventh week of the promotion, when New Mexico's seal graced the spoons, the American Memento Company expanded the operation, offering the service to newspapers in cities that did not conflict with Bladen's papers. Across the country, and in Canada, publishers grabbed at the opportunity.

The American Memento Company operated at full stretch until a month after America's entry into the war, a total of twenty-three months. When the last orders had been filled, Zalman worked out the final figures. He entered the study of his apartment at three in the afternoon, while his wife and mother-in-law went for a walk in the park with Helen and Jimmy. When he emerged, Jimmy was asleep, and the two women and Helen were sitting down for dinner. Four hours had passed.

"Guess how many spoons we sold."

"Ten million?" Julia asked. She knew the promotion had gone well, but had no idea of actual unit sales.

Zalman shook his head.

"Five million?" Frieda Bluestone ventured with less optimism.

"What about you?" Zalman asked Helen. "How many spoons do you think we sold?"

"Twenty million," replied the auburn-haired girl. "I know you're clever enough to have sold twenty million spoons."

Julia and her mother laughed at the enormity of the figure. "You have inherited your father's incredible imagination," Julia told Helen. "Do you understand how many twenty million is?"

"Helen is closer than any of you," Zalman said. He sat down at the head of the table and tore a slice of bread in half, salting it before popping it into his mouth. "The *Messenger* alone accounted for one hundred and thirty thousand complete sets. Over the remainder of Mr. Bladen's chain, two hundred and ten thousand sets were sold. Across the rest of the country and Canada, we sold another nine hundred thousand complete sets. Multiply those by the forty-eight spoons in each set . . ." Zalman's face broke into a huge grin as he surveyed the shocked reactions of his wife and mother-in-law. "Multiply by forty-eight for a total of fifty-nine million, five hundred and twenty thousand spoons. Add to that twenty million odd spoons—readers who wanted one specific state, or people who stopped collecting, for whatever reason, before the promotion was finished—and we have a grand total of just under eighty million spoons. You can stir a lot of tea with that."

Ten seconds of pure silence greeted Zalman's announcement. Frieda broke it by asking, "How much did you make on each spoon?"

"After all expenses? A fraction under two cents. Quick!" He looked at Helen. "At two cents on eighty million spoons . . . how much money did your father make?"

Helen screwed her eyes shut. She counted aloud, carrying zeroes and moving decimal points. Suddenly her eyes popped open. "One million, six hundred thousand dollars."

Zalman pulled a silver dollar from his trouser pocket and flipped it across the table to Helen. "Correct, my little accountant! There's your fee!"

Frieda gazed in awe at her son-in-law. "If only Louis were here to see this. He would be so impressed. He would say that you are a merchant after all."

Zalman smiled. It was amazing how differently people viewed you once you became a millionaire.

With the phenomenal success of the spoon promotion, Zalman's concerns extended far beyond Henry Bladen's *Messenger*. He bought interests in ventures from real estate to restaurants and bowling alleys. Most of his newfound capital, though, served to entrench him deeper in the newspaper world. He acquired news distribution companies in Baltimore, Detroit, Buffalo, and Cleveland.

For the first time, Zalman realized that each day comprised only twenty-four hours. No matter how hard he worked, he could not build up his own businesses, run the *Messenger*'s circulation department, and simultaneously be a father to his children and a husband to Julia. Something had to be sacrificed. In the summer of 1918, after trying unsuccessfully for six months to juggle all his responsibilities, he selected the obligation that had to go. He resigned from the *Messenger*.

Henry Bladen tried to change his mind. He poured compliments on Zalman, thrust increased sales figures in front of his face, promised him more money and greater status. Zalman refused to budge. As a last resort, the newspaper owner invited Zalman and Julia to dinner at his home on Riverside Drive.

The invitation in itself was stunning. Bladen kept his business and personal lives very separate. His friends were politicians, bankers, and industrialists, not reporters and circulation men. Although he worked closely with the heads of his newspapers and magazines, he rarely allowed that nearness to approach intimacy. Jake Thomson, the *Messenger* editor, was one exception. He had been with Bladen for more than thirty years, from young reporter in Chicago to editor in New York. Once a week, Bladen took Thomson to lunch or dinner at a restaurant or club. They were working meals, though, over which the two men discussed the *Messenger*. Not once did Thomson intimate to anyone that those meetings allowed him into Bladen's inner circle.

Bladen's home was a triplex apartment on Riverside Drive, above the Hudson. Waited on by a staff of six, he lived by himself. His wife remained in Chicago, close to the families of their two married sons. Bladen did not care for such warmth. As middle-age faded—he was now sixty-three—he placed more emphasis on empire- and influence-building than on nurturing family ties.

Zalman and Julia drove to Riverside Drive in a newly acquired Pierce-Arrow. A butler swung back the heavy oak front door. Following him inside, the visitors felt as if they were entering a museum. Silk tapestries hung from paneled walls. Statues filled every corner. Suits of armor punctuated imported flights of marble stairs. Julia watched her husband take it all in. He was seeing how the very wealthy lived, and he was impressed.

Bladen waited in the library, surrounded by walls of bookcases. Small sculptures and china pieces filled whatever shelf space was not occupied by books. The newspaper owner greeted his guests warmly, shaking Zalman's hand and, in a courtly gesture, kissing Julia's. Initial conversation centered on events in Europe. Bladen talked about the civil war in Russia, and asked Zalman what he thought of reports that the Czar and his family had been executed by Bolsheviks. Zalman surprised himself by answering that he had little emotion one way or the other. "When I lived in Russia, Mr. Bladen, I was radical. But it is fifteen years since I left. Away from repression, I no longer feel a need for radicalism."

Over dinner, Bladen used every wile to persuade Zalman

to stay with the *Messenger.* He offered to let him continue with his own businesses. He tried flattery, saying Zalman was the best circulation manager he had ever seen. He even brought Julia into the argument. "Perhaps *you* know if your husband is unhappy in my employ. I'm offering him more money than I've ever offered anyone. I'm offering him status. What else could he want?"

"He wants to work for himself, Mr. Bladen. The silver-spoon promotion whetted his appetite."

Sighing in resignation, Bladen accepted the obvious. As the butler poured after-dinner liqueurs, Bladen turned to Zalman. "I should never have been so generous in letting you set up your own company to handle that promotion."

"I never dreamed it would make so much money."

"Neither did I. I let you do it as a bonus for having the idea in the first place. I didn't think it would turn out to be your grubstake," he said with a chuckle. "Just remember, Zalman, if things don't work out, you've always got a place with me."

The two men parted friends.

Zalman drove home, his mind bubbling full of Henry Bladen's style of living. Emperors resided in such luxury. Zalman, the new millionaire, the refugee from Kishinev whose daughter took riding lessons in Central Park, was still a pauper by comparison. He vowed that such relatively impoverished circumstances would not last long.

Within a week of Zalman's departure from the *Messenger,* two other men followed him. Frank Brennan and Bill Regan. Zalman placed them in charge of his news distributorships in Detroit, Buffalo, Baltimore, and Cleveland. Money poured in.

Zalman paid attention to his other investments. Instead of dismantling the American Memento Company, he kept it operating, having its managers actively seek promotion work from newspapers. More money poured in.

As the war ended, he foresaw a dramatic increase in the number of automobiles. He used his real-estate interests to develop parking garages. Zalman possessed a Midas touch. Every venture produced wealth.

He controlled his diverse concerns from an office on Sixth

Avenue, in the same building as the American Memento Company. Much of the money he reinvested, but some he set aside for his family, to take them a few steps on the long upward journey to the rarified level Henry Bladen enjoyed. While maintaining the apartment at the Essex House, he bought a small estate at Glen Cove, on the northern edge of Long Island. Julia, her mother, and the two children spent the whole summer there. At first, Zalman joined them only on weekends; then, in August, convinced that his companies would function without his perpetual presence, he spent an entire two weeks with them.

Those two weeks constituted the longest period of time Zalman had taken off in his entire life. Even his honeymoon, thirteen years before, had lasted only one week. He didn't know what to do with himself. He got up at seven each morning to drive along narrow roads in the Pierce-Arrow and explore surrounding areas. When he found a place he considered interesting, he had Julia make up a picnic lunch, and the whole family went out there.

In the afternoon, he played with his children. Helen could swim already. Zalman, remembering how Julia had given him swimming instruction on their honeymoon, took it upon himself to teach four-year-old Jimmy to swim. In water little more than knee-deep, Zalman showed the dark-haired boy how to dog paddle. As his small arms and legs pumped and kicked, Zalman held him with both hands, then one, and finally none. Jimmy was delighted by his newfound independence. Zalman, expecting him to head for deeper water immediately, stood ready to block his path. He need not have worried. Jimmy was happy to use his new skill where his feet could always touch bottom. Zalman filed the information in his memory. During this vacation, he was learning more about his children than he had ever known before.

In the evenings, the children listened to their father spin his stories. Every so often, he would vary the diet of fiction with questions about his business. He never forgot that an inadvertent remark by his mother-in-law had given birth to the spoon promotion. All around him minds waited to be tapped, and Zalman was not about to waste such talent.

After the children were in bed, Zalman took Julia walking

on the beach. As waves lapped against their bare feet, she asked if he were enjoying his first real vacation with his family.

"I'm embarked on a voyage of discovery," he told her. "Helen is like one would imagine a son to be, ready to climb any tree, eager to accept any dare. Jimmy shows no such boldness. If anything, he is a very cautious child."

"He's four, Zalman. Give him time."

"A four-year-old should have no fear. It is now we should be watching him the closest, to make sure he does not do something foolish. It seems that he automatically knows his limitations and doesn't want to test them."

"Is that bad?"

Zalman was genuinely puzzled. "I don't know. If I had known my limitations, and respected them as Jimmy seems to do, where would I be now? Still in Russia? Or worse, dead?"

Julia, disturbed by such talk, clutched Zalman's arm. "There is nothing wrong with a little caution. When the time is right, Jimmy will show you all the daring you'll ever want to see."

When the two weeks were over, Zalman returned to his office. As he scanned reports from his companies, he felt vaguely disappointed that everything had worked so well in his absence. He told himself that he had set up the companies to work that way, but such self-assurance did little to relieve the niggling doubts that worked their way into his brain. Now that his businesses were operating smoothly under the supervision of competent managers, they no longer required so much of his time.

Facing boredom, he threw himself into the day-to-day work of his companies. That was a mistake. He could visualize profitable schemes such as the parking garages, but he was out of place participating in the daily real-estate routine. The same applied to the American Memento Company. The original idea had been his, but its routine business required less mercurial minds.

He felt at ease only in the news distribution companies. There, at least, the commodity was newspapers and magazines, items which he understood thoroughly. Accompanied

183

by Bill Regan and Frank Brennan, Zalman made visits to Baltimore, Buffalo, Cleveland, and Detroit. His agencies in those cities handled hundreds of papers and magazines, including some owned by Henry Bladen. It was good to be on familiar territory again. Good to spend time in the company of Regan and Brennan, newspapermen like himself. When he returned to New York, Zalman felt like a man going back to work after being on vacation. He decided to look further afield for more distribution companies.

Julia saw the transformation. With all the money coming in, Zalman was wealthier than he had ever imagined. He was also thoroughly unhappy. Energy no longer coursed and sparkled through his lean frame. The long, quick stride of a man in a hurry to get somewhere had been replaced by a solemn pace. His wavy hair, she noticed, showed the first streaks of gray at the temples. Since leaving Henry Bladen and the *Messenger,* Zalman had changed from newspaperman to businessman. She wondered if he understood the metamorphosis that had occurred.

She entered the study one evening to find him scribbling notations across that morning's *Messenger.* "If you're going to take the time and trouble to improve the paper, don't you think you should send your suggestions to Mr. Bladen?"

"I'm keeping in practice, that's all."

"Practice for what? For when you go back there?"

"Why on earth would I want to do that? I don't have enough hours in the day as it is."

"Are you trying to convince me or yourself?" She sat down next to him and looked at his marks on the newspaper. "I've seen you like this before, Zalman. After we were married, when you worked in Blue Stone. You hated it. You were like a caged animal until you got that job with the *Messenger.* Then everything changed. Suddenly you were excited."

"Julia, let me explain something to you. In Russia I was poor. So was everyone else. When I came here, I was determined to become wealthy. I used people I knew as yardsticks. First I wanted to be as rich as Paddy Mulligan, who owned the saloon where I worked. Then I wanted to be as wealthy as your father. When I saw how Henry Bladen lived, I decided I wanted to be that wealthy. With all the work I've done since leaving him, I'm on the way, but I've come to realize that the pursuit of wealth alone is meaningless. I cannot go through life just making money. That's too easy, and too soul-destroying. I need more than that. Much more. But I still need to find out what."

"Stop lying to yourself. You know already."

Zalman concentrated on expanding his news distributorships. Accompanied by Brennan and Regan, he crossed and recrossed the country by train, often staying away from New York for two or three weeks at a time. The three men passed the endless journeys by playing cards. When they reached their destinations, they purchased news distribution companies. By the summer of 1920, when he took off another two weeks to spend with the family at Glen Cove, Zalman owned fourteen distribution companies from coast to coast. Should he ever care to do so, he could operate his own censorship by dictating what newspapers and periodicals were available.

During his hectic dashes about the country, Zalman had ignored his children. He hadn't been there with the regularity they had come to count upon. He hadn't played with them or told them his wonderful stories. At Glen Cove, he did his best to make up for his neglect. He took them for rides, played ball with them, cavorted with them in the water. He was amazed at how well Jimmy swam now, even if his son's sense of caution continued to override any daring. And Helen . . . Zalman could see childhood slipping away from her, womanhood waiting in the wings to take its rightful place. Where had the time gone?

One afternoon he went fishing with the children in a small rowing boat. Helen willingly learned how to bait a hook. Jimmy, a fastidiously clean child, stared with such horror at the wriggling worm that Zalman burst out laughing.

In three hours of angling, Zalman had only one bite, a small bluefish. He reeled it in and freed the hook from its mouth. As the bluefish flapped frantically in the bottom of the boat, Jimmy turned away, unable to look. Zalman, inexplicably, became vexed with his son's squeamishness.

"Does seeing a fish caught bother you?" He grabbed the

boy by the shoulder and tried to turn him around. "You eat fish, don't you? You should know how they're caught!"

Jimmy struggled in his father's grasp. The boat rocked. Helen shrieked in fear and warning. The next instant, the boat tipped, throwing all three occupants into the Long Island Sound. Zalman surfaced immediately. Helen popped up next to him, holding the side of the boat as it rocked in the water. Of Jimmy there was no sign. Zalman dived beneath the water to search for his son. Something banged into him. He turned and saw Jimmy, eyes open wide in terror, bubbles streaming from his mouth and nose. Barefoot, in swimming costume, and in his depth, he could swim with confidence. Wearing shoes in twelve feet of water, he was drowning. Zalman grabbed the boy and kicked out hard. He surfaced by the boat. Helen helped to roll and shove Jimmy inside. Father and daughter followed. Jimmy coughed and spluttered and screamed in terror. Zalman turned him over onto his face and pressed hard against his lungs. Jimmy heaved. Water spewed from his mouth. The boat pitched as Zalman continued clearing his son's lungs. At last, he sat Jimmy up. Color returned to his face, his breathing slowed.

"I'm sorry," Zalman whispered. "I didn't mean for you to go into the water."

Jimmy gave his father a wan smile. "It was my fault. I should have looked at the fish like you told me to."

Zalman felt his stomach tremble. He'd heard Julia say she loved him. He'd heard Helen say the same thing. There was something different about hearing a son voice the feeling. That was what Jimmy had just done. He'd forgiven his father for almost drowning him. Pardoned him because he loved him, and Zalman was overcome by the knowledge.

At night when the children were in bed, Zalman sat reading on the porch. Invariably, he read newspapers. Just as invariably, Julia noticed, he made notes. He might have regained some of his old interest by becoming so heavily involved in coast-to-coast newspaper distribution, but distributing newspapers was not the same as working on them. He would not be happy, Julia knew, until he worked once more on a newspaper.

* * *

If Zalman had been surprised two years earlier to be invited to dinner by Henry Bladen, the newspaper owner's second invitation was shocking.

"Spend a day on the water with me," Bladen suggested in a telephone call the week after Zalman returned from his summer vacation at Glen Cove. "I've just taken delivery of a new yacht. I want to show it off. Make it this Saturday. Bring Julia and the children. I'm sure they'll all enjoy a day at sea."

Fittingly, the yacht was named the *Masthead;* eighty-five feet of shining white hull, polished decks, and gleaming brass, cared for by a permanent four-man crew. Bladen welcomed Zalman and Julia aboard and introduced himself to Helen and Jimmy. While the steward took breakfast orders, the captain guided the *Masthead* away from the dock.

"Where are we going?" Zalman asked. He marveled at how fit Bladen appeared, face ruddy, eyes sparkling. In his starched whites, he looked ten years younger than his sixty-five. Perhaps that was why moneyed Americans owned such boats; membership of the New York Yacht Club kept them young. Zalman made another mental note about the lifestyles of the wealthy.

"Out a few miles, that's all. Since Congress has decided that we can't drink in America, we have to leave the country every now and then if we want our libations to be legal."

By the time breakfast was over, the ship was in international waters. After the steward cleared the plates, Bladen said, "Why don't you show Mrs. Isaacson and the two children around the *Masthead?*" The moment they were out of sight, Bladen produced a bottle of cognac. "Too early in the day for you?"

"Well, as long as I'm in international waters . . ."

Bladen poured cognac into two snifters. "Here's to the success you've made of yourself since you left me. Oh, I kept an eye on you, don't worry about that."

"Is that the reason for the invitation, Mr. Bladen? To tell me you're surprised at how well I've done?"

"You'll find no surprise here. As well as being smart, you've got one great advantage over everyone else. We're all old men, Zalman, a bunch of graybeards. You're young." He

187

sipped the cognac, all the while gazing intently at his guest. "If anyone had any qualms, it was you. You had to find out for yourself just how well you could do on your own. Right?"

Grudgingly, Zalman nodded his head. Some of his drive had been self-doubt; he had needed to learn his own abilities.

"So now you know just how smart you are, how about stopping all this nonsense and coming back with me?"

Zalman bit back a laugh. He didn't want to offend Bladen. "Mr. Bladen, I own fourteen distributorships. I own valuable real estate and other assorted enterprises. I'm worth a couple of million dollars, and I earn more than three hundred thousand dollars a year. Of what possible interest to me is the job of circulation manager of the *Messenger?*"

"Not the *Messenger.* I'm talking about everything. Group circulation director, responsible for all my newspapers and magazines. I want you to increase the circulation of what we already have. I want you to learn where we should be starting newspapers. I want you to find out in what areas of interest we should be publishing magazines. Those three hundred thousand dollars you earn a year. You don't *earn* that money. It comes in because of something you set up, which other people, like Frank Brennan and Bill Regan, now run. What I'm offering you is a monumental job, and I'm only willing to pay you fifty thousand dollars a year. But you'll take it all right, because you're desperate to get back into the business end of newspapers."

"What makes you think that?"

"Why else would you spend time critiquing each edition of the *Messenger?*" Seeing astonishment steal across Zalman's face, Bladen smiled. "If you're going to analyze my newspapers, the least you can do is let me see your remarks. I value your judgment highly, you know that."

Zalman looked past Bladen, seeking Julia. Had she contacted the newspaper owner? Of course she had.

"Think how marvelously my publications will do with all the distribution you control," Bladen said. "Not to mention how much business your companies will get. Give me your decision by the time we berth. In the meantime, enjoy the cruise." He stood up and walked away, leaving Zalman sitting by himself.

Julia returned ten minutes later, alone. "What did Mr. Bladen offer you?"

"A whole lot of headaches for a lousy fifty thousand a year. And it's all your fault. What did you do?"

"I wrote him a letter. Will you take what he's offering?" Zalman leaned forward to kiss his wife. "Of course I will."

Zalman returned to Henry Bladen's fold as group circulation director. He was installed on the top floor of the *Messenger* building, next to Bladen's office in the boardroom. Bladen's instructions were simple. "Whenever you've got an idea, knock on the door and come in." Zalman was the only man in the group to have such carte blanche.

Bladen published a variety of monthly titles: magazines for women, that dealt with the home, with fashion, food, dressmaking; men's magazines concerning science, mechanics, sports. In his first week, Zalman suggested two more titles, concepts he'd been considering for a long time. One, as car production boomed, was for motorists. The other was a monthly magazine for amateur photographers. To promote them, he suggested a simple idea.

"Make a deal with car and camera manufacturers. When a motorist buys an automobile, he gets a year's free subscription to the motoring magazine. When a photographer buys a camera, he gets three months of the magazine for nothing. If we can't win them as permanent readers in that time, we may as well go into another business."

Bladen, loving everything about the ideas, told Zalman to get on with it. Six months later, in the spring of 1921, the first issues of both magazines rolled off the press.

When he had left Bladen two years earlier, Zalman had felt overcome by his many responsibilities. He was older, shrewder, now. He knew how to delegate. He didn't waste time on matters a subordinate could handle. Despite Bladen's description of the job as monumental, Zalman found time to keep an eye on his own businesses. Frank Brennan and Bill Regan met regularly with him to report on the distribution agencies. Zalman kept tabs on his other concerns by meeting managers for a drink. Sometimes a phone call sufficed. The trick, he told Julia one evening, was to surround yourself with people who were smarter than you.

"Only a frightened man surrounds himself with inferiors, and then he isn't doing himself any favors. I learned that from Henry Bladen. He sticks himself in the middle of the smartest people he can find."

"Are you saying you're smarter than Mr. Bladen?" Julia asked.

"I want to say yes. But then I remember Bladen must have been damned smart to do such a thing in the first place."

Julia laughed. "It's a tie. You're as smart as each other."

Zalman created time to be with his children, to share their growing up, which was occurring far too quickly for his comfort. He found he could relate to Helen better. That bothered him. He loved both children equally, as any father should. Favoritism was despicable. Yet he always felt he understood Helen more.

Jimmy was too fastidious for his father's comfort; he didn't fit Zalman's concept of a son. He was a polite, pleasant boy, yet something was missing. He lacked the spark of mischief other boys had. Or *should* have.

Helen was the opposite. At school, some boys had made fun of her bright auburn hair. Beacon head, they'd shouted, and flicked water at her to put the fire out. Helen had attacked the biggest bully with such unexpected ferocity that the boy had fallen over. She'd sat on his chest, choking him until he apologized. After telling her parents about the fight, she'd asked them to buy a punching bag for her next birthday. Julia had been horrified. Zalman had laughed, and had gone out to buy one there and then, setting it up in a small spare room. Simultaneously, he had bought gloves for both children. Jimmy had swung a couple of listless punches at the bag and quit. Helen had stayed there for ten minutes, slamming gloved fists into the bag until she was exhausted. Now, whenever she lost her temper, she retired to the spare room and donned her gloves.

During summer at Glen Cove, Zalman grew even closer with Helen. While they fished in the Long Island Sound, he began to tell her about Russia. About Kishinev, and before that, the expulsion of his family from Moscow. Helen listened raptly, captivated by the story. Zalman stopped in midsentence and took her hand.

"I'm not making this one up, princess."

"I know."

He continued his tale, wondering, as he described the days leading up to the Kishinev pogrom, why he was burdening his daughter so. Any knowledge the children had of their heritage came from their mother. Zalman bore his identity casually at best; he never discussed it with anyone. But now he wanted Helen to know of his background, to know how he had lost his entire family, how he had arrived in this country penniless.

If she fully understood how he had made something out of nothing, she would better appreciate everything he gave to her.

Zalman liked to gamble. It was a vice that had bloomed slowly, nourished by the surroundings of his new country. During quiet periods in Jimmy Doyle's circulation department at the *Messenger,* cards and dice had prevailed. Zalman had played rummy, finding it kept his mind alert. When he took over, he allowed the games to continue; they were for nickels and dimes, and harmless. He no longer played himself, though. As department head, he felt it proper to stay one level above the men who worked for him.

Cards occupied the long train rides with Frank Brennan and Bill Regan. Both men were keen gamblers. Zalman had no qualms about playing cards with them. They were more like partners in the news distribution business than employees. He recognized traces of himself in the men from Hell's Kitchen. Like Zalman, Brennan and Regan had fought their way up in life. Zalman had crossed a continent and an ocean to get where he was. Brennan and Regan had only crossed Eighth Avenue. Yet, symbolically, the journeys were analogous. Zalman viewed it as a quirk in his character that he could empathize with sharp but unpolished men like Brennan and Regan, and simultaneously identify with a wealthy sophisticate like Henry Bladen. An advantageous quirk.

The fondness for gambling was also advantageous. In July

of 1922, it paid a dividend to Zalman, the equal of which no gambler had ever seen.

Zalman reached his office before seven-thirty in the morning. Julia and the children had left the previous week to summer at Glen Cove. Zalman, who would be joining them for the weekend, felt jealous. Everyone was away. Even Bladen. Two days earlier, the newspaper owner had set off aboard the *Masthead* for the Bahamas. Zalman checked his diary. His only appointment was lunch with Brennan and Regan.

As the morning passed, Zalman dwelt on the fact that he was working while everyone else was enjoying the fine weather. By the time his visitors arrived, he had made up his mind to do something about it. When Brennan asked where they were eating, Zalman replied, "Outdoors. We're going to Belmont."

"Didn't know you liked the ponies."

"I want to spend a day in the sun like everyone else."

On the way to the parking garage where Zalman left the Pierce-Arrow, the three men stopped at a newsstand. "Give me a paper," Zalman said. Handed the *Messenger* without asking for it, he tipped the stand owner a dollar. Brennan picked up a copy of *Form Guide,* a daily racing paper, which he read during the journey out to Belmont. Zalman noticed that the thin racing sheet cost fifteen cents, compared with the two cents a daily newspaper cost.

They reached Belmont twenty minutes before the first race. While Brennan and Regan bet, Zalman studied *Form Guide.* He'd seen it before, but he'd never taken much notice. It carried the names of horses scheduled to run that day at tracks across the country, accompanied by results of their previous outings and *Form Guide*'s own selections. Zalman decided to bet the racing sheet's tips right through the card. By afternoon's end, he'd achieved a place and two shows, but no winners.

Regan drove the Pierce-Arrow back to Manhattan. Zalman, still reading the racing paper, sat alone in the back. Neither of the henchmen spoke unless Zalman asked a question. Their boss was hatching an idea, and no one disturbed him at such times.

"A man called Fred Schroeder's listed as publisher. Know anything about him?"

"Used to be a sports writer with the *World,*" Brennan replied. "He started *Form Guide* ten years ago."

Zalman vaguely recalled the name. "What kind of circulation does a sheet like this have?"

"Twenty-five thousand maybe. Racegoers and gamblers who use bookies and horse parlors. Not worth bothering about," Brennan added, mystified that his boss should be taking such an interest.

"How many racetracks do we have in America?"

"Twenty-five, thirty."

"If it's that many, it's worth bothering about. Did you see the size of that crowd today? Must have been twenty thousand. This country's gambling mad." Zalman returned his attention to *Form Guide.* "The information given here—past results, jockeys, weights. How could it be improved? You're both horse players. What other information would you like to see?"

"Instead of just knowing a horse won its last time out, I'd like to know what kind of surface it ran on," Regan answered. "Firm, soft, sloppy, it makes a big difference if you know that."

"Seeing how a horse ran over each part of the race is important," Brennan said. "That can tell you a lot. You see a horse comes dead last in a mile race and you forget about it. But if you notice it was leading through the first five or six furlongs and then faded badly, that tells you to watch out for when it runs in a shorter race. Likewise, you can see that a horse that finished out of the money in a mile race came from dead last to fourth in the home stretch. In a mile and a half, that horse will win going away."

Zalman instantly saw a way of achieving such detail. A man watching the race through binoculars from the grandstand roof could call out positions as the horses passed each stage: positions out of the gate; positions at each distance post. A clerk could write down that information. "How many other sheets are there like this?"

"A couple of dozen around the country," Brennan answered. "New York has two, *Form Guide* and another sheet called *Daily Odds.* Other cities have one or two."

"We handle distribution for some of them," Regan added.

"For now we do, Bill. For now."

Zalman threw himself into the new venture with customary zeal. He researched the market carefully. More than thirty tracks operated in North America, some for a few days each year, some for a few months. People who gambled regularly on horses, at the track or through bookies, numbered in the millions. Each gambler represented a reader for the new racing paper Zalman envisaged.

He took off the last two weeks in August to be with the family in Glen Cove. Even then, he wasted no time. He spent the afternoons at Belmont, not so interested in the actual racing as in the people who attended. He watched them bet, separating the serious players from the dilettantes. He kept a count of how many gamblers consulted a copy of *Form Guide,* or its rival, *Daily Odds.* The more he saw, the more convinced he became that not only was his idea of a national racing sheet plausible, but it might turn out to be the best idea he'd ever had. More profitable even than the silver souvenir spoons.

Julia sensed his excitement each time he returned to Glen Cove. She asked what he was up to. "I'm researching my first paper," he replied. "Bigger than anything Bladen has." But he never told her what kind of paper it would be.

When he returned to work, one question remained. Did he buy an established paper such as *Daily Odds* or *Form Guide,* or did he start from scratch? He chose to pursue the first alternative.

Daily Odds was owned by a man named Lew Schwartz. Its circulation was smaller than that of *Form Guide,* but at this stage, Zalman was unconcerned about readership. That could always be increased with smart promotion. Schwartz operated from the basement of a building on Canal Street. Zalman visited him at three in the morning, as *Daily Odds* went to press. In the street outside, two small trucks waited to deliver the paper. Zalman introduced himself to Schwartz, shouting to be heard over the rattle of machinery.

"Lew, I'm Zalman Isaacson, and I want to buy your paper. How much do you want for it?"

Schwartz picked up one of the first copies off the press, keeping Zalman waiting for an answer while he inspected the evenness of the printing. A tall, heavyset man in his early thirties, he had started the paper four years earlier, on his return from army service in Europe. Before the war, he had been a printer. "How much are you offering me?"

"A man who wants to sell a product should name his price," Zalman responded. "He shouldn't wait to see what he's offered."

"I don't want to sell anything. You want to buy." Schwartz knew Zalman by reputation. If he wanted *Daily Odds,* he'd have to pay through the nose. "When you show me how badly you want to buy, I'll let you know how badly I want to sell."

"That's not the way I do business. When you're ready to name a price, get in touch with me." He started to walk away, then swung around. "I'll see how interested Fred Schroeder is in selling *Form Guide* to me. Right now, you don't own the only racing sheet in town, Lew. But when I get into the business, I'll make damned sure that mine is the only sheet in town."

Schwartz jabbed an ink-stained finger at Zalman's face. "You don't frighten me with your threats. I stood up to the best the Kaiser could throw at me—do you really think your bluster is going to make me tremble?"

Zalman left. He waited the remainder of the day to hear from Schwartz. The next morning, he visited Fred Schroeder's *Form Guide* operation on the West Side. Schroeder was a different proposition from Schwartz. He put out *Form Guide* with the help of his wife. It occupied most of their time, leaving little opportunity for leisure. Schroeder was sixty-two, his wife a year younger. As they neared old age they viewed the paper as a ball and chain around their ankles. They were ready to sell, and when Zalman asked for a price, Schroeder responded with the first figure that came to mind. A nice round figure with enough zeroes to make him feel important.

"Two hundred and fifty thousand dollars."

"Done!" Zalman exclaimed before the offer could be retracted. He offered his hand to seal the bargain. Schroeder grabbed it, unable to believe his good fortune. He had intended the quarter of a million to be a starting point for negotiations. From there, he had expected to go down, perhaps to a hundred thousand, which would still have been a wonderful sum.

Zalman, too, was convinced that he had a bargain. It would cost him more to launch a racing sheet, and he would never be able to come up with a title as good as *Form Guide*. Or, for that matter, *Daily Odds*. His sole regret about the deal was that he would have preferred to buy *Daily Odds;* then he would only have Fred Schroeder's *Form Guide* to put out of business. Schroeder would have folded easily. Instead, he had walked away with a healthy retirement present.

Zalman suspected that it would be much more difficult to put Lew Schwartz out of business.

Zalman created a company for *Form Guide*. He placed Frank Brennan and Bill Regan in charge, giving each man fifteen percent of the equity. The remaining seventy percent belonged to Zalman.

He gave Brennan and Regan such power because he knew he did not need to look over their shoulders. With little guidance from him, they had done a fine job with the distribution companies. Zalman had faith in them. They returned that faith with diligence. The longer he knew them, the more he found they had in common. They had all graduated from the same school of publishing. The only difference was that Zalman's imagination, his ability to spot a profitable scheme at a single glance, put him firmly at the top of the class. Brennan and Regan respected him in the same way they had respected previous employers—Henry Bladen, and before him, William Randolph Hearst.

When work began on the new *Form Guide,* Zalman let Julia in on the secret. He showed her a dummy, make-up pages with columns of copy pasted down. She looked at it and turned her nose up.

"What's so wonderful about this? You told me you were

working on something big. Bigger than anything Mr. Bladen had."

"It will be. Give it time."

She looked again. Lacking Zalman's vision, she failed to see a finished publication. There were no ads, no pictures, none of the familiar appurtenances of a newspaper. Horse racing itself meant little to her, and gambling signified even less. She might just as well have been holding sheets of wrapping paper. "How much time?" she asked.

Zalman was not disappointed. He was accustomed to people not seeing what he could see. "A year."

By the end of 1923, when the year was up, *Form Guide* had changed dramatically. Each edition carried information for that day's racing in North America: horses, jockeys, trainers, track conditions, plus each horse's previous performance broken down into different stages of the race. To accomplish such detail, charting crews attended every meeting. Additionally, *Form Guide* carried articles on horse racing by specialist writers. Most important, the single *Form Guide* had blossomed into eight separate editions published in New York, Chicago, Los Angeles, Cleveland, Cincinnati, Detroit, Baltimore, and Toronto, in Canada. The same *Form Guide* carried by a gambler at Rockingham Park could be found at the Dufferin Park half-mile track in Toronto.

New York was the headquarters. Clerks collated and stored all the information sent in by the charters at the tracks. More clerks retrieved it to be used when a horse ran again. While typesetters and compositors put together the edition of *Form Guide* that went on sale in New York, the same details were wired to the other offices. The price of *Form Guide,* depending upon the distance of the point of sale to the printing plant, ranged from a quarter to half a dollar. Print runs were continually expanded to match the growing demand. The paper continued to baffle Julia, but she could appreciate its influence.

The cities where *Form Guide* published already had established racing sheets. More such sheets were published in areas where Zalman intended to introduce *Form Guide* in the future. He checked competing papers regularly, feeling flattered by the improvements he saw, evidence of his own successful enterprise. *Form Guide* demonstrated new heights in accuracy and information. If the other sheets wanted to remain in operation, they had no choice but to follow its example. Zalman decided to take care of the competition before any of them followed the example well enough to become a nuisance.

He paid a second visit to the basement in Canal Street that housed Lew Schwartz's *Daily Odds*. Schwartz was one of those who had improved his product in the face of Zalman's rivalry. "What do you want?" he growled when he recognized his visitor.

"If you'd have been smart, you could have made yourself two hundred and fifty thousand dollars like Schroeder did. Then I'd be talking to him now, instead of talking to you."

"We've got nothing to talk about."

"I'm offering you another chance to sell out to me."

"How much?"

"Fifty thousand." Zalman considered the offer generous. He didn't need to pay anything to rid himself of rivals, but he wanted to keep force and coercion only as a last resort.

"Fifty thousand? You must be crazy!"

"How long do you think you'll stay in business once I turn up the heat?"

"Quarter of a million. I'm worth as much as Schroeder."

"You were worth that much when I had a use for you. Now I'm offering charity."

"Two hundred and fifty grand."

"Forty thousand," Zalman said coldly.

Schwartz took a moment to realize that Zalman's counterproposal was below his original offer. He exploded. "Drop dead, you son of a bitch! You think you can force me out of business, you've got another think coming! Now get the hell out of here!"

Grabbing Zalman by the shoulders, Schwartz muscled him toward the door. Zalman did not resist. He could have handled the heavier man, but he wanted none of Schwartz's employees to recall a fight. He needed them to swear in court, if necessary, that he had never lifted a hand to Schwartz, had never made any kind of threat, had never intimated violence. His visit had been that of a businessman tendering an offer.

Revenge for this humiliating treatment would take other, more effective ways.

During the following week, Zalman offered to buy out competition right across the country. Owners of eight marginally profitable racing newspapers, understanding the writing on the wall, accepted purchase prices that fell between eight and twenty thousand dollars. Zalman turned the pressure up a notch. His own agencies, which had continued to handle distribution for many of the sheets, pulled the rug, refusing to do business with them anymore. Twelve more racing sheets, with no other means of distribution, folded.

For the sheets that were unaffected by either buy-out offers or the loss of distribution channels, Zalman conceived a special plan. A scheme that used his influence as Henry Bladen's circulation director. Eight such sheets remained in competition to him—seven in major cities across the country, and one in New York. Zalman reserved New York for himself. It was personal. He talked with shop and newsstand owners, and his message was ominously clear.

"Drop *Daily Odds,* or Bladen will drop you."

There was no choice to make. *Daily Odds* was a single paper with limited appeal. Bladen newspapers and magazines supplied a large part of a retailer's livelihood. Zalman returned to his office and waited to hear from Lew Schwartz.

He didn't wait long. First thing next morning, Schwartz stormed into the circulation director's office. "You son of a bitch! You've blackmailed my outlets. You told them you'd cut them off from Bladen unless they dropped me."

Zalman remained as cool as Schwartz was flustered. "Did you find one dealer who told you that?"

"Of course not! They're all too damned scared of your power to say anything. But I'm not stupid. You're doing it right across the country to racing sheets like mine. Those you couldn't buy out, you shut down."

"I'll give you one last chance to sell out to me."

At the prospect of money, Schwartz's fury lessened by a fraction. "How much?"

Zalman smiled inwardly. Normally he took no pleasure in bringing a man to his knees; he never knew when he might need that man's help. This was different, the settling of a score. He had Schwartz crawling now, and if he could get him to accept a pittance where once he could have taken a respectable sum, Zalman's vengeance for his humiliation at Schwartz's hands would be complete. "Five thousand dollars."

Schwartz's face collapsed. He started to come around the desk. Zalman stood up, hands clenched into large, bony fists. "I don't mind how many people see you being carried out of here."

Schwartz stopped. "Keep your stinking five grand! I'll have a hundred times that when I drag you into court, you wait and see!" He swung around and strode out of the office, leaving the threat hanging in the air like a thundercloud.

Lew Schwartz took more than a year to keep his promise. He brought legal action against Zalman, charging him with creating a racing sheet monopoly by forcing competition out of business.

Zalman was confident that he could beat the charge. The newsstand owners were loyal to him. Not one would support Schwartz's claim that they had been blackmailed into dropping *Daily Odds*. Besides, how could Schwartz even claim a nationwide monopoly existed when a handful of other racing sheets continued to print, even if they were in areas which Zalman had considered economically unfeasible for *Form Guide?*

Nonetheless, Schwartz's action generated unwelcome publicity. Other newspapers, glad to link Bladen and his circulation chief with anything that hinted of corruption, plastered Schwartz's allegations across their front pages.

Zalman soon felt the first effects of the storm. Henry Bladen summoned him. It was not the normal kind of invitation for a meeting, where Bladen would stick his head around the door of Zalman's office and ask if he had a few minutes. This was formal, delivered by Bladen's middle-aged secretary. A crisp "Mr. Bladen would like to see you in his office at eleven-thirty, Mr. Isaacson." It was the summons to an execution.

When Zalman entered the boardroom, Bladen sat at the head of the long table. Set out in front of him were opposition

200

papers. Every one, with the exception of the *Times,* carried a front-page story on Lew Schwartz and his monopoly allegations. Zalman braced himself.

"What are we going to do about this mess?" Bladen asked.

"Schwartz can't prove a thing."

"Perhaps not, but he can leave a lot of dirt sticking to us with these claims that you used your position in my company to further your own ends." Bladen rested his chin on his hands. Zalman thought he looked old. "You and I have been together what . . . twenty years? That's longer than many people live. I've given you more leeway than I've given anyone, because you produced, and that was all I cared about. But now I'm troubled."

Zalman perused the newspapers while he considered a reply. He and Bladen had shared a wonderful relationship. Because of the depth of that bond, Bladen was having difficulty saying the words he had to say. He didn't find it easy to fire the man he had hired twice. Zalman helped him out. "I'll resign," he said softly. "I'll resign as of"—he checked his watch—"midday today. That gives me twenty minutes to clean out my desk and make a couple of telephone calls."

"Thank you, Zalman." Bladen lifted his face. He looked relieved. "I knew what you were doing all along, using my name, my papers and magazines, to promote your *Form Guide.* I didn't mind that at all, just as long as I wasn't seen to be in the know. The same as that time"—his voice trembled—"that time I offered you Jimmy Doyle's job. I knew what you did. You arranged Hagerty's death. I knew what Doyle had done, the vandalism of rivals' trucks and printing plants, the deeds that were committed in the name of circulation. Of course I knew all that. Just as long as the world outside the *Messenger* wasn't aware that I knew. This is the same. Even at my age, I can't afford to be shown as knowing what all my people are up to."

Zalman understood perfectly. He shook Bladen's hand, cleaned out his desk, and went home.

Lew Schwartz lost in court. Among Zalman's witnesses were Fred Schroeder, owners of smaller sheets who had also sold willingly, and selected shop and newsstand operators

201

who swore that no pressure had ever been exerted on them. Zalman's counsel rebutted Schwartz's allegations with a counterclaim that his action was simply a spiteful revenge for Zalman choosing to buy *Form Guide* for two hundred and fifty thousand dollars instead of paying more for the inferior *Daily Odds*.

Schwartz failed to prove a single allegation, and Zalman was exonerated. On the way out of court, magnanimous in victory, he offered his hand to his adversary. Schwartz turned away. The cost of bringing the case had ruined him.

Zalman learned the cost to himself after the case ended. Julia had avoided mentioning the issue to Zalman, either in the time leading up to the case, or during the hearing itself, which she attended. As they drove home after the verdict, she asked Zalman one question.

"Was what that man claimed true?"

He laughed and put an arm around her. "The court found in my favor . . . how could it be true?"

"Courts aren't always right. Half the people at liberty right now should be in jail."

"But not this person. I am as innocent as a newborn lamb, Julia. Schwartz tried to hike the price and I wouldn't have any of it. I went somewhere else. He couldn't compete with me, so he tried to recoup his losses by having some judge order me to pay him damages."

"Helen and Jimmy have been asked questions at school about their father. From fellow pupils and teachers alike."

"Really?" Zalman didn't know that. Julia, fearing he would find such news distressing, had kept it from him. "What answers did they give?"

"I told them to say other people envied your success."

Zalman leaned across to kiss her. "This is what you get for giving the right answer."

The car swerved. From behind, a horn blared. He sat up, concentrating once more on the road. And thinking.

This whole episode was a warning. Bladen had sanctioned violence and blackmail to sell papers. Hearst, too. Every publisher had dirtied his hands at one time or another. But they all knew how to remain insulated from the mayhem. So many corporate layers separated the Bladens and the Hearsts from the filth in the gutter that no one could ever point a finger.

Zalman flicked a glance at Julia. He'd cheated her this time. He'd gone back on a silent promise never to cause her another moment of concern. He wouldn't do that again. He would be so respectable and clean, he'd squeak.

Chapter Nine

Rachel's position with Harold Parker soon took on more than the simple responsibilities of secretarial work. She impressed the agent with both a quick grasp of the variety-theater business and a fine judgment when it came to the merits of different acts. At the end of 1920, after she had been with him for nine months, Parker gave Rachel a raise and made her his assistant. When he was occupied elsewhere, she attended talent shows and visited theaters to see if certain performers were worth representing. She watched and listened carefully to everything that Parker did, and when the agent offered her the opportunity to negotiate a deal, she put what she had learned to good use.

She answered the telephone one morning, then looked across the desk at Parker who was reading the "Next Week's Calls" section of the *Performer*. "The Wimbledon Theatre. Someone's ill, and they need a specialty act for next week. They've only got thirteen pounds."

Parker pointed with his cigar to the file box. Rachel checked the cards. A juggler named Larry Wilde was available; on the card was the notation that he would work for twelve pounds. She got back to the manager of the Wimbledon Theatre. "We can get you Larry Wilde. He normally works for fourteen pounds, but we'll see what we can do." She broke the connection, then called the juggler. "Larry? This is Rachel Lesser from the Harold Parker Agency. The Wimbledon Theatre needs a specialty act next week, but

204

they're only offering ten pounds . . . All right, Larry, we'll try to get them up."

She waited two minutes, then called Wilde's home once more. "Larry, as it's an emergency, Wimbledon is prepared to go as high as thirteen pounds." Then she made a final call, to the manager of the Wimbledon Theatre. "Larry Wilde will work next week for only thirteen pounds." When she finished the negotiation, Parker set down his copy of the *Performer* and clapped his beefy hands. It was only a minor deal, a specialty act to fill a few missing minutes in a bill, but she had handled it in a manner that made Parker proud of her. She had absorbed from him the first and most important lesson of being an agent—leaving both sides believing they were getting a bargain.

A childless widower in his middle forties, Parker possessed a strong sentimental streak that centered around his dead wife. Five years after her death, he was as deeply in love with her as he had ever been. He missed her presence every moment of the day. Her framed photograph stood on his desk, a round-faced woman with tightly waved hair. Every morning, when Parker entered the office, and every evening when he left, Rachel watched him lift the picture to eye level, study it, then kiss it. Once he even revealed to Rachel that his wife's clothes still hung in the wardrobe, just as she had left them.

"I never had the heart to get rid of them," he admitted. "I couldn't throw them away like so much garbage, and the thought of giving them away or selling them so some other woman could wear them, well, that just chilled me down to the bone."

Rachel smiled gently and touched his hand. She was growing very fond of Parker. There was nothing sexual in that fondness, just the closeness of two people who worked together every day and found they liked each other. She accompanied Parker to an increasing number of matinees. He never asked her to accompany him to evening shows, because he knew she belonged with her family. Nor did he ever make demands on her that fell outside customary office procedure. He liked her company simply because it was company. And because she understood . . .

Jacob was not so understanding. With pride already injured by the need for Rachel to find work, he sought out further slights. In Harold Parker, he started to see not Rachel's employer, but a competitor for her loyalty. And then, as Rachel proudly described new responsibilities that Parker gave her, Jacob saw the agent as a rival for Rachel's affection. Slowly, his anger built. Until, fueled by the frustration of having to teach in a state school, it exploded.

"I don't want you working for that Harold Parker anymore," Jacob said. It was evening. Dinner was over, the dishes washed and dried. The boys were upstairs, doing homework. "If you feel you must work, I want you to work somewhere closer to home."

Rachel was doing needlepoint. She looked up from it. "What is wrong with my working for Harold?"

Jacob waved his left hand around, as though plucking an answer from the air. "This work is causing you to ignore your duties as a mother and a wife. Besides, you come home with your clothes stinking of that man's cigars. You smell disgusting."

"I am ignoring none of my duties," Rachel answered evenly. "And I don't come home smelling of tobacco. Harold knows I don't like his cigars. He always opens the windows when he smokes. Even on cold days." Rachel set aside the needlepoint. "What is really troubling you, Jacob?"

"I don't like you working for him. He is looking for another wife, and I think he has found *you.*"

Slowly, Rachel shook her head. Jacob's claim was so preposterous that she wanted to laugh. It was a scene out of one of the many revues she had seen during the past year, except these roles were being played by Jacob and herself. "You're wrong, Jacob. Nothing could be further from the truth. Harold will be in love with his wife, with her memory, until the day he dies. Like I'll always be in love with you." She walked across the room to kiss him. He held her with his left arm, but it was not the embrace of love; it was the grip of a frightened man clinging to a lifebelt.

In the summer of 1921, Emmanuel left school and began to work for a women's wear company in the East End. On his first payday, he handed his unopened pay envelope con-

206

taining thirteen shillings to his mother. "I'm grown up and I earn my own living. Now I can help you."

Rachel took the envelope and returned a shilling to Emmanuel for spending money. "The remainder goes away for a rainy day," she said. "That's the first thing you do when you earn money, put some away for a rainy day." She placed it in a savings account which she opened in Emmanuel's name, adding to it from each week's pay packet.

Emmanuel swaggered about the house, talking continually about his job. "Learning to operate a sewing machine's just the start of it. Next I'll learn cutting, then sales. You see, by the time I'm twenty I'll have my own company and we'll be making enough money to buy up every house in this street."

Emmanuel's boasting and his carefree attitude goaded Sidney and Bernard. They paid less attention to their schoolwork; their marks deteriorated. When Jacob asked them what the trouble was, Sidney replied, "What do our school marks matter? We're going to leave when we're fourteen, just like Emmanuel did."

Jacob, who had always dreamed that one of his sons would follow in his academic footsteps, was distressed. He blamed Rachel. If she had not gone out to work—if she had stayed at home to exert more parental control over the boys while their father was absent—none of this would have happened. Arguments developed, quarrels that followed a set course. Jacob said his piece and then rejected any of Rachel's reasoning by turning away from her. When she forced him to reply to questions, his answers were limited to a curt "yes" or "no." Rachel wondered whether Jacob's brooding attitude also prevailed at school. If so, how long would it be before the school decided that it no longer needed the services of such a sullen malcontent?

Sidney left school at the end of 1922 to learn to be a furrier. Like Emmanuel, he handed over his unopened pay envelope to his mother each week, receiving only pocket money. The remainder went toward the "rainy day." Sidney promised his mother that the first fur garment he made would be for her. After eight months, he brought her home a hat made of Persian lamb trimmings which she wore proudly throughout the winter.

207

Bernard left school in 1923, to enter the clothing business. Unlike Emmanuel, he started in the costing department, where he displayed a sharpness with figures that he had never bothered to show in school. He memorized the prices of buttons, materials, and trimmings that went into each piece of women's clothing. Within a few weeks, he could look at a finished garment and instantly know how much it could be wholesaled for.

Rachel was amused to see the changes working wrought on her sons. The characteristics that were always there became sharper. Bernard, the quietest of the three, was content to remain in the background. Emmanuel and Sidney jostled for position at the front, each trying to prove himself better than the other. It seemed to Rachel that they were always meeting on the narrow stairs, where there was only room for one to pass. They squared up, neither giving way, always resolving it by turning sideways and sliding past each other with triumphant smirks on their faces. Rachel told them that to pass like that on the stairs was to court bad luck, but they paid no attention to her. Their mother's old-country superstitions had no place in modern London. Only Bernard heeded his mother's advice. He never failed to leave the house without a piece of red ribbon in his wallet. He believed as deeply as his mother did that such a talisman would ward off ill fortune.

Rachel's relationship with Jacob worsened. When he returned home after teaching all day, he was withdrawn, given to long periods of silence. In bed, he was just as unresponsive. He fell asleep with his back turned toward her. She had forgotten the feel of his embrace. His kiss was now nothing more than the merest brushing of his lips against her cheek. There was no passion in it, no affection. It was habit.

When Jacob did want to talk, it was always about the old times. The good times, before the war. Before he had lost his arm. Rachel seized upon these opportunities, because they were the only times she could communicate with him. She drew her sons into these conversations. They understood their mother's reasons perfectly. If their father was ever to change, they had to show him the way. They asked about the

208

club, and gladly listened to Jacob tell the same stories over and over again. They knew that the most important thing was to make him talk; what he talked about was of secondary importance.

At the end of 1924, on the day the schools closed for the Christmas break, Rachel's worst dreams became reality. She came home from work to find Jacob sitting in front of the fire, staring morosely into the flames. In his hand was a sheet of paper. Before she could utter a word, he turned to her and said, "Is this how England treats its heroes? Look at me, I am a cripple, a man who lost his arm fighting for his country, and how does my country reward me? By dismissing me. I am no longer fit, they tell me, to shape the minds of the young. Can you believe that? A teacher for all these years, and now I am not good enough."

She took the sheet of paper from his hand. It was his notice of dismissal. "Did you expect anything else, the way you've been behaving? A teacher leads the way, he shows by example . . . as you once did! A teacher doesn't growl at everyone and find fault with everything, as you now do!"

Jacob, expecting sympathy in his plight, was stunned by the sharpness of Rachel's voice. "You, too! I gave for my country and now you also turn against me!"

Rachel felt her control slipping. She tried to hold back—criticizing Jacob would be like picking on a helpless child—but she could not help herself. Words of anger poured out. "You have no one but yourself to blame, Jacob. Do you remember when I asked you about your responsibilities as a father, you told me you had responsibilities as an Englishman? You were the one who wanted to run away and fight! You were the one who wanted to wrap yourself in the flag. What has happened to you is your own doing, and you have no one else to blame." Watching him sitting there, head bowed beneath the tirade, Rachel tried to picture the man she had married. She failed. This dismal image was all she could conjure up. The other Jacob—the strong, happy man with whom she had fallen in love—no longer existed.

Jacob rose from the seat, took the letter of dismissal from Rachel's hands and left the room. As he closed the door, Rachel heard him say, "If a man cannot find sympathy in his wife's eyes, where should he look for it?" Suddenly guilt-ridden, she ran after him, calling his name as he climbed the stairs to the second floor. He ignored her. As she reached the top of the stairs, she saw him enter the bedroom. The key turned, and the lock snapped.

He came down again for dinner but said nothing throughout the meal. Afterward, he went out for a walk before retiring early. When Rachel, an hour later, climbed into bed beside him, his body stiffened. In the bed where they had made love so many times, where they had conceived their three sons, Rachel now felt as if she were lying next to a total stranger. She whispered his name. His response was to get up and leave the room. He slept the night in a spare room. And every night after that.

Jacob remained uncommunicative for the entire Christmas period. He ignored Rachel and his sons. Rachel wondered how he passed his time. One day, as she rode home from work on the tram, she saw him walking aimlessly along the main road, head bowed, the empty right sleeve of his coat flapping helplessly by his side. She blinked back tears. He looked so desolate and yet, somehow, so familiar. Only when the tram had rolled past did she realize why. Jacob resembled a thousand other injured war veterans Rachel had seen, all lost, all wandering aimlessly through life, permanent casualties of a fruitless war.

The days leading up to the New Year were hectic ones for Rachel. All of Harold Parker's clients were busy, in variety, in revue, and in pantomime. The telephone rang continually with queries from theaters and performers alike. The instant one panic was settled, another arose.

"You should have told them to look on the bright side," Parker said, after Rachel had spent thirty minutes unraveling a problem concerning a dance duo that had been booked into two different London theaters on the same night. "We could have booked them into three theaters, not just two."

Rachel laughed and reached out a hand as the telephone rang again. Simultaneously, the office door opened. A man stood framed in the doorway, a walking stick clenched in his left hand. Rachel let the telephone go unanswered. "What are you doing here?" she asked.

Jacob, who had never visited the agency before, disregarded the question. He strode across the office to where Parker sat. "Parker?" When the agent failed to respond immediately, Jacob slammed the stick down across the desk with all his strength.

Parker's head snapped up. "What do you think you're doing?"

Jacob's mouth was a livid gash in a chalk-white face. He raised the stick and said, "I never wanted my wife to work! I wanted her to stop, to come home where she belonged. But she wouldn't listen to me. She only listened to you! Now I'm going to teach you a lesson!" The stick slashed down. Parker raised a hand in self-defense. The cigar in it flew across the room as the stick cracked across his knuckles. Parker yelled in pain and jumped back. Rachel threw herself on Jacob and tried to drag him away. She was no match for him. He shrugged her off and advanced on Parker, who cowered in a corner of the office. The stick came down twice across his shoulders. Parker's yelling changed to a terrified scream. Rachel tried again, flinging herself on Jacob and shrieking at him to stop. This time she had help. Two young men from the lawyer's office across the hall burst through the door, summed up the situation in a second, and pulled Jacob away. One wrestled the stick from his grasp while the other pushed him into a chair. Rachel leaped to Parker's aid. Two fingers of his right hand were twisted at crazy angles. He groaned in pain as Rachel touched his shoulder. One of the young men picked up the telephone to summon medical help.

Rachel watched Jacob. He sat in the chair, as peaceful now as he had been wild only moments earlier. Whatever devil had driven him had been exorcised by the attack on Parker. When he saw Rachel looking at him, he gave her a sheepish grin, as if apologizing for the mayhem he had wrought.

Jacob's attack left Harold Parker with two broken fingers and a fractured shoulder. When the police interviewed him, Parker refused to press assault charges; he claimed the incident had been the result of a misunderstanding, and he did not want it to go further. Rachel was grateful. The agent understood the private hell Jacob endured, and he was sympathetic.

In the moment that Rachel had seen Jacob sitting in the chair, smiling self-consciously, she finally acknowledged the truth of the situation: no future existed for them. Beginning with the loss of his arm, and ending with dismissal from his teaching job, events had telescoped until, at last, they had become too much for Jacob to bear. Deep within him, something had snapped. The man who shared the house with her—the man who had assaulted Parker—was not the man she had loved enough to marry. Nor was he the kind, loving man who had fathered her three sons. This man was a stranger, a twisted individual who could not come to grips with the simplest difficulties. She had weathered the mood swings, the anger, and the bitterness, but after the violent attack on Parker, Rachel was frightened to be close to Jacob. The only path she saw was separation.

She broached the subject to her sons. Sidney suggested converting the top floor of the house into a separate flat for Jacob, but Emmanuel instantly vetoed the idea. Putting an arm around Rachel's shoulders, he told his younger brother: "Mama's scared of being under the same roof as Papa, don't you understand that? She wants him right out of the house, not just living on a different floor."

"You're a right callous pair of bastards!" Bernard suddenly burst out. It was the first time Rachel had ever heard any of her sons swear; none of them ever even used a simple "bloody" in her presence. "Just listen to yourselves, talking about moving Papa here and there as though he's nothing more than a blasted piece of furniture."

Both brothers turned on him. "Have you got any better ideas then?" Sidney demanded.

Rachel stepped between them to exert a calming influence. Her two older sons had turned the discussion into a contest, the way they did with everything. Only Bernard seemed visibly upset at the prospect of the family splitting up. His eyes glistened with tears he could barely control. Emmanuel and Sidney had accepted the breakup as fact the instant Rachel had mentioned it. As much as it pained them, they felt as she did: the man who now lived with them was not the

212

father they had idolized. Which was best, Rachel wondered: Bernard's emotion-filled response, or Emmanuel's and Sidney's pragmatic, if cold, approach? And which method would she use when she saw a solicitor to draw up the necessary separation papers?

Jacob saved Rachel the trouble of visiting a solicitor. The day after her talk with the boys, he said he needed to speak to her. "Bernard told me what you had discussed, Rachel. Is that what you really want? For us to be apart?"

Rachel swallowed hard. She was not surprised that Bernard had told his father. Of the three boys, he was by far the most sensitive. At last she managed a faltering "I think that separation would be best, Jacob."

Jacob stood quite still for several seconds, face composed, blue eyes unblinking. "I still love you," he said.

"I know," Rachel whispered. "And I love you, too. Or at least, I love the Jacob I used to know. The Jacob I married. But the Jacob I know now scares me."

Jacob recoiled as though he had been struck. "Bernard mentioned that you were frightened of me. I didn't believe him. Now, hearing it from your lips, I know he spoke the truth. The last thing I want to do is frighten you, Rachel—"

"Then why did you attack Harold? Why have you acted so strangely? God only knows that you've been through terrible times, but you had no excuse to behave as you have done."

Jacob said nothing. He just shrugged his shoulders and gave Rachel the same embarrassed smile he had given her in Parker's office. The expression made up Rachel's mind. "We'll help you find work, and somewhere to live. But we'll all be better off if we're no longer together."

Rachel and Jacob separated. He moved into a small flat a mile from the house in Graham Road. Rachel dipped into her glass jar for money to buy furniture. She and the boys visited Jacob regularly. She took him food and asked him what shopping he needed. After a couple of weeks, she suggested that he start shopping and cooking for himself; she wanted him to gain some independence. Every Friday night, Jacob made his weekly visit to the house for dinner. It was the same

213

day that Harold Parker paid Rachel, and before Jacob left to walk home, Rachel always gave him enough money to see him through the next week.

After six weeks, Jacob found a job selling cigarettes, candy, and newspapers in a local shop. It was a far cry from teaching, but it was a giant step on his path back to self-esteem. He mixed with people all day long, discussing anything from the weather to front-page news. Some confidence returned. Rachel dropped by the shop once or twice a week on her way to work to buy a newspaper; the boys did the same. They all saw the improvement.

In the summer of 1925, after six months of working, Jacob told Rachel that he was taking off a week. "I'm going away, to Brighton. A working man deserves a holiday by the seaside."

Four days after Jacob left for his vacation, Rachel went to the glass jar to add some money to the family's reserves. Her heart dropped into an abruptly knotted stomach. The jar had contained almost forty pounds; now it contained nothing. Which of her sons had taken the money? And why?

Emmanuel arrived home first. Rachel asked if he had been to the jar. He denied all knowledge, as did Sidney, who arrived ten minutes later. That left only Bernard. Emmanuel and Sidney offered to wait with her for Bernard, but she rejected the idea. The theft of the money was between Rachel and her youngest son; it did not concern the other boys. She sent them out of the house, with instructions not to return for an hour.

Bernard's face dropped the moment he entered the house and saw his mother waiting for him. He did not need to look at the empty glass jar in her hands to know why she was waiting. "I took the money," he said.

"Why? Why did you steal it like a thief? If you needed money so desperately, why didn't you just ask?"

"You wouldn't have understood. I'll find a way to pay it back, don't worry about that."

"I'm not worried. I want to know why you took it. I want to know about this thing I'm not supposed to understand."

"It was for Papa."

Of all the reasons Rachel had considered for Bernard taking the money—gambling, the need to impress a girl, even just a compulsion to steal—Jacob had never entered her mind.

"Papa wanted to go away. He couldn't afford to."

Rachel could not believe what she was hearing. "You gave your father forty pounds to spend a week at Brighton? He can spend forty weeks there with all that money."

Bernard looked at his mother with something that resembled pity. "You don't understand, do you? He didn't go to Brighton. He just told you that. He's sailing to Canada."

"Canada?" Rachel repeated the word in disbelief.

Bernard nodded slowly. "He wanted a new start in life. He told me he had nothing left here. He felt his country had betrayed him. Even us . . ." Bernard's voice broke; he sniffed back tears. "I was the only one in the family he trusted enough to confide in. I was the only one he felt comfortable asking for help. That forty pounds was his fare money, and a little extra to get him started over there."

"When did he leave?"

"Three days ago."

Rachel set the jar on a table and reached out to hold Bernard. "Don't worry about the money," she whispered. "It doesn't mean a thing."

Had she really been so insensitive? Had they all been so callous that Jacob had no alternative but to ask Bernard to steal money for him? Her body trembled as she started crying.

"He said he'd write," Bernard said as he held on to Rachel. "He promised he'd write."

Eight weeks after Jacob's departure, Rachel received a letter postmarked Toronto. In it, Jacob mentioned that he had settled down and found a job teaching. He described the city as quiet after the bustle of London, and wrote that he was living in a furnished room in an area called Kensington. "Kensington is quite like the East End, Rachel. I feel at home here." Rachel did not reply because no return address was included with the letter. Each morning, as she had done when Jacob was in the army, she checked the mail for another letter. She wanted to know his address so she could write to him with news of England, of his family. But after six weeks, six months, and then a year, when no further letter came, she understood. Jacob did not want to hear about England. His new life was precisely that. New. Unencumbered by entanglements from his past.

That revelation saddened her, but it also brought peace. Jacob had finally found what he sought. He had a new life, new friends, perhaps even a new family. Rachel should not feel cheated. The Jacob in Canada was not the Jacob she had loved so passionately. That Jacob had died at Ypres. A different man had returned home with an empty sleeve, a man who reminded Rachel of her husband—and the boys of their father—but a different man nonetheless. They had tried to love him, but they had failed. Like so many other families, they had lost someone in the war.

By the autumn of 1926, the turmoil of Jacob's departure had abated. The household swallowed up the disruption and carried on. Emmanuel, at nineteen, and earning good money as a salesman in the women's clothing business, appointed himself the man of the family. His first act was to ask Rachel to call him Manny instead of Emmanuel. When she asked him why, he told her that outside of the house he was known only as Manny. He produced a business card which read Manny Lesser.

"Everyone in the trade knows me as Manny. It's an easier name to live with. Sidney and Bernard haven't called me Emmanuel for ages. They always call me Manny."

"I loathe the familiar shortening of names. I never called your father Jake, and he never called me Rach, and no one calls your brothers Sid or Bernie. Besides, Emmanuel is far more meaningful than Manny. My father's name was Mendel, and I was going to name my first son Emmanuel in his honor. Only that son was stillborn." This was the first time Rachel had discussed her dead son with any of the other boys; she was breaking ground. "So you became the first born. You became Emmanuel."

"You mean I'm really the *second* Emmanuel?"

"I suppose you are."

"I'd rather be the first Manny."

"Is it that important to you?" When he nodded, Rachel

said, "All right, from now on I'll try to remember to call you Manny. But if I forget, you'll forgive me, all right?"

Manny kissed his mother and hugged her. "You know I'll always forgive you. No matter what you do."

Rachel watched him walk away. No woman could have more devoted sons than she did. All loving her in different ways. Emmanuel—Sorry, she caught herself at once!—Manny! Manny loved her as an oldest son should love his mother. Seriously, as though it were a solemn duty. Sidney's affection was much lighter, that of a young man embarrassed at displaying such feelings. One day when he saw sadness on his mother's face, he came up to her, squeezed her shoulders, and said, "Stop looking so glum—we'll go out and find you another husband." She was horrified by his offer, but that did not stop her laughing.

The two older boys were as different as brothers could be. Sidney had grown tall and slim, a young man who liked to go dancing on the weekend so he could show off the elegant steps he had practiced all week long. Manny was shorter, stocky, with a barrel chest and a body that could blossom into obesity if he were not careful. The fair hair of both boys had darkened, but the blueness of their eyes could never alter. In Manny's eyes, the blue was colder, more calculating; even when he smiled, his eyes remained serious. Sidney's eyes shone with laughter, as if he were always enjoying some private joke. The eyes were truly the windows of the soul.

Then there was Bernard, who was nearing seventeen. Did every mother, Rachel wondered, automatically favor her youngest son? Or did she lean to Bernard because he displayed more sensitivity? He had been the most visibly upset about Jacob's problems; he'd been the one to help Jacob flee his past. Rachel was confident that Bernard could stand up on his own—didn't he already have a responsible position in the costing department of the clothing firm he worked for?—but he demonstrated a vulnerability that was missing in the other two boys. She found it touching.

Eight weeks before Christmas, Manny brought home a brown paper bag. While his brothers watched, he shook the contents onto the kitchen floor. Rachel, who was stirring a saucepan of soup, shrieked and dropped the ladle.

"Are you mad, bringing mice into the house?"

Manny picked up one of the mice and held it out to his mother. She backed away before seeing through slitted eyes that the animal was only a soft toy made of cloth trimmings with tiny black buttons for its eyes. "We want to go into business selling these," Manny said. "We can make small animals like mice, and bigger animals like lions with fur clippings for their manes."

"I've already been in touch with a couple of toy shop owners who have promised to take some for Christmas—" Sidney said.

"They cost next to nothing to manufacture," Bernard broke in. "We'll make a fortune this Christmas, and who knows what we'll be doing by next Christmas."

Rachel's eyes darted back to her eldest son as he took up the baton again. "We're offering you the opportunity to be a partner in this venture."

"You mean you're coming to me for some money?"

"Would you rather we went to a bank?" Sidney asked.

"We don't have enough in our savings accounts," Manny said. "We need help to finance the company. This is a certain thing. See how realistic these mice are. They scared you, didn't they? Children will have a great time with these things."

"How much do you need?"

Manny and Sidney looked at Bernard, who stood between them. "A hundred and fifty pounds," Bernard answered. "The material's the cheapest outlay. We're going to have to rent a room, hire a couple of machines, and pay people to operate them. Manny and Sidney will be out taking orders. I'll be keeping the records."

"You mean you're going to leave your jobs?"

All three boys nodded simultaneously.

"What if this scheme doesn't work? We would have lost a hundred and fifty pounds, and you'll be without jobs."

"How can it fail?" Sidney wanted to know. "Christmas is coming. These toys are a wonderful idea, and Bernard estimates they'll retail competitively. They'll be the biggest bargain of the whole season. The biggest success, you'll see."

Rachel mulled over the proposition. Three young men with an idea to get rich quick. Their business background was limited to work they had done for other people, and that was in the clothing industry, not in toys. But their zeal made up for any lack of experience. If Manny and Sidney couldn't sell it, and if Bernard couldn't manage it, then it wasn't worth selling and managing. One hundred and fifty pounds would put a major strain on the family finances, but the certainty in Manny's eyes made any risk seem minimal. "All right, I'll become your partner in this venture. What's this company going to be called anyway?"

Sidney handed her a card. "Rachel's Toys," she read aloud. "You were so sure I was going to help that you named it for me?"

"We were going to name it for you whether you helped us or not," Sidney answered.

The three boys quit their jobs and started their own company. They rented a room, leased machines, and hired operators. Manny and Sidney went out on the road with samples and order books. Bernard remained in the one-room factory, ready to supervise production of the sea of orders his brothers brought in.

The sea turned out to be a trickle. Small shops booked small orders. At larger shops and department stores, Manny and Sidney were told that Christmas orders had to be placed much earlier. The merchandise was attractive, well made, and competitively priced, but they had started their sales campaign far too late. Next year, was the advice they received, plan earlier.

A week before Christmas, they admitted defeat. They let the rented room go, returned the machines, and fired the machinists. Out of their initial capital, only three pounds, eight shillings, and twopence remained. Their stock amounted to two hundred and eighty assorted soft animals which filled a spare room.

Rachel surveyed the inventory: lions and tigers, cats and dogs, mice and elephants. She looked at the long faces of her sons. Dreams died hard. The business had collapsed, and they were all out of work. "No rich man became a millionaire overnight," she said. "You'll try again, and keep trying."

Manny answered her. "It wasn't the money. It was the challenge, to see if we could make something out of nothing."

"You'll find other challenges. Now we have to decide what to do with all these toys." She thought for a few seconds. "Take a couple of toys each. Keep them as souvenirs. I want you to give the rest to the Salvation Army—"

"The Salvation Army?" Bernard burst out in disbelief.

"That's right. More than anyone, the Salvation Army will know what to do with toys at Christmas. You might not be happy, but that shouldn't stop hundreds of other children from smiling."

Sidney's face brightened. "We'll get a pushcart. We'll be three Jewish kings bearing gifts. Just as long as the Salvation Army doesn't preach at us."

"They won't," Rachel promised. "They'll be so happy to get these lovely toys, they won't even care if you're atheists."

She watched the boys load the soft animals onto a borrowed pushcart. Their first venture had collapsed, but Rachel was not concerned. They were bouncing back already, as thrilled at the prospect of brightening up Christmas for poor children as they had been at starting their own company. They had good attitudes.

She recalled Manny's sentiment, that the challenge had been more attractive than the money. Her three boys were seeking mountains to climb, and Rachel knew they would do just fine when they found them.

Chapter Ten

In May 1927, America held its breath as a twenty-five-year-old aviator flew his Ryan NYP monoplane from Long Island's Roosevelt Field to Paris's Le Bourget Airport. The first New York–Paris flight took more than thirty-three hours, and Charles Lindbergh stayed alert at the controls of the *Spirit of St. Louis* by munching homemade sandwiches. At Le Bourget, a hundred thousand Parisians greeted him. In the following days, he was given the French Legion of Honor, and was received by both King Albert of Belgium and King George the Fifth of England.

The biggest, most traditional reception of all came a month later. Crowds lined the streets of New York to cheer Lindbergh's triumphant procession. Clouds of ticker tape cascaded down like snow. At every window along the route, faces pressed themselves against glass, eager for a sight of the young Midwesterner who had written aviation history.

Standing among the crowds were Zalman and Jimmy. They caught no more than a glimpse of Lindbergh before the procession passed, but it was enough for father and son to feel part of this historic day.

"What did you think of him, Jimmy?" Zalman asked, as the packed mass of people began to dissolve.

"He didn't look very extraordinary, did he, sir? I mean, he just didn't look like a hero."

"Very few outstanding people do. Take Calvin Coolidge, does he look extraordinary?"

"He's not outstanding. He's just the President. There have

been lots of those, whereas Charles Lindbergh did what no other man has ever done."

Zalman laughed and wrapped an arm around Jimmy's shoulders, enjoying a moment of closeness with his son that was all too rare. After twelve years, Jimmy remained something of a mystery to his father. He was a well-spoken, extremely polite boy who did well at the private school he attended. Anxious to please, was how the school's headmaster had described Jimmy during a meeting with Zalman and Julia. *What was that supposed to mean,* Zalman had asked Julia. *That we raised a toady for a son?*

The one area in which Jimmy exhibited little aptitude was sport. He cheered enthusiastically from the sidelines at school baseball and football games, but he never participated. Even if he had not been slightly overweight, with a roly-poly shape and a chubby face, it was doubtful that sports would have held any attraction for him. His interests lay in other directions. He played the piano well, and was a passable artist. Two of his paintings hung in Zalman's office. One depicted the Flatiron Building; the other showed the family's Glen Cove estate. He also loved animals. For the past couple of years he had kept hamsters and white mice as pets, often taking them out of the cage and carrying them around in his shirt pocket. Zalman remembered one dinner when two mice had jumped out of Jimmy's pocket and chased each other around the plates and dishes. Julia's shriek had been loud enough to shake the crystal chandelier above the dining table. Only Helen had found the scene amusing. Zalman's daughter had turned it into a game, laughing uproariously as she tried to trap the terrified rodents beneath dishes, while Jimmy pleaded with her to be careful.

Zalman often wondered what had happened with his children. Jimmy possessed the sensitivity and gentleness a girl should have, while Helen had the daring any father would want to see in a son. Helen was nineteen now and she still worked out her frustrations on the punching bag Zalman had bought her six years before. When she was annoyed over something, she'd tie her auburn hair in a bun, slip on gloves, and pound the bag. If Zalman were home, he timed the bouts. That way, he knew if Helen was just irritated or really upset.

222

Three months ago, after being jilted by a boy, she'd beaten the daylights out of the bag for seven minutes. That rated high on the really-upset chart. But it was nothing to the battering she'd given the bag a year ago, soon after the family had moved to a five-story townhouse on Fifth Avenue, just north of Eighty-second Street. Julia and Zalman had wanted their daughter to attend college after finishing school. Helen had other ideas. She wanted to go out to work—on a newspaper.

"A newspaper?" Julia exclaimed. "Why would you want to do something like that?"

"It's the most natural thing in the world for me to do. All I've ever heard is newspapers. I've eaten, drunk, and breathed them since I was old enough to stand up."

"It's no career for a young woman from a good home. Your father will tell you that."

Helen looked at Zalman. He knew he had to support his wife. "Never mind the awful stories you'll be expected to cover. They'll be nothing compared with the degenerates you'll work alongside. Most of the reporters are drunks—"

"They can't be. Drinking's illegal now. Don't you know about the Volstead Act?"

"And they're also lawbreakers," Zalman said without breaking stride. "You don't want to mix with people like that, Helen."

Julia took over. "Besides, soon you'll be thinking of getting married. You'll have to give up work then anyway."

"I'd have to give up college as well, wouldn't I?"

"That's not the same."

Helen turned accusingly to Zalman. "It's all right for you to mix with reprobates, but not me, is that it?"

"I don't mix with them. I supervise them."

"That's a double standard if ever I saw one. It reeks of hypocrisy." She swung around and headed for the room where the punching bag was installed. Zalman listened outside the door, one eye on his watch. Helen hammered the bag for thirteen minutes. When at last she stopped, he knocked on the door and entered. She was slumped on a stool in the corner of the room. Her breath came raggedly, and tears glistened in her hazel eyes.

"It's not fair," she said. "I don't want to go to college. I want to be a reporter. I don't want you to use your influence to get me a job. I'll find one myself, on my own merits."

Zalman could not fight his daughter's tears. "You find a job without my help, and I'll straighten it out with your mother."

Helen did. She banged on doors until the *World* hired her as a cub reporter. Only after she'd been there three months did anyone connect her last name with the owner of *Form Guide* and the former circulation boss of Henry Bladen. When Julia had expressed shock at the way Helen had disobeyed her parents, Zalman had soothed the troubled waters by persuading her to admire how Helen, instead of trading on her father's name, had carved her own path.

Walking with Jimmy away from the Lindbergh procession route, Zalman wondered whether his son would ever have the gumption to do what Helen had done. He doubted it. The boy was too gentle to push his way into anything. God help him if he ever had to face the challenges his father had faced. How would Jimmy have managed in Russia? How would he have fared as a penniless immigrant in New York twenty-four years before?

Father and son traveled to a new eight-story office block on East Forty-second Street, close to Second Avenue. The first three floors belonged to *Form Guide.* The printing plant was housed on the ground floor. Editorial, circulation, and clerical staff occupied floors two and three. Zalman's other businesses—souvenirs, real estate, some magazines he had acquired—were spread out over the next four floors. The top floor was given over to a company called the Rijndam Corporation. Zalman's office was there, with a northeast view across the East River to Welfare Island and Queens.

Zalman had brought Jimmy to this office several times to let him get the feel of business, but it had all been of little interest to the boy. As Zalman had yelled instructions over the telephone, or made decisions that affected the lives of hundreds of people, Jimmy had wandered around listlessly. Once, while Zalman had engaged in a twenty-minute negotiation that had sealed the purchase of a building on Madison Avenue, Jimmy had whiled away the time by sketching the

224

view through the window. Zalman didn't know what to make of him at all.

The one aspect of Zalman's office that fascinated the boy was the full-sized English snooker table. It occupied the center of the office much as a boardroom table might occupy the center of another businessman's office. Zalman used it to aid thought; playing stimulated his imagination. Jimmy had first tried the game a year before. His immediate grasp of the technique amazed Zalman until he came to understand that snooker went far beyond the normal definition of sport. It was geometry with its angles; art with its multitude of colors and dazzling combinations; and music with the crack of ivory against ivory. It didn't challenge Jimmy's body as sport normally did. It challenged his mind.

Zalman picked up a cue and chalked it. "You rack."

Jimmy slapped the rack around the fifteen red balls, spotted the black, pink, and blue. Zalman set up the green, brown, and yellow. "How much are we playing for?" Zalman asked.

"Two dollars, sir," Jimmy answered unhesitatingly.

"You sure? That's your entire weekly allowance."

"I'm sure." Jimmy chalked his cue and stood watching as his father positioned the white ball in the D behind the balk line. His father gave him two dollars every Friday, then nullified the gesture by buying Jimmy whatever he wanted. The knowledge that he had money of his own, even if it were only two dollars a week, gave Jimmy a feeling of independence. It also gave him a stake when his father challenged him to a game.

Zalman struck the cue ball. As it rolled toward the far cushion, he swore. He'd hit the ball too hard. Instead of coming back to gently kiss the triangle of reds, it bounced back with enough force to scatter them. Jimmy lined up a red for the corner pocket, and potted it with the minimum of fuss.

"One," Zalman said, sliding the marker along the scoreboard. The cue ball rolled to a stop directly in line with the black and the other corner pocket. Jimmy sank it for another seven points.

"You ever stop to think how lucky you are?" Zalman said,

as Jimmy replaced the black on its spot and lined up another red.

"This is a game of skill."

"I don't mean the game. I mean life. You ever realize how lucky you are to have a rich father?"

"I think about it sometimes, sir. But I prefer to believe that I chose my father very carefully." He sank the red and turned to the black once more. It went down.

Zalman laughed. Jimmy possessed a dry humor that was occasionally amusing. At other times, depending on Zalman's mood, it could be very irritating.

Father and son made an odd comparison. Zalman, tall and thin, paced around the table restlessly waiting for his son to finally miss. His curly hair was unkempt. His shirtsleeves were rolled high above his elbows; his tie was dragged down, shirt collar open. Jimmy, who continued to wear his jacket, was the epitome of composure. He lined up shots calmly, acknowledging each sinking with a slight smile. His dark-brown hair was as neatly brushed as it had been when he had left home. His black shoes were just as shiny. Somehow he had gotten through the entire day without a mark on himself.

Finally, after running up a break of forty, he missed. "About time," Zalman muttered sarcastically. The two dollars was as good as lost. Snooker required patience, and that, possibly, was the one area in which his son was better equipped. He made nine points before missing. Jimmy took over once more.

"You didn't choose me carefully, you just got lucky. Luck is what rules the world, Jimmy. Look at Lindbergh. Sure, he's a brave and fearless aviator, that's why his name will appear in the history books, but the main reason for his success was luck. He was lucky to be born with drive and determination, and a bent for flying. Take me. I was lucky to be born with imagination. And you're lucky to be born into money when you could have been born to some poor Negro family."

Jimmy enjoyed listening to his father's philosophy. He considered his father to be the wisest man in the world, far more intelligent than the teachers at school who prattled on dryly about theory. Jimmy was prepared to bet that no

226

teacher—no matter how many letters he had after his name—had done a tenth of what his father had done.

"When you see some vagrant panhandling money in the street, don't shy away because you think you're better than him, Jimmy. Always remember that you're only *luckier* than him. If he'd have had the luck, he'd be where you are, and you'd be where he is."

"I'll remember that," Jimmy said. He had often seen his father stop in the street to give money to some down-and-out soul. Now he understood why, even if he did not know that his father had learned to do that from his own father in Russia. He potted the ball that put the game beyond doubt. "I think you owe me two dollars, sir."

Zalman threw his cue down in disgust. He handed the money to Jimmy, who left the office immediately. When he returned ten minutes later, Zalman asked where he'd been.

"I went to find someone who wasn't as lucky as me."

"Did you?"

"Yes, sir. A tramp with everything he owned on his back. I gave him your two dollars."

Zalman smiled. If he told Jimmy to walk through fire, the boy would probably do it.

Always eager to expand his investments, Zalman constantly sought new ventures. Those who worked for him did the same. Frank Brennan and Bill Regan acted as chief scouts. As co-general managers of *Form Guide,* they visited the racing sheet's far-reaching branch offices. Regan might bring back news of a small newspaper group he thought would interest Zalman; Brennan might return with information about a magazine he considered a prime candidate for membership in the Isaacson domain. They would discuss ideas over the snooker table. Zalman never bet on the games he played with his henchmen. He reserved that practice for Jimmy. Making his son back his skill with money was a way of honing the competitive spirit that Zalman felt was lacking in the boy.

In Zalman's entire operation, Brennan and Regan remained the two men most important to him. He valued them not only for their work—for the way they viewed everything through the same perspective he did—but also for their sentimental significance. Sometimes Zalman felt that he, Brennan, and Regan were the only survivors of the old days. New York's own three musketeers.

Everyone else had gone, or faded into unimportance. Jake Thomson, editor of the *Messenger* had been struck down with a heart attack. Len Bennett had retired. Henry Bladen himself was sick. Now seventy-three, he was plagued with complaints. Arthritis had stiffened his joints; ulcers tortured his stomach. A less resilient man would have quit years before. Bladen's determination kept him going. Even so, he was a shadow of his former self. His pink scalp gleamed through thin white hair. His back was bent, and his hands were gnarled like an old tree root. Zalman was shocked whenever he saw his old boss. Age had no respect for anyone, not even the powerful. He was also distressed. He recalled the conversation aboard the *Masthead*. Bladen had told Zalman then that he had an advantage: he was young, while everyone around him was a graybeard. Looking at the deterioration of Henry Bladen, Zalman faced up to the fact that even the richest of men could not outrun the march of years.

For the first time, Zalman acknowledged his own mortality.

In May 1928, over a game of snooker, Frank Brennan introduced a new idea that grabbed hold of Zalman's imagination, shook it this way and that, and refused to let go.

"Giuseppe Salerno's looking for someone to take the Sporting News Agency off his hands."

"Where did you see him?"

"He telephoned me. He's old and tired and he wants to get out. Asked me to check if you were interested."

Zalman accepted the answer. Despite the many things he had in common with his henchmen, he moved in different circles. His interest in racing went little beyond the two million dollars he made each year from *Form Guide,* while both Brennan and Regan were keen fanciers of horseflesh. For them, mixing with a man like Giuseppe Salerno was quite natural.

He set down his cue, the game forgotten. Salerno wanted

to sell the Sporting News Agency. The bookies' lifeblood. The wire service that transmitted race results over telephone lines to bookmakers. Without the agency, New York's off-track bookies, from one-man handbooks to wire rooms and plush horse parlors, could not function.

A smile spread across Zalman's face. He already owned *Form Guide,* the horse players' bible. The Sporting News Agency seemed a natural progression.

"What kind of fees does the agency charge for its service?"

"Twenty dollars a week for a little street-corner handbook. Perhaps four hundred a week for a big horse parlor."

"How many bookies are there in America?"

Brennan remembered only too clearly a similar question about racetracks. "Thousands and thousands."

Using a hypothetical figure of fifteen thousand, Zalman did some quick arithmetic. The results shocked even him, a man accustomed to dealing in huge amounts. Based on an average weekly subscription fee of one hundred dollars a week—and he considered that conservative—a nationwide wire would bring in a million and a half dollars every week. He had no idea how much such a service would cost to set up; he didn't even know if a nationwide wire was feasible. But the cost had to be less than a million and a half. You could operate an entire country for that.

"Tell Salerno I'd like to meet him some time in the next couple of weeks. Better yet, tell him I'd like to meet him as soon as possible," Zalman added. Quite suddenly, he perceived himself exchanging the status of the simply wealthy for the less populated but far more satisfying ranks of the extremely rich.

Two days later, Zalman met Giuseppe Salerno for lunch at a restaurant in Mulberry Street. Zalman felt totally out of place. The air reeked with the smell of spices; garlic assailed him like a fog. Waiters took orders and gave advice on the food in tones other people used for arguments. The constant babble of Italian that deprived the restaurant of a moment's silence threw Zalman back twenty-five years to the turmoil of Ellis Island.

Salerno waited in a corner booth. He stood up as Zalman

approached. The two men shook hands. Zalman felt eyes boring into him, estimating the strength of a potential adversary. Zalman stared right back, doing exactly the same.

The owner of the Sporting News Agency was sixty-six years old, a small gray-haired man with a thick mustache and a warm sparkle in his brown eyes. Born in the Italian port city of Naples, he had come to New York in 1890. He had earned a living by being a bookie's agent among the Italian community. The manner of payment was simple: if the bets he collected lost, the bookie tipped him; if the horses won, the gamblers tipped him. Before long, Salerno came to know which bets had a good chance of losing. Those he kept. The risky ones he passed on. Soon, the bookmaker told Salerno he could no longer afford the business he brought in. They parted company, and Salerno went to work on his own as a bookmaker.

In 1906, he linked up with a telegraph operator named Harry Hemphill, who had devised a simple system of relaying racing results from the track to bookmakers. One man inside the track signaled by mirror code to a confederate in a nearby building, who then telegraphed the information to bookies. For two hundred and fifty dollars a day, Salerno bought the exclusive use of Hemphill's service, which the telegraph operator had named the Sporting News Agency. Salerno routed the service to pool halls and bookmakers who paid up to two hundred dollars a week. In 1911, when moralistic legislation closed the New York tracks, causing the bookmakers to go elsewhere, the Sporting News Agency fell silent. When the tracks reopened two years later, Salerno owned the wire service outright. He had bought Hemphill out.

"For seventeen years I ran the agency," Salerno told Zalman over lunch. "No trouble, no problems. I made sure the right people were paid off, the police and the bosses who own the streets. I bought peace like everyone has to. But the world is changing. A new breed is taking over. Not men from the old country, compassionate men who leave you with enough to live on, but hard, greedy men. They're not satisfied with bootlegging liquor, these men. They want everything. They want the liquor, they want the gambling, they want it all."

230

Zalman listened without interruption. He understood the problems faced by the wire service. *Form Guide* and the SNA both supported horse racing, but all similarity ended there. *Form Guide* was a legitimate publication; respectable racegoers read it. The wire service was different. While some of its subscribers were newspapers, needing the information for their sports pages, the majority were bookmakers, men who populated a shadowy world of big money that attracted predators like a dead animal draws hyenas. Giuseppe Salerno was too old to compete anymore. He was, to borrow Henry Bladen's description, a graybeard. The world belonged to the young, to aggressive men who would take it and make it in their own image. It didn't have patience for old, timid men like Salerno.

Salerno became unnerved by Zalman's silence. He had expected a torrent of questions. *He* certainly would ask them if he were interested in purchasing something as important as the wire service. What he did not know was that Zalman had spent every minute since his talk with Brennan finding out all he could. When he sat down for lunch with Salerno, he didn't feel there was much the Neapolitan could tell him.

"Mr. Isaacson, I thought from speaking to Mr. Brennan that you were interested in making a deal with me. Are you?"

"Sure. I'm interested." Zalman shoved a forkful of veal parmigiana into his mouth. "How much do you want for it?"

"Three hundred and fifty thousand dollars. For fifty percent of the shares."

Zalman lowered his fork. Salerno had just thrown him a curve ball. "What do you mean fifty percent?"

"I have two sons, Mario and Luigi. I intend to give them twenty-five percent each."

"I was under the impression that you wanted to sell the whole Sporting News Agency. I'm not interested in a partnership with people I don't even know."

"They are good boys. They work hard. They are smart. And they know the business." Salerno watched Zalman wipe his mouth. "Are you fortunate enough to have sons, Mr. Isaacson?"

"I have one."

"Would you reject him by selling your entire business

231

interests to a stranger, or would you leave him something?"

Zalman smiled. There was no comparison between his vast business interests and Salerno's wire service, but he saw little point in mentioning that. Salerno had reached Zalman with the comparison of sons. Jimmy was a strange boy, but Zalman would rather swim through burning lava than turn his back on his son. "Where are these boys of yours?"

Salerno lifted his head. "Mario! Luigi!"

Chairs scraped in the booth behind Zalman. Two heavyset men appeared. Salerno made the introductions and indicated for them to sit down. Mario, the older at thirty-five, took the place on his father's right. Thirty-year-old Luigi sat on Zalman's left. Zalman asked about other wire services. Mario answered that a couple of dozen existed across the country. "Some are so small that they operate out of the backs of restaurants and service maybe a dozen bookies."

Zalman noticed that the brothers' speech contained none of the poetic meandering apparent in their father's manner of talking. Individually pronounced consonants next to each other were enunciated without insertion of a gratuitous vowel. These men had been born in New York. They were American, not Italian. Young, ambitious. And, Zalman suspected, glad of the opportunity to operate out of the shadow of their father.

"I don't believe in equal partnerships, Mr. Salerno. I like to control what I own. I'll give you four hundred thousand dollars for sixty percent of the Sporting News Agency."

Salerno looked at his sons, then nodded. Zalman shook the hands of the three men and walked out of the restaurant.

Over dinner that night, he told his family that he was buying a major interest in the Sporting News Agency. Helen flung a hand to her mouth and stared in shock at her father.

"You can't!"

Stunned by the reaction, Zalman stared at his daughter. "Why on earth can't I?"

"Because it's dangerous. I hear stories at the *World* about the Sporting News Agency. The crime reporters say that sooner or later there'll be a gang war for control of bookmaking in New York, and the SNA will be right in the middle of the shooting."

Julia looked concerned. "Is that true, Zalman?"

"Of course it isn't. Do you think I'd spend four hundred thousand dollars to put myself in danger? The wire service is the same as *Form Guide,* for heaven's sake. It disseminates information on racing, that's all. One complements the other, it's a natural thing for me to buy." He looked at Jimmy, who, unwittingly, was the cause of his accepting only sixty percent of the enterprise. "Do you have an opinion?"

"Yes, sir, I do. Why do you have to involve yourself in something that Helen says is so risky?" Tears suddenly shone in Jimmy's dark eyes. "It's dangerous. Please leave it alone."

Zalman always became upset at the sight of tears. What had gotten into his family? What had happened to the trust they'd always shown, the belief that he could pick up a bag full of snakes and not get bitten? "Your sister's worked on the *World* for two years and already she knows all the answers, is that it? Don't you think I know any of the answers?"

The outburst created a minute of awkward silence. This was the first time they had questioned Zalman's decisions, and he had left them feeling like ingrates. But just when Zalman thought he had weathered the storm, Jimmy spoke up. "Don't you have enough already, sir? *Will* you know when you have enough, or will you keep collecting companies like a philatelist collects stamps? What obsession drives you to collect wealth in this manner?"

Zalman thought he was traveling in a time machine. Even ignoring the salutation of "sir," his thirteen-year-old son sounded like a character out of Victorian times, some proper young man from a Dickens book who had never learned to laugh or play. What kind of son had he fathered?

"The thought of you having to endure the poverty I knew when I was young, that's the obsession driving me." He lashed out as he had done eight years earlier, when a five-year-old Jimmy had turned his eyes away from a struggling fish. "I collect wealth because I don't ever want you to go through what I went through. I don't want you walking halfway across a continent, I don't want you sailing an ocean in some stinking steerage compartment, and I don't want you working in a bar. I don't think you've got what it takes to survive in that kind of rotten world!"

233

*　*　*

Under Giuseppe Salerno, the Sporting News Agency had operated from offices south of Greenwich Village. Zalman's real estate company purchased a small building close to *Form Guide.* Some of Zalman's companies occupied the lower floors. The top floor belonged to the SNA. Armed guards checked out anyone who came up by elevator or the stairway.

Zalman looked immediately to expand his new acquisition. Mario and Luigi Salerno, forced on him as partners, had ambitions equaling his own. "My brother and I talked of joining all the wire services across the country into a national organization," Mario said. "A system covering every race at every meeting, a system where bookies in Florida could lay off bets with bookies in New York. Our father was not interested. He made a decent living out of what he already had, and that satisfied him."

"That four hundred thousand dollars you paid for sixty percent of the agency was the biggest bargain since the Indians sold Manhattan," Luigi added. "If our father had listened to us, sixty percent of the SNA would have been worth ten million."

"It still can be worth ten million. I'm not without ideas for expanding the wire."

The three partners split up responsibilities. Mario and Luigi Salerno moved across the country. With one hand they offered money, with the other they intimidated. They walked into wire-service offices and requested to know the selling price. If one was forthcoming, they paid it, and transferred ownership of the company to the SNA. If the business was not for sale, they made other arrangements. Owners were threatened by locally hired thugs. Offices were vandalized, staff beaten up.

Zalman followed the Salerno brothers' trail of destruction with the means of rebuilding. He had Brennan and Regan link up the news distribution companies across the country to the New York wire, then sell the service to bookmakers in their areas. The nationwide gambling system took shape.

In October 1929, the gamblers of Wall Street lost billions of dollars as a bout of frenzied trading climaxed with an enormous crash. The Coolidge boom years had come to an end; the years of Depression were just beginning. Zalman was barely affected by the crash. Although much of his wealth centered around gambling, he owned no shares. He believed in investing money in things he could see and touch, not scraps of paper that jumped up and down in value every day.

The Wall Street crash occurred seventeen months after Zalman had bought into the racing wire. Now it covered thirty states. With hard times looming, Zalman knew that gambling—the chance to strike it rich—would be popular as never before.

By May 1930, the Sporting News Agency was the telephone company's fifth largest customer, paying almost half a million dollars a year for the use of its wire. It could afford to pay that much because it was clearing for its partners, after all expenses, an annual total of almost two million dollars.

More than enough to attract the attention of the sharks which swam in such rich waters.

Zalman's preoccupation with the racing wire was interrupted by a happy family event. Since the beginning of 1930, a young man from Brooklyn had been calling for Helen in the evenings. His name was Jerome Wolfe. Helen had met him at the *World,* where he was a lawyer in the newspaper's legal department. He was a good-looking young man, with straight dark hair, liquid brown eyes, and a strong aquiline nose. Julia liked the way he was so polite, always opening doors for Helen, and helping her into the Plymouth convertible he drove.

One June night, Jerome took Helen to dinner. Afterward they saw *Blue Angel,* with its sultry German star, Marlene Dietrich. They returned late to the townhouse on Fifth Avenue. Zalman and Julia were in bed. Helen rapped on their door. "Could you come downstairs, please? I have something important to tell you."

Fastening robes around themselves, they followed Helen to the drawing room that faced Central Park. Jerome Wolfe stood in the middle of the room. Helen joined him and held his arm. "I would like to introduce my fiancé."

Louis Bluestone's face flashed in front of Zalman's eyes. He heard his late father-in-law's voice asking if he had enough money to buy a decent engagement ring. Smiling broadly at the recollection, Zalman strode toward Jerome and stuck out his hand. "Welcome to the family, young man."

Julia invited Jerome's parents for dinner. Ben and Lottie Wolfe traveled from Brooklyn, where they lived in a three-room apartment above their business, a shop selling cigarettes, candy, and newspapers. They had come to America from the Ukraine thirty years ago. That their son had become a lawyer was already beyond their wildest dreams. That he was marrying a girl from Fifth Avenue—the daughter of a man who had to be a millionaire—terrified them. Zalman put them at their ease immediately. "It wasn't that long ago," he told them, "that I was responsible for making sure you got your copies of the *Messenger.*"

Following dinner, Zalman suggested to Jerome that they go for a walk. Julia watched them leave the house, remembering all too well how her father had taken Zalman into the dining room to offer him a job. She hoped Zalman would handle the situation better. Of course he would. Zalman approved of Jerome, which was more than Louis Bluestone had ever done of Zalman.

The two men walked south along Fifth Avenue, Zalman two inches shorter than his future son-in-law. The boy must make an imposing figure in court, he couldn't help thinking. "A man and wife should never work together, Jerome. Leads to trouble, their spending all night and all day in each other's pockets. Helen's mother and I worked together when we were first married. Believe me, we sometimes got on each other's nerves."

"Helen won't work on the *World* forever. When we're ready to start a family, she'll leave."

Zalman felt a momentary pang of anxiety. Just how well did Jerome know the young woman he was going to marry? Did he understand the strength of her will, and was he prepared to make adjustments? He decided to pursue the matter from a different angle. "There aren't that many good lawyers around, Jerome. I could always do with an extra one."

"In what area? Publishing, newspaper distribution, real estate, the American Memento Company . . . ?"

Zalman noted that Jerome did not mention the Sporting News Agency. Despite its success, the family still disapproved of the racing wire. They couldn't stop Zalman's involvement, but they could show their displeasure by pretending it did not exist. And by getting newcomers to the family, such as Jerome, to join their subterfuge. "I can use you in the Rijndam Corporation—that's the holding company for all my interests."

"Rijndam? What does it mean?"

"I named the company after the ship that brought me to America. Want the job?"

"Yes, please." The two men shook hands to seal the deal.

Helen and Jerome were married in late August. Zalman and Julia gave a wedding party for them at Glen Cove. Four hundred people attended. Jerome's family stood around gawking at the huge marquees set out in the estate's grounds, the dozens of waiters and waitresses, the quantity of food, the orchestra that had been hired for the occasion. They had never seen such splendor. Zalman made sure to talk with as many members of Jerome's family as he could. Just because they lived in Brooklyn, worked at jobs that barely paid for their small homes, and thought a day at Coney Island was the epitome of relaxation, he didn't consider them inferior to himself.

They were, as he had once told Jimmy, simply less lucky.

Jerome Wolfe began to work for the Rijndam Corporation for three times the salary he had received at the *World*. Zalman, like Louis Bluestone before him, wanted to be sure that his daughter lived in a style that befitted her.

At the same time, Zalman sent Jimmy away to a boarding school in Connecticut. The boy was fifteen now. In three years he would be ready to start university. Zalman had no doubt that Jimmy would qualify academically, but he still considered his son soft. He hoped that the boarding school's disciplined routine would drill into him a measure of toughness and independence to complement his intelligence.

Within a week of Jimmy leaving for boarding school, the business in which he had begged his father not be involved turned on Zalman.

Zalman had an unexpected visitor at the Rijndam Corporation's offices. The receptionist called through to announce the arrival of a Mr. Charlie Bruno. Mr. Bruno did not have an appointment, but he was sure that Zalman would see him.

Zalman knew the name well. Since the start of Prohibition eleven years earlier, violence had rocked the country as gangs fought for supremacy in the supplying of illegal liquor and beer. In New York, different names had surfaced as fortunes swung in favor of one organization, then another. First Masseria. Then Marranzano. And now, the newest name of all. Charlie Bruno, a criminal of vision who had welded different ethnic groups—Italians, Jews, and Irish—into one powerful syndicate. Charlie Bruno represented the kind of boss of whom graybeards like Giuseppe Salerno had been so terrified.

"Stall him," Zalman said. He checked around the offices. Frank Brennan was visiting the *Form Guide* plant in Chicago. Bill Regan was in Baltimore. Only the Salerno brothers and Jerome Wolfe were available. Zalman summoned Luigi and Mario Salerno to his office. Jerome he ignored; there was no way he would involve his son-in-law in the danger represented by Bruno's visit.

When Bruno was shown in to Zalman's office, the Salerno brothers were present. Mario leaned against a wall, watching his brother and Zalman play snooker. Only the black remained.

"Hey, I wish I had this kind of a racket!" Bruno said when he entered the office. "You must have some operation!"

Zalman, shirtsleeves rolled high above his elbows, lined up the black for the center pocket, slid the cue forward and watched the ball drop. He looked up at his visitor, taking in the dark complexion, the gleaming black eyes, the husky build disguised by the well-cut suit. "Rack, and you can play the winner."

Bruno waved away the offer. "You'd probably skin me alive. I came to talk, not play."

Zalman handed his cue to Mario. He dusted chalk from his hands, rolled down his shirtsleeves, slipped on his jacket, and sat behind his desk. Bruno took the chair opposite. The Salerno brothers started a fresh game.

"One thing always intrigued me about you, Charlie. Why did you change your name from Carlo Brunelli?"

Bruno's face shone in delight. "Hey, you remember me!"

"How could I forget when we went through so much together?"

"We did, didn't we?" Bruno turned around to the Salerno brothers. "Me and Zalman, we were pals back before you two could tie your own bootlaces. We made sure the New York *Messenger* made it into the hands of the public." Eyes alive, he swung back to Zalman. "We both served a tough apprenticeship, but it didn't do us no harm, did it? Me, I'm big-time now. And you . . . look at you with all you've got going. Who'd have thought twenty-four years ago that me and you, a Wop from Lercara Friddi and a Russian Hebe, would finish up owning New York?"

"Only in America."

Bruno leaned across the desk and pummeled Zalman's shoulder. "Only in America! Those were good days, none of the headaches that we've got today. Life was simple then, eh? Go out and sell papers. Anyone gets in the way, you knock 'em on the head with an iron bar wrapped around with a copy of the *Messenger*. That's how you use the power of the press to educate people!"

Despite the underlying gravity of Bruno's visit, Zalman could not help laughing. In all these years, the Sicilian had hardly changed. He was as irrepressible as ever. Just as irreverent. And still the sworn foe of the English language.

"But now, instead of talking about what we've been through together, we should be talking about what we're *going* to go through together. As partners."

"Partners in what? Bootlegging?" Zalman shook his head. "That's not my racket, Charlie."

"Who's talking about bootlegging? I mean partners here, in this Sporting News Agency of yours. What you've got is too much for you. You need a partner."

Zalman indicated Mario and Luigi, who had ceased their game to watch and listen. "I've already got partners."

"Giuseppe Salerno's boys? Not enough, Zalman. The merger I'm offering—as one legit entrepreneur to another—

will leave you free and clear to do business wherever you want, without fear of someone giving you a rough time."

"That sounds like protection, Charlie. I'm not buying."

Bruno looked offended. "Protection? That's a racket for two-bit hoods who don't have the guts to rob old ladies. You've got a million-dollar racket here, you don't buy protection for something like that. You buy *insurance.* And to make sure you don't get turned down, you go into partnership with the man who sells that insurance." He leaned across the desk, earnest, sharing a secret with the man with whom he had once shared danger. "I hear things, Zalman. A lot of people have got greedy eyes for this business of yours. With me as your partner, you don't have to worry about such things."

"You're pushing your policy to the wrong customer, Charlie. I went to the same college you did—the streets. How do you think I got my *Form Guide* everywhere, let alone the wire service? I've got all the insurance I need."

Bruno stood up. "I came in here an old friend," he said as he headed for the door. "I'm leaving as your competitor."

"Good luck!" Zalman called out. Bruno turned around and grinned. "You never answered my question. Why did you change your name from Carlo Brunelli to Charlie Bruno?"

Bruno's grin glowed even brighter. "Brunelli was too hard for my partners' lawyers to write on contracts. Bruno's easier to spell. *Arrivederci, goombah.*"

Zalman summoned Brennan and Regan back to New York. The instant they arrived, he held a meeting with the Salerno brothers. "Charlie Bruno's going to make a bid to take over the wire. My guess is he'll start in New York where he's strongest, and where we're headquartered. If he wins here, he wins everywhere."

"Muscle in?" Brennan asked. "Take over by force?"

Mario Salerno answered for Zalman. "Don't be fooled by Bruno speaking like some cheap torpedo. He's got more brains than all the old bosses put together. He knows that bodies in the streets make the cops unhappy, so he'll try a different way."

Zalman took no chances. He had the Salerno brothers increase security at the SNA's New York offices, and at the tracks where the agency's callers worked. Simultaneously, he had Brennan and Regan do the same for *Form Guide.*

The security proved to be unnecessary. No bombs were thrown, no guns were fired, no one on Zalman's payroll was threatened. Business carried on normally and profitably. Whatever cards Bruno had to play, he kept close to his chest.

Then, just before Christmas, a clue to Bruno's intentions appeared in print; three sentences buried deep in Walter Winchell's *Mirror* column.

Helen brought it to Zalman's attention that night over a crowded dinner table that included her husband Jerome and Jimmy, just home from his first semester at boarding school.

"Did you read Walter Winchell today?"

"I don't have time to look at gossip columns."

"You should find time. Sometimes they make very interesting reading." She pulled out a piece of paper, staring at her father over the top of it as she read. " 'Charlie Bruno, supplier of sauce to the rich and renowned, is finalizing plans for a racing information service to rival Zalman Isaacson's established Sporting News Agency. Watch out for sparks and short circuits when these two wires clash. SNA already has the troops out, but it might not be enough.' "

As everyone stopped eating, Helen folded the clipping and replaced it in her bag. "What do you have to say about *that?*"

"Are you asking me as a *World* reporter looking for a story?"

"Of course not. I'm asking you as a daughter who's concerned about her father."

"What does he mean," Julia asked, "that you already have the troops out?"

Helen shot her mother an exasperated glance. "The agency has men guarding the offices."

Zalman turned to his son-in-law. "Have you seen any guards?"

Jerome shook his head. "I haven't noticed anything out of the ordinary."

"Of course you haven't," Helen fired back. "My father keeps you insulated from what he does, like he tries to keep

241

all of us insulated. He thinks that what we don't know won't hurt us."

"That's not fair, Helen!" Jerome said. "I know everything that goes on at Rijndam Corporation. For God's sake, I'm one of your father's lawyers. I have to know."

"You know only what my father wants you to know."

Zalman sat back, watching his daughter and son-in-law fight it out. He wondered if he was witnessing their first argument. Too bad it had to be in public. Too bad for Jerome, anyway. He might be able to put on a show in court, but he was faring abysmally over the dinner table. He was no match for Helen's fire and righteous anger. Helen knew her father protected Jerome, just as he felt he had to protect all of his family. Angry now, because she thought her father was in danger, she was taking it out on Jerome. Taking it out on everyone. On her mother, her father, and her husband. The only person she'd neglected so far was Jimmy, and that was because he hadn't said a word.

When Jimmy did speak, it wasn't to enter the argument but to ask a question that had nothing to do with it. "Where would Walter Winchell get hold of information like this? From Bruno?"

"I doubt it," Helen answered. "They can't stand each other."

"Why not?" Jimmy enjoyed absorbing knowledge from his sister. Working on a newspaper, she knew so much.

"Bruno wanted to move into the St. Moritz. Winchell, who lives there, threatened to move out if the St. Moritz accepted a gangster as a tenant. He also threatened to publicize his reasons for leaving in the *Mirror.*"

"You're forgetting that politics make strange bedfellows," Jimmy said. "They hate each other, but they cooperate for their mutual benefit. Bruno gives Winchell the tip because he wants to frighten us. Winchell takes it because it gives him an exclusive." He looked at Zalman. "Does that make sense, sir?"

"Absolute sense, Jimmy." Zalman wondered if boarding school was such a wonderful idea after all. The boy seemed even more old-fashioned than ever. A truly Victorian gentleman.

"What about those guards?" Julia asked.

"Bruno's a businessman," Zalman answered. "He's going to try to bankrupt me by offering a better product. That's the American way. I don't need guards to handle that."

The rival wire service started operation in February. Called the Metropolitan News Bureau, it offered to the New York area a service identical to that provided by the Sporting News Agency. Except for price. Where the SNA charged a small bookie seventy dollars a week, Metropolitan charged sixty. Where the SNA charged four hundred a week to a horse parlor, Metropolitan charged three hundred and seventy-five.

After a month, the competition was keenly felt. Business in New York was off by twenty-five percent. Customers outside New York watched and waited. To the winner of the New York battle went all of North America.

For the first time in Zalman's business life, someone was doing to him what he had always done to others. He had Frank Brennan, Bill Regan, and the Salerno brothers visit bookies who had switched allegiance. They all returned to Zalman's office with the same story.

"The bookies are going with Metropolitan News because it's cheaper," Mario Salerno reported.

"Ten bucks a week makes such a difference?" Zalman asked in disbelief. "Why would they leave us for such a sum?"

"When a woman goes shopping," Regan said, "does she buy from the guy who charges fifteen cents for bread or ten cents?"

"Ten cents."

"Bookies aren't no different. Why should they pay more for the same loaf of bread?"

Brennan raised a hand. "Two can play Bruno's game. Let's drop our prices below his, see what he does about that."

"If we drop them in New York, we'll have to drop them right across the board," Zalman said.

"He might drop his prices again," Luigi Salerno pointed out. "Then what do we do? Keep dropping until one of us

243

runs out of money?" He looked at Zalman. "How are we fixed?"

"All right for the time being, but don't forget that we've got a phone bill of half a million dollars a year. We don't pay that, we go right out of business." He started to rack the balls on the snooker table. The four men watched as he broke with the most gentle of kisses that barely disturbed the reds while returning the cue ball above the balk line.

"Sweet shot," Brennan said.

"Thanks. Cut prices across the country."

The agency reduced its prices to below those offered by the Metropolitan News Bureau. Bookies who had been lured away returned. Within a month, Metropolitan responded by cutting prices even more. The wire war was coming down to a question of who had the deepest pockets. There, Metropolitan had a distinct edge. Bruno, with syndicate money backing him, only had to finance an operation in New York. Zalman was wealthy, but he couldn't match those kinds of funds. Either he found a solution to this war or he walked away from a million-dollar business.

In the middle of the war with Bruno, Zalman heard disturbing news from Julia. After only six months, Helen's marriage to Jerome Wolfe was on the ropes and ready to go down for the count. He wasn't surprised. He'd seen the argument that night when Helen had brought out the Winchell piece. And before that, the night Jerome had brought his parents to dinner. The way he'd talked so confidently during his walk with Zalman about getting Helen to give up work to start a family. That had been a tip-off that the young lawyer didn't know what he was getting into.

Zalman saw no point in speaking to Helen. Julia had already done that. He decided to try Jerome, inviting the lawyer to lunch. As they sat down, Zalman said bluntly, "What's this I hear about you and Helen?"

"She's being unreasonable. I earn enough money so Helen doesn't have to work. I told her I'd like her to stop. She didn't agree."

Zalman pitied his son-in-law. When Helen had moved out, she had left the punching bag at her parents' home. Jerome would have been better off if she'd taken it with her. "Is everything all right now?"

"Not really. And I would suggest"—a flash of rueful humor sparkled in Jerome's dark, soulful eyes—"that you're to blame."

"Me?" This was all Zalman needed. To be accused—in the middle of a business struggle that could destroy everything he'd worked for—of wrecking his daughter's marriage. The sympathy he'd shown for Jerome disappeared in a flash of heated anger. "What the hell do you mean I'm to blame? If you can't stand up to Helen, that's your problem, not mine!"

Jerome held up his hands as other diners in the restaurant turned to look. "I was paying you a compliment. A father's the first man in any girl's life. He's the first man she falls in love with. All other men are judged against her father."

"What are you trying to tell me?" Zalman asked. "That my daughter's in love with me?"

"I'm saying that no man on this earth can ever meet the standards you've set for Helen. They're impossibly high. What she's seen in you has spoiled her for any other man."

Zalman left the restaurant knowing that his daughter's marriage was already history.

Jerome and Helen separated. Jerome resigned from the Rijndam Corporation. Zalman barely noticed his absence. He was too involved in the battle against the Metropolitan News Bureau to be distracted.

As the wire war continued, Zalman found that a bookmaker's integrity was thinner than a minimum bet. It wasn't necessary for Metropolitan to undercut the Sporting News Agency by a full ten or twenty dollars a week. Five dollars would do. Likewise, a five-dollar cut by the SNA would regain them as customers.

By August, the SNA was running at a loss. Expenses eclipsed income. Money was borrowed from *Form Guide* to meet the bills. Charlie Bruno was winning the war, and the bookies were loving every competitive minute of it. What scrap of loyalty they had would go to the winner of this battle.

In the middle of the month Bruno telephoned Zalman. "Hey, you ready to talk about us being partners yet?"

"What's your panic?" Zalman responded. "Your funds low?"

"Not me! I've got plenty to go through yet."

"Me, too," Zalman lied before hanging up on Bruno's laughter.

A week after Bruno's call, Frank Brennan and Bill Regan marched into Zalman's office with a man in overalls "Charlie Bruno can keep this going far longer than we can," Brennan announced. "He's not paying his telephone bill."

"What are you talking about?"

"He steals our information. Meet John Guthrie, Zalman. John used to be an engineer for the phone company. Bill and I have had him checking over our system for the past few weeks."

Zalman turned his attention to Guthrie. "How does he do it?"

"Easy. He has men tapping into your lines. As the Sporting News Agency transmits results to its customers, Metropolitan siphons off the transmission to its outlets."

"That son of a bitch!" Zalman murmured, and simultaneously cursed himself for not even considering that Bruno would use such an obvious scheme. The SNA had been financing its own enemy. Given a similar situation, Zalman knew he might well have done the same thing. If he'd had the brains to think of it!

"What's so funny?" Regan asked. "Charlie Bruno's taken us for a seven-month ride and you're grinning like a hyena."

"You've got to admire a man who has that kind of gall."

"Admire him, hell! Give Frank and me the word and we'll put together an army to take care of Mr. Bruno and his wire-tappers."

"No!" The rebuke was sharp. "That's not the way to go about anything." Deep down, Zalman still had if not a fondness for Bruno, then a respect. A feeling of kinship. No two men shared what they shared without feeling that bond. Perhaps that was the reason Bruno had gone about his assault on the agency's wire in this manner. Not because violence would have created too many problems, but because he

246

also felt an affinity for Zalman. That notion threw up all kinds of possibilities. Two men who had succeeded in vastly different arenas—a businessman and a hoodlum—tied together for life, not by safeguarding copies of the *Messenger*, but by a single act of violence that had netted one man a thousand dollars, and the other man a career.

"What is the way then?" Regan asked.

Zalman walked to the snooker table and absently rolled the cue ball against the cushion, catching it as it bounced back, rolling it again. "We want to finish this once and for all. Using muscle will invite retaliation. What we need"—the first vestiges of a plot surfaced in his mind—"is something that will impress the bookies so much that they won't care if someone comes along in the future offering them a free wire service. They won't want to know because they'll want to stay with us no matter what happens." He continued bouncing the ball against the cushion, faster now as his thoughts moved into a higher gear.

"Our lines are being tapped, right? What's to stop us from passing along some bad information?"

"Nothing," Guthrie answered. "But what's the point?"

Zalman carried right on. He was thinking aloud, not seeking answers. If the engineer had known him better, he would not have offered one. "What's to stop us deadening the wire so the Metropolitan News Bureau can't supply results to its customers? Better yet"—Zalman's eyes began to gleam with excitement—"what's to stop us from bypassing the section of the wire he's tapping? We'll get the results to our customers some other way, and use that section for a special broadcast. A broadcast that's delayed by a couple of minutes. Enough time . . ." Zalman saw the entire picture spread out in front of him. Enthusiasm made his voice rise. "Enough time for our men to get down huge bets with Bruno's bookies on a horse we already know has won. He turned to Guthrie, now ready for answers. "Can that be done?"

"Anything can be done."

Zalman slapped Guthrie on the shoulder. "You're the kind of man I like to deal with."

* * *

While Guthrie arranged technical details, Zalman, Brennan, Regan, and the Salerno brothers picked out fifty Metropolitan News Bureau customers across New York, from small bookies whose daily handle might not eclipse a thousand dollars to luxurious horse parlors where bets began at a thousand. The only criterion was that each bookmaker had to be near an easily accessible public telephone. Then they selected a hundred men for the work, dividing them into fifty teams of two.

Guthrie announced that his work was complete. Two circuits were now available for use. The first bypassed the section of wire tapped by Bruno. The second went only to that section.

Zalman checked *Form Guide.* He wanted a full day's racing. Maximum traffic. Maximum confusion. Maximum opportunity for a stunning success. He chose the second Saturday in September. Belmont would be open. Churchill Downs. Rockingham Park. Pimlico, Riverside, and more. With that many meetings, there had to be at least one long shot.

He spent the day at the SNA main office. Extra phone lines had been installed, along with a special switchboard so operators could simultaneously contact the fifty teams in the field. Zalman stood behind the man transmitting results on the network that bypassed the tapped section. Five yards away, another man transmitted the identical results over the second circuit. There was a two-minute delay between the two transmissions.

The opening race at Belmont was chosen for a trial run. Emperor Pan came first, paying five dollars even. The operators contacted the fifty teams. One man from each team left to make a ten-dollar bet. Seven minutes later, return calls started coming in. Of the fifty men, twenty-eight had been shut out. The delay between transmissions needed to be longer.

"Double it to four minutes," Zalman ordered.

As each result came over the wire, the price was shouted out. Five to one. Three to one. Eight to one. Each time, Zalman shook his head. He was greedy. He wanted a real long shot, and if he didn't get one today, he would wait until next week, or the week after. Now that the system was set up, he would wait for as long as it took.

The fourth race at Rockingham supplied the horse he wanted. Hotspur, paying thirty-four dollars. Sixteen to one. Instantly the name went out to the men in the field. The second man from each team made a bet ranging from one thousand to ten thousand dollars. If the timing was right, the bets would go in just under the wire. There would be no time to lay off any of the risk. The bookies using Bruno's wire would be ruined.

Zalman held his breath during the delayed transmission. What if something went awry now? What if the agency's own information from the track was wrong? Such things had happened before, a faulty transmission, a genuine mistake when a horse had been disqualified following an inquiry. Never mind the battle with Metropolitan, he had a quarter of a million dollars riding on a horse he knew had already won. He hoped!

He barely breathed for seven minutes following the delayed transmission. The first confirmation call came in. Another. And another. And soon all fifty. Every bet had been placed. Four million dollars had been taken. Charlie Bruno's customers were reeling from losses that could drive them out of business. The roar of triumph that swept the wire office rivaled anything ever heard at Yankee Stadium.

Zalman let the bookmakers sweat it out over the weekend. On Monday morning, accompanied by Brennan, Regan, and the Salernos, he visited them all. He knew exactly how much money each establishment had lost on Hotspur. He repaid it personally.

"Let this be a lesson," he said as he handed over the money. "Don't ever rely on hand-me-down news again."

The gesture ensured each bookmaker's loyalty. Reports spread from city to city. The Sporting News Agency had won the wire war by using flair and ingenuity. Bookmakers across the country who had been waiting to see a victor emerge swung solidly behind the agency. No one would challenge it again.

Finally, Zalman contacted Walter Winchell at the *Mirror*. "You lifted the curtain. Now you can drop it."

The following day, Winchell ran a piece in his column that began: "New York's war of the wire is over. In a stunning coup, bookies learned the hard way that the only place to get reliable information is from the horse's mouth. What they got from the johnny-come-lately Metropolitan News Bureau came out of the horse's other end."

Zalman anticipated retaliation. Despite never paying a telephone bill, Charlie Bruno had invested a lot of money in his bid to take over the SNA business. Far more difficult to accept than the financial reverse would be the loss of face. His reputation had suffered; he had been made to look a fool. The wire-service guards remained alert.

Bruno surprised Zalman. No reprisal occurred. Not even the threat of one. The only contact between the two men took the shape of a package delivered ten days after the coup. The package was two feet high and weighed five pounds. A messenger brought it to Zalman's office, setting it down in the middle of the desk. Written across the packing was: "Caution. Handle with care." An attached card read: "Congratulations to a worthy winner. Charlie."

Zalman summoned Frank Brennan. The two men inspected the package from a distance of three feet. "You brave enough to open that?" Brennan asked.

"You brave enough to stand and watch?"

Brennan shook his head. "That's big enough to blow us both into the street. Let's soak it in boiling water."

Brennan cleared people from the top floor. He and Zalman stood the package in a deep bucket, covered it with scalding water, then joined the refugees on the floor below. After ten minutes they returned. The wrapping had softened. Brennan added more boiling water.

"How long?" Zalman whispered. He didn't know the first thing about bombs; he hoped that Brennan did.

"Let's give it thirty minutes to make sure."

They were halfway down the stairs to the next floor when they heard a small explosion. They climbed the stairs again. The bucket lay on its side, water soaking into the carpet. Across the floor, gleaming like dark jewels, were fragments of glass. Brennan went straight to the bucket. He picked up a piece of sodden paper and started to laugh.

"Our bomb was a magnum of vintage champagne."

Just then the telephone rang. Zalman answered. The caller was Bruno. "Did you get my gift yet?"

"We got it, thank you."

"I hope you know that's the good stuff, not some junk made in a tin bath under the light of the full moon. What you've got there's the real McCoy. From Epernay—that's a place in France."

"We just opened it." Zalman winked at Brennan. "Now we're passing it around and drinking to your health."

"You should have stuck it in the icebox for a while. Don't you know nothing about champagne?"

"You should have sent instructions."

"Sure. I bet you guys thought it was some kind of practical joke and stuck it in a bucket of water, right?"

Zalman laughed, and avoided answering. Instead, with Bruno in such an expansive mood, he decided it was a good time to mend fences with his onetime ally. "Charlie, I appreciate how well you're taking this."

"How else did you think I'd take it? I'm not some cheap hoodlum who don't know how to lose gracefully. Some of my partners who lost money on this deal, they weren't too happy. They ran off at the mouth about taking a piece out of your hide, but you don't have to worry. You and me, we go back too far for me to let anyone get a piece of you. I told them what they lost was the cost of doing business. Lookit . . ." Bruno's voice dropped to a conspiratorial whisper that Zalman could barely hear. "I'm a guy who believes big in honor. I only throw a friend to the wolves if I think it's going to save my own neck."

Zalman put the phone down with that sentiment echoing in his ears. He decided it would be an excellent idea to always know when Bruno's neck was in danger.

Zalman began to take an interest in the fortunes of Charlie Bruno. He learned nothing that caused him alarm for his own safety. Like other bootleggers, Bruno prepared for a post-Prohibition world by investing his profits in legitimate businesses. He seemed to have a particular penchant for the garment center, where he owned a piece of at least eight

251

different companies. That was in addition to the construction company and restaurants he also owned, all bought at bargain prices as New York staggered beneath the weight of the Depression.

After two years, when Prohibition was finally swept away, Zalman stopped concerning himself with the Sicilian. Respectable businessmen, no matter what their heritage, rarely had to worry about saving their necks; at least, not in the way Bruno meant. There existed little chance, as far as Zalman could see, of Bruno needing to throw anyone to the wolves.

As he neared fifty, Zalman took stock of what he'd achieved since stepping off the ferry at Battery Park thirty years before. He was well satisfied. The majority share of the Sporting News Agency brought him between a million and a million and a half dollars a year. *Form Guide* cleared another two million. Other concerns—the distribution companies, small newspaper groups and magazines which he had bought on the recommendation of Frank Brennan and Bill Regan—added two million more. He also owned several pieces of New York real estate, but he didn't put a price on those. At a time when unfinished skyscrapers dotted the skyline—abandoned by builders who had gone broke midway through the project—valuing real estate could be discouraging. Often he spent money as quickly as he earned it. He sold a winter home in Miami Beach for a huge loss only a month after buying it, when he found out that his next-door neighbor was Al Capone.

If Zalman's business interests were succeeding, the same was not true of his family life. Helen perplexed him. Her failed marriage to Jerome Wolfe, instead of being a learning experience, had simply been a paradigm for a second such marriage a year later. This one was to an architect named Alan Levine, a member of New York molder and shaper Robert Moses's staff. Helen had met him while interviewing Moses. Two months later, they married. Soon Levine, like Jerome Wolfe before him, found himself unwilling to compete with Helen's career. After four months, he acknowledged the fact and left her. She took his departure in stride. If she wept any tears at all, her father and mother never

252

knew. Now, single again, she lived in an apartment in Greenwich Village.

Helen's two husbands had been infatuations. Her one enduring love was her job with the New York *World*. Or *World-Telegram* as it was now called, after incorporation two years earlier into the Scripps-Howard chain. In seven years, she had risen from aspiring novice to a writer whose front-page byline was a common sight. She covered Fiorello LaGuardia's mayoral campaign with such zeal and empathy that the Little Flower once refused to start a press conference until he was certain Helen was present.

Only once did Zalman mention the broken marriages to Helen. That was at Julia's urging. For his own part, he felt that if his daughter did not want to discuss them with him, he certainly did not want to broach the subject to her. She was old enough at twenty-five to know her own mind. Nonetheless, he did as Julia requested, and met Helen one morning for breakfast.

"Loving your work is all well and good," he told her, "but you've got to know where to draw the line."

"You were just as involved. You still are."

"Never to the exclusion of my family. Your grandfather taught me that lesson very early on. He tried to take your mother back from me, a few weeks before you were due. I've never let work get in the way of family again."

"Jerome and Alan weren't the right men, that's all. I made a mistake. Two mistakes."

Zalman recalled Jerome's accusation, that Zalman himself had spoiled his daughter for any other man. "Does the right man exist, princess?"

"Of course he does. He's handsome, exciting, considerate, loving. A genuine knight in shining armor." Helen gave her father a mischief-filled grin. "Just one problem. Mama found him before I did."

Zalman took his daughter's hand and squeezed it. His first son-in-law had been right. Zalman accepted it as part of the special bond between himself and his daughter. The older Helen grew, the more of himself he could see in her. And the more of Rachel. Helen would have made it across Europe.

Just like Rachel, the sister she so closely resembled, had done.

If Helen was his troubling favorite, Zalman was completely confused over what to do about his son. The Connecticut boarding school which he had hoped would harden Jimmy served only to strengthen the characteristics already evident in the boy. Jimmy graduated in the summer of 1933 as a cultured, sophisticated young man who could talk at length about the arts. He started at Columbia in the fall, with little idea of what subjects he wanted to pursue. At the end of an unremarkable freshman year, he announced that he would not be returning as a sophomore. Jimmy Isaacson, a slightly overweight young gentleman with impeccable taste and manners, was ready to go to work for his father.

Zalman was furious. Didn't the boy understand the importance of a university education? Didn't he realize how lucky he was—in a time of great suffering—to be getting one? Instead, he was turning his back on it, as though it wasn't worth a damn!

"What do you think you're going to do for me?" Zalman yelled at his son. "The only experience you've got is having a good time! Finish university first. Get a good business degree, and then we'll talk about working for me!"

"Did you have a degree?" Jimmy responded. "What experience did you have when you began? Find me a job in one of your companies, and I'll prove my worth."

Zalman closed his eyes in angry frustration. How he wished he'd had the kind of opportunity Jimmy seemed intent on squandering. How much further could he have gone had the rough edges been smoothed over by education? If he could have learned at school the realities he had to master on the job? Jimmy was a fool if he thought he could make his way in his father's organization. What kind of work could he do? The people Zalman dealt with would eat a nineteen-year-old alive. Especially this nineteen-year-old.

Jimmy found an ally in his mother. Eight years before, Julia had fought against Helen's desire to begin work. This time, she supported Jimmy.

"Don't you see that he worships you?" she told Zalman. "He only wants to prove his worth to you."

Zalman understood that his daughter idolized him. He still found it difficult to acknowledge that his son did, too. No man could ask for more, but why could his son have not been built of sterner stuff? Strong and self-assured, not spoiled and lazy. Yet who had spoiled Jimmy? Who had bought him whatever he wanted? Who had sent him to Europe on the *Ile de France* the previous summer? And lazy? Was that really true? Or was it just an adjective Zalman applied to the boy because it went so well with spoiled?

"Create a job for him, Zalman. Surely one of your companies has a place for Jimmy." Seeing her husband waver, Julia pressed home the attack. "You gave Jerome a well-paying job. You would have given Alan one, too, had he wanted it. The least you can do is treat your son as well as you treated your sons-in-law."

Zalman pondered the problem. He considered sending Jimmy to California to work on a movie fan magazine he owned, then dropped the idea. In Hollywood, Jimmy would continue to have a grand old time. With all the money he wanted, not to mention the influence of the fan magazine, he would be able to bed any young actress he desired. That was all Zalman needed, for tales of Jimmy's escapades to drift back to New York.

He created a job for Jimmy in the Rijndam Corporation. Jimmy had an office of his own, and a secretary. His title was information manager. His function was to read every New York newspaper and business paper, and report on any developments which he believed would affect the companies held by Rijndam Corporation.

Jimmy arrived for work each day at Forty-second Street in exquisitely tailored clothes. Often, he wore a rose in his buttonhole. He was a pleasant-looking young man who enjoyed the attention he received from female members of the staff. All morning, he pored over newspapers. Before he went to lunch, he dictated his findings to his secretary, who had a draft report waiting when he returned. He spent the remainder of the afternoon polishing the report, and at five o'clock he presented it to his father.

It didn't matter what Zalman was doing at five o'clock. He always heard his son's report at that time. After listening, he tried to pick holes in Jimmy's reasoning. If he were in conference with one or more of his partners, he expected them to join in. Brennan, Regan, and the Salerno brothers were initially uncomfortable at picking on the well-dressed young man who had put his heart into preparing the report. But as they witnessed Jimmy argue against his father's criticism, timidly at first, then with a growing conviction—always eloquently—they joined in. Everyone knew what Zalman was up to. Jimmy had disobeyed his father by refusing to complete university. He didn't want to wait years before having to defend a thesis. So Zalman was making him defend one here. Not just once, but every day.

Zalman was intent on accomplishing on his own the toughening process that school had failed to do.

Chapter Eleven

In March 1930, Rachel completed ten years with Harold Parker. The agent bought her a cake with ten candles, which he lit for her during a ceremony in the Charing Cross Road office. After she blew them out, he gave her an envelope. "Happy anniversary," he said.

She pulled back the flap. Inside was a sheet of office stationery. Instead of the familiar letterhead announcing the Harold Parker Agency, Rachel saw "Parker and Lesser."

"Congratulations, partner, you deserve it," Parker said. "Without your organization, I'd have drowned in paperwork five years ago. And without your talent-spotting talent, I'd have passed up a dozen good acts."

Rachel glanced down at the threadbare carpet, the same carpet she'd walked on when she came to see about a job. Just a couple of months ago, it seemed. Then she looked at the candles on the cake. Ten years! Who would have thought that the job she had taken to augment a shrinking family income would become a career?

Over dinner that night, she told her sons that Parker had made her a partner. Manny reacted first. "About time!" Then Sidney chimed in with: "Why did you go to the trouble of making dinner for us? We should be taking you out!"

Rachel waved away the offer. "I wouldn't want to intrude on your social lives. I know how busy all three of you are."

"I'm not going out tonight," Bernard said. "I'll help you with the dishes."

Rachel smiled her gratitude at her youngest son. Manny

and Sidney went out nearly every night. Dancing mostly. They came home so late that Rachel often wondered how they got enough sleep to prepare for the next day. Bernard was the opposite. He spent four or five evenings a week at home, reading or doing odd jobs.

Manny and Sidney left immediately after dinner to go dancing at the La Boheme Ballroom in the Mile End Road, a favorite spot to meet girls. Bernard dried the plates his mother washed. As they worked, Rachel asked, "Why don't you go out with your brothers, Bernard? You won't find any girls staying at home."

"Manny and Sidney want to try out dozens of girls," Bernard answered. "They'll be so confused by the time they're finished, they won't know what they're doing. I'm only looking for one particular girl, and I'll know her the moment I see her."

"Oh? And how will you know?"

"She'll look just like you, a tiny thing with auburn hair and big bright hazel eyes. I'll know her, don't you worry."

Rachel smiled. A lifetime had passed since she looked like that. Her bright hair was now streaked with gray; her eyes, behind the glasses she used for close work, had lost much of their shine. "I hope you do find her, Bernard."

"I will, Mama, I will."

When they finished the dishes, Bernard gave his mother a hug and a kiss on the cheek, and she felt luckier than any girl Manny and Sidney would meet tonight.

For an hour, Rachel sat in the parlor, updating client lists she had brought from the office. She paused as she came to the name of Larry Wilde, the juggler for whom she had negotiated with the Wimbledon Theatre. Her first deal. She made many now. She came across another name that held a memory. Lenny Blount, the comedian who had guided the boys backstage at the Hackney Empire. A smile crossed her face as she recalled the Blount-inspired show her three sons had produced to raise money for the family. That show in the back garden had made pennies, but it was infinitely more successful than the soft-toy Christmas venture. Thank God the boys had found jobs after that debacle. All in the women's wear industry, Manny and Sidney selling, and Bernard costing. They never mentioned the soft-toy episode. Neither did Rachel. Everyone was allowed one mistake.

Her mind drifted from the sons to the father. To Jacob. Was he still in Canada? Was he alive? She had no way of knowing. Respecting his wish to be left alone in his new life, she had made no attempt to locate him. She supposed she was still married. She had not filed for divorce, and she had heard nothing from him. Remaining married suited her. No other man existed for whom she could feel the love she had once known for Jacob. She set down the file cards and stared out of the window. She could recall in detail every moment she had spent with Jacob. She had loved him so fiercely. His passionate patriotism had provided one of the attractions. Perversely, it was that love of country that had changed him. He could never understand why the country for which he gave so much granted him so little in return.

Late that night as she lay in bed, she heard her sons come home. Manny first, just after midnight, then Sidney. They held a whispered conversation in the hall, as if comparing notes on their visit to the La Boheme Ballroom. Sidney laughed out loud and Manny hissed at him to keep quiet. In the darkness, Rachel smiled. Perhaps Bernard was waiting until he found a girl who looked like his mother, but no such loyalty held back her other sons. They'd be married soon. Grandchildren would follow. Her sons would help to leave the promised footprint in history.

Rachel knew that a partnership with Harold Parker meant more to her ego than her bankbook. The agency handled small acts; it was not a major moneymaker. There were even times during the past ten years when Parker had taken nothing for himself so there would be enough money to meet Rachel's wages.

Parker and Rachel divided the responsibility of attending shows and talent competitions to search out new clients. Parker took evening shows, which provided him with opportunities to patronize the theater bar. Rachel preferred the matinees; despite being a partner in the agency, she still devoted her evenings to caring for her sons.

Four weeks after the start of the partnership, Parker met

with an accident, tripping over a loose paving stone. His injuries included a broken ankle and a concussion. He spent two days in the hospital, and was off work for an additional two weeks. Rachel assumed all of his duties. She called him every morning when she arrived in the office, and again before she left. When she asked for advice, Parker, more often than not, told her to do whatever she thought was right. "You're at the scene of the fire, Rachel. You know more than I do what size hose you need."

On the day before Parker was due to return, Rachel's calendar was full. She had a matinee at the Victoria Palace in the center of town, and a talent competition that evening at the Tottenham Rialto, in north London. She also had a headache. Parker was sympathetic when she called him. "Don't bother with the shows if you don't feel up to it. Especially the talent competition. There won't be much there."

"I'll see how I feel."

The headache persisted, and she passed on the matinee. At five-thirty, when she shut the office, she felt slightly better. She decided to go to the Tottenham Rialto.

The theater belonged to the Rialto Playhouse Partnership, which operated in London and the south of England. Formed a year before the war with the merging of two separate groups—Rialto Entertainment and the Playhouse Circuit—the Partnership staged annual talent contests at many of its theaters. Winners received twenty-five pounds and a two-week engagement.

The theater manager, wearing his customary tuxedo, stood just inside the theater lobby. With him was a tall gray-haired man in a dark-blue double-breasted suit. Rachel approached the two men. "Anything outstanding on tonight's bill?"

The manager started to say that everything on the bill was special. The man in the double-breasted suit cut him off. "No point in trying to soft-soap this lady—she's an agent."

"Thank you for the consideration, Mr. Prideaux."

James Prideaux was bookings manager of the Rialto Playhouse Partnership, responsible for putting together all the bills that appeared in the partnership's ten theaters. He drew Rachel off to one side and handed her a program. "You make up your own mind whether you're wasting your time. It's a talent show, that's all. You might see performers with a little potential that'll need years of hard work to bring out, but you can bet your last penny that you won't find another Stanley Holloway or Gracie Fields out there tonight."

Rachel took a seat in the stalls. She read through the program to familiarize herself with the dozen acts, then waited for the show to begin. The curtain rose. In front of a backdrop promoting local businesses, a young comedian named Bill Blenheim wove a first-person tale around the misfortunes of a man trying to rescue a cat from a tree, only to learn that the cat did not wish to be rescued. Noticing the rapport Blenheim established with the audience, Rachel put a mark beside his name.

The next act was a charleston dancer who billed himself as having lightning feet. Rachel rejected him. The charleston was old hat now, and she sought new blood. Likewise, she crossed out a two-man comedy act in which one of the men suffered from a horrendous stage stammer; she never found humor in a handicap.

An Irish girl named Rose Kinnear caught her attention. She sang "The Shepherd's Song" in a clear soprano which reached every corner of the theater.

She sat through the next half-dozen acts wishing she had taken Parker's advice and gone home. Her headache was returning by slow degrees, and the performers she watched were no substitute for aspirin. As the theater manager announced the eleventh and penultimate turn—a comedy sketch performed by a group called Less, Lesser, and Least—Rachel stood to leave. As she passed through the lobby, she heard laughter from inside. She stopped. Louder laughter followed. Despite the headache, she returned to the auditorium, feeling duty-bound to learn what entertainment could evoke such mirth.

Onstage stood three young men in army uniform. The tallest, wearing a general's insignia, kept tripping over his own feet. The middle man, stocky with a heavy face, played a bullying sergeant major. The third member of the act portrayed a hapless private undergoing the rigors of inspection.

"This man's boots are dirty," complained the general as he

peered at the offending footwear through an enormous magnifying glass. He pulled one boot toward him, sending the private crashing to the ground.

The sergeant major laid on the ground beside the private. "Did you 'ear that, you 'orrible little man?" he roared in the private's ear. "Your boots are dirty!"

The private, white-faced and visibly terrified, whispered something. The sergeant major turned to the general, who stood above them. "Sir, 'e says 'e polished them, sir!"

"Underneath, Sergeant. They're dirty underneath. We can't have that, you know. Never win wars wearing boots that are dirty underneath."

In the audience, men who had experienced tyrannical NCO's and ridiculous staff officers howled with laughter. Rachel made a note in the program beside Less, Lesser, and Least. They worked well together and had a feel for the audience. They most definitely had potential. She wondered what other routines they did, or whether this was the only string to their bow.

The sketch lasted six minutes, with the general becoming more quibbling, the sergeant major more abusive, and the private more flustered. The finale centered on inspection of the private's rifle. As the general twisted it this way and that to examine it with his magnifying glass, the weapon discharged. Gasps of fright from the audience turned to laughter as the sergeant major hopped around the stage clutching his rear like a wounded baboon.

Headache forgotten, Rachel sat through the final act and waited for the winner to be announced. The Irish singer Rose Kinnear possessed a beautiful voice; the comedian Bill Blenheim had a natural way to involve an audience; but if there was any justice in the world, Less, Lesser, and Least had to win the twenty-five pounds and the two-week engagement.

Justice prevailed. The comedian took third place. The Irish girl was voted second. Less, Lesser, and Least came first. Smiling proudly, they stood onstage to receive twenty-five single pound notes from the Rialto's manager.

Instead of visiting the three young men in the dressing room, Rachel waited outside the theater. They emerged ten minutes later. Rachel stepped forward to greet them. "Congratulations. I'm with Parker and Lesser, and I'd like to discuss the benefits of being represented by our agency."

The two young men who had played the general and the sergeant major stopped, but the private came up to Rachel and kissed her. "What did you think of us, Mama?" Bernard asked.

"You were good as any sketch comics in variety today. But I don't understand why you didn't mention this to me. Did you think I wouldn't find out?"

The three brothers looked uneasily at one another. "Things are lousy in the *schmatte* business right now," Manny said. "We thought we'd try something new. We didn't tell you because we didn't want you worrying. And in case we didn't win."

"We worked out this act using stories Papa told us about the war," Sidney added. "You remember, the idiot generals, the abusive sergeant majors, the hapless privates."

"I think it's wonderful that you want to make a living on the boards. Even if you weren't my sons, I'd want our agency to represent you. Less, Lesser, and Least. Which is which?"

"We go by height," Sidney answered. "I'm Less, Manny's Lesser, and Bernard's Least."

"What if Bernard ever grows another few inches?"

"Or if Sidney shrinks?" Manny asked.

Sidney laughed. "We'll worry about that when it happens."

Less, Lesser, and Least began their prize-winning engagement at the start of June, with a week of opening the bill at the Tottenham Rialto. The Partnership always placed talent-show winners in that spot; if they bombed, damage was slight. Rachel saw the first and last performances, and was delighted by the improvement. Gags were sharper, the slapstick broader. The final week of the engagement took them south of the Thames to another Rialto Playhouse Partnership theater, the Woolwich Playhouse. On the day they opened, Rachel contacted James Prideaux, bookings manager of the Partnership.

"If you've got time this week, Mr. Prideaux, I think you

should go to Woolwich. You've got an opening act there— Less, Lesser, and Least—that deserves much better."

Prideaux had been in the business too long to be affected by an agent's enthusiasm. "They're contest winners with no experience. In a couple of years, when someone else has smoothed out the rough spots, they might be worth taking a chance on. Right now they're just slightly better than the rest of the rubbish in that contest."

"That quote would look good in the *Performer*, wouldn't it?"

"Is that blackmail?"

"No. Persuasion. I really believe you should see them."

Prideaux was torn between annoyance at being pestered by an agent, and the awful possibility of letting a good act get away. "Forget your ten percent for a moment. How good are they?"

Rachel smiled. "I couldn't think more highly of them if they were my own sons."

Prideaux watched the second house that night. He remembered every detail of Less, Lesser, and Least's performance during the talent show—he could recall almost every detail of a thousand acts—and he was impressed with the improvements they had made. A week of opening the bill at the Tottenham Rialto had given the three young men the assurance of seasoned professionals.

Next morning, Prideaux telephoned the agency to discuss a summer contract. He offered an engagement starting the middle of July and running through the first week of September; a week at each of the Partnership's six seaside theaters, followed by a week at the London Playhouse, the circuit's flagship theater in Leicester Square.

"Fourth spot in the second half of the show," Prideaux said. "They'll have to stretch the act to eight minutes."

Rachel was delighted. The offer was everything she could have asked for, the set-up spot for the top of the bill. Manny, Sidney, and Bernard started work immediately on expanding the routine. Sidney's general became more ridiculous in his petty criticisms; Manny's sergeant evolved into a blistering caricature of a bullying NCO; and Bernard's luckless private developed into such a simpleton that Rachel wanted to intercede on his behalf. It was a crying shame that Bernard had to play such a character when he was by far the cleverest of her three sons. But the outgoing, assertive personalities of Manny and Sidney would never allow them to fill the role. It was Bernard's by default.

After a week of rehearsing at home, the three boys visited the agency. Harold Parker watched their act approvingly. When they finished, he picked up the latest copy of the *Performer*. A story was circled in ink. "Did you ever hear of Sammy Harris?"

"The comedian?" Sidney asked.

"That's him. A good one. He fell ill two weeks ago with heart trouble. Died a few days later. Here's his obituary. He was booked for the Partnership tour this summer. Someone else's misfortune has given you a golden opportunity. Don't waste it."

Bernard took the trade paper from Parker. "There's something distasteful about stepping into a dead man's shoes."

Sidney clasped his younger brother's shoulder. "There's nothing distasteful about it at all. Kings do it all the time."

Manny, Sidney, and Bernard left London on a Sunday afternoon to begin their summer season with the Partnership circuit. Brighton, on the Sussex coast, was the first stop. They telephoned Rachel to say they were staying at a small hotel used by Partnership performers. When Rachel asked if they each had a room, they laughed. They were all in one room, sharing toilet and bath with three other rooms on the same floor.

At rehearsals on Monday morning, they met their fellow performers. The opening act comprised two young dancers called the Simpson Sisters, Joanne and Linda, who were staying at the same hotel. Following them was a comedian, Harry Gregory, whose bill matter described him as the sultan of mirth. Next came an acrobatic team called the Flying Koronas, then Silver and Gold, a comedy duo. The final act before the interval was Henry Blalock, who sang and played the ukulele. The Simpson Sisters returned for another three-minute routine to open the second half of the show, after

265

which Leon Adams performed tricks on a unicycle. Then it was the turn of Less, Lesser, and Least. After their sketch came the star of the show, a popular singer named Betty Bailey, whose turn lasted twenty minutes. Closing the show so the audience would not rush for the exits during the star's performance was a juggler called The Amazing Derek.

Most of the cast ignored Manny, Sidney, and Bernard. They were newcomers. Respect was not given, it had to be earned. One act, however, went out of the way to be hostile; at least, half the act did so. In Silver and Gold, Gerry Silver played a cultured member of the upper class—complete with top hat and tailcoat—who vainly tried to improve Naomi Gold's scatterbrained stooge. Shaw's *Pygmalion* tailored to variety. The act was less than a year old and quite successful.

Sidney watched Silver and Gold rehearse. Both were in their early twenties. Naomi Gold held Sidney's attention. Beneath the portrayal of brainlessness was an attractive young woman with shoulder-length light-brown hair and the widest brown eyes he had ever seen. He gave her a big smile. Surprised by the approach from the young man in a general's uniform, she smiled back. Gerry Silver spun around immediately, determined to learn what had caused this departure from the script.

"Would you mind not interfering with our rehearsal?"

Sidney raised a hand in a peace gesture. "Sorry." Beyond Silver, Naomi Gold smiled at him again. Sidney reciprocated.

Silver gripped the cane that was part of his act. "You're playing with fire if you interfere with my fiancée."

"Your fiancée?" Sidney dropped his eyes from Naomi's face to her left hand. An engagement ring sparkled on the third finger. "She's only your fiancée because she never met me first."

Silver lifted the cane as if to strike. Sidney raised his own fists. He wasn't scared of this Gerry Silver. Before a blow could be landed, hands grabbed his arms and pulled him away. Silver returned to Naomi.

"Are you crazy?" Manny hissed. "Do you want to get us thrown off the Partnership circuit before we even get started?"

"I smiled at a girl—what harm is there in that?"

"None. As long as she doesn't belong to someone else. Now forget about her, will you?"

Of all the cast, only the Simpson Sisters were outwardly friendly. Joanne was twenty-five, Linda twenty-two. Although they shared the same surname, they were cousins, not sisters. After rehearsals, when Manny, Sidney, and Bernard stood around uncertainly, the Simpson Sisters suggested lunch at a nearby cafe, followed by a walk.

"Are you fellows nervous?" Joanne asked as they tramped over the pebbles that made up Brighton's beach. She was the prettier of the two, tall and slim with curly blond hair and blue eyes.

"Nervous?" Sidney scoffed at the idea. He held out his hand. "Do you see that shaking? Ice runs in those veins."

Manny held his hand alongside Sidney's. "More ice."

Linda, too, had curly blond hair, but she was shorter than the other girl, plumper. She reached out for Bernard's hand. "How about you? Have you got ice in your veins as well?" Bernard's hand trembled in her grasp. "My, you are a nervous Nellie, aren't you? Is it the thought of the show, or is it me?"

Bernard said nothing. He just snatched his hand away and shoved it into his trouser pocket. Unlike his brothers, he could not hide his anxiety. About the show, or about the closeness of these two young women. He stalked on ahead, kicking pebbles.

Linda started to laugh at his discomfort. Manny touched her arm and she stopped. Simultaneously, he looked at Sidney and winked. Sidney could forget all about chasing someone else's fiancée. They'd be in clover with these two girls.

The first show began at six-thirty. The three brothers stood in the wings and looked out. The auditorium was only a third full.

"First house on a Monday's always like this," Linda Simpson whispered. "The manager has to paper the house to get anyone to come in. Forty percent of the people out there are theatrical landladies on free passes. Another forty percent are probably unemployed men the manager found hanging around in the street."

267

"The manager gives tickets away?" Manny felt offended. If the audience didn't pay, how would he and his brothers get paid?

"Beats playing to an empty house. Second house'll go much better, you'll see."

The three brothers remained in the wings, watching the other turns. Sidney took special note of Silver and Gold. Gerry Silver played the Professor Higgins role off the stage as well as on it, coaching Naomi before the performance and criticizing her the instant it was over. Manny saw Sidney staring and nudged him. Sidney nodded and looked away; he had no intention of getting involved so close to his own performance.

The interval passed. The Simpson Sisters returned for their second routine, then the unicyclist amused the sparse audience. As he pedaled off, Manny hugged his brothers. "This is it. The moment of truth for Mrs. Lesser's little boys."

From the orchestra pit rolled a muffled drumbeat. A mournful trumpet played "The Last Post." Bernard dragged one weary foot after the other toward the center of the stage. He stood there, back hunched, legs bent, rifle dragging on the ground. Scattered laughter greeted him. In the wings, Manny threw out his chest, took a deep breath, and bellowed "Attention!" Bernard snapped upright. The trumpet sounded a lively march. Swagger sticks tucked beneath their arms, Manny and Sidney marched onstage. The inspection routine began. The laughs came in on cue, each louder and more sustained than its predecessor. At the end of the act, the three brothers ran off to applause.

Two hours and ten minutes later, they stood in the wings waiting for their spot in the second show. The auditorium was three-quarters full. Paying customers. Bernard's sloppy stroll into the center of the stage met with a solid roar of laughter, and all three brothers knew their real debut was a hit.

They returned to the hotel at midnight. Before eating the hot meal the landlady had waiting, they placed a call to London. As Rachel answered, Sidney yelled, "Don't worry, we're not at the station. We're still in Brighton and we're a smashing success."

Bernard took the telephone from his brother. "The audience loved us, Mama. They laughed and clapped and cheered—"

Sidney grabbed the telephone back. "It felt so good that when the colored bulbs in the footlights flashed, we carried on."

Rachel managed to get a word in. "Don't you dare do that! Better performers than you have ruined careers by deliberately overrunning time limits."

Manny took over from Sidney. "Don't listen to him. You know what he's like. Give him half the chance and he'll have you believing black is white."

After eating, the three brothers retired to their room. They sat on the beds, feeling the excitement drain from their systems. While Manny and Bernard reflected on the act, Sidney concentrated on Silver and Gold. He couldn't fathom how an attractive young woman could be engaged to a boor like that. Silver treated Naomi like a halfwit the whole time, showing her up in front of people. What did she see in such a heel?

Knuckles rapped on wood. Manny yelled, "Come in!" Joanne Simpson stuck her head around the door, waving a half full bottle of Scotch: "Look what the nice man at the theater bar gave us. Want to share it?"

Manny and Sidney stood up. Bernard remained on his bed, knowing he was not included in the invitation. Not that he wanted to be. His brothers wanted to sleep with every girl they saw. Bernard believed he had more respect for himself.

The Simpson sisters shared accommodation on the next floor up. Two narrow beds, a dresser, and a tiny table with two chairs filled almost all the available space. The girls took the chairs. Manny and Sidney dragged a bed up to the table. Joanne poured Scotch into four odd glasses.

"You looked really smart out there with your swagger sticks," Joanne said. "Know what to do with your swagger sticks, do you?"

"Give us the chance and we'll show you," Sidney answered.

"That brother of yours is a shy one, isn't he?" Linda said.

"He's only twenty," Manny said. "He hasn't learned to be anything else yet."

"Age doesn't mean anything. Even when I was fifteen, I wasn't shy like him."

Sidney looked at her over the top of his glass. "I just bet you weren't," he said.

Linda stuck out her tongue. Joanne reached back to the dresser and pulled out a pack of cards. "Play some poker?"

"What stakes?" Sidney asked.

Joanne's eyes gleamed impishly. "Whatever the pair of you are wearing. One hand for us girls, one hand for you fellows."

Manny took the cards and shuffled with a studied clumsiness. He saw Sidney start to grin. Joanne poured more drinks. Linda looked at the two young men. "You've got more clothes than we have. Not fair."

"We'll strip down to our underwear, all right?" Sidney offered. "We'll give ourselves a handicap."

"Is your underwear clean?"

"Cross my heart."

"You should always wear clean underwear in case you're in an accident," Linda said guilelessly.

Sidney laughed. "Nothing worse than having the entire hospital see you're wearing dirty underwear."

They stripped down to their underwear and argyle socks. Joanne's eyes wandered from Sidney's chest beneath the singlet, down to his narrow waist, and finally to the fly of his underpants. Linda's eyes did a similar exploration of Manny. He winked at her and began to deal. "Four of a kind or better wins it outright, okay?"

"If you say so."

Manny dealt five-card straight poker. Joanne and Linda won the first hand with a pair of kings. Manny and Sidney each ceremoniously removed one sock. Manny shuffled and dealt again. The girls won the next hand. The other sock came off. They won a third time; both young men removed their singlets. Joanne ran a hand across Sidney's chest and stomach, tugged at the waistband of his underpants. "Don't muck about with the goods until you've bought them, lady," Sidney warned. She laughed and put his finger in her mouth, nibbling gently on it.

"Shall I carry on dealing, or do you two want to stop for a snack?" Manny asked.

Joanne released Sidney's finger. "Deal. The way your luck's going, this will only take one more hand."

Manny dealt. The girls' eyes widened with glee. Manny looked at Sidney and winked.

"Four kings!" Linda burst out.

"Four of a kind wins outright!" Joanne shrieked. She lunged for Sidney's underpants, while Linda advanced on Manny. "To the victor go the spoils!"

"Wait a minute!" Manny roared. "This game's not over yet."

Both girls stopped. Manny turned over his cards. A five, and then, one after another, four aces.

"You cheated!" Linda said.

"Of course I cheated. How do you think you got four kings?"

Sidney began clapping his hands. "Strip . . . strip . . . strip!" Joanne undid her dress and stepped out of it. She rolled down her stockings and tossed them in Sidney's face. Her garter belt followed. She turned her attention to Linda, helping the younger girl out of her dress. Manny and Sidney watched, spellbound by the dance routine being staged for their benefit.

The girls stood in front of Manny and Sidney. They reached behind to unclasp their bras. Two pairs of breasts flopped into waiting hands. Joanne's hand slipped inside Sidney's shorts. "Ooh, look at that! I found where he keeps his swagger stick!"

"Me as well!" Linda squealed. As she grabbed Manny, he buried his face in her breasts. All this and money, too! What a job! What a way to earn a living! What idiots he and Sidney were for wasting all those years in the clothing business!

And Sidney, feeling Linda's hand close around him, forgot all about Naomi Gold.

Rachel traveled to Brighton on Saturday morning. Bernard met her at the station and took her out for lunch. When she asked about Manny and Sidney, he told her they were sleeping late.

"What time do they go to bed?"

"I don't know. They haven't slept in our room once."

271

Rachel met her other sons after lunch. Both looked worn out. "Enjoying Brighton?" she asked.

"Never knew any place could be so much fun," Manny answered.

"Let me give you a warning. You're in a new world. There's nothing wrong with a sleeping guide book, but make sure the pages aren't too dog-eared."

Sidney laughed, but Manny took offense. "It's a little bit late to be giving out motherly advice, isn't it?"

"I'm talking as your agent. You both look as though you could do with a good night's sleep. It only takes one bad performance to wreck everything you've achieved so far."

Later, in the dressing room, Manny and Sidney ganged up on Bernard. "Why did you tell Mama about us?" Manny demanded.

"She wanted to know why you didn't meet her at the station."

"Couldn't you have just told her we were sleeping late?"

"I did tell her that. But one thing led to another."

Manny pushed him away. "Make sure you don't lead somewhere."

Rachel watched the show before returning to London. Manny added brutal realism to his depiction of the bullying sergeant major. When he pushed Bernard around, he pushed hard, sending him staggering clear across the stage. Sidney was no gentler. Lifting Bernard's foot to check beneath his boot, he did it so sharply that Bernard had no time to brace himself for the fall. Among the audience, the hostility between the brothers served to create more laughter.

After the show, while Rachel was on her way to the station, Bernard stood up to his brothers. "One more performance like that and I'm through."

"There won't be any more performances like that," Manny answered. "We made our point."

Sidney flicked an imaginary speck of dust from Bernard's shoulder. "Just because you want to save yourself for your dream girl, don't ruin it for the rest of us, understand?"

After the final curtain that night, the cast left the theater for the last time. Bernard had the room to himself while his brothers spent the night with the Simpson Sisters. Joanne and

272

Linda had no work booked the following week, while Less, Lesser, and Least were traveling on to Portsmouth. Bernard wondered whose beds his brothers would find to share in Portsmouth. And in every town they played after that.

They finished the Partnership tour in September, with a week at the London Playhouse, on the south side of Leicester Square. In London, they stayed at home. Rachel welcomed their presence. The house was too big for one person. What would she do, she wondered, when they married? Find a smaller home? Or would Bernard—a smile crossed her face, only to be replaced by a worried frown—stay with her to make certain she needed nothing?

Sidney's general and Manny's sergeant major humiliated Bernard's private in theaters across England. After a year, they decided to change the act.

Different routines evolved. The most successful one portrayed Manny and Sidney as policemen and Bernard as a thief. "A policeman's lot is not a happy one," from *The Pirates of Penzance,* became the theme. A set with half a dozen doors allowed them to pursue each other in a wild, carefully choreographed chase. Each Saturday night when an engagement ended, the set was struck and taken to the station for shipment to the next city where Less, Lesser, and Least were appearing.

They no longer shared accommodation. Bernard slept on his own, undisturbed by Manny's and Sidney's liaisons. Never again could he reveal his brothers' movements to their mother. If she asked about their carryings on, he simply shrugged his shoulders.

Of the three, only Bernard felt less than comfortable on the stage. Manny and Sidney viewed variety theater as an adventure. Bernard regarded it as drudgery. He found no enjoyment in the spotlight. Mostly, he was tired of being pushed around for the audience's amusement. He might have forgiven his brothers for the episode in Brighton, but he had not forgotten. Each performance, whether as the army private or the thief—or whatever victim's role he filled—served to remind him. Suggestions he made to alter the roles were always turned down.

273

"The entire act rests on your character," Manny repeatedly told him. "Don't you realize how important you are? Without you in that role, we'll die."

"You get the most laughs," Sidney pointed out.

"The audience is laughing at me, not with me."

"That's better than having them swearing at you."

Once, Bernard took his case to Rachel. To his distress, she agreed with Manny and Sidney. "You've filled the role of victim for two years," Rachel said. "You can't change it now. The fans of Less, Lesser, and Least want you to keep things just the way they are."

His mother's opposition was, for Bernard, the most stinging rejection of all.

In the autumn of 1933, Less, Lesser, and Least returned to the London Playhouse in Leicester Square for a two-week engagement. This time, Rachel did not need to sell them to James Prideaux. The chief booker of the Rialto Playhouse Partnership had followed their career with interest. Prideaux particularly favored their policemen/thief routine. It had never been seen at the London Playhouse. He decided to rectify that oversight.

On Monday morning, they attended band call. When their rehearsal was over, they stood in the wings watching the other acts. Most were performers with whom they had worked at one time or another. One was not, a young woman whose four-minute juggling routine was scheduled to open the second half of the show. Her name was Rita Reynolds, and she was a late replacement for a specialty act who had been taken ill with appendicitis. Manny's interest rose as he watched her rehearse with Indian clubs. She couldn't be much older than twenty, a dark-haired slim girl who didn't look strong enough to throw the clubs into the air. She certainly had difficulty catching them. Three times in a minute, a club crashed to the stage. Each time, her face grew redder. Musicians shifted uncomfortably. In the stalls, Manny saw the theater manager slowly shaking his head.

"Miss Reynolds!" the manager called out. "Is everything all right? Perhaps you'd like to change the tempo of the music."

She switched from clubs to rings, and then to horseshoes. Her skill improved. Manny could feel the relief that flooded over her. When she came off, he touched her arm. "It'll go better when there's an audience out there, Rita."

"It's thinking about the audience that terrifies me. This is the London Playhouse. I've never worked in such a big theater."

"Audiences are the same everywhere."

She gazed at him in disbelief. "That's easy for you to say. You and your brothers have been creating your own special kind of craziness in big theaters all your lives."

Manny relished the flattery. "Stop worrying. Once your music starts tonight, you'll be just fine." He saw doubt remaining in her gray eyes and added, "That's the voice of experience talking—the voice of someone who's been creating his own special kind of craziness in big theaters all his life."

The anxiety became a weak smile. "My mother always told me to listen to people with experience. She said I'd learn."

"Give me the chance and I'll teach you everything I know."

Watching her walk away, Manny wished he had used a different parting line. His last remark was the kind of cheap innuendo he used on girls he was trying to pick up. Picking up Rita Reynolds had, admittedly, been his first thought. But after witnessing her anxiety, another feeling had superseded lust. He'd wanted to protect her. From the theater manager. From the audience. From anyone he felt might threaten her.

Sidney appeared at his elbow. "Any luck?"

Shaken from his musing, Manny could only answer, "With what?"

"With the girl. Will she drop them for you?"

Manny's blue eyes froze. "You know something? You can be a real disgusting pig when you put your mind to it."

The first night drew well. Less, Lesser, and Least filled second spot. Two tap dancers started the show, clicking their way through three minutes of Cole Porter's "Let's Do It." Bernard, wearing the striped shirt and mask of a stage villain and carrying an enormous gold watch, stood just out of the audience's view. Sidney, dressed in a policeman's uniform a size too small, stood next to him. Manny, in a uniform two sizes too big and stuffed with cushions to make him appear enormously fat leaned against a wall, observing backstage activity.

Spotting Rita Reynolds, Manny waved. "See how easy this audience is? They haven't thrown a rotten tomato yet."

"That's because they haven't seen me yet."

"You're going to win every heart out there. Besides, last week, the Variety Artistes Federation had the government pass a law making it illegal to throw rotten tomatoes at jugglers." His ears picked up as Cole Porter's music ended. "See you later."

"Is that true—?" She broke off, laughing. Of course it wasn't true. It was just something Manny had invented to take her mind off the butterflies cavorting in her stomach.

The opening act finished. The tap dancers ran off. The curtain lifted to reveal the six-door set. Paper shuffled in the orchestra pit. The tuba player launched into Arthur Sullivan's tribute to a policeman's pain and misery. Bernard ran to the center of the stage. From behind came a stentorian bellow. "Stop, thief!" A split second before Sidney and Manny charged onto the stage, Bernard darted through the nearest set door. A wave of laughter swept up from the audience as the sketch began.

Rita Reynolds was standing in the wings when the three brothers came off seven minutes later. "You were wonderful," she told all three, but her eyes singled out Manny.

"So will you be." Manny did not follow his brothers to the dressing room. He stayed with Rita, trying to calm her nerves. Only when the interval began did he join Sidney and Bernard, who had exchanged their costumes for robes.

"Better get back into your costumes."

"What?" Sidney checked his watch. "Second house doesn't begin for another ninety minutes."

"You might be needed long before then." In soft, earnest tones, he began to sell an idea.

"You're mad," Sidney broke in. "We'd be washed up, dead."

276

"On the contrary. If we do it right, the audience will love it. And whatever the audience loves, management loves."

The interval ended. Members of the audience returned to their seats. Rita stood in the wings waiting for her cue. Less, Lesser, and Least joined her. "Break a leg," Manny whispered, clutching her hand for support. Her skin felt warm and sticky. Manny guessed her heart was pumping like an express train.

"What are you doing back up here?" a technician asked Sidney. "You're not due on again until second spot in the next house."

"We want to watch the show. Is there a law against that?"

Rita's introduction sounded. She skipped out onto the stage, flipped her clubs into the air, and started juggling. Manny wondered how long it would be before she dropped one. No more than thirty seconds, he guessed.

His estimate was optimistic. After twenty seconds, she failed to get enough height on one club. Realizing her mistake, she tried to adjust her rhythm. The move caused instant disaster. Clubs crashed like thunder onto the stage. Rita stood horrified, wanting to run and hide from this embarrassment, but unable to transmit the command to her legs.

Before the audience could react, Manny shoved Bernard out from the wings. He stood perfectly still for a moment, arms spread out, mouth open. Then, as interest switched from the debacle in the center of the stage to the unexpected intruder, he jumped into action. He ran to where Rita stood, knelt down to pick up two clubs, whispered, "You're being robbed, call the police," and prayed she had enough initiative to catch on.

She did. "Help! Police! I'm being robbed!"

From stage right, in a reprise of the second-spot opening, came the roar of "Stop, thief!" Bernard clutched the clubs to his chest and dashed off stage left. The orchestra conductor pointed his baton at the tuba player. The opening bars of "A policeman's lot" drifted from the pit, speeding up as Manny and Sidney leaped out from the wings in pursuit of Bernard.

Gratitude gave Rita inspiration. She threw her hands above her head. "He went that way! No . . . that way! Or was

277

it that way? Oh, I don't know . . . he must have gone one of those ways!"

Laughter washed over the stage as the audience savored the chaotic activity. Manny and Sidney skidded to an exaggerated halt by Rita. "Which way *did* he go, madam?" Manny asked.

She pointed again in four directions.

"And what did he steal?" Sidney added.

"My clubs."

"Your clubs? Your rugby clubs, your bridge clubs, or your youth clubs? Exactly what kind of clubs?"

"My juggling clubs."

Sidney turned to Manny. "Imagine that. People join clubs to juggle these days."

"I *use* them for juggling."

"Aha!" Manny pulled out a coin which he dropped onto the stage; the orchestra drummer crashed a cymbal. "What was that?"

"I don't know," Sidney answered.

"The penny dropping."

The conductor motioned with his baton. The orchestra, in unison, groaned loudly. Sidney beckoned to a violinist who handed up his bow. "What's this for? To stir the plot when it thickens." The orchestra groaned again. The audience laughed. Returning the bow, Sidney looked to Manny for the next joke. During the interval they had agreed to improvise, confident they could carry on until the colored bulbs began to flash.

Instead, the joke came from Rita. "What do you call a puritanical policeman who juggles axes clumsily?"

"A defective detective?" Manny guessed.

"A proper copper chopper dropper."

The orchestra's groan was louder than ever. So was the audience's laughter. Manny looked at Sidney in amazement; they were being beaten at their own game.

Puns whipped back and forth, each one more painful than its predecessor. After thirty seconds, Bernard reappeared from the wings. A chase started, through the orchestra pit, along the center aisle—with the two policemen involving members of the audience in the action—and back onto the

278

stage, where Rita had four gold-painted balls in the air at one time.

"Good Lord!" Bernard grabbed for one of the balls, upsetting the entire act. "Do you know how valuable gold is?"

"No. How valuable is gold?"

"If I knew do you think I'd be asking you?"

The colored bulbs began to flash. "I'm all right," Rita whispered. She bent down to pick up the gold balls. "Let me finish off the act."

Sidney pulled out a notebook and pencil. "I must warn you that anything you drop will be picked up and used in evidence."

She didn't drop a thing. For the next twenty seconds, while the three brothers stood watching, she juggled perfectly. When the curtain fell, the applause lasted a full minute. Instead of a mundane second-half opener, the audience had been treated to the zaniest four minutes of entertainment they had ever seen.

"Thank you. Thank you all," Rita said as they ran off the stage. "I would have died of embarrassment without you."

"What about the second show?" Manny asked.

"I think I'll be all right." Rita gazed at him with gratitude, and adoration. "But will you be there, just in case?"

"We'll be there."

The theater manager waited in the wings. "Would someone mind explaining to me what just happened?"

"A little improvisation," Manny explained.

"The Partnership detests improvisation. Don't let me see it in the second show. And don't think you've heard the last of this. There'll be more said, I guarantee you. Much more."

The second show went without a hitch. Whatever nerves had plagued Rita disappeared. After the show, while his brothers returned to their mother's home, Manny escorted Rita to her lodgings at a bed-and-breakfast hotel. During the journey, he got her to talk about herself. She came from the port city of Bristol, and had been on the boards for two years.

"This was my first big chance in London, and I made a mess of it. Or I would have done if you hadn't helped me out."

When he said good night to her outside the hotel, Manny

shook her by the hand. "See you tomorrow. And stop worrying, will you? I told you no one would throw rotten fruit."

All the way home he wondered why he had shaken her hand instead of kissing her good night. Was it for the same reason that he had convinced his brothers to help? Because he felt Rita needed protection? And he wanted to be the one to protect her?

He smiled to himself. For the first time in his life, he had found someone who made him want to be a perfect gentleman.

When Manny, Sidney, and Bernard arrived at the Playhouse the next afternoon, the theater manager waited. "You're wanted in Mr. Martin's office," he said with a smugness that boded ill.

No doubt existed about the gravity of the summons. Leslie Martin was general manager of the Partnership. He supervised the business side while James Prideaux, the bookings manager, oversaw the daily operations of the theaters.

The Partnership's offices were located next to the theater. Prideaux and Leslie Martin had adjoining rooms. A receptionist with tightly waved iron-gray hair occupied a desk between the two offices. She told the brothers to sit down. On the wall behind the receptionist was the poster for that week's show. They tried to find some comfort in the knowledge that the names of Less, Lesser, and Least had not been scratched out.

After five minutes, the receptionist said the general manager was ready to see them. She knocked on Martin's door and ushered them inside. A smoky haze filled the room. Martin sat behind an oak desk. As the visitors entered, Martin crushed a cigarette into a crystal ashtray that overflowed with butts.

"Less, Lesser, and Least, who don't agree with the way the Partnership runs its bills, so they innovate." He stood up, a short, heavy man wearing a creased gray suit and scuffed black shoes. Martin had been involved with theater for thirty years, since starting fresh out of school as a clerk with Rialto Entertainment. Theater was his life, and he would allow no one to disturb its rhythm. "Who the hell do you think you

280

are? If you don't like the way we run our theaters, go somewhere else. We will not tolerate a bunch of bloody sketch comics who think they're bigger than the Partnership!"

Before they could answer, he strode to the door connecting with Prideaux's office. "Do you want to take a few bites out of these young upstarts as well, James?"

Prideaux's reprimand was delivered in quiet, calm tones, but it was just as effective as Martin's yelled rebuke. "I saw the show last night, both houses. In all my years in the business, I've never known performers to do what you did. Can you imagine what would happen if everyone did that? We wouldn't have a bill. We'd have outright anarchy."

Manny took it upon himself to offer a defense. "We did it because Rita Reynolds needed help out there."

"Other performers have flopped!" Martin shouted; he was beer to Prideaux's vintage wine. "She wouldn't have been the first to wet herself in a big house. You're lucky the orchestra conductor knew enough to go along, otherwise we'd have had four stranded idiots on the stage, not one." He fumbled on the desk for a pack of cigarettes, stuffing one into his mouth and lighting it in the same movement. Manny, Sidney, and Bernard took that as their cue to leave. Sidney reached for the door handle, grateful that they had not been dismissed for breach of contract.

"Just a minute." Prideaux's voice called them back. "We haven't finished with you yet. What you did last night was unforgivable, even if you did save Rita Reynolds's act. She might, once she conquers her nerves, turn into a passable performer, and she'll have you to thank. We're not interested in that. What does interest us is that, in your misbegotten chivalry, you might have stumbled on a unique device—coming on in the middle of other people's performances to liven things up."

That single compliment made up for all the reproach. "Shall we do it all week?" Manny asked. "If you saw both houses, you must know how flat the second show went."

"Ask Rita. If she doesn't mind, it's all right with us."

Manny did, the moment he left Martin's office and went backstage. Rita considered the idea before saying, "Will you let me get half a minute's juggling in before you come on?"

"Only if you promise not to drop anything." Then he kissed her for the first time.

Two days later, Manny called his brothers together in the dressing room and said he wanted Rita to join the act. "We've been together three years now. Even with different routines we're getting a bit stale. Rita will add a newness."

Sidney protested instantly. "You want her in the act because you're soft on her. What about when you go off each other? Do we drop her and go back to being Less, Lesser, and Least?"

Manny ignored his brother's objections. He looked to Bernard. "What about you? What do you think?"

"I don't care one way or the other."

"You don't care about a blooming thing, do you? Maybe Rita can replace you, and we won't have to change our name at all."

"Shut up," Sidney said. "Take your mind out of your groin for once and think what's best for the act. We got into enough trouble just going to her aid."

"Right! That's why we're doing it every night now, and the audience is lapping it up."

They took their quarrel where they had traditionally taken disagreements. To Rachel. She listened to Manny's argument that the act needed something new, and Sidney's claim that Manny cared only for himself. She was not shocked by the force of the dispute; it was a continuation of the battle that had raged for years. Nor was she surprised at Bernard's apathy. The longer the act went on, the more indifferent he grew. He did not belong in the spotlight. He liked to work behind the scenes. He'd be good—the idea flashed into her mind—as an agent.

At last, she said, "Manny's right, the act is getting old. Rita will add life. You can build new routines around her."

Manny's sharp expression of triumph matched his younger brother's bitter disappointment. Manny had gone one up on Sidney, and Sidney wouldn't rest until he had evened the score.

Rita became the fourth member of the act. "Less, Lesser, Least, and Rita" read the bill matter. "Mayhem at a mortal

282

level." Routines centered around Rita's strenuous efforts to accomplish something serious, and the brothers' equally vigorous attempts to foil her. She portrayed a maid setting a table, a teacher giving English lessons to foreigners, a secretary taking dictation from three people simultaneously, and a clerk in a china store. Whatever role she played, absolute chaos ensued.

The new act ran through 1934, tickling the ribs of audiences across the country. They drew more money. The style of living improved. On the road, they could afford a finer class of accommodation. But when they played in London, the brothers always stayed with their mother. The house in Dalston where they had been born offered a secure base that was missing in their nomadic theatrical lives. Rachel felt the same way about the house. The boys had talked often about buying a more modern home in a better neighborhood, but she was settled in Graham Road. Most of the memories comforted her.

Rita used a small flat in the West End of London as a base. Manny never stayed overnight, nor did he sleep with her when they were traveling. They spent hours together, petting heavily, but he always managed to show restraint, leaving before he crossed into a terrain that was as familiar with other women as the back of his own hand, but troubled him with Rita. The protective instinct that had originally made him rush to her defense remained as strong as ever, even to sheltering her from his own urges. One autumn night in Blackpool, in the middle of a twelve-week tour, she expressed confusion. "I've heard Sidney boast about the women you've both had. Is there something wrong with me? If I have bad breath, tell me. I'll change toothpaste."

Manny smiled at her joke and simultaneously damned Sidney's big mouth; for once, he wasn't proud of his sexual successes. "I feel differently about you, Rita. I want something more."

"Like marriage?"

He nodded. Marriage had crossed his mind every day for the past six months, ever since he realized he loved Rita. He just hadn't known how to approach it. Marriage wasn't a throwaway line, a gag you used onstage. It was serious, and

283

after four years of knockabout comedy he wasn't sure how to cope with a serious situation. "That's exactly what I had in mind."

Rita kissed him. "Good. It'll save me changing toothpaste. Who shall we tell first?"

"No one. We'll wait until we return to London in November. Let my mother be the first to know."

Then Manny remembered that immediately before London, they were booked for a week at the Bristol Hippodrome. Rita's hometown. She had not seen her parents for the year she had been based in London. She had barely spoken to them for the two years preceding that, ever since starting in the theater. Her family, headed by her schoolmaster father, regarded her as a black sheep. "Let's tell your parents first," he suggested. "Maybe such happy news will mend the rift."

Rita, realizing how much of a sacrifice it was for Manny to keep the news from his mother, was delighted by the suggestion.

In Bristol, she contacted her parents and arranged to meet them for Saturday tea at a restaurant near the Hippodrome. They were waiting when Manny and Rita arrived. Manny sensed tension instantly. This wasn't a family get-together; it was a meeting of strangers. Rita kissed her parents on the cheek before introducing Manny as the leader of the act. William Reynolds, a stiff, angular man, studied Manny through wire glasses perched awkwardly on his thin, beaky nose.

"Manny Lesser, eh? Is that a stage name?"

"It's my own name."

"What kind of name is it?"

"English."

"Really?" Reynolds turned to his wife. "Wouldn't you say, Emily, that Manny Lesser lacks the familiar, wholesome ring of a Smith or a Henderson?" He looked again at Manny. "What are your brothers' names? Are they English, like your own?"

"Sidney and Bernard. For your further information, my mother's name is Rachel and my father is Jacob." Perhaps this was why he had felt uncomfortable at the thought of marriage. The obstacles. This was just the first of two. What would his own mother say when he made known his plans?

Rita cut in quickly. "I've got you tickets for the first house. It's a wonderful show tonight—"

"I'm sure it is, but your mother and I have to be home early. I'm reading the lesson at tomorrow's service." Reynolds stared into Manny's eyes. "Perhaps you'd like to come along. With such an obviously English name, you'll feel right at home in church."

"Father . . ." Rita's voice quaked. "I asked you here because I wanted you to meet Manny. He is the man I'm going to marry."

Emily Reynolds gasped weakly. Her husband touched her hand. "You're over twenty-one, Rita. You can do as you please. You've proved that already by involving yourself in the debauchery of music halls. Just don't expect our approval." He stood up, pulling his wife to her feet. Before leaving, he tossed a handful of coins onto the table to cover his share of the bill.

The first house went terribly. Rita missed cues and bungled lines. In the dressing room, Sidney vented his anger in sarcasm. "Is appearing in front of the hometown crowd too much for you?"

"If you've got anything to say," Manny shouted, jumping between his brother and Rita, "say it to me!"

Sidney, loath to start a fight with his brother, turned away.

Second house went better. When it was over, Manny persuaded Rita to call her parents. Her father answered. When Rita announced herself, he said, "We told you already, do whatever you want to do. Just don't expect our blessing." Then he hung up. Rita started to cry. Manny held her tightly. "What about your mother?" she asked. "How will she react to our news?"

"We'll find out when we get to London tomorrow."

The four members of the act left Bristol by train the next morning. Reaching London, they separated. Rita went to her flat while the three brothers traveled to their mother's home. They fully expected her to have been cooking in preparation for their return, and they were not disappointed. The aroma of baking was overwhelming. After twelve weeks of eating in

285

restaurants and hotels, dinner promised to be a foretaste of heaven.

"I invited Rita," Manny told his mother.

"That's nice. She's part of the act, isn't she? A client of Parker and Lesser, just like the three of you are."

Rita arrived at six-thirty, bringing flowers for Rachel. Conversation during dinner centered around the just-completed tour and rehearsals beginning the next morning for a comedy revue called *Laughter Is The Best Medicine*.

Over dessert, Manny made his announcement. "Rita and I are getting married."

"When did you decide this?" Rachel asked.

"A few weeks ago, in Blackpool." Manny had no clue how his mother was taking the news. Surely not the way Rita's parents had done! Would she make some crass comment about names? Would she say that Reynolds lacked the familiar, wholesome sound of a Cohen or a Levy? He decided to push the issue. "Mama, you know that Rita's not Jewish, don't you?"

"Are you happy with each other?" Rachel asked, after a long moment.

"Very happy," Rita answered. Manny nodded his assent.

"That's all that matters," Rachel answered, her eyes brimming with tears. "No one can argue with happiness."

Laughter Is The Best Medicine brought together a dozen different comedy styles: sketches, stand-up comics, slapstick, double acts, and more. A production of the Rialto Playhouse Partnership, the revue was scheduled to run for six weeks, from the last week in November through the beginning of January 1935.

On Monday morning, when rehearsals began at the London Playhouse, Sidney said to his brothers: "This place is becoming our second home. Maybe we should start paying the management room and board." He looked down into the stalls where bookings manager James Prideaux sat, snapped his arm straight out, Nazi style, and shouted: "Everyone thinks Hitler's giving a salute when he does this! He's not, you know. He's asking to be excused. He wants to go to the toilet! Does it so often that maybe he should see a doctor!"

Prideaux roared with laughter, and Sidney decided to use the joke in the act.

Among the revue's cast were comics the brothers had worked with before, and some they had just seen. Backstage, they met a man whose shapeless jacket had bottles showing from every pocket.

"You inspired our first show," Manny said. "Remember us?"

Lenny Blount stared at them for a few seconds. "Hackney Empire, the summer of 1920. I showed you backstage. You've done pretty well for yourselves since then, haven't you?"

They walked to their dressing room, marveling at the comic's memory for dates. In fifteen years, would they be able to recall individual performances with such clarity? And would they still be doing the same act, as Blount obviously was? There was much to be said for longevity, but wasn't it also a sign of failure?

Sidney stopped. Coming out of the next dressing room was a woman he had not seen in four years. Naomi Gold had hardly changed. Fair hair rested on her shoulders exactly the way Sidney remembered. The brown eyes were just as sensitive. He saw tiny lines around those eyes, and thought they added to her beauty. He took her hand. "Naomi, what a lovely surprise . . ."

"I noticed your names on the bill," she answered. "With another name. Rita."

"We expanded a year ago."

Holding onto his hand, she searched his face for the marks of time. Creases crossed his brow. Character lines etched their way from his nose to the corners of his mouth. His eyes were still the same bright blue that had captivated her in Brighton.

"Are you still the funny half of Silver and Gold?"

"Gerry's the funny part of the act. He decides on subject matter and writes the scripts. I just memorize the lines and say them the way he directs."

"I don't believe that." Sidney saw another figure emerge from the dressing room. "Hello, Gerry, I was just saying to

287

your fiancée how pleasant it is to share the bill with you again."

Silver scowled. "For the past two years Naomi's been my wife. Come, Naomi"—he pulled her away from Sidney—"we've got work to do before we're ready to face an audience."

The dressing room walls were thin. Sidney heard Silver's voice, loud and angry, criticizing Naomi for some imperfection. Either Naomi was utterly stupid—and Sidney refused to believe that—or Silver was a rigid martinet. Each time Silver's voice rose, Sidney tensed, hands clenched as he stared at the separating wall.

"Ignore it," Bernard said. "There's nothing you can do, Sidney, so just disregard it."

"Someone should teach him some manners," Sidney replied. "It's not just in the dressing room. He humiliates her onstage when they're rehearsing in front of everyone."

Rita tried. "Sidney, some performers respond best to that kind of approach. Once they're away from the theater, they're probably a very different couple. Do you think she would have married him if he were like that all the time?"

Only Manny said nothing. He remembered pulling Sidney away from Gerry Silver in Brighton. Sidney had taken a shine to Naomi in that first brief meeting. Seeing her again had rekindled the feeling. Manny offered no advice because he knew words were empty. Sidney would do whatever he felt was right.

Final rehearsals were held next morning. Silver and Gold opened the second half of the show. Less, Lesser, Least, and Rita, who followed them, watched from the wings. The Silver and Gold routine centered around an invitation to a society garden party. Gerry Silver's cultured gentleman briefed the unsophisticated Naomi on what to expect, drawing laughter from her artless but skillfully constructed questions.

Throughout the five-minute act, Silver held Naomi's left arm in his right hand. Sidney felt his fury rise. Whenever Silver felt Naomi was unsatisfactory, he dug his nails into her flesh. She didn't wince. She just lifted her performance a notch to meet his expectations.

The act finished. James Prideaux made a couple of com-

288

ments from the stalls, then Silver and Gold came off. Sidney blocked Gerry Silver's path through the wings to backstage.

"I don't like your act, and I like you even less."

"Get out of my way."

Sidney stood his ground. He grabbed Naomi's arm and held it up to Silver's face. Nail marks gouged the skin. Fading bruises testified to earlier rough treatment. "If I see you lay a hand on her again, I'll lay both my hands on you." He shoved his way past Silver to join Rita and his brothers already onstage.

"Something wrong?" Prideaux called out from the stalls.

"Nothing at all," Sidney answered. Was Prideaux blind?

Following rehearsals, the cast left the theater. Sidney found Naomi standing alone by the stage door. He asked where Silver was. "Gerry's seeing Mr. Prideaux. He thinks Silver and Gold deserves a better spot on the bill. Better than you."

"Does he?" Sidney laughed, then turned serious. "Why did you marry him, Naomi? You can't possibly love a man like that."

She gave Sidney a wistful smile. "Gratitude, I suppose. We lived in the same building in Flower and Dean Street. Do you know that area?"

"I know it." Flower and Dean Street was part of the East End slum that the Dekker Boys' Club had tried to reach.

"Gerry was a wonderful dancer. He taught me everything. At eighteen we were winning charleston competitions. Then he had a new idea. Silver and Gold, a comedy double act."

"For that you married him?" Sidney asked in amazement.

"He got me out of Flower and Dean Street, Sidney. He showed me there was glamour in the world."

"And pain and humiliation to go along with it."

Naomi shrugged. "He's a perfectionist."

"You deserve more than Gerry's kind of perfect."

The show opened that night. From the wings, Sidney watched two performances of Silver and Gold. Gerry Silver never relinquished his grip on Naomi's arm. The Svengali of Flower and Dean Street did not work his wiles with hypno-

289

tism. He used pain and fear, and Sidney did not know how long he could contain his temper.

He lost control on the third night. He arrived last in the dressing room to prepare for the performance. As he walked in, he heard Silver's voice coming from next door. When he looked at Manny, Bernard, and Rita, they all turned away. Sidney left the dressing room and banged on the adjacent door.

"Would you mind keeping the noise down? You're not the only people in the theater, you know!"

The noise subsided. He returned to his own dressing room to change. Five minutes later, a timid knock sounded on the door. Rita answered the summons. "Sidney, Naomi wants to see you."

Sidney turned around. The left side of Naomi's face bore a vivid handprint. Tears filled the soft brown eyes. "May I speak to you, please?"

Manny, Bernard, and Rita filed silently into the corridor. Naomi entered the dressing room and closed the door. "Please leave Gerry alone," she whispered.

"Leave him alone? To do this to you?" He tried to push past her, but she blocked the door.

"You have to understand that Gerry lives on the edge. He worries about the act all the time. His nerves——"

"Nerves, hell! He's crazy."

Naomi carried right on. "He believes I asked you to threaten him in the wings that time. He thinks I put you up to banging on the door just now. He sent me here to tell you to stop."

"With that"—he brushed his fingers across her inflamed cheek—"as added incentive? Why didn't he come himself?"

"He thought you'd listen to me."

Sidney caressed her face with his hands. "Not when you're repeating his words."

Naomi's heartbeat quickened at Sidney's gentle touch. "Would you listen if I told you they were my words?"

He lowered his lips toward her own. "No," he murmured before kissing her.

She resisted. "I have to go back. If he finds out, he'll——"

Sidney cut her off with another kiss. "Leave him, Naomi.

Leave him and come to me. I'll treat you as well as he treats you badly." The offer sprang from his mouth so quickly that he knew it was right. He wrapped his arms around her waist, drawing her close. Her resistance ebbed. Slowly, she responded, sliding her hands down his back to his buttocks, pressing him to her. Her lips tasted sweeter than those of any woman he had ever known. He slid the bolt on the door and guided her toward the old couch that filled one wall. Voices sounded from the corridor, low, then raised. Neither Sidney nor Naomi paid attention. Their minds were occupied only with each other.

The door smashed open. Gerry Silver burst through, shaking off the attempts of Manny and Bernard to hold him. His face was scarlet with fury as he flung himself forward, arms outstretched.

Sidney swung around and straightened up. His fist flashed through the air. Silver ran straight into it. The shock of the punch shot along Sidney's arm, from his knuckles right up to his shoulder. It was nothing compared to the pain that ripped through Silver's face as the blow shattered his jaw. He gave a sharp scream and collapsed onto the floor, clutching his injured face.

Manny, Bernard, and Rita pushed through the doorway. Behind them came stagehands and other members of the cast. All parted moments later as James Prideaux pushed his way through.

"What in God's name is going on here?"

Silver writhed on the floor. Sidney stood over him. Naomi sat on the couch, hands to her face, crying softly. "He pushed Naomi around once too often," Sidney answered softly. "I pushed him back."

"And ruined the show! How do we open the second half now? Or didn't you consider that before you indulged your temper?"

"You could have stopped this if you'd spoken up when you saw what was going on during rehearsals."

"How dare you criticize me? My responsibility is to organize shows. How performers go about optimizing their talent is their concern." He turned around and clapped his hands.

"All right, everyone out. We'll take care of this, thank you very much."

The crowd dispersed. Prideaux swung back to Sidney. "We'll have to alter the entire schedule to compensate for this. God help you if it doesn't work," he said menacingly before striding out of the dressing room.

Ten minutes later, an ambulance arrived. Manny and Bernard helped Silver into it. Sidney held Naomi's hand. "I've sent your husband to the hospital and forced you off the bill. What else would you like me to do for you?"

Naomi smiled, as Sidney knew she would.

After the second house, Sidney visited the hospital. He met Naomi there, who told him that Silver's jaw was fractured in two places. At best, he would not be able to eat solid food for two months, and it was doubtful that he would perform for at least twice that long. Sidney escorted Naomi back to the Chelsea flat she shared with Silver. They said good-bye at the front door.

"I meant what I said before, Naomi. Leave Gerry and come with me. You'll never be sorry, I promise you."

"I can't leave him now, not while he's in a hospital bed."

Sidney knew his disappointment would have been greater had Naomi agreed. No man should be deserted while in the hospital, not even a scoundrel like Gerry Silver. "Do you need money?"

Naomi shook her head. "We have some put away."

"Call me every day. I want to hear your voice. I want to know you're all right." He kissed her and left.

The comedy revue lived by its own title, proving that in a period of economic misery, laughter was indeed the best medicine. Audiences packed each house. The engagement carried beyond the original closing date to the end of January, then into February. The Rialto Playhouse Partnership had a success on its hands.

Sidney heard from Naomi every morning. Gerry Silver came home, jaw wired. His diet consisted of liquids. Writing on a notepad comprised his sole means of communication. Two or three times a week, Naomi stole away to meet Sidney

292

for lunch or tea before he went to the theater. Each hour they spent together convinced Sidney he was in love with her.

The show closed the last day of February. The last house finished forty-five minutes late, as each act exceeded its time limit. When the curtain dropped for the last time, cast members assembled backstage to open bottles of champagne. They had plenty to celebrate; that week's trade press included a story about another "Laughter" revue being planned for next year.

The theater manager appeared. He made straight for Sidney. "Mr. Martin and Mr. Prideaux want to see you." When Sidney looked at his brothers, the manager added, "Just you. They only want to see *you.*"

This late at night, no receptionist guarded the Partnership's executive offices. Sidney knocked on the door of the general manager's office and entered. Leslie Martin sat at his oak desk. James Prideaux stood by a window overlooking Leicester Square.

"You wanted me?" Sidney said.

"Not any more," Martin answered. "You and your comedy act are finished with the Partnership."

"What?"

"Gerry Silver's solicitor contacted us today. He's suing the Partnership, and your hot temper's the cause of it all."

"Why is he suing *you?* If he should sue anyone, it should be *me.* I'm the one who hit him, and I did it in self-defense."

Martin erupted. "Self-defense? He caught you trying to have it away with his wife. Where's the self-defense in that?"

Prideaux seemed pained at his partner's crudity. "Gerry Silver's not suing you because, quite possibly, he believes you haven't got two pennies to rub together. He's suing us because we do have money, and because we carry insurance. We're liable, his lawyer claims, because we failed to afford a performer adequate protection while on our premises."

"Are you banning us in the hope of currying favor with Silver and his solicitor?"

Prideaux smiled enigmatically. "You caused us a lot of inconvenience. Now we're going to cause you some. You can tell your brothers and Rita Reynolds that you are persona non grata on the Partnership circuit. Then you can tell the same news to your agent. I think that will be the most exacting task of all."

Sidney turned and walked out of the office. At the door, he swung around, venom in his eyes and cold fury in his voice. "In six months time, you're going to realize just how much you miss us. You'll come begging on your knees for us to return, you'll see! And we'll tell you to go to hell! We'd sooner sell tickets for Stoll or Moss Empires than top the bill on the Partnership circuit!" He ran out of the office and down the stairs.

Damn Silver! Sidney knew exactly why he wasn't being sued personally. Such a judgment would come to a hundred pounds. Two hundred tops. Nothing. By suing the Partnership, Silver had accomplished much more. He'd forced the Partnership to get rid of the entire act. He had achieved complete and utter revenge.

Sidney returned to the theater with the news. Manny stared at him in disbelief. Anger slowly took over. "I should bloody well finish off what Gerry Silver started."

"If someone shoved Rita around, would you just stand by?"

"I wouldn't get mixed up with another man's wife!"

"No, you're bloody perfect, aren't you?"

Bernard pushed himself between his brothers. "Let's just collect our stuff and get out of here."

Manny grabbed Rita's arm and left. Sidney and Bernard traveled home by taxi. They arrived after midnight. Light shone in Rachel's bedroom. Sidney knocked on her door and went inside. She sat at the dressing table, brushing her hair. Sidney dropped himself onto the edge of her bed and related what had happened.

"What are you going to do?" she asked.

"The Partnership's not the only theater group in the world. We'll find plenty of work elsewhere."

She looked at his reflection in the mirror. "I didn't mean that. What are you going to do about Naomi?"

"Wait for her to leave Gerry Silver," Sidney answered. "Marrying Naomi will be my revenge on him."

Naomi telephoned early the next morning. "Gerry told me

294

what he did, Sidney. He's gloating because the Partnership's banned your act. I hate him."

Sidney breathed in deeply. He had reached a crossroads in his life; he could set off in one of two directions. "If Gerry's fit enough to gloat, and fit enough to unleash lawyers, he's fit enough to care for himself. Leave him."

"I will," Naomi answered immediately. "Right now."

An hour later, a taxi drew up outside the house in Graham Road. The driver waited while Naomi walked up the front steps and knocked on the door. Sidney opened it. Naomi's hair was unkempt. Her eyes were red; dried tears stained her cheeks. "Would you pay for the taxi, please?"

"Of course." Sidney walked down the steps to pay the driver. "Where are your things?" he asked Naomi when he noticed that the taxi's baggage rack was empty.

"Everything I own is on my back. This coat and hat and dress, my stockings, my shoes—these constitute all my worldly goods." Her voice took on an edge. Tears started to flow. "The moment I finished speaking to you, I told Gerry I was leaving. He wouldn't let me take a thing with me. He said he'd paid for it all. Everything I owned had been bought with his money. I was nothing until he met me, and I'd be nothing again. If you were going to take me, you'd have to take me in the clothes I stood in." She paused to wipe her eyes. "Gerry stood by the door to make sure I didn't take anything. He even searched my pockets. He made me feel like a criminal."

The taxi was just pulling away. Sidney yelled and the driver stopped. "I want you to take us to Chelsea!"

"No!" Naomi threw herself into Sidney's arms. "I don't want to go back there. I don't want to see him again, ever."

Sidney waved away the taxi. "We'll find a lawyer. You'll sue him for your share of everything you earned together—"

"Let him keep it," Naomi said. She sniffed back the tears and forced a wry grin onto her face. "I guess if you want me just like I am right now, then you really do want me."

"You're right. I really do."

By five that afternoon, Sidney had taken the first steps toward turning Naomi's life around. He gave her money to buy whatever she needed, then he took her to a solicitor to instigate divorce proceedings.

When Rachel returned home, Sidney introduced her to Naomi. "She left Gerry Silver. I told her she can stay here for as long as she likes."

Rachel's welcome was tinged with doubt. She understood how much the young woman meant to Sidney. No man did what he had done without some deep emotional stimulus. Yet at the same time she realized Naomi could spark the feud between her older sons. In the continuing battle for supremacy within the family, Manny viewed dismissal by the Partnership as a weapon. Sidney had caused it. Manny was not likely to let him forget it. And there was something else that bothered Rachel . . .

"Sidney." She drew her middle son aside, embarrassed for Naomi to hear what she had to say. "I don't care what you do while you're traveling, but in this house you don't get up to any hanky-panky. Understand?"

Sidney's face turned red. "I'm a grown man. I'm going to marry Naomi once she's divorced."

"When you're married, you can do what you like. But until then . . ." She smiled to cover her confusion at having to broach such a subject, but she would have been more disturbed had she said nothing. Much had changed since her arrival in England. Men flew the Atlantic. Women voted; they worked; they had a say in the way their lives were conducted. But morality remained morality. At least, in Rachel's home it did. Elsewhere people could do as they chose, but under her roof, she set the rules.

Naomi moved into a spare bedroom on the top floor of the house. The next morning, she told Sidney she was going out to look for a job. He was amazed. "Why do you want to work? I'll give you money for whatever you need."

"I need some pride. Gerry destroyed whatever self-respect I had. I want to prove that I can be independent." She softened her refusal of help with a kiss. "Now do you understand?"

Sidney wasn't sure that he did, but he nodded nonetheless.

Naomi found a job in a dress shop. On her first payday she handed money to Rachel for board and lodging. Rachel accepted the money. She understood Naomi's motivation better than Sidney did. And what she understood, she liked. Sidney, when he eventually married this young woman, would do well for himself.

A month after the closing of *Laughter Is The Best Medicine,* Less, Lesser, Least, and Rita prepared to go on tour again. The eight-week engagement with a provincial circuit had been booked six months earlier. It would begin in Leeds and work across the north of England to finish in Newcastle at the end of May.

A week before they left, Manny told his mother that he and Rita planned to get married when they returned from the tour. Rita wanted to be a June bride. Rachel started to ask Rita if her parents would come to London for the wedding. She stopped after the first two words, fearful of hurting her future daughter-in-law by reminding her of the family rift. Instead she asked, "What about your best man, Manny? Who are you entrusting with that responsibility?"

Manny had no doubt who his mother wanted him to choose. He could see the way her eyes drifted toward Sidney. She viewed such a choice as a way of healing. He turned to his younger brother. "Can I trust you not to lose the ring?"

"If you can't trust your own brother, who can you trust?" He shook Manny's hand. "You can do the same for Naomi and me."

Rachel smiled, pleased with herself for finding a way of bringing her sons together.

When they left for Leeds at the beginning of April, Manny was in an expansive mood. He and Rita had spent the past week making arrangements for their future. They had rented a flat near Regent's Park and bought furniture; they'd reserved a time at the registry office and booked a restaurant for the wedding breakfast. The good mood disappeared long before the train reached Leeds. The reason was Naomi. Although she remained in London, she dominated Sidney's thoughts. He waited until Rita left the compartment to visit the washroom, then said, "I think we could use another person in the act."

Manny looked sharply at his brother. "Four's company, five's a crowd. We're getting along fine now."

"Naomi's working in a dress shop. She doesn't belong there. The stage is in her blood, the same as it's in ours."

"So let her organize an act of her own. We're popular just the way we are."

Bernard got up and left the compartment. Standing in the corridor, he pretended to watch the scenery. He wanted no part of this argument. Neither Manny nor Sidney noticed his departure. "It's all right for you to have Rita as part of the act, but it's not all right for me to have Naomi, is that it?"

Manny smiled coldly. "You should have found a talented woman first. Then you could be telling *me* what I'm telling *you*. Or maybe you should have been smart enough to have been born first."

"Don't be such a smug bastard."

"And don't you keep on being such a stupid one! What are we supposed to do with this act—keep adding anyone and everyone? Soon there won't be a poster big enough to carry our name!"

Rita returned. Manny and Sidney lapsed into a silence which lasted for the remainder of the journey.

Ill feeling ruined the tour. Rehearsals became battle-grounds as each discussion developed into a row. Stagehands blamed it on artistic temperament. Theater people were an odd lot, especially comics; they could make everyone laugh but themselves.

When Sidney pointed out what he considered a weakness in Rita's performance, Manny bristled. "I suppose Naomi would do better, eh?" The remark quickly became a standard line.

Sidney retaliated by denying his brother and Rita privacy. Somehow he always managed to be eating at the same restaurant, walking where they were walking, busy in the dressing room when they hoped to have a moment together. Bernard, cast as a reluctant witness, wondered just how long the act could last when two of its members were constantly at each other's throats.

They returned to London at the end of May. Rachel had no need to ask how the tour had gone. She knew. Poor

298

reviews had appeared in provincial newspapers. The act had lost its gloss; its members marched through comedy with all the humor of undertakers. When she asked Bernard what had gone wrong, he told her about the interminable arguments.

"They've always competed fiercely with each other."

"Not this time, Mama. This was more than competition. I kept waiting for them to come to blows."

Had Rachel doubted Bernard's story, that skepticism soon disappeared. Not only did Manny and Sidney ignore each other, but Sidney announced that he no longer wanted to be his brother's best man. Bernard assumed the responsibility.

Manny and Rita were married at Caxton Hall Registry Office on the third Thursday in June. Bernard held the ring, ready to offer it the moment the registrar asked. Sidney stood with his mother on one side and Naomi on the other.

Rita's parents, William and Emily Reynolds, traveled from Bristol for the ceremony. They kissed Rita on the cheek, shook Manny's hand, and were formally polite to Rachel. They left immediately after the ceremony to return to Bristol. Rachel noticed that they had not given a present. She wondered whether they had made the long trip just out of curiosity. Certainly they had not come out of approval.

At the wedding breakfast, Rachel tried to play peacemaker between her sons. Holding Manny's hand, she guided him toward Sidney. "You formed one union today, Manny. It's time you mended another."

The brothers glared, each unwilling to yield first. "What's the matter with you two?" Rachel demanded. "You're carrying this silliness too far."

"Ask him," Manny said. "Ask the maniac here who got us kicked off the Partnership circuit."

"Ask *me?*" Sidney laughed. "What about *you,* a little Hitler bossing everyone around like you own the world."

"Stop it, both of you," Rachel said. She felt like she was settling a squabble between two five-year-olds, not a groom and his brother. "It's bad enough Rita's parents acted the way they did. We don't need similar behavior from you. Now shake hands."

Sidney extended his hand two inches. Manny reciprocated. Slowly, their hands advanced until they touched, shook. "That's better," Rachel said. She complimented herself on achieving the victory although she feared it was just a temporary triumph.

In December 1935, Harold Parker took a ten-day European trip, visiting cities in Holland, Belgium, and France to seek acts he could represent in Britain. Usually he returned from such trips full of enthusiasm. This time, he came back looking worn out.

"They're living on borrowed time over there," he told Rachel. "Sooner or later that madman in Germany is going to want all of Europe under his boot. God help us when it happens, because we won't be able to do a thing to stop him." He looked around the office he had rented for more than twenty years. "I worked my way right through one war in this place. I'm sixty, too old to do it again. I'm packing up the business."

Rachel took scant notice of the final sentence. She could only concentrate on Parker's first words. She asked a question she had once asked—it seemed like only weeks ago—of Jacob. "Do you really think there'll be a war?"

"Not tomorrow. Maybe not next year or the year after. But mark my words, there'll be one because we're all letting this maniac get away with whatever he wants to do. Did you hear what I said about the business? Do you want to buy it?"

"I'm almost fifty, Harold."

"What about your sons? They're not going to stay on the boards forever. I went into agency work from the stage; it's a natural stepping-stone. Besides, judging from the reviews they've had since *Laughter,* the act's dying."

Rachel moved her head in slow, regretful assent. That northern tour had been the precursor of trouble. The truce Rachel had negotiated at Manny's wedding had lasted for four weeks, until their next engagement. Bernard had relayed details of dressing-room squabbles. Sidney's irritation that Rita was in the act while Naomi worked in a dress shop continued to fester. He picked on his sister-in-law constantly. During a summer show at Southend, stagehands had been forced to separate Sidney and Manny. The odd thing was that while Manny and Sidney fought, Rita and Naomi remained good friends. Naomi held no grudges against Rita. Rita, in turn, tried to persuade Manny to soften his position. It was the one favor he would not grant his wife; he refused to yield where his younger brother was concerned, and his stand became tougher by the day.

"Well?" Parker asked. "Would your sons be interested?"

"Manny and Sidney fight all over theater circuits. In a small space like this, they'd kill each other."

"What about your youngest?"

Rachel recalled her thoughts at the time of the argument between Manny and Sidney—yet another row between them!—over taking Rita into the act. She had believed then that Bernard would make a wonderful agent. "I'll discuss it with him."

"If he wants to come aboard, I'll stay on until the end of 1936 to help with the changeover."

Rachel talked to Bernard about joining the agency. He grabbed at the opportunity. Less, Lesser, Least, and Rita had bookings through the summer of 1936. Bernard told his partners that he would leave the act at the beginning of autumn. For a moment, they buried their differences and turned on him.

"Who needs you?" Manny demanded. "You've been moaning all along. First you didn't like the role you had to play, you didn't like being the victim. Now when we all gang up on Rita and make her the stooge, you're still not happy."

"This is a comedy routine," Sidney chimed in. "It doesn't need a long face like yours. Become an agent stuck behind a desk. See who cares."

Bernard served out his notice. Once summer was over, he joined the agency. He arrived at the office before eight each morning, and stayed until after six. Harold Parker would retire at the end of the year, and Bernard wanted to learn everything he could from the experienced agent.

He soon realized that he did not have much to learn. Being an agent meant knowing people, establishing relationships with theater owners and the artists who graced their stages.

He already knew the owners and the bookings managers from his six years on the circuits. He also knew the performers; during those same six years, he had worked with most of them.

Before the first week was finished, he was on the telephone constantly, telling performers he knew of the advantages of being represented by Parker and Lesser and persuading bookings managers to hire his clients. One of the calls he made was to James Prideaux at the Rialto Playhouse Partnership.

"Mr. Prideaux, I wanted you to know that I've joined Parker and Lesser."

"I wish you luck, Bernard."

"I hope that luck extends to when I approach the Partnership with a proposal."

"As long as that proposal doesn't include your brothers' act. We have no use for hotheads. Anything else I'll listen to with an open mind."

"Listen to this." Bernard began to talk about a second-spot comic he had worked with during the summer. "He involves the audience by insulting them. Anyone walks in late, he gives them both barrels; asks if they had trouble with the car. Anyone goes to the toilet during his act, he calls out to remind them to wash their hands . . . That's right, and the audience just loves it . . ."

Parker watched Bernard for a few seconds, then turned toward Rachel. No mother could have looked prouder. The unwilling participant of a comedy routine had turned into a very willing agent. After six years of wandering in the wilderness, Bernard had found the promised land.

With Bernard gone, the act was changed to Less, Lesser, and Rita. The new name didn't work. Neither did the revised act. Bernard had provided a counterpoint to his brothers' aggression. Without him, there was no subtlety; only hammer blows.

Desperation altered Manny's perspective. The act was dying, and he sought a cure wherever he could find it. Two months after Bernard's departure, he told Sidney he needed to speak to him urgently. "We can count ourselves lucky to have Christmas bookings. But if we flop, no one will touch us again. Let's change the act while we've still got an act to change. What do you say to us working Naomi into the routine?"

Sidney held back a smile of triumph. For eighteen months he had tried to change his brother's mind. Now Manny was where Sidney had always wanted him: on his knees, begging. Sidney waited a full minute, luxuriating in his brother's obsequiousness before saying, "Look at it from Naomi's perspective, Manny. If she ever decides to return to the stage, it wouldn't look good for her to have been involved in the death throes of this act."

"You haven't even asked her!"

"I don't have to. I can talk for her."

"You bastard!" Manny shouted before storming away.

The act died the week after Christmas in a small Manchester theater. During the first house on a Monday, Less, Lesser, and Rita failed to establish themselves with the audience; silence greeted their gags. Panic set in. The second-house audience was subjected to flubbed lines and missed cues. Relief came with the dropping of the curtain. After the show, the manager paid them off for the entire week. They traveled back to London on the overnight train. Manny shared one compartment with Rita. Sidney occupied another. Despite the voluntary separation, their thoughts during the long journey were identical. Both brothers knew that they had just participated in funeral rites.

The news came as no surprise to Rachel. No act could survive when its participants pulled so hard in so many different directions. On New Year's Day of 1937—the first day of Harold Parker's retirement—she called her two older sons together.

"You had more than six years on the stage; that's longer than a lot of acts. Now you've got to decide where you go from here. Bernard needs help in the agency. Business is increasing and he can't handle it all on his own, besides which I'd like to stop working. Which one of you wants to go partners with him?"

Both Manny and Sidney understood why their mother had

chosen that particular phrasing. She wanted to separate them. She did not want their state of war transferred from the stage to the agency. They also realized that whoever chose to go into the agency would be Bernard's junior partner.

Sidney answered first. "I'll pass, thank you." He had no intention of being subordinate to anyone; he'd already had his fill of not getting his own way.

Right on the heels of the rejection came Manny's acceptance. "I'll give it a try. I always did envy the way agents collected ten percent for doing absolutely nothing."

Rachel did not smile; the situation was too serious for jokes. "What are you going to do?" she asked Sidney.

"Take time off to make plans. Business plans and marriage plans." He pulled an envelope from his pocket. "Naomi's divorce from Gerry Silver becomes final this week. I promised I'd marry her the minute that happened, and that's one promise I'm not going to break."

Sidney married Naomi four weeks later. It was the beginning of February, and miserable. Instead of a traditional honeymoon by the sea, they spent a week at the Dorchester Hotel in Park Lane.

By day, they concerned themselves with material matters. They leased a flat in Bayswater, and arranged for it to be furnished. At night, pampered in luxury, they made love with a furious passion that compensated for all the time they had denied themselves the pleasure of each other's bodies. Before falling asleep each night, they discussed how Sidney would make a living. Such debate was redundant because they already knew the answer. The entertainment business was in his blood, just like it ran through the veins of his brothers.

During that week, Sidney took one other step. He officially adopted his stage name; he didn't want anyone confusing him with Manny and Bernard.

From the Dorchester, they took a taxi to their new home in Bayswater. The next day, Sidney rented a small office in Shaftesbury Avenue, in the heart of the theater district. He ordered a telephone, a desk, and chairs. Lastly, he had a signwriter paint in gold on the office door the words: Sidney Less, Ltd., Theatrical Agent.

Whatever his brothers could do, Sidney was sure he could do it just as well.

Chapter Twelve

When Jimmy turned twenty-one in 1936, his father made him a birthday present of his second transatlantic voyage. The first had taken place three years earlier, when he had sailed on the *Ile de France* and traveled by train across France, Switzerland, and Italy. This time, Jimmy enjoyed first-class passage aboard the *Queen Mary,* on the return leg of the Cunard liner's maiden voyage. He spent more than two months as a guest at London's Hyde Park Hotel, from where he immersed himself in England's history and culture. He visited museums and galleries, bid at art and antique auctions, attended theater, ballet, and opera, strolled in famous parks, and ate in the finest restaurants. With him he carried a letter of credit. Whenever he needed money, banks obliged.

Returning to New York at the end of August on the *Queen Mary*'s Blue Riband voyage, Jimmy brought with him two steamer trunks full of antiques—including a silver tea service once owned by Disraeli—a Gainsborough drawing, and a new maroon Bentley tourer with its steering wheel, distinctively, on the right-hand side. He also came back a confirmed Anglophile.

When Zalman saw the quantity of baggage, he realized he had raised the world's most sophisticated and indulged twenty-one-year-old. He could not help feeling a little jealous. With the exception of completing university, Jimmy was doing everything Zalman would have wanted to do had he been given the chance. One generation away from the Pale, Jimmy was a young gentleman of impeccable taste and manners. How far such refinement would take him in real life, Zalman could only guess.

On Jimmy's first night back, over dinner at the Fifth Avenue townhouse, the entire family quizzed him about the trip. With the exception of Zalman's original journey from Russia, none of them had ever been outside North America. Zalman himself had always been too busy to take such a lengthy trip. Julia got sick on the Hudson ferry, and Helen, since leaving school, had focused all her attention on her newspaper career.

Zalman's main concern was how the British felt about Hitler. "Are they still as eager to ignore his expansionism as they were when he marched into the Rhineland five months ago?"

"A few members of Parliament, such as Winston Churchill, call for action, but he is an isolated figure. The British prefer to believe that everything will work out in the end. However, I think they are becoming resigned to the fact that they will have to confront Germany eventually. A program began while I was there to make enough gas masks for every citizen. Also, the Royal Air Force is being modernized with new fighter aircraft."

"What about those in Britain who would like to see their country follow the path set by Germany and Italy?"

"Mosley's fascists?" Jimmy shook his head. "Britain is too stable for that kind of political extremism to become popular. They draw people to their rallies, but I doubt if they will experience a lasting success."

Julia's questions were of a less complex nature. She wanted to hear about the shows Jimmy had seen, and what did he think of women's fashions in London? He answered his mother's questions with as much detail as he had his father's, describing at length the different styles he had seen worn.

Helen kept her questions for last. They concerned British reaction to the civil war in Spain, which Helen saw as the year's major story. Far more important than Italy's invasion of Abyssinia, or Germany's march into the demilitarized Rhineland. And certainly of greater significance—although a hundred and thirty million Americans might disagree—than Jesse Owens' triumphs in Berlin. She hadn't told her parents, but she hoped to go to Spain to report on the war. If the *World-Telegram* wouldn't send her, she'd pay her own way. The Loyalists were fighting for fairness and justice. They needed all the help they could get. In bullets or in propaganda, it didn't matter which.

At ten o'clock, Helen left to return to her Washington Square apartment. Julia went to bed. Father and son settled in the library, where Jimmy expressed his gratitude for the trip. "Thank you for my birthday present. I had an absolutely wonderful time."

Zalman tried to see if he could rattle his son's poise. "You spent sixty thousand dollars of my money in London. Did you at least get laid?"

Blushing, Jimmy slowly nodded. Zalman roared with laughter. Sixty thousand dollars had been worth that single blush.

The following morning, Jimmy was back in his office at the Rijndam Corporation, diligently reading newspapers and business magazines and compiling the report he would present to his father at five o'clock. Information manager might be a job created to keep him busy, but Jimmy firmly believed that his work was of value to his father. Zalman, in turn, might criticize his son's softness, but he could never fault his dedication.

Nor could he stop spoiling him. Soon after returning from England, Jimmy decided that no young man of his age should be living with his parents. He approached his father for the money to buy a house for himself.

Zalman was amused at his son's ambition. "Why buy? And a house as well? Why not rent an apartment as your sister does?"

"You own property. As a landlord, you make money. Why should I fill the pockets of some other landlord?"

"Find a house," Zalman said, unable to criticize his own logic. He was curious where such a proper young gentleman would choose to live. Helen felt at home among the unconventional people of Greenwich Village. With two failed marriages, and political ideas that grew daily more sympathetic to the intellectual left, she fit in perfectly. Zalman could not see Jimmy settling for the same kind of atmosphere. Jimmy understood money, even if it was his father's he spent, and not his own. He would want to be among people who shared that understanding.

Jimmy bought a redbrick house in Irving Place, in Gramercy Park. The area reminded him of a London square. His neighbors were writers, actors, painters, musicians. At night, when he drove to one of his favorite cafe society haunts, his companion in the maroon Bentley was, more often than not, one of the many attractive, arty young women who resided in the neighborhood. The sixty-thousand-dollar lay in London had sparked an appetite.

In December, Helen left for the Spanish Civil War. Her mother's protests and her father's concern had no effect. Nothing, she told them, would stop her from reporting on the struggle against fascism. Only Jimmy shared his sister's excitement. On the day she sailed, he had delivered to her cabin an enormous bouquet of flowers and a silver necklace in the shape of a horseshoe. The attached card read: "Keep upright, so your luck never runs out. Fondly, Jimmy." Helen wore the necklace all the time.

In Madrid, as Franco's rebels pounded the city, Helen took shelter in the Florida Hotel, the base for writers whose stories favored the Loyalists. There was no need to write letters to her family in New York. Her stories in the *World-Telegram* vividly depicted the sights she witnessed. And if those reports were not terrifying enough, there were always the accounts of Helen's fellow guests in the Florida: Hemingway, and Herbert L. Matthews of *The New York Times* to name but two.

Julia's defense against worry was faith. Each night and morning she prayed for her daughter's safety, for the war to end, for all mankind to live in peace. She even took to going to the temple once a week, hoping her prayers would be more acceptable coming from such a holy place.

Zalman, who scorned religion in America as strongly as he had ever done in Russia, found protection from anxiety in his work. He created even tougher schedules for himself. He made surprise inspections of his businesses, taking a perverse pleasure in the increased activity that heralded his arrival.

Even the normally frantic racing wire increased its tempo when he walked in.

The five o'clock ritual with Jimmy continued, but the rules changed. When Jimmy read, he no longer sought only news that affected his father's concerns. He was now expected to be an expert on the Spanish Civil War as well. He briefed his father on a series of setbacks for the Republicans, including the fall of Malaga—where the rebels had been aided by fifteen thousand Italian troops—the tightening grip on Madrid, and rebel gains in Bilbao. Brihuega was the only place where loyalists stemmed the tide, but that victory was soon forgotten in the savage bombing of the Basque capital of Guernica by aircraft of the Luftwaffe.

"Hundreds of farmworkers were cut down in the fields," Jimmy told his father. "German warplanes strafed the marketplace and bombed houses. According to Helen's story in the *World-Telegram,* fires burned for twenty-four hours after the raid."

"German planes bombing civilians," Zalman muttered. "Italian troops fighting at Malaga. This is a rehearsal, Jimmy. A dress rehearsal for a war between the forces of good and evil."

"Good and evil?"

"Never before has evil been defined so clearly. These instruments of the devil—Germany, Italy, and now Japan—have even formed their official alliance."

Jimmy smiled. Zalman asked what was funny. "Your reference to the devil. You always told me that there was no such thing as God, that religion was a device used by kings to keep their subjects submissive. Therefore if there is no God, it stands to reason that the devil doesn't exist, either."

"I don't believe in God, Jimmy. But I do believe in the forces of good and evil. That's what I meant by the devil. And right now, the devil's getting the upper hand."

High above Zalman's concerns for the future of the world was his anxiety for Helen. What was she doing in Spain? What drove her to be in the middle of the fighting? Did she want to wake up America? Shock it into doing something? And did the American people, reading their newspapers in the comfort of home, ever appreciate the danger reporters

310

faced to publicize the savage toll taken when the devil joined forces with modern warmaking technology? Zalman doubted it.

He just hoped that trying to awaken American consciousness did not cost his daughter her life.

Death touched Zalman a month later. At eighty-two, Henry Bladen slipped away peacefully in his sleep. He had spent the last two weeks of his life in the hospital following a stroke that had completely paralyzed his right side. Arrangements were made by Bladen's two sons, Arthur and Albert, to ship the body back to Chicago for interment next to Bladen's wife who had died eight years before.

A special train carried a hundred and fifty of Bladen's friends and associates from New York to Chicago. A postal car carrying the casket followed the engine. Behind stretched eight Pullman Glen Summits, two dining cars, and an observation car. Among the men who traveled to Chicago to pay their last respects to the newspaper magnate was Zalman. He renewed many of the connections he had made during his years with the *Messenger,* and soon the solemn trip took on the feeling of a wake, where the departed was remembered in bursts of laughter and his soul wished on its way with toasts.

After the train changed engines in Pittsburgh, Zalman went to bed in the compartment he shared with a New York state senator and a delegate from the mayor's office, who would be representing LaGuardia at the interment. He couldn't sleep. The constant drumming of wheels kept him wide-awake. As the train pulled into Cleveland, he left the compartment and entered one of the car's three drawing rooms. He sat there, contemplating how Henry Bladen's life had affected his own. Zalman had received his first real chance working with Bladen. Selling subscriptions. Then the trade-off, the death of Wilfred Hagerty for the job of circulation manager, and the influence he had used in that position to create power for himself. Zalman looked toward the front of the train, where Bladen's body rode in the postal car behind the engine. Where would I be if it hadn't been for you?

311

He wondered. Still selling toys and dolls' houses? You saved me from that, Henry Bladen, and I'll be forever grateful.

For five minutes, he had the drawing room to himself. Then he was joined by a tall, bony man with fading ginger hair and a thin mustache. His back was slightly stooped and his face wore an anxious frown. Zalman tried to summon the lightheartedness that had characterized the earlier portion of the journey.

"Stop looking so worried, Edward. Henry Bladen can't criticize your front pages anymore from where he is now."

Instead of chasing the gloom from Edward Beecham's face, Zalman's comment served only to increase it. "I was worried when he was alive. The truth is, I'm worried more now that he's dead."

Zalman sat forward in the seat, intent on the man who had replaced Jake Thomson as *Messenger* editor ten years before. Beecham had served his apprenticeship editing one of Bladen's smaller Midwest papers, and had been brought to New York on Thomson's death. Like all editors Bladen favored, Beecham believed in giving the public what it wanted. His one failure was poor timing. He was unfortunate to have been favored by Bladen when Bladen was already old, and much of his power gone.

"I sometimes feel that I was hired for the *Messenger* not as editor, but as a priest to administer last rites. It's been going down like a rock. Daily circulation's at four hundred thousand, and Sunday's down close to half a million."

Zalman shuddered. In his day, the figures had been much higher. "What would stop the decline?"

"Some good people would be one hell of a step in the right direction. I need half a dozen reporters to compete with the other papers and some money to send them where the news is happening. The other papers run exclusives from Spain, while the *Messenger* has to make do with agency reports. My budget's cut to the bone. I've barely enough staff to put out an unremarkable paper, let alone a good one. Bladen lost interest with age and illness. Word got around, and it became impossible to hire good staff. They don't want to risk their time and reputations on something that might fold. And now, with Bladen's sons taking over, it sure won't get any better."

Zalman had met Bladen's two sons, Arthur and Albert, on half a dozen different occasions. Each time they had failed to make any impression on him. They were both accountants, cardboard men who didn't have an ounce of their father's red blood between them. Zalman wondered if such men ever experienced real emotion. Had they ever really loved their wives and children? Had they ever really laughed? Had they ever known genuine fury? He suspected not.

Beecham's words echoed Zalman's thoughts. "Bladen spent his last twenty-five years in New York because his family was a disappointment. They grabbed everything and gave nothing. The moment Bladen's safely in the ground, Arthur and Albert will sell off every paper he ever owned. Mark my words, they'll take the money and run, and a great publishing empire will simply cease to exist. When you think of the blood and sweat it takes just to get one lousy edition onto the streets, you realize how much Bladen must have sweated to achieve what he did. And just like that"—he snapped his fingers with the clear, sharp sound of a pistol cocking—"it will all be gone."

Returning to the compartment he shared with the state senator and mayor's representative, Zalman dozed fitfully. He couldn't rid his mind of Beecham's misery. An editor mourning the demise of his newspaper resembled a parent grieving for a child. Zalman could appreciate Beecham's pain. He, too, had blood and toil invested in the *Messenger*.

A fleet of thirty cars and a single hearse met the train. Bladen's casket was removed from the postal car and set on the hearse. The train passengers boarded the cars. The cortege moved off. At every intersection, police cleared the way. Chicago was witnessing its biggest funeral procession since the days of Al Capone. All through the ceremony, Zalman kept his eyes on Arthur and Albert Bladen. They looked enough alike to be twins, in their fifties with gray hair and pallid faces. Neither showed the least sorrow. Their pale, lifeless blue eyes followed the casket to its resting place in the family vault. When the journey was complete, Arthur nodded as if in satisfaction.

After the service, Zalman joined the line of people forming to speak with the two brothers. He shook hands first with Arthur. "I'm Zalman Isaacson. I knew your father for thirty years and respected him greatly."

"Thank you." Arthur's eyes stared blankly at Zalman before flicking on to the next man.

Zalman received the same treatment from Albert. Neither man knew him. Neither showed any sign of recognizing his name. He joined the line again. Three minutes later, he offered his hand once more to Arthur Bladen. "I want to buy the *Messenger* and all of its assets. How much do you and your brother want?"

The answer came right back. "Eight million dollars."

Edward Beecham had been right, Zalman thought. Between Henry Bladen's death and his funeral, his sons had priced his entire empire. They had an emotion after all. Greed. "Far too much. Four million."

Ignoring the other people in the line, Arthur turned to his brother, who was shaking hands with the sheriff of Cook County. "Will we take four million for the *Messenger?*"

Albert dropped the sheriff's hand. "Five."

"Four and a half, and that's my final offer. You can reach me in New York." Zalman walked away, knowing he had succeeded in one area where Bladen had failed. He had a son who loved him. Bladen, for all his wealth, had never known that pleasure.

On the return journey to New York, Zalman sought out Edward Beecham. The editor's face was even more dismal than on the outward journey. "Did you get an opportunity to ask Arthur or Albert about the future of the *Messenger?*"

"I didn't have to ask. Arthur ran after me to say they'd already received an offer. He suggested I start thinking about another job, in case my face didn't fit with the new owners. I looked at that vault and I saw old man Bladen turning over. If he could only see what's already happening to all he worked for . . ."

Zalman didn't need to wait to hear the brothers' answer. They had already made up their minds to take his offer. He could begin to make plans. "Are you sure you didn't see him smiling?"

Beecham stared uncomprehendingly at Zalman.

"How many people do you need to run the *Messenger* properly?"

"Half a dozen reporters. Maybe a couple of good editors."

"When you get back to New York, start looking for them. And tell them that the *Messenger*'s got an owner who knows what it takes to put out a damned good newspaper. An owner who's prepared to spend money to get what he wants."

"You?"

"Me. And don't worry any more about having to run secondhand news of the Spanish Civil War. I've got just the person to give us firsthand accounts."

While Beecham mulled over the change in his fortunes, Zalman sat in the drawing room, considering the irony of life. He had traveled west on this special train to pay a final tribute to Henry Bladen. He was returning as Bladen's successor.

An even greater paradox struck him. Thirty-four years after decrying the power of the *Bessarabatz,* he owned a major daily newspaper that was every bit as influential.

Arthur and Albert Bladen contacted Zalman the day after he returned to New York. Lawyers met. Details were worked out. In return for four and a half million dollars—two million cash and two and a half million in notes—Zalman would receive the title of the New York *Messenger,* the building it had occupied since 1907 near Union Square, and all the newspaper's assets.

The final meeting took place in the boardroom on the top floor of the *Messenger* Building. Jimmy witnessed every signature his father made. Zalman noticed that Jimmy didn't look at all overawed by the occasion. The young man belonged at the table where seven-figure deals were consummated. When the last document was signed, the Bladen brothers and their lawyers left. Zalman's own advisers followed. Only Zalman and Jimmy remained.

"That office outside, Jimmy. Once it was my office. Now it's yours."

"What will I do there?"

"I haven't decided yet. There's a lot needs doing to turn

315

this paper around. I'll find you something important. But right now I want you to do me a favor and let me be by myself."

Jimmy left to sit at the desk which had once belonged to his father. In the boardroom, Zalman walked around the long table, pausing to touch each of the eight chairs, then sitting in the chair that had been Bladen's. It was in this chair, seventeen years before, that Bladen had accepted his resignation as group circulation director. And it was in this chair, twelve years before that, that Bladen had accepted a gold ring with the initials W.H.

He remained in the chair for fifteen minutes, until the imprint of his buttocks was fixed firmly into the red leather seat. Now it truly belonged to him. He got up and called for Jimmy to come back in.

"I've just made my first decisions as owner of the *Messenger*. I want you to send a wire to Helen Isaacson, Florida Hotel, Madrid. Text is as follows: 'You now work for the *Messenger*. Expect you to sever other connections immediately. File all stories attention of Zalman Isaacson, Chairman, New York *Messenger*.' And when you've done that, get a truck and some guys with muscle, and get my snooker table sent over from the Rijndam Corporation. Tell them if they have trouble fitting it in here, throw out this table. It's too damned big and pretentious for my liking anyway."

Jimmy was grinning broadly as he left the boardroom.

Zalman created a company called Messenger Publications. Into it he placed all of his publishing enterprises, with the exception of *Form Guide*. The dozen magazines and two small newspaper groups he owned now had a major daily to head them up.

Helen's reports from Spain began to appear three weeks later with a story about the Nationalist victory at Santander. By then, Zalman was working at full speed to turn the *Messenger* around. With Beecham, he wrote an editorial position declaring that the *Messenger* was the paper of the people of New York. It would fight injustice and intolerance, hypocrisy and corruption. With every word, it would support the rights of individuals.

While that promise appeared every day in the bottom left-hand corner of the front page, Zalman increased the *Messenger*'s news section by four pages. The six extra reporters hired by Beecham had strong city backgrounds. They went out seeking wrongdoings in local government. Graft had sold papers in 1907. Zalman was sure it would do the same in 1937.

With the editorial content gaining pace under Beecham's guidance, Zalman turned his attention to the one area where no one excelled him. Promotion. Using a budget of thirty thousand dollars a week, he launched a promotional blitz that shoved the *Messenger* into the public eye. Advertisements ran everywhere. Complimentary copies were delivered to homes across the city. He even overhauled a successful attention-grabber from twenty-six years earlier. In 1911, he had gone up in a balloon to launch tiny, numbered parachutes across New York. Now he went aloft in a biplane, dropping coupons to be matched against lucky numbers that would appear in the *Messenger* for the four weeks leading up to Christmas. The only person who did not like the promotion was Julia, but her dislike was not for the idea. It was for the thought of Zalman going up in the plane.

"Don't you have anyone else you can send?" she asked him.

"A job like that requires experience. I've done it before."

"You were twenty-seven then. Now you're fifty-three."

"It would not matter if I were a hundred and fifty-three. I'll never tire of doing things to sell my paper."

"Your paper?" The words threw Julia's memory down a long tunnel, to a day thirty years before when Zalman had declared how much pride and pleasure he got from seeing people read his paper.

"That's right." He held her close and kissed her. "It is my paper now."

"Did you ever believe it would be?"

He contemplated the question. "Deep down I think I always knew that one day I would own it."

"The same excitement shines now in your eyes that shone there when you worked with Jimmy Doyle." Her finger traced the contours of his face. His cheeks were sharply outlined; a fold of sagging skin softened his jawline. "Do you think he knows?"

"He knows. The day we closed, I went to the cemetery where he lies. I told him what I'd done. And I heard his Irish accent telling me to make it the best bloody paper in New York."

Julia did not poke fun at Zalman's story. He had heard Doyle's voice because he'd wanted to hear it. "What about our Jimmy? Have you found a role for him yet?"

"He's my personal assistant. He attends meetings with me—"

"He's too intelligent to be an errand boy, Zalman. Give him a chance to do more."

Zalman chuckled at the way Julia stood up for their son. She was so accustomed to Zalman criticizing Jimmy's softness that she automatically sprang to his defense. "Julia, I bought the *Messenger* for Jimmy, but I can't turn it over to him just yet. He's only twenty-two, for heaven's sake."

"You were only twenty-four, with even less experience, when Henry Bladen made you circulation manager."

"I stepped into a dead man's shoes," Zalman said quickly.

"Jimmy still deserves a chance. It's not enough that he knows you love him. He needs to know you respect him as well."

"All right. In the New Year we'll be reorganizing the *Sunday Messenger.* He'll have his chance there."

"Thank you." Julia gave Zalman a kiss. She was sure he'd be in for a pleasant surprise when Jimmy showed what he could do.

The Sunday edition of the newspaper contained a pictorial news magazine called *Cavalcade* that had not been changed in ten years. Zalman put Jimmy in charge of updating the magazine. "Give me some suggestions for a new look. Think up story ideas. I want the new *Cavalcade* out by the end of February."

Jimmy set to work enthusiastically. He discussed stories with writers and photographers. He had the art department create dummies which he showed to his father. Zalman added suggestions of his own, but on the whole he was

318

pleased with what he saw. Jimmy's appreciation of elegance was paying dividends. The new *Cavalcade* would be as classy as the old one was stale.

By early February, Jimmy had the contents for the first issue ready. He presented them at a meeting with his father and Edward Beecham. Zalman glanced through the photographs, then looked sharply at his son. "Who the hell is Andrés Segovia?"

"The world's greatest classical guitarist. He just performed at the Town Hall."

Zalman raised his eyebrows. "Has he sold as many records as Bing Crosby?"

"Quality doesn't appeal to the masses."

"Quality might not, but a newspaper damned well should!"

Jimmy defended his position. He waved a photograph under his father's nose. "Look at that expression on his face. Look at the emotion there, the love of beauty—"

"You want expression?" Zalman yelled. "You want emotion?" Grabbing Jimmy's arm, he ran him downstairs to the newsroom, motioning for Beecham to follow. Zalman started rummaging through files until he found pictures of the Luftwaffe bombing of Barcelona the previous month that had killed two hundred civilians. He shoved a batch of photographs into Jimmy's hands. In front of Beecham and a dozen shocked reporters he shouted: "That's the only kind of expression and emotion that's worth seeing! And that's the only kind I want to see!"

Jimmy looked at pictures of dead bodies stretched out and survivors staring about them in numb shock. How could his father be so callous? Only last month, when he had seen the pictures for the first time and read Helen's story about the bombing, Zalman had been frantic with worry. He had sent Helen wire after wire, urging her to put caution before the need for a good story. Now he was using the pictures of carnage as an example.

"When your classical guitar player gets mentioned in the same breath as Crosby, you can include a feature on him. A *small* feature. In the meantime, I want to see features that'll grab people's attention, not send them to sleep."

Head down, Jimmy walked away. Zalman turned to the reporters who had watched him chew out his son. "What are you lot gawking at? Nothing worth writing about today?" When they hurriedly returned to their typewriters and telephones, Zalman looked at Beecham and winked. "I've got a daughter who's one hell of a newspaperman. I'm going to make one out of my son as well."

Cavalcade came out every Sunday with Jimmy's name as editor. When he was lucky, he managed to squeeze in a short pictorial essay about an art exhibit. Most of the space, though, went to Zalman's idea of what the readers wanted to see. One Sunday, the magazine carried a grisly color spread entitled "Night Out With the Police," which showed in gory detail accident victims, a man burned to death in a house fire, and blood pouring from a robber fatally wounded in a shootout with police. The next edition gave subscribers an in-depth look at Sing Sing's death row. The cameraman even sat in the electric chair to take a photograph called "Murderer's Last View," while an artist graphically depicted every detail of a man writhing in the current's grip. Zalman could never hope to eclipse the *Daily News* front page of ten years earlier, when a photographer in the death chamber had strapped a camera to his ankle to capture the execution of a murderess named Ruth Snyder. But he came close.

Jimmy wondered why he seemed to be the only member of the staff who was out of step. He was interested in quality, while everyone's else's priority was quantity. Edward Beecham agreed with everything Zalman suggested, and Zalman almost always concurred with Beecham's ideas. Either walking the floors of the *Messenger* Building or hunched over Zalman's snooker table, the men batted ideas back and forth to push circulation higher. Only Jimmy was convinced that their concepts belonged in the jazz-journalism era of the twenties. Those days were finished. Readers wanted a responsible press now, not a sensational one. They wanted to be informed and educated, not shocked and titillated. Or so Jimmy thought . . .

Zalman and Beecham's favorite targets were city and state government departments for whose excesses the taxpayers of

New York footed the bill. The paper attacked the park commissioner's office for building playgrounds in every part of New York except Harlem, Stuyvesant Heights, and South Jamaica. "Don't Negro Children Have the Right to Play?" thundered one headline. It unearthed scandals in the city's sanitation and transportation departments. It forced an investigation into promotion practices at the fire department. Only one agency was spared editorial wrath. Zalman forbade Beecham to let his reporters loose on the police. Police cooperation, assured with payoffs, allowed bookmakers to operate. Bookmakers, in turn, were the lifeblood of the Sporting News Agency, and staunch supporters of *Form Guide*. A million-dollar fraud could take place in the police department, and the *Messenger* would look the other way.

Despite Jimmy's pessimism, the mix of promotional stunts and crusading stories yielded the results Zalman expected. By the end of March, seven months after the change of ownership, daily circulation had risen from the low of four hundred thousand to a new high approaching six hundred thousand. The Sunday edition now sold almost seven hundred thousand. The newspaper wasn't making money yet, but it was on the right track. Zalman was pleased enough with the results to let Jimmy include in *Cavalcade* a preview of the new Cloisters Building in Fort Tryon Park, scheduled to open in eight weeks time. To balance such cultural exposure, Zalman preceded the Cloisters piece with a spread of pictures smuggled from Moscow showing the executions of eighteen men charged with subversion.

Helen wrote her last report from Spain in April. The war was going badly for the Loyalists. As hard as she tried, she found it increasingly difficult to send back encouraging news. With German might thrown behind Franco's rebels, the end was in sight.

It came for Helen at Tortosa, on the Mediterranean coast. She was there to write about the American Lincoln-Washington Battalion. What she wrote was an epitaph as Nationalist forces crushed the American volunteers.

She returned home aboard the *Queen Mary* at the end of May. Zalman went to meet her at the dock. He spotted her

321

high up at the rail, auburn hair standing out like a blazing beacon against the white backdrop. He waved, happy beyond measure that after seventeen months his daughter had returned. And then, as she came down the ramp, his stomach began to tremble. She wasn't walking. She sat in a wheelchair, dependent on the Cunard officer who gently pushed her. She held her arms out to her father. Zalman bent to kiss her.

"What the hell are you doing in a wheelchair?"

"The bullets at Tortosa weren't selective. I got hit twice."

He touched her right leg, swatched in plaster of Paris. "Who patched you up?"

"The Nationalists."

"Franco's fascists?"

"Amazing, isn't it? They took me prisoner, along with what remained of the Lincoln-Washington Battalion. The bone was shattered. They treated me and put me out of the country, across the French border. They realized I was a reporter and let me go, I think, to score some points over here."

"Spanish doctors?" Zalman shook his head. "We'll get that leg checked right away."

"I didn't trust them, either. I had it examined while I was in London. I'm going to be in a wheelchair for a couple of months, then I'll be as good as new." She pulled her father down and kissed him again. "God, I never thought it would feel so good to be home again."

Zalman took Helen back to the Fifth Avenue townhouse. Julia saw the wheelchair and shrieked. "You've got dozens of other reporters working for you, Zalman. Why did you have to send Helen where there's a war going on?"

"He didn't send me anywhere," Helen said. "I volunteered."

"If your father ever lets you write about anything more dangerous than a church fete, he'll have me to deal with."

Helen stayed at the townhouse for three months. Once the plaster was removed, she started therapy to rebuild the wasted muscles. She walked every day in the park and exercised strenuously. A slight limp remained. Zalman made appointments with specialists. They all told him the same.

322

The right leg, the injured leg, was marginally shorter than the left. She could compensate for it easily enough by wearing a built-up right shoe.

"Goddamned Spanish doctors," Zalman muttered.

In August, Helen returned to her apartment in Greenwich Village. She felt strong enough to be on her own once more. She went to work at the *Messenger* for Edward Beecham. Zalman told the editor to make certain that she was not assigned to anything remotely dangerous; he was still catching hell from Julia about Helen coming home in a wheelchair.

Mostly, Julia was concerned that Helen, nearing thirty, was still single. She worried that the two failed marriages, to Jerome Wolfe and Alan Levine, had soured her daughter against marrying a third time. Zalman, eager to soothe his wife's concerns, smiled and answered that when the time was right, Helen would fall in love again. He just wished he felt as confident as he sounded. Jerome Wolfe's accusation that Zalman had set Helen impossibly high standards was never far away.

It wasn't Helen who fell in love, however. It was Jimmy. In the middle of November, he began dating an up-and-coming Broadway actress called Lee Robins. A tall blonde with stunning violet eyes, Lee was two years older, but age did not matter. At the newspaper, or, for that matter, in any situation controlled by his father, Jimmy might suffer feelings of inferiority. Away from his father's scrutiny, he carried himself with a dignity and sophistication that most men twice his age never attained.

Lee had a small role in a play at the Morosco. Two or three times a week, Jimmy took her out after the show. By Christmas week, they had been dating for a month. Jimmy had bought her several gifts, among them a sapphire necklace to match the color of her eyes, and Lee was happily anticipating this wealthy young man continuing to be her generous lover for some time to come.

After a Saturday-night performance, Jimmy and Lee visited the Cub Room at the Stork Club. Next to their table sat another young couple whom Jimmy knew, Ira Schatz and his wife, Paula. Ira was a tall, dark, intense-looking lawyer. In contrast, Paula appeared not to have a care in the world, a young woman who smiled and laughed at the slightest pretext. Jimmy introduced Lee to the Schatzes. They had seen the play at the Morosco a week earlier, and complimented Lee for her part in it.

As they spoke, another person sat at the Schatzes' table. "This is my cousin, Sonya Cushman from Montreal," Paula said. "Sonya turned twenty-one last week. She's celebrating by doing the grand tour of New York."

Jimmy stood up, hand outstretched. "Sonya, I'm delighted to make your acquaintance." His first impression was that Paula's cousin was one of the most beautiful young women he had ever seen. Dark-brown hair curled gently to shoulders left bare by a black evening gown. Her face was heart-shaped, lips full and moist beneath a fine, straight nose. Dark-brown eyes smiled a greeting. His second impression, made only moments after the first, was that Sonya Cushman was *the* most beautiful young woman he had ever seen.

When Jimmy sat down again, he paid little attention to his own date. He spoke across the space separating the tables. "I understand that Montreal, with its European influence, is a very handsome city."

"It is. You should visit. But not now, not in winter."

"How long do you plan on staying in New York?"

"Until the New Year. Paula has arranged many things for me."

Jimmy gazed reproachfully at Paula. "I hope you aren't taking up every minute of your cousin's time. That would be most unfair, you know."

"Sonya's an adult, Jimmy. If she chose to do something on her own, I couldn't stop her."

Jimmy felt a hand touch his arm. "Remember me?"

Jimmy blushed. The last thing he had intended was to slight Lee, but he had been so smitten by the girl from Montreal. "I'm terribly sorry. Truly I am."

"That's all right." Even as he spoke to her, Lee could see his mind was elsewhere. She knew it was time to rethink plans, start afresh. "I think I just heard my exit cue, Jimmy. The role was fun while it lasted, but any good performer knows it's fatal to overstay a welcome. Good luck."

She stood up to leave. Jimmy grabbed her arm. For a

moment she thought he might beg her to stay. "Let me give you cab fare home." He peeled off a fifty from a roll of bills.

"Always the gentleman, Jimmy. Always the gentleman."

Before Lee had gone five paces, Jimmy had returned his attention to the Schatzes' table.

"Ten thousand men would give their right arm for what you just sent home," Ira Schatz remarked.

Jimmy smiled. Only if they hadn't seen Sonya.

"Why don't you join us?" Paula said. "You look kind of silly sitting there all by yourself."

Jimmy took the chair next to Sonya. At first she felt vaguely uncomfortable at the attention paid to her by this young man with the round smiling face and the warm brown eyes. No man had ever sent a date packing on her behalf before. Certainly not an attractive actress. But then her young men had not been in New York; they'd been in Montreal. Slowly, the discomfort changed to interest, and soon the two young people were unaware of anyone but each other.

The waiter presented the check. Ira paid it, then coughed to attract Sonya's attention. "Paula and I are leaving . . ."

"I'll escort Sonya home," Jimmy offered instantly. He sensed Paula's uncertainty. She felt responsible for her Canadian cousin. "If Sonya's visiting New York, don't you think it's only fair that she sees the city at its best? At night? We won't be late, don't worry."

Jimmy and Sonya left shortly after the Schatzes. From the Stork Club, they went dancing at El Morocco. Holding Sonya tenderly, Jimmy covered the floor. He considered himself an excellent dancer; this time, knowing he would be judged by everything he did, he went out of his way to be better than excellent. When Sonya complimented him, he shrugged modestly and replied that his partner made him look good.

From El Morocco, Jimmy drove Sonya to Ira and Paula Schatz's East Side apartment. Outside the building, they sat in the Bentley and talked. Sonya spoke of Montreal, where she lived with her parents in the Outremont district. "That means the other side of the mountain."

"What mountain?" Jimmy asked.

"Mount Royal, after which the city is named."

"Of course. Mont Real." Jimmy nodded his head and waited for Sonya to continue. He enjoyed listening to her talk; her accent was refreshing.

She spoke about her family. Her father owned a clothing factory in Montreal. Her mother was active in charity work. Her only brother, three years older than herself, worked with her father in the factory. Jimmy knew he could have been listening to the story of any family in New York, but Sonya made it sound far more interesting. The entire family spoke French as well as English. Jimmy like that; it demonstrated a cosmopolitan attitude toward life.

The outside chill entered the car. Sonya shivered. Jimmy helped her out of the Bentley and walked her into the lobby of the apartment building. At the elevator, he kissed her good night. All the way back to Gramercy Park, he thought about her. He had started the evening with one date—a Broadway actress for whom ten thousand men would give their right arm—and he'd finished it with another. As far as he was concerned, he'd made one hell of a deal.

The last thing he did before going to bed was write a note in his diary to telephone Sonya the following day. As if he could have forgotten. He'd been in love with her from the moment Lee Robins had walked out. Picking up the diary again, he wrote in parentheses next to Sonya's name: "The girl I'm going to marry."

Sonya remained in New York until the third day of January. Jimmy saw her every evening. He took her dancing and to the theater. On New Year's Eve, she attended a party at his Gramercy Park home that had been planned a month before. She acted as his hostess, a role Lee Robins would have filled had not she and Jimmy gone to the Stork Club that Saturday night. Everyone asked Jimmy who the dark-haired girl was. "A very dear friend from Montreal," he answered, always emphasizing the "very dear."

On the evening before Sonya returned to Montreal, Jimmy took her to his parents' home for dinner. He made no bones about the reason for the invitation. "I want to see if they approve of you as much as I do."

The bold statement unnerved Sonya. Until now, she had looked on the relationship as a little added spice to her vacation, a romantic interlude that would end when she boarded the train. Jimmy was the most interesting man she had ever met, cultured, sophisticated, equally at home discussing a Renoir in an art gallery or a bottle of 1928 Margaux at "21." Nonetheless, she had no intention of taking the friendship further.

Zalman and Julia did approve of Sonya. They thought Jimmy had brought her home for the obvious reason, and they went out of their way to make her welcome. Julia asked if Sonya thought she would find life in New York much different than Montreal. Before she could answer that question by saying she had no intention of finding out, Zalman said, "No wonder Jimmy thinks you're special. You're the first girl he's dated who's not an actress, singer, or musician."

Sonya became flustered under all the attention, but not so unsettled that she failed to notice the change that came over Jimmy. He seemed to shrink in stature. The suave habitué of cafe society became, in his father's presence, an uncertain young man. In all their dates, he had shown a sharp wit and a keen understanding of many subjects. Now he was quiet, speaking only when spoken to. Just once did he interrupt his father. That was when Zalman jokingly offered Sonya a job.

"When you go back home, you can work for me. You can check how my business interests in Montreal are doing."

"You have interests in Montreal?"

"One of my father's newspapers is sold all over North America," Jimmy said quickly. "*Form Guide,* it's a racing paper."

"You publish that, Mr. Isaacson?"

Zalman nodded. He knew why Jimmy had dived in so quickly. To cut his father off before he could mention the racing wire that went into Montreal. Jimmy did not mind Sonya knowing about *Form Guide,* but the wire was too risky. Zalman could appreciate that; he tried to keep his own family isolated from it.

The following morning, Jimmy saw Sonya off at Grand Central Station. As she leaned through the window to kiss him good-bye, he said; "Have dinner with me next Saturday."

"I can't. I don't know when I'll be back in New York."

"I meant in Montreal. I'll come up."

"Just to have dinner with me?"

"Just to see you."

Sonya didn't know how to answer. While she thought about it, the train began to move. "If you don't meet me at the station," Jimmy yelled, "I'll be hopelessly lost."

Sonya met him the following Saturday in Montreal. By doing so, she understood that the idea of Jimmy as an enjoyable part of her New York vacation was no longer true. No girl could afford to treat the pursuit of such a charming young man as nothing more than an amusing interlude. The Jimmy Isaacsons of the world were too few and far between to be regarded in such cavalier fashion.

On Saturday night, they ate dinner in Jimmy's hotel room. As they finished, he gave Sonya a small velvet-covered box. Inside was a diamond brooch in the shape of a butterfly. She pinned it to her dark-green dress.

Jimmy spent Sunday at the home of Sonya's family in Outremont. Her parents, Ben and Sarah Cushman, wanted to meet the suitor who had traveled all the way from New York to be with their daughter. Even her brother, Joseph, turned up for a look. Jimmy felt like a soldier on parade. The Cushmans, finding it fascinating that Jimmy's father owned a daily newspaper, asked a whole succession of questions about it. Every so often, Joseph, a tall, powerfully built young man who had played football for McGill University, tried to swing the conversation around to *Form Guide.* He often went to the track, he explained, and found the racing paper of enormous help. Each time he raised the subject, Jimmy directed conversation back to the *Messenger.* He wanted to impress Sonya's parents. The mention of gambling would do the opposite. He could always impress Joseph later.

He left by Pullman that night to return to New York. Sonya accompanied him to the station. "Same situation, different roles," Jimmy joked as he prepared to board the train. "Will you be here to meet me next weekend?"

Sonya's heart leaped. "You're coming again?" Surprised

that Jimmy would consider making another such trip filled her voice. Then she revealed how she had hoped for such an event by saying, "My parents want you to be their guest next time. There is more than enough room at the house."

"Thank them for me. I'd be delighted to accept."

Jimmy repeated the journey the following weekend, and the weekend after that. Each time, Sonya met him, brown eyes alight with joy and excitement. When they parted on Sunday evening, no matter how brave a smile she wore, her eyes reflected sadness.

At the beginning of February, after four successive weekends on the train, Jimmy told Sonya he could not continue. "Customs officers are becoming suspicious of me. They see me so often they think I'm running the biggest smuggling racket in North America. Only they haven't figured out what I'm smuggling yet."

"Tell them you're smuggling love."

"I've got a better idea. Why don't we get married and let the customs officers get on with their work?"

They were married at the end of March at the same synagogue where Jimmy's own parents had been married thirty-three years earlier, New York's Temple Emmanu-el. Though the temple had moved uptown since the old days, there was still a comforting sense of continuity. A party was held at the Hotel Pierre. As a wedding gift, Zalman made Jimmy an officer of the Rijndam Corporation. Other than countersigning checks, he had no real function there. The promotion was as much a gift from Zalman to Julia as it was to Jimmy.

Coincidentally, Jimmy's and Sonya's marriage took place on the same day as the marriage of Clark Gable to Carole Lombard. Zalman made sure his son got better billing in the *Messenger* by having Jimmy's wedding photograph—*Cavalcade* Editor Ties Knot to Canadian Beauty—placed above Gable and Lombard's.

Marrying Sonya was the first thing Jimmy had ever done of which Zalman approved wholeheartedly. Being married might just make a man out of him.

Jimmy and Sonya honeymooned for two weeks at Havana's Hotel Nacional. They returned in the middle of

April to a New York completing preparations for the 1939 World's Fair. The gold Trylon and the crystal-ball Perisphere stood ready. Final touches were made to welcome the millions of visitors who would tour the world of tomorrow.

The attention of most New Yorkers, however, was not on the upcoming spectacle at Flushing Meadows. Nor were they concerned with Italy's invasion of Albania, the mutual-aid treaty between Britain and Poland, or Holland's reinforcing of its border with Germany, all signs of Europe's drift toward war. What thrilled New Yorkers in the spring of 1939 were the juicy findings of the McKinnon Committee.

Charles McKinnon was a Kansas senator who headed a year-long investigation into criminal infiltration and control of industry. The committee had completed its work a month before, and was now revealing its findings. For many in the New York area, where much of the investigation had focused, the report constituted a trip down memory lane. Following the repeal of Prohibition almost six years before, familiar names had disappeared from the pages of newspapers. Anastasia, Adonis, Costello, Genovese, Lepke, Siegel, Zwillman, and a hundred other such names had ceased to be the household words they were during the free and easy days of Prohibition. Under the McKinnon Committee, many old names resurfaced. Stories of union corruption, blackmail, protection, and extortion titillated newspaper readers. Circulation soared as extra editions were run off each time a committee member opened his mouth and mentioned a name.

One name appeared far more prominently than most. That name was Charlie Bruno . . .

Jimmy went back to work the day after returning from Cuba. He felt the excitement sweeping through the *Messenger* Building. Reporters sat with telephones jammed to their ears as they followed leads. Edward Beecham impatiently awaited each new fact, each new name pulled from the McKinnon hat. Only Zalman seemed aloof from the frenzy. He sat in the *Messenger* boardroom with a worried expression on his face.

"Why do you look so unhappy?" Jimmy asked when he saw his father for the first time. "You should be delirious with all the extra papers you're selling over this McKinnon Report."

Zalman's response was an angry "What the hell do you know about selling papers?"

Jimmy jumped back as though he had been struck. What kind of welcome home was this?

Zalman calmed down. "I'm sorry, Jimmy. It's just . . ." He indicated a pile of newspaper clippings scattered across the snooker table. Every headline mentioned Charlie Bruno's name. "I'm just waiting for the other shoe to fall."

"I don't understand."

"Charlie once told me he never threw his friends to the wolves unless by doing so he could save his own neck."

Jimmy still didn't comprehend. "What could he throw you to the wolves about?"

Zalman's face relaxed in a smile, but it was the expression a brave man might give as he lay beneath the guillotine. "I've spent the last twenty-four years keeping you from finding out."

Jimmy asked his mother, then his sister for the meaning of Zalman's words. Both women shook their heads. Zalman had concealed the nitty-gritty of his dealings from his wife and daughter as efficiently as he had concealed them from his son.

The McKinnon Committee turned over its findings to the attorney general's office. Federal lawyers began to build cases; where hard evidence of specific crimes was difficult to obtain, they settled for tax-evasion charges. The case against Bruno was the easiest of all to build. Sitting high at the top of the pile, he was an obvious target. Testimony implicated him in a dozen crimes, including construction union vote-rigging, a restaurant protection racket that passed itself off as a trade association, and the bombing of a coat company that competed too successfully with a manufacturer in which he had an interest. A grand jury indicted him on ten counts. Press reports claimed that enough proof existed to put Bruno away for life.

Charlie Bruno examined the prospect of spending the remainder of his days behind bars and didn't like what he saw. Two weeks after the indictment, he summoned his attorneys.

"Don't fight the case," he ordered them. "Just find out what kind of a deal you can make."

The attorney general's men laughed at the offer. Bruno, they said, had no cards to deal with. He sent back another message. Maybe he had no bargaining power on the charges he faced, but he could recite chapter and verse on illegal gambling. "I used to run a racing wire before I had to get out of it," he told a suddenly interested audience.

"What made you get out of it?"

"I squared up against a guy smarter than me."

A deal was made. In return for information, a recommendation for leniency would be made. Bruno began to talk. The government lawyers listened to him describe the history of the racing wire, how the Sporting News Agency once owned by Giuseppe Salerno had been expanded through intimidation and coercion to incorporate all small wires into one continent-wide system. They smiled understandingly when Bruno related how the SNA had outwitted him by feeding his customers delayed results. Lawyers could appreciate foresight and cunning more than any other profession.

After Bruno finished talking, the lawyers were still smiling. Cooperation existed between the branches of government, and Bruno had given them plenty to cooperate on. Internal Revenue Service investigators took up the baton. They spent the summer studying information about the SNA. Then they studied *Form Guide* and Zalman's other business interests. They passed on information to the Federal Bureau of Investigation. Some of Zalman's methods of promoting his own concerns seemed to violate antitrust laws.

The other shoe began to fall.

On the day war erupted in Europe, a team of IRS agents entered the offices of the Rijndam Corporation and demanded to see the books. Other agents descended on Zalman's Fifth Avenue townhouse and the Glen Cove estate, seeking more records.

The tax agents were not made welcome at the Rijndam offices. When the chief investigator, a man named Lawrence Cohen, requested space in which to work, he was given a utility room in which cleaning equipment was kept. Sitting at a table surrounded by mops and brooms, Cohen and his team waded through sets of books, compiling a list of discrepancies that indicated fraud.

As the inspection progressed, Zalman's health betrayed him. All his life he had been a fit, energetic man. The tax problems sapped his spirit, as if he understood that he faced a problem his strength and shrewdness alone could not resolve. He lost weight. In six weeks his face became gaunt, his skin ashen, his eyes, behind gold-rimmed glasses, more deeply sunk than ever.

Julia became concerned with the physical change. "Zalman, you look terrible. Please see a doctor."

Zalman hated doctors. The last time he had seen one was five years ago, when influenza had temporarily deprived him of the vitality to go to work. "No doctor can help with what I've got."

Julia's face paled. "What have you got?"

"Aggravation. Julia, I always dreamed of spending the latter part of my life as a respectable businessman, not some two-bit operator with his finger in a thousand pies. What's more respectable, I ask you, than being publisher of a daily newspaper? It was something worthwhile I could leave to Jimmy. Now, instead of being allowed to enjoy my success, I've got the FBI trying to build an antitrust case against me, and Treasury Department sleuths going through my records with a fine comb."

"What will they find?".

Zalman made no reply. To Julia, his silence was more terrifying than any answer could have been.

The Internal Revenue Service won the race. Lawrence Cohen's team of investigators assembled a tax-evasion case to take to the grand jury before the FBI could decide on an antitrust suit. Six men were named in the action. Zalman. Mario and Luigi Salerno, his partners in the Sporting News Agency. Bill Regan and Frank Brennan, Zalman's longtime associates who, between them, owned thirty percent of the equity of *Form Guide* and were officers of the Rijndam Corporation. And Jimmy.

Immediately, the Salerno brothers offered to assist the

333

government and make reparations of any taxes they owed. The offer was accepted.

Zalman cared little about the Salernos' defection. While they had been useful, he had never regarded them as anything more than junior partners taken on in a sentimental moment. He was the government's main target, and if the Salernos wanted to protect themselves, who could blame them? But he was horrified at Jimmy's involvement. That came as a total shock and was decidedly unfair. His son's recent presence on the Rijndam board was a token gesture, a salve for Julia. Jimmy had as much to do with the actual running of the company as the window cleaner.

The grand jury convened in May. Government lawyers claimed that between 1931 and 1937, Zalman had concealed eight million dollars of income from the Sporting News Agency. In that same period, Zalman, Brennan, and Regan had failed to report another four million dollars income from *Form Guide.* More allegations followed: hundreds of thousands of dollars worth of gifts disguised as legitimate expenses; vacations paid for out of business funds; the short-lived winter home in Miami Beach charged as renovation work to a New York office building; weekly housekeeping costs of four hundred dollars billed to *Form Guide* as racing expenses; Jimmy's home in Gramercy Park concealed as a write-off of worthless property to Zalman's real-estate company. Zalman, Brennan, and Regan showed no emotion, but Jimmy flinched at each accusation. He couldn't believe that the father he worshipped could be guilty of such dishonesty. Instead of driving a wedge between father and son, however, each new barb only served to increase Jimmy's devotion.

The accused men's lawyers claimed that no duplicity had ever been intended. Zalman's attorney, a graduate of Harvard Law School named Bernard French, admitted that his client did owe back taxes, but this was due to an error caused by sloppy bookkeeping that had failed to keep pace with the swift expansion of the business. The members of the grand jury were unimpressed by the excuse. Government attorneys celebrated with tight-lipped smiles as the grand jury indicted all four men.

The next week, Zalman, Jimmy, Brennan, and Regan surrendered to federal authorities in New York. They were formally charged with income tax evasion, fingerprinted, and released on bail, pending a trial date. It was the most degrading experience of Zalman's life. As badly as he felt for himself, he felt even worse for his son, who stood like a robot—face torn with pain and embarrassment—as a deputy marshal inked his fingers and rolled them on the card. Nothing in Jimmy's sheltered, spoiled life had prepared him for this degradation.

As they drove away from the federal building, Zalman turned to Jimmy. "I'd give everything I own to avoid you being put through this. I made some mistakes, but I never meant to hurt you in any way."

Tears shone in Jimmy's eyes. In the stress of the moment, he reverted to the ponderous formality of his youth. "I understand that, sir."

Zalman blinked back tears of his own. He held little hope for his own future, but he had to find a way for Jimmy to avoid further prosecution. A public trial would leave scars. A prison sentence would destroy Jimmy. He would never live to enjoy the respectability his father had planned for him.

A trial was set for February, seven months in the future. Zalman tried to forget about his troubles by throwing himself into his business. Many loose ends needed to be tied up. The first thing was to rid himself of the majority interest in the Sporting News Agency. He cursed the wire service as the cause of his troubles. His family had been right to fight him over it; he should have listened to them. The only offer came from Mario and Luigi Salerno, who owned the other forty percent. Zalman held no grudge against the brothers. Besides, he needed quick cash. He sold them his share for eight hundred thousand dollars.

He sold his interests in news distributorships, and hurriedly liquidated his real-estate holdings at a loss. By Christmas, he had almost five million dollars in cash. More than enough, he hoped, for his plan to spare Jimmy the trauma of a trial. He summoned Bernard French, the attorney who had represented him before the grand jury. Although only in his late thirties, French had acted for Zalman for more than five years. Zalman liked the thin, bespectacled young man

335

enough to engage him for this matter over older, more highly qualified lawyers.

"The trial's two months away. What chance have I got in front of a jury?"

"The best we can hope for is fifty percent."

"Even money? Those are lousy odds." Zalman recalled another well-publicized tax trial: that of Al Capone, who had pleaded not guilty to far lesser charges and received eleven years. "Bernard, you know how I feel about Jimmy. He's my only son. To spare him this ordeal, I'm willing to make a deal with the government."

"What kind of a deal?"

"I'll accept all responsibility for tax violations as long as the charges against Jimmy are dropped. I'll plead guilty, offer to make payment on what I owe, and serve whatever time the judge gives me. A year or two in jail is worth it to me."

"Have you talked this over with anyone? With your wife? Your daughter? Jimmy?"

Zalman shook his head. "They'd all fight me. The last thing I need is division in the family as well. I'll present it to them as a *fait accompli.*"

French met with representatives of the IRS commissioner's office. He presented Zalman's deal and offered a settlement of two million dollars. He returned to Zalman with mixed news.

"They'll deal all right. For you to plead guilty, they'll drop all charges against Jimmy and the other defendants, Brennan and Regan. But they want eleven million dollars in back taxes, interest, and penalties."

Zalman was stunned. He had stripped and sold businesses to come up with almost five million. To find another six million meant selling off even more. You never got a good price when you sold in a hurry. "Bargain with them," he told French.

The attorney offered three million. The Treasury agents came back with ten and a half million. The negotiations continued over the course of two weeks, a hundred thousand here, ten thousand there. The largest moves were always made by French; the smallest by the government. At last French returned to Zalman with a final offer.

"Eight and a half million. They won't go lower. If you refuse eight and a half, they'll proceed with the case against all four defendants."

Zalman sighed. He'd have to mortgage his remaining companies. If he dropped dead now, at fifty-five, he wouldn't leave Jimmy respectability; he'd leave him a pile of debts. What kind of legacy was that?

"What do you want me to do?" French asked quietly.

"Accept their offer," Zalman answered in a dull voice. "It's the best we'll get."

The deal was made. Four million dollars up front, the remainder to be paid off over the next five years. Zalman told his family what he had done. Before any of them could argue, he said; "If I'd fought the charges, I might have been far worse off."

"You might have been cleared," Helen said.

Zalman shook his head. "The government is too determined to crucify me to let that happen."

"How long do you think . . ." Julia started to ask.

"A year, perhaps two. You'll be able to visit me every week. It'll be like when we were dating each other."

To please Zalman, Julia forced a smile on her face.

Only Jimmy said nothing. He sat motionless in the chair, staring at his father. Zalman understood exactly what was going through his mind. Jimmy was horrified that his father had made this sacrifice on his behalf. Sure, Brennan and Regan had slipped away as well, but the taxmen hadn't been interested in them. They were only supporting players. Zalman had agreed to pay a massive fine and spend time in jail just to help Jimmy, and Jimmy wasn't sure he was worth such a sacrifice.

Jimmy sat next to his father during the court proceedings. Every so often, he placed a hand on Zalman's shoulder, offering support. Each time, Zalman turned and nodded appreciatively.

Now that the uncertainty was over, Zalman's appearance had improved. He had regained some of the weight he'd dropped. His skin had lost the pallid color. He even joked to

337

reporters during one recess that he was looking forward to a short vacation at the taxpayer's expense.

"When this is all over, I'll be the biggest taxpayer around, so you could say I'll be paying for my own room and board."

The joking stopped when sentence was handed down. Zalman had already accepted the eight and a half million dollars. The prison sentence jolted him. No agreement existed on that. Instead of the two years maximum he thought he would get, the judge handed out four years.

Zalman heard Jimmy's sudden intake of breath. He squeezed his son's arm reassuringly. If Jimmy was ever going to show that he was Zalman Isaacson's son, there was no better time than now.

The sentence was to be served at the federal penitentiary closest to New York—Lewisburg, in Pennsylvania. Zalman made his farewells to his family. He kissed Julia and held her tightly. Then Helen. Finally he came to Jimmy, who had tears glistening in his eyes. Zalman hoped his son wasn't about to cry.

"I'm leaving you a real mess, but you'll have plenty of help. If you've got problems on the *Messenger,* Edward Beecham's your man. Anything on *Form Guide,* see Frank Brennan or Bill Regan. Any legal problems, Bernard French'll be there. And once a week, you see me. Don't forget, I might be a guest of Uncle Sam, but I'm still running the show."

Jimmy threw his arms around his father. Embarrassed by the show of affection, Zalman tried to fight him off. In the end, he hugged him back. "Jimmy," he whispered, "if all this doesn't make you start shouldering responsibility, nothing will."

When Zalman had gone, Jimmy walked between his mother and his sister, an arm around each woman's shoulders. His father's last words weighed heavily on him. He was the man of the family now. He had to start proving it right away.

Chapter Thirteen

Early in August 1940, eleven months after the outbreak of war, Germany launched an intense air assault on British coastal defenses. In the middle of the month, the attack switched to inland airfields. Bombs fell for sixteen consecutive days as the Luftwaffe tried to destroy the Royal Air Force and set the stage for Operation Sea Lion—the invasion of Britain. When that failed, the Nazi high command used lessons it had learned in Spain and refined at Warsaw and Rotterdam: that indiscriminate bombing of civilians destroyed the will to resist. In the first week of September, London's enormous civilian population became the target for Herman Goering's Luftwaffe. The blitz began.

Rachel's three sons begged her to leave London. She refused. "German bombs are falling everywhere. Why should one place be safer than another? Besides, no one is going to drive me from my home a second time. I'll leave here when I'm ready, not a moment before." When Manny, Sidney, and Bernard argued that she had no reason to stay in the city, she told them they were crazy. "My family is in London. What do you mean I have no reason to stay?"

The three brothers ceased trying to change their mother's mind, and Rachel remained where she was.

When she first heard sirens, Rachel ran to the bottom floor of the house, where the parlor and dining room were located. Built partly below ground, it was the safest place; only a direct hit would cause damage there. As the bombing increased, she took to sleeping in the parlor, while Bernard made a bed for himself in the dining room.

Most nights she slept well, certain that a bomb would never hit the house. At least, not as long as she had the scrap of red ribbon stitched to her nightdress, and the gold-and-enamel watch and the copper penny with Edward the Seventh's likeness beneath her pillow. Rachel was convinced the talismans really worked, because the closest anything fell was three hundred yards away. An incendiary bomb dropped onto a building in a short residential street called Stannard Road. The builder who rushed out from the house opposite to extinguish the fire received no mention in any newspaper. Such courage and tenacity were too commonplace to merit special attention in the fall of 1940.

One night at the beginning of October, when aircraft activity was particularly busy, Rachel couldn't sleep at all. She lay for an hour listening to the drone of planes overhead, the thunder of antiaircraft fire from nearby batteries, and the crash of bombs. At last she got up and looked into the dining room. There was no sign of Bernard. She climbed the stairs to the middle floor, and then the top. She found her youngest son standing at the open window, viewing the aerial battle through binoculars. He handed them to his mother. She watched a German bomber frantically trying to wriggle free from the embrace of three spotlights, while all around it antiaircraft shells exploded; then she lowered the glasses to study the red glow filling the horizon. The docks in the East End were ablaze. She wondered if the building that had housed Tobias Dekker's club still stood. Or was that just a pile of rubble now, like so much else of London?

"Do you remember Tobias and Hannah, Bernard?"

"Of course I do."

"One day they came to this house in a new car. A bright yellow car."

"We went for a ride in it, all of us."

"That's right." Rachel was amazed that Bernard remembered so well. He couldn't have been five at the time. "Later that day we sat in the parlor, discussing over tea the possibility of war with Germany and Austria-Hungary. A war with motor cars instead of horses. I recall saying that the generals

340

would probably be able to find some devastating use for aircraft, like dropping rocks on each other's heads." She stopped talking while a series of thunderous explosions from two miles away made the ground tremble. "I wish I'd been right," she said, handing back the glasses, "and rocks were all they dropped."

Instead of returning to bed, Rachel sat up in the parlor. Thirty-five years she'd spent in this house. Thirty-five years, and now two world wars. She recalled changes she'd witnessed in the neighborhood. The biggest one, surely, had been the ripping up of the streetcar tracks, and the replacement with macadam of the tar-covered wooden road surface. What a day that had been! She smiled at the memory. Like a carnival, the street crowded with local people pushing wheelbarrows full of tarred wood blocks home for their fireplaces. No one had gone cold that winter.

Thirty-five years! On the day she had inspected this house with Jacob, while the first Emmanuel grew inside her, could she have ever dreamed she would remain so long? Four children had been born here. Four sons. Three had grown to manhood. Two had left. One remained. Rachel knew why Bernard stayed. Not because he liked the old-fashioned house in which he'd grown up, or because he didn't have money for a place of his own. He could easily afford a nice flat in a good part of town. He simply refused to let his mother live by herself. Repeatedly she told him that she wasn't really alone; a woman came in twice a week to clean. Bernard wouldn't listen, though. Until he married, to begin a family of his own, he would not desert his mother.

The entire family got together once a week, on Friday night, when Rachel's children visited for dinner. Even during the bombing, public transport remained remarkably efficient, which was just as well since gasoline could not be used for pleasure trips. Sidney and Naomi came from Bayswater, where they lived in the flat they had leased before their marriage three years ago. Manny and Rita came from their new house on the Broadfields Estate in Edgware, a district in northwest London once famous for its coaching inns but now blossoming into a thriving suburb. They had given up

341

the flat near Regent's Park on the birth of their son, Jonathan, in January 1938.

Jonathan, with his curly brown hair and his father's blue eyes, was the joy of Rachel's life. She spoiled him incessantly. Every Friday, she baked cookies specially for him, sometimes in the shape of a rabbit, at other times sculpted like a fish or an elephant. When Manny and Rita jokingly complained that the boy was beginning to expect such pampered treatment at home, Rachel quashed their protests by claiming that every grandmother had an inalienable right to indulge a grandchild. If they wanted her to spoil Jonathan less, they should give her more grandchildren so she could share her love around.

"We're planning to do just that," Manny answered. "Why do you think we bought such a big house with four bedrooms?"

Then Rachel looked at Sidney and Naomi, now in their early thirties, and asked what they were waiting for. To make her point, she even managed to joke about the war. "Don't you know that with all the people dying, it's your solemn duty to help repopulate the world?"

"When we're ready, Mama," Sidney answered. "Right now, Naomi's too busy helping me in the office to have time to be a mother. You're not going to argue about that, are you?"

Rachel shook her head. Sidney was struggling to keep afloat the business he had started four years ago in Shaftesbury Avenue, and Naomi's assistance was vital. At the outbreak of war, Sidney and every other agent had faced disaster because of a government decision to close all sports stadiums, theaters, and cinemas for fear of massive casualties should they be bombed. The ban was replaced after two weeks by a ten o'clock curfew. People with money in their pockets and scant opportunity to spend it flocked to shows and movies. Entertainment thrived.

Not everyone shared the boom. Big agencies, with top stars on their books, put entire bills into theaters. Smaller, newer agencies like Sidney's had to exist on the crumbs that fell from the rich man's table.

Manny and Bernard, working together as Lesser Brothers,

342

fared much better. They had taken over Harold Parker's established business. Some of the complete bills that went into smaller theaters belonged to them.

The success of Lesser Brothers galled Sidney. He had nothing against his younger brother, Bernard, but he hated to see Manny doing so much better than himself. The large house in Edgware and the new Rover Manny had driven until fuel rationing crimped his style added to Sidney's rancor. Manny, in turn, made little attempt to hide his dislike of Sidney. He poked fun at Sidney's fight to stay solvent in front of theater people he knew would relay his words to his brother. He wanted Sidney to know he was laughing. The break-up of the act four years ago had pushed a childhood competition into the realm of adult bitterness.

The continuing feud between the brothers distressed Rita and Naomi. No ill feeling existed between the sisters-in-law. Naomi often bought a small gift for Jonathan, and Rachel was sure that Rita would do exactly the same if the child was Naomi's. The resentment existed solely between the brothers. God alone knew what it would take to break it down.

Under the National Service (Armed Forces) Act, passed by Parliament on the first day of the war, all men between the ages of eighteen and forty-one were subject to conscription. Manny, Sidney, and Bernard registered as they were obliged to, then returned to their normal lives. As normal as could be under wartime conditions. Sidney, with Naomi's help, continued to place small acts, while Bernard and Manny had two complete shows touring the country.

In May 1941, the finger of conscription reached out to touch Bernard. He was the youngest of the three brothers, and unmarried. Theatrical agent was not a reserved occupation. He was a prime candidate for a uniform. He left early one morning for his medical examination. When he returned home, he had a question for his mother.

"Do you realize that you produced an inferior specimen when you had me?"

"You failed the medical examination?" Before she jumped for joy, Rachel wanted to hear what the doctors had found wrong with her youngest son.

343

"They told me I couldn't march on flat feet, and I might not be able to hear vital orders with a perforated right eardrum."

"So that's why you never listened to me." She wagged a finger in Bernard's face, as though reprimanding him for some long-distant incident. Then she kissed him. At least one son would be spared. He didn't look very happy, though. "Why are you so miserable? Nine men out of ten would like to have your ailments if it got them out of active duty."

"I don't feel that I'm unfit. We're in a war for survival and I should be doing something."

"You want to do something? Make people laugh. Give them pleasure, and you'll do more good than a thousand soldiers drilling." All these years later, thought Rachel, some of Jacob's flag-waving had surfaced in Bernard. She thanked God for tempering the patriotism with flat feet and a perforated eardrum.

A year passed before conscription beckoned to the Lesser family again. In June 1942, six months after the conflict had become a true world war, Sidney's turn came. Unlike Bernard, he passed the physical. He waited for dinner the next Friday at his mother's home before sharing his news.

"What service will you be in?" Bernard asked.

"Royal Air Force."

"What will you be doing?"

"Some officer asked about my background. I told him about the agency and being on the boards, and said I could help the war effort by organizing entertainment for the troops. He said the Air Force needs bomb-aimers and gunners, not song-and-dance men."

Rachel glanced at Manny to see his reaction to his brother's news. She was gratified to see that he wasn't gloating. But neither did he show concern, as Bernard did. "What about the agency?" she asked.

"Naomi will have to carry on. She certainly can't live on the money the government pays soldiers' wives."

"How much is that?"

"Seventeen shillings a week, plus another seven shillings out of my pay."

Manny made his first contribution. "I've spent more than that on lunch."

"We'll look after your clients," Bernard offered. "Naomi can work out of Lesser Brothers' office."

Sidney, who had been hoping for such an offer, looked at Manny to see if any contradiction was forthcoming. Manny nodded. "You could have saved yourself all this trouble, you know."

"How?" Sidney asked.

"By having a child, like Rita and me. By the time they call up married men with children, this war will be over."

Sidney knew Manny was needling him. "Not if we're going to win it, it won't be," he shot back. "You'll get your turn to serve your country, don't you worry about that."

The following week, Sidney entered the RAF. After initial training, he became a supply clerk at Hendon Aerodrome, just three miles from where his older brother lived. Every day when Manny traveled into town by train, he passed right by the aerodrome. Whenever he saw men marching or running, he smiled. If it was raining at the time, he smiled a little more.

Manny's amusement lasted only until the end of September, when his own call-up papers arrived. The army took him. Once his training finished, he was posted as a driver with a transport unit in Reading, west of London. He managed to get home to see Rita and Jonathan one weekend out of four. The other three weekends, Rita took her son to Reading.

With Manny's departure, Bernard was left on his own to handle Lesser Brothers' business and help Naomi with Sidney's clients. The added workload proved too much. Rachel offered help, which Bernard immediately and gratefully accepted.

For five days a week, Rachel slipped back into the world of variety theater. It was both a return to familiar ground and a journey of discovery. The theaters were the same—those that had escaped the bombs—but the artists had changed. Many well-known names were in the forces. Newcomers had taken their places. Rachel set about memorizing new names, fresh acts. The work provided good therapy. It was better than staying at home and worrying about Manny and Sidney being shipped off to some awful place where armies fought and young men died.

In the early summer of 1943, more than two years after failing the medical examination, Bernard still did not understand why he had been rejected for military service. Flat feet or no, he felt he could walk as well as any man, and his hearing seemed perfectly adequate. Had it not been for the doctors, he would never have known he was partially deaf in his right ear.

With each day, he saw more uniforms. Not only British and Commonwealth, but French, Polish, American. In suit and tie, Bernard felt out of place in wartime London. Those soldiers, sailors, and airmen were doing their bit; he wasn't doing his.

He visited James Prideaux at the Rialto-Playhouse Partnership offices in Leicester Square. The bookings manager was sixty-seven now. At an age when other men retired, he remained deeply involved with the theater. "I've got a proposition for you, Mr. Prideaux. Any show I put together for a Partnership house, on Monday nights allied troops get in for nothing."

Prideaux checked a wall chart showing upcoming productions. Lesser Brothers had a comedy show called *Laughter on Parade* starting in August. "We supply the theater—what do you supply?"

"Lesser Brothers will donate twenty percent of its fee to a wartime charity."

Prideaux mulled over the proposition. Much was already being done for troops. At the top was the Entertainments National Service Association, the British equivalent of the USO. ENSA as it was known for short—or Every Night Something Awful, as one comedian had nicknamed it—sent professional entertainers as far away as North Africa to amuse the troops. Army and air force shows used artists in uniform. What Bernard proposed was novel. Free admission once a week to a commercial theater. Prideaux liked the idea. His group, certainly, was doing enough wartime business to hand a little back. "All right. No charge for servicemen on Monday nights. How long will this last?"

"Right through to the end of the war."

"Do you have a fortune teller on your books who happens to know when that will be?"

Bernard shook his head. "I like a long run as much as you do, but already I'm looking forward to the day this folds."

Bernard contacted military officials. Allied personnel on leave or pass in London were informed that they would be able to pick up free tickets on the day of the performance.

On the first Monday of *Laughter on Parade,* the line at nine o'clock in the morning outside the Playhouse box office stretched for twenty yards. Tickets for both first and second house were gone by ten o'clock.

Bernard watched the first show with James Prideaux in the bookings manager's private box. Men in every imaginable uniform filled all fifteen hundred seats. They clapped and cheered enthusiastically as the curtain rose. A cockney double act began the show. Too late Bernard wondered how well such dialect would be understood by foreign troops. He need not have worried. Eager for any diversion, the audience—British and ally alike—roared with laughter at anything and everything.

"We could have Henry the Fifth on the stage," Prideaux whispered to Bernard, "and this audience would still love it."

Bernard nodded excitedly. He was finally doing his bit.

Chapter Fourteen

Most small towns have nothing to bring them to public notice. The small town of Lewisburg, Pennsylvania, situated in the heart of Pennsylvania Dutch farming country, is luckier in that respect. It has two distinct claims to fame. One is Bucknell University, chartered in 1846 as the University of Lewisburg. The other is the federal penitentiary opened some eighty years later as part of the creation of the Federal Bureau of Prisons under the Hoover administration.

Every Sunday, Jimmy Isaacson traveled from New York to Lewisburg to visit his father. The round trip of more than three hundred miles consumed the entire day. To Jimmy, the long journey was the least unpleasant part of the whole business. Far worse was the actual visit. That shattered him. No matter how many times he saw his father clothed in the drab gray uniform, the shock never lessened. For the first few months of his father's incarceration, the vision of Zalman in prison uniform roused Jimmy sweating and shouting in the middle of the night. Sonya, lying beside him in bed, could do nothing.

Jimmy understood the reason for the nightmares. No matter how sick he felt about seeing his father in Lewisburg, he had to bottle up the feelings. His mother and sister accompanied him on those weekly trips. They were allowed to express their emotions; they could let tears flow when they saw Zalman. Jimmy, the man of the family while his father was away, could not. No matter what pain and misery tore at him, he had to preserve a face of stone. His father expected

348

that of him, and Jimmy obeyed. Only when he was asleep, his guard relaxed, did his suffering surface.

During the visits, Zalman told the family about his job in the prison library. "Because I'm a publisher, they thought I'd be good at cataloguing books." He listened patiently to Julia's list of what needed repairing in the house. He asked Helen about the stories she'd covered. He told Jimmy to organize a series on federal prisons. "You don't get your ordinary thieves and rapists here. You get a really interesting class of criminal."

Fifteen minutes before the end of each visiting time, Julia and Helen left father and son alone. During that time, the two men discussed business matters. Incarcerated or not, Zalman still controlled what remained of his empire after he had sold off so much to pay the government. He stayed current through letters and visits from Bernard French, Edward Beecham, Frank Brennan, and Bill Regan. Zalman's edicts to Jimmy concerned the *Messenger.* He had bought the paper for his son, and now was the perfect time for him to develop from simply editing *Cavalcade,* a Sunday pictorial magazine, to understanding the entire operation.

Sometimes the instructions concerned circulation. The *Messenger* was one of many papers available at the prison. Zalman, always on the lookout for an edge, noticed that the Sunday edition often arrived on Monday. "Do you know how embarrassing it is to have convicts asking how come all the other papers get here Sunday, and your own paper's a day late?"

Jimmy promised to look into it.

At other times, Zalman was more concerned with editorial content. As the spring of 1941 passed into summer, he became increasingly interested in the war in Europe. "The sooner we get involved, the better. Tell Beecham to start slamming Lindbergh, McCormick, and the rest of the America First disciples. Useful idiots to Hitler's cause, that's all the isolationists are."

Jimmy was all for American involvement. He deeply admired his brother-in-law, Joseph Cushman, who was a lieutenant in the Canadian army. Sonya kept a photograph of him in uniform on the bedside table, taken just before he had

349

left for assignment in England. Whenever she received a letter from him, Jimmy insisted on reading it.

Despite his sympathy toward Britain and his respect for his Canadian brother-in-law, Jimmy queried his father's orders. "McCormick's another publisher. Are you sure you want to lock horns with him?"

Zalman shrugged ambivalently. "What can the Chicago *Tribune* do to me that hasn't been done already?"

Jimmy returned to New York and relayed his father's orders to Edward Beecham. The *Messenger* editor brought up the same caveat Jimmy had raised. "Making a personal attack on another publisher is very questionable practice."

Jimmy picked up a copy of the *Messenger* and pointed to his father's name. "That is the only publisher we care about here, Mr. Beecham. Please do as I ask."

Beecham had always regarded Jimmy patronizingly, a spoiled young man doing a job any vaguely competent person could have performed. For the first time, he noticed steel in his voice.

The next day, the *Messenger* carried a scathing attack on America First supporters. The article even carried Zalman's "useful idiots" description of Charles Lindbergh and Colonel Robert McCormick, owner of the Chicago *Tribune*. When Jimmy visited Lewisburg the next Sunday, his father congratulated him.

"Do you recall that day when you remarked about Lindbergh not looking much like a hero?" Zalman asked. "Well, you just made him look really ordinary. That was one hell of a piece. You might have a newsman inside you after all."

Jimmy blushed. He could never remember receiving such a compliment from his father. It made the miserable business of visiting the prison almost worthwhile.

On the first Sunday in December, Jimmy took good news to Lewisburg. "You're going to be a grandfather," he told Zalman, expecting to see his father's face gleam with joy.

Instead, Zalman appeared disconsolate. "How can I bounce my grandchild on my knee when I'm stuck in this lousy place?"

"The baby's not due until June," Julia said. "You might be out of here by then."

350

Zalman shook his head. "Bernard French was here. He doesn't think the parole board will do me any good. I kept too much back from the government. They want to make an example of me so other people don't get sloppy with their bookkeeping."

Jimmy's prison face slipped. His father had been sentenced to four years in prison, but no one had expected him to serve it out. Eighteen months, everyone had figured, and then parole.

While Zalman's family sat absorbing the news, a ripple of excitement began sweeping through the prison. Guards whispered urgent phrases to each other. Heads shook; faces whitened. Zalman swung around as a guard walked past.

"What's going on?"

"The Japanese just bombed Pearl Harbor in Hawaii."

The news took a moment to register, then Zalman turned back to his visitors. He didn't seem to notice Julia and Helen. Only Jimmy. His brown eyes sharpened, bayoneting his son. "Why are you still sitting there? You should be in New York helping Beecham put out the paper. Go on, get out of here!"

As Jimmy walked away, Zalman called his name. "We need a patriotic front page tomorrow. Frame it with flags! Tell Beecham to run a border of Old Glory around the entire page!"

Jimmy nodded. His father's mind was always working. Even in prison, he never missed a trick when it came to selling papers.

In June, Sonya gave birth to a girl. When Jimmy visited her the following day, a photographer from the *Messenger* accompanied him. Jimmy had the man take four pictures of the baby in Sonya's arms. He framed the best picture and carried it with him on the next trip to Lewisburg.

Zalman was thrilled at being a grandfather. He sat staring at the photograph for fully two minutes. "Does my granddaughter have a name?"

Jimmy gave an embarrassed smile. "Sonya and I haven't made up our minds yet. We were both so sure we'd have a son that we never considered names for girls."

Zalman laughed. The first question he asked the following

351

Sunday was whether a name had been chosen for his grand-daughter yet.

"Leah," Jimmy answered.

"Who's Leah?"

"Sonya's grandmother was named Leah."

Zalman nodded in approval. He liked it when a person was remembered with enough fondness to have another human being named after them. He'd named Jimmy in the honor of a good friend. One day, he hoped, someone would name a child after him. But not for a long time yet.

"What about a middle name?"

"We're still working on it."

Each Sunday after that, Jimmy came to Lewisburg with new photographs of Leah. Zalman studied them intently, comparing them with previous pictures and joyfully indicating differences. "Look how her face is filling out. That dimple, see it? That wasn't there last week. And look how much thicker her hair's becoming!" Then tears would burn his eyes as he realized that he was only admiring pictures when he should have been holding his granddaughter in his arms.

In the middle of August, Jimmy arrived at Lewisburg by himself. He had no pictures for his father to cherish. "What's the matter with you?" Zalman asked, noticing his son's red, puffy eyes. "Where's your mother? Where's Helen?"

"New York. They're looking after Sonya."

"Sonya?" Zalman's face took on Jimmy's expression of misery. "What's the matter with Sonya?"

"Her brother Joseph was killed at Dieppe."

Zalman's voice turned loud enough to bring guards hurrying to where he sat. "What the hell are you doing here? You belong with your wife, not here with me! Go home and help Sonya! She needs you! I don't!"

Jimmy ran toward the door, embarrassed and hurt by his father's sudden fury. By the time he was clear of the prison grounds, he knew his father's tirade had been prompted by concern, not anger. Zalman had shouted at him out of love.

Two weeks passed before Jimmy returned to Lewisburg. Sitting with his mother and sister, he told his father that he had been to Montreal with Sonya.

"That's where you belonged," Zalman replied. "Once

you're married, your parents come second—your own family comes first." After giving Jimmy a few seconds to digest that thought, Zalman asked how the visit to Montreal had gone.

"The house was filled with grief," Jimmy said. "Sonya's mother just sat there, like she was in a trance. All over the place were clippings from newspapers about the Dieppe raid. Her father, old Ben Cushman, showed the clippings to visitors. There must have been hundreds of visitors. Sonya's mother kept telling him to stop, but he carried right on. You know what he said to people when he showed them the clippings?"

"Tell me."

"He said if his son had to die, at least he thanked God he was chosen to die for a worthwhile cause."

"Every man's a poet."

"I wrote a short piece about my visit to the Cushmans. It ran in the *Messenger* two days ago."

"I read it." Zalman sighed. "You know, Jimmy, life's an odd experience. I'm unlucky because I'm sitting here in prison. Yet compared to a man like Ben Cushman, who has seen his only son die on the beach of a foreign land, maybe I'm not so unlucky after all. Life's just a matter of how you look at it, I guess."

As always, Julia and Helen left Zalman and Jimmy alone fifteen minutes before visiting ended. Instead of discussing business, Zalman talked some more about his son's visit to Montreal. "You're finally growing up, Jimmy. Two years ago, you couldn't have made that trip in those conditions. You would have looked to me for help. You would have asked me how to go about comforting a wife who'd lost a brother."

Jimmy didn't argue because he knew his father was right. These eighteen months without his father's constant presence had matured him. There was more to it than being able to help Sonya and the Cushmans through the loss of Joseph. More to it than the way his mother and sister came to him for advice. Jimmy saw his maturing in Edward Beecham's manner. When Zalman had first gone away, the *Messenger* editor had dismissed Jimmy as the owner's pampered son.

353

Now, when Jimmy made a suggestion, Beecham listened. Even when he knew the idea hadn't come from Zalman.

Before he left his father that day, Jimmy had one more piece of news. "We finally decided on a second name for little Leah."

"What's that?" Zalman asked, amused that the choice of a middle name could have taken two months.

"Josephine. In honor of Sonya's brother."

"That's nice. Leah Josephine Isaacson, that's a really pretty name."

Jimmy smiled. Even in the choice of his daughter's name he needed to hear his father's approval.

The baby's names became reversed. The birth certificate read Leah Josephine, but once the middle name had been chosen, the original given name was relegated to second spot; the memory of a beloved brother was dearer than that of a half-forgotten grandmother. Jimmy and Sonya began calling their daughter Josephine. Helen and Julia followed suit. Zalman was the last to switch, and even then he accepted only half the name. He referred to the granddaughter he had never seen as Jo. Each time Jimmy brought new photographs, Zalman would always talk about how much his little Jo had grown.

"You'd better not call her that when you get out of here."

"Why not?"

"First of all, she won't answer to it. Secondly, Sonya will have a fit to hear her daughter called that."

"Josephine's too much of a mouthful for an old man like me."

"Fifty-nine's not that old."

"There's fifty-nine and there's fifty-nine," Zalman said philosophically. "To some men it's old, to others it's not. I think it's old because I've put more into my fifty-nine years than most men put into a hundred and fifty-nine."

Jimmy believed that. His father had always been larger than life, with his big deals and unusual businesses. The fathers of Jimmy's friends worked in banking and law; they were doctors, merchants. Eminently respectable, and quite boring. Only Jimmy's father had owned a racing paper, a daily newspaper, and a wire service to bookies. No matter how much he had criticized Zalman's original purchase of the wire, Jimmy had still taken a private, perverse pride in the fact that his father owned it.

But he never thought of his father as old. Zalman's age, unless you knew it, had always been difficult to tell. His lean body and bony face defied guesswork. Despite the gray, his curly hair remained thick. He could be anywhere, Jimmy thought, from fifty to sixty. Only his eyes placed him closer to the upper figure. Behind the gold-rimmed glasses, they gleamed with the pointed cynicism it took a lifetime to acquire.

"Like you say," Jimmy told his father as he stared into that sardonic gaze, "you've put plenty into your fifty-nine years."

Zalman made the best out of his time in prison. He exploited his job in the library by reading almost every book on the shelves. He taught himself about photography and plumbing, farming and building. He even became the acknowledged prison expert on American history, from the Pilgrim Fathers to Pearl Harbor. Each week he proudly showed off some new area of proficiency to his visitors. If he had to spend up to four years in jail, he was determined to come out a more educated man than he had gone in.

In August 1943, Helen brought her father news that shook him. "I'm going to England for the *Messenger.*"

Zalman looked at his wife. Her face was rigidly composed. He had no need to ask what Julia thought of Helen's decision. Furthermore, he could see that she blamed him. Because the *Messenger* belonged to Zalman, it was all his fault. For Julia's sake, he tried to change his daughter's mind. "Wasn't one war enough for you, Helen? Your right leg's shorter than your left leg as it is. Are you so eager to even them up?"

"England's the big story. It's the Grand Central of the entire war. Everything starts or finishes there—"

Jimmy interrupted her. "The CBS broadcasts are heard in millions of homes. The New York *Times* and the *Herald Tribune* have big staffs there. If we're to compete for readers, we can no longer afford to settle for stringers or agency stories. It's time we stopped counting pennies and started spending them. We need someone there to write really good human-interest stories, and I can't think of anyone better qualified than Helen."

Zalman noted how his son took over the conversation. He also observed how Jimmy began by using the editorial "we" before replacing it with the personally responsible "I." The boy exhibited more confidence with each passing week. Zalman couldn't fight them both. "When are you leaving, Helen?"

"Tomorrow."

Zalman turned to his wife. "Did you hear that, Julia? Are you going to wish Helen luck, or is she going to have to remember you looking like a quart of sour milk until she sees you again?"

"I'd be much happier if she didn't go at all."

"And your parents would have been much happier if you hadn't married me, but you still did it, didn't you?"

Some of the ice fell from Julia's face. "This is hardly the same situation."

"It doesn't matter. Helen's thirty-five years old, Julia. You can't tell her what to do anymore."

"I never could. You made a tomboy out of her from the moment she could walk."

Zalman returned his attention to Helen. "Did you ever want to be anything else?"

"I wanted to be exactly the way I turned out."

"Make her promise," Julia said, "that she won't go where the fighting is."

"You heard your mother."

"I promise. No war stories. Just people stories."

Zalman regarded his daughter fondly. The brightness of her shoulder-length auburn hair was starting to fade; a handful of gingery-white strands highlighted the red. Delicate lines worked their way out from the corners of her eyes. He took in every detail, storing them in his memory. That was all he'd have until he saw her again. Memories. He felt a hard lump forming in his throat, and he sought relief in humor.

"I've got another parole hearing coming up before the end of the year, and Bernard French is confident that this time we'll make it. Jimmy might not know the difference between mediocre and outstanding," he said with a wink in his son's direction, "but you can bet your last dime that I do. When I get out of here, you'd better be sending me nothing but your best. Otherwise I'll get the accounts department to start checking your expenses carefully."

Helen threw her arms around her father's shoulders and hugged him as tightly as she could. Tears streamed down her face. She didn't know when she would ever see him again. Or *if.*

And what a lousy way that would be to say good-bye. In a federal penitentiary.

Chapter Fifteen

The London that greeted Helen in the summer of 1943 was very different from the city she had passed through on the way home after writing her articles about the Spanish Civil War.

The people had altered beyond recognition. Five years before, Helen had found Londoners friendly, eager to help when asked for directions, happy to stand and talk about subjects as complex as world affairs or as simple as the previous Saturday's football game. Now, many of the people Helen met were listless zombies trudging forward from one day to the next. The only emotion they showed was a vengeful bitterness. Helen saw it illustrated sharply in the way they grabbed at the latest editions of newspapers, or listened avidly to radio broadcasts to learn what damage allied bombers had done to Germany. The cheers they gave on learning casualty figures turned Helen's stomach.

The city had also changed dramatically. Newsreel films Helen had seen of bomb damage told only part of the story. Witnessing the destruction firsthand, even after human tragedy had become clinical memorabilia, appalled her. Piles of rubble and gaping craters ran one into the other to create a charred and lifeless desert. It took all of her imagination to realize that much of the debris had once been homes. Only when some striking piece of evidence presented itself—a broken doll, a piece of a china plate, a dented saucepan—was the transformation easier to make. Then, when she heard the satisfaction in Londoners' voices as they discussed the saturation bombing of Hamburg, she began to understand. Her American stomach had no business turning. Londoners . . . the entire British nation which had suffered so grievously through the blitz . . . had the right and privilege to feel just as satisfied as they wanted to feel.

After settling into a small apartment in Portland Square, Helen used her *Messenger* credentials to join the Correspondents Association. By themselves, American reporters had little leverage when dealing with allied officialdom. As a group, they represented most of the reading public in the United States. General Eisenhower, the allied commander, fully appreciated the power wielded by the press. He bent over backward to help.

Every day and night, Helen ate and drank with American writers and radio broadcasters who scoured the war's front line for news. Sometimes she felt jealous of the camaraderie of danger that bound such elite journalists. What it must be like to fly with the bombers that raided Germany! How it must feel to use a nonchalant lead like Edward R. Murrow's "Last night some young men took me to Berlin . . ." Then she remembered the promise she'd made to her parents, and the brief from her brother Jimmy. The *Messenger* wanted human-interest articles, stories about American soldiers, sailors, and airmen stationed in England. The paper didn't want her being taken anywhere near Berlin. She'd been shot at and shot in one conflict. Her dues as a war correspondent had been paid in full. She didn't have to risk her neck again.

She visited American bases to talk to men and women whose activities and views made good reading back home. Twice a week she filed her stories. Whenever the New York office had a special assignment for her, they wired instructions. Otherwise, Edward Beecham and her brother gave her a free hand.

In early January, she filed a series of stories called "The Love Invasion," which dealt with American servicemen falling in love with British girls. A week after she filed the series she was startled to receive a highly critical memo from New York.

"In case you haven't heard," she read, "there's a war going on. What do moon-eyed GI's and man-hungry British girls who'd trade their virginity for a pair of nylons have to do with it? Suggest you start sending in real stories before we find someone to replace you."

In the middle of a rising fury at Edward Beecham and her brother for having the gall to send such a memo, Helen noticed that neither of their names filled the sender's block. She started to laugh. The name and title of Z. Isaacson, Publisher, stood out in bold capitals. He was out of jail and showing he was back in charge.

She taped the memo to the mirror of the dressing table in her bedroom, as proud of it as any family portrait.

Bernard Lesser was equally proud of his work for servicemen. The agreement with James Prideaux for free admission on Monday night to men in uniform had set a precedent. By the beginning of 1944, Lesser Brothers had three shows touring the country. Included in the contracts with each theater was a clause stating that on Monday nights admission was free to troops.

Looking forward to the spring and warmer weather, Bernard began formulating plans for open-air shows. Just as long as the rumored invasion did not rob him of his audiences. And if it did, maybe he could take one of his shows across the English Channel to Europe.

Instead of robbing him of the opportunity to play a mundane part in this most massive of human dramas, Bernard's flat feet and perforated eardrum had given him the chance to do much more.

All through spring, Helen saw evidence of the coming invasion. The troop and equipment build-up increased. Entire areas were closed off for maneuvers. She saw men of the First Infantry Division, who had fought in North Africa. The presence of this battle-hardened unit alone indicated the imminence of the jump across the Channel. Censorship curbed Helen from mentioning in her reports what was clear to anyone with a decent pair of eyes.

As spring passed, and invasion fever gripped the country, Helen's memory of her promise to her parents dimmed. She sought desperately for a way to become involved. "I don't expect to be in the first wave of troops going ashore," she told her father in a transatlantic telephone conversation. "I don't *want* to be among them, but I want to be a part of it somehow. I'll be damned if I'm going to sit here trying to create human-interest stories when the rest of the reporting world's watching the German army get the hammering it so richly deserves."

"We hope," Zalman answered. "Your mother and I don't want the aggravation we suffered while you were in Spain. Especially me. I get it from two sides, Helen. I worry about you, and I catch hell from your mother if anything happens to you. So the answer's no."

"What am I supposed to do then?"

"Find a new angle."

"There *are* no new angles. As well as being troop-saturated, this island is press-saturated. Whatever can be written about has been written about."

"Has it? There's one thing I haven't seen many column inches on. The awkward problem of keeping hundreds of thousands of men occupied. British soldiers can go home on pass or leave; maybe their girlfriends and wives can visit them. French and Polish servicemen based in England are buoyed up by the hope of seeing their homes again soon. What do Americans have to look forward to? How do all these men, so many thousands of miles from home, pass the time? Their commanders can't fill every waking moment with training activities. There has to be relief somewhere—some form of entertainment—otherwise there would be a revolution. Write about that."

"Entertainment?" Helen couldn't believe it. She'd come to England as a war correspondent, and now her father expected her to be a movie critic. He wouldn't take no for an answer, either. He was in charge of his newspaper again, and making everyone aware of the fact. It had taken him no time at all to get back in control; he'd shaken off the experience of prison like a duck shakes off water. She wondered what Jimmy was doing now? Was he back to editing *Cavalcade*? Back to living in his father's shadow as he had done before Zalman went to jail? That would be a pity, because he'd proven himself to be a very competent young man. With his father away, he'd grown up in one hell of a hurry.

"That's right. Entertainment. There must be hundreds of stories. Glenn Miller's gotten most of the headlines, but there are thousands of additional singers, dancers, and comedians in uniform. Write about the shows these people are putting on. Write about the USO. Show America how its stars have another face. The face of patriotism."

The operator informed Helen her time was up. The connection broke as Helen told her father to give her mother a kiss. She sat staring at the telephone for almost a minute, wondering where to begin. Entertainment! She could see it now, a future journalism class studying war reporting, comparing Ed Murrow's "Last night some young men took me to Berlin," with Helen Isaacson's "Yesterday afternoon, I saw an awful matinee."

Nonetheless, she did as her father ordered. She tracked down entertainers in uniform. Among the men she met was a comedian she had once applauded at a New York night club; now he cooked chow in an infantry battalion. The *Messenger* carried her articles side by side with hard war news. She wrote about shows arranged by the USO and the British ENSA organization. As she became interested in the subject, she found enough material to fill a dozen newspapers. Most exciting was the knowledge that many of the young artists appearing in such shows represented the next generation of stars. Young men and women were getting the kind of exposure in six months that they would have to wait ten years for in a world at peace. Helen wrote about them under a collective heading of "Remember these names."

When D-Day came on June 6, she was so engrossed in her new assignment that she didn't even miss the thrill of witnessing firsthand the single greatest blow struck against evil in the history of the world.

Within a week of D-Day, as optimists began a countdown to the end of the war, the first V1 rocket fell on London. More of these terrifying missiles followed, their distinctive sound earning them the name of buzz bombs. Women and children were evacuated from London in a reprise of reaction to the blitz.

Bernard remained the only man in the Lesser family out of uniform. Sidney was now stationed at an RAF base near Cambridge, from where bombers flew on missions over Germany, while Manny's army transportation unit waited to be ordered into Europe. When buzz bombs exploded with a deadly regularity, Bernard did not wait to be asked by his brothers to send their families out of London. He acted on his own, finding rental accommodation for Rita, Jonathan, and Naomi in a farmhouse near Oxford. Rachel refused to join her daughters-in-law, and Bernard didn't argue. He knew his mother's feelings about being driven from her home. Besides, in the sudden terror-stricken days of flying bombs, he was glad of her company, both at home and in the office.

The rain of buzz bombs coincided with final preparations for a new musical revue Bernard was organizing. Called *Broadway Tribute,* it featured scenes from *Show Boat* right through to the previous year's huge hit, *Oklahoma.* The schedule called for *Tribute* to start with a month's run at the London Playhouse in mid-August, followed by a tour of provincial theaters. As always, servicemen would be allowed in free on Monday nights.

On the morning before *Tribute* opened, the cast held a final rehearsal. Bernard entered the darkened auditorium toward the end of the rehearsal. Onstage, a tall black man sang "Bess, You Is My Woman Now" in an echoing bass-baritone. Bernard watched for a few seconds before joining James Prideaux, who sat in the center of the eighth row. Three other people sat with him—his secretary, the show's musical director, and a woman in some kind of a military uniform. Bernard slid into the seat behind the bookings manager. "All going well, Mr. Prideaux?"

"Yes, thank you. I think we're going to have quite a success with this production." He turned his attention back to the stage, ignoring Bernard until the scene from *Porgy and Bess* ended. "I hope you'll join us for lunch, Bernard. This young lady"—he gestured to the uniformed woman—"is asking questions that you're probably better qualified to answer. Helen, meet Bernard Lesser, whose show this is. Bernard, Helen Isaacson's a war correspondent doing a series of articles about entertainment for the troops."

In the dimness of the theater, Bernard could barely make out the woman's features. The two noticeable things about her were the cap sitting jauntily on shoulder-length hair, and the bright brass US insignia on the lapels of her jacket.

Helen offered her hand. "I represent the New York *Messenger*. Mr. Prideaux tells me that all your shows give free performances on Monday nights for servicemen. How did that come about?"

"I was medically unfit for military service. I felt I could do my bit in other ways."

Helen memorized the modest answer; it would make a good quote. "Nothing serious, I hope."

"Hardly. Flat feet and the inability to hear dogs barking five miles away."

The sound of Bernard's voice appealed to Helen. Too many Englishmen—army officers and civilians alike—spoke in such condescending tones. Condescending to what? A woman, or Americans in general? Bernard's voice had a gentle warmth that Helen found attractive. She just wished she could see him better. "Is it so important to hear dogs barking?"

"That was just another way of saying the doctors found a perforated eardrum."

Prideaux swung around in the seat. "Please, could the interview wait until lunch?"

Bernard returned his attention to the stage, where a tall blonde wearing a long shimmering turquoise dress taken from the pages of a Civil War history book sang "Can't Help Loving That Man of Mine."

Two more songs from *Show Boat* completed the rehearsal. The theater lights came up. Prideaux had a short discussion with the musical director. He made a couple of comments to his secretary, which she noted in the stenographer's pad she carried. At last, he turned to Helen and Bernard. "Ready to eat?"

Bernard barely heard the question. His attention was riveted on Helen's heart-shaped face, the hazel eyes and auburn hair, her entire deportment. He couldn't believe the information his eyes relayed to his brain. The uniform worn by this woman threw him. So did her voice. He had never pictured her in any kind of uniform; he had never imagined her speaking with an American accent. He remained confused for only a moment. She could have been clad in a suit of armor, and spoken in ancient Latin, and Bernard would still have recognized her.

Instead of feeling embarrassed by the intense appraisal, Helen was flattered. Ever since hearing Bernard's voice she had wondered what he looked like. Now that she could see, she felt pleasantly surprised. There was an empathy about him that she welcomed. He didn't have the pallor she normally associated with Englishmen, the fair skin that turned lobster red after just five minutes exposure to the sun. Bernard's dark complexion, the curly brown hair, and deep brown eyes, spoke of a heritage far from England. His appearance would have fit better, Helen decided, in the melting pot of New York rather than London. She had seen many there who looked just like him. Perhaps that was why he seemed so familiar.

Prideaux coughed into his hand. "I asked if you were ready for lunch." He led the way toward the exit, glancing once over his shoulder to be sure his two guests were following.

They ate at a small restaurant in Soho. Over the meal, Prideaux felt increasingly like the odd man out. He could see the mutual attraction between his two guests growing stronger with each passing minute. Helen asked a dozen questions about Bernard's work, but she made no notes of his answers. It was as though, Prideaux concluded, she was asking him questions just to hear him speak. He also concluded that, despite lunch being his idea, he had no business at this table.

Midway through the meal, Prideaux made a show of glancing at his watch. "Good Lord, is it one o'clock already?" He dabbed his lips with a napkin and started to get up. "You will have to excuse me. I'd clean forgotten about an appointment I had. If you need any more information, Miss Isaacson, please feel free to contact me. However, I think Bernard here will be able to tell you anything you need to know. Good day." He stopped at the cash register to pay for the lunch party and left.

"He thinks very highly of you," Helen remarked.

"We've had a long association, one way or the other."

"Tell me about it."

Bernard did, all the way back to the talent show fourteen years before when Less, Lesser, and Least had gained their foothold in variety. Helen listened raptly, speaking only when she needed clarification on a point, or when a British term confused her. "Each time you talk about variety theater," she said, "I have to make a mental transformation to vaudeville. That's what it's called in the States."

"Vaudeville." Bernard tried out the word, unsure whether or not he liked it.

"It's a better term," Helen claimed. "At least, it's better in that it meets with a newspaper's style guide of never using two words when you can use one."

"I'm not sure that newspaper style is the criterion one should use." He looked at his own watch, surprised to see that it was one forty-five.

"Are you going to use Mr. Prideaux's ploy to get away from me? Surely I'm not that much of a bore."

Bernard shook his head. "On the contrary. I'd like to sit here all day and talk to you. Unfortunately, I *do* have an appointment. At two o'clock. Also, I left my mother alone in the office, and she must be wondering what's happened. I told her I'd only be gone for half an hour." He stared down at the tabletop, uncertain what to do next. He'd waited all his life to meet this woman, and he didn't want it to end with just a few words over a meal. Her memories of him should be more meaningful than information to be used in a story; his own recollections of her should be deeper than just the knowledge that vaudeville meant variety theater. He desperately wanted to know how to contact this woman again, but he didn't know how to go about it.

Helen helped him out. "Do you have a business card, Bernard? A number where I can reach you if I need more information?"

"Of course." He pulled out his wallet. As he opened it to extract a card, a snippet of red ribbon dropped onto the table.

366

He tried to snatch it back before Helen noticed it, but he wasn't quick enough.

"What's that?"

"A good-luck talisman. I carry it to please my mother who's the most superstitious person in the entire world."

"Red ribbon?"

"It wards off the evil eye." Bernard's chagrin mounted. What must this sophisticated woman think of him, a grown man who carried lucky charms? "My mother is convinced red ribbon will shield me from harm. It'll keep me safe from bombs, she says."

Helen laughed. "Don't be so embarrassed, your mother might be right."

"You believe in these daft old wives' tales?"

"I didn't notice any bombs falling on you during lunch."

Just one, thought Bernard. But that was you. "How can I contact you? In case I think of something else that might be of interest for your story."

Helen wrote down the telephone number of her flat in Portland Square. "I'd best not keep you any longer, otherwise you'll be late for your appointment."

Reluctantly, Bernard pushed back his chair and stood up. At the door of the restaurant, he turned around. Helen sat watching him. He smiled at her. In that moment, seeing the expression soften the sharp lines of his face, she realized why he looked so familiar. He reminded Helen of her father. Bernard didn't possess Zalman Isaacson's drive and vitality. No man did. But the thinness of his face, the curly brown hair and gentle brown eyes recalled for Helen the years of childhood, when her father had woven those magic tales for her and her brother.

Once outside the restaurant, Bernard walked quickly in the direction of the office. Suddenly he stopped; subconsciously he fingered the piece of red ribbon inside the wallet. From above came a terrifying buzzing. He looked up. Streaking low across the sky was the stub-winged shape of a V1 rocket. He half turned in the direction of the restaurant. The engine noise continued. The flying bomb passed overhead, continuing in the direction of Fleet Street. Twenty seconds later, and two miles farther on, the buzzing stopped. Deprived of power, the rocket's motion changed from graceful flight to a clumsy, tumbling fall. The explosion shook the ground on which Bernard stood. A plume of smoke rose into the air. He touched the piece of ribbon one more time and continued on his way.

Rachel was white with anxiety when Bernard returned. "Where have you been? I heard that buzz bomb explode, you were so late, I didn't know what had happened to you! Where were you?"

Bernard did something he never normally did. He laughed at his mother. Then he kissed her. And then he hugged her. "What are you so worried about? Don't you know I'm safe from bombs when I'm carrying red ribbon?"

"Don't be so silly."

"I'm not. It really works. It worked twice today."

"Twice? I heard only one bomb. What was the second time?"

"I met the woman I'm going to marry."

"How are you so sure?"

Bernard kissed his mother again. "She looks just like you."

That evening, before leaving the office, Bernard tried the number Helen had given him. It rang unanswered a dozen times before he hung up. No doubt she was constantly on the run. He wondered how long it would take him to catch up with her. It was one thing to find the woman he was going to marry. It was another thing entirely to catch her.

At ten o'clock the next morning, Helen telephoned Bernard. "I still need answers to a couple of questions for my story."

"Ask."

"Would you believe that I'm one reporter who hates using telephones? If you're not busy, why don't we meet for lunch today? My treat. I have a good expense account."

Bernard, never having felt so flattered in his life, agreed. Before leaving the office, he told Rachel he was having lunch with the woman he was going to marry. "She asked me, no less."

"Will you give me at least five minutes advance warning of this marriage? I'd like to make sure I have a handkerchief to dry my eyes." She watched him go through the door, amused at the sudden change. Almost thirty-five years he'd waited. Now he was making up for lost time. Rachel just hoped that he was right, and this woman—whoever she was—was the mate intended for Bernard. Rachel wasn't sure that after all this time Bernard would know how to handle disappointment.

Bernard met Helen at a restaurant in Coventry Street. She wore her war correspondent's uniform again. Bernard decided it suited her, especially the cap perched gaily on top of her auburn hair. As they sat down, he asked what information she needed.

She smiled shamefaced across the table. "I lied. There are no questions I need to ask. I just wanted to see you again."

Bernard felt his heartbeat quicken. "I telephoned you yesterday evening. There was no answer."

"I had a dinner date. With a very pompous British colonel who used to be musical director of some theater and is now an army bandmaster. When he decided that the dinner invitation included a pass, I told him where to put his baton."

Bernard's initial envy turned to laughter. He could imagine this self-assured American woman telling some colonel just that. "Why does a woman want to be a war correspondent?"

"Because she can do it as well as a man," Helen answered in all seriousness. Then she smiled. "I've done it before, in Spain. I got shot there. This time my father made me promise that I'd stick to writing 'safe' stories. I had to say yes, because it's his newspaper."

Bernard nodded understandingly and waited for Helen to continue. Yesterday over lunch, he had done all the talking. Now it was her turn. She obliged, telling Bernard about living in New York, about her family, about all the businesses her father had owned at one time or another. In the hour lunch took, she told him about everything except Zalman's tax problems and what they had led to. Bernard presented a fascinated audience. The world Helen spoke of existed for him only in the few Bogart, Cagney, and Edward G. Robinson movies he had seen.

Despite Bernard's protests, Helen paid for lunch. "I told you, I have a good expense account."

"I know, your father signs the checks. Nonetheless, I feel embarrassed at having a woman pay for me. I insist on buying you dinner to even things up."

"Just to even things up?"

"And because I like your company."

Smiling, Helen decided not to push Bernard any further. Since meeting him the previous day at the London Playhouse, he'd hardly left her thoughts. Even when she'd been fighting off the lecherous army bandmaster, half her mind had been concentrated on Bernard. He wouldn't have tried to force himself on her, as the bandmaster had done. Helen sensed a shyness about the Englishman that was refreshing amid a wartime mentality of instant gratification in case tomorrow never came. No, not shyness. Reserve, she decided, was a far better word. Bernard was reserved, as all Englishmen were supposed to be. But in a much warmer, more gentle manner.

"Pick me up at seven-thirty," she said. "I've got an apartment—sorry, flat—in Portland Square."

"I know what an apartment is. I've picked up enough American culture from films."

"If that were really true, you'd say movies." She stood on tiptoe to kiss Bernard on the cheek. "Thank you for letting me take you to lunch. You answered my questions perfectly."

Hands in his pockets, Bernard strolled back to the office, smiling and nodding at complete strangers. If a buzz bomb passed low over his head today, he wouldn't even bother looking up. His mind could only cope with one topic at a time, and the topic that filled it now was Helen Isaacson.

Bernard saw Helen almost every evening for dinner. The rare times he missed was when she had an assignment she could not avoid. Then she would find her telephone ringing no matter what time she got home as Bernard called every fifteen minutes until she answered.

Rachel viewed Bernard's helpless slide into love with a mixture of emotions. She was happy because his constant failure to become serious over any girl had always been a worry; what would he do, she had often pondered, when she died? She could see humor in the way he repeatedly checked his appearance in the mirror before venturing out, the certain sign of a man hopelessly in love. And she felt anxious in case the future held disillusionment.

When the romance was two weeks old, Rachel traveled to Oxford to spend Saturday and Sunday with her daughters-in-law and grandson. Manny was also there, on a thirty-six-hour pass. Rachel told them about Bernard's mystery woman. Manny laughed at the idea of his youngest brother finally being involved, but Rita and Naomi showed more sympathy for Rachel's concerns.

"Don't you know anything about her at all?" Naomi asked.

Rachel shook her head. "He hasn't told me her name. I don't know where she comes from, what she does, where she lives."

"Haven't you spoken to her on the telephone?"

"How could I? Bernard answers the phone the instant it rings. He spends all his time at home and in the office hovering over the thing, waiting for it to ring."

"If this is really the first time he's fallen for anyone," Rita said, "he's just being a very normal jealous lover. He's probably so terrified of losing her that he won't share her with anyone. Even with his family." She looked at Manny as he held Jonathan. He filled out every inch of his uniform. "Especially you. The last thing Bernard wants is for you to make some bad joke about his girlfriend."

"Would I do that?"

"You and Sidney both," Naomi said.

Manny turned his attention to his son. He didn't like to hear himself compared with Sidney.

"When Bernard's ready to tell you all about his ladyfriend he'll tell you," Rita said simply. "In the meantime, don't start worrying over something that might never happen."

The Saturday night Rachel was away in Oxford, Bernard did not sleep at home. He and Helen went dancing at a night club. They left the club just before eleven, walking through dark streets to Portland Square. Helen invited Bernard inside. She poured drinks from a bottle of bourbon a fellow member of the Correspondents Association had brought back from a visit to the States. Bernard sat on a sofa in the living room, sipping bourbon while Helen busied herself in the apartment's single bedroom. When she came out, she no longer had on the black dress in which she'd danced at the club. She wore a pale-green silk dressing gown that clung to her body as she moved.

She sat down next to Bernard on the couch. "Aren't you uncomfortable with all that stuffy clothing on? Relax. Take off your jacket. And take off that tie as well. Even a banker doesn't wear a tie at midnight."

Bernard tugged at his tie knot. He started to slip out of the jacket of his blue suit. Helen moved closer to help him. He felt his skin start to burn as he realized she had nothing on beneath the green silk gown.

"That's better. Now undo a couple of buttons on that shirt. You'll feel a lot cooler."

Bernard undid the top two buttons. Helen knew that if anything was going to happen, she would have to take charge. She wanted something to happen, just as badly as she sensed Bernard did. His reserve—his shyness—held him back. If the English were really so reserved, God only knew how they managed to repopulate the country from generation to generation.

"Not just two buttons. Undo them all." She reached toward him. Bernard's hands closed around her own. For a moment she thought his bashfulness had won out and he was going to stop her. She was wrong. He lifted her hands to his mouth, kissing each fingertip in turn. She drew herself closer to him, slid her hands inside his shirt. His fingers tugged at the fastening of her robe. His hands glided across her waist and stomach, caressed her breasts and moved on. Her body felt on fire, a roaring, blazing inferno that threatened to burst through her skin and engulf them both.

Haste precluded them from going to the bedroom. They made love right there on the sofa, a hurried, frantic coupling that left them gasping from blissful exertion. Bernard collapsed, spent, on top of Helen. He slid down her body. She cradled his head to her breasts, listening as his breathing slowed to a regular pace. Contentment flooded over her, soft

372

and gentle to cool her flaming skin and soothe the nerve ends that had screamed out, moments earlier, in tortured ecstasy.

Suddenly, just as Bernard seemed on the verge of falling asleep, his entire body stiffened and he cried out as if in pain.

"What is it?" Helen whispered. "What's the matter?"

"Nothing." He closed his eyes to blot out the terrifying scene that filled his vision. Instead of Helen lying beneath him, he had seen his mother.

Helen kissed the top of his head. "Go to sleep."

Bernard closed his eyes and let his taut muscles relax. He had done nothing to be ashamed of. Wasn't finding a girl as special as his mother what he had dreamed of doing his entire life?

When Rachel returned from her weekend in Oxford, she found a note from Bernard saying he would not be home that night. He would explain all when he saw her the next day in the office.

Bernard's explanation was blunt. "I'm moving out," he told his mother. "I'm moving into a flat in Portland Square."

"With your girlfriend?" Rachel told herself she shouldn't be surprised. Anyone as smitten as Bernard had to make some such gesture. It didn't seem possible, but Rachel could swear he had changed since she'd last seen him a couple of days ago. He seemed taller, broader. There was a confidence to his walk, a swagger that she'd never noticed before. "You could at least tell me the name of this woman who's swept you off your feet."

"I'll tell you everything about her in good time. And you'll be amazed. This is a very extraordinary woman."

"If you're in love with her, I'm sure she is," Rachel answered. She did not pursue the subject further. Bernard would be thirty-five in just a couple of months. He was entitled to all the privacy he wanted.

When Bernard finished work each evening, he went straight to Portland Square. If Helen were free, they ate out. If she were working, he made himself something to eat, then listened to the radio or read until she returned. The time he spent with her opened a new world. He explored the pleasure of intimacy, the joy of sharing, of being part of a union based on love. He found security in her embrace. When he lay in her arms, he felt safe from everything. Even the regular explosions of V1's, and the new terror weapon, the V2—which arrived with no warning whatsoever—couldn't harm him while Helen's arms provided protection. Her love was more effective than a mile of red ribbon.

With each day that passed Bernard's love for Helen grew deeper, until at last he could keep her to himself no longer. "I want you to meet my mother. I want you to come with me to her home on Friday night for dinner. She doesn't know a thing about you, and it's driving her absolutely mad."

"Are you putting me on display, Bernard?"

"I can think of nothing I'd like to display more."

"Have you really told her nothing about me?"

"I didn't want to share you with anyone until I was certain I wouldn't lose you."

She hugged him. "You won't lose me, Bernard, don't worry about that."

A thought occurred to him. Did her selfishness match his own? "Have you told your family in America about us?"

Helen laughed. "Of course not. All my father expects from me is war news. He didn't send me over here to enjoy myself, or, God forbid, to fall in love."

"You're going to get a tremendous surprise when you meet my mother," Bernard promised, deciding to share his secret for the first time with Helen. "When you see my mother's wedding picture, you'll think you're looking in a mirror."

The laughter disappeared. In its place was confusion. "Is that why I attracted you?"

Bernard feared he had made a mistake. How did a woman feel when told an initial attraction rested on her similarity to another woman? "Is it wrong that I should have liked you originally because I thought you resembled my mother?"

To Bernard's relief, Helen shook her head. "No. Not at all. It's just that . . . I felt so comfortable with you because you reminded me of my father."

Rachel could not hide her excitement when Bernard told her he was bringing his mystery woman to Graham Road for dinner on Friday night. She dusted off her best china, shined the silverware, set out good linen, and splurged ration coupons at the butcher. She contacted Manny and Sidney at their respective military bases and begged them to get passes that weekend. When her youngest son—her baby—finally brought home his intended bride, Rachel wanted to make sure she got a real family welcome.

Helen had an assignment on Friday afternoon, interviewing injured GI's who'd been brought back from Europe. Bernard had a six-thirty appointment with James Prideaux concerning *Broadway Tribute,* which would end its London run the following day. He thought the meeting, to discuss a return engagement, would last no more than half an hour. He and Helen arranged to meet outside the Playhouse at seven o'clock, and travel together from Leicester Square to Rachel's home.

Manny and Sidney arrived at their mother's home almost simultaneously, a few minutes before seven. Manny carried a bunch of flowers for Rachel. Sidney had managed to acquire a box of chocolates. The house smelled comfortably of baking.

"Where is he?" Manny wanted to know.

"Where's our future sister-in-law?" Sidney demanded. "Wait until we tell her a thing or two about our brother."

"They won't be here until seven-thirty or so. Bernard had a six-thirty appointment with James Prideaux." She saw Sidney make a face. "And don't either of you dare say anything to Bernard's lady friend. It's taken him a month to bring her here, and I don't want you two to frighten her off."

Manny touched his chest in a dramatic gesture. "Cross my heart and hope to die."

Rachel led her sons into the front parlor, where they could watch through the window. It would be just like old times, her three sons all home together again. Her two older sons weren't even arguing. They hadn't been together for so long that their animosity for each other had dulled.

Seven-thirty came and went. No couple climbed the steps to knock on the porticoed front door. At five minutes to eight, Sidney looked at his watch and sighed impatiently. "Where are you, little brother? Dinner's getting ruined."

"You said he had an appointment with Prideaux?" Manny

asked his mother. "I'm going to try the Playhouse. Maybe his meeting went on a long time." He went to the telephone in the hall. Two minutes later, he returned to the parlor, shaking his head. "I can't get through to the Playhouse."

"The number's engaged?" asked Rachel.

"No. I keep getting this high-pitched whistle."

"Must be something wrong with the line," Sidney said.

"We'll wait another fifteen minutes," Rachel said. "You know how difficult traveling around London can be."

Next to Sidney's chair stood a radio. He switched it on as the eight o'clock news began. The announcer's emotionless voice belied the gravity of the news he had to impart. "Shortly before seven o'clock this evening, a Vee-two rocket hit the London Playhouse in Leicester Square and exploded. A line had just started to form for tonight's performance of the show, *Broadway Tribute*. Up to two hundred people, inside and outside the theater, are feared dead. A Civil Defense spokesman said the death toll would have been far higher had the explosion happened fifteen minutes later when—"

Sidney turned off the radio with a click that sounded like a gunshot in the suddenly silent parlor.

Rachel shrank into the chair. "Oh, no . . . Please God, no . . ."

Manny knelt beside his mother, hugging her as he felt her body shake beneath the onslaught of tears. His own breath stuck in his throat to choke him.

Sidney dropped to his knees on the other side of the chair. He put his left arm around his mother's shoulders. His right arm hung in the air for an instant before dropping onto Manny's shoulders. Manny looked into his brother's tear-filled blue eyes and saw his own grief mirrored there. All their fighting, all their bickering, all their years of rivalry . . . what idiots they'd been to waste such time hating each other when they could have been helping each other instead.

They hugged each other tighter, an inseparable trio that nothing would ever break apart again. Tears fell freely for five minutes. When at last they began to cease, Rachel started a fresh deluge with the words:

"He never even told us her name."

The death toll ran higher than early predictions had estimated. Two hundred and thirty-five people died in the V2 explosion at the London Playhouse. Among the dead were Bernard Lesser and James Prideaux, killed instantly as they sat and talked in the booking manager's office, general manager Leslie Martin, who had been working next door, and an American war correspondent named Helen Isaacson, who had been standing outside the theater.

Both Sidney and Manny took emergency leave to attend their brother's funeral and spend the traditional week of mourning with their mother. Unshaven, they occupied low wooden chairs on either side of Rachel, shielding her protectively from the visitors who filled the house.

When the mourning period finished, Rachel rose for a final time from the low chair, looked around the parlor, and said, "I've lived in this house long enough. I'm more than ready to move now."

Fate chose Edward Beecham, editor of the New York *Messenger,* to be the bearer of bad news. Just after ten o'-clock, a reporter telephoned Beecham at his East Side apartment to apprise him of a wire-service report that had just been received. Weighed down with sorrow, Beecham took a taxi to Fifth Avenue and knocked on the townhouse door.

A maid answered. Beecham apologized for being so late and asked for Mr. Isaacson. The maid left him waiting in the library while she called Zalman.

Moments later, Beecham heard the sound of running feet. The door flew open and Zalman burst into the room. There was no need for Beecham to say a word. His unexpected presence so late at night told everything.

"What happened?" Zalman demanded.

"A rocket bomb hit a theater called the London Playhouse. Helen was either inside or waiting nearby, I don't know."

Behind Zalman came Julia. She heard the last sentence and screamed as though in physical pain. "Helen! No! Not Helen!"

Zalman swung around and held her tightly, cheek to

cheek, tears mingling. He'd let her go over there. He'd let her have her own way again. A theater . . . How do you keep hundreds of thousands of troops happy? Do a series on troop entertainment, he'd told her. And this had happened.

Beecham shifted from one foot to the other. "Is there anything I can do? Would you like me to inform Jimmy?"

"No," Zalman answered. "I'll take care of that myself. You go to the newspaper. I don't care what's happening in the world. I don't care if that bastard Hitler dropped dead. I want you to put together a front page that'll make everyone who reads my newspaper remember my daughter for all time. Have you got that?"

Beecham left. Still holding Julia, Zalman called for the maid and instructed her to fetch the doctor. When he arrived, he gave Julia a sedative. Zalman telephoned his son's home in Gramercy Park. "I want you to meet me at the *Messenger*, Jimmy. Helen died tonight, and we're going to make a memorial out of the front page." As he hung up, he thought he heard Jimmy sobbing. That was all right; this was one night when Zalman could appreciate sensitivity.

Jimmy was waiting when Zalman arrived at the newspaper. He hugged his father tightly and asked about his mother. Zalman replied that she was sleeping. He explained how Helen had died, continuing to place the blame upon himself. "If I hadn't told her to do that series on troop shows, this would never have happened. She wouldn't have been within five miles of that stinking theater. I should have let her go across into Europe. She'd have been safer there."

Jimmy felt a huge emptiness swelling up inside him. He'd always looked up to Helen, admired her nerve and determination, and now she was gone. He'd cried when he'd first heard the news. He felt like crying now, but he knew he had to stand firm. Tears could come later, after he'd helped his father. "Helen was there because she wanted to be there, not because you sent her. When did my sister ever do anything she didn't want to do?"

They met with Beecham. The editor typed a factual account of Helen's death, followed by a four-paragraph tribute. Zalman made a couple of suggestions. Jimmy added another. Beecham edited the piece with a blue pencil. He sent the tribute to be set, then sorted through the file pictures of Helen. Zalman chose one that had been taken the week before she left for London. She had a serious expression on her face, eyes looking straight into the camera lens, jaw fixed stubbornly. That was the way *Messenger* readers would remember her.

As Zalman and Jimmy watched, Beecham created Helen's memorial. Not of stone, but of paper. The major story was to have been the breaching of the Siegfried Line by the American First Army. Now it was the death of one of the *Messenger*'s own.

"Black border," Zalman said. "Don't forget a black border."

Beecham nodded, and indicated where one should be placed.

Zalman and Jimmy stayed at the newspaper until the first edition rolled off the press. Only then did they leave, arms draped around each other's shoulders like two dear friends.

Helen's death did what incarceration at Lewisburg had failed to achieve. It knocked the fight clean out of Zalman, destroying the spirit that had driven him furiously for sixty years.

Jimmy had seen his father age in the hours they had waited for the paper containing Helen's tribute. The excitement of making sure that his daughter received such a send-off had carried Zalman past the first few hours of shock. Finishing the work had yanked the prop away.

Zalman sat at home with Julia, neither speaking, their minds too full of memories and pain for words. Jimmy took it upon himself to arrange a resting place for his sister's body. None of the soldiers killed in Europe were being brought back; at least not until the war was over. Jimmy thought it proper that Helen should receive similar treatment.

He booked a telephone call to the Correspondents Association in London. His instructions were for Helen to be interred in England. Later, he would discuss with his parents a more permanent resting place.

"Did your sister have a religious preference, Mr. Isaacson?"

379

Jimmy knew how his father would reply, but Zalman was not making the decisions now. Jimmy was. He pondered the question. Like the rest of the family, Helen had never made an issue of her background, but both of her marriages had been performed in a liberal temple. Jimmy couldn't remember now whether Helen or her husbands had made that choice. It didn't really matter.

"She came from a Jewish family," he said at last.

"We'll get in touch with a Jewish burial society," promised the representative from the Correspondents Association. "All necessary documents will be forwarded."

"Thank you."

Jimmy received the documents four weeks later. He went with Sonya and two-year-old Josephine to Fifth Avenue. It was October, autumn. While Sonya took Josephine to play in Central Park, Jimmy showed Zalman and Julia the documents.

"Helen lies in a Jewish cemetery in a place called Willesden. That's a district of London. The grave is marked with a plain wooden stick. Tombstones are consecrated after a year. We'll be notified when the time comes. We'll make a decision then."

"If the war is over," Zalman answered, "I want my daughter brought back here."

"It will be over," Jimmy said. "We captured our first German city yesterday. Aachen. Didn't you read the report?"

Zalman shook his head. "I don't read war reports anymore."

"You should. The news gets better every day."

Jimmy looked at his mother. Her face wore grief. Lines split her skin as though etched by acid. Her eyes were bloodshot from crying. His father's appearance was little better. Zalman's back was bent, shoulders stooped; animation had fled from his eyes. In the last four weeks, they had barely stepped outside the house. They had lost a bright star in their universe, and they didn't know how to carry on.

Jimmy had also lost. Helen had been his sister. Knowing he would never see her again, he had cried for her more than once. Sonya had comforted him as he had consoled her when

380

Joseph had died at Dieppe. His parents lacked that solace. How could one comfort the other when they had both lost so much? Jimmy knew he had to be their comfort. If he did nothing, they would stay in this house forever. It would become their tomb.

"Sonya's across the road, playing in the park with Josephine. You should see how my daughter runs. Sonya can barely keep up."

Julia looked over Jimmy's shoulder, through the window, and across Fifth Avenue to the park. The trees, turned red and gold by fall, blocked her view. "Why don't you bring them here?"

"This house is no place for a child."

Zalman looked strangely at his son. "Since when?"

"Since you turned it into a mausoleum." He pointed to a picture of Helen on the mantelpiece, two more on the tops of coffee tables. His parents had brought every picture of their daughter into this room, so they could sit and look at them all day long. "Surrounding yourselves with pictures of Helen isn't going to bring her back. If I thought it would, I'd do it myself. After a week, you stop preoccupying yourself with the dead and you start thinking about the living again. You start thinking about your granddaughter and the living people to whom you mean so much."

"When did you take charge of the world?"

"When you abdicated."

Zalman thought that over. "Does Jo really run so fast?"

"Don't let Sonya hear you call her by that name."

"You hear that, Julia? Jimmy's telling me what I can and what I can't call our granddaughter."

"She won't answer if you call her Jo."

"No? How much money have you got in your pocket, bigshot?"

"A couple of hundred dollars."

"I bet you two hundred dollars that she does answer to Jo."

"And I bet you she doesn't."

Zalman hoisted himself out of the chair, then offered a helping hand to his wife. "Come on, Julia. We're going across the road to the park. I'm going to show you how easy it is to make two hundred dollars from some kid who's still wet behind the ears." Arm in arm with Julia, Zalman walked toward the door. Passing Jimmy, he gave him a playful punch on the arm. "You sure you've got no more money you want to lose, bigshot?"

Jimmy followed his parents across Fifth Avenue to the park. The first step was always the hardest. Now they were walking on their own.

Chapter Sixteen

The cemetery in Willesden was busy. The war in Europe had been over for four months. The war against Japan had ended less than a month before; suddenly, with the dropping of two atomic bombs. The sorrow of those visiting the resting places of loved ones on this cool and damp Sunday afternoon was softened by the knowledge that the gravediggers were working fewer hours these days.

A large group of people gathered around a grave in the newer section of the cemetery. A tombstone consecration was taking place. Many of those attending were show business people, entertainers who performed in theaters around the country. Without their stage makeup, they looked quite ordinary.

At the front of the crowd stood Rachel. Beneath the black hat and veil, the once-red hair was gray. Her eyes, as she surveyed the spot where her youngest son rested, brimmed with tears. She dabbed at them with a lace handkerchief, wishing that this day was over. No feeling in the world equaled the misery and despair of outliving one's child.

Manny and Sidney flanked her, their military uniforms lending them the appearance of guards. Next to them stood Rita and Naomi. Their attention was riveted on the white marble stone on which was written: "Bernard Lesser, loving son and brother."

The service finished. People began to drift away. Rachel, her sons, and her daughters-in-law remained beside Bernard's grave until the very last. Before leaving, they each picked up a couple of smooth pebbles and set them gently on the marble.

Still shielded by her sons, Rachel walked along the path toward the cemetery entrance, passing between rows of marble tombstones that stood rigidly erect like soldiers on parade. How many of those who lay below were soldiers? she wondered. Or even civilians, killed, like her son, in the war? Pebbles rested on many stones. People never died completely; they lived on as long as there were loved ones to remember them.

"What's going on there?" Rita asked, indicating two men in hats and light raincoats who stood beside another grave. This one had no stone, only a thin wooden marker warped by rain and sun. Workmen carefully raised a pine coffin from the ground, brushed it free of clinging clay, and set it gently on a trolley.

Manny stopped to watch, grateful for the diversion that took his mind off his dead brother. "Maybe there's been foul play."

"There'd be police here if that were the case," Sidney said.

The workmen pushed the coffin-laden trolley toward the path. The Lesser family stepped back. Rachel surveyed the two men who followed the trolley, one in his thirties, the other sixty or so. The brim of the older man's hat was pulled low, keeping much of his face in shadow. All Rachel could see as they drew level were thin gold-rimmed glasses and a deeply lined, tight-lipped face frozen in grim determination. By contrast, the younger man appeared quite affable. He smiled pleasantly as he noticed the curious gazes that followed the trolley and tried to dispel the tension with a weak joke.

"We must look like grave robbers."

At last, Manny understood. The man's American accent told the story. "Your brother?" he asked, assuming the body in the coffin was that of an American soldier killed in the war. It never occurred to him that such a body would have been interred in a military cemetery.

"My sister. She was a war correspondent based in London for the New York *Messenger*."

The older man spoke for the first time. "Perhaps you heard of her? Helen Isaacson. She was a well-known reporter."

Manny and Sidney shook their heads. Rita and Naomi stood quite still. Only Rachel showed any reaction. Behind the veil, her face creased in thought. Then she said, "The name sounds awfully familiar."

Zalman's face thawed. "One of those rocket bombs the damned Germans used toward the end of the war—my daughter Helen was in the wrong place at the wrong time."

"So was my youngest son, Bernard. He died the same way." Rachel found herself warming to this man who had traveled so far to collect the body of his daughter; they seemed to have so much in common. "I always thought Bernard was the lucky one of my three sons. He had flat feet and a perforated eardrum which made him unfit for military duty. He wasn't a soldier, what reason did he have to die?"

"My daughter had no reason to die, either. She had no reason even to be here. But being an excellent reporter, she wanted to be where the stories were happening. The odd thing was, I wouldn't allow her to go into Europe after D-Day. I wanted her to be safe, so I ordered her to stay in England."

"You ordered her . . . ?"

"The *Messenger* belongs to my father," Jimmy explained.

"I see," Rachel said, nodding.

"So instead of being safe, she was blown to pieces by a rocket that landed in Leicester Square." Like many Americans, Zalman pronounced it "Ly-cester Square."

Rachel could scarcely believe the words she heard. "My son died in that same explosion."

Zalman's face folded into a smile bereft of humor. He held out his hands to clasp Rachel's. "Dear lady, what a tragic waste of life."

"Your daughter, was she married?"

"No. Was your son?"

"No."

"A small mercy—they didn't leave behind families to grieve."

"Except us."

"That's right, except us." He squeezed her hands again,

then let go. As if recalling the terrible reason for visiting this cemetery, his features turned once more to rock. He no longer saw Rachel or her family. He acknowledged only the mission he had to accomplish. "Come on Jimmy, we've got a lot to do yet before we can take Helen home."

Jimmy reached into the breast pocket of his jacket and extracted a business card. He held it out. "Perhaps we might meet again one day in happier circumstances."

Sidney accepted the card without looking at it.

Jimmy and Zalman doffed their hats to Rachel. "Good day," Jimmy said. Then he and his father followed the trolley toward the cemetery office to sign for the coffin on the first leg of its journey to New York.

"Did you really know that reporter's name?" Naomi asked her mother-in-law.

"No. I just thought it might make the poor man's task a little easier if he believed his daughter hadn't died unknown in a foreign land."

Manny felt tears burn his eyes. He blinked and stooped down to kiss his mother on the cheek. "You're one of a kind, you know that? No one else would even think to help a complete stranger."

"That man was no stranger, Manny," Rachel said as she resumed the walk toward the cemetery gates. "I knew him. I knew him very well, in fact. He's family."

"Family?"

"The family of parents who have attended their children's funerals. Unfortunately, we've become a very large family."

Sidney, lagging behind the others, felt something in his hand. Looking down, he saw the card. He couldn't even remember accepting it. Jimmy L. Isaacson, Messenger Publications, followed by an address and a telephone number in New York. Sidney glanced back at the vacated grave, then far ahead to the two figures in raincoats and hats who followed the coffin-laden trolley. The son held his father's arm supportingly. Sidney identified with the scene immediately. He and his brother were doing exactly the same for their mother. She was right. In a tragic way, they were all one family.

He slipped the card into his wallet and hurried after his mother and brother.

PART TWO

Chapter Seventeen

In Britain, the period immediately following the war bore a bitter parallel to the aftermath of the earlier world conflict, when the promised land fit for heroes became a nightmare of depression and unemployment. As the rubble of World War Two disappeared, so, too, vanished the heady optimism originally generated by peace. The cost of six years combat had been astronomical. Once the world's mightiest power, Britain now bordered on poverty. The standard of living plummeted. Food was scarce. Necessities were rationed. Nonrationed goods, under the country's newly elected Socialist government, were subjected to a one hundred percent purchase tax.

Gradually, the will to carry on took hold. The determination that had carried the country from Dunkirk to victory resurfaced. People complained incessantly, but while they grumbled they worked at setting Britain back on its feet. Damaged buildings were repaired, roads resurfaced. Houses were painted, windows washed; flowers waved brightly in small front gardens. People seeking entertainment packed concert halls and theaters. Customers, more aware of ration coupons than money, jammed shops. Everywhere could be seen lines. Women queued to buy fruit. Men waited for combs sold by a street-corner trader. Families stood patiently to catch a glimpse of the gifts received by Princess Elizabeth and Prince Philip on the occasion of their wedding in November 1947. Wherever there were products to be bought, exhibits to be seen, or music and drama to be heard, people waited willingly in line.

The single event that most sharply defined the return to

normality occurred in the summer of 1948. After a twelve-year lapse, the Olympic Games resumed. The last Games had been held in Berlin. Fittingly, the 1948 Games were staged in London. In their own way, the London Games were just as political as the Berlin Games. Iron Curtain athletes deserted in droves. Barely a day passed without newspapers heralding the defection of a competitor from Poland, Hungary, Czechoslovakia, and Yugoslavia to seek a better life in Britain, Canada, or the United States.

Unlike 1908, Rachel Lesser did not attend the opening of the Games. That omission did not quell her interest. The first London Games—when she had seen King Edward the Seventh, cheered for the Finns, and booed the American athlete who refused to lower his nation's flag for British royalty—had solidified her allegiance to her adopted country. The 1948 Games, with the memory still so fresh of Britain standing alone against tyranny, reaffirmed that bond. Rachel scanned the results avidly, finding pleasure in the infrequent instances of British success. And if Britain could do no better than a handful of golds in rowing and yachting, Rachel could always forget her earlier animosity over the flag incident and find some degree of satisfaction in the United States' continuing domination of Olympic competition. The two nations had been allies, after all.

Despite her expressed desire following Bernard's death to leave the house in Graham Road, Rachel had remained there until the autumn of 1945, when both Manny and Sidney were discharged from the service. Brimming with enthusiasm, the two brothers had returned to civilian life, picking up the theatrical agency their mother had kept running for them. Bookings were brisk, and very soon they sought new places to live. What they'd had before the war was no longer good enough.

Preferring the bustle of the city, Sidney and Naomi took a large apartment near Marble Arch. Manny and Rita moved twenty miles west of London, buying a spacious country house called The Paddocks, near High Wycombe in Buckinghamshire. Then Rachel's sons asked her in which home she wanted to live: the apartment near Marble Arch or The Paddocks. Rachel chose The Paddocks. There she could spoil her grandson Jonathan more than ever, and do the same to her second grandchild, a girl with dark hair and solemn brown eyes born exactly nine months after Manny's demobilization from the army and named Bernice, in memory of Rachel's youngest son.

As Rachel followed the Olympics, one athlete captured her imagination. A seventeen-year-old Californian, Robert Mathias, scored more than seven thousand points in a gruelling Decathlon event mocked by pelting rain, a waterlogged track, and slick jumping and vaulting runways. Rachel read the account of Mathias's triumph half a dozen times, amazed that so young a man could have risen so high above such miserable conditions.

"Where does a boy of seventeen gain the confidence to achieve so much?" Rachel asked Manny when he returned home to The Paddocks that night from the theatrical agency.

"He's too young to know any different," Manny answered, amazed that his mother would even be interested in athletics. He wondered if living in the country was starting to bore her. He certainly wasn't bored, but then he traveled into town each day to work. "At seventeen, Mama, you don't understand that you're supposed to be frightened of bigger, older opponents. Look at Sidney and me, and Bernard, when we were that age. We started our own business making and selling soft toys. That went bad, so we tried going on the boards. We had no nerves in those days, we'd try anything. I'm forty-one now, and you couldn't pay me enough to get up on a stage and perform."

"You don't have to. You and Sidney arrange for other people to do such things."

Rachel brought up the subject again, over dinner. This time she angled it in a direction Manny could understand. "Imagine how proud that boy's mother must feel back in America. Her son representing his country and doing so well."

Rita looked across the dinner table at her mother-in-law. "Any prouder than you are of your sons?"

Rachel shook her head. "No, of course not." Since the war, her sons had worked ceaselessly to build up the agency their mother had inherited from Harold Parker. Despite their different surnames—Manny Lesser and Sidney Less—they continued to operate under the name of Lesser Brothers. They had moved to much larger premises in Haymarket, and had taken over half a dozen smaller agencies. They still disagreed, but Rachel heard none of the anger and vehemence that had characterized the rows during their stage career. Now the arguments were constructive, dealing with the agency, not with personalities. Bernard's death had been the catalyst. It had shocked the two surviving brothers into realizing that family members should be supportive friends, not bitter enemies.

Their preference and expertise differed. Manny stuck to representing individual acts, while Sidney, showing a far more extroverted and adventurous streak, preferred to lease theaters and put on his own shows. He had started along that path in 1946 by producing a revival of Sigmund Romberg's *The Student Prince*. In 1947, staying with Romberg, he produced a revival of *Desert Song*. Now he had a production of Cole Porter's *Anything Goes* in rehearsal. Rita was right: Rachel had much to be proud of.

And then she felt sorry for Rita, whose parents had never shown any pride in their daughter's life. Rita and Manny had enjoyed a wonderful marriage for thirteen years. They had two healthy, lovely children, and a beautiful home. Any parents should be delighted that their daughter had done so well, but not Rita's mother and father. Their home in Bristol was a hundred miles away, but for all the times Rita saw them, it might just as well have been the moon. At the wedding they had made it quite clear that they did not approve of their daughter's choice of husband, and their ill feeling had not lessened.

Too bad, Rachel thought. It was their loss.

The new offices of Lesser Brothers were spread across the entire floor of a building at the top of Haymarket, between Piccadilly Circus and Leicester Square. Compared with the single room in Charing Cross Road, where Lesser Brothers had taken over the agency run by Harold Parker, the new home was a palace. Manny and Sidney and the half-dozen agents who worked for them had their own rooms. Clients no longer had to be taken to a pub or restaurant to ensure privacy and quiet.

When Manny arrived just before nine the next morning, his secretary, a dark-haired Welsh woman named Carol Jones, had half a dozen messages waiting for him. She also had a large white mug of tea, without which Manny never started the day. The mug had twice the capacity of a cup. As Manny drank the equivalent of eight cups of tea a day, the mug cut down on the necessity for refills. The sheer size and practicality of the mug impressed people who came to see him. It was the choice of a man who had no time for airs and graces.

Manny spent the first half hour of the day on the telephone. At nine-thirty, people entered his room for the daily meeting. First came Sidney, elegant in a new dark-blue suit. Manny felt a moment of envy as he watched his brother lower himself gracefully into a chair. Sidney had stayed in fantastic shape. His hair, combed straight back with a slight natural part in the center, was touched by gray at the sides. Other than that mark of age, he was as slim and debonair as when he was young. Manny wished he could say the same for himself. He'd blown up like a football when air is pumped in. He liked to claim that army cooking had ruined his body. The simple truth was that he enjoyed eating. With his mother sharing kitchen duties with Rita, his appetite was doubly indulged. Also, he got very little exercise. Funny that, he reflected. I live out in the country and Sidney lives in town. Being out in all that fresh air, you'd think I'd get the exercise. Instead it's the other way around. I ride everywhere, and Sidney walks. Weather permitting, he even walked the couple of miles to work each day.

Naomi followed Sidney into Manny's office, sitting down next to her husband. Since the day the business had gotten back to normal, Naomi had worked as Sidney's personal assistant, a title that took in everything from secretary to . . . to . . . Manny smiled. All the old jokes were true when it came to the relationship between his brother and Naomi, but who better than husband and wife? Like Sidney, Naomi had found kindness in the passing years. She was closing in on forty now, yet her figure was still shapely, her fair hair as lustrous as it had ever been. Manny knew that his own wife hadn't worn so well. Rita's dark hair was streaked with gray, and, like himself, she'd gotten plump. But she'd had a couple of children; her life hadn't been as easy as Naomi's. Manny caught himself. Naomi's life hadn't been any bed of roses, either, certainly not during her time with Gerry Silver. Or, for that matter, when she'd first lived with Sidney. God, how Manny wished he could turn back the clock and alter his earlier relationship with his brother. Still, he supposed he should be grateful they were friends now. Some brothers hated each other until their dying days.

Carol Jones followed Naomi into the office, steno pad in hand to take down notes. Next came David Best, a man in his early thirties, tall and thin with rounded shoulders. His fair hair was sparse on the crown, and his face was bisected by a pair of wire-framed spectacles. Behind him, closing the door as he entered the office, came Barry Levy. In his late twenties, Levy was short and dark, with oily black hair, sharp eyes, and a pencil mustache. Both Best and Levy had been agents themselves, picking up the pieces of businesses their fathers had operated before the war. Of the six agencies Lesser Brothers had taken over, those owned by Best and Levy were the biggest. The fathers of both men had built up strong European connections, bringing unique circus and specialty acts to Britain. Once the war was over, Best and Levy renewed those relationships. Manny, who made his own trips to Europe to check out the talent in dozens of small towns, offered the clients of Levy and Best greater opportunities. Then, impressed by the two young agents, he had offered them the chance to join Lesser Brothers.

The meeting began in the traditional manner. "Any panics last night?" Manny asked, looking around hopefully.

His optimism was shattered when Barry Levy raised a hand. "The Flying Cassinis are threatening to go back to France on the next boat unless we get them better billing."

Manny winced. The Flying Cassinis were a troupe of acrobats Levy had brought over from Marseilles for a three-month circus engagement. "Have a word with the circus management, persuade them to bump someone else so the

396

Cassinis can move up. Explain to them that the Cassinis are too popular to risk upsetting."

"Any suggestion as to who they should bump?"

"Any act not represented by Lesser Brothers," Manny retorted instantly. When the laughter died down, Manny saw David Best's pencil beckon. "What's your problem?"

"We're signing our European clients to British and American rights. A couple of them are starting to ask questions about when we're going to get them some American exposure."

"So are our British clients," Levy added.

Manny nodded. He'd had the same experience with his own clients. America was the golden land beckoning, like the sunset, from the west. Its cities had not taken the same battering as European cities. Its theaters were larger, its people had more to spend. Entertainers made far more money there than they could ever earn in Europe. Sadly for Lesser Brothers, the gateway to America was controlled by one English agency which, long ago, had made connections across the Atlantic. This agency sent European artists to America and, in return, brought American acts to London. No one else got a look in. In disgust—mingled with jealousy—other firms refused to mention this particular agency by name. It was always referred to as the Association.

Sidney's voice filled the office. "We can't change the situation from over here. The Association has got too tight a grip on the business. So Manny and I are planning a trip to America to put together a deal with a New York agency to be their European representatives and have them represent Lesser Brothers in the United States."

In public, Manny made it a point never to question his brother. They might disagree in private, but in front of the other agents they always presented a united front. This time, though, Manny was so surprised that he barely managed to stop himself from saying such a trip was news to him.

The meeting broke up shortly after. Manny followed Sidney into the office he shared with Naomi. Unlike Manny's office, which was decorated simply with two still-life paintings, and a photograph of Rita and the children on the desk, Sidney's office was a tribute to the man. On the walls were posters from the days of Less, Lesser, and Least. Manny always felt a lump in the throat when he saw Bernard's name and picture. Other bills advertised Sidney's clients. Set directly behind Sidney's desk to impress visitors were posters for the two Sigmund Romberg revivals Sidney had produced. At the very top, above the title, were the words: Sidney Less Presents.

"When did we decide to become transatlantic travelers?"

"About two seconds after David broached the subject of American representation."

"It'll take a month. A week each way on the boat, and we'll need a couple of weeks there. Can we afford to be away a month?"

"We can't afford not to. America's where the future lies. Our European clients want to appear there, while Americans are becoming in demand over here. And don't worry about us both being away together. We've got enough competent people to handle the business in our absence."

Manny looked at Naomi. "Are you going to let your husband go away for a month?"

"If Rita will let you go, I'll have no choice."

Manny pursed his lips. He'd always wondered how life would have been had his mother gone to America as she originally intended, instead of England. Perhaps he and Sidney would now have the opportunity to find out.

Manny and Sidney booked October passage on the *Queen Elizabeth,* two months in the future. Then they picked the brains of their own contacts for the names of agents and theater owners to approach in New York. The first person they saw was the man who, since the end of the war, had been managing director of the Rialto Playhouse Partnership. Gordon Prideaux.

Gordon Prideaux was the only son of James Prideaux, the Partnership bookings manager who had died in the Leicester Square V2 explosion in September 1944. Gordon, too, had been in the theater that day. Miraculously, amid all that death, he had suffered only a broken right leg, three cracked ribs, and facial lacerations. Trapped by tons of rubble, and pinned by a steel girder for thirty-six hours before being freed, he had kept up his spirits by singing show tunes, going through the score of every musical he had ever seen. As rescuers reached him, he passed out. Only when recovering in the hospital did he learn that his father had been killed.

There had never been any question that Gordon would follow the older Prideaux into theater management. In 1922, fresh from school, he worked as a stagehand. From there, he moved to the box office, then to assistant manager of one of the Partnership's smaller houses, and finally to manager. Following twelve years in operations, he moved to the talent side of the business, booking acts for the Partnership and working toward the day when he would eventually take over from his father. After the V2 wiped out the top management of the Rialto Playhouse Partnership, a new board was constituted. Its first act was to appoint Gordon Prideaux as managing director.

Gordon's major assignment following the war was to rebuild the London Playhouse. The Partnership, with only seven theaters remaining, had lost much of its prewar status. It needed an imposing flagship. The new Playhouse, with a capacity of more than two thousand seats, provided it. The doors opened at the beginning of 1948. It was immediately evident that a fresh hand was at the tiller. Instead of settling for the security of familiar English acts to top the bill, Gordon gambled by importing American stars. The gamble paid off. Within six months, Americans who would never have dreamed of crossing the Atlantic to perform were lining up for a shot at the Playhouse.

When Manny and Sidney visited Gordon at the Partnership's offices next to the rebuilt London Playhouse, they took a trip back through time. Architects had followed the original design as closely as possible, and the walk up the stairs to Gordon's office was the same as the walk had been to his father's office. It brought back memories for Sidney, sharp recollections he would just as happily forget of a night thirteen years before when he had been told that the act was no longer welcome in Partnership theaters. Times and attitudes, fortunately, had changed.

Gordon Prideaux came out from behind a large oak desk to greet his guests. Tall and slim with wavy black hair, two mementoes of that September afternoon had robbed him of his father's handsomeness and elegance. The broken leg had left him with a noticeable limp, and the right side of his face bore a wide, curving scar that stretched from the corner of his mouth to above the eye. Because of it, his right eye remained in a permanent quizzical squint.

"Fleeing from the misery of Britain, are you?"

"More like trying to bring a little brightness back to it," Manny answered. He sat down, noticing that Gordon's desk was badly scratched. He wondered if it was a relic of the original office; perhaps even James Prideaux's own desk.

"We can do with all the brightness we can get."

"We want to set up an American connection, get our clients work over there, and arrange to represent some of their agencies over here. You've had success with American stars, haven't you?"

"Only here. London might be ready for the likes of Danny Kaye, Jimmy Durante, and Jack Benny, but the rest of the country still wants the kind of entertainment they had before the war. Provincial tastes change very slowly."

Manny nodded in agreement. The more sophisticated the stars he brought over from Europe, the less chance he had of booking them into smaller towns. "Bing Crosby could come over here next week, and outside of London he wouldn't even cover the deposit."

Gordon passed across several envelopes. "Those are letters of introduction to American agencies. I can't promise they'll welcome you with open arms. They already have connections well established over here."

"Sure, with the Association. At least after this trip they'll know our name. Thanks."

While Manny glanced through the letters, Gordon turned to Sidney. "How are rehearsals going?"

"For *Anything Goes?* No trouble at all. You know"— Sidney looked around him—"I think one of my productions would go down really well in this house."

"Can you guarantee filling every seat?"

"I'm in the business of producing revivals, not miracles."

"And I'm in the business of hiring star quality, the only thing that will keep a house this size filled. I'll make a deal

400

with you, Sidney. When you have a first-run show with a star cast, I'll give you special consideration."

"You're making a promise in front of a witness, Gordon."

"I'll testify on behalf of whoever pays the most," Manny said without looking up from the letters of introduction.

"I mean it," Gordon said earnestly. "Offer me a good show, and I'll offer you a stage for it."

Sidney stared at the Partnership's managing director. "Gordon, you inherited your father's love and understanding of this business, but I'm glad you didn't inherit his vendetta."

"What was between you and my father died with him. Besides, I knew Gerry Silver. I couldn't stand him, and even though my father threw you out for hitting him, I was applauding like hell in the background. I never told you before, Sidney, but I always thought Naomi was far too good for Gerry. I'm glad you broke his jaw *and* stole his wife."

Sidney glanced down at the hand that had done the damage. He hadn't hit anyone before or since. It did not even seem possible now that he had hit Silver. He'd done that out of love, the most violent passion of all. "You ever have any dealings with him?"

"His agent tried to get him and his latest female stooge on the Partnership circuit a couple of summers ago, but that act belongs in the museum. If he wants any proper work, he'd better come up with something new."

Manny finished reading the letters and placed them carefully in his jacket pocket. "Thanks for your help, Gordon."

"My pleasure." Gordon shook hands with both men. "I wish you luck in your endeavors."

Manny followed Sidney out of the office. At the door, he turned back for a quick, final look. Gordon was already involved in another matter, fountain pen in hand as he scanned a contract. Manny couldn't help wondering if Gordon ever felt nervous about sitting in the exact spot where his father had been killed. But then, of course, he and Sidney had just been sitting in what must have been the very place where Bernard died.

Manny could not make up his mind whether that was a good omen or not.

*   *   *

On the day of the sailing, Naomi and Rita accompanied Manny and Sidney to Southampton. Rachel remained at The Paddocks to look after her two grandchildren, ten-year-old Jonathan and his two-year-old sister, Bernice. Rita had wanted her mother-in-law to share in the excitement of seeing Manny and Sidney off, but Rachel preferred to stay behind. She didn't like farewells. She had experienced too many to be fond of them, even temporary ones.

A party atmosphere prevailed at Southampton. As guests of passengers, Rita and Naomi were allowed on board the *Queen Elizabeth*. They took tea with Manny and Sidney and walked along the deck, looking down at the busy dockside far below. When the call came for visitors to disembark, both brothers made their farewells reluctantly.

"Don't let my mother spoil the children while I'm away," Manny told Rita. "You know what she's like if you give her half the chance."

Rita's brown eyes misted with tears. "Don't fall in love with America and stay there forever, all right?"

"Fat chance. I miss you and the children already."

Sidney held Naomi tightly. He'd never told her what Gordon Prideaux had said about Gerry Silver. Now, facing a month's separation, it seemed like a good time. "Are you glad I broke Gerry's jaw and stole his wife?"

Naomi regarded him oddly. "What a funny question."

"It's a funny time." He held her tighter as the message for visitors to disembark was repeated. "Tell me, are you glad?"

"Of course I'm glad."

"I always knew you were." He kissed her, broke away, then kissed her again. "Make sure the office works smoothly while we're gone."

As tugs nudged the mighty liner away from the dock, Manny and Sidney looked down over the rail. Among the crowd waving good-bye, they spotted Naomi and Rita. Shouting and laughing, they waved back. Moments later, a steward interrupted their fun by instructing them to prepare for lifeboat drill. The farewells were over. The voyage had begun.

* * *

The *Queen Elizabeth* sailed from Southampton to Cherbourg to pick up more passengers, then steamed west across the Atlantic toward New York. Sidney mixed easily with other passengers, swapping stories and raising laughs with tales about the theater. Manny was happy to stay in the background. When Sidney nagged him to enter the ship's talent contest as a double act, he refused.

"You go on alone," he told Sidney. "You'll win hands down."

Manny felt uneasy aboard the ship. He sensed a class structure. Not first and second class, or even the social distinction between upper and middle class. Rather, he noticed a difference between American and British passengers. Americans spent lavishly while the British counted pennies. Government currency restrictions, even for business trips, made foreign travel an exercise in fiscal restraint. As he joined the penny-watching game, Manny debated the wisdom of visiting America. Among the free-spending Americans on the *Queen Elizabeth,* Manny, for possibly the first time in his life, felt out of his depth.

He shared his fears with Sidney as they leaned on the rail at the stern of the ship, watching the wake spill out behind them. "We're going to arrive in New York like two paupers visiting a nation of princes."

"You think the people on this boat are typically American? Forget it. These people are as typical of the average American as Churchill is representative of the average Englishman."

Manny remained unconvinced. He studied the wake wistfully, a part of him wishing he were back home with Rita and the children.

Watching the wake became a favorite pastime. The brothers spent a couple of hours each day leaning over the stern rail talking. "All this rail had to be refinished, you know," Sidney said. "A steward told me there wasn't a square inch without some American serviceman's initials carved in it. Cunard even sent a section of the rail to the American army as a souvenir of all the troops the *Queen Elizabeth* carried across the Atlantic."

Manny chuckled. Ferried into battle on the world's greatest liner, he would probably have done the same thing.

Sidney shared more information about the *Queen,* gleaned from the ship's officers. At other times, standing at the stern, he repeated to Manny stories of New York that he'd picked up from American passengers.

"I wish I had your ability to sit down with a bunch of perfect strangers and chat with them like you've been the closest friends for twenty years," Manny said.

Sidney stared at his brother. "You have the same ability. You use it every time you pick up a phone and book a client."

"That's different. That's work. I don't do it for pleasure." Manny stared out over the water, realizing that he was confessing envy of Sidney. He'd never done that before.

The next day, Sidney came back with a confession of his own. During a conversation about Manny's children, Sidney said, "Each time I see you playing with Jonathan and Bernice, I think you're the luckiest fellow who ever lived."

"What's stopping you from having children of your own before it's too late? I know that you're aware of what you're supposed to do—remember, I was in Brighton with the Simpson Sisters."

Sidney, embarrassed by sudden memories of that first tour, shielded his face with a hand. "Don't even mention that."

"So what's the problem then?"

"Naomi. She can't have any."

Manny's heavy face creased into a mask of sadness. "I'm sorry. Why did you never say anything before? Mama was always upset that you and Naomi had no children. She thought you were both more interested in the business than in having a family."

"I wish."

"Have you ever considered adopting?"

"Not the same, is it?"

"Better than nothing."

Sidney said no more, but Manny could see him thinking.

During their time hunched over the stern rail, they covered dozens of subjects. They discussed their mother's struggle to keep the family together after their father's return from the Great War and his subsequent disappearance. They talked about their stage careers, and Bernard's death. They spoke openly for the first time about the adolescent rivalry that had blossomed into such destructive dislike. And they agreed that if they had pushed personalities to the rear, instead of parading them up front, their stage careers could have gone on much longer. Perhaps even to real star status.

"But then we wouldn't be where we are now, would we?" Sidney wanted to know.

"Is this where you want to be?" Manny asked.

Sidney swung around to face his brother. "Producing my own shows? Finding work in America for my clients? Trying to bring American talent to Britain? You're damned right this is where I want to be."

By the time the *Queen* steamed into New York, a metamorphosis had occurred. The two brothers whose youthful rivalry had changed to mature loathing—who had been drawn together only by their younger brother's death—had become the best of friends.

Manny and Sidney stayed at an unpretentious midtown hotel called the Parkview. To stretch funds, they shared a small room for the first time since they were children. The lack of space didn't bother them; it was no worse than their cabin aboard the *Queen Elizabeth.* The hotel room was just a base, a camp from which they would sweep out and conquer New York.

After just two days, the room at the Parkview came to mean much more. It represented a tranquil retreat where they could lick the wounds they'd collected that day and prepare themselves for the rigors of the next. New York treated them with the same disrespect it reserves for all newcomers. It intimidated them, scared them, and beat them down. Towering buildings nourished feelings of insignificance. Automobiles and trucks blasted their ears with a deafening decibel chorus. Policemen answered requests for directions with a sharpness that made Manny and Sidney feel guilty for asking. Crowds swept past like ocean waves. The frenzied pace of the city made both brothers want to keep looking down at their feet to see if they were standing still. On top of that, an election campaign was in full swing. Accustomed to British politics, Sidney and Manny thought the chaotic hijinks they witnessed in New York belonged, not in an election, but in a circus.

Nor was New York's theatrical world waiting to greet them. Using their letters of introduction, they visited agencies and theater owners. The proposal to join forces with Lesser Brothers was invariably greeted with polite interest, followed by: "We appreciate you taking the trouble to call on us, but we're happy with the arrangements we have already." Occasionally, the people they saw were not so courteous. One man named Sol Bateman, who owned the four-thousand-seat Ionic Theater in Times Square, which combined live entertainment with movies, kept taking telephone calls during the twenty minutes Manny and Sidney spent in his office. After the sixth call, he spread his hands apologetically and said, "Look, I'm sorry about these interruptions, but you've got to understand that I'm in the middle of putting together a real big deal. You two, you're just a couple of Limeys looking for a piece of the action, and I'm trying to book Frank Sinatra."

They left Bateman's office fuming. In London they were regarded as professionals. In the United States, they were dismissed as a joke.

When they weren't being rejected, they toured the city's sights. Sidney wanted to walk from one end of Manhattan to the other. Manny made him compromise by riding the bus. In the evenings, when they ate dinner, they never ceased to be amazed by the size of the servings. The prime rib Manny had the first night would have made three portions in a London restaurant. Provided, Sidney pointed out, you could find such quality meat. Manny, especially, enjoyed himself, eating Chinese one night, Italian another, and Jewish deli the next. On two nights, they followed dinner with a show, watching talent they would not be bringing to Britain, and sitting in Broadway theaters where their clients would never appear.

Halfway through their stay in New York, Manny, who had been doing the bookkeeping, reached a distressing conclusion. "We're running short of money. I've worked it out that if we see no more shows, eat in moderately priced restaurants, and spend money only on essentials, we'll have just enough to see us through."

Sidney whistled through his teeth. The trip they'd anticipated so eagerly was turning into a minor disaster.

It became a full-scale disaster two days later. Manny awoke early in the morning, sweat-covered and feverish, with a knife skewering through his stomach. He climbed out of bed and staggered into the bathroom. Sidney, disturbed by the noise, followed. He saw his brother bent over the toilet bowl, one hand supporting himself, the other grabbing his stomach as he vomited.

"What's the matter with you?"

Manny managed to turn around. Eyes rolled up in pain, he croaked, "Call a doctor!"

Sidney took one look at his brother's face and grabbed the bedside telephone. Even as he yelled for help, Manny, groaning softly, collapsed onto the bathroom floor.

A doctor arrived within five minutes. He knelt down on the floor beside Manny, touched his forehead, and pressed gently on his abdomen. Manny's moan became a shout of pain.

"What is it?" Sidney demanded.

"Appendicitis, I think. Acute. I'm getting this man into a hospital immediately."

Minutes later, ambulance attendants removed Manny from the room. He was barely conscious, face white, his abdomen a sea of fire. Sidney, clothes thrown hurriedly over pajamas, followed.

By the time the ambulance reached the hospital, Manny had thrown up twice more, heaving dryly when nothing was left to bring up. He also had diarrhea. The doctor retracted his first, hasty diagnosis.

"Where did you eat last night?" he asked Sidney.

"Some small Italian restaurant on Seventh Avenue. Mario and someone or other." Sidney and Manny hadn't been interested in the name. Watchful of their distressed budget, they had chosen by price, not name or reputation.

"Did you order the same dishes?"

"I had veal. Manny had oysters something or other." Sidney's face reflected his own distaste for seafood. Unlike Manny, he remained true to some of the Jewish dietary laws he'd learned from his mother; not from any religious feeling, but because a few of them made sense.

"We'll do some tests on your brother. He may have eaten oysters that fought back."

Sidney remained at the hospital all morning. From a pay phone, he canceled the two appointments he and Manny had with agents that day. Judging from his experience so far of New York, he did not believe the cancelations amounted to much of a loss.

Just after midday, another doctor approached Sidney. "It's not appendicitis. Just a serious dose of plain old-fashioned food poisoning."

Sidney breathed a sigh of relief. "Are you going to let him out now?"

"Tomorrow or the day after. He's very weak, lost a lot of fluid. It won't do any harm to keep him under observation."

Sidney shook the doctor's hand. "Thanks for all your help."

Traveling back to the hotel, he thought it ironic that the first piece of decent treatment in America should come from a hospital.

Manny was discharged two days later, the same day America went to the polls to choose between Thomas E. Dewey and Harry S. Truman. Sidney, oblivious to all the excitement, took fresh clothes to the hospital.

"How do you feel?" he asked his brother as they left Manny's private room and walked downstairs to the hospital offices.

"Absolutely awful. They told me it might be a week or so before I feel really well again. I'm dreading the thought of getting on that boat. Once it starts moving . . ." He rolled his eyes expressively and mimicked a man suffering from seasickness. From somewhere he found the strength to smile.

The hospital cashier also smiled when she asked Manny how he wished to pay: cash or check. Manny perused the bill. Two nights in a private room coupled with doctors' fees, medication, ambulance service, and half a dozen other incidentals he didn't for a moment comprehend came to more than three hundred dollars.

"I'll give you the name and address in London of the company that issued our travel insurance. Send this to them."

The cashier's smile turned stony. "That is not the way we do business with foreign patients. We charge you, then *you* collect from your insurance company."

Sidney felt himself go over the edge. Face flushed with a sudden burst of anger, he pushed his way between Manny and the cashier. "We don't have the money to pay you. We've got just enough to see us through our last five days in New York, settle the hotel bill, and get a taxi to the Cunard dock. And maybe we'll have enough left over to buy a drink on board so we can toast leaving this lousy city!"

"Unless Mr. Lesser's account is settled, he might not be leaving to go anywhere."

"Just watch us!" Sidney grasped Manny's arm and helped him toward the hospital door. They took a taxi back to the Parkview. When they arrived, a message was waiting from the cashier to say that the hospital would have no qualms in seeking legal redress. That included pursuing a court order to stop Manny from boarding the *Queen Elizabeth* the following week.

"Can they do this?" Sidney asked the desk clerk.

The man shrugged. "Hospitals can do whatever they like."

Sidney saw Manny up to the room and told him to stay there. He didn't want his older brother delaying his recovery by worrying about how the bill would be paid. Sidney would do enough worrying for both of them.

Missing the voyage home was all they needed, he thought as he returned downstairs. They didn't have the money to pay for extra nights in the hotel. If the hospital was any example of American goodwill, the Parkview would throw them out and keep their baggage as payment for whatever they owed. They'd finish up sleeping on benches in Central Park like a couple of tramps. They'd never get home. They'd just disappear, two London agents who went to New York and were never seen or heard from again.

Chilled by that vision, Sidney sought help at the British consulate. A reedy young man with a school tie and an impeccable Oxbridge accent told Sidney it was not the consulate's function to pay hospital bills for British holidaymakers foolish enough to travel abroad without adequate funds.

"We are not holidaymakers," Sidney spat through gritted teeth. "My brother and I are businessmen, trying to drum up some export trade to help pay the wages of *civil servants* like you."

Offended at being called a civil servant, the consular officer shot back a sneering "Real businessmen manufacture goods such as cars, electrical equipment, and clothing for export. Your kind of businessman, Mr. Less, can be found on any street corner, playing a musical instrument for pennies."

Sidney stormed out of the consulate, mind already forming the letter he would write to the Foreign Office about the rudeness of consular staff once he got home. If he ever got home!

He returned to the Parkview and went up to the room. "The consulate was no bloody help whatever."

"What are we going to do? Get the office to wire us some more money? By the time they find their way around the maze of currency restrictions, we'll be out on the street or in jail."

Sidney waved away Manny's picture. He had created enough depressing visions of his own.

Manny continued complaining, turning his anger into a comparison of England and America. "No one would be treated this shabbily back home, would they? Say an American visitor to London's taken ill. He'd be looked after properly. He'd be allowed to go home and settle the bill once he got there, right? It wouldn't matter that he didn't have any cash on him, or didn't know a single soul in London . . ."

While Manny talked, Sidney pulled out his wallet and leafed through the cards and scraps of paper that filled every pocket. He was usually fastidious when it came to his wallet. Every Friday evening, at the end of the workweek, he emptied it out, made notes in his diary or address book of important names and dates, and threw everything else away, so he could begin fresh the next week. For some reason, he had kept this particular business card, placing it securely inside his driving license. Why? So he could say yes, he did know someone in New York?

"We do know one single soul here, Manny."

Manny stopped talking. "Who?"

Sidney waved the card. "Willesden Cemetery, remember?"

Manny held out little hope. "He's going to remember us after three years? Sure he will, and I'm Lord Louis Mountbatten!"

Chapter Eighteen

By the fall of 1948, Jimmy was riding the crest of a wave. In January, he and Sonya had become parents for the second time, with the birth of a son named Harold. In August, Jimmy cleared the final debt incurred by his father's tax trial. Money owed to the government in delinquent taxes, penalties, and fines had been repaid four years before; loans secured by Messenger Publications stock had taken longer. Now, the company belonged free and clear to the Isaacson family again. Just as important, under Jimmy's stewardship, it showed a sound profit.

When Zalman was released from prison at the beginning of 1944, after serving a little less than three years of his four-year sentence, he had returned to New York to find Jimmy running the business efficiently. Confronted by a problem, Jimmy was neither afraid nor too proud to ask for help from people who knew more than he did. Zalman's incarceration had spawned a silver lining after all: his son had matured from a playboy into a shrewd businessman who understood and accepted responsibilities.

Back in New York, Zalman prepared to take over the reins once more. His name, after all, remained on the *Messenger* masthead as publisher and president, left there by a son who refused to see his father's contribution forgotten. Zalman assumed that Jimmy would simply step aside and allow his father to become publisher once more in action as well as in name.

Zalman was wrong. Jimmy resisted fiercely, reluctant to

relinquish control, especially of the *Messenger*. During Zalman's absence, Jimmy had transformed the give-the-public-what-it-wants *Messenger* into a respected newspaper. The sensational stories and gory pictures that had characterized Zalman's dominance had been replaced by responsible reporting, crisp news photographs, and insightful comments. Even Edward Beecham, once slavishly loyal to Zalman for resurrecting his career, now looked to the far younger Jimmy as the boss.

Helen's death had shattered Zalman's plans of stamping his own personality once again on the *Messenger*. While he mourned at home with Julia, surrounded by pictures of their daughter, Jimmy carried on resolutely, stifling his own grief in the interests of Messenger Publications. When Zalman did eventually return, he knew the torch had been passed. By weathering two patches of turbulence—his father's trial and his sister's death—Jimmy had come of age. Zalman moved back into his former office, complete with the snooker table over which he had conjured up some of his most lucrative ideas. Jimmy remained in the office that, during Henry Bladen's reign, had been his father's. But the balance of power had shifted. It lay with Jimmy. And Zalman, ready, in his early sixties, to slow down the hectic pace that had carried him since arriving in America, gradually realized that there was also pleasure in living vicariously through his son. Wasn't Jimmy, at little more than thirty, the son Zalman had always wanted?

Understanding the sacrifice on his father's part to allow someone else to guide the company he had created, Jimmy never failed to consult Zalman before making a decision. As likely as not, he sought his father's guidance while they played snooker. Zalman no longer insisted his son back his skill with money. Jimmy had enough strength and independence for a dozen sons.

The first major matter to be broached over the snooker table came in the spring of 1946 when Jimmy asked Zalman's opinion about moving Messenger Publications to a midtown location.

"Why do we need to move?" Zalman wanted to know.

413

"This place was good enough for Henry Bladen, and it's been good enough for us all these years."

"Union Square's not the center of New York anymore," Jimmy answered. He understood his father's sentimental attachment to old areas. He would feel the same if those places had been as meaningful to him as they'd been to Zalman. "Everyone's moving to midtown. It's more central."

"How long will it take to line up new premises?"

Jimmy interrupted his shot long enough to extract a sheaf of papers from his pocket. "It's all here. East Forty-second Street, between Second and Third Avenues, near *Form Guide*."

Zalman skimmed through the papers. Everything was there—reports, studies, costs. "Why bother asking me if you've done the research already?"

"Because I want to hear your opinion."

"What if I said no?" Zalman decided to test his son. What was strongest—loyalty to his father, or business acumen? "What would you do with all your studies and reports if I told you I thought your idea was garbage and we were better off staying where we've always been?"

Jimmy took back the papers, holding them between his hands as if to tear them to shreds. "Tell me."

Zalman's stomach trembled. Jimmy might have changed from man-about-town to hard-nosed businessman, but he would still walk through fire for his father. "It's a great idea. We've been here so long even the cockroaches are sick of the sight of us."

Two months later, Messenger Publications, with its daily and Sunday newspapers and a dozen assorted magazines, moved to its new ten-story quarters in midtown. Jimmy assigned his father the largest office on the executive floor, an airy paneled room with a huge picture window that looked north, while he took the adjoining room for himself. Zalman watched the smoothness of the move approvingly. Not an edition was late, a deadline missed. But then he had come to expect nothing less of his son.

Of the men who had worked for Zalman, only Edward Beecham remained. He was now approaching sixty and considering retirement. Frank Brennan had died of cancer the previous Christmas Day. Bill Regan, who had lost a son at Iwo Jima, retired soon after, and Bernard French, the counsel who had represented Zalman's interests for a number of years, had gone into private practice. Jimmy had replaced Zalman's favorites with his own hand-picked men. Not, perhaps, as rough and ready as men Zalman would have chosen; men more in keeping with Jimmy's sense of what was socially proper. But solid men nonetheless. No other kind of men, Zalman thought appreciatively, could have organized a move of such magnitude without a slipup somewhere.

Messenger Publications had barely settled into its new home when Jimmy broached an idea to his father. "Sonya and I walked along Fifth Avenue last night looking in shop windows, and do you know what we noticed?"

Zalman shook his head. He felt like Henry Bladen had done when a much younger Zalman had broached the silver-spoon circulation scheme to him. Excitement and anticipation caused tiny tremors in his stomach.

"A lot of the fashions are aimed at girls, young women between sixteen and twenty."

"Of course. They've got the money. They're working. And probably living at home, with low expenses, so they can spend their spare cash on clothes."

"Right. But Sonya pointed out that there are hardly any magazines available for this group of girls. There were none at all when she was that age in Montreal, she said, and just one or two now."

"What would you call such a magazine?"

"*American Miss. A.M.* for short."

Zalman repeated the name once before deciding he liked it.

"I've already got the art department working on a dummy. The ad department will start circulating it next week."

"When do you hope to have it on the stands?"

"Two weeks before Christmas. That's"—Jimmy looked at the calendar on his father's desk—"twelve weeks from now."

"Don't you think you'd better start advertising for an editor and some staff?"

"I've gone one better. I've been asking store buyers who's the best fashion writer in the city. They told me Pauline

Fulford of *Vogue*. I had lunch with her yesterday, and offered her the job. She called me ten minutes ago to accept."

Zalman nodded slowly. He was familiar with Pauline Fulford, a tiny, vivacious woman in her early forties who knew every square inch of every office in the garment district. Seeking the advice of fashion buyers was the kind of move Zalman would have made. Never mind the obvious method of advertising the position. Use your contacts and ask around. Pride and pleasure shared equal space in Zalman's smile. Jimmy's mind ran more and more like his father's with every passing day.

"Two weeks before Christmas?" Zalman asked. "Twelve weeks time? Why the hell will it take so damned long?" When Jimmy looked at him in shock, he laughed and slapped his son on the shoulder. "I'm teasing you, that's all."

American Miss made it to the newsstands right on schedule, chock full of sparkling editorial, scintillating fashions, and bright advertisements. Edited by Pauline Fulford, Jimmy's acquisition from *Vogue,* it was a success from the very first issue, reaching out to inform and entertain a whole section of the American public that was largely ignored. The second issue carried even more ads, and the third more yet.

Constantly increasing sales and advertising figures formed only part of Jimmy's pleasure at the triumph of his first proper foray into publishing. His greatest joy came from hearing his father boast about *American Miss* as if it were a publication he himself had launched. Above all else, Jimmy still needed to hear his father's praise. He would never outgrow that yearning. Nor would he ever want to outgrow it.

In the early summer of 1948, Jimmy sought his father's advice on an idea outside of publishing. Television.

Zalman grimaced at the word. "It's a fad, that's all."

"People said the same thing about radio. At one time the military wanted to keep radio strictly for its own uses." Jimmy walked across to the new Emerson he used for monitoring news broadcasts. He turned it on and waited for the tubes to warm up. Then he swept the needle across the dial, pausing for a moment each time he heard music or voices. "Television will be like that one day, you see. A dozen or more stations, and we've got the opportunity to get in on the ground floor."

Zalman looked at his son through a new emotion. Envy. Jimmy would see so many things that Zalman could not even begin to dream about. Zalman had grown up in a Russia struggling to get out of the Middle Ages, and here was his son talking about getting in on the ground floor of television. "Send away for a license. It's your two-cent stamp."

The very next day, Jimmy formally applied to the Federal Communications Commission for a license to build a television station in New York. It would be named WMES.

Once a publication was established, Jimmy left it to operate in the capable hands of those he hired. He had learned from his father the value of employing the best people and letting them do the job they were hired to do. Why buy a dog and bark yourself? He only involved himself when the profit curve began to dip. The same applied to the new television station. He hired men with experience in broadcasting, paid them well, and expected them to get on with it.

The one exception to this rule of noninvolvement was the *Messenger* itself. A major daily metropolitan newspaper was far more meaningful than even the most successful fashion or photography magazine. It was the heartbeat of the city, a finger on the nation's pulse, able to dictate trends and influence thought. Supporting or criticizing those who sought power, either on a national or local level, was far too important to be left to the paid help. Jimmy attended both the Democratic and Republican conventions in Philadelphia in the summer of 1948, and when the *Messenger* endorsed Thomas E. Dewey as the man to lead America into the postwar future, the Republican candidate invited Jimmy for breakfast. When Dewey tried to pin down Jimmy on the reason for his unqualified support, Jimmy answered that he believed Dewey's experience as governor of New York put him in a far better position to govern a country as diverse as the United States than Truman's Kansas background. Never would Jimmy admit that he supported a Republican candidate because it had been a Democratic administration that had persecuted his father.

Jimmy was shocked and disappointed when Truman, against all predictions, squeaked into the White House. Late on the morning after the election, he met with Edward Beecham to devise a commentary saying that the people had spoken, and it remained only to congratulate Truman and wish him well.

"We might have backed the loser, Mr. Beecham," Jimmy said, "but I find some comfort in the fact that we don't look one percent as ridiculous as the Chicago *Tribune* does this morning."

The *Tribune,* seeking a scoop, had come out early with a massive banner headline proclaiming "Dewey Wins." Beecham chuckled dryly. "It'll be a long time before they live that down, Mr. J."

"It will indeed."

Beecham had been the first to label Jimmy with the title of Mr. J. When Zalman had been in charge, the editor, regarding Jimmy rather patronizingly, had called him simply by his given name. The first time he used the familiar name after Zalman's imprisonment, he faced an icy glare. Jimmy's sense of propriety would no longer accept such familiarity. Beecham, trying to recover the situation, thrust forward the formal appellation of Mr. Isaacson. The softening of the glare was accompanied by a slight shake of the head. "My father is Mr. Isaacson." Then Beecham tried the semiformal title of Mr. J. Jimmy smiled and nodded. He liked it. The title had just the right ring of respect and cordiality to suit him. That same day, Beecham sent out a memo to all staff on Messenger Publications that Zalman's son was to be referred to as Mr. J. When Zalman returned, Jimmy began calling him Mr. Z.

In the middle of Jimmy's meeting with Beecham, the telephone rang. The caller was Brian Gilbert, Jimmy's personal assistant. "Mr. J., there are two men at the downstairs desk wanting to see you. Manny Lesser and Sidney Less."

"You know better than that, Brian. I don't see anyone without an appointment. Check them out. If they've got anything useful to say, put aside ten minutes in my diary for them. Otherwise get rid of them."

Gilbert came back a minute later. "They say they know you."

Annoyance sharpened Jimmy's voice. "I do not know them."

"They were wearing uniforms when you met them, they told me to say. You saw each other at a cemetery in London."

A shiver rippled down Jimmy's back. His tone softened. "I'll see them, Brian."

"Shall I have them brought up?"

"No. I'll go down to meet them personally." He hung up on an assistant puzzled by this sudden departure from the norm. In Jimmy's world of rigid protocol, where courtesies were exchanged and expected, he saw no one without an appointment. Going downstairs to the lobby to meet with two strangers who had walked in off the street represented a noticeable breach of rules.

"Please excuse me, Mr. Beecham. I'm wanted downstairs."

Beecham collected his notes on the election editorial. "I'll take care of this, Mr. J."

"Thank you." Jimmy walked through the outer office, in which Brian Gilbert sat, and entered the elevator. When the doors opened at the ground floor, he saw two men waiting at the reception desk. One was tall and slim, elegant in a tailored overcoat, sure of himself. The shorter, stocky man by his side fidgeted nervously; an unhealthy pallor bathed his face. Jimmy would have passed both men on the street without a second glance, but knowing now who they were, and understanding the instant of tragedy they all shared, he strode across the marble floor like a man approaching long-lost friends. Manny Lesser and Sidney Less . . . Jimmy did not remember which was which—he could not even recall if they had introduced themselves properly at the cemetery in London—but he knew how to find out without letting them recognize his ignorance.

"Manny . . . ?"

The shorter man offered a hand. Jimmy grabbed it, then used his own left hand to grasp the taller man's hand. "And Sidney . . . ! How are you both? What are you doing in New York? And why, for God's sake, didn't you let me know you were coming?"

Both brothers were set back by the effusive welcome.

419

Sidney recovered first, recognizing the ploy Jimmy had used to identify them. He felt pleased that the young American had gone to such trouble. It was a good sign. "We had business appointments to deal with first. Work before pleasure, you know. Besides, that card you gave me was out of date. You've moved your offices."

"A couple of years ago, to centralize our operations." Jimmy ushered his surprise guests toward the elevator. "So this isn't a vacation then? What kind of work are you doing over here?"

"Theatrical agents, getting bookings here for our European clients, and seeking American clients to represent in Britain."

"Theater, eh?" Jimmy's face brightened with understanding. "Is that why you're brothers with different names?"

Manny replied before Sidney could, omitting any reference to a family split. "With our late brother, we had a variety act called Less, Lesser, and Least. When we went into agenting, we kept our stage names."

The elevator deposited its occupants on the top floor. As Jimmy passed Brian Gilbert's desk, he said, "What time is my lunch appointment?"

Gilbert, a slim, smooth-faced man, five years Jimmy's junior, perused a diary. "The police commissioner's expecting you at twelve-thirty."

Jimmy checked his watch; it showed five after twelve. Face set in an apologetic smile, he turned to his visitors. "I would stand up anyone but the police commissioner so I could take you to lunch instead. But that's one appointment I can't break."

"We wouldn't expect you to," Sidney assured Jimmy. "We just dropped by to say hello."

Jimmy ushered them into his office. "Coffee?" When they nodded, he lifted the telephone and gave an order to Gilbert. Then he turned back to the brothers. "Is this your first time in New York?"

When Manny answered yes, Jimmy asked for first impressions. Manny spoke carefully, not wishing to offend the man from whom they sought help by criticizing his country. While Manny and Jimmy discussed the city, Sidney looked around the office. The business card that read Jimmy L. Isaacson, Messenger Publications had not even scratched the surface. Sidney sensed power. Lots of it. Even the authority that James Prideaux had once wielded paled into insignificance beside what Sidney saw here. Framed front pages decorated the walls: Pearl Harbor; VE Day; VJ Day; and one with a black-bordered story headlined "The *Messenger*'s Loss." The James Prideauxs of the world had the power to make or break entertainers. The Jimmy L. Isaacsons, Sidney suspected, could do the same to figures of national stature.

Brian Gilbert brought in three cups of coffee on a tray. Jimmy, who took his black, waited for his guests to add cream before asking, "Have your endeavors over here met with success?"

"We made some good contacts," Sidney answered.

"But no firm commitments, huh?"

Sidney shook his head. There was no point in trying to deceive Jimmy. He gave a brief rundown of the brush-offs they'd received from agents and theater owners. "My brother and I have come to know one American expression very well. Don't call us, we'll call you."

"This is a tough city. Far tougher, I would imagine, than London. And certainly not as gentlemanly."

"It's even tougher if you're sick," said Manny.

Jimmy recalled noticing Manny's pallor when he'd met him in the lobby. "I'm sorry to hear that," he said sympathetically. "What was wrong?"

Manny described being taken ill and rushed to the hospital. As he recounted the altercation at the cashier's office, and the threats that had followed, Jimmy's compassion yielded to outrage.

"That is reprehensible! A respectable businessman visits New York only to be treated in such a shabby fashion! What kind of opinion will he take home with him?"

"*If* he ever gets home," Sidney remarked dryly.

"Mark my words, he will," Jimmy promised in a tone that left neither Sidney nor Manny in any doubt. "My sister Helen passed through London on her way back from covering the Spanish Civil War. She had been shot twice in the leg and patched up by some Spanish sawbones. In London, she visited a specialist to have the leg properly treated. He did not hold her ransom until his bill was paid. She told him it would be taken care of once she reached home. Being a gentleman, he accepted that."

Jimmy paused long enough to glance at the framed front page dedicated to his sister's memory. "And I know full well that had Helen been injured by that bomb, and not killed, she would have been cared for professionally in a British hospital without anyone worrying where the money to pay the bill was coming from." He lifted the telephone and gave instructions to Brian Gilbert to contact the hospital and settle the bill.

"We'll repay you the moment we get home," Manny vowed.

"Whenever it's convenient." The stiffness and anger departed in a flash as Jimmy brought the conversation back to a social level. "Tell me, as theatrical agents, how do you feel about television? How is the industry in Britain? How will it affect your business?"

"It's a novelty at the moment," Manny replied, noticing for the first time the RCA set Jimmy had installed against the wall. "Very few people have the sets. Neither of us has."

"It will never replace live entertainment," Sidney added. "Who in their right mind would choose a tiny black-and-white box in the corner over a stage with real people on it?"

"Don't make the mistake of thinking it will remain a tiny black-and-white box in the corner forever. Movies changed from black-and-white to color, and screens got bigger. I firmly believe that one day television will cause a major decline in the fortunes of movies and live theater. Newspapers certainly feel threatened by it. Most don't even carry program listings."

"How do people find out what's on then?"

"Magazines are published in different cities. Television owners subscribe to them."

"Does your newspaper carry the listings?"

Jimmy smiled. "My father and I believe in television. We believe that instead of being enemies, newspapers and television can coexist. We own a license, and we are in the process of opening our own station."

422

Manny remembered the thin, angular man, face shaded by his hat, from the cemetery. "How is your father?"

"Very well. He has an appointment with an optician this morning, otherwise I'd take you to see him. His office is just outside. And your mother, how is she?"

"Also very well, thank you."

The telephone rang. The caller was Gilbert, reminding Jimmy about his lunch appointment. Jimmy turned regretfully to his guests. "I'm afraid that I have to leave you."

"You've been of tremendous help," Sidney answered as he stood up. "We really appreciate it."

"I'm just sorry our time together was so short." He walked them through Gilbert's office to the elevator. As the operator started to close the door, Jimmy snapped his fingers. "Wait, are you busy tomorrow night?"

Sidney looked at Manny. "We've got nothing planned."

"I'm having a small dinner party. Nothing fancy—my parents and a few friends. I'm sure my father would like to meet you again. I'll have my driver call at your hotel at seven."

Before Sidney and Manny knew it, they were standing on the street outside the Messenger Building. Men and women hurried by, oblivious to anything but their own haste to reach a destination. There was color in Manny's face now, and when he grinned at Sidney the color deepened.

"What's the matter with you?" Sidney asked, even as he felt his mouth begin to widen in a smile of his own.

Manny's grin grew even wider. "Just call me Lord Louis Mountbatten," he said.

The car that called at the Parkview hotel the following night was the same maroon Bentley Jimmy had brought back from his visit to England. Twelve years old, it looked like it had just rolled off the showroom floor. Paintwork gleamed, bumpers and headlights shone, the interior woodwork radiated a soft luster. Manny and Sidney sank into polished leather upholstery as the uniformed chauffeur closed the door.

"A right-hand-drive Bentley," Manny whispered. "Makes me feel right at home."

423

Sidney chuckled. "We'll never feel at home in cars like this. You have to be born rich to be at ease in such luxury."

"I could learn," Manny said. He fell silent as the chauffeur climbed into the driver's seat, started the engine, and joined the flow of traffic, heading toward Jimmy's home in Gramercy Park.

Manny gazed out of one window, Sidney out of the other. They had walked the streets of Manhattan and ridden them in buses. Now they felt as though they were seeing the city for the first time. Everything appeared more interesting, and definitely less hostile, from the seat of a luxury automobile.

As the Bentley pulled into Irving Place, its passengers recognized the quaint, old-world appeal that had drawn Jimmy to the area twelve years before. Suddenly they were a world removed from the pressure cooker that was Manhattan.

Jimmy met Manny and Sidney at the door, welcoming them to his home as warmly as he had welcomed them to his office. In the large entry hall, he introduced them to Sonya. Jimmy's Montreal-born wife held a young girl with shoulder-length dark brown hair whom Jimmy introduced as his daughter, Josephine.

"Josephine's been waiting up especially to meet you," Sonya said. "When we told her we had dinner guests from England, she wanted to know if you'd ever met the King."

Manny, unthinkingly, shook his head. Sidney, seeing disappointment grow in the little girl's brown eyes, sought help in a lie. "I've met His Majesty often."

The girl's eyes widened in awe. "What's he like?"

"Well, he has to take a lot of aspirin, because he keeps getting headaches from having to wear his crown all the time."

"You stayed up to ask your question, now it's off to bed," Sonya told her daughter. "Say good night."

Josephine solemnly shook hands. "Do you just have the one?" Manny asked Jimmy.

"Two. We had a son, Harold, in January. Yourself?"

"The same, a boy and a girl. Jonathan and Bernice."

"And you, Sidney?"

Sidney shook his head.

"A shame. You get on well with children." Positioning himself between Manny and Sidney, Jimmy guided them into the drawing room. "Let me introduce you to my mother and father."

Zalman and Julia sat together on a loveseat in the corner of the drawing room. As Jimmy approached with the English guests, Zalman stood up and came forward, hand outstretched, to greet them. His curly hair was steely gray. The dark-brown eyes behind the gold-rimmed glasses sparkled with vitality. Age had slowed his body, but his mind was as energetic as ever.

"Mr. Z., you remember Manny Lesser and Sidney Less—"

"Or course I remember them. From that damned cemetery in London. Your mother was with you that day. How is she?"

"She's fine, thank you," Sidney answered.

"Good. I hear from Jimmy that you've had quite a time in New York so far."

"Quite a time. If it wasn't for your son's help, we might have been here forever."

Laughing, Zalman drew them toward Julia on the loveseat. In contrast to her husband, Julia appeared old and tired. Her hair was tied in a bun, much the way it had been when Zalman had first met her more than forty years before, but now it was thin and almost pure white. Her face bore lines of age and grief. The once-luminous brown eyes had dimmed, and a wire connected her right ear with a hearing aid attached to her black dress. Zalman pointed his mouth directly at the hearing aid and spoke loudly. "These are two of Jimmy's business associates, Julia. From England. Manny Lesser and Sidney Less."

Julia smiled and held out a hand. "I hope you're enjoying your stay in New York."

"Very much, thank you," Sidney replied.

After a few seconds, Jimmy moved them on to the next guests. "It's best that we don't mention how we met in front of my mother. She's never gotten over losing my sister. My father could numb some of his grief by working, but my mother didn't have such an outlet. She lives a lot in the past, I'm afraid."

"I'm sorry," Manny murmured.

"So are we. We've tried everything to snap her out of it. The best doctors, changes of scenery. My father even sold the townhouse on Fifth Avenue where I grew up because he thought my mother might be seeing my sister in every corner. They moved to an apartment on East Eighty-sixth Street. No stairs, all comforts. It hasn't helped. My mother lives in a little shell she's created for herself. It's heartbreaking." Jimmy sighed loudly, then forced his face to brighten. "I've no business burdening you with my troubles. Come and meet our other guests. Maybe you can tell them about the King needing to take lots of aspirin."

Jimmy's guests comprised an odd mixture of publishing, the arts, and politics. At dinner, Manny sat between Pauline Fulford, the editor of *American Miss* and her latest escort, a tall, saturnine French actor named Claude Lavigne who had left France in 1938 and was now an automatic choice for romantic leading-man roles in movies and stage shows.

Sidney, sitting opposite, found himself inserted between a husband and wife in their late thirties named William and Thelma Baron. Thelma, a thin, talkative blonde, used the meal to tell Sidney her family history. During hors d'oeuvres of pâté de foie gras, he learned that the Barons, from Upstate New York, had been college sweethearts at Syracuse University, marrying shortly after graduation. Over a spicy mulligatawny, Sidney discovered that Thelma had gone on to become a teacher, while William had been awarded a scholarship to study law at Harvard. Admitted to the Bar, he had worked for a small law firm in Syracuse before moving to a larger firm in New York City. By the time the main course of Beef Wellington was served, Sidney knew that William Baron had joined the army in 1942, serving for three years. But it was only when the after-dinner cognac was poured that Sidney realized William Baron was more than just a lawyer.

Jimmy rapped on the side of his snifter with a knife. "A toast, to William Baron who, two days ago, was elected to his second term as Republican congressman for the Silk Stocking District of New York."

Sidney turned to his neighbor. "Pardon me, I didn't know I was sitting next to royalty."

Baron's dark face creased into a smile. "Hardly royalty."

426

"But a politician. You make the country work."

"My sole contribution so far has been membership of the House Un-American Activities Committee. That's looking for Communists under the bed," Baron added quickly when he saw the blank expression on Sidney's face.

"I see. What's your connection with Jimmy?"

Baron didn't need to answer. Jimmy did it for him, by raising his glass for another toast. "A salute to the *Messenger* as well, for having the good sense to endorse William Baron. Not once, this past week, but two years ago as well. And to future endorsements, when he runs for the Senate and when he decides to run for the White House."

Sidney raised his glass toward Baron. "I never thought I'd be hobnobbing with a future President."

Thelma replied for her husband. "I tell fortunes for a hobby, and I can see you getting to sit next to more than your share of national leaders. You and your brother."

"Fortune telling?" Manny asked from the other side of the table. "If you're any good, we'll sign you up to our agency."

Thelma laughed. "Thanks. I'll keep my options open."

Jimmy's parents were the first to leave. Zalman held Julia's arm all the way to the limousine that waited outside. Manny and Sidney followed fifteen minutes later. Jimmy saw them to the large entry hall where they had left their coats. "I'm glad you got in touch with me."

"So are we," Manny answered, shaking Jimmy's hand. "You've been a tremendous help, not to mention a wonderful host."

"It hasn't been a one-way street. Read tomorrow's *Messenger* and you'll see what I mean."

Sidney turned toward the front door, then stopped by a large picture that hung above a half-table. The scene was a Venetian canal, and the picture was done in cross-stitch embroidery. "This is beautiful."

"That's Sonya's hobby. She does a lot of it."

"Naomi, my wife, took it up a couple of years ago, but her work's nothing like this."

Jimmy smiled proudly. "On behalf of Sonya, I thank you."

As he walked Manny and Sidney to the waiting Bentley, Jimmy said, "Don't be surprised if you get some unexpected telephone calls before you leave. I consider myself to be an ambassador for my country and my city, and I hate to see anyone leave in a bad frame of mind."

Letting Sidney and Manny dwell on his words, Jimmy said good-bye and returned inside the house.

When they got up the next morning, they made sure to buy a copy of the *Messenger*. Somehow it all seemed much more personal now, the name of Zalman Isaacson listed as president and publisher, and Jimmy L. Isaacson as chairman of the board. It became even more personal when they saw an editorial broadside against mercenary hospitals that acted as the worst possible advertisement for both the city and the country.

That afternoon they had a telephone call from Sol Bateman, the owner of the Ionic Theater in Times Square. Did they have time to see him again before they sailed? Of course they did, Manny answered, seeing Jimmy Isaacson's face dancing in front of his eyes. He started to understand Jimmy's definition of an ambassador's duties. No one left New York unhappy.

Sidney and Manny met with Bateman the following morning. The theater owner's attitude was still curt, but his words were more welcome this time. "I have forty-five minutes to fill between movies. What have you got for next September that's worth two grand a week?"

Manny reeled off a list of specialty acts, ending with a popular ventriloquist named Allen Barnett and his dummy, Muldoon. "Will an American audience be able to understand a Limey ventriloquist?" Bateman wanted to know.

"You've got my word on it."

Bateman shook Manny's hand. "You send me good talent from the other side of the pond, we'll find a place for it."

They returned to the Parkview knowing that the trip to America hadn't been a total disaster after all. One arrangement for a ventriloquist was better than nothing. A message waited. An agent named Irving Kreeger wanted to see them.

"We paid him a visit already," Sidney told Manny. "He wouldn't even give us the time of day."

Sidney remembered. Kreeger had made two phone calls

while the brothers had been in his office. He'd talked in numbers rather than words. Sidney was convinced both calls had been to bookies.

Kreeger's office was located on West Fifty-seventh Street. Manny and Sidney visited him the day before they were due to sail. Kreeger, gray-haired and overweight, with a cigar stuck permanently in the corner of his mouth, looked at them through a haze of blue smoke.

"You two have some pluck, coming all the way across the ocean to look for business. Moxie like that deserves encouragement."

"That's not what you said when we spoke to you before. You were the first person to say don't call us, we'll call you."

Kreeger shrugged. "So I called you. So what? A man's entitled to change his mind. The thing is, I'm tied up with the Association."

"Everyone over here is," Manny pointed out.

"Yeah, but I was thinking that I'm only tied up with them until someone shows me something better. All of a sudden, this new London Playhouse is a hot number. I've got singers and comedians, big names, who want to work there. You get me some bookings at the Playhouse, and we've got a deal."

"We'll get you bookings, Mr. Kreeger."

"Irving. My business associates always call me Irving."

When the *Queen Elizabeth* sailed the next day, Manny and Sidney stood at the stern rail looking back at the diminishing Manhattan skyline. They were glad to be going home, and, simultaneously, a little sad. America had greeted them with open jaws, ready to crush and swallow them whole the instant they cleared customs and immigration. They'd been treated to every facet of the legendary New York rudeness. Manny had even been poisoned into the bargain. And somehow, everything had turned out for the best. All thanks to a powerful young man named Jimmy Isaacson. Neither Sidney nor Manny knew what wiles, what blackmail, what coercion Jimmy had used on Sol Bateman and Irving Kreeger. They didn't care. All that mattered was that they were returning home with some business. Not much, but certainly more than had seemed likely only a few days before.

Sidney fingered his wallet, wondering why he had carried

429

Jimmy's business card these past three years. Fate? A knowledge that one day it would prove useful?

Those were the kind of answers his mother would give. Who knew, with her miles of red ribbon, and her imprecations whenever she saw an ambulance, maybe she had something after all!

Chapter Nineteen

The *Queen Elizabeth* berthed at Southampton in the early morning. By midday, Manny and Sidney were speeding by train toward London, telling Rachel and Naomi, who had met them at the dock, about their adventures in New York.

"The whole trip was a disaster until Sidney remembered that business card he'd been given at Willesden Cemetery. Contacting Jimmy Isaacson was like saying Open Sesame. He knew everyone. We even met some politician at Jimmy's home . . . What was his name?" Manny asked, looking to his brother for help.

"William Baron. He's a congressman. That's the equivalent of a member of parliament, I suppose. Don't forget, Manny, the first thing we do when we get home is arrange to send Jimmy what we owe him."

"I'll take care of it," Manny promised.

Rachel cast her mind back three years, bringing into focus the two Americans they had met on the day of Bernard's tombstone consecration. "Is his father still alive?"

Sidney nodded. "He was at the house with Jimmy's mother."

"How was he?"

"Very fit, very lively. He must be in his midsixties and he still puts in a full day on that newspaper they own."

"And Jimmy's mother? What's she like?"

"Not very well," Manny offered. When Rachel regarded him questioningly, he touched a finger to his temple. "Up here. Her daughter's death affected her badly. Jimmy says she lives in her own little world."

Rachel glanced through the window at the passing countryside. The green of the fields was muted by drizzle and mist. God had given her the strength to weather the loss of a child. He had obviously given that same strength to Jimmy Isaacson's father, but not to his mother. Rachel felt an overwhelming pity for the poor woman.

The train reached London in time for Manny to visit a bank and arrange for money to be sent to New York. From the bank he went straight to the office, eager to be back in the swing of things as soon as possible. He wanted British bookings for his new American clients; he had American bookings to arrange for his British clients. He couldn't wait to get to work.

Sidney had more on his mind than returning to work. Much more. While Manny had returned from New York all set to conquer America, Sidney had come back knowing that he was running out of time to begin a family.

Manny's comment about adoption on the outward trip aboard the *Queen Elizabeth* had focused Sidney's mind on the possibility. And Jimmy Isaacson's remark that it was a shame Sidney had no children of his own because he displayed an obvious empathy with them had pushed Sidney even further along the route. It was not a new direction. He and Naomi had discussed adoption several times. Each time it had lost out to the hope of a miracle, a chance, no matter how faint, that the specialists who had examined Naomi and pronounced her barren could be wrong. But now, with Sidney forty years old and Naomi only a year younger, the hope of a miracle had just about run out. If they did not do something soon, it would be too late.

Instead of returning to the office, Sidney wandered around Hatton Garden, perusing jewelry displays until his fancy was taken by a thin gold necklace with a heart-shaped locket the size of a shilling. He gave it to Naomi that night, over dinner in a restaurant near their Marble Arch apartment.

"I wanted to bring you back a souvenir of New York, but we were so broke we barely managed to bring ourselves back."

"What did you do, go out shopping this afternoon?"

When Sidney nodded, Naomi leaned across the table to kiss him. She opened the heart-shaped locket and looked inside. It was empty. "I'll put a picture of you in there, a tiny portrait picture, so whenever you go halfway around the world again, all I'll have to do is look down to see you."

"Wouldn't you rather have a picture of our children?"

The gaiety dropped from Naomi's face. "More than anything, but fate keeps teasing us."

Sidney reached out to cover Naomi's hand. "It's about time we stopped trying to fool ourselves, darling. Fate's not teasing us—it's saying no with a capital N. I think we have to decide now what we're going to do about it."

"Do? What can we do?"

"We can adopt."

Naomi fidgeted uncertainly. The idea of raising another woman's child made her uncomfortable. That wasn't the way nature had intended it to be. A woman should mother her own children, not someone else's. And what if, once they adopted, the miracle happened? Would she favor her own natural child over the adopted child? Painful questions plagued her, just as they always did when this subject arose.

Sidney recognized the torment on his wife's face. "I know it's unfair for some women to be unable to bear children. It's just as unfair for some children to have no mothers. Adopting is the only way to redress the wrongs both sides suffer."

"Will you be able to love an adopted child as dearly as a child of our own?"

"It *will* be a child of our own. We would have just gone about acquiring it in a different manner. And not a child, but children."

"You want more than one?"

"At least two. We'd spoil one child silly."

Naomi considered Sidney's proposition. Not one adopted child, but two. She looked down at the locket again, picturing two tiny faces there. A few minutes ago, the idea had scared her. Now it was beginning to appeal. Was that because two children were somehow less frightening than one?

"Adopting might have some advantages after all," she said.

Sidney's heartbeat quickened as he recognized the surrender in Naomi's words. "How's that?"

"We'll get to choose whether we have sons or daughters."

Sidney and Naomi visited an orphanage in South London. Their hearts were torn by the sight of children with no family other than the orphanage staff. Were it possible, they would have adopted every child. Instead, they tried to establish a friendship with two sisters named Andrea and Linda.

Sidney felt an immediate kinship for the two young girls. They came originally from Dalston, the very area where he had been brought up. Only their childhood had been far less happy, and far shorter. It had ended in the fall of 1944 when a flying bomb had destroyed the library where their father worked. Their mother had also died in the explosion. The two girls, Andrea then four, and Linda only a year old, had been staying with a neighbor at the time. Not only could Sidney relate to their geographic background, he could relate to the means of their loss; his own brother had died in similar circumstances.

With no other family to care for them, the two girls were taken in by the orphanage. Linda made the adjustment far better than her older sister. Andrea, a dark-haired, soulful girl, remembered her parents clearly while Linda, a mischievous imp with bright red hair, soon forgot the few memories she might have harbored. Andrea understood that she lived with other children in a place that was not her real home. Linda, after a few weeks, did not even realize that she had ever lived anywhere else.

Sidney and Naomi began their courtship of the two sisters by taking them out on Sunday afternoons for lunch and then a movie. Laughter, Sidney noticed, always came easier from Linda. Andrea, whenever she thought anyone might be watching, kept a rigidly straight face. Only in rare, unguarded moments did she smile. And then the smile disappeared as quickly as it had bloomed when she realized someone might see.

The two sisters soon began to refer to Sidney and Naomi as aunt and uncle. One afternoon, a month after they first met, Sidney and Naomi took them to the Corner House for

434

tea. During the meal, Andrea set down the piece of cake she was eating and asked, "Why do you and Auntie Naomi take us out every week?"

"Because we're very fond of you," Sidney answered.

"Why? We're not your children. We're not even your *real* nieces."

Naomi saw Sidney's face flush as he tried to find a way around the awkward questions. She helped him out by using his own rationalization. "Andrea, some husbands and wives don't have children, just as some children don't have parents. It's very wonderful when those people can get together like this."

Andrea dredged up the word that always floated alluringly around the orphanage like some magical charm. "Are you and Uncle Sidney going to adopt us?"

"Would you like us to adopt you, Andrea? Linda, would you like to live with us?"

Linda nodded happily, red curls bouncing up and down. Andrea considered the question at great length before saying, "That wouldn't make you our mother and father, would it?"

"No. No one can ever replace your real mother and father."

"Do you remember them?" Sidney asked.

"Of course I do." Andrea's eyes misted over; a tear appeared like magic in the corner of her right eye. "My father was the most handsome man in the world, and my mother was beautiful, like a queen." The single tear became a deluge. "They were much more handsome and much more beautiful than you!" Andrea pushed back from the table, jumped from the chair, and ran toward the exit.

Sidney ran after her, grabbing her arm just as she reached the door leading to the busy street. "Stop it! Auntie Naomi and I don't want to take the place of your mother and father. No one ever can! We just want to be your friends, that's all."

Some of the anger disappeared. Sidney lifted Andrea into his arms and carried her back to the table, dabbing at her tears with a handkerchief. When she sat down again, Naomi kissed her on the cheek and hugged her.

After tea, Sidney and Naomi took the girls to their home for the first time. Pulling Linda behind her, Andrea inspected the flat. She sat in chairs, bounced on beds, fingered the heavy drapes, and looked out of the window toward Hyde Park. It was all very different from the orphanage. Even different from what she remembered of Dalston. "Would we share a bedroom? We share a bedroom now, you know."

"Would you want to?"

"Yes. I want to be with Linda. I have to look after her. I always promise our parents that I will."

"You promise them? When do you make this promise?"

"Every night when I speak to them in my prayers."

Naomi felt a lump in her throat. For an eight-year-old girl to show such responsibility wrung tears from her. "Of course you can share a bedroom. You can do anything you want to do."

When they returned Andrea and Linda to the orphanage that evening, Sidney and Naomi knew they had found the children to make their lives complete.

In the weeks that followed, Naomi and Sidney introduced the two girls to other members of the family. Rachel took to the sisters immediately. If her younger son and his wife could have no children of their own, it was only right that they should adopt. She began buying presents for the two girls, spoiling them as much as she had ever spoiled her natural grandchildren. Watching Rachel's reaction made Sidney and Naomi even more certain that they were doing the right thing.

Manny, too, was delighted by Sidney and Naomi's decision. He pummeled his brother's arm and said, "I'm glad you listened to me for once. Congratulations!"

"I just got fed up buying birthday presents for my brother's children. I figured it was about time he bought some for mine."

"With pleasure," Manny said, beaming, and Sidney knew he meant it. "With absolute bloomin' pleasure!"

The very next week, when Andrea and Linda were once again in Marble Arch, Manny turned up with an enormous teddy bear for Linda and a rag doll for Andrea that was as big as she was.

Manny's children reacted as warmly as their parents did. Eleven-year-old Jonathan paired off instantly with Andrea, showing her card tricks he had learned from his father. Linda took up with Bernice, who was eighteen months younger than herself. She let the little girl play with her toys, and patiently showed her how to dress the dolls Sidney and Naomi had given her. When the time came to part, tears glistened in the eyes of adults and children.

In the spring of 1949, Sidney and Naomi, certain they were making the best decision of their marriage, officially adopted Andrea and Linda.

Almost a year after their trip to New York, Manny and Sidney began to see the dividends. Allen Barnett, the ventriloquist the brothers had sold to Sol Bateman, took his dummy Muldoon onto the stage of the Ionic Theater in Times Square and thoroughly captivated four thousand people. Less than an hour after Muldoon and Barnett convulsed the audience, Irving Kreeger, the Lesser Brothers representative in New York, was on the telephone selling the ventriloquist and other British and European acts to major theaters across the country.

Lesser Brothers honored its part of the bargain by finding work for Kreeger's clients in Gordon Prideaux's London Playhouse. The first American star Lesser Brothers brought over in the fall of 1949 was Tony Marino, a singer who had started out as a band vocalist with Artie Shaw before striking out on his own with a dozen hit songs and a handful of successful musical films. As well as a reputation for singing, Marino was known as a hell-raiser and womanizer. Simultaneous with his arrival in London, the Fleet Street press ran specials on the entertainer's life, from his affairs with Hollywood's most beautiful actresses to his legendary brawls with journalists and photographers. Interest soared. Tickets were snapped up by British fans eager to see if the American crooner sounded as good in the flesh as he did on the records that were played constantly on the radio. Outside the theater, scalpers worked double-time.

Manny, Sidney, Rita, and Naomi watched the opening-night show from Gordon Prideaux's private box. They felt as nervous as any novice. The occasion affected Gordon, too. Usually during a show, he sat hunched forward, concentrating with every muscle and nerve on what was taking place onstage. On Tony Marino's opening night, Gordon talked nonstop to his guests.

"Instead of keeping the band in the pit, we put it on the stage. That should make him feel at home, shouldn't it?"

"That's the way he's used to singing," Manny replied.

"You know, we've changed our whole format around for him. We're giving him forty-five minutes. That's twenty, twenty-five minutes more than the top of the bill usually gets. I hope he can last that long."

Sidney patted Gordon on the shoulder. "His shows in the States run an hour at least," he said reassuringly, although his own stomach was twisted into an uncomfortable knot. God help him and Manny if Tony Marino did not live up to expectations. Marino would get bad reviews, nothing more. He'd go home swearing never to appear again in front of a Limey audience, while the two agents who had brought him to London would spend the next five years repairing their badly battered credibility.

An all-British cast carried the first half of the show. The audience applauded each turn, but their impatience was obvious. They had come to see only one person; everything that preceded him was window dressing. During the break, excitement and anticipation mounted. When the curtain rose again, the band was in place. Tommy Trinder, one of the country's most popular comedians, made a brief introduction. "Ladies and gentlemen . . . ! The Yanks are coming . . . again! You lucky people!"

Tony Marino stepped out from the wings. Slightly built, with hunched shoulders and a thin face in which blue eyes glowed, he stood perfectly still in front of the band, peering out into the silent auditorium as though seeking a friendly face. In Gordon Prideaux's box, Manny gulped nervously. Rita clutched his hand.

Tony Marino remained like a statue for fully five seconds. It was the longest five seconds Manny and Sidney had ever known; mountains grew and oceans evaporated. In the darkness of the auditorium, someone coughed. Marino's right hand moved. White cuff shot out from the sleeve of his dark blue jacket. The gold of a cuff link gleamed dully. His fingers snapped, his foot tapped softly. The band swung into "Begin The Beguine," a number Marino had sung with huge success during his days with Artie Shaw. Recognizing the opening bars, the audience applauded. Eyes half closed, Marino caressed the microphone and began to sing in a lightweight baritone that was simultaneously tender and attractively rough around the edges. Every woman in the audience felt the words were meant only for her, and every man felt the ugly ache of jealousy.

"He's good," Manny whispered as though surprised.

"Damned good," Gordon answered.

Manny sat back, enjoying every note Marino sang. He and Sidney would not have to repair their credibility after all.

Marino filled the Playhouse for six weeks. Manny and Sidney fussed over him, both at the Playhouse and the Dorchester where he had a suite. Marino was a perfect gentleman. Only once did Manny and Sidney see evidence of the famous Marino temper. After one show, with Rita and Naomi, they took the singer to dinner at an Italian restaurant in Soho. As they left the restaurant, a flashbulb exploded in Marino's face. A photographer from one of the tabloids tried to dart away. He wasn't quick enough. Marino pounced on the man, grabbed the camera, smashed it against a wall, and warned the photographer that he'd be next. The man tarried only long enough to collect the camera pieces.

"What the hell do I have to do to get some peace and privacy when I go out for a meal?" Marino demanded of his companions.

"Being famous has a price," Rita answered.

"So does being a press photographer," Sidney said. Even Marino laughed.

The next morning, the tabloid pictured the shattered camera on the front page, alongside an open letter to the American singer. "Perhaps," the letter ended, "such thuggish behavior is acceptable in America, Mr. Marino, but different rules apply here. The rules of a civilized, cultured people."

Marino hit back with a lengthy telegram, attacking the tabloid and all newspapers that sent reporters and photographers out like attack dogs to harass celebrities. "You talk of civilization and culture" ran part of the telegram. "Since when is it civilized and cultured to shove a camera in a man's face while he is engaged in conversation with other people and blind him with a flashbulb? If newspapers want people to act in a civilized manner, they should instill those same qualities in their staffs. Apes are very trainable, I have been told."

The wire, enlarged for easy reading, filled the entire front page of the tabloid. That night, when Marino stepped onto the stage, the audience gave him a standing ovation.

After Marino returned to America, Lesser Brothers rounded out 1949 by bringing over another American to top the bill at the Playhouse. Buddy Beck, a zany, rubber-faced comedian, kept Playhouse audiences in stitches, doing a routine he had perfected in a career that had taken him from a Brooklyn tenement to Hollywood stardom. On opening night, he had the audience on his side within a couple of seconds. He stumbled out from the wings and stood forlornly in the center of the stage, wringing his hands. "I'm frightened to death," he said. As people began to laugh, he added, "I'm standing here in front of you all, absolutely terrified, and you're laughing at me."

After the performance, Beck's agents and Gordon went backstage to congratulate the comic. "That was a great routine," Manny said. "From the moment you staggered out from the wings, you had the audience in the palm of your hand."

"*What* routine? I was terrified. I didn't stagger from the wings. I had to be pushed out. I heard my cue and I couldn't move. So help me, I was stuck there like a statue."

"You?" Sidney could barely believe his ears. "You starred at the Flamingo in Las Vegas. How could you have nerves?"

Beck dismissed the comparison with a wave of the hand and the facial expression of a man stepping in dog's mess. "That's the Flamingo! This is the London Playhouse. How can you compare them?"

"But you earn more there," Gordon pointed out.

This time, Beck's expression was of a man who had not only stepped in dog's mess, but had felt with his hand to see what he'd trodden in. "The hookers earn more there as well.

440

Money's not everything. Class is important, too. And believe me, the Playhouse has got class."

Gordon's smile of pride stretched the scar on the right side of his face into a broad band.

Both Marino and Beck proved so popular, even among newspaper critics who had originally complained about Americans receiving preferential treatment at the Playhouse, that Gordon Prideaux decided he wanted them back for a return engagement the following September. Not for an ordinary run, but for the Playhouse's annual autumn extravaganza—the Performing Artists' Gala.

The gala was the major fund-raiser of the Performing Artists' Benefit Society, a charitable body founded in 1910 to assist music hall artists who fell on hard times. Since then it had expanded to help the families of entertainers. It also operated a retirement home in the resort town of Bournemouth called Second House, which accommodated fifty elderly variety artists who could no longer care for themselves. Society funds came from donations and the proceeds of the annual gala. Traditionally, royalty attended the gala, and it was the ambition of every performer to be invited to participate. The inconvenience of working for nothing was more than compensated for by the public relations coup of being presented to a member of the Royal Family.

During the 1930's, James Prideaux had won the right for the Rialto Playhouse Partnership to produce the gala, working with the society's board of management to put together the best possible show. As well as a charity event that raised money for a cause with which Prideaux was entirely sympathetic, the gala, with its link to royalty, represented a trophy for the London Playhouse. Other theater groups waited for the standard to slip, so they could offer the society an alternative. Prideaux worked hard to make sure the standard never wavered. The annual gala would leave the Playhouse only over his dead body.

The war suspended production of the gala. When peace returned, with James Prideaux dead and the London Playhouse in ruins, the Performing Artists' Benefit Society renewed the gala at another theater in the West End of London. As Gordon Prideaux supervised the building of the new Play-

441

house, he met with the society's board of management to plead his case for taking over his father's responsibility of producing the annual event. He succeeded. The first gala at the new Playhouse was held in September 1948. Lesser Brothers placed one act in that show—Allen Barnett, the ventriloquist they later sold to Sol Bateman's Ionic Theater in New York. In 1949, they placed two acts—a comedy duo named Sherwood and Forrest, and a popular singer called Laura Lane. For the 1950 Performing Artists' Gala, Gordon Prideaux wanted to establish control of the show beyond reach of any competition. The success he'd had with Tony Marino and Buddy Beck would assure him of it. Simultaneously, it would establish Lesser Brothers as a major international agency.

Rachel attended that year's Performing Artists' Gala, wearing a pale-green evening dress that had been specially made for the occasion. At a reception following the show, she watched Gordon Prideaux introduce the artists to that night's guests of honor, the King and Queen. Rachel noticed that the Queen had a couple of extra words for the two Americans brought over by her sons.

"Why is Gordon making the introductions and not you?" she whispered to Manny and Sidney, who stood with their wives. "You're responsible for the two biggest names being here."

Manny felt himself blushing and wondered if anyone else had heard. His mother's voice carried further than it once did; he suspected she was becoming hard of hearing. "You know full well why, Mama. Gordon is the Partnership's managing director. This is his production. We're just agents who work behind the scenes, not on center stage. Would you have ever tried to upstage James Prideaux?"

Recalling the older Prideaux's no-nonsense attitude, Rachel smiled at Manny's question. She glanced up at Sidney who stood staring at Gordon Prideaux chatting with the royal couple. Sidney hadn't answered her question, and Rachel understood why. He was too busy picturing himself in Gordon's shoes. Manny might want to work backstage, but Sidney saw himself in the limelight. That was the reason he preferred to produce his own shows, why he took financial risks leasing theaters when he could live comfortably off the agency's commissions.

She turned back to watch the royal couple. She had worked with James Prideaux, and now her sons worked with Prideaux's son. That satisfied Rachel's sense of propriety. She had seen too much upheaval in her life not to appreciate continuity.

After the performance, Manny drove his mother and Rita back to The Paddocks. Sidney and Naomi traveled the much shorter distance to Marble Arch by taxi. Despite the speed of the journey, Sidney used the time to reach a momentous decision. He would resign from Lesser Brothers in order to pursue his own career as a producer.

He shared his news with Naomi as they gratefully slipped out of their formal clothes.

"There's not just ourselves to think about anymore. We've got two daughters to care for as well." He paused long enough to kick off his dress shoes, sighing with relief as he wiggled his toes. "This family needs more than a partnership in Lesser Brothers can give us."

Amusement brimmed in Naomi's wide brown eyes as she regarded her husband. It wasn't the sight of him in stocking feet, with his dress shirt flapping down to his boxer shorts, that made her smile. It was the oddity of his claim. "Sidney, you make more money now than you ever have. What with the American deals, your income from the agency has doubled in the past year."

"There are more expenses."

Naomi fell silent. She loved Sidney too much to contradict him further. If he wanted to believe he was making a move to better himself financially, she wouldn't argue. In his own good time he would admit the real reason to himself.

The next day, after the regular morning meeting in Manny's office, Sidney cornered his brother. "I want to concentrate on producing. Those Romberg revivals I put on made money. So did *Anything Goes* last year, and *Show Boat* this year. I'm not cut out to be an agent. Bernard was. You are. But I'm not."

443

"Eventually you're going to run out of revivals."

"They just gave me a taste for putting on my own productions. Now I want to start producing first-run shows."

Manny did not look at all surprised. He had frequently wondered how long it would be before shows became his brother's sole concern. Sidney was right—he was too much of a showman to hide behind an agent's smile and handshake. "Why the decision now, on the day after the gala of all days?"

"Coincidence."

Manny shook his head. "You were turning green last night when Gordon was hobnobbing with His Majesty. I saw it. Mama saw it. Rita and Naomi saw it. It's a miracle the King himself didn't see it."

Sidney smiled artfully at his brother. "Tony Marino and Buddy Beck made that show something special last night. They got the loudest applause, they had the biggest spots. And it was you and me, Manny, who brought them over. It was you and me who turned a mundane gala into a real spectacular. And it should have been you and me presenting Tony and Buddy to the King and Queen. If you're too shy to take the credit, then I'll happily accept it on my own."

Manny roared with laughter. "You want to produce full-time, Sidney, go ahead. You know I'll help you in any way I can."

"May I keep my office here?"

"Of course. Don't you know that no agency's complete without its own resident impresario?"

The two brothers shook hands. For the second time in their lives, they were going separate ways. Only this time they wished each other nothing but the best.

Chapter Twenty

The New York *Messenger* severed a major connection with the past when, at the end of 1949, Edward Beecham stepped down as editor.

During Beecham's final week, Messenger Publications honored him with a farewell dinner at the Waldorf-Astoria attended by more than a hundred middle- and top-management executives. Following dinner, and the presentation of a gold watch on which was inscribed the *Messenger* logo, Beecham uncoiled his lanky body from the chair.

"I spent twenty-two years as editor of the *Messenger.* During that time I served three chiefs: Henry Bladen, Zalman Isaacson, and Jimmy Isaacson. Henry Bladen, may he rest in peace, believed in filling every column inch of the paper with sensationalism. Garish stories, blood and guts, and scandals of a sexual or political nature; both together, more often than not. Mr. Isaacson"—he inclined his head toward Zalman, two seats away—"who, like me, learned his trade from Henry Bladen, also believed in giving the public what they wanted. Nothing wrong with that. Newspapers have to be sold and read before they mean anything. But it was Mr. J. who showed me that while giving members of the public what they wanted, you could also educate them to want something better."

Beecham glanced down at Jimmy, who sat next to him, and there was a certain fondness in the editor's mien. "When you took charge of the *Messenger,* Mr. J., I didn't think you had what it took. I believed your appointment was blatant nepotism. Your father once told me that he had a daughter who was one hell of a newspaperman, and he was determined to make one out of his son as well. I never dreamed he'd be able to do so. I was wrong. You surprised me, Mr. J., and you pleased me. And for that, I thank you."

Jimmy sat back, face flushed with pleasure. He looked at his father and saw Zalman smiling. That single expression meant more than all of Beecham's compliments. Jimmy could not recall his father making such a statement to Beecham, but he could believe it. The old editor had witnessed many confrontations between father and son when Jimmy had tried to bring class and culture to the *Messenger*'s Sunday magazine. Now Beecham was thanking Jimmy for polishing the *Messenger* into a sophisticated newspaper, and Zalman was smiling in proud agreement.

As Beecham continued speaking, Jimmy's gaze moved from his father to the petite middle-aged woman with the bright brown eyes who sat across from him. Pauline Fulford was another whose expertise had added to the success of Messenger Publications. Her *American Miss* was now one of the top young women's magazines in North America, its sparkling fashion coverage and bright editorial content keeping it streets ahead of the half-dozen imitators that had sprung up in the past three years, all trying to cash in on the popularity of *A.M.*

Jimmy's eyes traveled on, past the well-dressed figure of Brian Gilbert, his personal assistant, to a tall, gaunt man whose thin face had lost its battle with acne. Not that it mattered. Marvin Baker was not a man you looked at. He was a man you listened to because he knew so much. Especially about broadcasting. Baker had been lured a year earlier from his position as manager of a small radio station to direct WMES, Messenger Publication's fledgling television station, and seek areas of expansion, either by acquiring existing stations or opening new ones in promising locations. An FCC freeze on new licenses soon after approval of the WMES application limited expansion temporarily, but Jimmy was still satisfied with Baker's achievements. WMES had gone on the air in February of that year with a breezy mix of news and entertainment. Especially satisfying to Jimmy was that two weekend programs created by WMES had become instant hits. With *Music Makers* and *Appearing Tonight,* WMES served notice that it would create, not follow.

Beecham began to reminisce about the day he and Zalman had ridden on Bladen's funeral train to Chicago. The story brought a smile to Jimmy's face. He knew how his father had stood twice in line at the cemetery to shake hands with Bladen's two sons, the first time to offer his condolences, the second to ask how much they wanted for the *Messenger.* Only Zalman Isaacson would have the nerve to do that, Jimmy reflected, but if he had not taken the bull by the horns that day, would they all be sitting here now, so honorable and beyond reproach? The *Messenger* wasn't the biggest money-maker in the group. *Form Guide* held that title; the national racing paper produced money like a treasury printing press. But the *Messenger* was the publication that had added respectability to the Isaacson empire, and Jimmy was the last person to denigrate respectability.

As Beecham continued talking, Jimmy's mind drifted back to the newspaper's television station. *Appearing Tonight* had been his own suggestion, a series that showcased both established and emerging talent. Hosted by a man named Bill Delaney, it had instantly become the show for any entertainer to be seen on. An appearance with Bill Delaney meant national attention. The idea for *Music Makers,* a dance show for teenagers, had come from Sonya. She had broached it the same way she'd floated the idea for *American Miss,* saying that she'd noticed there were no programs suitable for youngsters who wanted to hear the latest music while they watched people of their own age dancing to it. Jimmy had immediately seen the possibilities of such a program. So had Marvin Baker, the station manager. Three months later, the first *Music Makers* aired. Youngsters loved it. More important, so did sponsors.

The longer Jimmy was married, the more he understood that he was wed to a very special woman. Sonya expressed herself artistically with her needlepoint work. At least two galleries had offered to buy all she could make, but money held no appeal. She either gave her creations to friends or let them be sold for charity. Her artistic nature was complemented by shrewdness, especially where her husband's business was concerned. She had the ability to see where a certain program or magazine would succeed. On top of that, Jimmy thought smugly, she was one hell of a wife to him and a mother to Josephine and Harold. He didn't know where she found the time. What he did know was that the money he had paid for that first train ticket to Montreal more than ten years ago was the smartest investment he had ever made.

Edward Beecham neared the end of his speech. "All that remains now, before I type 'thirty' for the final time, is to wish Richard Hartford, my successor, all the luck in the world."

Sitting next to Marvin Baker, Richard Hartford, the new editor of the *Messenger,* inclined his head in acknowledgment. Tall and thin like Beecham himself, Hartford had been Beecham's understudy for the past year, since coming over from the *Journal-American,* where he had been city editor. He knew the city, he knew newspapers. The transition of power would be smooth.

As Beecham sat down to ringing applause, Jimmy looked around the room at the people who held key positions in the company. Like a good general, he had his best troops on the front line. Should battle ever be joined, he was sure of victory.

Following Edward Beecham's farewell dinner, Jimmy accompanied his father to the apartment on East Eighty-sixth Street which his parents had occupied since moving from Fifth Avenue. His mother sat in the living room, a shawl wrapped around her shoulders. There was no need for the shawl, for there were no drafts in the apartment. Every window was tightly closed, the heavy drapes were drawn, and the radiators kept the room at a steady seventy-eight degrees. Jimmy tugged at his shirt collar. Zalman, accustomed to the heat his wife preferred, dropped into a chair next to her.

"We just had Ed Beecham's farewell dinner, Julia. You should have come. You would have had a lovely time listening to his recollections. He even paid Jimmy a few compliments."

"Ed Beecham?" She adjusted her hearing aid, as though having trouble with it.

"You know, editor of the *Messenger.*"

Julia nodded. "He brought news of Helen that awful night." She looked between Zalman and Jimmy to a coffee table on which rested the photograph the *Messenger* had used in its tribute to Helen. Her eyes turned dull. She cocked her head as if listening for some faint sound. Her voice altered, becoming lighter, shrill, more like that of a young girl. "I spoke to her only a few minutes before you arrived. She wanted to let us know that she's all right, and we shouldn't worry. She'll be home the moment she's finished the story she's writing. You shouldn't send her so far away, Zalman. You know how it frightens me to have Helen where fighting's going on."

Zalman and Jimmy exchanged glances. Without the slightest warning, Julia had slipped away, trading reality for the dream world her mind found so much more comfortable. There was no knowing when she would return. Sometimes she went to bed in that strange and troubled state.

Jimmy stayed for half an hour. When he kissed his mother good night, she was relating a conversation she'd had that very afternoon with her own parents, Louis and Frieda Bluestone. She laughed when she explained to Zalman how she had ribbed them about their opposition to him. "I told them not to worry about you being a bartender. You wouldn't remain one forever. One day you'd own a famous newspaper."

On the journey home to Gramercy Park, Jimmy blinked back tears. All the success in the world could not insulate him from the family tragedy that was taking place. His mother's health, shaky at best since Helen's death, was deteriorating rapidly. She had become a total recluse. Jimmy visited her every day, finding time in his busy schedule to sit with her for ten or fifteen minutes and try to engage her in conversation. Sonya, too, did her share, taking Josephine and Harold to see their grandmother twice a week. It was a duty visit. Josephine did not enjoy being in the musty living room where Julia always sat surrounded by photographs of Helen, and Harold, though not yet two, sensed the depression in the room and grew cranky.

Jimmy remembered how old his mother had looked on the

evening of the dinner party to which he had invited his English friends. Her white hair had been stringy, her face lined. She'd been sixty-three then and appeared ten years older. Jimmy wished she looked so good now. Her hair came out with every brush stroke; her face, deprived of sunlight and fresh air, resembled parchment. She looked like a woman of ninety. No one could get through to her. Neither Zalman, who spent almost every evening sitting by her side until she went to bed, nor the full-time nurse could make contact. Doctors gave long-winded reasons for her condition, but Zalman and Jimmy understood the real malaise. Julia was pining away. She was dying of a broken heart.

At the end of the Christmas holidays, Josephine showed off her father to her three best friends from school.

Television itself was still something of a novelty. To simply own a set was a step up the social ladder. Josephine's father not only owned a television—he owned a television station that Josephine's friends watched, not to mention a newspaper and magazines that their parents read.

Jimmy arranged for the four girls to visit his office in the early afternoon so they could have lunch before touring the newspaper and the television station. Sonya brought them to the newspaper offices. Brian Gilbert, playing up to the occasion, met them in the downstairs lobby and escorted them up to the executive floor.

"Mr. J., your lunch appointments have arrived."

"Show them in, Brian." Jimmy got up from behind the desk, straightened his trousers, and tugged down at the jacket of his charcoal-gray suit. Josephine must have made up a thousand stories about him. He couldn't let her down.

Gilbert held the door open for Josephine and her friends. Not one of the young girls, Jimmy noticed, seemed the slightest bit awed. For a moment he envied them their youth, their innocence, and their lack of fear.

"Daddy, this is Alison, Sharon, and Nancy."

Jimmy bent forward at the waist as though being introduced to royalty. "My pleasure, young ladies. I took the liberty of booking a table at the Stork Club. Of course, if that's not suitable, I can make other arrangements . . ."

"Oh, Daddy, don't be so silly!" Josephine burst out. "You know you promised us spaghetti!"

Brian Gilbert, still standing by the door, looked sharply at the seven-year-old girl. He had never heard anyone speak to Jimmy Isaacson like that. But Jimmy did not appear to mind. He was laughing as he shook the hand of each girl before giving his own daughter a hug and a kiss on the cheek.

They lunched at a nearby Italian restaurant, a favorite among *Messenger* staff but one in which Jimmy had never eaten. He nodded to half a dozen people he saw sitting at the red-and-white-topped tables. Surprised stares followed him to a corner table. Playing the gentleman to the full, he helped each girl into her seat. Josephine's three friends were pretty children. Alison and Nancy had straight fair hair that fell to their shoulders, while Sharon's dark-brown hair was fixed in braids that thumped against her back. In Jimmy's eyes his own daughter was by far the prettiest. Her shoulder-length brown hair shone with a healthy luster, and she had her mother's deep brown eyes, full of warmth and sensitivity.

After lunch, they returned to the Messenger Building. First, Jimmy took his daughter to see her grandfather. Josephine's friends were immediately drawn to Zalman's snooker table. He racked the balls and let each girl have a few shots, smiling sympathetically when the cue proved too big and unwieldy for them to manage. Next, Jimmy introduced the girls to Richard Hartford. The new editor played along by taking time out of his busy day to walk them through the newsroom. Above the clatter of typewriters and the ringing of telephones, Hartford explained the workings of the newspaper. A man with a huge press camera stepped in their path, blinding them with a flash. Jimmy promised the girls they would each have a photograph by the time they left the building.

A linotype operator set each girl's name in type. The moment the metal cooled, they clutched their prizes in their hands, as if they were made of gold. In the composing room, a man with ink-stained hands set up a dummy page with a banner headline proclaiming the visit of the four girls to the paper. He ran off a copy for each girl, which they rolled up and carried carefully.

The final visit was to the pressroom. The girls stared at the silent mechanical monsters. "Is this where the paper comes from?" Alison asked. "The paper we get at home each morning?"

"This is where it comes from." Jimmy cupped a hand to his mouth. "Start 'em up!"

A press operator flicked a switch. The rolling presses filled the air with sudden thunder. All four girls shrieked and clapped their hands to their ears, dropping the lines of type and dummy pages. Jimmy laughed and signaled to the operator. The noise died.

"Want to work here when you grow up?" Jimmy asked.

Without exception, the girls shook their heads vehemently.

When they returned upstairs to Jimmy's office, Brian Gilbert had four black-and-white photographs waiting for them. Carrying their spoils in large envelopes, the girls rode with Jimmy through the first flakes of a snowstorm to a television studio on West Fiftieth Street. The journey provided another thrill. Jimmy had replaced the old maroon Bentley with a new black Rolls Royce. While Josephine's friends reveled in the spaciousness and luxury of the car, Jimmy watched the windshield wipers sweep away the gathering flakes. He asked the chauffeur to slow down. The responsibility of four children made him nervous.

At the studio, when a uniformed doorman saluted sharply, Josephine turned and smiled at her friends. Hadn't she told them how important her father was?

Marvin Baker was another of the Messenger Publications family in on Jimmy's scheme to entertain his daughter and her friends. The manager of WMES took the girls on a tour of the studio. On one set, an educational program was being aired. The girls watched, spellbound, eyes flicking from the monitors above them to the participants.

"Would you like to be on television?" Baker whispered. All four girls nodded. "Come with me." He took them to an empty room which contained a single television camera. Baker turned on lights and operated the camera himself. Josephine led the girls as they clowned around in front of the monitor, which was mounted high on the wall. Next to Baker, Jimmy stood smiling happily. He knew he was spoiling his daughter, but if you had the money and the power and you didn't spoil your kids, what kind of a father were you?

From the studio, Jimmy returned the girls to the Messenger Building. Sonya collected them at five-thirty. Half an hour later, Jimmy accompanied his father to the apartment on East Eighty-sixth Street. The snow was heavier now, settling on the road and sidewalk. Today he would have lots to tell his mother. He could try to break through her wall with the story of how her granddaughter had shown him off to her friends. That might do it, he mused; that might just make his mother smile.

The nurse was sitting with Julia in the living room when they arrived. Excusing herself, she got up to leave. Jimmy and Zalman took her place. To their delight, Julia listened attentively to the story of the girls' visit. When Jimmy mentioned the photograph that had been taken of Josephine and her friends, Julia asked, "Do you have one for me? I could put it"—she looked around speculatively before pointing to the mantel—"right there, next to Helen's picture."

"I'll have one sent to you tomorrow."

Zalman held Julia's hand in his own. "What have you been doing today, darling?"

"Just sitting here, thinking."

"Have you looked out of the window at all? It's snowing, Julia. You should look, it's really beautiful out there."

Julia stood up and walked to the window that overlooked the street. She pulled the heavy drapes wide open and looked out at the snowflakes drifting downward, entranced by the sight. When she turned around, her eyes were misty.

"Do you remember the way we used to walk in the snow, Zalman? When we were courting?"

"Of course I remember."

"We walked in Central Park, hand in hand, kicking up the freshly fallen snow with our feet. They were lovely times, weren't they?"

Zalman moved a few steps closer, his arms held out. "They were, Julia, they were indeed."

Jimmy watched his mother and father embrace. They weren't aware of his presence. Especially his mother. Even as he watched, he could see her beginning the journey back in time.

Zalman saw it, too, and allowed himself to join her. "Would you like to walk with me in the snow?" he asked softly.

Jimmy watched his mother consider the proposition. "I don't think so," she said at last. "Not now. Later on, perhaps, when it stops. We'll dress up warmly and go to the park and watch the skaters. I'd like that." Her eyes sharpened; color seemed to glow in the waxy skin of her face. "And when we come back, I'll make hot chocolate and we'll sit in front of the fire."

"Yes, darling." Zalman kissed Julia on the forehead and led her tenderly to the chair. He saw Jimmy staring and gave him a slow, sad smile. Perhaps joining Julia on her trips was the best way to communicate with her. The one difference was, Jimmy knew, his father could return whenever he chose. His mother, once she entered her fantasy world, had no control. She returned only when the ruler of that world released her troubled mind.

Jimmy left for home shortly afterward. He and Sonya had tickets for that night's performance of *Death of a Salesman.* While sitting in the back of the Rolls on the way to the theater, he told her about the visit to his mother. In return, Sonya told him how excited Josephine and her friends were about their visit to the newspaper and the television studio.

"They didn't stop talking about it all the way home. Alison, Nancy, and Sharon think you're absolutely wonderful because you have control over so many things, and Josephine thinks you're even more wonderful because you made her friends think that."

"Stop it. I'm getting carried away with all the wonderfuls."

"Here's one more," Sonya said and kissed him. "I think you're wonderful, too."

Jimmy blushed, embarrassed that the chauffeur might see.

The play consumed only half of Jimmy's attention. The rest he focused on the odd comparisons the day had brought. He had found joy by bringing pleasure to his daughter, and sadness at his mother's distress. Life was a trade-off. Too many people were loaded down with sadness. He, at least,

454

had much for which to be grateful. Hadn't his father told him many years ago that he wasn't better than anyone else—just luckier?

Following the show, Jimmy and Sonya ate a late dinner at Sardi's. They did not get home until after one. The downstairs lights were on. As they walked from the car toward the front door, it flew open. The housekeeper stood there, a heavy woolen coat covering her nightgown.

"Oh, Mr. and Mrs. Isaacson, thank goodness you're home!"

Sonya clutched Jimmy's arm. "What is it?" he asked. The housekeeper, an Irish woman prone to theatrical exaggeration, had only been with them for three months. Jimmy hoped she was acting that way now. "What's the matter, Eileen?"

"Your father telephoned not fifteen minutes ago, Mr. Isaacson. He said your mother had been rushed to the hospital."

Jimmy grabbed the woman by the arm. "What hospital?"

"Lenox Hill."

"I'll go with you," Sonya offered immediately.

"No. You stay here." He pushed her into the housekeeper's arms. "Call the hospital. Try to get hold of my father. Tell him I'm on my way." Before Sonya could argue, Jimmy ran back to the car, giving the driver instructions to get him to Lenox Hill Hospital as quickly as possible.

Jimmy found Zalman striding around a waiting room, hands clasped behind his back, head bent forward. "What's the matter?"

"Me!" Zalman jabbed himself in the chest. "My fault! You remember I asked her if she wanted to go for a walk in the snow? Well, she went for one. At eleven o'clock!"

"What are you talking about?" Jimmy stared uncomprehendingly at his father. He'd expected it to be a heart attack or a stroke, or perhaps even a terrible accident, and his father was talking about walks in the snow.

"We thought she was in bed. Instead she slipped out of the apartment, took the elevator downstairs, and went out in just a nightgown and bare feet."

"Why didn't anyone see her? What about the doorman?"

"She found some back entrance, slipped out that way. Walked a couple of hundred yards along an alley in the snow until she reached the street. Then she collapsed. Someone called a policeman, he called an ambulance. They brought her here."

"How did they know to call you?"

Zalman took a deep breath. "She had her handbag with her, just like she was going out for a real walk in the snow in Central Park. Me!" He jabbed himself in the chest again. "I put the crazy idea into her head, and this is what happens!"

Jimmy wrapped his arms around his father and hugged him. "It wasn't your fault. You've done everything you can for her." He could feel his father shivering in his arms. He hugged him tighter, trying to quell the shaking. "She must have felt happy when she went down there. She wasn't miserable, she was happy, don't you understand that? Happy because she was young again and going for a walk in Central Park with you."

Footsteps sounded. Jimmy released his father and turned around. A doctor approached. "Mr. Isaacson?"

Both father and son answered. "Yes?"

"Mrs. Isaacson is resting comfortably. She doesn't seem to be suffering from exposure and I'm confident that in a day or so she'll be able to return home." He looked from Jimmy to Zalman, as though uncertain which Mr. Isaacson he wanted. "Why would she do something like this?"

Jimmy let his father answer. "My wife, I'm afraid, is not a well woman. She suffers from hallucinations. Sometimes she seems to live in a world that she inhabited many years ago."

The doctor nodded. "Why don't you both go home? There's nothing to be gained by staying here."

"I'll take you," Jimmy offered.

Zalman shook his head. "You go. You have Sonya and the children to worry about. I'll wait here." He accompanied the statement with a fierce expression that neither Jimmy nor the doctor cared to contest.

Jimmy returned home. For the remainder of the night he lay beside Sonya, but he couldn't sleep. He could not drive from his mind the notion that he had seen his mother for the last time; that his father was waiting in the hospital not for news but so his wife would not die alone.

At eight in the morning, Jimmy telephoned the hospital. Fearing the worst, he was relieved to hear that his mother had spent a comfortable night and was now awake and in stable condition. When he asked about his father, he was told that Mr. Isaacson had left half an hour ago. Jimmy began to dial Zalman's number, then stopped. His father would be asleep, exhausted after the long night's watch at the hospital. Let him sleep.

By nine o'clock, he was in the office. To his surprise, he found his father. "What are you doing here? You should be at home getting some rest. It's bad enough *one* of you is in the hospital. I don't want you both there."

Zalman dismissed Jimmy's concern by saying, "Your mother's going to be all right. Our generation, we came from a tough school. We can walk barefoot in the snow and get away with it."

"I'll have my driver take you home."

As Jimmy reached for the telephone, Zalman's hand stopped him. "What am I going to do at home? Talk to the walls? I'm better off here, finding something to occupy my mind. I'll stay until midday when I go back to the hospital. And if I feel tired, I can always catch some sleep in my own office. No one's going to fire *me* for sleeping on the job, are they?"

Jimmy recognized the sense of his father's words. "There's something I need your advice on. I've got a meeting at eleven with Richard Hartford. He's proposing that we make major changes to our political coverage by adding a new columnist and a new cartoonist. He's already drawn up a short list of names."

Zalman pursed his lips. "The new broom sweeps clean, eh? Maybe it's time. Our current people have been here since I was running the show."

The meeting with Hartford lasted forty minutes. When it was over, Jimmy accompanied his father to Lenox Hill Hospital. The same doctor who, the previous night, had sug-

457

gested that they both go home was back on duty. He greeted the Isaacsons with a smile.

"Too often I'm the bearer of bad tidings. For once it's a pleasure to offer good news. Mrs. Isaacson is much improved. I saw her fifteen minutes ago and she was asking for both of you."

"Does that mean you'll be letting her go home?" Zalman asked.

The doctor crossed his fingers. "Tomorrow morning."

Zalman squeezed his son's arm. Joy filled his voice. "Let's go see her."

"You go in alone. I'll follow in a minute."

Zalman entered Julia's private room. Just inside the doorway he stopped in astonishment. Years had fallen away. Julia's skin, though still heavily lined, had a healthy pinkish hue. Her eyes were sharp and her hair, somehow, seemed thicker. Her face beamed in welcome when she recognized Zalman. She inserted the hearing aid into her ear, eager to hear his voice.

"If you've come to tell me what a silly old fool I am, you're too late. I already know."

"I came to tell you nothing of the sort." Zalman approached the bed, knelt over it, cradled Julia in his arms, and kissed her. "I just want you to promise that if you ever feel like walking in the snow again, ask me to come with you. It made me jealous, you going off on your own like that."

"Did you think I was going walking with another man? Now it's you who's being a silly old fool."

Zalman held her tighter, grateful to Jimmy for giving him these few moments alone. Julia was rational, lively, better than he had seen her in ages. Could the walk in the bitter cold and the fall in the snow have jolted her out of her make-believe world? Zalman had no idea; he was a newspaperman, not Freud.

When Jimmy entered the room he found his father and mother wrapped in an embrace. He stood smiling for a few seconds, then coughed discreetly. Zalman barely turned his head.

"Think your parents are too old for a bit of romance?"

"Isn't this where you're supposed to give me a quarter to go see a movie, Mr. Z.?"

Zalman broke the embrace and stepped away. Jimmy, bending over the bed to kiss his mother, noticed the same improvement his father had seen. "You look like you've been sitting out in the Florida sun, not tramping through the New York snow."

"I feel like it as well. It was the fresh air, Jimmy. I should have breathed it years ago instead of locking myself away in that dungeon of a living room."

Jimmy's eyes met those of his father. The recovery was too sudden for either man to be able to accept easily. After five years of watching Julia deteriorate, seeing her whole again proved difficult. Jimmy probed. "I've got that photograph of Josephine and her friends at the newspaper yesterday. You said you wanted to put it on the mantel next to Helen's picture."

"Thank you." Julia's brow creased for an instant. "I've been lying here all morning, wondering about redecorating the apartment. Especially the living room. It really needs it, you know. What do you think?"

"The moment you're home, we'll have decorators come around," Zalman answered quickly. "We'll get wallpaper samples, paint charts, drapery swatches. Whatever you want, Julia. Tell us and we'll get it for you."

Julia's eyelids began to drop. "I'm tired now. Let me sleep on it all for a couple of hours."

Jimmy kissed his mother good-bye, then stood back while his father embraced her. This time he didn't cough discreetly, nor did he make any reference to being sent to the movies. He just watched, happy that his mother was so much better; happy that she would be coming home prepared to face life again; and happy that his father and mother still cared so deeply for each other.

"I'm hungry," Zalman stated as he and Jimmy left the hospital. "I haven't eaten a damned thing since dinner last night, and seeing your mother looking so well for the first time in years has given me one hell of an appetite."

"We'll have lunch somewhere. And then I'm taking you home and you're going to bed. No more arguments."

459

"No more arguments, bigshot."

Father and son stopped off at a restaurant. Zalman finished off a steak, then amazed both Jimmy and the waiter by ordering another. "You're going to get indigestion, eating so heavily and then sleeping," Jimmy said.

"You worry about you, and let me worry about me. Besides"—Zalman's eyes twinkled mischievously—"you look as though you could do with taking some of your own advice about diet. Either Sonya's feeding you too well, or you're treating yourself to too many snacks during the day."

Involuntarily, Jimmy looked down at his stomach. Always having a tendency to gain weight, he had become noticeably pudgy during the past year, as though celebrating the fact that he had taken Messenger Publications out of debt and made it completely independent once again. "It's all paid for."

"So's this." Zalman tapped his own stomach. Beneath the vest of his brown suit there wasn't a spare ounce of flesh to be seen. "I weigh now just about what I weighed when I married your mother forty-three years ago. You should look so good when you've been married that long."

Jimmy welcomed his father's aggressiveness. It showed a return to normality that he'd gotten over any feelings of guilt about sending Julia out into the snow. "This time of year I'd rather have a bit of insulation than be a walking skeleton like you."

"Walking skeleton, am I? Pick any physical activity you like—walking, running, lifting weights, boxing—and I'll pin your damned ears back!"

Jimmy grinned and shook his head. His father's determination alone would carry him to victory. "Let's begin with sleeping. I'll see you home and you can get some sleep."

"You see me home. *I'll* decide if I'm going to sleep."

Jimmy took his father home. Outside the door, he did something he rarely did. He kissed Zalman. A deep affection for this man who was so proud of weighing what he'd weighed forty-three years ago welled up inside Jimmy. He loved his father more than he had ever loved anyone. Even Sonya. His father was the most precious person in the world. No one else came close.

"Go back to the office," Zalman whispered, overcome by Jimmy's sudden display of emotion. The grown man would walk through fire for him just as the young boy would have done, and the realization still made Zalman tremble. "Damned place'll fall apart without you."

Jimmy climbed into the Rolls. He whiled away the journey back to the Messenger Building by composing a prayer of gratitude for his mother's recovery. Not that he ever intended offering it up to any deity. In that respect he followed his father, although his disdain for religion did not approach Zalman's vehement loathing. The prayer was just a simple thank-you to no one in particular, a note of appreciation to a benevolent fate.

Still musing on the prayer, he rode the elevator up to the executive floor. When the operator slid back the door, Brian Gilbert was waiting to say that the hospital had telephoned five minutes ago. Moments after Zalman and Jimmy's departure, Julia had suffered a massive heart attack. While Zalman had been ordering his second steak for lunch, his wife had died.

Julia's funeral was held two days later. After the service, Jimmy took his father to Irving Place. Although there was no formal mourning period, no sitting unshaven on low chairs with all the mirrors covered, Jimmy and Zalman remained at Gramercy Park for a week. Well-wishers visited from morning to night, men and women associated with Messenger Publications, members of New York's business community, politicians and policemen, actors and authors, anyone whose life had been touched by the Isaacson family. On the last day of the week, William Baron, the Republican congressman who represented New York's Silk Stocking district, called to pay his respects. Baron traveled up from Washington just for the day, arriving at the Isaacson home with his wife.

"Thelma and I just found out about your mother," Baron explained to Jimmy. "Otherwise we'd have been here much sooner. We would have attended the funeral had we known earlier."

"We're very grateful that you came." Jimmy felt both

honored and pleased that Baron should have made the trip from Washington. The *Messenger* had twice supported the congressman. Now Baron repaid that support with friendship and respect. Jimmy hoped that somehow his mother knew. She would be so proud.

The most regular visitor was Brian Gilbert, who came twice a day, in the morning and again in the evening to bring Jimmy up to date on Messenger Publications business. Just thirty, Gilbert had been Jimmy's assistant for three years. He had been with the *Messenger* for seven years before that, first as a reporter, then as an advertising salesman. Jimmy named him personal assistant, with a salary in the middle-management range, after Gilbert had made two major contributions to the *Messenger*. The first was to suggest a weekly fashion series which gained both readers and advertising dollars. The second, and far more important in Jimmy's view, was exposing a *Messenger* advertising rep who passed details of a department store's weekly special promotions to its rival in time for the rival to undercut. Jimmy had fired the unethical rep immediately, and blackballed him on every newspaper in the city. It took the rep four months to find another job, and that was in Des Plaines, Illinois.

Gilbert meant more to Jimmy than a resourceful personal assistant. He was a young man worthy of esteem because he exhibited qualities Jimmy admired. Gilbert dressed impeccably in custom-made suits that enhanced his slim body. He drove stylish sports cars rather than run-of-the-mill sedans. He understood good food and wine, appreciated art and music, took expensive vacations, and lived in a luxurious Park Avenue apartment. In a word, he had class. Jimmy knew that Gilbert came from a wealthy family—both of his parents were doctors—but he never fully understood how the young man managed to live quite so well. During one of Gilbert's visits to the house, Jimmy decided to ask him.

"A plethora of wealthy girlfriends, Mr. J." Gilbert produced a photograph from his wallet and handed it to Jimmy.

Jimmy studied the picture. Taken at a country club, it showed Gilbert and a tall blonde dressed for tennis. Gilbert smiled at the camera, while the young woman never took her

462

eyes off her companion. "You mean you take money from women?"

Gilbert smiled disarmingly. "In all my life, I have never asked a woman for anything. But for some reason they just want to buy me things. This young woman, Millie Spencer, she gave me that new Jaguar you see me driving."

"Why don't you marry one of these women?"

"What? And slaughter all the geese that lay the other golden eggs?" Gilbert shook his head. "No, sir, Mr. J. For the time being, I like things just the way they are."

Jimmy laughed. From anyone else such a confession would be horrifying, but from Gilbert he could accept it. Somehow it made him even more likable.

All through the week, Jimmy kept a close watch on his father. When Zalman sat downstairs, Jimmy made sure to sit nearby. When Zalman went out for a walk, Jimmy decided that exercise would suit him, too. And when Zalman was in bed, Jimmy would peek in. Once Zalman caught him quietly opening the bedroom door and remarked sharply, "You think I'm a kid you've got to keep checking on me?"

Jimmy, red-faced, didn't know what to say. At last he blurted out, "I thought I heard you coughing, that's all."

Zalman's face softened. "I wasn't coughing, but thanks anyway. Your mother would be happy to know you're taking such good care of me."

At the end of the week, Sonya, who had managed the task of supplying hospitality to all the people who thronged the house, drew Jimmy aside. "You can't let your father go back to that apartment. He'll see your mother in every corner, just like they saw Helen in every corner of the townhouse."

"What do you suggest, that he move in permanently with us?"

Sonya shook her head. "Your father would never be happy with a room in someone else's home, and we don't have the space to give him much more than that. Why don't you both take a complete break? God knows you need it. Instead of going back to work, start looking for a new home. One we can all live in."

"All of us?"

"Children grow up healthier in the country than in the

city. Especially a city that's going to top eight million people in the not too distant future."

Such a figure staggered Jimmy, and pushed him firmly toward Sonya's way of thinking. A population of eight million might be one hell of a market for a newspaper, but it wasn't much of a place in which to raise a family. That night, long after Sonya had fallen asleep, he contemplated the subject. He tried to understand what his children would need by delving back into his own childhood. He recalled the estate at Glen Cove, on the north shore of Long Island. He had liked that house, it had been a wonderful place to spend the summer. If he had liked living in such a house, surely his own children would have similar tastes.

The next morning he told his father they were going for a ride. "We're going to find a new home. For all of us."

"How do you know I want to leave my old home?"

"You don't have any choice. I've told my assistant to pay off the staff there and have the furniture covered. Once we find another place, we'll get everything moved."

"You're presenting me with a *fait accompli,* is that it?"

"No. Sonya and I just think it's time we moved. For the children's sake mainly—we think they'd be better off growing up with grass instead of concrete. I remembered how happy we were in Glen Cove during the summer. Somewhere like that, on the Sound perhaps, would be ideal. And when we find it, we'd like you to move in with us."

"Put like that, it sounds a whole lot more inviting."

Jimmy and Zalman toured communities bordering Long Island Sound, both on the Island and in Westchester County. Each time they saw a property they liked, they took Sonya back for a second, more critical examination. The first property they all agreed on was a Kings Point estate, but any possible deal fell through when a pest inspector unearthed termite infestation that had gone unchecked for years. The second property to appeal to everyone was a stone-built mansion in the Westchester County town of Rye, little more than twenty miles from New York and served by both road and rail. Tucked away at the end of an imposing drive, the house overlooked three acres of lawns and trees and flowerbeds. On the ground floor was a self-contained one-bedroom apartment. On the second floor was a studio, filled with natural light, where Sonya could do her needlepoint.

Jimmy didn't quibble about the cost. He simply accepted the asking price and said he wished to move in as soon as possible. Like his father, once he made up his mind to do something, he wanted it done immediately.

The move from Gramercy Park to Rye was set for mid-April, giving Sonya time to supervise the work of interior decorators who transformed the old-fashioned stone mansion into the kind of warm and comfortable home she wanted for her family.

Until the move, Zalman stayed in Irving Place. He kept to himself a lot, spending time with the family only to eat. When Jimmy and Sonya sat down after dinner to watch the WMES news, Zalman excused himself and went to his room. The death of his wife was far too recent to allow him to resume normal life. Also, he felt he was imposing on his son and daughter-in-law by staying in their home. At sixty-five, Zalman was as fiercely independent as ever. He didn't want to take anything from anyone, even his son.

"What do you do all evening in your room?" Jimmy asked one day as they drove to the Messenger Building.

"I look through the *Messenger,* I read all the magazines you publish to find the mistakes." He gave his son a weak smile. "I look for ways they can be improved."

Jimmy didn't know whether to believe his father or not.

The day of the move dawned cool and blustery. Instead of going to work with Jimmy, Zalman said he wished to remain at home. "I want to keep an eye on the movers," he told his son. "Make sure they don't steal anything. You've got some valuable paintings and pieces of silver, you know."

"They're not going to steal anything, Mr. Z." Nonetheless, Jimmy let Zalman have his way.

The move took all day, and Zalman watched every piece loaded onto the two trucks that were used. His favorite articles of furniture from the apartment on East Eighty-sixth Street had been taken out to Rye the previous day, to fill his own apartment.

When the last item had been loaded, Zalman asked Sonya

for a favor. "Drive me past the old house on Fifth Avenue, will you? I want to take a last look."

Sonya obliged. She parked across from the townhouse. Zalman climbed out of the car and stood in front of the house for fully two minutes, looking up and down the front as if seeking changes made by the new owners. At last he turned around and came back to the car.

"We moved from here, Sonya, because Helen died. Now I'm moving from Eighty-sixth Street because Julia's no longer with me. I guess the only way I'll leave your new home—"

"*Your* new home as well," Sonya said quickly.

Zalman inclined his head. "I guess the only way I'll leave my new home is feet first."

"Stop feeling so damned sorry for yourself. You've had a damned good run for your money."

Zalman's eyes opened in shock. He stared at Sonya for a few seconds, as if unable to accept the sharpness in her voice, the sudden use of harsh language. Then he recovered. "With the exception of Lewisburg, New York City has been my home since I came to this country forty-seven years ago. I lived in slums and I lived in style. I felt pain and I enjoyed pleasure here. I've had some of everything. Forty-seven years is long enough. Start the engine and let's get out of here. I'm sixty-five, and eager"—a smile grew wide across his face—"to see how I'm going to enjoy the next forty-seven years in Rye."

As the car pulled away, he looked back at the townhouse a final time. "Rye? What kind of a name is Rye? Whoever thought I'd spend my latter years living in a loaf of bread?"

Zalman took time to settle down in Rye. Instead of going into work every day, he accompanied Jimmy in the Rolls Royce only a couple of times a week. He claimed the long journey to New York was tiring. He wanted time to explore the new house. Never, he declared, had he seen such a place. He would make a map so that everyone would know how to get from one room to another.

Spring in Rye was a novelty to Zalman, who was accustomed to watching seasons change through concrete, steel,

466

and glass. He spent time in the grounds, recalling springs of many years ago, in Russia, outside the crowded realm of Kishinev. This was how spring had been there, clean and clear with the promise of summer not far behind. Not like New York, where increasing pollution from cars and trucks deadened one's senses and appreciation of nature's miracles.

In the spacious grounds, he played games with Josephine and Harold, and sometimes, when the sun shone too strongly for any kind of physical exertion, Zalman told his granddaughter stories of Russia, as he had once told such tales to his daughter. He did not draw pictures of terror and suppression. Instead, he wove magical tapestries of family life in the face of hardship. So many years later he remembered his story-telling mentor, and as he spun his tales, he thought fondly of Jimmy Doyle.

Zalman also took an interest in the work of gardeners who toiled ceaselessly on rose gardens and flower displays. He asked questions, and learned through using a trowel himself to plant a shrub, or cutters to prune a rosebush. One day he told Jimmy: "You should think about launching a magazine on gardening. Run a regular gardening section in the *Messenger* as well. Not everyone lives in an apartment with no green space, you know."

"I'll get someone to look into it," Jimmy said.

"*You* look into it."

"Mr. Z., I'm busy. In case you haven't noticed, there's been a war going on for the past three months—"

"A police action, Jimmy. A good newspaperman should always get his facts straight."

". . . and elections are coming up. We've got to put our weight behind the people we think will do the best job."

"Are you supporting William Baron again?"

"Can you think of an alternative?"

Zalman shook his head. "He visited us after your mother died. Give your support to the man who respects you."

Under Jimmy's guidance, the newspaper promoted Baron as a conservative in a period when conservatism was necessary, while lambasting his opponent as a woolly-minded liberal stronger on ideals than common sense. Baron retained his seat. His election to a third term coincided with the entry

467

of Red China into the Korean War. When Jimmy watched papers carrying the news spill off the press, he felt satisfied that he had thrown his weight behind the right man.

A week after the election, Baron visited Rye to thank Jimmy personally for the *Messenger*'s help. Jimmy accepted the gratitude with a modest courtesy rather than the acknowledgment that such appreciation was his rightful due. He was more satisfied with knowing that as a man with the power to cause change, he had simply done the proper thing.

Chapter Twenty-one

Sidney found the transition from partner in the Lesser Brothers agency to producer an easy one to make. On the surface, little really changed. His morning walk from the flat in Marble Arch to Haymarket was the same, perhaps a trifle quicker now, his stride a trace more purposeful. He continued to occupy the office he had used as an agent. Naomi still worked with him, although her hours had been curtailed by the arrival in the family of Andrea and her sister Linda. The main difference Sidney found was his omission from the regular morning meetings that took place in Manny's office. Only then, when the rest of the floor was as quiet as a cemetery, did he fully understand that he was no longer part of the bigger operation.

Manny cooperated fully in his brother's dream. Knowing that Sidney was risking every penny he had in going out alone, Manny offered him the use of all office facilities, from telephones right down to Carol Jones, his own secretary, for those times that Naomi was busy at home with the two girls. When both brothers were in the office, Manny always made sure to pop into Sidney's room each day and spend a few minutes with him. He knew that Sidney wanted to keep up to date with Lesser Brothers, and he wanted just as much to know what was happening in the world of impresarios. Manny found it hard to believe how much he cared about his younger brother; his baby brother now. He wanted Sidney to succeed in the venture as much as Sidney himself wanted to succeed. Manny's elation when Sidney put together a series of shows to tour seaside theaters during the summer of 1951 was as great as his brother's. And it was Manny who rushed out to buy a bottle of champagne when Sidney won the rights to bring to London an English version of *D'Artagnan,* a popular French musical based on Dumas' *The Three Musketeers.*

By early summer, as Sidney Less shows played to holiday-makers around the country, and rehearsals began for *D'Artagnan,* there was no longer a need to share facilities with Lesser Brothers. With a staff of his own, Sidney sought new offices. Being close to his brother held appeal, and he leased space in the same building, on the floor above the agency. Instead of wandering along the corridor to pay daily visits to Sidney, Manny now climbed a flight of stairs, breathing heavily from the unaccustomed exercise. It was worth it. Every week, new bills seemed to appear on the walls of Sidney's office, shows Sidney was after or ones he had succeeded in acquiring rights for. "Coming here," Manny said during one visit, "is a cross between working out in a gymnasium and visiting an art gallery."

Manny found the daily talks with his brother refreshing. When they discussed agency business, Sidney's viewpoint— so often very different from what he heard downstairs—gave Manny a better overall picture. Similarly, Manny's opinion shone a new light on Sidney's operation, especially when he grumbled about late payments or unsatisfactory conditions encountered by Lesser Brothers clients appearing in Sidney Less productions.

"I can't keep my finger on every pulse," Sidney protested after Manny aired the complaint of a singer who had been promised her own dressing room in Southend and subsequently found she had to share with four other people. "I lease the theater, put a manager in charge of the show and let them go. I'm not supposed to know everything that goes on."

"You are, you know, as long as your name's out front," Manny replied. "You can be sure that Gordon Prideaux knows every single thing that happens in Partnership theaters."

Sidney winced. "That's unfair, throwing Gordon in my face. He's been in the business longer."

"That's how he stayed in the business longer. He didn't overlook anything."

Sidney jotted down a note to call the manager in charge of that particular show and tear a strip off him. Manny was right. If his name was out front, he was responsible for everything.

Just as often, the exchange went in the opposite direction. Once, Sidney put his brother wise to a popular comedian who was slipping further and further down the road to alcoholism. Another time he told Manny about an actress whose bitchy behavior was driving everyone else in a show to desperation. "It's either her or the rest of the cast," Sidney said. "And I'm not going to let an entire cast go just for one prima donna."

"I'll have a word with her," Manny promised.

And sometimes the conversations were of a personal nature, especially when Sidney, who considered himself a new father, sought advice from someone more experienced in the role.

"What do you do, Manny, when either Jonathan or Bernice don't seem to take to you?"

Manny chewed his lip thoughtfully. "I don't think it's ever happened. Jonathan got mad once because I made him pay out of his own pocket for a window he broke with a ball, but he soon got over that. And Bernice runs out to meet me every day when I get home from here. Who's not taking to you? Andrea or Linda?"

"Andrea. She always keeps a distance. It's been two years since we made everything official, and in all that time I'm not sure I ever once got through to her. She's polite, friendly on the surface, and always willing to please, but whenever I try to get close, things go haywire. For a moment or two, it looks like we're going to be the greatest of friends, then she gets this standoffish look in her eyes and tells me I'm not her father."

"What about Linda?"

"Linda never knew her father so she can't compare. She's like Bernice, always waiting for me to get home. But I swear that Andrea tells her about him, or how she thinks she

471

remembers him. Sometimes I think Andrea's trying to turn Linda against me as well."

"How about Naomi? Does Andrea say she's not her mother?"

"No. She saves the bitterness for me. I tell Naomi, and she says maybe it's all in my mind. It's crazy, but sometimes I think Andrea blames me for taking her out of that damned orphanage. She couldn't have liked it there, could she?"

Manny shrugged, feeling truly sorry for his brother. After all the trouble he and Naomi had encountered trying to have children of their own, they deserved better luck than this with their adoption. "Bring them over to us more. Being with Jonathan and Bernice might help. Maybe seeing more of Mama will do the trick. Who knows, if Mama could handle you, me, and Bernard, *olova sholom,* she can handle anything."

During the last week of the summer break, Sidney and Naomi sent the girls out to The Paddocks for a few days. Each morning, Manny brought Sidney a progress report. Andrea and Linda were having the time of their lives in the country. They played with Jonathan and Bernice, went for walks with Rita, picked fruit, and were given riding lessons by a neighbor who operated a small stable.

"Jonathan and Andrea are so thick with each other," Manny said, "that there might be a budding romance there. Would that be kosher?" he asked as an afterthought. "You know, they're not real cousins, are they?"

Sidney smiled at the thought, but his heart was not in it. He could not understand why he failed where others succeeded. On the day he and Naomi collected the girls from The Paddocks, he took his mother aside to ask what he was doing wrong. She smiled and said, "You're doing nothing wrong. Nobody ever claimed that raising children was easy. You don't win a child's love just by being there. You have to keep working at it, all the time."

"Is that what you did with us?"

"I never stopped trying."

Looking back, Sidney could only agree. His mother had never stopped working to win her children's love, from the moment they were born right up until the present day. Some-

472

how she had always found a way to contribute where contributions were needed most.

On the journey home to Marble Arch, Naomi asked the girls if they had enjoyed themselves. Linda answered, happily describing all their activities. Sidney listened for a minute, smiling to himself at the younger girl's enthusiasm. "How about you, Andrea? Did you have a good time?"

"It was all right."

The simple, grudging reply stunned Sidney. Andrea had been laughing when she'd left The Paddocks. Now she was frowning, uncommunicative. He looked at Naomi as if to ask her whether she still thought Andrea's behavior existed only in his imagination.

"What's the matter, Andrea?" Naomi asked. "Suddenly decided you got out of bed on the wrong side?"

Andrea stared blankly at Naomi as if failing to understand the meaning of the question. "I'm going back to school tomorrow. I'm wondering what's going to happen, that's all. I'll be in a different year."

Sidney glanced at Linda. The red-haired girl was smiling as if recalling some special event at The Paddocks. Sidney could not help thinking that the younger sister was as different as chalk to Andrea's cheese. Were they really sisters? Or did Andrea have some deep psychological problem that prevented her from accepting her new parents as readily as Linda had done?

He sighed. He hadn't adopted Andrea to drop her in midstream when he learned she had a personality quirk he didn't like. He'd persevere. He'd follow his mother's advice and keep on trying to win her love.

In the fall of 1951, Manny stopped concentrating on Sidney's family problems and fixed his attention on a predicament that threatened to undermine Lesser Brothers' American business.

It began with an afternoon telephone call from Sol Bateman in New York. Manny, who had never gotten over the wonder of being able to speak to someone on a different continent and in a different time zone, responded the way he always did to such calls. "Sol, how's the weather in New

York? Ours is beautiful today, a real Indian summer, but of course over here it's three in the afternoon while it's . . . what is it where you are, Sol?"

"Ten in the morning. I'm drinking my second cup of coffee, I'm halfway through my second pack of Lucky Strikes, and it's bucketing down outside. So much for the weather report, now let's get on to the serious news. Manny, are you aware of Irving Kreeger's troubles?"

"What troubles?" Manny asked, sensing a portent of doom.

"He's into the bookies for big bucks. It's all over town that no one will take his action anymore, and unless he starts coming up with the green stuff to pay off some heavy debts real soon, he's going to be signing contracts with crutches."

Manny translated Bateman's New York colloquialisms into everyday London English. "What do Kreeger's gambling habits have to do with me?"

"Plenty. He's desperate for money. He's pushing his own people above yours. Some booking agents who've shown interest in your acts have been sidetracked by Kreeger. He's gone all patriotic, tried to make them sign American talent, his talent, in preference to your British clients. That way he doesn't have to split commissions. If that doesn't work, he offers to pull the kind of shady deal that gives agents a bad name."

"Go on," Manny said, certain he could see what was coming.

"Say you've got a singer who'll earn five thousand dollars. Kreeger will make a deal with some theater owner to sign the singer for four thousand, and he'll swear blind to you and your client that it's the best deal available. Then he'll split the odd thousand dollars with the owner. An extra bonus is that he also gets to pay you a smaller cut."

Manny felt his face burn. He couldn't care less about losing a few dollars in commission. He was outraged that his clients would be cheated. "Has he made this kind of offer to you?"

"He wouldn't dare. He knows you've dealt directly with the Ionic. He does it with people he thinks won't ever have any direct contact with you."

"And these people oblige?" As he asked the question,

Manny dug through his memory for recent deals Kreeger had concocted. The money was down! Each time Kreeger had come back with less than Manny had anticipated. He'd said the market was bad and Manny had believed him. It wasn't the market that was bad, it was Kreeger's damned luck!

"Someone offers to cut you in on a thousand dollars for doing nothing more than saying yes, wouldn't you oblige?"

"No," Manny answered. "I wouldn't. Not if I knew someone else was paying the bill for me. Thanks for letting me know, Sol. I appreciate it."

"You're welcome. Weather doesn't look so much like Indian summer there anymore, eh?"

"No, Sol, it's suddenly become very cold." Manny sat staring at the picture of Rita and the children on the desk. He'd been to the United States only three months before, on a trip that took in Las Vegas and California. He did not fancy making the lengthy journey again. The majority of his work was done from this desk, juggling two or three telephones at one time as he kept as many conversations going. This problem was one he could not solve from the desk. He could not simply dictate a letter to Irving Kreeger voiding the agreement the two agencies had. For a matter as serious as this, he required firsthand information; he needed to see for himself. "Sol, I'm going to book a flight to New York. Get someone to meet me at the airport, will you?"

Manny flew to New York the following day. Sol Bateman waited at Idlewild Airport with an enormous pale-blue Cadillac that had enough gleaming chrome to bounce signals to Mars and back. Manny wasn't surprised that Bateman himself had driven out to meet him. Since their first meeting three years ago, the two men had done enough satisfactory business to become good friends.

"I booked you into the Astor."

"Thanks. How badly in debt is Kreeger?"

"I heard more than a hundred thousand, and that's after selling off almost everything he owns to pay some of the debt."

"If he owes that much, what good is a five-hundred-dollar split from some shady deal?"

"He uses whatever he can raise to rush out to the track and try for one big score. Hopes he can pay it all off with one huge daily double. The track's the only place he can still bet. No New York bookie will take his action." Bateman concentrated on driving for a few seconds. "You planning to see him?"

"No." Manny glanced down at his heavy hands, like bunches of pink bananas when he clenched them. "I might do him physical injury for cheating my clients."

"You think a lot of your clients, eh?"

"They feed and clothe me. I never forget that I'm only an agent, Sol. Without my clients' talent, I'm nothing. Without an agent, they still have talent."

"That's a refreshing thought."

Manny checked into the Astor and went straight to bed, tired from the long journey and the five-hour time difference. He awoke early the next morning, ate breakfast, and then went for a long walk in the park. When he returned to the hotel, he telephoned Messenger Publications and asked for Jimmy Isaacson. Although he called Jimmy on each of the three visits he'd made to America since that first one in 1948, Manny rarely found time in his hectic schedule to see him. This trip was different. He had made it for the express purpose of meeting the publisher.

Jimmy came on the line immediately. "What's this, the second coming? You were only here a couple of months ago."

"An emergency. There's a fire blazing out of control, and I'm looking for a hydrant."

"I see. How can I help?"

"It's about Irving Kreeger. I hear he's in deep trouble over gambling debts. I also hear that to buy himself some time he's operating in a manner which is not in the best interests of the clients of mine he represents."

"Come on over. In the meantime, I'll get my bloodhounds on the scent."

Manny traveled by taxi to the Messenger Building and rode the elevator up to the publisher's floor. He found Jimmy talking with a tall, elegantly dressed man. Brian Gilbert. Manny congratulated himself for remembering the man's name. Gilbert left the office and Jimmy indicated a chair for Manny to sit in.

"Whoever your sources are, they're good. Irving Kreeger's dug himself a deep hole with some very nasty characters. He owes"—Jimmy consulted a yellow sheet of paper Gilbert had left with him—"one bookie in excess of sixty thousand dollars. Another some forty thousand. On top of that he's into loan sharks for almost thirty."

"Loan sharks?"

Jimmy smiled at Manny's confusion. Britain, despite enduring six years of war, remained a very genteel country. Perhaps that was why Jimmy liked it. "A modern term for usurers. Usurers who employ extremely distasteful business methods."

"Like making a man use crutches?"

"At the very least."

"Where do you learn all this?"

Jimmy waved at the door. "On a newspaper you have someone who knows something about everything. Crime reporters, show-business writers, gossip writers, you name it. The world's greatest pool of information. Now, how can I help?"

"I want proof that Kreeger's cheating me. Your television station has a show called *Appearing Tonight,* right?"

"The title's just been changed to *The Bill Delaney Show.* It's a network show now."

"Will Mr. Delaney do me a favor?"

Jimmy did not ask what the favor concerned. He just said, "I'll introduce you to Bill, and you can ask him yourself."

Bill Delaney saw Manny that afternoon, fitting him in between rehearsals for the show that would go out live the following Sunday evening. Delaney was thinner than Manny, and taller. A young woman with a clipboard followed him around, diligently noting everything he said. When Manny began to explain the situation, Delaney interrupted. "I know all that already. Jimmy Isaacson told me. Just tell me what it is you want me to do."

"Among our clients Kreeger has booked in America is a comedian named Brian Baylor. A really funny man who'll make you laugh just by standing in front of you." Delaney did not appear at all enthused at the description. He stood there, arms folded across his chest, a dour expression stamped on his face. "Brian will be here in four weeks. He's going to be appearing at the Latin Quarter for a couple of weeks, then he's going to play spots in Chicago and on the West Coast. Would you contact Irving Kreeger and say you'd like him on your show. Then see if you can cut any kind of an underhand deal with him."

"That's called entrapment in legal circles over here."

"Where I come from, it's called protecting your clients from thieves and rogues."

Delaney smiled for the first time, a thin, tight-lipped expression. "I'll do it. I'll do it now." He turned to the young woman with the clipboard. "Get Irving Kreeger on the phone. Tell him Bill Delaney wants to talk business."

Manny eavesdropped on the conversation through an extension. Delaney began by telling Kreeger he'd heard good reports about a British comedian named Brian Baylor who was coming over for a tour. "I'd like him on my show."

"No problem. Those Limeys would kill for the opportunity to be on your show. Raises interest for the rest of the tour."

"How much do you want for him?"

Kreeger turned coy. "We're always open to offers."

Delaney glanced over to the extension, where Manny was biting his lip to stop himself from shouting out in anger. He never did business that way. He asked a price and usually got it; he did not bargain like some street trader. "How about we cut a deal, Irving? I'm short for the next couple of months, the sponsor's reassessing its goals—you know the kind of crap we go through every few months. You talk this Brian Baylor into coming on my show for nothing and I'll slip you five bills."

Manny bit down hard on his lip. He could actually hear Kreeger salivating at the thought of five hundred dollars for doing nothing more than lying. What horse would he bet that money on? What track would he spend it at?

"Leave it with me, Bill. And remember, there's plenty more where this Limey came from."

Delaney looked toward the extension again. Manny nodded. He would take it now. "Don't bet your last penny on that, Irving."

For a moment there was pure silence. Then came a faltering "Who's that?"

"Me. Manny Lesser, chairman of the British agency you used to represent."

"What's the matter, you can't take a joke?"

"I'm not laughing, Irving."

"Delaney! Was that Delaney, or was that someone you put up to sucking me in?"

"It was me," Delaney said. "And I'd say he's got you dead to rights."

Kreeger ignored Delaney's interruption. "Hey, think about this, Manny! You drop me and you get no more of my people for the Playhouse. Or anywhere else in Limeyland for that matter!"

"The way you're going, you soon won't have anyone worthwhile left," Manny said, and hung up. "Thanks, Bill. I hated to ask someone to do this, but I needed to see with my own eyes, to hear with my own ears, before I could break our relationship."

Delaney nodded. "Just remember, when you have some singer who's a runaway success in Europe, the first place he appears in the USA is *The Bill Delaney Show.*"

"You've got a deal," Manny said, and shook Delaney's hand to seal it.

That night, Manny invited Jimmy and Sonya to dinner. Sonya arrived carrying a flat parcel wrapped in corrugated paper. "For your home," she told Manny.

He opened the wrapping and discovered a picture of the Manhattan skyline, painstakingly created in needlepoint. "Thank you, I've never seen anything quite like this before."

"It's a Sonya Isaacson original," Jimmy said proudly. "You won't find it in any art gallery."

Over dinner, Manny described the confrontation with Irving Kreeger. When he tried to thank the publisher for helping out, Jimmy waved aside the gratitude. "That time in '48, when you came with your brother and no one would give you the time of day, I had the *Messenger's* theater critic contact some people and persuade them to give Lesser Brothers a

479

chance. Kreeger was one of those people. Therefore I feel partly responsible for any problems."

"What will you do now for representation in the United States?" Sonya asked.

"I'll try to set up appointments with other agencies while I'm here," Manny answered, not relishing the prospect. The business with Kreeger had depressed him. He wanted only to go home. Traipsing around New York to knock on doors held no appeal, even if he were assured a far warmer welcome than that of three years ago.

"Why don't you open a branch of your own agency over here? What it would cost to operate will be more than offset by no longer having to split commissions with American agents."

Manny stared at Sonya as if she had suddenly revealed the secret to eternal youth. "Lesser Brothers, London and New York, Limited," he said softly, already seeing the gold-lettered sign.

"Companies aren't limited over here," Jimmy said. "They're incorporated."

"Lesser Brothers Inc." Manny tried it a couple of times, giving it both a London and a New York inflection. "That sounds even better. I'll see a lawyer tomorrow about setting up the business. Can you recommend one?"

"Of course."

"And an office?"

"Try 250 West Fifty-seventh Street," Sonya suggested.

"What's that?"

"An enormous building on the south side of the street, between Broadway and Eighth Avenue." She looked at Jimmy. "Mr. Z. once said that if 250 West Fifty-seventh ever burned down, the entire entertainment business would be running around like a chicken without its head."

"Mr. Z.?" Manny asked.

"My father," Jimmy explained.

"Of course. How's he getting on these days? Does he still work now that you've moved so far out of town?"

"He comes in for a couple of days each week, otherwise he finds plenty to occupy himself at home. He's taken up gardening, and he reads voraciously. He reads every word of everything we publish, and God help me if he finds a mistake."

Sonya laughed. "And then God help whoever made it."

The next day, Manny inspected vacant offices in the building Sonya had suggested. He leased one on the fourteenth floor, then went to keep an appointment Jimmy had made for him with a lawyer. When he flew back to London, he was as excited as he had been nervous and worried on the outward journey. Irving Kreeger's perfidy had come with its own silver lining.

Lesser Brothers Inc. took two months to set up. Barry Levy, whose small agency had been acquired by Lesser Brothers shortly after the war, volunteered to move to New York to manage the branch office. Once there, he would hire people as necessary.

On the day the New York office opened, Manny had a case of champagne delivered to the main office in Haymarket. At three in the afternoon, the office was crowded with agency staff and people from Sidney Less Productions. Rachel had come into town for the day and stood proudly between her two sons, a glass of champagne bubbling in her hand.

"I can't help thinking," she whispered so that only Manny and Sidney would hear, "that my brother Zalman's dream has finally come true. In Rotterdam, he wanted us to go to America. Now, at last, the Isakharov family has reached America."

Manny squeezed his mother's arm, thinking how strange it was the way everything worked out in the end. And how wonderful.

One of the telephones on Manny's desk rang. Carol Jones, his secretary, answered it. She listened for a few seconds, then looked at her boss.

"A call from New York is coming through. Mr. Barry Levy, of Lesser Brothers Inc., wishes to speak to Mr. Manny Lesser, of Lesser Brothers Limited." The secretary smiled mischievously. "Should I tell him you're in? Or should I say you're out?"

Beaming, Manny took the receiver. He waited for the connection to be made. "Barry, how's everything in New York?

481

How's the weather over there? You're lucky you're not here right now, it's raining cats and dogs."

"Our weather's clear and crisp. It's a perfect day, in fact, to open a business."

Manny raised his own glass and toasted everyone in the room.

Days later, Manny received an envelope full of press clippings concerning the opening of Lesser Brothers Inc. from Barry Levy. He read through the accounts, pleased at the good coverage, then mystified when he realized that none of the clippings came from the *Messenger*. He put down the omission to an oversight, either by Levy, or on the part of Jimmy Isaacson's newspaper.

A complete copy of the *Messenger* arrived on Manny's desk the very next day. Turning to the theater page, he found a story about the expansion, including an interview with Levy concerning the agency's objectives. Wondering why Levy had sent the entire newspaper, Manny leafed through the pages. On page two, he noticed that a story had been circled in red ink. As he started to read, he felt his stomach contract. Theatrical agent Irving Kreeger had been found dead in his apartment. A police spokesman said that an empty bottle of sleeping pills and a note found beside Kreeger's bed indicated suicide. The story included quotes from friends who said Kreeger was heavily in debt and had been severely depressed after his business had suffered several serious setbacks.

Manny set down the paper and leaned back in the chair. Kreeger's death had taken the edge off his joy.

Chapter Twenty-two

In the general election of 1952, Jimmy pushed the New York *Messenger* along the same political road he had taken it four years earlier. Only this time, the result was different. In 1948, he had supported a surprise loser in Thomas E. Dewey. In 1952, he backed a runaway winner in Dwight Eisenhower. Equally impressive was the performance of another Republican endorsed by the *Messenger,* William Baron. It was the fourth such endorsement for Jimmy's friend, only this time Baron was not running for the House. He was running for the Senate.

After the election, the freshman Republican senator for New York visited Rye. He sat with Jimmy and his father in the library, sipping coffee and watching flames leap across logs in the masonry fireplace. "You've supported me four times, Jimmy, and I've won four times. I feel like an ingrate, because I've never given you anything in return."

"You have. So far you've given six good years of your life in the House of Representatives. That was why we endorsed you, and that was all we expected."

Baron looked from son to father. "Can you believe your son? Fifty million people in this country would kill for the chance to hear what I'm offering him, and he gives me an answer that would have made George Washington proud."

"Make that fifty million and one," Zalman answered. "Twelve, thirteen years ago, I would have killed to be asked that question by a friend in government who could have done something."

"Mr. Z. . . . !" Jimmy held up a warning hand. He didn't want his father musing on his income-tax evasion trial. That was long in the past; it didn't need to be brought up now. Especially in front of Baron. He had to know about it, of course, unless he'd been blind and deaf during 1940 and 1941. He was tactful enough never to mention it, but he might question his friendship with the publishing family if he was reminded of Zalman's history.

Baron's face broke into a grin. "Don't worry about family skeletons with me, Jimmy. I don't hold grudges. I only care about what a person does now. I'm not interested in some baggage from the past that ten thousand other people got away with because they paid off the right people. Now, is there anything I can do for you? Or your father?"

Jimmy prepared to turn down the offer once again. Then, knowing how badly Zalman would have wanted this opportunity twelve years ago, he looked at his father. It wouldn't do any harm to let him have it now. "Mr. Z., how about you?"

"Yes, what about it, Mr. Z.?" Baron echoed.

Behind the glasses, Zalman's dark-brown eyes sparkled. "If you'd have asked me six weeks ago, Senator, I'd have said two front-row seats for the Marciano–Walcott fight in Philadelphia."

Jimmy laughed. At sixty-eight, his father still liked a good scrap, even if he could only watch.

"If there's a rematch, will you be interested?" Baron asked.

"If there's a rematch, I'll be looking for an envelope addressed to me in your writing, and postmarked Washington, D.C."

After Baron's departure, Jimmy turned to his father. "I'm disappointed in you. I always thought you were ambitious, a man with grand ideas, yet when you have the chance to ask for anything in the world, you settle for a couple of tickets to a fight that might never take place. A man with real aspirations would have asked for a dinner invitation to the White House, and a bed for the night thrown in."

Zalman gave his son a patient smile. "Supplying two tickets for a Marciano–Walcott rematch is not beyond your friend's ability. Room and board at the White House once

President Eisenhower and Mamie take up residence is, I think, out of the senator's reach. Always remember, Jimmy, when a man says he'll give you anything you ask for, make sure you ask for something you're reasonably sure he'll be able to provide."

Jimmy reached out to hug his father. No matter how old he got, how wise he thought he had become, or how powerful others viewed him, he could still learn a trick or two from the old man.

In the middle of November, Zalman altered the habits he had formed since Julia's death and the move from New York to Rye. Instead of going into the city a couple of times a week, he started making the journey in Jimmy's black Rolls Royce every day. Once at the Messenger Building, he sat in the office going through Audit Bureau of Circulation figures and working with a secretary he had taken from the steno pool.

Whenever Jimmy asked his father what he was up to, Zalman wagged a finger in his son's face and told him he would know in good time. Curiosity piqued, Jimmy frequently stopped outside his father's door to listen in. Occasionally, he caught a murmur of voices; other times, he heard the click of snooker balls. When Jimmy asked the secretary what was going on, she told him that Zalman had sworn her to silence. Only on Thursdays and Fridays did this pattern change. Then Jimmy saw his father outside the building, loitering by a newsstand. He swore that Zalman was studying what people bought.

On the journey home, Jimmy tried to trick his father into giving himself away. "I heard those balls rattling away all day. You must really have ideas popping out of your brain."

"No, I just like to keep in practice. Can't let my fingers stiffen up."

"And what about hanging out at the newsstand? What schemes are you dreaming up in that room?"

"Big schemes" was all Zalman would say.

Two weeks after the start of this odd behavior, Zalman marched into his son's office clutching a folder full of papers and three magazines. He dumped everything on Jimmy's desk and sat down. "The shops are getting ready for

Christmas," he announced. "Any idea what the big gift will be this year?"

Jimmy glanced at the magazines and immediately knew the answer. They were publications listing television programs in three different cities. "Television sets, right?"

"Right. There's a boom on. The industry's in a state of transformation. Fifteen million sets are in use in this country, and the number's going to double within a year or two. You know what this nation's biggest area of interest is right now?"

"Korea?" Jimmy wondered what that had to do with television.

"Korea, hell! More Americans are interested in whether Lucille Ball will have a boy or a girl than ever cared about Korea. Even Eisenhower cares. He's worried that she'll take the spotlight away from his inaugural in January by having the damned thing on the same day! And you know something else?" Zalman picked up the three magazines and tossed them contemptuously onto the floor. "There isn't one magazine in the country that does any kind of justice to the potential of television."

"Those do all right."

"One's circulation is a hundred and ninety thousand, another sells a hundred and sixty thousand, yet another tops two hundred thousand. You call that all right? It's peanuts, Jimmy. Peanuts! Television networks span the country. We should have a television magazine that does the same thing, and all we have are these, run by amateurs who are so busy trying to make a quick buck that they can't see beyond the end of their nose. Thirty years ago, I went to Belmont one afternoon with Frank Brennan and Bill Regan. One of them, I can't remember which, bought a racing sheet called *Form Guide*. It was like those magazines, a spit in the ocean, covering just one tiny area."

Jimmy knew how his father had made *Form Guide* a national racing paper; he had done the same with the racing wire, turning that from a sloppy group of independents into a tightly run, profitable operation that linked the entire country. "This isn't so simple, Mr. Z. With *Form Guide,* you had the identical paper coming out in eight different locations. A weekly television magazine that's good for New York will be useless for Chicago or Los Angeles."

Zalman regarded his son with annoyance. "Do you think I'm stupid? I know all that. What I'm proposing is that we first clear the way by taking over whatever magazines there are, then we publish one weekly magazine to cover the entire country. We print the editorial section on our own presses. It'll carry stories about network shows, and it can be shipped ahead of time to major cities where local listings can be wrapped around it."

Jimmy quickly caught his father's vision, just as Zalman had hoped he would. He caught it and ran with it. "We maintain advertising and editorial staff in each city. Advertising can be taken for both national and local accounts, Chesterfield cigarettes and Joe's Car Wash on the corner of Fifth and Main."

"That's right," Zalman said eagerly. "Fifteen million television owners are out there, Jimmy. Pretty soon there'll be thirty million, and then fifty million. We're going to jump on the biggest circulation bandwagon of all time before it even starts to roll."

"What's in the folder?"

"A couple of dummies I made up." Zalman spread them across Jimmy's desk. One was the size of *Time*. Inside, columns of type were mixed with pictures, listings, and advertisements clipped from other magazines. The second dummy was much smaller, no larger than a pocket book. Editorial was confined to the first dozen pages; then the listings began. It was obvious from the way Zalman positioned the dummies on Jimmy's desk that he favored the smaller one.

"What's so special about this odd little size?"

"It's distinctive," Zalman answered. "I want to call this magazine *TV Diary*, so why shouldn't we have something the size of a diary?"

Jimmy looked from the small dummy to the larger one, then back again. The old man hadn't lost it. He started to smile. "When you talk about taking over magazines, Mr. Z., I hope you understand that what was all right in the twenties isn't so acceptable now."

"I'm too old for that kind of takeover action. Besides, I no longer have the kind of dependable men I used to have. And I certainly wouldn't want to do anything that might embarrass my fancy-pants son with his respectable ideas and his hoity-toity friends in Washington. We'll buy whatever we need to take over."

Calculations danced in Jimmy's head. He spoke the results aloud. "Expenses first. It'll cost maybe a million and a half dollars to acquire existing magazines. We'll have to hire staff to run the operation in perhaps ten major cities and lease office space for them. We can estimate an initial circulation of ten percent of television owners, which means the cost of printing between one and a half million and two million copies a week. Now for income. Sales of one and a half million copies each week, and whatever advertising our people can drum up." He gazed at his father. "We'll start out well behind the eight ball on this one. Nor will we get it back in a hurry. It'll take time to gain acceptance among readers and advertisers."

"Save money by using already existing space wherever you can. Double up *TV Diary* staff in *Form Guide* offices where the cities coincide. In New York, you can find space in any one of a dozen offices for *Diary* staff. *American Miss,* alone, has enough extra space to run two more magazines. They're loaded with space."

Jimmy nodded. Pauline Fulford had created an empire for herself on the sixth floor of the Messenger Building, and because of *American Miss*'s outstanding success, he had allowed her to do so. Now, more urgent priorities required the empire be pulled back to its original borders. "Did you do all this research for mental exercise, Mr. Z.? Or did you do it because you want to run this operation?"

"What do you think?"

"You've got it." Jimmy felt excited. The idea of *TV Diary* thrilled him, and no one was better qualified than his father to run it. It was a carbon copy of what Zalman had done with *Form Guide,* and if it were as successful it would make the company's other magazines look like . . . like peanuts! More exhilarating still was the knowledge that his father had finally found something to challenge him. Coming in two days a week, reading at home, and playing gardener hadn't been anywhere near enough to occupy his mind and stop him thinking about Julia. This, a new magazine with the potential to become the biggest money-spinner in Messenger Publications' arsenal, would do the trick.

Zalman threw himself into the challenge. The years seemed to fall away; he worked with the energy of a man half his age. He contacted the owners of the three magazines he had shown Jimmy and invited them, one after another, to the Messenger Building. Flattered by the summons, and not a little intimidated, the three magazine owners were asked to name a price. None made the mistake of a racing sheet owner named Lew Schwartz who, thirty years before, had told Zalman that it was his responsibility to make an offer. Two of the owners, without any consultation, chose an identical sum—half a million dollars. It was paid without a murmur. The third owner asked for a nice round figure: one million dollars. Ten minutes later, the check was ready.

While Zalman eliminated competition, Messenger Publications' personnel department hired editorial and advertising staffs in the ten major cities across the country where *TV Diary* would publish. At the end of January, eight weeks after the idea had been broached, Zalman had a launch date for Jimmy to consider.

"I want the first issue out on Thursday, May 14, 1953, giving program listings for the week of May seventeenth through the twenty-third."

Jimmy checked the calendar. "Our ad salesmen start selling this week. That gives us three months. Have you thought about editorial content for that first issue? It has to be special."

"Do you forget who you're talking to? I used to own a couple of movie magazines. I know what the fans want to read."

"*TV Diary* is not going to be a fan magazine, Mr. Z. It's going to be a serious—"

"Whose idea was this magazine?"

"Yours, but that doesn't mean a damned thing. This magazine is going to be a serious publication, with searching articles about the networks, about the industry, about the programs. It is not going to be some star-studded 1930's movie

489

fan magazine. It's going to be the bible of the television industry."

Zalman laughed at his son. "You want a bible, go find Moses or Jesus to run it for you."

As Zalman turned to go, Jimmy called out: "Remember, I get the final look at every single piece of copy that goes in. And our printing schedule gives me enough time to change anything!"

Not everyone at Messenger Publications was as in favor of *TV Diary*. Marvin Baker, general manager of WMES, made known his opposition to the idea the moment Jimmy asked for his opinion.

"Such a book will be obsolete before the ink dries on the first edition."

"Obsolete? What does that mean?"

"You're a newspaper publisher, Mr. J. You carry television listings as part of the newspaper's service. Most of those newspapers that saw television as threatening competition, and subsequently didn't carry the listings, are changing their minds about it now. Once more papers carry listings, why would anyone in their right mind pay extra for a magazine like *TV Diary?*"

Baker found an ally in Brian Gilbert. "It's a funny little publication," Gilbert told Jimmy. "Looking at it certainly doesn't send any shivers down my spine."

"Didn't anyone warn you against judging a book by its cover?"

"To throw a cliché back at you, Mr. J., didn't you ever hear that you never get a second chance to make a first impression?"

Jimmy laughed. "Why don't we talk about it over lunch?"

Gilbert was one of the few company people with whom Jimmy socialized. If he had no lunchtime appointment, Jimmy often asked his assistant if he fancied something to eat. He liked to hear Gilbert's opinions, but he also enjoyed ribbing him about the never-ending stream of generous girlfriends. He asked Gilbert about the clothes he wore—who had bought him the suit, the tie, the shirt, the gold cuff links. Gilbert always took such ribbing in stride. He knew he had his boss's loyalty and affection, and the teasing was the price he had to pay.

Over lunch, Gilbert argued eloquently against *TV Diary*. "Advertising agencies are accustomed to investing their clients' money in big glossy magazines. Can you imagine an account executive at J. Walter Thompson, for example, explaining to a national account why they should spend a million dollars on some stunted little runt of a publication that carries what anyone can find in a newspaper for nothing?"

Jimmy respected Gilbert's opinion, but he refused to be deterred by the criticism. His father believed in the little magazine. So did he. And that was all that mattered. If Baker and Gilbert didn't agree, that was their prerogative; he had never made a practice of hiring men who concurred with his every utterance. But when disapproval of the scheme came from another source within Messenger Publications, Jimmy was stung badly.

Pauline Fulford made an appointment to see him. She breezed into his office, as bright and cheery as ever, but with a hard set to her normally shiny dark eyes. "Mr. J., strange things are occurring at my magazine. Would you please tell me why?"

"What strange things?"

"*American Miss* is losing its identity. It's being merged with another magazine. With *TV Diary*." She coated the name of the new publication with contempt, as though it were beneath her dignity to even utter it.

"Nothing's being merged, Pauline. *TV Diary* and *American Miss* are two completely separate entities."

Pauline smiled grimly. "Then would you please explain to me why advertising people from *TV Diary* are being placed in offices belonging to my magazine."

"Financial reasons. You have plenty of extra space. The *TV Diary* people need space. Ergo, they take yours." He saw Pauline's cheeks flush crimson as she prepared to fight for every square inch of space she had acquired for her magazine. He tried to head her off with calm reason. "Pauline, getting *TV Diary* off the ground has left us short of cash. Certainly we have many highly profitable publications, yours among them, but we also have some properties that are a drain on the company's finances. I believe that *TV Diary,* in the very near future, will be the biggest thing this company has ever done, but to get it on the stands requires us to cut back wherever we can. That means doubling up. I've always let you have more space than you really need. Now I'm taking some of it back."

Pauline stood up. "I'm sorry, but I will not tolerate working in conditions that a sardine would rebel against. Either *American Miss* retains all of its space and facilities or you find yourself another editor."

Jimmy didn't move. He just sat behind his desk, staring calmly at Pauline on the other side.

"Did you hear what I said, Mr. J.? I would rather leave this company than be expected to produce a quality magazine from a dingy corner of some communal working space."

Faced by such a threat, Pauline fully expected Jimmy to retreat from his cost-cutting position. She was the founding editor of *American Miss.* She had been with the company for more than six years; they couldn't afford to let her go. Surely he understood that. Yet as she stared back across the desk, she began to realize he understood nothing of the kind.

Finally Jimmy spoke. "Go ahead, Pauline. Do whatever you think is best."

Pauline's mouth started to drop. She caught herself just in time, maintaining the poise that was her trademark. He hadn't rolled over at the threat of resignation. He had simply accepted it. "Mr. J., let's not rush into something we might regret . . ."

Jimmy was no longer listening. His decision was made, and now he was wondering how best to replace the magazine editor. The obvious choice was promoting Pauline's assistant, a woman in her early thirties named Cheryl Walker. The appointment would be temporary, until Cheryl either proved herself or Jimmy found someone who could do a better job.

"Mr. J., did you hear what I said?"

He smiled at her. "Thank you for everything you've done for us, Pauline. You helped make *American Miss* the success it is, and we'll be forever grateful. Good luck in whatever else you decide to do."

Pauline left the room in a daze. She had found out that at Messenger Publications, no one was indispensable.

Pauline's contract required a month's notice, running through the end of February. In the first day of the notice period, while rumors ran like wildfire through Messenger Publications over the editor's impending departure, Jimmy met with Cheryl Walker.

Jimmy had never taken much notice of the woman. Pauline had done the hiring, bringing Cheryl over from *Cosmopolitan* three years ago. If Pauline was satisfied, Jimmy, too, was satisfied. Now, as she entered his office, he paid close attention to her for the first time. He had to admit that Cheryl Walker fitted the role of editor of a magazine that influenced the lives of young women. Tall and slim, she walked gracefully toward his desk, her long blond hair falling in a soft pageboy onto the shoulders of her dark-green dress. Green seemed to be her favorite color. She wore an emerald necklace that complemented not only the dress but her eyes, which were the most brilliant shade of green Jimmy had ever seen.

She sat down, carefully crossing one leg over the other, and regarded her employer expectantly. Jimmy changed his initial opinion. Instead of a glamorous magazine editor, Cheryl Walker looked more like a hungry tigress closing in on the kill.

"No doubt you know that Pauline Fulford will be leaving us at the end of February. Until we formally appoint a new editor, I want you to be interim editor."

"Thank you." Cheryl almost leaned over the desk in her eagerness. "But the magazine doesn't need to look any further than its own staff for a permanent editor."

"I'm sure, but a position as prestigious as this will attract considerable interest. It's only fair to both our readers and our own people that we hire the very best person available."

"I see." Cheryl appeared irritated at the reply, as if she had already assumed the position would be hers. She recovered quickly. A smile drew her lips back from even, white teeth. Again Jimmy was struck by the tigress comparison. "Mr. J., I think you're a man who appreciates frankness, so I'll be very open with you. If I'm appointed editor, you'll never have cause to regret it."

"Thank you, Miss Walker. We'll let you know." Jimmy stood up and walked quickly to the door, holding it open for Cheryl. The woman had put him on the defensive from the moment she'd entered the office, and Jimmy was unaccustomed to feeling that way in anyone's presence. Her last statement, and the promise he thought it contained, added to his discomfort.

On the journey to Rye that evening, he discussed the meeting with his father. "Any moment I thought she was going to leap over the desk and go for my jugular."

"Or something else," Zalman said, and nudged his son in the ribs. "You know, there's a lot of men who'd give their right arm for a chance with that young woman."

"Someone told me the same thing at the Stork Club on the night I sent a good-looking actress home in a cab so I could spend some time with a very lovely Canadian girl I'd just met. That girl was Sonya, and I feel the same now as I did then."

"Good. You don't know how glad I am to hear that."

"Did you ever cheat?"

"On your mother?" Zalman looked genuinely shocked. "Of course I didn't! I couldn't have looked at myself in the mirror again if I had."

"Good. And you don't know how glad I am to hear that." Jimmy turned in the seat to smile at his father. "Couple of real faithful husbands, aren't we?"

"Best way to be," Zalman answered. "I just hope you and Sonya stay as happy as Julia and I did."

"It's our fourteenth anniversary next month. I'd say we're off to a flying start."

"Are you going to give the green-eyed tigress the job?"

"I don't know what to do. She's right—she is perfectly qualified, but her attitude unnerves me. I used that story about our responsibility to readers and employees as a ruse to get rid of her. This whole business with *American Miss* has come at a lousy time. I've been so busy with that, I haven't had a chance to talk to you about *TV Diary.*"

Zalman patted his son's knees. "Relax. As long as I'm in charge, you've got nothing to worry about."

"What's going to be in the editorial section?"

Zalman ticked off topic on his fingers. "I've commissioned an in-depth feature on *I Love Lucy*. A feature on *The Honeymooners*. An article on Milton Berle. And . . ."

"And what?"

"I don't know yet. I'm still looking for something out of the ordinary to balance the serious stories. Don't worry, I'll come up with it."

"I'm sure you will, Mr. Z. I'm sure you will." At least, with his father in charge, Jimmy knew he had no worries where the new magazine was concerned. He could concentrate his attention on other problems.

Replacing Pauline Fulford occupied Jimmy's mind for the rest of the week and into the weekend. It snowed on Friday night, and even when Jimmy watched his two children toboggan across the white wasteland on Saturday morning, his mind dissected the problem. An advertisement would run in that Sunday's papers, the *Times* as well as the *Messenger;* additionally, feelers had been put out to the staffs of other magazines to see if anyone would step forward. Still Jimmy did not know whether he was doing the right thing. Promoting Cheryl Walker seemed so simple, so automatic. Jimmy always liked to promote from within, but he couldn't get the hungry tigress out of his mind. The woman actually frightened him.

After lunch, he wandered into the daylight studio where Sonya worked on her needlepoint. Earlier examples of her art covered the paneled wall and Jimmy stopped to admire them. Forest scenes, street scenes, buildings; in Jimmy's eyes, they were as good as any painting by one of the old masters. He wondered which friends or charities would be lucky enough to receive these. With her skill and sharp mind, Sonya could probably open a gallery and make a fortune selling nothing but her own art.

Footsteps sounded behind him. "Are you interested in buying any particular work, sir?"

He turned to face Sonya. She didn't like anyone entering

the studio when she was creating, and she had a work in progress on the table, left there before she'd broken for lunch. Jimmy glanced at it—the Rialto Bridge in Venice. "Actually, madam, I'm seeking inspiration and I thought I might find it here."

"Oh?" She stepped closer. "What kind of inspiration?"

Sonya knew about Pauline's resignation. Jimmy hadn't told her about Cheryl's expectations. He rectified that omission now. "I might be grossly slandering her, but I could swear she was making a pass at me."

"At least that shows she has good taste. Isn't good taste a prerequisite for that particular job?"

Jimmy grinned. "When I told my father about it, he said I was turning down what a lot of men would give their right arm for. I reminded him that your cousin's husband said pretty much the same thing before the war, when I dumped an actress named Lee Robins for you."

Sonya stepped into her husband's arms and looked up into his eyes. He hadn't changed very much in fourteen years. His face was a shade fuller, perhaps; a trace of gray had crept into dark-brown hair that was thinner than she first remembered it. His brown eyes were still as gentle, just as sensitive. Gazing into them, she found it easy to bring into clear focus that night at the Stork Club, when he'd chosen her over the actress. She could remember every wonderful minute of that night, how he'd taken her dancing at El Morocco before driving her back to her cousin's East Side apartment. He'd seen her every evening for the rest of her stay in New York, as gallant a Sir Galahad as ever there was, and then he'd followed her up to Montreal. "If I worked for Messenger Publications, I'd make a pass at you as well. And I'd be very put out if you gave me the brush-off."

He pushed her back so suddenly that she wondered what had happened. When he stared intently at her, she looked down at herself to see what was wrong. "Why don't you work for Messenger Publications?"

"What?" Sonya started to laugh. "The only work I've ever done was in the Montreal clothing factory my father owned. I ran errands for him, and he called me his personal assistant."

"I don't need a personal assistant. I already have an excellent one. I need an editor for an influential magazine called *American Miss*."

"I wouldn't know how to edit anything."

"The magazine was your idea, remember? We walked down Fifth Avenue one evening and you said there was no magazine to help a girl become a young woman. You can handle it, Sonya. You're more artistic than any other woman I've ever known, and behind that lovely face is a brain Einstein would envy."

The proposition tantalized her. She would be able to leave her artistic signature on more than just needlepoint. "What about the children?"

"Josephine's ten, Harold's five. They go to school. We have servants to look after them when you're away. You won't have to put in the same hours I do. And if need be, you can always work from here."

"I don't know." She wrung her hands. "I just don't know. What will the staff think of such an appointment? They'll put me down as a family member given a glamorous job and they'll expect me to make a complete mess of everything I touch."

"I haven't seen you make a mess of anything yet. You've got the weekend to think it over, Sonya. I'll need to know before I leave for work on Monday morning."

Sonya threw her arms around Jimmy's neck and kissed him. "You're a tough guy to work for, you know that?"

Jimmy knew. Just as he also knew that he would not have to wait for Monday morning for his answer.

The appointment of Sonya as editor-in-chief of *American Miss* drew stunned surprise. Questioning looks met Jimmy when he made the announcement, but no one had the nerve to challenge his decision out loud. After making arrangements for the children to be picked up from school, Sonya started traveling into the city each day. She worked for three weeks alongside Pauline Fulford, then, when Pauline left the magazine, she took over the top spot.

Sonya's first act as editor was to call a staff meeting. "I might be sitting in the editor's chair, but I fully realize that

I'm still the new kid on the block. I'll need help before I know my way around. That's on the debit side. For credit, this magazine was originally my idea. I know fashion, I understand current trends, and I've been told that I'm one heck of an artist. All in all, I know I'll make a fine editor."

Jimmy instructed Brian Gilbert to keep an eye on the situation at *American Miss*. After a couple of days, Gilbert reported that the majority of the staff had accepted Sonya, although there was some muttering about dilettantes and nepotism. She was proving herself to be both likable and competent. She earned further respect before the first week was out by returning to a regular contributor a feature on setting up one's first apartment that she considered unsubstantial.

At the end of the first week, Jimmy asked Sonya how she felt she'd done. "I only had trouble in one area," she answered. "On Wednesday, I asked Cheryl Walker to lunch. She was Pauline's assistant, and I thought she could explain a few things to me. She told me she was too busy to have lunch anytime that week. I'm going to have trouble with her, Jimmy, and I think it would be best for the magazine if she left."

"You're the editor. That means as well as putting the magazine together, you have the power of hire and fire."

The instant Sonya reached the office on Monday, she sent for Cheryl Walker. "If you go to the accounts department, you'll find your salary check made out to the end of the month. Have a vacation on us."

"You're letting me go?" Cheryl couldn't believe it. "Just because I wouldn't have lunch with you?"

"No. I'm firing you because you thought my husband might be tempted to cheat on me. There is no room on this magazine for people who make errors of such magnitude."

Jimmy watched Sonya's confidence grow with each passing day. She was not afraid to ask questions, but like her husband she only asked them once. And after the example she made of Cheryl Walker, no one else on the magazine questioned her authority.

With the *American Miss* situation under control, Jimmy

turned his attention once more to *TV Diary*. Initial reports on advertising revenue were anything but heartening. In cities across the country, his salesmen met fierce resistance. Some agencies quoted the subject matter of the publication as a reason for their reticence to involve clients' money; others claimed the odd diary size made the magazine physically unattractive. Jimmy shielded himself from the bad news by remembering his own words that the magazine would not be an instant hit. It would need time to gain acceptance.

He switched his concentration from advertising to editorial. The articles his father had commissioned were arriving. Jimmy took them home for Sonya to read. She was a huge fan of *I Love Lucy,* and she thoroughly enjoyed the feature on the show that would be the cover story of *TV Diary*'s first issue. Jimmy liked the stories on *The Honeymooners* and Milton Berle; both struck the right combination of entertainment and news value.

The final story for the first issue arrived in the middle of March. Zalman dropped a buff folder on Jimmy's desk. "This wraps it up. Starting today, we're working on the next issue."

Jimmy opened the folder and saw a black-and-white photograph of a human mountain wearing nothing but high-topped boots and striped briefs. The man weighed at least three hundred pounds, with shoulder-length blond hair that looked as if it had just left the beauty parlor. "What do you call this?"

"That's Dazzling Dan Dixon, the wrestler."

"What's Dazzling Dan Dixon doing in *TV Diary?*"

Zalman looked pained at his son's ignorance. "He's on every Saturday. Dazzling Dan's the biggest draw in professional wrestling. Advertisers have wars to sponsor his bouts."

Shaking his head in wonderment, Jimmy began to read. He supposed even the bible of the television industry had to include some token genuflection to bad taste. Trust his father to come up with a story like this. Dazzling Dan! Suddenly, Jimmy's amazement turned cold. "Wait a minute! We can't carry this."

"We can't carry what?"

"The fact that he wrestles to support twelve children."

"What's wrong with that? Can you think of a more noble reason to work?"

"According to this, Dazzling Dan's never been married. All his children have been born out of wedlock, to twelve different women no less. What's the headline? Dazzling Dan's Dirty Dozen? This is a family magazine, Mr. Z. I want any person from eight to eighty to be able to pick it up and enjoy it."

"The *Messenger*'s a family newspaper. That never stopped you putting in some juicy scandals."

"You mean it never stopped *you* putting them in. I consider carefully whether a story has meaning and value before I use it."

"You're trying to build circulation for a new magazine. To do that, you've got to appeal to the lowest common denominator, and a story on Dazzling Dan Dixon will hit the bull's-eye." Zalman walked toward the door. As far as he was concerned, the discussion was over.

Jimmy chased his father through the open door and into the next office, where Brian Gilbert sat talking on the telephone. "If you feed readers garbage, they'll expect more garbage. If you offer them something better, they'll come to expect that, too. And eventually they'll thank you for it."

Zalman waved a hand in derision at his son. "Stop spouting theory at me. You never had a dime's worth of common sense when it came to selling newspapers and magazines. People don't want to be taught refinement. They want a good old belly laugh. You want to feed them vintage champagne and caviar, and all they want is beer and hot dogs." He strode toward his own office.

Jimmy was determined to have the last word. "In the thirties they wanted beer and hot dogs because there was a Depression. Basics counted more than luxury. We're in a boom period now, Mr. Z. People are ready for a little luxury, some refinement, and I'm going to damned well give it to them."

Zalman slammed his office door. Jimmy breathed out loudly and turned around. For the first time he noticed Gilbert, a hand clapped over the mouthpiece so no one would hear the argument. A look of astonishment covered his face.

"Don't worry about it, Brian. I had a sister who was one hell of a newspaperman, and I'm determined to make one out of my father as well."

"Now where have I heard that line before?" Gilbert responded.

Chuckling, Jimmy returned to his office. He stared at the story for fully five minutes before reaching a decision. He'd let it run, but first he would delete any reference to Dazzling Dan's dozen little bastards. The wrestler's own story, how he'd risen from the slums of Cleveland to become a celebrity in the new world of television, was entertainment enough.

William Baron kept his promise. On the night of May 15, Zalman and Jimmy had front row seats at the Rocky Marciano–Jersey Joe Walcott rematch in Chicago for the heavyweight championship of the world. Jimmy made sure to pay Baron for the tickets; he wanted no accusations of receiving favors—no matter how small—for throwing editorial support behind the senator.

Marciano needed less than two and a half minutes to finish the contest. Despite the controversy of the quick finish, Zalman talked about the bout with gleeful relish on the flight back to New York. He remembered every punch, every feint, every step each boxer took. Jimmy listened halfheartedly. His mind was on what had happened yesterday, when the first copy of *TV Diary* had come out. Sales had met expectations, in excess of one and a half million, but advertising was far below initial predictions.

"Do you think the doubting Thomases might be right?" he asked his father.

"About what? The fight?"

"*TV Diary.* And please don't hand me a line about things getting better if only we'd include more blood and guts."

"We both knew we'd need patience, Jimmy. *TV Diary* covers a different subject matter. It's an odd size. Advertisers will have to get used to it. One and a half million readers is nothing to be sneezed at. When that increases, advertisers will have to support us. They wouldn't dare miss out."

Jimmy felt reassured by his father's words. Some things never changed; he could always look to him for comfort.

501

"Sonya and I are planning to go to England in a couple of weeks, take the children for a few days."

"Why?"

"There's a major news event taking place over there. The coronation of Queen Elizabeth the Second. I'm going for the *Messenger*, and Sonya's planning on writing a piece for *American Miss*. Will you come with us?"

Zalman shook his head fiercely. "There's nothing in England I want to see. Not even a coronation."

Jimmy understood. England held bad memories for his father.

Chapter Twenty-three

D'Artagnan, the French musical based on *The Three Musketeers,* pushed Sidney into the vanguard of British impresarios. Past productions—shows in seaside theaters, revivals of nearly forgotten musicals—meant nothing anymore. Future productions would be judged against the spectacular success of *D'Artagnan.*

The show contained everything for an audience to savor: a storyline; a memorable score that people whistled and hummed each time the theater emptied; spectacular sets; and dashing swordplay resulting from hours of painstaking rehearsal. *D'Artagnan* opened in October 1951 at the Admiralty Theatre, off Trafalgar Square, and ran for a year. It closed only because the stage was needed for another Sydney Less production, a British play this time called *A Breath of Death.* Bitingly satirical, the show concerned three brothers from a farming community sent into the trenches during World War I.

The entire family attended the opening night of *Breath.* It recalled for Rachel the time she had first seen her sons on a stage. The domineering NCO's, absurd staff officers, and luckless privates seemed to be lifted straight from that first skit.

During the first-night party that followed the show, while Sidney gloried in his second straight triumph, Rachel mentioned the similarity. He smiled and nodded. "That was the first thing that struck me when I read the script. I saw Bernard, Manny, and myself winning the talent competition

503

at the Tottenham Rialto all over again. I knew I had to produce it. And I knew that the public was ready for a vehicle that showed the futility of war."

Even before *Breath* completed its first sold-out week at the Admiralty, Sidney was busy seeking fresh material. He flew to New York to see a show called *Desire,* a bawdy, risqué musical about the life of a prostitute. When he made the return flight, he had contracts for the British production safely in his pocket.

Success gave Sidney confidence to chase a fantasy. One dream above all had always tantalized him. From the moment he had stepped onto the stage at the Tottenham Rialto, a single form of entertainment had remained his favorite. Variety. While professional interest guided his observation of musicals and plays, he watched variety strictly for enjoyment. He loved the broad tapestry of talents, the mix, the variety itself. It was no longer the business he and his brothers had worked in. That was amateur hour compared with the slick productions of the postwar era. Modern variety relied heavily on musical turns. More often than not, big-name, big-money American artists topped the bill. Nonetheless, it remained the most exciting entertainment of all. Sidney could think of no better way to spend an evening than to sit in the London Playhouse, watching Gordon Prideaux's latest production. Each time he came out, the dream was sharper. Above all else, he wanted to create a major variety show.

He even knew where. Among the theaters Sidney passed on the walk from home to office was the Showcase in Coventry Street. The old theater had changed ownership three times since the war. Diverse productions had been staged there—drama, comedy, musicals. Nothing had worked. Each time he walked past, he considered ways to make the Showcase profitable. One answer always came to mind, the one entertainment form that had not been used. Variety. He understood why no one else had tried. The Showcase was a short walk from the London Playhouse, the city's premier variety theater. To compete from such close range was the theatrical equivalent of putting your head in a noose. Unless you had the ambition and self-confidence of Sidney Less.

Sidney controlled the dream until the fall of 1952. The day after he returned from the States with the British rights to *Desire,* his morning walk paid off with more than exercise. Nailed to the exterior of the Showcase he saw the sign of a London estate agent. The theater was for sale again. Sidney stood staring at the sign for fully two minutes, the dream alive and dancing in his head. In front of his eyes, the dirty brick building became sandblasted clean; the entrance shone with fresh paint; glass gleamed, lights shone. Biting his bottom lip with excitement, he turned away and strode toward Haymarket.

When Manny arrived, he found Sidney waiting in his office. "The Showcase is up for sale!"

"That's right. The current proprietors owe us more than six thousand pounds. They can't pay until they sell and recoup their investment. If they can't sell, they go into liquidation and we join the line of creditors."

"Why didn't you tell me it was up for sale?"

"I didn't know you were interested—" Manny broke off as the door opened and Carol Jones entered with the day's first steaming mug of tea. "You want some?"

Sidney waved away the offer. He was too excited to hold a cup without spilling it. Manny took a sip of scalding tea and smacked his lips in satisfaction. "Why are you interested in that dump? No one's made a go of it since before the war."

"I want to turn it into a variety house."

Manny regarded his brother as though he were mad. "Will you listen to yourself? Why would you want to open a variety house when variety's dying? Radio struck the first blow, television's finishing it off. Theaters are closing all over the country."

"This isn't the rest of the country. This is the West End."

"Right, where one variety theater rules unchallenged. Sidney, you cannot hope to lock horns with Gordon Prideaux and win. He's got the power of the Rialto Playhouse Partnership behind him. He'll have you on toast for breakfast, just like his old man did. You've got hit musicals and plays coming out of your ears and you're going to risk money and your friendship with Gordon for some stroke of lunacy! What's the matter with you?"

505

"I never appeared in a play or a musical, Manny. Neither did you. We began as variety artists. You might have forgotten, but I haven't. My heart's still there, on the boards, entertaining people. And I want to produce the kind of variety in the kind of theater I would have loved to appear in."

Manny sipped his tea thoughtfully. "You got the money to buy that place?"

"What I don't have I can borrow. I'm good for it. I need something else from you."

"What?"

"Clients. You represent major stars, European and American. If I take over the Showcase, I don't want to be blacklisted by Lesser Brothers because you're scared of upsetting Gordon."

"Sidney, you pay what Lesser Brothers' clients are worth, and I promise you they'll appear at any theater you own."

Sidney bought the Showcase. He had owned shares in theaters before—he had a fifteen percent interest in the Admiralty—but he had never owned a theater outright. On the day he took possession, he stood with Naomi on the stage and looked out into the auditorium. "What do you think?" he asked.

She tried desperately to say something encouraging, but all she could manage was: "I never worked in a theater that looked as badly in need of repair as this place does."

"Neither did I. My mother would never have allowed it, but then she was a good agent. All it needs is a coat of paint—"

"And the reupholstering of every chair, not to mention some cosmetic work for the entrance."

"Dressing rooms aren't anything to write home about, either," Sidney said. "The surveyor's report says the plumbing's not much good, and if we ever turn on all the lights at the same time, we stand a good chance of starting the second Great Fire of London."

"Then why did you risk everything we own, not to mention whatever you could beg or borrow, to buy the place?"

"So Lesser Brothers could be paid the six thousand pounds they were owed by the mob who ran this place."

"Brotherly love doesn't run that deep."

"My dream does. Soon, the best singers in the world, the most popular dancers, and the funniest comedians are going to be performing on this stage." He held a hand in front of her eyes, blocking her vision. "Can you hear Jimmy Durante making people laugh, and Edith Piaf wringing tears with song? If you believe in something strongly enough, Naomi, it'll happen."

She clutched his hand, believing in his dream. "You can make it all come true, Sidney."

But when Sidney stood on the same stage the following day, he had second thoughts. The chairs looked even shoddier, the carpet more threadbare, the walls and fixtures more decrepit. Needing a tonic, he did to himself what he had done to Naomi. He closed his eyes and made believe. And he prayed that he hadn't let ambition push him into making the biggest mistake of his life.

Soon the Showcase echoed to the bang of hammers, the rasp of saws. Builders labored to knock the old theater into shape. Seats were removed for reupholstering, carpet replaced, circuits rewired, plumbing repaired. Sidney spent every spare minute at the theater. He didn't want to be presented with a completed renovation—he wanted to see improvements as they happened. He was rarely alone. Sometimes Naomi watched with him, sharing his excitement and his trepidation. Manny popped in to see how work was progressing. Rachel, too, stopped by, when she came to town to visit with her adopted granddaughters.

As Rachel watched the work, she remembered another renovation project from almost fifty years before. The Dekker Boys' Club. She didn't even know if the building still stood, whether it had been bombed during the war or torn down afterward to make way for new development. Since moving out to The Paddocks, she had no reason to visit London's East End. In Sidney's eyes, she saw the same gleam she had witnessed in Tobias's. Two men with a dream. She prayed that Sidney's had a happier ending.

"Do you want me to supervise the workmen for you, Sidney? I did such work for Tobias Dekker."

Sidney hugged his mother. "You could probably do a bet-

507

ter job than me, Mama, but I can't afford to have the men downing tools because you're demanding too much."

Another time, Rachel visited the Showcase with Andrea and Linda. Seeing Sidney at work, she thought, would help the girls, especially Andrea, to draw closer to their adoptive father. Linda was excited by the visit. While Sidney and Rachel watched, she stood in the center of the stage, curtsied to an imaginary audience, and began reciting a T.S. Eliot poem she had learned at school about a mysterious cat named Macavity. She completed the poem flawlessly. Sidney and Rachel's applause was echoed by the work crew who had stopped to listen.

Andrea, despite being told not to go where men were working, wandered away during her sister's recital. Moments after Linda finished, a man's voice called out from backstage. A piercing shriek was followed by a crash. Sidney leaped onto the stage and ran through the wings. Andrea lay beneath a ladder, screaming for help. The building foreman arrived before Sidney and lifted the wooden ladder from the girl's legs.

"You all right, love?" the foreman asked.

The screaming calmed to a rapid sobbing. Gingerly, Andrea got to her feet. She was white-faced and badly shaken. As Sidney reached out to her, she backed away. Rachel stepped forward and wrapped her arms around the girl. "That isn't what's meant by bringing the house down, darling. There, there, you're all right now. Nothing broken, nothing worth crying over."

Sidney tried to cover his pain at Andrea's rejection by drawing the foreman aside and asking what had happened. "Your daughter started climbing that ladder, Mr. Less. I warned her to get down, but she didn't listen. Youngsters, I guess, they've got more daring than common sense."

"Thanks." As he watched the man right the ladder, Sidney wondered how much time had to pass before Andrea accepted him. He did everything he possibly could to make her regard him as her father, and still she backed away. But then, he supposed, no matter what he did, he could never really be her father.

* * *

The frantic pace of restoration continued. Costs outstripped the budget as more defects became visible. All income from the production company went into the Showcase. Forced to return to the bank for more money, Sidney, after years of comparative affluence, was learning again that every barrel had a bottom.

Financial worries failed to darken his dream. Assured by the builders that all work would be completed by the end of April, he looked beyond that, to opening date. He intended to coincide the reopening of the Showcase with the coronation of Queen Elizabeth II. London would be full of tourists that week; they'd flock to the city from all over the world to catch a glimpse of British pageantry and tradition. It would be the brightest spectacle since before the war, the perfect time to open a theater.

Manny agreed. "If you don't fill every seat of every house that week, you might as well go back to being a furrier."

"Before I fill any seats, I need a good bill. Let's talk."

Manny checked a calendar. Coronation week was the beginning of June, five months away. He'd have no trouble casting the first half of the show, but the really big names—the stars who'd draw crowds by performing the entire second half—were all booked well ahead. He wasn't sure he could pull an Edith Piaf or a Vera Lynn out of the hat at such short notice. "I'll talk to Barry Levy in New York, see if he has anyone who wants to visit London for the coronation. Remember when we went to a coronation?"

"Us? You and me?" Sidney searched his memory. "George the Sixth? We weren't there. We were probably having a knock-down, drag-out fight in some flea-bitten theater in Manchester or Sunderland when that happened."

"Try George the Fifth's coronation. Nineteen eleven. I was almost four, you were two and a half. We sat on the barricades and waved flags. A mounted policeman stopped to talk to us."

Sidney shook his head. "That's too far back for me to remember. I'm not even sure I was born back then."

"Take my word for it, you were."

"Imagine that, if you count Edward the Eighth, this will be our fourth coronation. At least, we'll make a profit from this one, as long as you get me someone outstanding to top the bill."

Manny's son Jonathan turned fifteen three weeks later. His parents made him a party on Saturday afternoon at The Paddocks, inviting a dozen of his schoolfriends and his adopted cousins. Sidney and Naomi drove out for the day with Andrea and Linda.

After Jonathan, helped by his six-year-old sister Bernice, opened his presents in the sitting room, the youngsters went to play elsewhere in the large house. The adults remained in the room, clustered around the fireplace. They could see rain falling through the window; tree branches, bare of leaves, swayed in the wind. Like most January days in England, it was meant to be spent inside.

"Not much doubt whose son Jonathan is," Naomi said. "He's got your hair and skin, Rita—"

"And the poor devil's got my figure," Manny broke in.

Naomi laughed. She had noticed that similarity, too. The boy's solid, chunky body was a duplicate of his father's. "I was going to say he had your big blue eyes."

"Sure you were," Manny said with a grin.

"Who do you think Bernice takes after?" Rita asked.

Naomi glanced at a photograph of the young girl that stood on the mantel. The long dark hair and sensitive appearance came from her mother. "You. Except for the eyes. You've got gray eyes, Rita. Manny has blue. Bernice's are brown."

Rachel supplied the answer. "She has the eyes of the person she was named after. Bernard. The same deep brown eyes my brother Zalman had."

Sidney watched Naomi study the photograph of her niece. A lump lodged in his throat as he realized that no one would ever see a family resemblance in the two girls he and Naomi had adopted. Andrea's dark-brown hair and melancholy brown eyes and her sister's curly red hair would be eternal evidence that no true blood link existed between the children and the people who acted as their parents.

"I keep telling Manny he should help you do up the Show-

510

case," Rita told Sidney. "Maybe then he'd get as slim as you."

Sidney touched his ribs. He'd lost ten pounds in the past two months, running around and worrying about every tiny detail that went into such a major undertaking as refurbishing a West End theater. He saw the change each morning when he shaved. Naomi called him gaunt; she'd even hinted that he see a doctor. He calmed her concern by saying he had never felt better. It was true. Excitement and anticipation lent him energy. He'd be a lot happier, though, if Lesser Brothers came through with a star turn for the Showcase's reopening. So far, in three weeks of trying, Manny had come up with nothing suitable for such a grand occasion. The big names were already booked; the less famous names Sidney didn't want.

"Did you read last Sunday's *News of the World?*" Manny asked his brother.

"We take the *Express.*"

"Did it mention Hollywood's latest scandal?"

"I didn't notice anything."

Manny chuckled. "That's why I buy the *News,* less empire saluting and more good old-fashioned gossip." He pulled the week-old copy from a newspaper rack. "Tony Marino got himself some more bad headlines."

"For what? Breaking a photographer's camera? Hitting a reporter? Starting a fight in a bar?" Sidney's mind reeled at the possibilities. Marino's voice could tempt birds from the trees, all right, but once he got them on the ground he was just as likely to shoot them as feed them. Nor was he a bad actor, but the stories that reached England painted him as totally undisciplined. Half the time he didn't bother with rehearsals, and his late-night parties ruined shooting schedules and plunged budgets deep into the red.

"Nothing so exciting. He's putting together a new television show in the States, and he hired a certain writer for it, a man called Alfred Mintz. Unfortunately, Mr. Mintz was blacklisted four years ago because of alleged Communist sympathies—you know how they are over there. Marino was told he couldn't use him."

"So?"

511

"Telling Tony Marino he can't do something is like sticking a camera into his face and asking him to smile. He blew up. If he couldn't have Mintz, he wouldn't do the show. That was all the *News* carried. On Monday, when Barry Levy telephoned from New York, he told me the rest of the story. The show was canceled, and Marino then went and did some canceling of his own—a movie, some recording dates, and a whole series of concerts through spring and summer. If the American people were going to tell him who he could and could not use as a writer, he'd be damned if he'd even bother to work in America."

"Which means . . . ?" Sidney held his breath. Did he even dare to hope?

Before Manny could answer, the telephone next to him began to ring. He lifted the receiver. The operator was on the line, putting through a call from New York. "Barry Levy wants to speak to you, Sidney, but before he even opens his mouth I can tell you what he's going to say. He wants to know if you'd be interested in having Tony Marino top the Showcase bill for six weeks?"

Within an hour of announcing to the press the following day that Tony Marino would headline the Showcase's grand reopening, Sidney received a telephone call from Gordon Prideaux. "Sidney, I was interested in what you were doing with the Showcase. I was even pulling for you a little bit, wishing you luck."

"Because you didn't think I'd make a go of it, eh?"

"You haven't made a go of it yet. You're still four months from your opening date, and a lot of work has yet to be done."

"It doesn't seem quite so much now that I've got Tony Marino."

"Can you rely on him?"

"You did, when you started bringing Americans over to the Playhouse. And he didn't do badly by you."

"Sidney, the man's unstable. You can see for yourself how he's walked out on half a dozen commitments. How do you know he won't do the same to you?"

"Stop being so concerned for me, Gordon. I know how to

512

handle Marino—I'll remember not to tell him who he can and who he can't use."

"All right, Sidney. Let me phrase it another way. I cannot afford another variety theater so near the Playhouse, so I'm going to do everything in my power to drive the Showcase out of business, Tony Marino or no Tony Marino."

Sidney felt no animosity for Gordon. He had the right and the responsibility to protect his own interests, and Sidney never doubted that his methods would be aboveboard. Gordon would try to destroy the Showcase by putting on better performances, hiring bigger stars, giving the public more entertainment for their money. He would try to win through competition, which was exactly what Sidney intended to do.

Contracts with Marino's signature arrived two weeks later. Sidney held them in his hands and shouted for joy. Those first six weeks would be a sell-out. Confidence booming, he returned his attention to the renovation. Maybe it was his imagination, but the work seemed to be going faster. He noticed changes even as he watched. Before he had seen only destruction—seats removed, carpet ripped up, heavy flock paper stripped off walls. Now he witnessed construction. Deep red carpet went down, ornate chandeliers were hung, newly upholstered seats were set in place.

The Showcase was ready at the middle of April, six weeks before its official reopening. When the last builder left, Sidney walked to the center of the stage and looked out. It was magnificent, a theater fit for the greatest entertainers in the world. "Gordon Prideaux!" Sidney pitched his voice so that it reached every corner of the auditorium; the acoustics were wonderful. "I challenge you to do your damnedest. We can take whatever you and the Rialto Playhouse Partnership can dish out."

Queen Elizabeth II's coronation was set for the first Tuesday in June. Five days before that, the Showcase was scheduled to open, with a bill topped by forty minutes of Tony Marino.

Marino sent Sidney details of his requirements. He wanted a full band on the stage behind him. Sidney would see to the hiring of the band, and Marino would supply the arrangements he used for his shows and recordings in the States. He could arrive in England a week before the first performance, giving ample time for vocalist and band to get to know each other.

Two days before Marino was due, Sidney received a wire from Palm Springs. "Wish me luck, pal. I'm getting married. I'll be a couple of days late. Tony."

Sidney stared at the wire. Marino's words danced in front of his eyes; Gordon Prideaux's warning echoed in his ears. He had spent a fortune buying and refurbishing the Showcase, and now the entire investment rested on the whimsical fancies of Tony Marino.

Sidney had Manny telephone Lesser Brothers Inc. in New York. The instant Barry Levy came on the line, Sidney grabbed the receiver. "What the hell is going on, Barry? I got this telegram from Marino. How late is he going to be?"

"If he said he'll be a couple of days, he'll be a couple of days. He married Gayle Carson last night. The papers over here are full of it. Must have happened too late for the English morning papers to pick it up."

Sidney knew Marino's bride. He'd seen her in movies, a tall, dark-haired actress with a soft southern accent that guaranteed her a role in any Civil War movie ever made. "Get hold of him, Barry. Remind him he has a contract with me."

"He's already walked out on a lot of contracts this year, Sidney. Just leave him alone. He'll turn up."

"He's got to rehearse with the band."

"Let them rehearse. You gave them the arrangements, right? As long as they know what they're supposed to be playing, that's all that matters."

Levy's assurances did little to cheer Sidney. Especially when another wire arrived the next day, this time from Las Vegas, to beg two more days. Weighted down with gloom, Sidney watched rehearsals. The band he had hired to back Marino played the American arrangements faultlessly. Oh well, he supposed he could always have the band top the bill. Maybe everyone wouldn't want their money back. Maybe he'd be able to salvage some of it to put toward the vast debt he'd incurred.

Sure, and maybe pigs would sprout wings and fly.

*   *   *

Tony Marino sent one more wire, promising to arrive two days before opening night. Sidney met his Stratocruiser at London Airport. The airport was busier than usual as London began to fill with visitors for the coronation in seven days time. Every day, newspapers and the country's single television station carried pictures of the famous, the powerful, and the strangely dressed—kings, queens, premiers, and sultans. Adding to the color were Malayan soldiers in white uniforms and green sarongs who shared security duties with red-coated Canadian Mounties.

Sidney waited for half an hour as passengers emerged from customs. He saw no sign of Marino. In desperation, he grabbed the arm of a passing customs officer, explained who he was, and asked if anyone had not yet come through. The customs officer smiled grimly and motioned for Sidney to follow him. They walked through the customs area toward a room from which came the sound of raised voices.

"I'm not putting up with this bullshit! I'm getting on the next damned plane out of here and I'm going home!"

"No!" Sidney heard himself shout the single word as he broke into a run. Bursting into the room, he saw four people. Two customs officers stood on one side of a table. On the other side stood Gayle Carson and a red-faced, furious Tony Marino. Between them were four open suitcases and a cardboard carton. Three more cases and two trunks rested on the floor.

"About time you got here," Marino told Sidney. "These jerks are trying to charge me duty on my own personal belongings."

"Don't worry, Tony, I'll take care of it." Sidney smiled at Gayle Carson. "Congratulations on your marriage, Miss Carson," he said, then turned his attention to the customs officers. "I'm Sidney Less, owner of the Showcase Theater, where Mr. Marino's due to appear. What seems to be the problem?"

One of the officers tipped the cardboard box for Sidney to see inside. It contained twelve bottles of Grant's Standfast. "And there's this," said the other officer, opening a small

515

case. Inside, Sidney saw a dozen cartons of cigarettes. "Mr. Marino seems to think that our laws don't apply to him."

"I'm not importing the stuff to sell it!" Marino yelled. "Gayle and I are going to be in this godforsaken place for more than six weeks. We smoke. We drink. How are we supposed to know if your shops stock what we like? I don't mind paying excess baggage—I expect to do that, the way I travel—but I'll be damned if I'm going to pay duty on my own booze and smokes!"

Sidney cut through the argument with a single question. "How much is the duty on the whiskey and the cigarettes?"

"Thirty-two pounds, eight shillings."

"I don't want you paying it!" Marino said.

"Call it a gesture of Anglo-American cooperation," Sidney answered. Then, to the customs officer: "Will you take a check?"

"Yes, sir."

"Thank you." Sidney wrote out the check and passed it over. "I've booked you a suite at the Dorchester, Tony. I'll get a taxi to follow us with all your baggage."

In the car, Marino's anger subsided. He started to tease Sidney. "I bet you were having kittens over my being late."

"You'd win."

"How did the band do with my arrangements?"

"They sounded fine."

"I'll just drop right in with them."

"There's a rehearsal tomorrow."

"No problem. Now tell me the truth, Sidney, if you'd married Miss Gayle Carson here, wouldn't you have tried to steal a couple of days as well?"

Sidney glanced at Gayle in the backseat. He wouldn't steal a couple of days—he'd steal a year. Movies had not done her justice. Sensuality colored her broad-boned face; a tight dress struggled to contain a ripe figure. Sidney understood what Marino saw in her, but he failed to see what she found attractive in him. Gayle Carson looked the kind of woman who hung on the arms of men who lifted weights five hours a day. She did not belong with a skinny little guy like Tony Marino.

Popular newspapers the next day carried stories of

516

Marino's problems with customs. Sidney was not surprised; every time an entertainer of such stature sneezed, it was news. In the afternoon, Sidney watched the rehearsal. He expected the worst. No man who led such an undisciplined life could hope to get up on a stage and perform professionally. They would have to work all day. Tomorrow as well, before the curtain rose.

Instead, Marino sang just one song—Cole Porter's "I Get a Kick Out Of You." When it was through, he stood gazing into the air as if following the flight of the final note. Then he looked down to where Gayle sat, next to Sidney.

"Well, lover, what do you think? Do I need to rehearse some more, or did I sound okay?"

"Wonderful, baby." She turned to Sidney who remained sitting quietly. "He did, didn't he? He did sound wonderful."

Sidney shook himself out of the trance Marino's singing had created. He couldn't believe it. The man was magic, absolute magic. Marino could have turned up at London Airport an hour before the curtain rose on the first show and Sidney would have forgiven him. "You sound better than I've ever heard you."

Marino snapped his fingers. "I'll give your Showcase an opening night to remember, Sidney."

On the morning of the opening, Sidney gave complimentary tickets to a dozen people he owed favors. Lastly, he sent two by messenger to the London Playhouse. Gordon Prideaux telephoned the moment he received them. "Thank you, Sidney. Do I read confidence into this gesture?"

"Supreme confidence." Sidney looked at the newest poster on the office wall, the same poster that was plastered across the city. Sidney Less Presents Tony Marino at the London Showcase. Soon Sidney Less would be presenting Bing Crosby, Frank Sinatra, Lena Horne, Edith Piaf, Louis Armstrong. He'd be presenting every star worth seeing. Tonight, Gordon Prideaux would understand that.

"My wife and I will try to be there."

Sidney continued to stare at the poster. His name was a size smaller than Marino's, and now he wondered whether he had made a mistake. The two names should be the same size. They were equal partners after all. Without Marino, Sidney

517

would have no show. And without Sidney, Marino, after burning all his bridges back home, would be collecting unemployment.

The office door opened. Manny walked in, visiting from his downstairs office. "Let me have two more comps for tonight."

"I just gave away my last two. To Gordon Prideaux. Who do you need more for?"

"Jimmy Isaacson just telephoned. He's in London with Sonya and the children for the coronation. They're staying at the Dorchester, same as Marino. When he got in touch, I offered to get him two tickets for tonight. His wife's a big Marino fan."

"No problem. He and Sonya can sit in my box."

"How many people have you got there already?"

"Me, you, Naomi, Rita, Mama, Gordon and his wife, and now the Isaacsons. So it'll be a tight squeeze."

"That's the understatement of the year," Manny responded as he turned to leave. He knew his brother would find space for as many people as he could. He wanted everyone to be a part of this special night.

Sidney leaned back in the chair, hands clasped behind his head. Jimmy Isaacson couldn't have come to London at a better time. The Lesser family would repay all the good turns, starting with clearing that hospital bill and then helping the agency get established in America. Simultaneously, they'd show him that they were just as influential in England as he was in New York.

Tony Marino was electrifying. Wearing a midnight-blue tuxedo, he picked his way through familiar ballads, coaxing tears with heartwringers like "I'll Never Smile Again" and "September Song," setting toes tapping with "A Foggy Day" and "All Of Me," and getting people swaying in their seats as he belted out "Sunny Side Of The Street" and "How About You?"

Each time thunderous applause greeted the end of a song, Sidney turned to the people who crowded his box. "Well?"

Sonya was the most enthusiastic. "I've seen him in New York several times, and he was never this good."

"He's trying to prove a point," Jimmy told her. "He's showing America what it's missing. If he does six weeks here like this, he'll be able to hire Joe Stalin and Karl Marx as scriptwriters when he goes home and no one will dare oppose him."

As if hearing Jimmy's remarks, Marino stopped singing and began to talk. He spoke of his troubles in America over the blacklisted scriptwriter, then he asked for any Americans in the audience to make themselves heard. A roar went up. Marino grinned. "They heard that noise back in Washington. That's where they want to hear it, with their idiotic ideas about who can and who can't write for television. I've done pretty good by singing Irving Berlin songs, but according to the criteria of those stupid SOB's who want to blacklist everyone, Irving should probably be banned as well because he was born in Russia."

The audience laughed. Marino snapped his fingers and the laughter died. He looked over his shoulder. The band played the opening bars of "Sweet Lorraine." The political harangue was over; the concert was continuing.

"He'd do us all a favor if he stuck to singing," Jimmy said.

Sidney turned around. Marino's request for support had been answered by Sonya, who had leaned over the edge of the box to call out something, but Jimmy had remained silent, arms folded stoically across his chest. "You don't approve, eh?"

"I have a love-hate relationship with Tony Marino. I approve of him as a singer. There is no finer interpreter of Berlin, Gershwin, Cole Porter, *et al.* But as a human being, Tony Marino leaves much to be desired. He doesn't have an ethic to his name. He's not putting on a tremendous show because he wants to give you value for money. He wants to give America the finger. He's already said as much. He'll probably do half a dozen encores instead of his usual two for that very reason. Just to show America what it's missing."

Jimmy was right. After the twelfth song, Marino drew breath. "This is where I usually take a couple of requests, but I feel good enough tonight to keep on singing until dawn. Of course, if any of you have to leave to catch the last bus or the last subway train, I'll understand. But it'll be your loss, not mine." Marino looked up at Sidney's box. "You won't mind paying overtime to the band and theater staff, will you, Mr. Less?"

Sidney, blinded by the spotlight that suddenly swung in his direction, waved a hand in acknowledgment.

"Seeing as how generous you are, Mr. Less, I'll ask you for the first request."

Sidney turned to his guests. They all sat perfectly still. He looked at Gordon Prideaux and his blond wife, Elena. "Do you have anything you want him to sing?"

"How about it, Mr. Less?" Marino called out. "Or has the prospect of paying overtime shocked you into silence?"

Sonya saved the day. She leaned over the edge of the box and shouted: " 'Begin The Beguine,' Tony! Sing 'Begin The Beguine!' "

Marino snapped his fingers. "You heard the lady," he told the bandleader. "Let's start playing 'Begin The Beguine.' "

In all, Marino sang thirteen numbers on top of the original program, interspersing them with a rambling monologue covering everything from Italian food to baseball. Instead of ten-thirty, the show finished at midnight to a five-minute foot-stomping, hand-clapping barrage of applause. Sidney swore he could feel the building shake. Marino's extended performance had wrecked plans for the opening-night party, but Sidney could forgive him.

When the audience started to file out, Gordon Prideaux took Sidney's arm. "Thank you for a most exciting evening."

"Are you still going to drive me out of business?"

"I told you I can't afford to have a variety theater so close to the Playhouse. Especially now, when I can see exactly how good you are. You put on one hell of an opening night, Sidney, and I'm convinced that you'll go on to even better things. Which makes my job even harder, but I'll do it."

Sidney and Naomi invited Jimmy and Sonya back to Marble Arch for a drink. The American couple deferred, saying they had to return to the Dorchester. "Why don't you all come out to The Paddocks next Sunday for the day?" Manny asked. "The English countryside will make a nice change after the rush of London."

"Thank you. We'd like that."

After making arrangements to collect them from the Dorchester on Sunday morning, Manny took his mother and Rita home. Sidney walked around the empty theater, thoroughly pleased with how opening night had gone. His only complaint was that he had been cooped up for too long. He needed fresh air.

"Would you like to walk home?" he asked Naomi.

"I'd rather take a taxi. My heels weren't made for hiking."

They compromised. Sidney walked while Naomi sat in a taxi that crawled along the curb, keeping pace. Through the open window they talked about the evening. Sidney mentioned what Gordon had said. Naomi laughed. "He paid you a compliment by saying you've made his job harder. Do you think Marino will do a show like this every night?"

"No man has that much energy. Tonight was special—our opening, his opening. I'll be more than happy if he sings just a dozen songs in the future, with one or two encores."

The taxi stopped at a traffic light. Sidney opened the door and climbed in. "Have you changed your mind?" Naomi asked.

"I just remembered that I have to get up early in the morning to read the reviews. I'd better get home and get some sleep."

Reviews of Tony Marino were better than anything Sidney had hoped for. The *Mirror* described it as: "America's loss and Britain's gain." The *Express* claimed that Marino had gotten coronation week off to a flying start, while the *Observer*'s critic welcomed the Showcase to the ranks of London's top theaters and described the opening show as the "finest piece of popular musical entertainment in many years." Sidney had his secretary paste the clippings into the office scrapbook. When he grew tired of looking at posters on the walls, he could always read reviews.

Marino's shows on the next two nights were equally exciting. He cut down the extra songs to two, but no one felt cheated. He put more energy and talent into fourteen numbers than many singers mustered in their entire life. After the Saturday performance, Sidney asked if Marino and Gayle Carson wished to spend Sunday at Manny's country home.

521

Marino said no. They were taking a tour of London to see the coronation finery. Sidney didn't repeat the offer. It had been based on courtesy alone; he hadn't really wanted to shove Marino and Jimmy Isaacson together.

On Sunday, Manny drove into town to collect Sonya and Jimmy, their two children, and the maid they had brought with them from the States. By the time he returned to The Paddocks, Sidney, Naomi, and the two girls had arrived. The New Yorkers proved a novelty for the English children. Jimmy endeared himself by passing out American coins. When Bernice pointed to Washington and asked what king that was, Jimmy answered, "He's the man who got rid of the king for us. We don't believe in royalty."

"That's why we come over here to watch your coronation," Sonya added. "We have none of our own."

After lunch, rivalry erupted among the children. Jonathan boasted about his father finding work for the world's most famous entertainers. "On top of that, my uncle Sidney owns theaters. He's got Tony Marino working for him in the Showcase, and he's putting on an American show called *Desire* at the Admiralty Theater in September. Americans would rather work for my uncle and earn pounds than stay in their own country and work for dollars. That's because they aren't worth so much. It takes three dollars to make one pound, you know."

Josephine was not short of American bragging material. "My father owns newspapers, magazines, and a television station. You've only got one television station in this entire country, haven't you? We've got dozens and dozens."

Even Andrea joined in, her competitive spirit overcoming, for once, the wall between herself and Sidney. "Who wants to watch television when you can see real people on a stage? What your father does and what my father does are like chalk and cheese."

Naomi, overhearing that remark, walked away to share it. Sidney listened, amazed that Andrea would have found something in his life to boast about, let alone refer to him as her father. He wondered if a breakthrough had occurred. Or could it be something else? He didn't try to push forward, just in case his fear was true—that she had referred to him as her father simply because it was too awkward to call him Uncle Sidney.

For the remainder of the day, it fell to Sonya to carry most of the conversation for the American guests. Jimmy grew silent, listening to everything that was said, but offering little. Sonya talked about her new job as editor of *American Miss* and how she was in England to write something on the coronation. Only when she mentioned Messenger Publications' latest magazine, *TV Diary*, did Jimmy become animated.

"Let's all take a break from that damned thing," he told Sonya. "We're three thousand miles away from it, let it rest."

Manny glanced at Jimmy, guessing that the American was acting in opposition to his own advice. His silence hinted at a hidden unhappiness, and Manny thought he understood what it was. Jimmy had carried worries over this new television magazine with him to England, and they were eating him away.

Sonya swiftly changed the subject. "I heard one of the children talking about Sidney putting on *Desire* in London. Is that the *Desire* from Broadway?"

Sidney nodded. "I saw it last year, decided I liked it, and bought British rights. I'm also producing another American show in London in the autumn of 1954. *Painting The Town.* It's a musical comedy."

"Jimmy and I saw it the week it opened. It's wonderful."

The Isaacsons stayed at The Paddocks until just after six. Manny drove them back into town. Outside the Dorchester, he shook hands with Jimmy and kissed Sonya on the cheek. "Enjoy the coronation parade. Telephone us before you leave."

"We will," Sonya promised. "Thanks for everything."

Sonya kept the promise. She called on Wednesday morning, as the Isaacsons prepared to leave for the airport. Excitement filled her voice as she told Manny about the wonderful position they'd had on the coronation route. "I think there were more Americans than anyone else. We even saw American sailors waving placards that read 'Liz Is A Whiz.' "

"I saw them, too, on television. Disrespectful, but we'll overlook it this time. On the whole, Americans behave well."

"Unfortunately, one American hasn't been so well behaved. There was some trouble here around midnight when Tony Marino and Gayle Carson decided to throw their own coronation party. They had a full-scale lovers' tiff, shouting and screaming until other guests complained. When someone from the hotel went up to their suite, Gayle threw a bottle at him. Somehow it's all been hushed up, but I thought you'd better know."

"Thank you. I'll tell Sidney. That should make him very happy. Have a good flight home."

Sidney was anything but happy when Manny passed on the information. He sent his secretary out to buy copies of all the newspapers. He and Manny scanned the pages, grateful when they found no mention of the incident. Tony Marino, the delight of reporters, had gotten lucky for once.

When Marino and Gayle arrived at the Showcase that evening, Sidney was waiting. "I hear there was some trouble last night." Seeing Marino's face tighten, he added quickly. "Nothing got into the papers, don't worry."

"What business is it of anyone's if my wife and I have an argument?"

"None. I just want to be sure everything's all right."

"It's fine." Marino looked at Gayle. "Tell him everything's fine, honey, before he gets worry lines all over his face."

"It's fine."

Sidney could see it was not. Tension sparked between Marino and his wife. After only two weeks, the marriage was trembling. The stress carried over into Marino's performance that night. He sang like an automaton, with none of the feeling he had put into earlier performances. Applause was more polite than deafening, and when, after his standard dozen songs, he asked for requests, there was a noticeable pause before one came. Marino took that as a signal. He didn't ask for another. He walked off the stage the moment he finished the first encore and left the theater.

Sidney caught up with him at the Dorchester. "I can't sing in front of a hostile crowd," Marino explained. "That's why I canceled everything in the States—people were hostile. I can't perform when I feel hostility."

"The audience wasn't hostile. They were just disappointed

524

because you didn't seem as brilliant tonight"—Sidney chose his words with care in case he, God forbid, appeared unfriendly to his star—"as you were the first few nights. You've got to face it, Tony, you're a hard act to live up to. You're so great so much of the time that on those rare occasions when you slip, people are shocked."

Marino appeared mollified by Sidney's words "Maybe you're right. To tell you the truth, I've got a problem."

"Oh? What's that?" As if I don't know, Sidney thought.

"Gayle. She flirts with other guys. She knows it drives me nuts, that's why she does it. Says she likes to see how deeply I feel for her—figures the madder I get at her, the more I love her. That was the trouble the other night, she was giving the eye to a waiter in a restaurant."

Sidney's manner became businesslike. "Tony, when I hired you for six weeks, I hired your voice, your stage presence, your singing style, and your popularity. Nowhere in the contract does it say I hired your personal life and any troubles it contains. Please remember that, and keep your personal life off the stage. It doesn't belong there."

The reprimand had the desired effect on Marino's performance. The verve returned to his singing. He strutted around the stage like he owned it. When he asked for requests, the audience roared out the names of songs. Sidney congratulated himself. He'd taken the action a theater owner had to take. He'd put his foot down and set a temperamental star firmly in his place.

The ideal situation lasted for one week. Sidney had no forewarning of trouble. Marino performed faultlessly. He and Gayle arrived at the Showcase and left it each night holding hands. Then, at three o'clock on a Thursday morning, Sidney's bedside telephone rang. He drew the receiver beneath the covers.

"Yes?"

"You've got to get over here right now!" a woman screamed. "He's locked himself in the bedroom and he's threatening to blow his brains out! He's got a gun! He'll do it!"

"What's going on?" Naomi asked as Sidney jumped out of bed.

"Tony's threatening to commit suicide. Gayle says he's got a gun, God alone knows from where."

"Let him do it."

"That statement shows a distinct lack of compassion."

"Marino doesn't deserve compassion."

"But *I* do. If he doesn't complete six weeks, the Showcase's first production might be its last."

The Dorchester was less than half a mile from Sidney's Marble Arch flat. He ran all the way. "Mr. Marino's expecting me," he called out to the desk clerk as he raced past. He rapped once on the door of Marino's suite. Gayle pulled it open immediately. She was wearing nothing more than a flimsy black nightgown.

"Has he done anything?"

"Not yet."

Sidney breathed a silent sigh of relief. "Where is he?"

She pointed to the bedroom door. Sidney walked toward it. "Tony, can you hear me?"

"What do you want?"

"I want to stop you killing yourself."

"She rang you, eh? How did she know to get hold of you? Has she got a thing going with you as well?"

"She doesn't want you to hurt yourself." He looked back at Gayle. "Where did he get a gun?"

"He brought it with him from the States."

"Jesus Christ! What did he think customs officers would do if they found a gun in his baggage?"

"They were too busy with the cigarettes and the whiskey to worry about looking for a gun."

"What started him off this time?"

"Some guy downstairs asked for my autograph, said he'd seen me in a couple of movies. Tony went crazy."

Sidney turned back to the door. "Tony, you hurt yourself and you're going to hurt thousands of your English fans."

"Screw my English fans. This country's for the birds. Take away your royalty and your fish and chips, and the damned place would sink into the ocean."

"Do something!" Gayle screamed. "He's going to kill himself, Mr. Less. I know he is."

The terror in the woman's voice panicked Sidney. He rattled the door knob. "Open this bloody door and come out, Tony. We've all had enough of your nonsense."

A sharp explosion eclipsed the last words. Sidney jumped back from the door, stunned. "He's killed himself!" Gayle shrieked. "He's really gone and killed himself!"

"Call downstairs," Sidney told her. With Marino dead, there was no longer any point in worrying about publicity hurting his concerts. "Tell them to get an ambulance and the police."

The bedroom door opened. Tony Marino stepped out. His hands were empty and the biggest lunatic grin Sidney had ever seen covered his face. "Had you scared that time, didn't I?"

"Oh, baby, you had me so worried," Gayle cried as she threw herself into his arms.

Sidney walked into the bedroom. The bed had been stripped of all covers. In the center of the heavy mattress lay a revolver. One side of the mattress was scorched and torn where Marino had fired at point-blank range. Sidney inspected the mattress. He could find no exit hole. The bullet was still inside. Pocketing the gun, he walked out of the bedroom, past Marino and Gayle who were still embracing, and left the suite. Downstairs, he spoke to the desk clerk.

"There's been some trouble in Mr. Marino's suite. You can make fifty pounds for yourself if you get the mattress replaced in the next fifteen minutes and dream up a plausible explanation for any guests who might have been disturbed."

Sidney walked along Park Lane to Marble Arch, pausing only to drop the revolver down a drain. He could barely believe what had happened. Producing major shows should reward him with prestige and respect. Instead he was dropping guns down drains in the middle of the night. This was not how it was supposed to be. A thousand Tony Marino sellouts were not worth such aggravation.

Next morning, Manny found Sidney waiting for him. "I've got a complaint about a client of yours."

"Marino?"

"Who else?" Sidney related what had happened. Manny's heavy face paled at the mention of the gun. "I dropped someone fifty pounds to switch the mattress and keep a lid on the whole thing because I didn't want publicity. I was frightened what it might do to Marino, and through him to me. But when I tossed that gun down the drain, I started thinking. I'm in business to produce shows, entertain people, make some money. I'm not in business to nursemaid madmen. You're Marino's agent, so I'm telling you he's through. Last night was it. We'll pay off the supporting turns, of course. I've already instructed my people to put canceled stickers over the bills. We're booking ads in newspapers. Any moment now the phones will start ringing off the hook with reporters wanting stories. We'll issue refunds—"

"Do you have the money?"

"Touch and go."

"If you need any, I'll help."

"You don't have to feel liable because he's your client."

"Don't be a fool. I want to help because you're my brother, not because of Marino. Does he know yet?"

"He will the moment reporters start calling him. I think you, his agent, should tell him first."

Manny made the call. The telephone rang for almost a minute before being answered. "I left a wake-up call for noon. It's nine-thirty, for Christ's sake!"

"This isn't the desk. It's Manny Lesser."

"Don't you ever sleep?"

"I sleep when I'm supposed to. I don't stay up all night threatening suicide and then shooting holes in mattresses. If it wasn't for my brother keeping the peace, you'd have slept in jail last night."

"He's got a big mouth . . . And, hey, where is that gun?"

"In the sewer, where my brother threw it."

"He threw my gun in the sewer? He had no right. I've got a permit for it."

"Only in the States. Not here."

"Only in the States, not here," Marino mimicked. "You can't do a damned thing here. You need a license to breathe."

"You won't have to worry about it anymore. The show's been canceled as of now. You can catch a plane home when-

528

ever you feel like it. I'll settle up your British tax details and send you the money for the shows you did."

"You can't do this. I'll sue you sons of bitches. I'll get my fans to sue you."

Manny hung up. "He'll get his fans to sue us."

Sidney spread his hands. "So sue us."

Tony Marino flew out of London the next day. Before boarding the plane, he held a press conference engineered to reopen doors he'd slammed behind himself only a few weeks before.

"The grass always looks greener on the other side of the fence," he told reporters. "That's how the British grass looked to Gayle and me." He slipped his arm around his wife's waist and hugged her. "We were mistaken. There's no place like the good old USA. There might be a couple of things wrong with it, but it's paradise when compared with a burg like this."

"Did you at least enjoy the coronation?" one reporter asked.

"Coronation?" Marino laughed. "I've seen better Columbus Day parades down Fifth Avenue!"

British newspapers took Marino to task for his comments. Some record shops even organized ceremonial smashings of Tony Marino discs. Sidney found little to cheer him in the outbreak of hostility toward the American. The Showcase remained dark for the next four weeks, and when the lights came on again, they shone only on a mediocre show originally booked to finish out the summer season. Marino had been Sidney's big gamble, and the gamble had failed abysmally.

Sidney's luck continued on a downward slide. The shows he'd booked for autumn at the Showcase did not draw the houses he had expected. Fortunately, the British production of *Desire* at the Admiralty played to full houses every night. That, and profits from a couple of smaller shows, furnished him with funds to keep the Showcase running. Taking from Peter to pay Paul, though, could not last forever. Sidney knew he had to start booking top international stars for the

Showcase. This year was already ruined; he had to concentrate on 1954, 1955, and beyond.

He did, and ran straight into Gordon Prideaux's promise to drive the Showcase out of business. Prideaux's method of suppressing opposition was simple yet effective. Backed by the financial strength of the Rialto Playhouse Partnership, he offered the highest salaries. The Playhouse booked top-rate stars, while the Showcase had to be satisfied with second best.

Sidney went to see his brother. "Gordon's skimming the cream of the talent from every agency. I'm being left with water. Can't you, at least, give me some kind of a break?"

"Make believe you're with Lesser Brothers again and pretend someone asked you that question."

Sidney's answer was immediate and honest. "I'd tell them to go jump in the lake. I'd tell them my responsibility was to my clients, not to theater owners. Whoever offered my clients the best conditions got their services."

"Precisely."

The crunch came for Sidney in the early summer of 1954. The Showcase continued to run at a loss, with little improvement apparent for the future. His major successful show, *Desire,* began to lose momentum. Soon, he had to begin rehearsals for the musical comedy *Painting the Town,* and he did not have enough money to cover all expenses. He resembled a juggler struggling to keep one ball too many aloft. Which would be the first to crash? And once one fell, would the others follow?

Early one Monday morning, as he made the customary walk from home to office, he heard another set of footsteps matching his own. Looking to his left, he stopped walking in shock.

"Mind if I join you?" Gordon Prideaux asked. "You always seem so fit from all this walking, I thought I'd give it a try. Perhaps while we walk, we can even talk a little."

Sidney resumed normal pace. "As long as you don't gloat."

"Do you think I would?"

"You'd have every right to. You said you'd drive the Showcase out of business and you've just about done it. Another couple of weeks like I'm having now, and I'll have to decide which theater to give up. Or which theaters . . ."

"That bad, eh?"

Sidney realized that Gordon did not know just how much of a fix he was in. "I've got far more money going out than coming in. It's been that way for a while, and it's going to continue that way for the foreseeable future."

"So, you've discovered Mr. Pickwick's definition of misery. What are your plans?"

Sidney shrugged. "I've been broke before and I'll be broke again. But you can bet your last sixpence that I'll never book Tony Marino again."

"If you remember, I did question your wisdom in using him."

"I thought you were trying to deter me from following a course that would help the Showcase succeed."

Gordon laughed. "I was."

Sidney smiled as well. "I appreciate the honesty. The real aggravation is *Painting the Town*. We're supposed to open in the autumn, and the way things are going, I don't think I'll be able to afford to raise the curtain. Shame, it would have been my biggest show ever."

"Why don't you put it on at a Partnership theater instead?"

"Pardon?"

"Make it a Sidney Less Production at a Partnership theater. You can't have the Playhouse; that's booked, of course. But we can make room for you in another West End theater."

Sidney turned to face Gordon. There was no smile on the scarred face, no hint of mischief in the gray eyes. "How could Sidney Less produce at a Partnership theater?"

"Quite easily—if he were joint managing director of the Partnership with me. I made such a suggestion to my board some time ago, Sidney. I told them that if you ever fell on difficult times—and, to be honest, I believed you would—we should offer you a position on our board immediately. You're too valuable to leave floating around where you might come back to haunt us again. My board agreed with me."

"Joint managing director with you? How would that work?"

"Unlike my father, my feeling is for the business side of theater. I want to concentrate on that. Your responsibility would be your strength. You would focus on consolidating and expanding Partnership entertainment, seeking new opportunities, and strengthening the current roster of stars."

"My first contribution could be *Painting the Town*."

"We were hoping it would be," Gordon said, offering his hand. Sidney grabbed it and shook it heartily to seal the bargain.

Sidney moved from Haymarket to Leicester Square, occupying the adjacent office to Gordon Prideaux, just as Leslie Martin had once inhabited the next office to Gordon's father.

On his first day as joint managing director, one thought filled his mind: how sweet and fitting it was for him to be on the board of the company from which he had been banished nineteen years before. When Gordon entered the office and found Sidney with a broad smile covering his face, he asked to be let in on the joke. "I was just remembering what I told your father on the night he threw us out."

"Is it repeatable?"

"Of course. I told him we'd rather sell tickets for Stoll or Moss Empires than head the bill on the Partnership circuit. A lot changes in nineteen years, doesn't it, Gordon?"

"Only if you allow it to change. Just make sure you sell plenty of tickets for the Partnership."

"I will, Gordon. I will."

Sidney relished his new responsibilities. The Partnership offered greater scope for his talents. Aside from theaters around the country featuring everything from variety to pantomime and serious drama, it operated a nationwide chain of movie houses. New vistas opened to Sidney. Live entertainment, though, remained his initial love. His first task was to assign his rights in *Painting the Town* to the Partnership. His second task was to find a theater he considered suitable for its production. The solution was simple. He brought the Showcase into the Partnership fold.

Summer passed in a flurry of activity. If Sidney thought he'd been busy before—on the boards, as an agent, or as a producer—he soon learned he didn't know the meaning of the word. He traveled all over the country to work with Partnership theaters in the planning of future bills. Some theater managers he already knew; they'd been with the Partnership when Sidney had been part of Less, Lesser, and Least. Sidney had no doubt these managers remembered the uproar of the act being banned, but no one ever mentioned it.

In London, Sidney spent much of his time overseeing *Painting the Town* preparations. Rehearsals satisfied him; he always left the theater whistling one of the show's half-dozen catchy tunes. When the show opened at the beginning of October, he was sure it would be an instant success.

For the first time since the war, Sidney had no time for a summer vacation. That didn't stop him sending the rest of the family. In the middle of August, he put Naomi, Andrea, Linda, and the family's new housekeeper, a Spanish woman named Maria, on the train to the Kent seaside town of Cliftonville, where Manny had taken his family for two weeks. He joined them on Sunday, traveling to the coast early in the morning and returning to London at night. Naomi understood, but the two girls did not.

"They think you care more about your work than you care about them," Naomi said on the second Sunday he spent at the seaside. They were sitting in deck chairs on the beach, watching Manny, Rita, and the four children play at the water's edge. Rachel, preferring to be out of the sun, sat in a shelter on the promenade behind them.

"Andrea said that?"

"No. Linda did. She wanted to know why Manny and Rita were here all week while you weren't."

"Doesn't she know how busy I am?" Sidney watched Andrea and Jonathan dash into the water and swim toward a fixed diving platform some thirty yards out, racing each other with a swift overhand crawl. The boy was sixteen, two years older than his cousin, yet she was almost matching him stroke for stroke. Only when they turned and headed back toward the beach did Jonathan pull away. Now who had taught Andrea to swim like that? Not him, that was for sure. For an instant, he felt guilty about neglecting the girls.

"She knows, but she doesn't understand."

It seemed odd to Sidney that the complaint would come from Linda. He wondered if Andrea had put her up to it. After six years, he still couldn't fathom the older girl.

"Linda pointed out that Manny has his own business, yet he finds time to take two weeks off with his children. You work for someone else now, and you can't spend even a week here."

"I *work* for someone else? I've never worked so hard in my entire life."

"But you like it, don't you?"

"No." He smiled at Naomi's surprise. "I love it." He got up from the deck chair and walked to the water's edge, determined to compensate for any neglect. He wore only swimming trunks. The sun warmed his bare shoulders. "Who wants a race?"

"I'll race you, Uncle Sidney!" Jonathan called out.

"How about you, Andrea? You looked pretty good just then."

She shook her head. "That last race wore me out."

Sidney bit back disappointment. Andrea's excuse might sound plausible to others, but to Sidney it rang hollow. He dwelled on it for the rest of the day and during the journey back to London. In the morning, fully occupied once more with Partnership business, he gratefully allowed it to slip from his mind.

Painting the Town was set to open at the Showcase in the middle of October. Three weeks before that was the London Playhouse's annual presentation of the Performing Artists' Gala, the only production with which Gordon Prideaux remained involved. He had inherited responsibility for the gala from his father, and he guarded it zealously.

It was also the only aspect of Gordon's life that Sidney coveted. He clearly remembered 1950, when Lesser Brothers had brought Tony Marino and Buddy Beck over for the gala. Manny had accused him of envying Gordon's duty of introducing the stars to the King and Queen. Sidney had not denied it; nor had four years lessened his envy. After the show, the same old jealousy welled up as he watched Gordon introduce the cast of international stars to that night's guest of honor, the Queen Mother.

"Is my face turning green?" he whispered to Naomi.

"A lovely shade of emerald, darling. But don't worry, in three weeks time when *Painting the Town* opens, Gordon's face will be just as green."

Sidney smiled, then shook his head. "Gordon's jealous of no one. He's like his old man, too secure and too confident in himself to ever envy any other man."

"Are you saying you're not confident?"

"Sometimes I worry that this"—he made a sweeping gesture with his right hand to encompass all the men and women in evening dress—"is just a dream. I'm the son of a penniless refugee. How can I possibly mingle with royalty?"

Naomi squeezed his hand, finding the trace of insecurity touching. "You probably mean more to British royalty than some man whose family tree resembles *Debrett's Peerage*. You're proof, Sidney, that Britain is a country where people can make something of themselves. Even the children of penniless refugees."

Sidney remembered Naomi's words three weeks later when the curtain rose on *Painting the Town*. The show songs, played constantly over the radio, were already hits. Sidney swore he could hear the audience tapping its feet in time with the music. Of all the shows he'd put on so far, this was by far the biggest. In New York, it was still running after more than a year. He hoped it would do as well in London.

Following the performance, Sidney and Naomi had planned a first-night party at Isow's, the show-business restaurant in Soho's Brewer Street. They were about to leave the Showcase when the telephone began to ring.

Manny, lifting the receiver from the rest, called out, "Shall I tell them there are no tickets left for opening night?"

"Are you crazy?" Sidney called back. "Tell them they can have as many as they want!"

Manny put the receiver to his ear. The grin faded from his face. "Sidney, it's your housekeeper."

Fear gripped Sidney's heart with icy fingers. He grabbed the receiver from his brother and spoke only three words. "What's the matter?" He listened intently before replacing the receiver and turning to Naomi. "Maria was asleep. Something disturbed her. She got up and looked around. When she checked the girls' room, Andrea and Linda were gone."

"Gone? Where?"

"Wherever it is, they've taken clothes with them. Maria said their closets were open, clothes were spilled everywhere."

"Call the police," Rachel suggested. "They'll find two girls wandering around by themselves in the middle of the night."

"Maria already telephoned them." He looked at the people who had been expecting a triumphant first-night party. "Why don't the rest of you go on over to Isow's?"

"While you're worrying yourself sick over two missing daughters?" Gordon Prideaux said. "Some hopes!"

"What are you going to do? Help us look for them?"

"Why not? We've all got cars. How hard can it be to spot two girls walking along the street in the middle of the night?"

"He's got a point," Manny said. "Sidney, you take Naomi and Mama to Marble Arch. The rest of us will cruise the streets. We'll telephone every half hour to see if you've heard anything."

Sidney saw sense in the suggestion. He returned with his mother and Naomi to the flat. The housekeeper was distraught, blaming herself for the girls' disappearance. Naomi assured the woman it was not her fault. Sidney sat with his mother in the living room, amazed at how quickly triumph could become disaster.

"Did you have any idea they would run away?" Rachel asked.

"None whatsoever." He stared at the carriage clock on the mantel. Five minutes to one! Young girls shouldn't be walking the street at five to one in the morning!

The telephone rang. Sidney snatched at it. Coins dropped, then came Manny's voice. "You hear anything?" When Sidney answered no, Manny said, "We've just been all up and down Oxford Street, Wigmore Street, and up to Regent's Park. Nothing."

"Thanks. Keep looking." The instant Sidney hung up, the telephone rang again. This time it was Gordon Prideaux. He had spent the past half hour cruising Regent Street, then

536

combing the nest of small streets running northeast of Oxford Circus.

The telephone continued to ring at half-hour intervals. By three in the morning Sidney's heart no longer quickened at the sound of the bell. Each time he hung up, he looked at his mother and his wife, who shared the vigil with him, and shook his head.

"Why don't both of you get some rest?" he asked, twenty minutes after the three-thirty calls had come in. "Naomi, go to bed. Mama, lie on the couch. You both look worn out."

"How can we sleep when those girls are out there somewhere?" Rachel asked. She walked to the window and looked out, not wanting Sidney to see the flush she could feel creeping across her face. He had enough on his plate right now without having to worry about her as well. She wiped sweat from a forehead that was alternately cool and burning. Her heart pounded; the meal she had eaten before the show lodged painfully in her chest. The anxiety was upsetting her physically as well as mentally. She loved the girls as much as she loved her natural grandchildren. If anything should happen to them . . . !

Another bell rang. Not the telephone this time, but the doorbell. Sidney strode down the hall and flung back the door. Naomi followed, with Rachel bringing up the rear. A police sergeant stood outside. With him were the two girls. Linda hung her head. Andrea, a small suitcase pulling down her right arm, stared straight ahead, unrepentant about running away, uncaring about the worry she had caused.

"Mr. and Mrs. Less? Would I be correct in assuming these two young ladies belong here?"

Sidney's legs trembled. "You'd be correct indeed, Sergeant."

"Where were they?" Naomi asked. She took the girls from the policeman's care and hugged them.

"Sitting in Victoria Station, madam. Their wanderlust must have urged them to take a train somewhere. Fortunately, there aren't any for a few hours yet."

"Thank you," Sidney said. "Thank you very much." Desperate to show appreciation, he started to dig into his pocket.

The sergeant frowned and gave the slightest shake of the head.

"That's not necessary, sir, but I would suggest you have a good talk with your daughters. Bad things can happen to young girls, as I'm sure you know. Good night." He touched his hand to his helmet and walked away.

Sidney shut the door. He remained calm for a few moments, then relief burst forth in a surge of anger. "You had us scared to death! Why did you run off like that?" Naomi backed away, leaving the girls exposed to Sidney's fury. "I should shake some sense into the pair of you!"

Rachel stepped in front of her son. "Let me speak to them."

Sidney stared down at Rachel, and his anger increased at the aggravation the two girls had put his mother through. Her face was pale and sweaty; her eyes had an unhealthy, glassy sheen. Sidney could never remember his mother looking so tired, so worn, not even on that terrible night that the flying bomb had hit the Playhouse. "Mama, go and lie down. This is between Andrea, Linda, and me."

Rachel stood up straighter. "Sidney, let me talk to them."

"Sidney . . ." Naomi's voice broke in. "Let your mother have five minutes with them." She was frightened by his wrath. Loud words and angry tones would only separate him further from Andrea; and with her, Linda. Naomi had little doubt that Andrea had been the instigator. Linda would never have done it on her own. If Sidney screamed at them now, he would alienate both girls forever. He would accomplish what he feared the most.

Sidney nodded. Rachel smiled feebly. She turned to the girls, took them by the arm, and guided them toward the bedroom they continued to share. The door swung closed behind them like the final curtain dropping on a play. Naomi, tears spilling down her cheeks, held out her arms. Sidney stepped into them.

"I've never seen you so angry. I thought you were going to hit them."

"So did I," Sidney answered, ashamed of himself now for even considering such a thing. He had held his hands by his

538

sides in case he raised them to the girls; at the very least, to shake some sense into them, as he had threatened to do.

"Your mother will get to the bottom of it all, you'll see."

"I wonder if even she can."

The telephone rang. It was Manny. "It's okay, they're home. A policeman brought them back here after they'd been found at Victoria. Thanks for your help."

"What about Mama?"

"She's talking to them. She'll sleep here, there's no point in having her travel all the way out to The Paddocks now."

Moments later, Gordon Prideaux called. When Sidney related the good news, Gordon said, "You can now boast that you're a true theater person, Sidney. You've worn both of its faces in a single night."

"Believe me, I don't want to do it again. See you tomorrow."

For fifteen minutes, Sidney and Naomi sat together in the living room, holding hands and wondering what was taking place in the girls' bedroom. At last, the door opened. Rachel's footsteps, slow and unusually ponderous, approached the living room. Sidney released Naomi's hand and stood up.

"Well?"

"They've gone to bed," Rachel replied. She dropped down into a Queen Anne chair and let out her breath in a long sigh. "Leaving home was Andrea's idea. She talked Linda into it."

"But why?"

"Sidney . . ." Rachel looked directly at her son. "Andrea's terrified that what happened before will happen again. She was only four years old when her father died. She loved him like every girl loves her father, and he died. She can't forget that, and in some twisted logic she can't forgive him for dying, for leaving her. She's terrified about having to go through that wrenching feeling of loss again."

"You mean she won't let herself like me because she's scared that I might die?"

Rachel gave a weary nod. "That's why she never let you in."

"She let *me* in," Naomi said.

"She loved her mother, but not as much as she loved her father. He was some kind of magic figure who went off each

539

morning and came home each evening. Her mother was with her all the time. When they were both killed, it was her father she missed the most."

"And she passed this fear on to Linda," Sidney whispered.

"She saw it as her duty to do so. She was the older sister. She was responsible for Linda. That responsibility included protecting her from all kind of harm, all kind of pain—"

"Including the pain, no matter how unlikely, of loss."

"Where were they going?" Naomi asked.

"They didn't know. They were just going to get on the first train and leave London far behind."

"With what?"

"They've been saving their pocket money for months and months, Andrea told me."

Sidney stood up and walked past his mother toward the girls' bedroom. When Naomi tried to follow, he waved her back. "I want to speak to them alone."

The bedroom door was shut. He knocked gently on it, knocked again, then pushed it open. The bedroom was large with a south-facing double window. Andrea's bed was next to the window. Linda's bed was close to the door. When Sidney entered, the two girls were already in bed, covers pulled up to their chins. Sidney placed a chair in the middle of the room and sat down.

"I want you to listen to me carefully. What you did tonight frightened us terribly. Anything could have happened to a couple of young girls wandering the streets late at night. You had no right to put us through such fear and anxiety, but that's all I'm going to say about it. Right now I want to discuss something else. Do you know what an adage is?"

"It's a saying," Andrea answered. "A truism."

For the first time since leaving the Showcase, Sidney smiled. "Very good. Believe me, when I was fourteen I had no idea what the word meant. You must both pay more attention in school than I did." His eyes flicked from sister to sister, pleased when he saw a trace of a smile first on Linda's face, then on Andrea's. He didn't know whether they were smiling at the joke or in relief at not being punished for running away; he didn't care. It only mattered that they *did* smile. "Listen to this adage and tell me what you think it means. 'If you touch life only with your fingertips, you'll never hold anything in your hands.'"

Silence filled the room for several seconds, then Andrea said, "Unless you become fully involved in life, you'll never have anything worthwhile."

"That's precisely what it means, Andrea." He turned to the younger girl. "Do you understand that, Linda?" He saw she did not. "If you go through life avoiding making friends, avoiding commitments to others, avoiding giving anything of yourself, you might save yourself pain, but you're going to lead an awfully empty life. It's a very uneven exchange."

"I have friends," Linda responded.

"Of course you do. They help you enjoy life. But supposing one of your friends broke her arm. You'd be upset, wouldn't you? You'd be even more upset if something worse happened to her . . ."

"Like *dying*." Linda whispered the word fearfully.

"Perhaps. If you could avoid being upset for all time simply by avoiding liking people, would you do it?"

"No."

Sidney turned back to Andrea. "It's not worth it, Andrea. We understand what you tried to do for Linda. You wanted to spare her pain, but you've heard for yourself that she wouldn't want such an exchange. And neither should you, unless you're prepared to go through life as a very unhappy person."

Tears bloomed in Andrea's eyes. "I don't ever want to lose a father again. Not until he's very old and gray."

"I don't want you to, but there's no way I can promise you it won't happen. We can't control our own fate. You have to take chances, Andrea, that's what makes life exciting. What you have to decide now is whether you're prepared to take those chances."

Andrea bit her bottom lip. Tears cascaded down her face. "Will you promise me one thing?"

Sidney nodded.

"Promise you won't do anything dangerous."

Sidney raised his right hand. "I promise that I'll look right, left, and right again before crossing the road. I promise that

541

I won't drive a racing car. I promise that I won't jump out of an aircraft unless it's on the ground—"

"You're being silly."

"Haven't you been just as silly?" He stood up and walked toward the bed by the window. On the bedside table was Andrea's handkerchief. Sidney wiped her tears with it. "The pair of you had better get some sleep. You've got school tomorrow."

"Do we have to go?" Linda protested.

"How else will you know what an adage is?" He walked toward the door. As he grasped the handle, Andrea called out to him.

"I'm sorry for causing all this trouble."

"It's all right. My brother and I probably caused your grandmother even more. Good night." A lump lodged in his throat as he watched Andrea hold out her arms toward him. It was the first time he had seen the older girl display any kind of affection. He returned to her bed to hug and kiss her on the cheek, then did the same to Linda. Outside the bedroom, he had to blow his nose and dry his eyes. It wouldn't do to let his wife and mother see tears in his eyes. And then he thought, why not? Tears could mean happiness as well as pain.

He returned to the sitting room. The scene was just as he had left it, Naomi on the couch, Rachel occupying the Queen Anne chair. He sat down next to Naomi and put his arm around her shoulder. "Congratulate me, I've just become a father."

"*Mazel tov,*" Rachel said. She had to concentrate all her faculties to see Sidney sitting on the couch with Naomi. Her head was a hydrogen-filled balloon, floating high above her body. She felt terrible. If she tried to stand, she was certain she'd fall flat on her face. "Now be a good boy and call a doctor for me before you become an orphan."

Sidney met Manny at the Middlesex Hospital early the following morning. Rachel, who had been rushed there at four o'clock in the morning, suffering the classic symptoms of a heart attack, was in serious but stable condition. Both brothers were told that they could probably visit her in the afternoon.

"She must have been sitting there with this pain in her chest the whole time we were looking for Andrea and Linda," Sidney said as they came out of the hospital onto Mortimer Street.

"Don't blame the girls."

Sidney looked shocked. "I'm not! If anyone's to blame, it's me. I saw she didn't look good, but I was so concerned about everything else it didn't register."

"Don't blame yourself either. You know Mama. She would have kept quiet no matter what until your problem was resolved."

They stopped in at a restaurant. Manny, who had left home before dawn, had not eaten breakfast. Sidney sipped a cup of tea. "We've got to think about moving Mama back to town," Manny said. "This rushing back and forth is too much for her. She needs to be here. Maybe Rita and I should sell The Paddocks and move back, get a big house so Mama can stay with us."

"No. I agree with you that she should be back in London, but I think she values her independence."

"Independence? After a heart attack?"

"Let's get her an apartment in one of the big hotels. She'll be cared for, we'll be able to visit her regularly, and she'll be at the center of things again, which is where she wants to be."

Manny thought it over. "You're right. She can't do much for herself out at The Paddocks. In town she'd be able to walk in the park, go shopping, do whatever she wanted to do."

They visited Rachel at the hospital that evening. Propped up by pillows, she looked frail and weak, but her eyes held far more life than they had the previous night.

"How do you feel?" Manny asked.

"I'm told it was a small attack."

"You're a small person," Sidney told her. "Why didn't you say anything earlier?"

"I thought it was all the excitement. Only after you came out from talking to Andrea and Linda did I realize something was wrong. How are they?"

"Worried about you. They asked me to give you this."

Sidney kissed his mother on the forehead. "They want you to get better quickly, so they can visit you in your new home."

Rachel seemed puzzled. "My new home?"

"Manny and I thought you'd be happier back in town. We've leased a lovely flat for you at the Grosvenor House. You can move in there the moment you feel strong enough."

Rachel's eyes saw pictures of a new life among the bustle she loved. Never had she come right out and told Manny and Rita that she did not fully enjoy living with them. Even after eight years she found it difficult to grow accustomed to the country's calm. She visited the city frequently enough to overcome the boredom of country life, but visits were no substitute for living there.

"I'll be able to walk in Hyde Park, go shopping."

"And you'll be able to attend opening night of every production Sidney puts on," Manny said.

"Not to mention being able to work for Manny in the agency whenever he gets short-staffed," Sidney added.

Rachel found strength to wag a finger. "I've done my share of working to keep you both in business. When I move into the Grosvenor House, I intend to be a lady of leisure."

They stayed ten minutes before a nurse said Rachel needed to rest. As they reached the door, Rachel asked, "Sidney, how is it with you and the girls? Is everything all right?"

He winked and raised a thumb. Rachel lay back, satisfied.

Chapter Twenty-four

Manny had been right that Sunday at The Paddocks, when he'd considered Jimmy Isaacson's increasing silence to be a symptom of his obsession with *TV Diary*. The weekly magazine that his father had built in the image of *Form Guide* had overshadowed the entire coronation trip for Jimmy.

The odd combination in that first issue of good circulation with advertising well below predictions presaged what was to come. Despite his father's assurances that revenue would increase when advertisers became accustomed to the new magazine, Jimmy was even more disturbed by the second and third issues. Advertising revenue fell, while sales positively plummeted. Jimmy took the problem to London with him. Every spare moment of his time there was taken up with fretting about it, with wondering why *TV Diary* had not only failed to live up to expectations but had failed so abysmally.

All the fretting in the world did not help. Sales hovered around the million mark all through summer. Advertising contributed little to the cost of producing the magazine. Jimmy became gloomier and gloomier, and more than once he confided to his father that he would like to kill the magazine stone dead.

Zalman fought such feelings on his son's part. "Do I need to remind you of your own words when you first agreed with me that this would be a wonderful idea? We'd be starting out well behind the eight ball on this one, you said. Nor would we soon get back our investment. Time and patience would be needed to succeed."

"I remember. Only there's one thing I never reckoned with."

"What's that?"

"Being laughed at. This is the first magazine we've ever published that advertisers treat as a joke, Mr. Z. I hear from ad reps that they couldn't get a bigger laugh if they took Groucho Marx along on their calls. Advertisers want to know why they should waste good money in some scrawny little publication when they can spend it in any one of a thousand magazines that looks like something."

"You think no one laughed at Henry Ford, the Wright Brothers, Marconi, and all of them? Idiots who couldn't see farther than their own noses laughed at me when I started *Form Guide*. They laughed again with the racing wire. In a few months they were laughing on the other side of their faces, and the fools who laugh at *TV Diary* will be doing just the same. Jimmy, look me in the eye . . . Do you think I'd waste my time on it if I thought the magazine was no damned good?"

Jimmy had no further argument. When it came to understanding what the public wanted, his father was the most astute man he had ever met.

On Labor Day, Jimmy hosted a party at Rye for employees. It was a tradition started the first year the family moved to Rye, an enormous catered barbecue where Jimmy could mingle with the men and women who worked for him. The idea for such a party had come from Sonya, who claimed it was far more personal than the company's annual Christmas celebration in the Messenger Building. Some people drove out to Rye. Most, however, traveled in one of the special buses chartered by Jimmy, which collected passengers on East Forty-second Street at midday and returned them in the evening.

When the food was served, Zalman walked among the picnic tables, talking to people, telling jokes, happily sharing in the enjoyment. Zalman had always considered Messenger Publications to be his extended family, and he was glad that his son had inherited the feeling of fondness.

Jimmy joined his father. "Having a good time?"

"Sure. So should you be. You're with your people. You

should be close to them all the time. There's got to be more between the boss and his people than just hours worked and wages paid. In my day, I always knew how everyone's families were, who was doing well in school, who was sick."

"But you never did this."

"No, I used to take my people out to the track on a nice day, or go to a bar with them. You can't do something like that, of course. My little Sir Right-and-proper would never be seen in a bar, let alone mixing with a bunch of degenerates at the track."

Jimmy laughed. "Do you ever wonder if I'm your son, Mr. Z.?"

"I used to wonder, Jimmy. I don't anymore. You've proved you're mine in many, many ways."

"Thank you."

As the barbecue wound down, Jimmy stood on a table to give his customary Labor Day talk. He expressed the hope that everyone had enjoyed the summer. He welcomed new people, and mentioned the names of personnel who had left. Lastly he spoke of the company's achievements since the previous Labor Day. Circulation and advertising revenue had risen on the *Messenger* itself and on most magazines. WMES, the company's television station, had also shown increased income. "Our major venture this year was *TV Diary*. We really got in on the ground floor here. Of course"—he tried to think of a positive message—"this is not the kind of publication that takes off overnight, as those of you who work on it understand. We fully expect slow sales until people across America become accustomed to the unusual size and the novelty of the content—"

He broke off as Brian Gilbert stepped up to the table and tapped his leg. Gilbert handed up a sheet of paper. "Mr. Z. asked me to give you this."

Jimmy read the words scrawled on the paper, then carried on talking as though no interruption had occurred. "I'm glad to report that such acceptance has not taken long. Sales last week of *TV Diary* leaped by more than a hundred and fifty thousand."

Applause began. Jimmy sought out his father. Zalman stood with Sonya at the back of the crowd. Jimmy stuffed the note into his pocket and joined in, directing his applause toward his father. If anyone deserved acclaim, it was Mr. Z. He must have known about the sales increase all weekend, but he'd kept it from his son until this moment.

Labor Day was the breakthrough. Sales of *TV Diary* rose steadily. At first, Jimmy failed to understand the reason. Marvin Baker, the station manager of WMES, enlightened him. "We rerun old programs in the summer when everyone's away on vacation. New programs begin in the fall when people come back." Jimmy felt like kicking himself for failing to understand such simple rationale.

Circulation continued to rise until, in the summer of 1956, three years after the little magazine's launch, it stood above four million copies a week. Jimmy had no trouble now understanding the reason for the tremendous increase: the magazine reflected the increasing ownership of television sets across the country. The Labor Day boast that Messenger Publications had gotten in on the ground floor was nothing more than the tip of the iceberg. Every second of the day, someone, somewhere, bought a television set. Every one of those people represented a reader. *TV Diary* was more than a magazine: it was a license to print money.

The effect of the magazine's success on Zalman was extraordinary. It seemed to Jimmy that years fell from his father's body. His walk became more sprightly, his back straighter, his eyes sharper. At one time Jimmy even wondered if his father had taken to darkening the iron gray of his hair. At seventy-two, he appeared in far better shape than many men ten years his junior.

"Have you got a portrait of yourself hidden away somewhere, Mr. Z.?" Jimmy asked during a visit to his father's office. "A portrait that's growing horribly old while you become younger."

Zalman lifted the latest copy of *TV Diary* from his desk. "My portrait's right here. For every circulation jump of a hundred thousand, I drop a year from my age. I was like an old boxer, Jimmy, who had been written off by everyone but who still believed he had one good fight left in him. This was it."

"*I* never wrote you off."

"Didn't you? Didn't you write me off after Helen died? And after your mother died?"

"I worried, but I never wrote you off. I just wish . . ."

"Yes?"

"I just wish that you'd come with us to England that time. I stood where Helen died. You should, too. It might clear all the resentment inside you."

"I'm not angry any more, Jimmy. Helen died because she was unlucky, nothing else. Twelve years later, who am I going to be mad at? The Krauts? The British? Myself, for not putting my foot down and forbidding her from going over there in the first damned place?"

Jimmy heard hostility bubbling through the voice, and he turned away. Even if the father failed to understand his own emotions, the son did.

As he grew older, Jimmy found himself understanding his father better. Even events from the past that had once mystified him now made sense. On the evening Zalman had mentioned he was buying a controlling interest in the Sporting News Agency, Jimmy remembered asking if he didn't have enough money already. *When will you have enough,* he had asked. *Will you know when you have enough?* Now he realized why his father had sought wealth and power. When a man endured such experiences as Zalman had—the years of want, the flight for life, starting again in a strange country— he could never have enough to satisfy him. And all those tricks Zalman had used to strengthen the son he believed to be a weakling . . . Now that he understood his father so well, Jimmy sometimes speculated that the entire tax-evasion trial had been a ruse to make him accept responsibility. If so, it had achieved remarkable results. Zalman's years at Lewisburg had matured Jimmy quickly. Some ruse, Jimmy thought. Such guile and sacrifice were beyond even Zalman Isaacson.

With greater understanding came the realization that his father's attempt to shape his son in his own image had been a rare example of failure, even if only partial failure. Jimmy would never have his father's strength and boundless energy. That emanated from Zalman's spare, athletic frame, a physical characteristic the son did not share. Zalman had suc-

549

ceeded, however, in molding his son's mind. He had given him ideas far more precious than physical attributes.

Jimmy realized that sons frequently became diametrically opposed to the beliefs of their fathers simply because those beliefs came from their fathers. He was different. He not only accepted many of his father's values, he tried to pass them on to his own children. He refused to let a background of wealth and luxury spoil his son and daughter. Josephine and Harold had to work for their pocket money. Harold shined his father's shoes while Josephine dusted and vacuumed the downstairs room Jimmy had made into his office. When Sonya complained that they paid the staff to perform such work, Jimmy held up a hand.

"If it was good enough for my father to act this way, it's good enough for me."

"My father never made me do such things."

"That was Canada, my dear. This is the United States. Here you *earn* money."

Sonya didn't like it, either, when Jimmy told the children that they were no better than other people, just luckier. In winter, when they rode in one of the Rolls Royce limousines Jimmy continued to buy, he often told the chauffeur to stop by a group of derelicts clustered around a fire and give them enough to buy food and clothing. Sometimes he had either Josephine or Harold hand the money to the men.

"A lot of people hate the poor because they feel threatened by them," Jimmy explained to his children. "Those people are terrified that one day the poor will rise up and take what they have, so they hate them and try to keep them suppressed. That's nonsense. Don't hate the poor, and never look down on them. Do you understand why?"

Josephine nodded. "Because we're no better, only luckier."

"That's right."

Sonya disliked Jimmy's social messages. As children, she and her brother had been given everything by a doting father who had made enough money in Montreal to indulge his family. She had not been brought up the same way as Jimmy, who, as a child, had been made to understand that position in life depended to a great extent on luck, and she could not comprehend his obsession in teaching the same lesson to Josephine and Harold.

Zalman appreciated it, though. Jimmy had learned well how to deal with both his family and his employees. He used Brian Gilbert as his finger on the company's pulse. Gilbert relayed news of people who could use help. A *Messenger* compositor whose eight-year-old son was killed in a car crash found the funeral parlor bill paid; a receptionist at WMES whose mother died after a lingering illness that called for round-the-clock nursing discovered the considerable medical bill had been taken care of.

As the children grew, Jimmy found it easier to spot family traits. Physically, Josephine resembled her mother. She had Sonya's thick brown hair and dark-brown eyes, but her independent personality reminded Jimmy of his sister Helen. Josephine stood up to her parents, arguing fiercely for what she thought was right. As with Helen, the traditional discussion-ending statement of "Because I said so!" had little effect; everything had to be resolved through reason. Additionally, she had a streak of adventure that she indulged by climbing the highest trees, riding her bicycle at breakneck speeds, and galloping across the countryside on the horse she kept at a nearby stable. Sonya claimed that such daring and self-assurance came from her brother Joseph, who had died at Dieppe eight weeks after the girl's birth. Jimmy knew better. The characteristics came from Helen. He even considered buying Josephine a punching bag on which she could take out her frustrations.

Jimmy's eight-year-old son was the opposite. Harold was a quiet, almost shy boy who usually looked as though he had just stepped out of a bath. His brown hair was always neatly combed, his face sparkling clean. He never got into the trouble boys were expected to get into. He never came home from school with his knees scraped, or an eye closed from fighting. Whenever Jimmy and Sonya visited Harold's school, the teachers expressed satisfaction with the boy. He excelled at every academic subject and never misbehaved. Jimmy wondered what was wrong with him.

"Nothing's wrong with him," Zalman explained one morning as he, Jimmy, and Sonya traveled into the city. Then he started to laugh. Jimmy asked what was funny. "You're just seeing the curse in action."

"What curse?"

"The favorite curse of parents—that their children should have children just like themselves." He winked at Sonya. "Didn't your mother and father ever wish that on you?"

"I can remember it."

"I wasn't like Harold—"

"You were just like Harold," Zalman told his son. "You were artistic, you were gentle, you even carried pet mice around in your shirt pocket! You worried the living daylights out of me because you did nothing I thought a boy should do."

"If Harold turns out like Jimmy," Sonya said, linking arms with her husband, "I don't think anyone will complain."

Zalman smiled. "Neither do I."

In Jimmy's eyes, the resemblance between Josephine and Helen flourished with each passing day. That summer of 1956, while Harold learned about nature at day camp, Josephine traveled into the city with her parents and grandfather. Instead of going to camp, she wanted to work; she was fourteen, she declared, and old enough to learn something about the family business.

On her first day, Jimmy instructed Brian Gilbert to find small jobs for her. At the risk of upsetting every union member in the building, Gilbert let her write a cutline for a picture. He changed a couple of words around and pushed it through. Proudly, Josephine pasted that cutline into a scrapbook. Underneath she wrote in block capitals: "My First Story."

Another day, she spent with her mother on *American Miss,* where she ran errands and assisted one of the fashion staff on a photographic assignment. She returned from that with such a deep interest in photography that she asked to spend the rest of her summer working with *Messenger* press photographers. Jimmy indulged her as Zalman had once indulged Helen. He asked the *Messenger*'s longest serving photographer, sixty-year-old Fred Harrup, to teach Josephine how to use a camera. Harrup, who had been with the newspaper since the end of World War I and was close to retirement, was happy to oblige. A kindly soul who saw nothing wrong in giving preferential treatment to the boss's daughter, he did more than just show Josephine how to use different types of cameras. He taught her how to develop film and print photographs. When summer was over and Josephine returned to school, she started to save toward her own darkroom. Jimmy gave her extra jobs so she could earn more money. Finally, as Christmas drew near and she was still short, Jimmy went out and bought everything she needed. To show her father the money was well spent, she created a family portrait. Jimmy liked it so much he displayed it in his office.

As he watched his children grow, Jimmy understood that he had much to be thankful for. Most of all, he was grateful that he had not erred in asking Sonya to replace Pauline Fulford as editor of *American Miss*. He had never shared Sonya's doubts that she was unsuited for the position; he had known with every ounce of certainty that she'd be perfect. His only worry had been that the family might suffer through her absence. That hadn't happened. Sonya tailored her working hours around the children's school times. On occasion, she even worked from home. And like both her husband and her father-in-law, she recognized the value of delegating tasks. Pauline Fulford had kept much of the responsibility to herself, regarding it as a privilege not to be shared. Jimmy had occasionally wondered if such an attitude signaled insecurity. Had Pauline been scared of jeopardizing her own position by letting an assistant demonstrate expertise?

He teased Sonya as they lay in bed late one night, cuddled up spoon in spoon. "Are you insecure like Pauline, scared that one of your own people might show you up?"

"Not at all. I'm far too confident of my own abilities to worry about silly little things like that. It wouldn't frighten me in the least"—she rolled around to face him in the dark, wrapping her arms around his body and kissing him—"if one of my assistants caught the boss's eye. Not when I've got everything else that belongs to him."

While *TV Diary* developed into the brightest jewel in the Messenger Publications crown, Jimmy became more involved in the city of New York. His city.

So far, his one friend in politics was William Baron, who was just starting his fifth year as Republican senator for New York. Now Jimmy sought to increase his group of influential friends. He lunched and dined with the men who ran New York, giving a platform in the *Messenger* to those with whom he agreed, and ignoring those with whom he did not. Many office-holders, he confided to Sonya, were distinguished only by their capacity to bore. The remainder, he told his wife, using a philosophy garnered from his father, were money-grubbers willing to sell their influence to the highest bidder.

Of all the men Jimmy met, one stood high above the rest. That man was Frank Kinsella, a deputy inspector in the New York Police Department. Tall and burly, with silver-streaked black hair and sharp brown eyes dominating a swarthy face, Kinsella came into Jimmy's circle through an incident in a bar. A scuffle broke out between two men. Frank Kinsella, in civilian clothes and having a drink with a friend, stepped in to break up the fight. When it was over, Kinsella had a cut head and bruised knuckles. The two men who had started the fight spent the night in the hospital, with fractured ribs, broken noses, and a hundred and twenty-eight stitches between them. Once everything stopped hurting, they pressed charges against Deputy Inspector Frank Kinsella, claiming he had savagely beaten them for no apparent reason, and without any warning.

Kinsella, a former amateur boxer and a veteran of twenty years on the force, enjoyed a reputation as a tough cop that went back to his days as a patrolman. He had brought criminals into the station house bruised and bloody, always claiming self-defense. As a sergeant, he had singlehandedly broken up a potential riot in Harlem by sorting out the ringleader and smashing his heavy flashlight into the man's skull. While a lieutenant and then a captain, he had given his men leeway in carrying out their duties. His credo was simple: violence was the best way to deal with violent criminals; their primitive brains understood nothing else. Kinsella's many defenders in the department described his methods as no-nonsense. His detractors, who were just as numerous, liked to portray him as a thug who got his kicks through brutality. They saw the fight in the bar and the ensuing charges as an excuse to get him off the force.

As Kinsella's future swayed in the balance, *Messenger* editor Richard Hartford told Jimmy that two of his reporters wanted to talk to him. The reporters' names were Harry Allen and Jack Green. Jimmy saw them in Hartford's office. Allen got straight to the point. "Frank Kinsella's being railroaded, Mr. J."

"How do you know?" Jimmy did not really care one way or the other about Frank Kinsella. Although he had never met the man, he knew of his reputation. Some of Kinsella's escapades had met with Jimmy's grudging approval; others had shocked him.

"Jack and I were there," Allen answered. "We were in the bar that night, and these charges they're making against Kinsella are a load of hogwash."

"Did he break up a fight? Did he beat those two men so badly they spent the night in the hospital?"

"Yes. But an awful lot happened in between that no one's caring about."

"The two guys were having a scuffle," Green said. "Pushing and shoving each other, swearing and shouting. Kinsella stepped in between them, held them apart, and advised them to go home and cool off. One of the guys told Kinsella to keep out of it."

"His exact words," Allen cut in, "were, 'Why don't you mind your own goddamned business, you stupid Mick bastard?' "

Green carried on past the interruption. "As Kinsella turned toward that man, the other guy lifted a beer bottle and smashed it over his head. That's when Kinsella went crazy. He took them both on, Mr. J., and they weren't small guys, either. He took them both on and beat the living daylights out of them, which is what they deserved."

Jimmy looked at Allen. "That's exactly what happened?" Allen nodded. "I suggest we carry an eyewitness story, Mr. Hartford, that sheds a better light on this incident."

The story ran on the front page the next morning. Just before lunchtime, Brian Gilbert told Jimmy he had a visitor. Deputy Inspector Frank Kinsella.

Kinsella wore a uniform, oak leaves gleaming, chest covered with ribbons. He shook hands with Jimmy, sat down, and came right to the meat of the matter. "I want to thank you for that article in this morning's *Messenger*, Mr. Isaacson. You printed the truth, which is good for you. And you got me off the hook, which is good for me. Which is one of two reasons why I'd like to buy you lunch today, if you're not busy."

"As it happens, I'm not."

The two men went downstairs. Standing next to the policeman in the elevator made Jimmy, for one of the rare times in his life, feel insignificant. Not only was Kinsella three inches taller, he was at least fifty pounds heavier, and all of it solid muscle. He was a bull of a man who filled every inch of his dark-blue uniform. Jimmy guessed the uniform was custom-made. Off-the-rack was never intended to fit men with Kinsella's physique.

Outside the Messenger Building, in a no-parking zone, stood a police car. "Mind riding in one of these?"

"Not at all." Kinsella held open the passenger door and Jimmy climbed in, looking with fascination at the equipment that filled the interior of the car. Kinsella settled into the driver's seat. "You just made a dream come true," Jimmy said.

"If you've got any more dreams about the department, just let me know. Italian food sound all right?" Without waiting for an answer, Kinsella set the car in motion. He drove down to Little Italy, parking the car on Mulberry Street. The two men entered a restaurant called Alberto's, already full with lunchtime trade. As if by magic, a table opened up. The restaurant manager led them past half a dozen people waiting to be seated.

As they ate, Kinsella pointed out different characters to Jimmy. "See him, the guy in the gray suit with the mustache? Runs a bookie operation out of a restaurant over on Canal Street that handles maybe a million, million-five a week. And him, that guy in the scruffy beige pants and the black shoes . . . doesn't look like much, does he? He's got a numbers beat that pulls in more than your advertising."

"If you know these things, why don't you do something?"

"Bookmaking, numbers, gambling . . . they don't harm anyone. Take numbers. The odds against winning are nine hundred and ninety-nine to one against a payout of six hundred to one. No official government lottery pays such good odds." Kinsella chewed thoughtfully on a mouthful of chicken parmigiana. "There's two guys I know who run numbers in your outfit."

"Give me their names."

"What the hell for? So you can throw them out and make a bunch of your people unhappy because they can't get any action?"

"What do you classify as harmful then?"

Kinsella's eyes narrowed; his face turned to rock. "Drug addicts, prostitutes and their pimps, the muggers and rollers, the garbage that don't make it safe for people to walk the streets of their own city. That's the scum I want to see behind bars. And that's the scum I'm going to put behind bars, just as long as the city leaves me alone to do it my own way."

The pure honesty of the speech appealed to Jimmy. He saw a lot of himself in Kinsella's approach to his work. Both men were guardians of the city. Kinsella did it with his fists, with his badge, and, if necessary, with his gun. Jimmy did it with his newspaper. Just as appealing to Jimmy was the respect with which this much decorated police officer treated him. Never once during their lunch had Kinsella tried familiarity. Other men of similar rank and influence would have resorted to using his first name, believing such informality was their due. Kinsella had done nothing of the kind. "You can rely on the *Messenger,* Inspector, to do all it can to make sure the city leaves you alone to get on with your job."

"Thank you, Mr. Isaacson. Getting your continued support was the second reason I asked you to join me for lunch."

Kinsella returned Jimmy to the newspaper. As eager as any young boy, Jimmy asked questions about the equipment inside the police cruiser. He wanted to know the meaning of the different codes that came over the radio; he wanted to know how fast the car would go.

"Would you like to go riding in a patrol car one evening, Mr. Isaacson?" Kinsella asked as he let Jimmy off outside the

557

Messenger Building. "You can find out what this city's really like just below its respectable surface."

"You bet."

"I'll arrange something."

Kinsella kept his promise. During the following month, he took Jimmy on weekly tours of New York by night. He pointed out hookers plying their trade on the sidewalk, pawn shops where last night's stolen goods turned up today, bars and restaurants where loan sharks plied their trade. Once Jimmy stood excitedly by the car as Kinsella chased a man he'd seen snatch a woman's bag. He lost sight of the deputy inspector when he flew around a corner. Two minutes later, he returned with both the man and the bag. The purse-snatcher, face contorted in agony, clutched his right arm. Jimmy watched Kinsella hand the bag back to the surprised woman, then shove the purse-snatcher into the back of the patrol car. The man yelled in pain as he fell on his injured arm.

"What happened?" Jimmy asked.

Kinsella fished something out of his pocket and tossed it to Jimmy. Jimmy caught it and pressed the button halfway down the handle. His heart leaped as a shining six-inch blade flashed into view. "He swung at me with that. I swung at him with this," Kinsella said, rubbing the edge of his hand.

When Jimmy arrived at the office the next morning, he called Brian Gilbert into the office. "I want us to start a police-beat column. I'll write the first one, about what I saw last night."

The police-beat column became a regular weekly feature. So did Jimmy's rides in patrol cars, sometimes with Kinsella, at other times with a sergeant handpicked by the deputy inspector. Sonya made fun of his sudden infatuation. "No one warned me before we married that when you reached forty-two you'd enter a second childhood."

Zalman didn't laugh at his son's newfound excitement. He felt jealous, because he had never shared this kind of community involvement. He'd been too busy running the paper to enjoy the privileges that came with the position of publisher.

"Don't you think you're giving this policeman too much publicity?" Zalman asked after one of Jimmy's columns had compared Kinsella to an old-fashioned western sheriff facing outlaws in single combat.

Jimmy gave his father a wide grin. "Is that an objective criticism or does it mean you'd like to take a ride in a police car now and then?"

Zalman pretended to give great thought to the question. "If someone asked me, I wouldn't say no."

Jimmy asked, and the next time he rode with Frank Kinsella, Zalman made a third. When Sonya joked that two men deep into their second childhood was too much to accept, Jimmy had an answer ready. "Our delivery trucks park illegally, do you ever see them get ticketed? Do you ever see our drivers pulled over for making illegal turns or running the lights? The *Messenger* gets onto the street quicker because Frank Kinsella makes sure the police look the other way."

Sonya could not argue with that logic. Kinsella gained some welcome sympathetic publicity while Jimmy had gained a very useful friend.

In the summer of 1958, Jimmy found out just how useful it was to have friends in the hierarchy of the police force.

The *Messenger* was hit with an industrial action that divided the entire staff. It began with a dispute among the reporters on overtime pay. Just under half the reporters walked out. The rest remained to face the taunts of their striking colleagues as they arrived for work each day. The situation deteriorated when some pressmen and mechanics joined the picket line. Jimmy was prepared to tolerate the striking reporters. They were taking action over what they considered a justifiable grievance, which was their privilege. When others struck in sympathy, he issued an ultimatum. The pressmen and mechanics had no grievance, and he would endure no job action on their part. If they did not return to work within an hour, they would be replaced. The sympathy strike continued, and Jimmy kept his promise. He fired the strikers and hired new men.

When the first replacements arrived for work, war broke out on the picket line. Fists flew, banners became weapons. A single telephone call was made to the police. Within five minutes, a force of thirty uniformed police officers, led by

Deputy Inspector Frank Kinsella, descended on the Messenger Building. They remained in evidence for the twenty-one days the strike lasted, and when publication of the *Messenger* returned to normal, the newspaper carried a lengthy editorial thanking the police department and Deputy Inspector Frank Kinsella for preserving law and order.

Jimmy thought it fitting in the spring of 1960 when Kinsella exchanged his oak leaf for the eagle of a full inspector. The Irishman deserved such success and recognition. Jimmy was just sorry that another friend, William Baron, was not so fortunate in his quest for promotion. In 1960, as a second-term senator, he threw his hat into the ring for the Republican presidential nomination. The *Messenger* endorsed him wholeheartedly, but it was not enough. He lost out to Richard Nixon.

Originally, Jimmy had planned to host a victory party for Baron and his wife at Rye. Instead, the gathering was more in keeping with a funeral. Zalman tried to lighten the gloom by forecasting trouble for the man who had beaten his son's friend.

"Nixon will come unstuck against this Senator Kennedy, mark my words. Kennedy's got youth and good looks. He'll score big with women voters. Nixon's got a face that'll turn milk."

Baron's wife, Thelma, caught on to Zalman's drift. "Maybe it's just as well that we didn't get the nomination this time. Let tricky Dicky take the fall, and we can come up to the plate again in four years when your second term's up."

"That's right," Jimmy added. "This isn't going to be the year for Republican lawyers anyway. Let Nixon, and not you, be the one to find that out."

Baron cheered up a fraction. "If I ever get to the White House, I'm going to owe your family a hell of a lot, Jimmy. Not only for the backing of your paper, but for the moral support. One day I'm going to find a way to repay you, and I won't accept a request for a couple of front-row seats to a fight that you wouldn't even let me pay for."

"I'll have at least four years to think about it," Jimmy answered. He glanced at his father and saw Zalman smiling, and Jimmy knew they shared the identical thought. Who would have thought it—a presidential candidate offering favors to the son of a man who had fled from Russia.

Late that night, when the house was quiet, Jimmy sat out on the patio, enjoying the mild summer night. He thought about William Baron's offer, and he thought about the favors Frank Kinsella had already done for him. Both men had prospered through the good graces of the Isaacson family, and both men were gracious enough to want to show their appreciation.

If Baron ever made it to the White House, what would Jimmy ask him for? What position would he want? Jimmy had no doubt that he would want a prominent post rather than some business offering that would make him more money than he had already. A man only needed so much money. After that, social acceptance became far more important. He chuckled to himself; he'd think about it, hard and long.

His thoughts turned to his children. Josephine would be off to Vassar in a few weeks. That was social acceptance, all right. Like Helen, whose personality she had inherited, Josephine wanted only one thing: to work for her father. Not as a reporter, as Helen had desired, but as a photographer. But before she set one foot inside the darkroom as a *Messenger* employee, Jimmy was going to make damned sure she had a good degree from a good school.

Then he focused on his son. At twelve, Harold was the same as he had been at eight. Shy, tidy, an exceptional scholar, and a poor athlete. He was, in a phrase, egghead material. The boy's dry preciseness irritated Jimmy, just as his own little quirks had bothered his father. It was the curse. He was merely being plagued by the curse every parent threw at every child. How long would he have to wait before it was removed?

Then he saw a solution to all his problems, a way to kill two birds with a single stone. If William Baron really wanted to perform a favor, Jimmy would ask him to remove the curse!

Chapter Twenty-five

Moving Rachel back into London, with her own apartment at the Grosvenor House Hotel, was the best thing her sons could have done for her. Despite being with Manny's family, she had found country life monotonous. Living on Park Lane, a short distance from anything she could possibly want to visit, rejuvenated her.

Rachel did all the things her sons had said she would do. On sunny days, she walked across Park Lane to sit in Hyde Park. She went shopping at the many fine stores that were suddenly, if not in walking distance, certainly no more than a short cab ride away. Rarely did she buy anything for herself; she always seemed to return to the hotel with gifts for her grandchildren, for Andrea and Linda who now lived so near that they popped in to see her at least twice a week, and for Jonathan and Bernice who came into town with their parents every weekend. And when Sidney had a show in rehearsal, or when one of Manny's clients was appearing in a production, Rachel always made sure to attend. She never waited to be asked for her opinion—she just came right out and gave it. Her sons listened, just as she expected them to. No matter how old they were, or how successful they had become, they could still learn from their mother.

In March 1956, Rachel celebrated her seventieth birthday with a party at her apartment. As well as being a special day for Rachel, it was a momentous occasion for her grandson. Jonathan, who had passed his driving test a few weeks earlier, drove into London for the first time in a white MGA convertible his parents had bought for him. He drove with the top down and, though huddled in a sheepskin coat, arrived at his grandmother's apartment shivering with cold. He kissed Rachel on the cheek and said, "I've got a special birthday treat for you, Grandma—a ride in my new car."

Manny charged in to protect his mother. "Wait until summer before you ask your grandmother to risk her life and limb."

Rachel stilled the protest. "Jonathan always promised that I'd be the first person he took for a ride when he got a car. I never stipulated that it had to be a Rolls or a Daimler." She went to the window and looked out. "Which one's yours, darling?"

Smiling proudly, Jonathan pointed to the open white sports car. Rachel nodded grimly and disappeared into her bedroom. She returned five minutes later wearing fur-lined boots, a black Persian lamb coat, a cashmere scarf wrapped around her head, and thick woolen gloves. "I'm ready," she declared with fervor. Riding in an open sports car in the middle of winter was not one of the things she'd sworn to do before dying, but she was not about to disappoint her grandson by letting him know.

Rachel's guests gathered around the window to watch. Jonathan opened the door of the low-slung car and helped his grandmother inside. She gripped the top of the door with one hand and braced herself against the dashboard with the other. Jonathan settled behind the wheel, started the engine, and tore along Park Lane to the rasp of the MG's exhaust bouncing back off the buildings. He drove south to Hyde Park Corner, swung around, then came back up along Park Lane to Marble Arch, circled that and returned to where he'd started.

"What do you think, Grandma? Splendid, isn't it?"

Rachel allowed her grandson to help her from the car. Her legs felt like she'd been at sea for a week, and her face was numb. Yet, determined not to disappoint the boy, she managed a weak if frozen smile. "Exhilarating, Jonathan."

"Do you want to go for another spin?"

"I think you should ask one of your cousins if they want

563

a ride," Rachel answered as she led the way into the hotel. "It wouldn't be right for me to go again."

When they got back to the apartment, Manny rushed forward with exaggerated worry. "Are you still in one piece, Mama? Jonathan here thinks the speed limit means minimum speed."

Rachel waved away her son's concern. "He drives beautifully, like a regular Stirling Moss." She took off her coat and sat down, grateful for the cup of tea that Rita gave her.

"I'm taking Andrea for a spin," Jonathan called out. "We'll see you in a few minutes."

Watching them go, Rachel felt a peculiar little flash of jealousy toward Andrea. She hoped the girl realized just how lucky she was to be taken for a ride by such a handsome young man. Rachel knew it was wrong to favor one child over another, but she could not help feeling an extra fondness for her oldest grandchild and only grandson. In the past two years, he had shot up. No longer was he chunky like his father. Now he stood tall and straight. His curly brown hair and the spark of adventure in his vivid blue eyes lent him a devil-may-care appearance. He was in his final year of school. In the autumn he would begin working, not for his father, but for the Rialto Playhouse Partnership, where his uncle was joint managing director. He might be Manny's son, but in numerous ways he resembled Sidney. Outgoing, daring, he belonged at the front, not wheeling and dealing behind the scenes like his father.

Rachel grew philosophical. If the biblical three score years and ten were all she would be allowed, she wouldn't grumble. She'd come from a bungled suicide attempt in a Rotterdam canal to being at the center of a warm and loving and highly successful family. No person could ask for more than that from life.

As another year passed, Rachel's feelings of contentment grew stronger. Now that he worked in town, Jonathan, her handsome favorite, visited her two or three evenings a week before driving back home to The Paddocks. Sometimes the visits lasted only ten minutes; at other times, he took her out to dinner, telling her everything that was happening at the Partnership.

564

Rachel found just as much pleasure in the visits of her other grandchildren. Since overcoming the barriers she had erected, Andrea, along with her sister, sat for hours in Rachel's apartment, listening to her stories. They didn't want to hear about her early days as an agent; they heard enough show-business talk at home. They wanted to learn about her years in Russia, the story of how she and her brother had escaped only to be separated a final time at Rotterdam.

"You should write about your life," Andrea said one day.

"A million people made such journeys, darling. They could all write books. Who would want to read mine?"

"I would," Andrea said. "I'd buy it, and I'd tell all my friends how good it was. I wouldn't lend it to them, either. I'd make sure they bought their own."

"And then Daddy could produce a play about it," Linda said in all seriousness. "There are plays about Jewish people, you know. Look at *The Diary of Anne Frank*. Perhaps the actress who played that role could play you as well."

Rachel smiled. Linda might not be Sidney's biological child, but she certainly had his big ideas.

She saw Bernice, her youngest grandchild, only on weekends, when she either came into London with her parents, or on those rare occasions that Rachel traveled out of London to spend a day at The Paddocks. Bernice was an introspective, quiet girl who liked to read. Whenever Rachel saw the young girl, she always had a present of a book to give her. Bernice liked to write poetry as well, simple verses about people she knew. She wrote one called "Darling Grandma" that Rachel pressed in a book so she would never lose it.

Also, Rachel drew pleasure from her daughters-in-law. Both women were interested in children's welfare, Naomi because her daughters came from an orphanage, and Rita because she recalled a childhood made unhappy by an imperious father and a timid mother. They talked Sidney into giving them a Partnership theater for two afternoons during the Christmas season, then they persuaded Manny to ask his clients in circus and pantomime to work for nothing on those afternoons, amusing children from orphanages. Rita and Naomi attended the shows. Afterward, as they supervised the distribution of presents to every child, they looked at each other and realized that their family had just increased a thousandfold.

Toward the end of 1957, just when Manny, at fifty, believed he would remain a theatrical agent for the balance of his working life, he discovered a new career. In television. A group of investors led by a banker named Nicholas Rawlinson approached him with the proposal of becoming chairman of a newly formed production company.

"Rawlinson's people want to produce shows to be sold here and to other English-speaking markets," Manny explained to Rita.

"And they want you as chairman because you've got contacts and you'll be able to pull in stars. What will happen to Lesser Brothers without you?"

"I'll still be able to put in time there. Besides, the agency's like a huge locomotive—even when the engine stalls, momentum keeps the whole thing rolling."

When Manny asked his mother's opinion, she had only one comment. "If you're going to produce television programs, please produce better than the garbage that's on already. The few times I watch a show, I want to throw something through the screen."

"I promise, Mama."

The new company, with its offices in Regent Street, was called White Hart Productions. Manny had money at his disposal and a brief to find productions to spend that money on. Proposals poured in. Eager for his first decision to succeed, he studied each idea carefully. Finally, he chose an adventure series based on Baroness Orczy's fictional hero, the Scarlet Pimpernel, and authorized production of twenty half-hour episodes at a cost of half a million pounds.

Immediately, the ceiling collapsed on Manny's head. His partners in the venture, those who had put up the money he had spent, demanded to know why he had taken such action without first getting the approval of the board.

"Because I never worked with a board before!" Manny answered. "Whatever I wanted done was done, and I thought that was why you asked me to be chairman of White Hart Productions. Because you trusted my judgment."

"Can production be stopped?" Nicholas Rawlinson asked.

"Technically, yes. Ethically, no. I made a commitment, and as far as I'm concerned, that makes it final."

Rawlinson turned to the other members of the board. "Manny's right. We asked him to be chairman because we trusted him."

The decision was a sound one. The Pimpernel series was sold in Britain on the strength of the first four episodes. It aired to enthusiastic reviews as an adventure suitable for both adults and children. Before the ink had dried on the reviews, Manny sold the entire series to Australia, then to Canada and the United States, where it was equally well received.

Looking around for further projects, Manny realized he was doing nothing different from what he had done for most of his life. Selling. He had sold clothing, then stuffed toys during the short-lived business venture with Sidney and Bernard. As an agent he had sold talent. First he'd spotted it, of course, then built it up, but in the end he had packaged it and sold it. Now he did the same with television shows. He supposed he could sell anything—even ice to eskimos.

While Manny combined agency work with producing television programs, Sidney, too, sought areas of expansion. In four years with the Rialto Playhouse Partnership, he had produced several successful shows. In addition, he had brought a couple of new theaters into the Partnership fold. As joint managing director of a company that operated eleven theaters and a nationwide chain of movie houses, he knew he was a someone. But it wasn't enough. The country had plenty of other theaters and movie houses. Sidney wanted to create something original.

In the spring of 1958, Sidney stood outside the Vanity Theater, on the north side of Leicester Square, across from the London Playhouse and the offices of the Partnership. The Vanity was an independently owned old house now fallen on hard times. The exterior was shabby; paint peeled from wood, grime covered the windows.

Sidney studied the old house in much the same manner as he had once surveyed the Showcase, wondering to what use it could be put. With him was his nephew Jonathan, Manny's son, who worked on the stage crew of the London Playhouse, learning the business from the ground up. "If this place belonged to you, Jonathan, what would you do with it?"

"Clean it up and get my uncle Sidney to put a show in there" came the immediate reply.

Sidney smiled at the compliment. Jonathan was the only boy in the family, and Sidney treated him more as a son than as a nephew. "Cleaning this place up isn't going to be enough. I've heard that the gallery's been condemned, and the rest of the place isn't in any great shape. It'll need to be rebuilt, maybe to the cost of a couple of hundred thousand pounds. You'll need something more than a show to recoup that kind of money. Even a Sidney Less show."

Jonathan stared at the dirty exterior once more, wracking his brains for an idea. He knew that his uncle already had one, and he wanted just once to demonstrate that he had inherited some of the family perception when it came to show business.

"Think about dinner theater," Sidney suggested. "A theater restaurant—a good meal, a good show, and dancing all for a price the average man in the street can afford."

Jonathan visualized it immediately. "You could leave the stage as it is, but make the dance floor an extension of it. Set the dance floor in the middle of the dinner tables, and have one side of it adjoin the stage. It can be raised up to stage level for the show and returned to floor level for the dancing. It could be like a catwalk, with the performers able to walk among the audience like models in a fashion show."

Sidney, thrilled at his nephew's vision, clapped him on the shoulder. He had only just discovered the idea, and already the young man was charging on ahead. "What shall we call this place, Jonathan?"

"Chez Sid?"

The clap on the shoulder became a light clip on the ear. "Have some respect for your father's brother."

"But Chez Sid's got a certain ring—"

"For a Marseilles bordello. If it's all the same to you, I'd prefer my name to be associated with something a little more elegant."

Jonathan came back with "Why not call it London Lights?

That name evokes a lot of images—London itself, the bright lights of the city, and the luminaries of the entertainment world who'll appear there."

Sidney regarded his nephew with unconcealed affection. "My brother Manny's a nice fellow, don't get me wrong, but it never stops amazing me how he had such a smart son. When your mother was expecting you, she must have been thinking a lot about me."

Sidney took the idea for a theater restaurant on the site of the Vanity to the board of the Rialto Playhouse Partnership. He used the name Jonathan had created, and he used his nephew's idea for a major special effect—a stage that could rise like a catwalk for the show and later drop down to floor level for dancing. For entertainment, he had his own ideas: an opening floor show at nine o'clock that would rival anything seen in Paris, followed two hours later by the star turn.

The Partnership board approved the proposal. An offer for the Vanity was made and accepted, and Sidney was authorized to spend up to two hundred thousand pounds, the same figure he had mentioned to Jonathan, to convert the Vanity into London Lights. He conferred with architects on the task of transforming the old house into a unique theater restaurant. He consulted with caterers over menus and dining arrangements. And lastly, after stories on the new project had filled trade newspapers, he met with his brother. Sidney wanted to open London Lights in November, and he wanted to open with a big name. When he sat down with Manny, he had only one question.

"Who are you going to get for me?"

"Tony Marino's willing to come over for the opening."

"Are you serious?"

"London Lights is big news over there as well as over here. Marino's agent contacted Lesser Brothers Inc., and intimated to Barry Levy that his client would appear at the opening providing the money and the conditions were acceptable."

"After what happened with that lunatic five years ago?" Sidney sat back and rocked with laughter. Marino hadn't been back to England since the coronation, nor would he be

569

welcome back. Following his remarks at London Airport before leaving the country, he'd given American reporters plenty of copy the instant he landed at Idlewild. One quote still stuck in Sidney's mind. When asked what he thought of London as a cultural center, Marino had snarled that it was nothing more than a stopover for the fish-and-chip crowd.

"Do I take it that means you're not interested in having Marino for the opening of London Lights?"

"You can tell the agent where to put his intimations. And while you're at it, you can let him know that Tony Marino can put his money and conditions in the same place."

"Who do you want for your opening then?"

Sidney threw out the first name that popped into his head. "Get me Judy Garland."

"Judy Garland . . . why not?"

The opening of London Lights in November 1958 was a glittering affair. Sidney, prouder of this venture than anything he had ever done, chose his first-night guests carefully. Although he had intended the nightspot to be a place for the average man, opening night was special. After much deliberation, he invited a who's who of British show business, mixing in friends and family and members of the press. Sidney's own table was by the dance floor. His personal guests were family, his mother, Naomi and the two girls, Manny and Rita, Jonathan and Bernice, and a girl named Kathryn whom Jonathan had asked if he could bring.

Rachel took in everything with a sense of wonder. She remembered the Vanity from the 1920's and her days with Harold Parker, whose office had been just around the corner. A frumpy old house was how Parker had always described it; a good place for shows that were going nowhere. And look what Sidney had done with it. Tables and chairs covered plush carpet where once rows of seats had stood mute witness to a hundred unremarkable productions. Sparkling chandeliers hung from the high ceiling. The virgin dance floor gleamed like burnished gold.

While the first-night crowd settled down with aperitifs, the club's two bands—one traditional, the other Latin-American—took turns playing. Several couples gathered on the dance floor. As a waltz began, Rachel felt a hand on her shoulder. She looked up to see Jonathan standing behind her.

"Give me a dance, Grandma?"

"Is that how young men ask ladies to dance with them these days? When I was young, you asked if you could have the pleasure of this dance."

Jonathan smiled. "It might not be a pleasure for you. I don't waltz very well."

"He waltzes like he drives," Manny said from the other side of the table. "Fast, faster, and very fast." Despite the joking criticism, he was pleased that his son had asked Rachel.

"What about your girlfriend, Jonathan? Why don't you dance with her?"

"She doesn't waltz well, either. She says I can have all the waltzes with you as long as I save her the jives and cha-chas."

Rachel allowed her grandson to lead her onto the dance floor. Although she hadn't danced for years, the steps returned quickly. She might be seventy-two, but age didn't stop her from enjoying one dance. As she circled the floor in Jonathan's arms, she saw people she knew. Famous people, members of the theater world of which she had been a part for almost forty years; stars who were represented by Manny or booked by Sidney. Tonight, the opening of another triumph for one of the Lesser boys, was more like a family affair.

The waltz ended. A quicker tune began. A samba. Jonathan started toward the family's table. Rachel held him back. "Can't you do a samba, Jonathan?"

He shook his head.

"Would you let your grandmother show you?"

"*You* can do it?"

"Of course. Then you can show Kathryn." She demonstrated the basic steps. He caught on quickly. "Your uncle Sidney said some of the best suggestions for London Lights were yours."

"The name was my idea."

"What else?"

"You're standing on it."

"The floor?" Rachel looked down to the gleaming wood. She didn't understand what was so special about it.

When they returned to the table, everyone stood up and applauded. "Not bad for an old lady," Sidney said, kissing his mother. Manny gave his son an affectionate pat on the shoulder as he sat down.

The band played another two songs, then waiters came around checking that none of the chairs touched the dance floor. Rachel heard machinery whir into soft motion . . . and then the floor began to move. She gasped in fright, and then, when understanding came, she turned to look at Jonathan. "This was your idea? A floor that makes you think you're seeing an earthquake?"

Sidney answered for him. "The best idea any of us had. It makes London Lights something very special."

An hour-long floor show of dancers, conjurers, and acrobats continued through dinner. When it finished, the floor was lowered. For an hour afterward, the two bands played dance music. Waiters came around once more to check that nothing impeded the rising stage. Rachel heard the sound of machinery again. The stage rose and clicked into place. A pianist picked out the first notes of "Somewhere Over the Rainbow." Applause exploded, and Judy Garland, the first star turn of London Lights, stepped out onto the stage. Hands clasped nervously in front of her, she stared into the lights for a few seconds, then she began to sing "The Man That Got Away."

She sang for an hour, interspersing songs with confessions about how scared she felt topping London Lights' first bill. She alternated between standing in one spot and roaming around the vast stage, looking down at the audience. Sometimes in the middle of a song she spotted a familiar face; between lines, she waved and called out greetings, spontaneous exhibitions of warmth that endeared her to the audience. Halfway through a belted-out version of "The White Cliffs of Dover," the wartime song popularized by Vera Lynn, Judy waved a hand at the band and stopped singing. She stood close to the table occupied by the Lesser family.

"Hi, Mr. Less, how are you tonight?"

"Just fine, Judy!" Sidney called back.

Instead of continuing singing, as she had done after earlier greetings, the singer had a suggestion for Sidney. "Mr. Less, why don't you take a bow?"

Sidney waved away the offer, a little uncomfortable at the sudden attention.

"Come on, Mr. Less." Judy turned to the audience, knowing she could find support among the other artists out there. "Let's hear it for the gentleman who's made London Lights into such a wonderful place!"

Roars of approval greeted the request. Sitting next to Sidney, Naomi dug him in the ribs and whispered, "You'd better acknowledge them. She's not going to sing again until she gets what she wants."

Sidney stood, gave a half-wave, half-salute, then sat down.

"Let's not forget Manny Lesser, either, who persuaded me to come over here. Not that I needed much persuasion to appear in a palace like this."

Manny stood, self-consciously, and waved acknowledgment. The music continued as Judy Garland returned to the business she knew best. Entertainment.

"I believe you're blushing," Naomi told Sidney. "You should be used to taking bows in the spotlight, you and Manny both."

"We were too busy fighting in it to be taking bows," Manny said. "Right, Mama?"

Rachel nodded but said nothing. She was too overcome by emotion to speak. Seeing her sons honored from the stage by such a world-famous performer, and then watching Manny and Sidney respond to the applause of the British show business elite, brought home to Rachel exactly how far they had all come.

The Lessers were the first family of British entertainment, even if one of them was a Less.

The reception given by the press to the theater restaurant was everything Sidney and the Partnership could have hoped for. The *Evening News*'s description of London Lights—"At little more than two pounds a head, it offers world-class entertainment tailored to the average pocket"—summed up the feeling adequately. The public flocked to London's newest nightspot.

After Judy Garland, Sidney brought in another American star: Sophie Tucker. Although in her seventies, she turned in an electrifying performance. Like Judy Garland, she made a point of stopping, midway through her show, at the table where Sidney and Naomi sat with their guests. Instead of calling out a greeting to Sidney, the last of the red-hot mamas singled out Rachel.

"Your sons requested this song especially for you, Mrs. Lesser." Sophie began to sing the number for which she was most famous: "My Yiddishe Momma." It brought the house down, and it brought more than a single tear to Rachel's eyes.

After the show, Rachel visited the American star in her dressing room to thank her for the salute. "We're the same age, Miss Tucker, so why should you singing 'My Yiddishe Momma' make me so emotional?"

The singer laughed delightedly. "Two reasons, Mrs. Lesser. The first is that no one ever sang that song like I do. The second is that you knew I was singing on behalf of your two wonderful sons."

"Yes," Rachel said softly. "They are wonderful sons, aren't they?"

The opening of London Lights launched the two brothers on another bout of competitiveness—to see who could own the largest chunk of show business. Manny was chairman of Lesser Brothers, an international agency, and also chairman of White Hart Productions. Sidney, with Gordon Prideaux, was joint managing director of the Rialto Playhouse Partnership, and personally responsible for all the acts that appeared at London Lights. Each new television production deal that Manny swung was immediately eclipsed by Sidney's news of another big-name star for London Lights. And each new signing by Sidney, it seemed, was overshadowed by another of Manny's deals.

After all the early struggles, life had become a ride on an express elevator that went in only one direction—up. Success followed success until both brothers felt they could easily become jaded. What thrill could a new achievement bring when so many notable exploits had gone before? But late in the spring of 1962, Sidney found a new thrill. One he had anticipated for years, and one which would never lose its excitement.

It began with Gordon Prideaux asking Sidney to lunch. "A business lunch," he stressed. "We need to resolve an issue." Gordon took Sidney to Gennaro's in Soho. During the meal, he said nothing of importance. He stuck with world events—the trouble in Algeria, the execution in Israel of Adolf Eichmann, the coming World Cup soccer championship in Chile. Sidney wondered what was troubling his partner. Gordon never normally rambled on like this, but Sidney made no attempt to push him. At last, as they lingered over coffee, Gordon came to the reason for the lunch meeting. "It's hard to believe we've been together eight years now, Sidney."

"Ever since the Partnership took pity on a brilliant but broke impresario."

Gordon laughed. "Believe me, no one took pity on you. You represented valuable property which we wanted. Has it been a good eight years?"

"It's been a fantastic eight years. We've had numerous top shows, we've expanded the Partnership's area of operation, London Lights is the biggest thing to hit British entertainment since talking pictures."

Gordon nodded in agreement with every claim. "Much of it's been due to you, Sidney. You carry the talent side of the Partnership, I carry the business. Now I'm asking you to shoulder the responsibility for one more piece of work."

"Go on."

"This year's Performing Artists' Gala, we've lined up a marvelous cast—"

Sidney began to run through the cast, names to be spoken with pride and pleasure. "Edith Piaf, Danny Kaye, Tony Hancock, Maurice Chevalier . . ."

"That's right. Possibly the finest gala ever. I want you to handle every single aspect of this year's gala."

"Everything? You mean . . . ?"

"Yes. I believe you deserve the honor of introducing the cast to our royal guest of honor. And if memory serves me right"—Gordon's scarred face split into a wide smile—"Her

Majesty the Queen has graciously accepted the invitation to attend this year's gala."

Sidney practiced his bow in front of a mirror for days before the gala. Was it too obsequious and groveling? Or was it too shallow, as though he didn't give a damn? He rehearsed offering his hand; he didn't want to shove it in the Queen's face, nor did he want to extend it too little and make Her Majesty come to him. He used Naomi, Andrea, and Linda as stand-ins. Once he even astonished the housekeeper by bowing to her, taking her hand, and saying with careful enunciation, "Good evening, ma'am."

Naomi did her best to calm him. She tried soothing words and when they didn't work, she used humor. "When you greet the Queen, you'll be trembling so much she'll think you're having an attack of palsy. You'll frighten her right out of the theater."

"This thing has got me more nervous than any first night, Naomi. Than stepping onto any stage."

"Gordon was never nervous."

"He's used to the pressure, he's done it so many times."

"One of those times had to be his first."

Sidney was not about to yield to logic. "He inherited iron nerves from his old man."

"You inherited some pretty sound characteristics as well."

"From my mother?"

"Who else? You'd better make sure she's at the Playhouse that night. She wouldn't want to miss this for anything."

Sidney made sure. Rachel attended the show with Manny and Rita. Her greatest pleasure came not from watching the two dozen international stars who had come together for the gala, but from looking at the royal box, where Sidney and Naomi sat with the guest of honor.

Following the show, Rachel attended the reception where Sidney presented members of the cast to the Queen. Afterward, brimming with pleasure, he turned to Naomi and his mother.

"How did I do?"

"Like you've been hobnobbing with royalty all your life," Naomi answered.

"My mother left Russia to avoid such hobnobbing." He turned to Rachel. "Well, Mama?"

"I noticed that before the show a bouquet was presented to the Queen."

"That's right."

Sidney's success emboldened Rachel. "Next year I would like to be the one who presents the bouquet to the royal guest."

Delighted at the way his first gala had gone, Sidney answered, "And so you shall be."

Two days later, Rachel received four copies of a contract from the Rialto Playhouse Partnership in the mail, booking her services as bouquet-presenter at the 1963 Performing Artists' Gala. All four were signed by Sidney and witnessed by Naomi. Rachel signed her name to the contracts, had them witnessed by Manny, kept one, and returned the rest. At seventy-six, she only hoped it would please God to keep her alive one more year so that she could honor this unusual contract.

Chapter Twenty-six

Watching his daughter and son grow, Jimmy found himself dwelling more and more on the parents' curse—the wish that all children became parents to children exactly like themselves.

The curse had not come back to haunt him with his daughter. Josephine, in 1962, just finishing her sophomore year at Vassar was everything a father could hope for. Seeking a degree in liberal arts, she worked hard to gain consistently high grades. During vacations, she worked just as hard. While other Vassar girls enjoyed the summer or performed field work related to their studies, Josephine returned to New York to work as an assistant on the *Messenger*'s picture desk.

It was with Harold that the curse came home with a vengeance. Every time Jimmy felt infuriated with his teenage son, he could see and hear his own father. When Jimmy said, "You're fourteen, Harold, it's time you started giving some serious thought to what you're going to do with your life," Zalman's voice, repeating the same words, echoed in Jimmy's ear.

At school, Harold's work began to deteriorate. He displayed interest in the arts—painting, music, and drama—but rigid disciplines such as math and science failed to raise enthusiasm within him. "Do you know what use subjects like art and music will be to you in real life?" Jimmy demanded when Harold brought home an uninspiring report card at the end of the summer semester. "You'll be able to work as a waiter somewhere, providing you don't drop the plates."

"Josephine's going for a liberal arts degree."

"She's a girl, she can," Jimmy shot back. "A man's got to have a much stronger grip on life. Besides, Josephine knows exactly what she wants to do. She's going to work on the *Messenger* as a photographer. She's only getting a degree because her mother and I insisted on it."

"Would you like to work on the paper during the summer?" Zalman asked.

"No thanks, Grandpa. I'm going away to camp, remember?" Harold smiled happily at the prospect and left the room.

Jimmy turned in exasperation to his father. "I know, it's the curse."

"How many times do you want me to say you were just the same? And you *stayed* the same until you were far older than fourteen. You're sending him to camp. I sent you to Europe."

"I changed because I was forced to change, but I'll be damned if I'll get myself into trouble just so Harold can understand the meaning of responsibility. Besides, I don't want Harold going through any kind of trauma; I'm not sure he could cope."

"I never thought you'd be able to cope, either," Zalman said. "I was wrong, and you're probably wrong as well."

Jimmy left it at that. The curse existed, and all he could do was wait until circumstances lifted it.

Like the rest of the country, Jimmy sweated through the events of that October as the United States and Russia squared off over the presence of offensive missiles and bombers in Cuba. Jimmy, at least, did not have to wait for news to be printed or aired. He kept constantly up to date with wire reports that came into both his New York office and his study in the house at Rye. As he scanned the increasingly grave reports, he wondered whether Josephine would finish her junior year at Vassar. Would she even finish this semester? Would Sonya bring out another issue of *American Miss?* Would Harold ever have the opportunity to understand what life was all about?

Zalman provided an anchor for Jimmy in those troubled

times. "First, Jimmy, you've got to understand the Russian mind. This Kruschev, he's painted himself into a corner over Castro and he desperately wants to get out of it without starting a nuclear war, but he can't be seen grabbing at the first opportunity. That won't do him any good here or in his own country. He's got to be seen to get out of it on his own terms."

With those words ringing in his ears, Jimmy wrote one of his editorials for the *Messenger*. He praised President Kennedy's firmness in standing up to the Soviets by blockading Cuba, and he explained the necessity of understanding the Russian psyche. The Soviets would bargain, he said, but only when they could be seen to take something away from the bargaining table.

Jimmy was at the *Messenger* when word came that Cuba-bound ships had changed course to avoid confronting the American fleet. He went around the entire newspaper, shaking hands with everyone he saw. When Kruschev, after a week of nail-biting tension, agreed to dismantle all bases and ship the missiles back to Russia, Jimmy wrote another commentary, congratulating Kennedy for combining resolution with perception. Kruschev had removed his missiles, but he had gained a promise that America would cease its blockade of Cuba and would not invade the country; he had left the bargaining table with something in his hand.

That year, Thanksgiving was a special holiday. Jimmy believed every American had good reason to give thanks. He did something he had never done before: he arranged for each employee of Messenger Publications to receive a turkey. The gesture was so well received that Jimmy decided to make it an annual display of the fondness he felt for those who worked for him.

Thanksgiving at Rye was a family affair. Josephine came down from Vassar to join her parents, brother, and grandfather. As Jimmy carved the turkey, he asked Sonya, "Does it still confuse you that our Thanksgiving comes later than the Canadian one?"

Sonya just smiled. After twenty-three years of marriage, she was accustomed to Jimmy's teasing about her Canadian background. He knew the dates of all Canadian holidays, and on those days she would invariably receive a bouquet or small gift with an attached card that read "Happy Dominion Day!" or "Happy Victoria Day!"

"You know," Jimmy continued, "I'm never sure that Canada has any reason to have a Thanksgiving holiday. After all, what do Canadians have to be thankful for? They live in a country bigger than the United States, yet only a tiny strip of it is habitable. Even then, they freeze for six months of the year."

"They're thankful that they're not Americans," Sonya replied. "Especially during the past few weeks. They're thankful that the rockets were aimed at New York, Chicago, and Washington, not Montreal, Toronto, and Ottawa."

Josephine spoke up, taking her father's side. "Read Neville Shute's *On the Beach*. If someone's stupid enough to press the button, there won't be any safe havens. If the explosions don't kill everyone, radioactivity will."

"Did anyone give thanks when you lived in Russia, Grandpa?" Harold asked.

Zalman gave a sour grin. "Sure, the *muzhiks* gave thanks that they had enough to drink. The Jews gave thanks that, no matter how destitute their surroundings, they weren't *muzhiks*. And the country's rulers gave thanks for the ignorance that shielded them from seeing their own impending downfall."

"What's a *muzhik?*" Harold asked.

"A peasant, an oaf, a man with no class or breeding but perhaps enough cunning to pull the wool over some people's eyes. Kruschev, he's a *muzhik*. Only a *muzhik* would bang his shoe at the United Nations." He looked at Jimmy. "Remember when I told you about the Spanish civil war being a rehearsal for a full-scale conflict between the forces of good and evil? Remember I said the devil was getting the upper hand?"

Jimmy had to think, then he nodded, amazed that his father could recall something that had happened more than twenty-six years ago.

"Well, he almost got the upper hand again. If it hadn't been for Kennedy's resolve, and that little *muzhik* Kruschev blinking, hell would have broken loose. You know, if I really believed in anything, I'd say this Thanksgiving would be a perfect time to offer up a prayer of gratitude."

"To the force of good?" Jimmy asked.

"Of course. What else?"

Jimmy looked down at his plate to hide his smile. For the second time in twenty-six years, his father had come as close as he had ever come to admitting that some supreme being kept an eye on the world's affairs.

Jimmy's grateful Thanksgiving mood lasted for almost a month. Until, on Christmas Eve, a shattering event made his gratitude yield to disappointment and disbelief, and caused him to speculate on whether any of his achievements had significance.

On Christmas Eve, Jimmy had a lunch appointment with Frank Kinsella. It was one in a series of monthly lunch dates between the publisher and the police inspector. Jimmy always eagerly anticipated the meetings. Kinsella made an interesting friend, taking Jimmy to restaurants in unusual areas of town and pointing out, between bites of food, questionable characters. Kinsella, likewise, knew that after these lunches he could always anticipate favorable exposure in the *Messenger,* invaluable to him in his search for the one star of a deputy chief.

When Kinsella arrived, he whetted Jimmy's appetite immediately by saying, "Today I'm going to introduce you to a particularly despicable class of criminal—a blackmailer."

In the outer office, Jimmy told Brian Gilbert that he would be gone for a couple of hours; he had no further appointments that afternoon. "Will you be here when I get back or will you be taking off early?"

"I'll be here, Mr. J. I'm meeting someone for lunch, then I'll be around for the rest of the day."

"Good. I want to see you," he said with a wink that hinted of a surprise. Gilbert guessed rightly that his boss's summons concerned a Christmas gift.

Jimmy rode the elevator with Kinsella to ground level. This time, the policeman had a plain blue Chrysler. Jimmy felt vaguely disappointed. Like a boy, he enjoyed his rides in a police car. "Where are we going?"

"We'll drive around first. I want to tell you all about blackmailers. I've got a special hate for them. They belong on the same slime level as the pimps and the pushers, and they deserve nothing short of a one-way trip to the dog-meat factory."

Kinsella drove up and down avenues and back and forth along streets while he educated Jimmy on the business of blackmail. "It comes in all forms. There's the simple, harmless kind of blackmail where a wife won't come across until her husband agrees to paint the damned kitchen the eggshell-blue she wants it. There's the complex kind, government-level spy stuff, where the Russians put the pressure on some American diplomat after they get pictures of him fooling around with a fag. And then there's the real slimy, grimy kind of blackmail, which is where we come in. Much of the time it doesn't come to light because the victims are too frightened to complain, too scared that public exposure of their secret will cause them even more pain and grief than the actual blackmail. Our hands are tied then, and so it goes on ad infinitum."

"This blackmailer you're going to show me, has his victim come to you? Is that how you know about him?"

Kinsella stopped the car for lights at the intersection of Sixth Avenue and West Fourth Street. A stream of people surged across the road. "He came to us a couple of weeks back. Which is very surprising, because this victim happens to be a crook."

"What kind of a crook?"

"Embezzler. His name's Larry Flynn and he works for a Wall Street brokerage firm. He found a system of sticking to some of the money that passed through his hands. Nothing monumental, a thousand here, a thousand there. Our blackmailer"—Kinsella set the car rolling as the lights changed—"learned about this scam and got his teeth into Flynn. Everything Flynn took he's had to pass to the blackmailer."

"He was taking the risk of stealing, but seeing none of the profit, eh?"

"Precisely. And our piece of garbage isn't content to wait for Flynn to choose his own time—he gives him instructions on when to steal. That's why he came to us. We made a deal.

583

We wouldn't prosecute if he helped us put this blackmailer out of business."

Pulling into a no-parking zone, Kinsella turned off the engine and stuck a badge in the window. Jimmy followed the burly policeman into a large self-service delicatessen. It was the kind of restaurant Jimmy would never normally patronize, but in the company of Kinsella, such places promised excitement. The two men ordered sandwiches and took them to a booth at the rear from where they could watch the entire restaurant.

Kinsella took a large bite out of a pastrami sandwich. "Flynn, it turns out, isn't the only victim dangling on our blackmailer's string. He has a dozen other similar victims, small men caught with their hands in the cash register. And he's milking every one of them for a tidy sum. There's Flynn now."

Jimmy saw a thin, pale-faced man with sandy hair approach the counter and give his order. Flynn glanced once at Kinsella, then looked away. When his sandwich was ready, he took it to a booth at the other end of the restaurant.

"How does the blackmailer locate his targets?"

"He uses snitches, informers to pass information on anyone who's doing what they shouldn't be doing. He pays by results."

Jimmy found that funny. "Isn't that how the police work? Maybe this blackmailer's a cop. Do you have any blackmailers in the department?"

"Why should I look in the police department?" Kinsella answered deadpan. "Newspapermen work the same way, don't they?"

The smile fell from Jimmy's face. "A newspaperman?"

"Sure. Think of it as public relations in reverse. Instead of paying some guy to get your name in the paper, you pay him to keep it out."

"A newspaperman?" Jimmy repeated numbly.

"Here's Flynn's man now. See for yourself."

Jimmy looked, and his heart plummeted through the pit of his stomach and onto the floor. Entering the restaurant, looking distinctly out of place in his custom-made suit and cashmere topcoat, was Brian Gilbert. Jimmy's personal as-

584

sistant did not go to the counter. He slid into the booth opposite Flynn and the two men began to talk.

"Flynn's wired," Kinsella explained. "You'll be able to hear later on what was said."

"I don't want to. I just want to get out of here before I throw up. Is there a back door, some way I can leave without having him see me?"

Kinsella indicated the door leading to the washrooms. Jimmy walked through to the alley that ran behind the restaurant. Kinsella joined him and the two men returned to the car.

Jimmy sat in the car, breathing deeply as he tried to control his jumping nerves. The new clothes Gilbert always wore, the new cars, the fancy apartment. Now Jimmy knew the truth. "What are you going to do?" he asked at last.

"Listen to what was said. Flynn had money on him, money we marked. When we pull Gilbert in, we'll find some of that money on him as well."

"Do me a favor."

"Sure."

"Don't arrest him until later today. Let him come back to the office. I want to fire him first. I don't want him to be an employee of Messenger Publications when he's arrested."

"Leave it with me."

At the Messenger Building, Jimmy went upstairs. He passed through the outer office without glancing at Gilbert's empty chair. Once inside his own office, he sat down at his desk and closed his eyes in pain. He felt betrayed. A man he had liked and trusted, a man with whom he had worked so closely—exposed as a blackmailer. Right there on the same slime level, to use Kinsella's description, as pimps and pushers. Jimmy opened his eyes and stared at the memorable front pages that were fixed to the paneled walls. His eyes fastened on Helen's picture. This was the blackest, bitterest day of *Messenger* history since Helen's death.

Gilbert returned just after two, sticking his head into Jimmy's office with a cheerful "I'm back, Mr. J. What did you want to see me for?"

"Originally"—Jimmy took a package from his desk drawer—"to give you this."

Gilbert stepped into the office and picked up the package. He opened it to find a pair of gold cuff links engraved with the *Messenger* logo. "Thanks a lot, Mr. J. They're—" He broke off, his gratitude frozen by the odd expression on Jimmy's face, the mixture of fury and anguish that contorted his features into a mask of misery.

"No reprehensible son of a bitch is fit to wear those!" Jimmy shouted, snatching the cuff links from Gilbert's grasp and tossing them into the trash can.

"What are you talking about, Mr. J.?"

"Don't Mr. J. me! You used your position as a platform for your loathsome extortion scheme! You used sources you cultivated as a newspaperman to make yourself rich! All those stories about wealthy girlfriends . . . ! I believed you because I had no reason to do otherwise. And all the time you were putting the pinch on miserable little people who, next to you, are saints!"

Gilbert's face had been growing progressively paler. He stuffed his hands into the pockets of his coat to stop them from shaking. "How did you—?"

"Find out? I'm a newspaperman. I have sources. And you can bet your last extorted dollar that those sources are going to stick you in jail where you belong. Now get out of here! I don't want to see you or hear from you ever again!"

Gilbert left. Jimmy slumped down into his chair and buried his face in his hands. What a lousy way to begin Christmas!

If Brian Gilbert had worked for any of the departments within Messenger Publications, heads would have rolled. Jimmy, on the principle that superiors should know what their people are doing, would have held responsible those immediately above Gilbert, and he would have fired them. As it was, Gilbert had worked for no one but Jimmy, and because of that, Jimmy carried the blame alone.

His paternalistic attitude altered sharply. The people he once referred to as his extended family he now regarded with suspicion. Gilbert's shortcomings made Jimmy view everyone with a new perspective. If a fashion editor on the *Messenger* wore a fur coat Jimmy felt was above her means, he made inquiries into her background. If a business writer was seen driving a new Cadillac, Jimmy ordered Richard Hartford to learn how the man could afford it on his salary. There was not to be a hint of a *Messenger* journalist taking bribes to get something into print. In turn, reporters who had once regarded the *Messenger* as the best paper to work on in New York began to change their minds. Rather than explain how they could afford to live a certain style, many left. Such desertions did not stop Jimmy from widening what he termed his campaign of ethics. He told Marvin Baker to carefully vet programs produced by WMES; he didn't want anyone getting airtime because of a kickback to a producer.

While the *Messenger* carried only token reports of Gilbert's arrest and subsequent trial, other newspapers had a field day. Anything of an unsavory nature in the company's history was dragged up and rehashed. Jimmy, to his horror, saw references to his father's tax troubles. And before that, to the establishment of *Form Guide* and the racing wire, and Zalman's association with a gangster called Charlie Bruno. At home, among the only people he now completely trusted, he complained bitterly about what he considered the lack of ethics in the newspaper industry. Sonya was sympathetic, but Zalman just laughed.

"It's a dog-eat-dog world out there, Jimmy, that's what I've always tried to tell you."

"But we're a newspaper, just like the *Times* or the *Post.*"

"You're only correct about the first syllable. Forget the paper, right now we're just *news.* Tell me something, if Brian had worked for the *Journal-American* and he'd done the same shady deals there, would you have stopped the *Messenger* reporting it?"

Jimmy considered the question for a long time. "Yes, I think I would have done exactly that."

"Then I've failed miserably," Zalman responded, "because I didn't make any kind of a damned newspaperman out of you at all."

Taking his father's words to heart, Jimmy lifted his ban order on stories about the Gilbert case. Full reports started to appear. They only added to Jimmy's embarrassment as other newspapers described the about-face as a publisher's belated attempt at public breast-beating.

Jimmy took comfort wherever he could find it. Rare messages of support were read over and over. Some, from public figures, appeared on the letters page. One letter Jimmy particularly appreciated came from William Baron in Washington. It praised both the *Messenger* and the Isaacson family, and stressed that no sound establishment should be tainted by one bad egg. Jimmy ordered it placed prominently in the newspaper.

The scandal even touched Jimmy's children, but in totally different ways. At Vassar, Josephine found her family's checkered history created celebrity status for her among her fellow students. But at the school Harold attended, the fifteen-year-old boy encountered hostility and derision. He came home one day close to tears.

"This was on my desk," he said, holding out a piece of paper.

If the note had not been addressed to his son, Jimmy might have laughed. It was that childish. Letters cut from newspaper headlines spelled out a death threat. Below the message was a crudely drawn black hand.

Zalman took it from Jimmy's grasp. "Someone in your school's been watching too many episodes of *The Untouchables.*" He screwed the piece of paper into a ball and threw it away.

Jimmy was unable to treat the matter so lightly. He had no doubt the message was just some adolescent's idea of a joke, but it was ill-intended and ill-received. Harold was too sensitive to cope well with such derision; he couldn't take pressure the way his sister could.

What kind of quirk was it, he wondered, that dictated the women in the family were strong while the men, with the exception of Zalman, were weak? Or had his own father, by being so vital and willful, somehow kept for himself the strength of future generations of Isaacson men?

The bleak days of Brian Gilbert's exposure and trial, leading to a five-year prison sentence, caused Jimmy much introspection. He had reached the nadir of his professional life.

Everything he had achieved was overshadowed by the acts of one man.

Instead of eagerly anticipating the future, as had been his custom, Jimmy began to look back. He studied what Messenger Publications controlled, and he asked himself what had been his achievements? What had he started? What had he envisioned, and what had he built?

The answer was depressing. The *Messenger* itself had been in New York long before he was born. *Form Guide* had appeared when he was in short pants. Nor could Jimmy claim responsibility for *American Miss* and *TV Diary,* two of the biggest moneymakers in the company. Sonya had dreamed up the magazine she continued to edit, and his father, running rampant through a second youth—or was it a third?—had conceived the television book. Of the other two dozen magazines, some were Jimmy's some were not. None was particularly notable. Jimmy found himself left with one major achievement only. WMES, the television station. And that, in truth, was nothing more than a minor tooth in the gear.

As he neared fifty, Jimmy Isaacson wondered, with his life more than half over, whether he should look for some more meaningful endeavor.

Chapter Twenty-seven

Sidney honored the contract he had made with his mother, and at the 1963 Performing Artists' Gala, Rachel's wish came true. Listed in the program, beneath the names of the stars who would appear in the charity show, was the brief note that a bouquet would be presented to the Queen Mother, that evening's guest of honor, by Mrs. Rachel Lesser.

Sidney made the introduction, then stood back to give his mother her moment of glory. She had been practicing for weeks, a mirror of Sidney himself a year earlier when he had learned that Gordon Prideaux was turning over responsibility for the gala to him. Restraining a smile, Sidney watched his mother present the bouquet, a frail, petite woman in a pale-green dress, her white hair still carefully groomed from that morning's trip to the salon, eyes sparkling behind thin gold glasses. A few words were passed. Rachel smiled. Some more words, and the Queen Mother smiled. Then the moment was over.

"What did she say to you when she accepted the bouquet?" Sidney whispered.

"She told me I had every reason to be very proud of my children, of you for putting on this wonderful show, and of Manny for selling British stars and British television abroad."

"And what did you say to her?"

"I told her she had every reason to be very proud of her children as well."

Sidney turned away before he burst out laughing. His

mother was perfectly capable of making such a comment. She wouldn't have made it out of disrespect. If anything, just the opposite was true. It was an example of the love Rachel felt for her adopted country and its establishment.

Presenting the bouquet lent Rachel courage. Before she returned to the apartment in the Grosvenor House Hotel, she took Sidney aside. "When the Queen is the guest of honor, may I present a bouquet to her as well?"

Sidney stared into his mother's eyes. How could you refuse a woman of seventy-seven a request as simple as handing a bouquet to the Queen of England? "Of course you can, Mama. Of course you can. Do you want me to send you another contract?"

"No. I think I can take your word for it."

The excitement of the evening triggered a stream of memories for Rachel, taking her back to when it had all really started. Sixty years ago, to that one instant in her life when she had been utterly alone, the moment fate had sent the carriage of Tobias and Hannah Dekker clattering across the bridge in Rotterdam in time to save a young Russian girl from drowning.

Instead of sleeping, Rachel lay staring up at the ceiling as though it were a screen, watching those sixty years unfold. Among the scenes there was much to be proud of, and just as much to make her sad.

The greatest single moment of heartbreak was the loss of Bernard, but in some kind of bizarre compensation, his death had served to bring his two warring brothers together. Children to be proud of, wasn't that how the Queen Mother had described them? As one mother to another, who should know better?

On her imaginary ceiling screen, a familiar room materialized. Rachel recognized the office where Harold Parker had plied his trade. She had enjoyed her years there, first with Parker, and then with Bernard. Just one bad moment stained the memories. She saw a door open. A tall fair-haired man stood in the doorway, his one good hand gripping a heavy walking stick, slamming it down across Parker's desk, then using it as a weapon to bludgeon Parker.

Whatever, Rachel wondered, had become of Jacob?

Since that single letter back in 1925, she had never heard a word from him. Thirty-eight years! That was how long had passed. Strange, it seemed much shorter. She thought of him often, but she had respected his unspoken wish to be left alone to go about his new life in his new country. Both Manny and Sidney had visited Toronto. Unable to quench their curiosity, they had looked up the name of Jacob Lesser in the telephone directory and made inquiries at Jewish community centers. They had found four men with that name, men who differed in age from twenty-four to seventy. All immigrants, from different parts of Europe. And all with one common characteristic—all four men had two good arms. Rachel's Jacob had done one of three things: he had changed his name, moved, or died before Manny and Sidney had made inquiries about him. Rachel could not fault her sons for looking. Despite his troubles, Jacob was still their father. But when they had reported their failure, Rachel had not been unhappy. Such meetings all too often yielded bitterness and confusion. It was better, sometimes, to let sleeping dogs lie.

The screen above her bed turned blank before filling with a familiar structure that had meant so much to both her and Jacob. A building with a blue-and-white sign that read "The Dekker Boys' Club." Rachel hadn't been to the East End for so long. The last time had been a couple of years ago when Manny and Rita had come into town one Wednesday to take her to dinner at Bloom's restaurant. Afterward Manny had driven around Whitechapel, asking Rachel if she recognized any of it. Where the club had been stood an anonymous office building.

Tobias and Hannah Dekker, the two most important people in Rachel's life. More meaningful even than Manny and Sidney, for without Tobias and Hannah none of this could have come about. Her life would have finished at seventeen, a drowning victim in Rotterdam, buried in some unmarked pauper's grave. Now she was a somebody, a woman with sons who arranged for her to be in the same room with royalty. Rachel felt an overwhelming gratitude for the couple who had been like parents to her. Dead these forty-four years, they still lived on in Rachel and all she did. They would be

592

so proud if only they could know. As proud as Rachel was herself.

Rachel panicked. She started to perspire. Her heart thumped inside her chest. Her hands clutched the covers. She was seventy-seven. How long did she have left? How long in which to perform the one act she must before death took her? For in that moment of remembering the Dekkers, sharp understanding had come. When she, the only memorial to the lives of Hannah and Tobias, died, there would be nothing to signify that they had ever lived.

Long ago, Tobias had visualized and built his own memorial. Through circumstances beyond his control, he had known the heartbreak of losing it. It was up to Rachel to build it once more. It was her responsibility to make sure the Dekker Boys' Club lived again.

Rachel wasted no time in sharing the dream with her sons. She called them to the apartment and said, "I want to create a memorial to Hannah and Tobias. You remember the boys' club, don't you? I'd like to build it again."

Sidney shook his head. "Mama, those kinds of clubs aren't necessary anymore. They were designed to help newcomers blend into British society during a period of great immigration."

"Immigrants coming here today find the red carpet rolled out for them," Manny said. "It's not like when your generation of immigrants came over, Mama. You might have had help, but all the other immigrants had to fight every inch of the way. Their first question was where they could find work. When modern immigrants arrive, the first thing they want to know is where to sign on for national assistance."

Rachel understood, and she could sympathize with the views of her sons. People entering Britain now expected handouts from the welfare state. The flood had become so great that only the previous year an Act of Parliament had been passed to restrict immigration. But no legislation could restrict Rachel's vision. "Animosity toward newcomers continues, only instead of referring to the new immigrants as 'bloody Jews,' the British now call them 'bloody wogs.' To stop this hatred, you have to begin with the children. That's the kind of club I'm thinking about. A youth club for boys and girls of all ethnic backgrounds. And I think it should be in the East End of London, because that area has been the focal point of immigration into this country since the Huguenots came here three hundred years ago."

"Will you let us think about it, Mama?" Sidney asked. Both he and Manny had full schedules; they could not spare time to invest in philanthropic schemes that might never see fruition.

"I'll be seventy-eight next birthday," Rachel warned. "Don't think about it too long."

Manny and Sidney promised they would not.

Rachel took her own warning seriously. God had already given her time to realize one ambition—presenting a bouquet to the guest of honor at the Performing Artists' Gala. She hoped He would grant her enough time to perform the same act for the Queen. Now she wished for time enough to make her dream of a youth club come true. Waiting for her sons to do everything was pushing her luck. She would have to do the groundwork herself. Then, when they saw how serious she was, they would find the time to help her.

The very next morning, Rachel stepped out of the Grosvenor House into a taxi. "Please take me to the East End."

"Any particular address?"

"Just drive me around. I haven't had a good look at the East End for many years. I want to reacquaint myself with it."

"East End it is." The driver pulled away from the hotel, his mind full of questions. People he picked up at the Grosvenor House usually gave swanky addresses. He'd never had a fare who asked for a tour of the East End of London.

Rachel settled down in the back of the taxi, looking at the driver's profile each time he turned sideways. After a mile, she asked his name.

"Daniel Kaye."

"Are you any relation to *the* Danny Kaye?"

The driver chuckled. "I *am the* Danny Kaye, lady. If you ever see the American comedian, ask if he's any relation to me."

Rachel smiled, and wondered what the driver would think

if he knew that one of her sons had once arranged for Danny Kaye to appear in London. "What was your name before it was Kaye?"

The taxi stopped at lights. With no interior mirror, the driver had to turn around to look at the elderly woman sitting primly in the back of his cab. "Kopelovitch."

"Why did you change it?"

"It wouldn't fit on my driving license." He looked forward again as the light turned green. "Why does anyone change a name? What was yours?"

"Once it was Isakharov. Now it's Lesser."

"Pleased to meet you, Mrs. Lesser. Are you looking for memories in the East End?"

"Perhaps. Don't you have any?"

The driver shook his head. "I was born in Stoke Newington. My father left the East End the day he married my mother."

"Pity. You don't know what you missed."

Rachel spent four hours in the taxi, having Kaye ferry her up and down every street she had known as a young woman. Outside the office building that had replaced the club, she stood on the sidewalk and looked around, trying to recall what had been there before. It was so hard remembering. Perhaps if she had a picture, something to jog her memory, it would be easier. Everything seemed so new and antiseptic. She didn't know if bombs had fallen in this street or if everything had been torn down after the war as a matter of course.

The taxi returned her to Park Lane. She paid the amount on the meter and handed the driver a five-pound tip. "That's for being so patient with an old lady."

"Thank you. Did you find what you were looking for?"

"Not really. Before I find it, I have to know what it is."

Rachel made the trip again the next day, and every day after that. Sometimes she rode in the taxi all afternoon, other times she got out and walked, letting the taxi follow her. She came to know the area once more. She walked along streets with familiar names: Brick Lane, Wentworth Street, Middlesex Street. Many of the buildings were still there, as depressing now as they had been sixty years ago. Somehow, they had been lucky enough to escape the German bombs, and then she questioned whether that was so fortuitous after all. She only had to close her eyes and breathe in deeply and she could turn back the clock.

Each day she asked the new driver his name. When she thought he was Jewish she asked if he were familiar with the East End, not as a cabdriver but as a resident. Invariably, the older Jewish drivers had lived there at one time or another. One of them, a middle-aged man named Sonny Scheff, was even familiar with the Dekker Boys' Club. His father, he said, had belonged to it. Ben Scheff his name was. Rachel dug deeply into her memory to recollect the name. And when she did, she gasped.

"Did your father ever mention Harry Myers, Nathan Rabinowitz, or Morris Bloom?"

"They were his best friends. I remember as a boy watching the four of them play cards every Saturday night. Solo they played. They're all dead now. You knew them?"

"I thought they'd all been taught a very good lesson about gambling, but obviously I was wrong."

The driver laughed. "You mean when the club manager dealt from the bottom? I heard that story often. He lost an arm in the First World War, didn't he? And then he disappeared, Canada or somewhere."

"That was my husband." The driver bit his lip, and Rachel felt sorry for the man. "It was all a very long time ago."

The driver nodded, glad of Rachel's acceptance. "Too bad that club had to close. I heard it did a lot of good."

"I'm hoping to reopen it. That's what I'm doing now, looking for suitable premises."

When Sonny Scheff returned Rachel to the Grosvenor House, he refused to take her money. "Think of it as my contribution toward the new club."

Rachel entered her apartment with tears in her eyes, and knowing that everything would work out.

Gradually, Rachel drew up a list of half a dozen premises throughout the East End that she thought would be suitable for the club. Empty warehouses with lease or sale signs fixed to the wall; vacant office buildings; disused factories. She turned the list over to her sons who promised they would look into it. Rachel held out no great hopes. She understood how busy they were. If the club were to become reality, she would have to shoulder the bulk of the work. Just as she had done some sixty years before when she had debated the finer points of flooring with an Irish building foreman . . . and won!

On a cold and miserable October day at the end of her third week of traveling back and forth to the East End, she stepped once more into a taxi. As always, she asked the driver his name.

"Gerald Silver" came the reply.

"Can you remember what the East End used to be like, Mr. Silver?" She guessed this driver could. A tall, thin man, he appeared to be roughly the same age as her own sons.

"I try to forget it."

"Why?"

"Because when I came out of a dingy flat in Flower and Dean Street, I had a head full of big ideas."

"So did a lot of people."

"Maybe their ideas worked out. None of mine did." He peered through the rain-spattered windshield for several seconds before saying, "I didn't do half as well as your sons, Mrs. Lesser."

Rachel looked sharply at the driver. She could only make out part of his profile. A thin face with a sharp aquiline nose. Beneath his tweed cap, oily brown hair was streaked with gray.

"You don't remember me, do you, Mrs. Lesser? Let me give you a clue . . . my ex-wife's married to your son."

Gerald Silver? *Gerry* Silver! From Silver and Gold!

Rachel sat bolt upright and clutched at the door handle. She would have passed him on the street without recognition. She hadn't heard the name for fifteen years or so, not since Manny had once mentioned hearing he was trying to revive the old act. Obviously he had failed. Instead of being on the boards, he drove a cab. "Please stop the taxi. I want to get out."

"Here, Holborn in the middle of a downpour? You'll wait a week before you find an empty cab, Mrs. Lesser."

"It doesn't matter. I'll get the train. A bus."

Silver paid no attention. He drove on, accelerating as traffic thinned. "Believe me, Mrs. Lesser, I don't hold any grudges. Whatever happened twenty, twenty-five years ago, is water under the bridge. And probably my fault as well."

Rachel relaxed a fraction. "Your fault?"

"That double act with Naomi was going nowhere in a hurry. It was one-dimensional, nothing else. But rather than admit the truth to myself, I blamed Naomi. I hated her for a long time after that. I hated your son Sidney for breaking my jaw and stealing my wife. I hated your whole family for years."

"What changed your mind?"

"Hearing about your son being killed. I lost a brother, too. A younger brother. He was a commando, really enthusiastic. He was going to kill every German between the English Channel and Berlin. He died in the first wave that went ashore on D-Day."

Rachel had thought she was long past offering condolences for losses suffered during the war. She was wrong. "I'm sorry."

"Thanks. I'm sorry about Bernard as well."

"You tried to carry on the act after the war, didn't you?"

"Tried? That's a good word for it. Failed is a better one. I needed to make a living, so I cycled through London for six months. Instead of memorizing lines, I memorized street names and shortest routes. Now I'm a cabdriver like my old man before me." He slowed for a policeman on point duty. "Do you still want to get out, Mrs. Lesser?"

"No, thank you. I'm beginning to think our meeting like this is a fortunate coincidence."

Silver chuckled. "It's no coincidence at all. All the drivers get together now and again over a cup of tea. Sonny Scheff mentioned taking you around the East End. So did a couple of other lads. For the past four days I've been cruising by the Grosvenor House in case you came out. Today I got lucky."

"Are you married, Gerry?"

Silver plucked a small photograph from his wallet and passed it through the open partition. Rachel saw a dark-haired woman and two boys in their teens. "They look like a nice family."

"They are. This time I married for the right reason, because I was in love and I wanted a family. Not because I wanted to keep a chain on my partner in a second-rate variety act."

"Naomi couldn't have any children, you know. She and Sidney adopted two little girls. Well, they're not so little anymore. Andrea's twenty-three and Linda's nineteen."

"Naomi couldn't have children . . . ?" Silver seemed lost in thought as he drove. "I had no idea," he said at last. "But then there was an awful lot I had no idea about."

"Why were you waiting for me to come out?"

"Sonny said you were seeking premises for a new club. I thought I might be of assistance. I help manage a youth club where I live now, in Ilford. And that's not so far from the East End, is it?"

Rachel understood. All these years later, Gerry Silver was trying to make amends. Had remorse started when he heard fellow cabdrivers talk about taking Rachel to the East End, or had it been a sentiment he'd nursed for a long time, unable to do much about it until an opportunity surfaced? Rachel believed the second alternative to be true. No matter how much Silver wanted to redress earlier wrongs, doors would have been closed. Her two sons, especially Sidney, would never have entertained meeting with him. Rachel decided to appoint herself as peacemaker. With a family of his own—a wife and sons he obviously loved—Gerry Silver represented no threat to Sidney and Naomi's marriage. Rachel doubted that he ever had. His only interest in Naomi had been business.

"That's kind of you to offer, Gerry. I'd like that a lot."

Silver switched off the meter. When Rachel asked what he was doing, he said, "It's my cab. If I don't bring in any money, no one's going to moan at me."

"Not even your wife?"

"She'll understand."

Rachel sat back, wondering if Sidney and Naomi would be so understanding.

During the next few days, Gerry Silver checked out the premises Rachel had marked as possible sites for the club. He found fault with every one, explaining in detail to Rachel why he considered them unsuitable. One warehouse was too

599

close to the river; it would certainly have damp problems. An office building was unacceptable because there wasn't a single area large enough for dances to be held in.

"Dances?" Rachel asked. "There were no dances at the Dekker Boys' Club."

Silver laughed. "Pardon my saying so, Mrs. Lesser, but that was the dawn of history. These days youth clubs have dances."

"I suppose they do."

Silver drew up his own list from premises he'd spotted while driving his cab. One place he particularly liked was a small, vacant clothing factory in Stepney. He took Rachel to see it, pointing out what he considered the advantages. "It's an old building, but it's good and sound, with just the right mix of small and large areas."

Rachel inspected the three-story building. It was in far better shape than the building Tobias Dekker had purchased for the boys' club. Most of the windows were intact, the heating system worked, plaster was not falling from the walls and ceiling. What struck her most of all were the floors. They didn't sag or squeak when she walked across them. The building would suit her purpose very well.

"I wish we had a place like this in Ilford," Silver said.

"May I see your club one day?"

"Of course. I always manage it on Tuesday nights. Why don't I take you then?"

Rachel accepted, all the while wondering how she was going to break this news to her own family. First, that she had found a building she wanted; and second, that, in doing so, she had become friendly with the man who had once caused them to be thrown off the Partnership circuit. And most difficult of all, how was she going to bring them all together?

The next Tuesday, Silver collected Rachel at six-thirty in the evening and drove her to Ilford. The club was affiliated with a local synagogue. Silver's wife Betty was one of the helpers. Considerably younger than her husband—no more than forty-five, Rachel guessed—Betty was a chubby, dark-haired woman with bright brown eyes.

"Because of space restrictions, we have different age

600

groups on different nights," Silver explained. "Tonight belongs to the sixteen- to twenty-year-olds. It's my favorite group because it's so varied, some still at school or college while others are out working."

Diverse activities filled the first part of the evening. Rachel watched a group of amateur guitarists practicing. Next door, chess games were in progress. In another room, club members lined up to play at two Ping-Pong tables. Down in the building basement, boxing instruction was being given by a middle-aged man whose broken nose and flattened ear attested to experience in the sport. Wherever Rachel went with Silver, she noticed how the youngsters treated him with a cordial respect. It reminded her of the regard Jacob had been held in at the Dekker Boys' Club. Never would she have believed that Gerry Silver could be held in the same esteem. But then she had never imagined having sons who mingled with royalty.

At nine o'clock, the activities ceased. More than a hundred young men and women squeezed into the club's small assembly hall. From the stage, Silver read a couple of announcements regarding upcoming events, then he introduced a band whose name Rachel didn't catch. Judging from the applause, though, it was obviously familiar to club members. Behind Silver, a curtain rose to reveal four young men. Three held guitars; one sat behind drums. Silver stepped off the stage and the band began to play.

Silver rejoined Rachel. "Like the band?"

"I didn't hear the name."

"The Easterners. Four local boys who met right here a couple of years ago. They're talented, write their own songs. I helped get them into a couple of small clubs in the West End. They've been getting some work at American military bases as well, here and in Europe. Whenever they're home, they always make sure to do at least one date here. For nothing. For old time's sake."

"That's nice. I like people who don't turn their backs on humble beginnings." Rachel began to understand the respect Silver had among these young people. He cared about them. In turn, they cared about him. It was a pity this side of his personality had not surfaced earlier. And then again, she thought, perhaps it wasn't such a pity. Things had a way of working out for the best. "Who handles them?"

Silver mentioned the name of a small agency with which he had once worked. "That won't last much longer. Sooner or later, the Easterners are going to come to the notice of a major agent—"

"Like Lesser Brothers?"

"Or the Grades, or Harold Davidson, or whoever. And then they're going to take off like rockets."

Rachel turned her attention to the stage. The four musicians looked like any other group, suits with tight trousers and boxy jackets, hair cut in a mod style. But there was no denying that they had talent. Rachel's eighteen years out of the agency business had not dimmed her eye for that most rare of attributes. "Gerry, did you bring me here tonight to see the Easterners?"

He shook his head. "Normally on a weeknight, everyone dances to records. I only heard yesterday from Alan Jacobs—he's the drummer—that the group was back in town and free tonight."

Rachel smiled at the answer. She had just found a way of tying everything together.

Rachel wasted no time. The very next morning, she arrived at Manny's office and told him that she had just seen an outstanding musical group. "They're called the Easterners, and with the right management they'll be the next big pop stars. I think Lesser Brothers should offer that management before someone else gets in first."

"Since when are you interested in pop, Mama?"

"I was talent-spotting for you."

"Where is this group?"

"I saw them in Ilford."

"What were you doing out there?" Manny realized that he had very little idea what his mother got up to, where she went, whom she saw. For all he knew, she could have half a dozen boyfriends bringing flowers to her apartment. She told him only what she wanted him to know, otherwise her life was a private affair. At seventy-seven, she was as independent as ever.

"Ilford has a youth club I was interested in seeing. While I was there last night, this group played. They travel all over Britain and Europe, but they always come back to play for nothing at the club, because that was where they all got started."

Manny called for Carol Jones. The Welsh secretary had been with Lesser Brothers for seventeen years, and often second-guessed her boss. This time, when she came in with a fresh mug of tea, she was wrong. Manny wanted information, not tea. "Find out what you can about a group called the Easterners."

Carol returned two minutes later, with essentially the same information Rachel had already given her son. "When are they going to be playing again?" he asked his mother.

"This Saturday."

"I'll send someone to have a look at them."

Rachel shook her head. "I think you should go. It's more than just seeing this group. I also want you to see the premises I think are suitable for the new Dekker club."

"In Ilford?"

"Stepney. But the man who'll help to run it lives in Ilford. He's one of the managers of the club there. He helped me find the premises."

"The new club, that I'll help you with, Mama. Sidney and me, we'll organize a fund-raising concert. But count me out of the pop business, will you? I know nothing about it. For me, pop is Bing Crosby, and that maniac Tony Marino. I know nothing about these new groups, this Mersey sound, and whatever other sounds are coming up through the pipeline. We've got agents who specialize in the music the kids like. I'll send one of them."

"I still think you should go."

This time, Manny had no doubt. His mother was issuing an order, just like when he had been a child. She had never shouted, never raised her voice a fraction. But the steel was evident in her tone. He checked his diary. For once he had an empty Saturday, a free evening he could have spent at home with Rita. He couldn't remember the last time she had cooked dinner on a weekend for him at home. They always seemed to be on the run. "Why don't we go out to eat on

Saturday night, Mama, and then we'll go to Ilford to hear your discovery. If Bernice has nothing planned, we'll bring her as well. That's her kind of music. Perhaps she'll be able to advise me."

"And Jonathan?"

"You have to make an appointment to see Jonathan these days. He's too busy running around with his girlfriends to bother with us old fogies."

Manny and Rita called for Rachel early on Saturday evening. With them was Bernice. Rachel's seventeen-year-old granddaughter anticipated the evening eagerly, not so much for the chance to hear the Easterners, but to witness her parents attending such a show. Jonathan had told her to remember everything her father said, to document every complaint, every moan. They would all be able to laugh about it later.

After eating, they drove to Stepney, where Rachel pointed out the empty factory she wanted for the club. Manny climbed out of the car and walked around the building. "What's the name of the man who recommended this place to you?" he asked.

"You'll know soon enough." She wanted to keep Silver's name secret as long as possible. If Manny knew his identity so soon, he might refuse to visit Ilford on principle alone.

Manny recognized his mother's obstinacy; she would tell him only when she was good and ready. "This fellow must be a real Sir Galahad. He helps you out, he helps out this club in Ilford, he's trying to help this group. How did you meet him?"

"He's a cabdriver. He drove me around the East End and he became interested in my idea."

"He's a cabdriver," Manny repeated to Rita as he started the engine once more. "Because of a cabdriver, my mother's got us wasting our one free Saturday night of the year."

"You're not wasting anything," Rachel said.

"We'll see," Manny grumbled, but his heart wasn't in it. He still had faith in his mother's judgment. If she said she'd been talent-spotting, she'd been talent-spotting. If nothing else, he might get a new client out of the visit.

They reached Ilford when the club dance was almost an hour old. The hall was even fuller than Rachel remembered it from the previous Tuesday, groups of teenagers clustered around the perimeter, while bodies bounced and jumped in the center. The Easterners occupied the stage, playing a song Manny had never heard before.

"What happened to Bernice?" Rita asked, as, quite suddenly, she realized her daughter was no longer with them.

"Some handsome young man asked her for a dance the moment we entered the hall," Rachel answered. She spotted Gerry Silver standing close to the stage. He wore a dark-gray suit and looked very different from the time Rachel had seen him in the taxi. Now he was slim and elegant, the way Rachel remembered him from the days of Silver and Gold. He waved when he spotted Rachel and started to walk toward her. "There's the man who's been so helpful to me, Manny."

Manny put a smile on his face and flexed his right hand, ready to greet the other man. He was always happy to meet people who helped his mother. "Doesn't look much like a cabdriver, does he? In fact," Manny said as the man drew near, "he looks very, very familiar."

"Good God," Rita whispered. "It's Gerry Silver."

Silver joined the group just in time to hear his name. "Thank you for coming, Mrs. Lesser. Manny . . . Rita . . . how are you?"

Manny recovered first. "Just about speechless. What are you doing helping my mother? What are you doing helping here? Why are you, of all people, helping anyone?"

Instead of defending himself against Manny's abuse, Silver waited for Rachel to step in. "Manny, what happened between you all is history. Like most history, it's best left undisturbed."

"Only if you're not interested in learning anything from it," Manny fired back.

Rita touched his arm. "Why don't you listen to what your mother has to say?"

His wife's calm tone mollified Manny. Once, after Less, Lesser, and Least had been kicked off the Partnership circuit, Manny could have happily torn Gerry Silver to pieces with his bare hands. But twenty-eight years later, the animosity no longer existed. His opening, bitter fusillade had been nothing more than reflex, the shock of seeing for the first time in years a man he had once hated. When he tried digging for more of that bitterness, he struck empty. There was nothing left inside him, no feeling at all.

Silver used a soft, conciliatory tone. "I can understand you being angry at me. I'd also be mad at someone who got me banned from some of the best houses in the country. But if you really want my opinion, I think I did the biggest favor anyone has ever done for you."

"How's that?" At last, Manny felt some ill feeling. The very suggestion that he owed a man like Gerry Silver a favor instantly fanned the flames. His two-word question formed a hostile challenge.

"Being banned was the beginning of the end for your act. When it fell apart eventually, you had to do something else with your lives. If you hadn't been banned, if you'd have stayed together, you'd have kept on plugging away at the same old act with maybe a variation here or there, and you'd have finished up as a cabdriver, just like me. Instead, look at you. You and Sidney. I'd say I did you both a favor."

Despite trying to maintain the angry pose, Manny heard himself beginning to laugh. "That's the most cockeyed piece of logic I've ever heard. Lesser Brothers and Sidney Less Productions owe it all to Gerry Silver, well, what do you know!"

"Don't laugh," said Rita. "There might be more than a grain of truth in that statement. I'm not sure we would have stayed together if the act had continued much longer."

Staring at her, Manny knew she was telling the truth. He'd been so wrapped up in the act in those days he had barely noticed what was going on around him. The thought of Rita leaving stunned him. Where would he be now, without her? Without Jonathan and Bernice? And he had Gerry Silver to thank? To some small degree, he supposed, he did. A minute degree, the tiniest proportion imaginable, that was all. But like a single link in a lengthy chain, it carried its own importance.

Slowly, he nodded. "Looking back on everything, I might not have been much to shout about in those days, either." He felt Rita squeeze his arm and knew he had made the proper appeasing gesture. "My mother tells me the Easterners are going to be the next big stars of pop."

"If they get the right breaks, they will be. I can't give them those breaks. They need an agent. A good one."

Manny took note of the music. The group was playing another tune with which he was unfamiliar, a spirited melody that made him want to snap his fingers. "What's the name of this song?"

" 'Liking Loving,' " Silver answered. "It's an original, one of many I might add. Do you want to meet them?"

"That's the reason I came here."

After two more songs, the Easterners took a break. Silver led Manny to where the four musicians sipped cold drinks. When he introduced Manny, the eyes of all four boys opened wide. It was obvious that Silver had not warned them that they might have a very important guest that evening. Manny appreciated the consideration. Such anticipation would have affected their performance. As it was, he liked what he'd heard. They played tunes a man could whistle, which was Manny's way of judging music. The lyrics were more than just moronic rhymes; they were clever poetry, often with an underlying message.

Manny spent no more than five minutes with the Easterners. In that time, he learned that he liked them personally as well as professionally. They were four unassuming young men who were having a grand time doing what they enjoyed. If it made them rich, so much the better, but wealth was not their main goal. Having fun was. Manny made the promise that they would hear from Lesser Brothers.

When the Easterners returned to the stage, Manny remained in the small room with Gerry Silver. "Thanks for coming," Silver said. "I appreciate the help you're offering those boys."

"I appreciate your help as well. To my mother."

"Will you do me one favor?"

Manny felt his stomach tighten. Maybe Gerry Silver hadn't changed after all. All his kindness and consideration might stem from some ulterior motive. "What?"

"Apologize to Naomi and Sidney for me."

Manny's mind was full of the unusual evening as he drove back to town. He couldn't get over Silver's transformation. From total scoundrel to a decent, sincere man who put himself out to help others. Manny didn't know what to make of it; he was only certain that Silver's metamorphosis was genuine.

He noticed that the evening's events were affecting everyone in the car. Rita stared straight ahead, trying, like Manny, to understand the change that had overtaken Silver. In the mirror, Manny saw his mother smiling like she'd just singlehandedly negotiated the end of the Cold War. In a way, he supposed, she had. And above the car's noise, he heard Bernice humming a song the Easterners had been playing. "Liking Loving." Catchy song, catchy title. It could be their first big hit.

Manny just wondered how he'd break all this news to Sidney and Naomi.

Sidney still liked walking to work from his home in Marble Arch. Sometimes he walked along busy main thoroughfares full of shops and people. At other times, he cut through back streets, past embassies and fashionable homes. In a few weeks he would turn fifty-five, an age when most men preferred to ride everywhere. Not Sidney. His step still had a spring to it; his slim body was filled with an energy that many younger men envied. And whenever he saw the traffic getting worse with each passing day, he thanked God that he walked. He failed to understand how Manny drove in every morning from The Paddocks. That was a day's work before he even sat down to the first mug of tea Carol Jones handed him. Manny had often talked about buying a home in town so he could stay over if he felt too tired to drive to Buckinghamshire, but he'd never done anything about it. The truth, Sidney knew, was that his brother was always too busy to look.

Today Sidney walked through Grosvenor Square, past the American Embassy and along Grosvenor Street to New Bond Street. The morning was filled with a hint of winter and he breathed deeply of the crisp air. He passed along Savile Row, stopped to admire a display of cashmere sweaters in the window of an outfitter in Burlington Arcade, then emerged

608

into Piccadilly. A hand touched his arm and he swung around, amazed to see his brother. On foot no less!

"What are you doing, taking up exercise in your old age?"

"I spoke to Naomi fifteen minutes ago. She told me you'd mentioned coming through Burlington Arcade, so I waited for you. I needed to catch you and pass on a message. An apology, to you and Naomi."

"Oh?" Sidney kept walking at his normal pace. "From who?"

Manny, breathing heavily, struggled to keep up. "Will you slow down, for crying out loud? Gerry Silver."

Sidney stopped. Incredulity covered his face. "Where did you see him, and what did you do to him to make him apologize?"

"Ilford. Mama and her club idea." Briefly, Manny related what had happened. Sidney never lost his amazed expression. Like Manny, he tried to find within him some spark of the fury that had once raged at the very mention of Gerry Silver's name, but time had dulled the fire. "I think he'd like to see you and Naomi. I really think he'd like to apologize in person."

"Do I have to tell him I'm sorry for breaking his jaw—?"

"And making off with his wife." Manny shook his head. "He never mentioned it. He just wanted to clear his account."

"Let me talk it over with Naomi. She suffered more than anyone at Gerry's hands. We just lost a job, which was probably my fault anyway for belting him. Naomi had to put up with his abuse all those years." He resumed walking, but at a pace Manny could cope with.

"Talk to her. Maybe it's because I'm getting older, Sidney, but I'm becoming more forgiving. Gerry was a right bastard in his younger days, but if he wants to salve his conscience and make amends, who are we to say no?"

Sidney wrapped an arm around his brother's shoulders. "I seem to recall that we weren't any great bargains, either, were we?" He felt terrific, and it wasn't just the walk pumping oxygen through his system. Manny was not the only one who had grown more forgiving with age. Sidney, also, welcomed the opportunity to pour oil on one particular spot of troubled water.

Naomi's emotions ran the gamut when Sidney told her about Gerry Silver. Remembering how he had treated her, she felt revulsion. Pity followed when she understood how his dreams had eluded him. Then she felt interest, and finally satisfaction that Silver had found some pleasure with a new family. She was glad to know that he had eventually made something of his life.

She did not want to see him, though. "I'll accept his apology," she told Sidney, "but I want nothing to do with him."

Sidney could not help teasing. "Frightened some of the old spark might remain?"

"What could remain after Sidney Less? No . . ." She shook her head. "Gerry belongs to a part of my life I should forget. Only one decent thing happened during my time with him. I met you."

"The least you could do is thank him for that."

"I don't think he'd see the joke."

Sidney remembered his conversation with his brother. "Manny and I were saying earlier that we were no bargains back then, either. We all had our own priorities, and too often we followed them with little regard for anyone else."

"You want me to see Gerry, don't you? You want me to tell him face-to-face that I accept his apology."

"If he's good enough to make it, the least we can do is accept it."

Naomi sighed. "All right. Maybe I'll be able to put a few ghosts of my own to rest."

The meeting took place at a small restaurant in Soho. Gerry Silver sat with his wife, Betty. Sidney sat with Naomi.

Silver got down to business even before Sidney could order drinks. "I'm glad you agreed to this meeting, Naomi. You're giving me the chance to get an awful lot off my chest. Telling your mother-in-law and Manny how badly I felt wasn't enough. I needed to tell you."

Naomi reached under the table to squeeze Sidney's hand. "It was long ago, Gerry. We all made mistakes. Be grateful we didn't have to pay for them the rest of our lives." She turned to Betty, trying to bring the woman into the conversation. Betty spoke about her small home in Ilford, the job of bringing up two sons, her membership on a couple of charity committees. Naomi listened carefully, puzzled. She had imagined Gerry marrying an exciting fashion plate, someone he would want to be seen with. Betty was more sensible than glamorous, practical rather than dazzling. But then, Naomi reminded herself, this was the new Gerry. The old one had died with his stage character.

Dinner passed quickly. Sidney checked his watch and saw it was nine-fifty. "Matt Monro's singing at London Lights. Why don't you join us? I'm sure they'll be able to find us a table somewhere."

"I'm sure they would, too," Silver replied. "Unfortunately, we have to get home. We told the boys we'd be back by eleven."

Naomi shook Betty's hand, then turned to face Silver. "I'm glad we got together, Gerry. I prefer this memory of you to the one I've carried all these years."

"I also prefer this memory. Good night, Naomi."

Sidney watched them walk toward the door. As they reached it, he called out: "Gerry!"

Silver turned around. "Yes?"

"Sorry I broke your jaw that time."

Silver laughed and waved good-bye.

Naomi returned his wave. "Betty's nice, don't you think?" she asked Sidney.

"Maybe she's the one who straightened him out."

"Does that mean I straightened you out? And did Rita straighten Manny out?"

"Perhaps. Want to hear Matt Monro?"

"Some other night. Let's go home instead. You know, I'm glad you persuaded me to see Gerry. Now I feel quite good about myself, and I want to share it with someone special."

Rachel began 1964 by putting a deposit on the vacant factory in Stepney. Manny talked big-name clients into donating their services to a fund-raiser for the club. Sidney, acting for the Partnership, offered the London Playhouse for a special Sunday performance at the beginning of March.

The show raised enough to buy the building outright. Further donations from corporations and individuals underwrote the cost of renovation. Manny and Sidney each gave ten thousand pounds. Rachel hoped to have the club operating by the fall of 1964.

One of the biggest hits of the show was a four-man group named the Easterners. They played three numbers. The third was "Liking Loving." Released four weeks earlier, it was now third on the British hit parade, with expectations of being number one when the next chart was published.

Two weeks later, the record was released in the States. The very next day, Manny received a transatlantic call. He expected it to be Barry Levy from Lesser Brothers Inc. Instead it was Bill Delaney.

"How's the weather in New York?"

"Never mind the blasted weather" came Delaney's curt reply. Manny could see the American show host sitting there with his arms folded, just like he appeared in front of the cameras. He was probably holding the telephone receiver between his ear and shoulder. "I'm wondering when my friend Manny Lesser's going to keep the promise he made to me some thirteen years ago."

"What promise?"

"That when he's got a singer who's a runaway success over there, that singer's first American appearance will be on the *Bill Delaney Show*."

Manny remembered—the handshake following Delaney's help with that unfortunate business over Irving Kreeger. "You've put my people on your show."

"They were run-of-the-mill entertainers. This is different. All I've heard from the moment I got up yesterday morning was this dumb ditty called 'Liking Loving' by this equally dumb Limey group called the Easterners. Now when do I get them on my show?"

Manny hadn't even considered an American tour for the group. First things first—he wanted them to have two or three hits before he sent them across the Atlantic. "What's the big hurry?"

"We're in the middle of the British invasion and I don't want to miss out. Neither should you. Besides, it's a damned good song. I've been humming it all day long."

"I never break a promise, Bill. I'll tell Lesser Brothers Inc. to start arranging a tour for them, with the first stop on your show." He said good-bye and hung up, delighted by the call, delighted by the way everything was going. All of it stemmed from his mother's knack for spotting talent, and her fortuitous meeting with a transformed Gerry Silver. And her insistence that he and Sidney accept Silver's gesture of apology. Manny smiled. He might be almost fifty-seven, but he could still learn a point or two from his mother, bless her.

The Easterners started a six-week American tour in June with a Sunday-night appearance on the *Bill Delaney Show*. Manny was prevented from going by a family affair. On the same weekend as the group's television appearance in New York, Manny and Rita attended their son's wedding. Jonathan's bride was a slim blond girl called Susan Parnell, who worked as a secretary for a film company in Wardour Street.

The ceremony took place at Caxton Hall, recalling for Rachel an earlier wedding, that of the groom's parents. Manny had wed Rita at Caxton Hall twenty-eight years before. This time, though, the bride's family was well represented. No qualms existed among Susan's family about the profession of the groom or his background. At twenty-six, Jonathan was well established. After eight years with the Partnership, he was assistant manager of London Lights, the nightclub he had helped conceive. And as for his religion . . . ? Rachel reminded herself for the first time in many years that her only grandson—her favorite grandchild—was not Jewish. His father was Jewish, but his mother was Episcopalian. Jonathan had been brought up as a little of each, or nothing at all, depending upon which way you looked at it. All his life he had received Christmas presents from his mother, and Chanukah *gelt* from his father, but he had never been circumcised or bar mitzvahed as Jewish tradition dictated, nor had he been christened or confirmed. Rachel supposed her grandson really had no religion at all.

What Rachel missed most in her grandson's marriage was

the warmth of the Jewish wedding ceremony. Without the traditional breaking of a glass and the shout of *"mazel tov!"* it didn't seem like a wedding at all.

Six weeks later, Rachel witnessed all the tradition she could want. The occasion was Andrea's wedding at the New West End Synagogue in St. Petersburg Place. Twenty-four-year-old Andrea, who worked as a receptionist for an advertising agency, married Robert Goldman, one of the agency's partners. Rachel could have been no happier had Andrea been her natural grandchild.

When the bride walked toward the *chuppah* on her stepfather's arm, Sidney's face shone with pride and joy. Watching the ceremony, Rachel remembered Andrea's early hostility to her adoptive family. No one, she'd claimed, could take the place of her real mother and father. She'd tried to imbue that feeling into Linda, her younger sister, who today was maid of honor. Rachel wondered how Andrea felt at this moment. Perhaps no adoptive parents could take the place of natural parents, but Sidney and Naomi had come within a hairsbreadth of doing so. Just as Tobias and Hannah Dekker had once done with Rachel. Now they were reaping their reward.

Rachel's monument to the lives of Tobias and Hannah opened the first Sunday in September. Standing in front of the converted factory, Rachel tugged at a cord. A piece of fabric dropped away to reveal a white board with blue lettering— The Tobias and Hannah Dekker Youth Club. A year had passed since she had first pictured a way to memorialize the Dekkers. Now the dream was reality.

The next night, she exchanged London's East End for its West End, and the annual Performing Artists' Gala. Sidney had kept yet another promise to his mother. The royal guest of honor was the Queen, and in the program was the note that a bouquet would be presented to Her Majesty by Mrs. Rachel Lesser.

Sidney had a car bring Rachel to the London Playhouse. He was amazed to find his mother so calm. "How can you be so cool and collected?" he asked her. "Don't you know what tonight is?"

"Of course I know," she answered. "The difference between us is that you've had weeks to worry about tonight, while I've had no time at all to get nervous. That club kept me busy right up to yesterday afternoon."

Sidney smiled affectionately at his mother, and kissed the wrinkled skin of her cheek. "You're seventy-eight, you're not supposed to be so busy."

"If I stopped being busy, I'd stop living," she replied. Sidney believed her. When you got to be as old as his mother, you didn't listen to other people tell you what was good for you and what wasn't. You already knew. His mother's best medicine was staying occupied. She'd spent her life keeping active, and she wasn't about to change now.

Chapter Twenty-eight

Jimmy's depression over Brian Gilbert did not dissipate quickly. All through the summer and fall of 1963, Jimmy remained filled with a burning bitterness at the betrayal by a man he had trusted and admired. When Gilbert wrote from prison to express regret at any distress he had caused, Jimmy crushed the letter into a tight ball and threw it into the garbage. He did not know whether the communication was prompted by genuine remorse or whether Gilbert viewed such an apology as the first step in returning at some future date to Messenger Publications. He did not care. He wanted nothing to do with Gilbert, either in person or by letter.

When the rest of America was flung into shock and despair by the assassination of President Kennedy, Jimmy was already there. Kennedy's death represented another burden in a life that had suddenly gone awry. In a moment of introspection, he considered William Baron. Had Baron won his party's nomination three years before and gone on to succeed in the national election, would Jimmy now be mourning a friend as well as a President? He wrote an editorial for the *Messenger,* saying that the country had reached a sorry pass when pledging one's self to public life required a man to volunteer as a target in a shooting gallery.

In the year's final week, Sonya asked her husband how much longer he intended to carry the cross Brian Gilbert had fashioned. "Kennedy died five weeks ago and the country's recovering," she said as they traveled by chauffeured Rolls into the city. "How long do you plan on wearing sackcloth and ashes?"

Jimmy didn't answer. He just stared out of the window, eyes slitted as if he were deep in thought. He'd taken to doing that a lot of late, Sonya thought. He'd become very quiet, both at home and in the office. Messenger Publications rumbled on regardless, churning out titles and money, but Jimmy had lost much of his interest. He worked like a robot. At first, she had waited for him to get over it in his own good time, but how long was that supposed to be? Six months, surely, was time enough to be eaten up with anger and sorrow over a trusted friend's shortcomings.

"You used to be a good traveling companion," Sonya told him. "I enjoyed going to work with you. But lately you've become a downright bore. The only time I enjoy these rides is when your father comes into the city. He still talks to me."

Jimmy smiled and reached out to hold Sonya's hand. "Have a little respect for a man's midlife crisis."

"Is that what this is? When do you expect midlife to end?"

"When I become old." Had his father ever suffered such a malady? Even now, nearing eighty, Zalman maintained his health and energy. He came into the city two or three times a week to roam the building and keep up to date. Jimmy always listened for the click of snooker balls, and wondered what his father's next brainwave would be; he was quite certain the old man hadn't finished yet. No, Zalman had never gone through a midlife crisis—or any kind of crisis, for that matter. He had never stayed still long enough to contemplate where he had gone wrong, what he had missed, what he should have done differently. Except, perhaps, for those three years in Lewisburg. Even then he had put the time to good use by reading and learning.

"You'd better become old very quickly then," Sonya warned. "Because if you don't remove that perpetual frown from your face, the editor of *American Miss* is going back to becoming a full-time housewife and needlepoint artist."

As 1964 dawned, Jimmy's bleak mood finally began to pass. A new year meant new opportunities, and he had much to anticipate. Most of all, he had Josephine's graduation from Vassar to look forward to, followed by her full entry into the family of Messenger Publications. With Zalman, Sonya, Josephine, and himself, the ride into the city would be a family outing.

Josephine graduated from Vassar with a degree in liberal arts. After a month's vacation in Europe, she returned to the United States ready to take up the position she had craved from the moment she picked up a camera.

No happier person existed than Josephine on the morning she entered the *Messenger* as a full staff member. Dressed in a navy-blue trouser suit with a shiny new Nikon hanging around her neck, she presented herself to Mo Jackman, the paper's picture editor. "I'm all ready, Mr. Jackman," Josephine announced proudly.

Jackman, a veteran of thirty years with the newspaper, saw Josephine's serious expression and immediately felt sorry for the young woman. She was raring to go, all wound up to rush out and take the electrifying news photographs that would win awards and catapult her to the top of the profession in a year. Unfortunately she wouldn't be doing any of that. At least, not for a very long time. "I'm afraid you're not at all ready. First of all you've got to do something about that advertisement you're wearing."

"Advertisement?"

"The camera."

Josephine lifted the Nikon away from her chest. "What's the matter with it?"

"Perhaps a reporter wants to be seen and heard, but a photographer's greatest asset is anonymity. Rush in, get the picture, and rush out. You're not anonymous with a gleaming camera hanging around your throat like a thousand-dollar pearl necklace. Carry it like this." Jackman lifted a Pentax from the desk where he worked and draped the strap over his shoulder, letting the camera hang hidden between his side and his arm. "That way it's not so visible, and you can grab hold of it in a hurry for when the shot presents itself."

Josephine shifted the camera to the approved position. "How's that?"

"Fine. But you're still not ready." Jackman's gray hair,

618

round face, and bright blue eyes lent him a kindly, grandfatherly appearance. He used his looks to their best effect, smiling at Josephine as he said, "Before you step outside that door, you've got to do some basic training in here. You can begin by working with me on assigning the jobs. You'll see who specializes in what kind of photography, you'll pick up pointers. After that, you can help out in the darkroom—"

"I've done enough darkroom work to qualify as an expert."

"That was while you were a part-timer, vacation help. Now you're on the staff and you start from scratch."

Josephine bit back her pride. She worked with Jackman on the picture desk, grading assignments by importance, collating the activities of photographers, evaluating pictures. Despite her own impatience, she grew very fond of the picture editor. He was an amiable man who lived in constant confusion. He was forever asking Josephine if she remembered where he had placed something. His desk epitomized his life, seven drawers that resembled miniature rummage sales. Beneath the clutter, though, Josephine discovered a man who understood more about news photography than anyone she had ever met. He talked willingly about the field, answering every question Josephine had. He did everything she could have wanted—except give her a chance to go out on her own.

After two months, she moved into the darkroom, where she printed and developed other people's pictures. Once a week she asked Jackman when she would receive an assignment. Each time he smiled and assured her of the need for a sound background. Other photographers she talked to echoed his words. Every one of them had started out the same way. On the journeys between Rye and the city, she feigned satisfaction with the way work was going. Whenever her parents asked how she was getting on, she answered enthusiastically. On the surface, she was content. Underneath she seethed with disappointment and impatience.

On Christmas week, after more than four months at the newspaper, Josephine received her first photographic assignment. Mo Jackman told her to cover the retirement of an official in the fire department. She did. The picture was printed but never used. She did not get another job for two weeks, at which time she was assigned to the presentation ceremony of a valor commendation in the police department. This time, at least, the picture was used, tucked away inside the paper and cropped down to nothing more than a mug shot.

Josephine's disillusionment grew until it peaked in February. In a month when New York was littered with news stories—the crash of a DC-7 off Jones Beach that left eighty-four dead; the firebombing of Malcolm X's home followed a week later by his murder; a plot to blow up the Statue of Liberty; and the arrest of Vietnam protesters blocking the entrance to the United Nations—Josephine's assignments amounted to nothing more newsworthy than presentations, portraits for the files, and shots of society matrons going about their giddy lives.

"You can hire some kid with a Kodak Brownie to do what you have me doing," she complained to Jackman. "When am I going to start doing some real work?"

"It's a pity patience comes only with age, when one doesn't really have enough time left to fully utilize it. Young people could put it to much better use than the old."

Josephine wasn't satisfied with Jackman's wisdom. She wanted work. She vented her dissatisfaction on the way home that night. "You'd think there was a plot to stop me doing anything," she complained to her parents. "I've been on the picture desk for six months, and my only assignments are presentations, someone shaking hands with someone else, someone sticking a medal on someone else's chest."

"Regard it as an apprenticeship," Jimmy answered. He turned to his father who had made the trip into town that day. "What did you have me doing when I started?"

"You were the company's first and last information manager. Every morning you read all the papers, and every evening you gave me a summation of all the news that might affect me."

Jimmy was thankful that his father's memory remained sharp. He looked triumphantly at his daughter. "See? Even *I* started out on the bottom rung. You've got to be patient, Josephine."

"Patient!" She gave a shrill, cynical laugh. "Did you tell

Mo Jackman to hand me the patience lecture as well? I don't know how much longer I can carry on being patient when all I get to photograph are clutch-and-grinners!"

Zalman watched his granddaughter through half-closed eyes. Like Jimmy, he could see his daughter in Josephine. Not in looks but in temperament. The young woman had taken all the learning she would accept. Now she wanted to fly, and God help anyone who tried to clip her wings. Zalman prayed Jimmy could handle Josephine better than he had handled Helen. Otherwise grief waited like an ambush.

Josephine continued working in Mo Jackman's department, splitting her time between darkroom tasks and administration details. Perhaps her father and Jackman were right, she reasoned, and patience *was* a virtue. Then, during a very slack period, her reasoning underwent a drastic change, and any patience she had accumulated died abruptly.

With nothing else to do, she offered to clean out Jackman's cluttered desk. "Think of it as an attempt to bribe you into giving me more glamorous jobs, Mo."

"Go ahead. Do a good job, and I'll let you do my apartment."

Laughing, Josephine emptied the contents of each drawer onto the desktop. She made a small mountain of curling photographs, strips of negatives, memos, notepads, pens and pencils, a couple of camera lenses, and an unopened packet of very stale gingersnaps. She even found an old Zeiss Ikon Super Ikonta, which she opened up and extended.

"What do you want me to do with all this stuff? Throw it away so you can start afresh?"

Jackman regarded the pile. "Figure out a filing system for it." Someone called his name, and his attention was diverted. "Put the memos in one drawer, the pictures in another," he said as he walked away. "Then figure out what to do with the rest."

Josephine started sorting the debris into categories. A scrap of paper caught her eye. It wasn't typed like a regular memo. It was handwritten, featuring a distinctive, wide-nibbed script. She read it, and her heart pounded as she understood why her career stagnated. Hearing Jackman return, she thrust the note into the middle of the memos and shoved them in a drawer.

She said nothing to Jackman, nor did she make a scene on the way home in the Rolls. Her grandfather and mother were present. She did not want to involve them. Her argument was solely with the man who had signed the note to Jackman. Her father. She waited until after dinner, when Jimmy had retired to his study. She knocked on the door and called out, "May I see you for a minute?"

"Of course. Come in."

Josephine entered her father's private domain, the room she had once vacuumed and dusted for pocket money. That experience had taught her independence, just as her father had intended it to. Now she was going to use it. Closing the door behind her, she stood just inside the room, watching her father earnestly scan a news report that was coming over the wire.

"Anything interesting?" she asked.

"Ed Murrow died."

"That's a shame. He wasn't very old, was he?"

Jimmy consulted the report again. "Fifty-seven, not old at all. Lung cancer killed him. Smoked four packs of cigarettes a day. My sister worked with him, you know. They were both in London during the war."

Josephine recognized her cue. "And because of what happened to your sister, you don't want to take a chance of anything happening to me through work, is that it?"

Jimmy looked up sharply, unable to follow the conversation's sudden shift.

"We weren't very busy today, so I did Mo Jackman a favor by cleaning out his desk before he fell into it and disappeared forever. I found that note you sent him."

"So?"

The question's abrasive tone shook Josephine. She'd expected some contrition on her father's part, a sense of regret that he had gone behind her back. Instead, he was challenging her, as though she were in the wrong. The single word shook her and angered her. "In four months time I will be twenty-three years old. I don't need wet-nursing anymore, thank you very much!"

"Who said anything about wet-nursing?"

"How else would you describe a note that threatens poor Mo with instant dismissal if he so much as lets me near a dangerous situation? You're the reason I'm only getting to shoot banal presentations. You've got Mo so scared out of his wits, he's terrified I might even slip in the darkroom and twist an ankle!"

Jimmy pointed a finger at Josephine. "Don't raise your voice to me, young lady—"

Josephine ignored the warning. "If I wanted to shoot clutch-and-grinners all day long, I'd have worked in a portrait studio. As it is, I want to be a news photographer because I know I can be a good one, and you're deliberately standing in my way."

"I am doing what I think is best for you."

"You stopped knowing what was best for me the moment you got in the way of my dream!" Josephine walked out of the study and slammed the door behind her. By the time her father opened it, she was running upstairs to her bedroom. Jimmy let her go. She'd get over her pique the instant she realized that her father had nothing but her welfare at heart.

Josephine did not ride with her parents the next morning. She took her own car, a green MG convertible, saying she intended going out after work. At lunchtime, she disappeared for two hours. On returning, she gave a week's notice to Mo Jackman.

"I'm going free-lance. If you need a good photographer, you can reach me here." She gave the astounded picture editor a sheet of paper with an address in Sullivan Street. "Sorry, but I haven't had a chance to get business cards printed yet."

"Have you told your father?"

"I'll leave that to you."

Within five minutes, Jimmy summoned his daughter to his office. "What do you think you're doing, Josephine?"

"Leaving the nest. It's the only way I can live the way I want to live. If I can't be a photographer on the *Messenger,* I'll be one somewhere else. Are you going to wish me luck?"

Jimmy embraced her and kissed her on the cheek. "Good luck. But don't come looking for any favors."

"I wouldn't dream of it. If the *Messenger* buys my stuff, it's because it's good enough to buy."

Jimmy watched her leave the office. It was Helen all over again. Instead of a typewriter, Josephine carried a camera. She should have been Helen's daughter. Then she would have been Helen's curse, a daughter exactly like herself. But Helen was dead, so the curse had been passed on to her brother. As if Harold wasn't enough of a curse to cope with already, Jimmy reflected; now he had Josephine to worry about as well.

He wasn't happy about it, but he would not try to stop her. To do so would only drive her farther away. He would let her find out for herself just how tough it was out there. Then she'd come back. He hoped.

Josephine searched out subjects for her camera. At night she returned to her apartment on Sullivan Street to develop film she had shot that day and print up the results in the darkroom she had fashioned from the small second bedroom. Compared with the darkroom at her parents' home in Rye, Sullivan Street was a primitive affair. A sheet of plywood covered the window. The enlarger was tucked away into the corner. A table held trays of developer, stop bath, and fixer. Next to the table was a large bucket of water into which Josephine dropped the prints after immersion in the fixer. A print drier was set up in the kitchen.

Despite the awkward arrangement, Josephine loved the apartment and the work she did. She created photographic essays of Greenwich Village, which was now her neighborhood. Moving farther afield, she captured the different ethnic mixes of Manhattan. She photographed people, buildings, animals, cars, anything she thought might contain an element of human interest. She visited newspapers and magazines, displaying a constantly updated portfolio, offering her business card to editors, and crossing her fingers that someone would bite.

In three months Josephine pressed the shutter release button of her Nikon three thousand times, made a thousand prints, saw more of Manhattan than she ever knew existed, and met every picture editor worth meeting. On the credit side, she knew her work had improved immeasurably. On the debit side, she had not yet sold a single picture. Once a week she went to Rye for dinner with the family. Conversation covered everything but her decision to go free-lance. Jimmy knew she had sold nothing, but he saw no point in mentioning it. Josephine would think he was trying to push her into rejoining the *Messenger*.

In August, two days before her twenty-third birthday, Josephine discovered the secret of successful news photography: being in the right place at the right time. At ten in the morning, while walking along a busy Sixth Avenue, just north of West Fourth Street, she heard shouts, followed by two sharp explosions. People parted. Twenty yards away Josephine saw three men running from a bank. Two men dived for the white Pontiac Parisienne idling at the curb. The third man collapsed on the sidewalk, dropping the bag he held. Josephine whipped the Nikon to eye level, focused swiftly through the short telephoto lens, and hit the shutter release button. The motor drive jacked the next frame into place. The shutter snapped again. Motor drive . . . shutter . . . motor drive . . . shutter . . . Before she realized it, she had gone through the entire roll of thirty-six exposures. Her final frames caught the Pontiac speeding away and a guard running out of the bank to stand over the wounded robber.

Sirens wailed. Police appeared. Josephine flagged a taxi, rewinding the film as the driver sped north. Ten minutes later, as first details of the bank robbery flashed across the wire, she was offering the film to the *Journal-American*. While she waited, the film was developed and contacts made. She inspected them through a magnifying glass. A flush of pleasure crept across her face. Not only did she have the faces of the men who had jumped into the Pontiac in sharp focus, she even had the driver as he turned around to urge his comrades to hurry.

The *Journal-American* carried the pictures in its next edition, turning from the front page to a dramatic center spread. Most exciting for Josephine was the sight of her name in the story, and her description as an enterprising free-lance photographer who had the presence of mind, while others dived for cover, to capture everything on film.

By four that afternoon, the three men who had escaped were in custody. Police credited their capture to the *Journal-American* and a hitherto unknown photographer named Josephine Isaacson. Josephine, though, knew nothing of the robbers' capture. At the time it became public, she stood in her father's office following his urgent summons.

"Congratulations on your first success. Now would you mind explaining to me why you embarrassed the *Messenger* by giving these photographs to another newspaper?"

"I didn't *give* them. I sold them, for five hundred dollars. There's also the probability of some reward money for helping to apprehend those men. As for embarrassing anyone, the *Messenger*'s a morning paper, already on the street when that opportunity occurred. Do you think I was going to wait almost an entire day to see my work in print?"

"You could have at least sold the damned things to the *Post*," Jimmy muttered. "Everyone knows the *Journal-American*'s on its last legs. You've probably kept it going another few weeks."

"Thanks for the advice. I'll cash the check immediately."

She turned toward the door. Jimmy called her back. "I spoke to Mo Jackman before. He was praising you to high heaven. Said he could really use a photographer of your ability."

"No more notes from the proprietor?"

"No more notes."

Josephine thought it over. The prospect tantalized her. Not many people made her father back down. Then she shook her head. "I like what happened today. I became fully independent. You should like it, too. That's what you always wanted for me."

Jimmy watched his daughter leave with pride in his heart and a sour feeling in his stomach. Despite his attempts to cosset her, she was going to take on the world and all its dangers. She'd make a name for herself, just as her aunt had done.

The bank-robbery exclusive opened doors. Photographic essays Josephine had once hawked futilely around town suddenly found buyers. Picture editors dialed her number when work came up. During the next few months, Jimmy saw his daughter's pictures in half a dozen newspapers as well as *Newsweek*, covering everything from John Lindsay's mayoral victory to Vietnam War protestors burning their draft cards. Of all Josephine's pictures, one perturbed her father. Appearing in the *News*, it depicted the immolation of a war protestor at the United Nations. Jimmy stared at it many times during the day. He took it home that evening to show his father.

"What are you so upset about?" Zalman wanted to know. "It's a damned good news picture."

Sonya, also, could not understand Jimmy's uneasiness. The *Messenger* had carried a similar picture. So had every other paper. "What's the problem with it?" she asked. "Does it bother you that Josephine should see such horror? That she could be unfeeling enough to photograph it?"

"Look beyond the young man who's committing suicide. Check the background. Take a good look at those two cops." He waited while Zalman scrutinized the picture. "Tell me if you can't see what I see. One cop's got a grin on his face a mile wide, and the other one's gesturing as though he's saying good riddance to that young man."

Zalman nodded. "So what's the matter with that?"

"I didn't see those cops in any other picture. I think Josephine did it deliberately. She slanted the shot to get her own message across—that America is fighting a wicked war and the Establishment couldn't give a damn. Josephine uses the occasion of a young man's antiwar suicide to gain sympathy for him and ridicule those on the other side. And I am one of those people she ridicules."

Zalman nodded in understanding. The *Messenger* frequently criticized antiwar protesters for forming a fifth column. "She's young. She's flexing her muscles, tilting at windmills. Let her get on with it. She'll run out of steam eventually."

Jimmy found little comfort in his father's advice. After twenty-three years, a split was developing between himself and his daughter. Her loyalty to the values of her generation was stronger than her loyalty to her father.

Relief came from an unexpected quarter. Harold, who had graduated from high school in June, started Columbia, which his father had attended for one year. He lived in student housing in New York and came to Rye only on Friday evenings. Although delighted that Harold had been accepted by Columbia, Jimmy expected the young man to go through the university the same way he had gone through school, doing well in the arts and caring about little else. He wondered if the boy would ever graduate.

Harold surprised his father. College opened his eyes to the real world. Music, art, and drama continued to hold his interest, but he began applying himself to math and science, subjects he had practically ignored before. In addition, he displayed his first spark of interest in Messenger Publications by questioning his father about circulation promotions.

"Why do you want to know about circulation?" Jimmy asked.

"We're doing an essay on business. I thought I should write about our family business."

"Go talk to your grandfather. He's forgotten more about selling newspapers than the Hearsts ever learned." Smiling, Jimmy watched his son walk away. Maybe a rift had developed between father and daughter, but it could not detract from the bond that had suddenly formed between father and son.

The bond strengthened. Jimmy took immense pride in his son's achievements. In turn, Harold showed an increasing curiosity about the business he would one day be part of. Instead of being ambivalent about his future, he told his father that he intended doing postgraduate work toward an MBA.

"Grandpa started Messenger Publications," Harold told his father. "You streamlined it. With my MBA, I'll prepare it for the twenty-first century."

The boy was changing before his very eyes. Just eighteen, he was turning into a man so quickly that Jimmy was frightened to blink in case he missed part of the transformation. He felt he'd missed too much already.

"When did he become so tall?" Jimmy asked Sonya as they traveled to New York one morning. "What happened to the skinny little kid who looked forward to piano lessons? All of a sudden my son is a husky young man, taller than me, and I don't remember any of it happening."

Sonya had the answers Jimmy lacked. "You spent too much time telling him how he should be and not enough time watching him turn out that way."

"But when did the curse get lifted?"

Sonya laughed. "You're as bad as your father! The curse was lifted somewhere between the time Josephine left home and quit the *Messenger* and Harold left home to go to Columbia."

Jimmy understood now. Harold had always been in Josephine's shadow, just as he, Jimmy supposed, had been in Helen's. With the obstruction removed, the sun shone through.

Harold finished his freshman year at Columbia with enviable grades. Jimmy offered him a summer vacation anywhere he wanted to go. Harold chose New York and Messenger Publications. He didn't learn photography like Josephine, or reporting as Helen had done. Harold worked in advertising, learning from the men and women who brought in the bulk of the company's revenue.

While Jimmy chose summer to impress his father, Josephine used it to embarrass him. Not with a picture this time but with an action. Late one afternoon, Jimmy got a telephone call from Frank Kinsella. "A dozen protesters got arrested for burning draft cards outside the induction center on Whitehall Street," Kinsella told Jimmy. "Your daughter was taken away as well."

"For burning a draft card?"

"She was taking photographs. When the police moved in, she assaulted one of the officers. Nothing serious, just a push."

"Can you take care of it for me?"

"I was going to offer to do just that."

Josephine was released without charges being filed. Kinsella himself brought her to the Messenger Building. Instead of thanking her father for his intervention, she was furious with him. "I can't even get arrested for a good cause, can I? I might not live with you anymore. I might not work for you, but that still doesn't stop you trying to control my life."

"No one's trying to control your life, Josephine."

"Then why did you have me released?"

"So I could give you a lecture about professionalism. Yours, I might point out, leaves much to be desired."

Josephine's face whitened. Jimmy could not have wounded her more deeply. "What?"

"You've got to make up your mind whether you're going to be a photographer or a demonstrator. You can't be both." He smiled grimly as he watched her consider that. It would not stop her tilting at windmills in the future, but it gave her something to think about right now.

When Harold returned to Columbia to begin his sophomore year, Jimmy knew beyond all doubt that the curse had indeed been lifted. The son had overtaken the father. Jimmy's formal education had ended with his freshman year. Harold was treading a virgin path. Suddenly Jimmy felt frightened for his son. Before he had hardly worked at all; was he now working too hard?

Jimmy broached the subject one Friday night when Harold came to Rye. "College isn't meant to be all work and no play. You're supposed to put a little time aside for fun."

Harold's eyes twinkled. "Don't worry, I have fun."

"What's her name?" Sonya asked.

"Carol Partridge. We share a couple of classes."

Zalman gazed over the top of his glasses at Harold. "Is that all you share?" When Jimmy looked sharply at his father, Zalman said, "What's the matter? The boy will be nineteen soon. Even you knew what you had it for by then."

"Mr. Z.!" This time the exclamation came from Sonya.

Only Harold appeared to enjoy the moment. He found a certain richness in an old man asking such questions; as if he were trying to recapture a lost youth.

No one in the family saw signs of impending trouble. Harold continued to visit his parents' home every Friday for dinner. He was eager to share any scholastic triumphs with his family, and even when Zalman unfailingly teased him about the girl called Carol Partridge, the young man never displayed any irritation. Then, on the Friday before the start of the Christmas vacation, on one of the rare evenings that

630

Josephine was present, Harold sat down and quite calmly shocked his family into silence.

"I won't be returning to Columbia in January," he said.

Sonya recovered first. "Are you in some kind of trouble?"

"No. I just decided that I've had enough education." He smiled as though enjoying a huge joke. "It's time to go to work and earn some money."

Zalman remembered his anger when Jimmy, more than thirty years before, had done just as Harold was now doing. Would Jimmy recall it, too? Jimmy's reaction was identical to his father's. "If you think four semesters of Columbia entitles you to a job at Messenger Publications, you'd better think again."

"I won't be working for Messenger Publications."

"Oh? And who will you be working for?"

"The army. I'm going to enlist for three years."

"You're going to do what?" Sonya whispered.

Jimmy exploded. "There's a war on, for God's sake! Once you graduate you'll get called to active duty soon enough, but at least you'll go in with a commission."

Josephine cut in before Harold could answer. "You're always at him to shoulder responsibility," she told her father. "What better way is there to learn how than in the military?"

Jimmy's mouth dropped at the incongruity of his antiwar daughter supporting his son's decision to enlist.

After Josephine and Harold had gone and Zalman had retired to his own apartment, Jimmy remained at the dining-room table, chin cupped in his hands. "Something happened, Sonya, to make him change like this. And I'm going to find out what it was."

"How? He won't tell you anything."

Jimmy touched the side of his nose. "I've got a newspaper full of reporters who'll find out for me."

Within three days, Jimmy knew the reason for his son's odd behavior. Harold's rush to arms was prompted by the oldest motivation of all. A woman. Jimmy shared the details with Sonya the moment he knew them.

"Harold's girlfriend, Carol Partridge, gave him the brush-off in favor of a fellow called Larry Towson."

Sonya felt offended on behalf of her son. "What's so special about this Larry Towson? What makes him better than Harold?"

"He's attending Columbia under the GI Bill. Twenty-four years old, and recently back from Vietnam with a chest full of medals, including a Silver Star for bravery, and a Purple Heart for being wounded in action."

"All those ribbons swept Carol off her feet, and left Harold looking for a way to get his own back?"

"That's right. Just when we thought he was maturing."

"Can you stop him?"

"I suppose so, but I've been thinking about what Josephine said. I was always at him to grow up, so how can I be opposed to him volunteering for a regimented life that'll show him the way? Besides, how can I ethically prevent him from enlisting when at least once a week the *Messenger* praises the young men who willingly serve their country?"

"But he isn't thinking straight, Jimmy. He's joining the army on the rebound, like a jilted lover running into the arms of the first woman he sees."

"Maybe this particular woman will make a man out of him."

In January 1967, as he turned nineteen, Harold left home one Monday morning carrying a briefcase that contained personal belongings. That evening he was at Fort Dix, New Jersey, sleeping for the first time beneath a brown blanket on which was stenciled a heavy black "US." The briefcase was delivered five days later to the house in Rye, removing from Harold his last shred of individuality.

Harold telephoned his parents the first Sunday. His processing period had finished, and he would begin basic training proper the following day. He had one favor to ask: on Sundays, when families visited trainees, he wanted his own mother and father to stay away. He would see them when he received his first pass toward the end of the training cycle.

Sonya, listening on an extension, was upset, but Jimmy thought he understood the reason for the odd request. "We won't show you up by arriving in a chauffeur-driven Rolls Royce."

"It's not that. I don't want you seeing how I change from

week to week. I want you to see what a month or more does."

Six weeks into the basic training cycle, Harold's platoon received weekend passes. Harold rode the bus from Fort Dix to New York City. Jimmy, Sonya, and Zalman met him at the bus station. They could see the change immediately. Harold Isaacson had been a slim young man. Muscles rippled beneath Private Isaacson's dark-green uniform. He seemed taller, straighter. He shook his father's hand with a firm grip, kissed his mother, and hugged his grandfather.

"How do I look?" he asked as he settled in the back of the Rolls. He removed his hat to exhibit closely cropped hair through which his scalp gleamed.

"You won't have to worry about Carol Partridge anymore," Jimmy answered. "You'll have dozens of girls chasing you now."

Harold appeared startled. "You knew?"

"I own a newspaper. I find out all the news."

Harold laughed. "I should have known that no one keeps a secret from you."

Sonya wanted to ask her son if he now realized how hastily he had acted. She was unable to ask anything. All she could do was stare at him and try to accept the change that had taken place. He had been right to refuse to see them. Week to week, they would have noticed little. In almost two months, the change was dramatic. She squeezed his upper arm. Harold laughed.

"Lot more muscle than there used to be, eh? I can do sixty push-ups now. When I went in, I couldn't do ten. And I can run a mile in six minutes and fifteen seconds."

"That's not so wonderful," Zalman said. "A fellow called Jim Ryun ran it last year in three minutes and fifty-one seconds."

"Wearing fatigues and combat boots?"

Zalman chuckled and slapped his grandson's leg.

Sonya saw that the changes went far beyond muscles. Harold's voice was deeper, his laugh more resonant. For possibly the first time in his life, her son was truly enjoying himself. Another change became evident that evening, after Josephine arrived from the city. The entire family went out for dinner. During the meal, when Josephine asked her brother what he intended doing once he finished training, Harold demonstrated that he had volunteered his mind as well as his body.

"Advanced infantry training, and then airborne."

"Do you want to come back from Vietnam with a row of medals?" Jimmy asked. "Do you think that'll impress Carol?"

"Carol who?" Harold turned to face his father. "You were right when you told me there's a war going on. There is, and it's a war we've got to win. Otherwise we can watch the whole of Southeast Asia turn Communist. You say the same thing often enough in the *Messenger.*"

"It's not a war," Josephine argued. "It's murder, and it's lunacy. Americans have no business being there, and they certainly have no business dying there."

Harold swung around on his sister. "We have every business being there. We were invited by the lawful government of a country that is fighting outside enemies."

"We are supporting the government of a country that is so corrupt it makes the Mafia look saintly."

Sonya clapped her hands. "This is a restaurant, not a debating hall. Harold, you're with us for one night. Josephine, you're here for the evening. Let's try to make it pleasant."

Josephine left for the city the moment the family returned from the restaurant. Harold went up to his old bedroom soon after, claiming that he was no longer accustomed to late nights. Jimmy, his father, and Sonya sat in the living room.

"I don't care what you say," Jimmy told his father, "but I never did any of these things he's doing."

"No, you didn't. But then Sonya never had eyes for a man in uniform, either."

"Never mind what you did or didn't do," Sonya said. "What are you *going* to do about Harold?"

"Absolutely nothing. Just because he wants to go airborne doesn't mean he'll qualify. There's more to it than being willing to jump out of an aircraft. A lot of hopefuls wash out."

"And if he doesn't wash out?" Zalman asked.

"I'll worry about it then. But in the meantime, I'll let him have his head."

Harold completed basic training at the end of March. After the customary two-week leave, he returned to Fort Dix for advanced infantry training. From there, he went to jump school at Fort Benning, Georgia. Jimmy waited for him to flunk out, to fall by the wayside because of physical short-comings, or yield to an attack of nerves when the time came to jump, either from the tower or that first time out of a moving aircraft. Jump school separated the wheat from the chaff, and Jimmy—despite Harold's newfound strength and dedication—did not believe his son was paratrooper material.

Harold proved his father wrong by graduating. He remained at Fort Benning for two more months, helping with the next training cycle, then, in the late fall, he was assigned to the Eighty-second Airborne Division at Fort Bragg, North Carolina. Before reporting, he took a week's leave. Jimmy could never remember feeling prouder than the moment he first saw his son with paratrooper's silver wings on his chest. Broad-chested and firm-jawed, he had become a truly handsome young man. As he hugged Harold, Jimmy felt a sudden twinge of conscience at the deceit he knew he must perform.

The instant Harold left for North Carolina, Jimmy placed a call to Washington. William Baron always maintained he owed favors to the Isaacson family. Jimmy was about to call one in.

The senator was delighted with the opportunity to repay the support Jimmy had always given him. After listening to the request, he said, "No problem. I'll have it taken care of."

"Thank you, William. Thank you very much. It'll mean a lot to me." As he hung up, Jimmy wondered if the senator had made up his mind whether or not to toss his hat into the ring for next year's Republican primaries. After losing to Nixon in 1960, he hadn't challenged Goldwater in 1964 because he believed, rightly so, that any Republican would be swept aside in a tidal wave of Democratic sympathy so soon after Kennedy's death. If Baron was as good as his word, and Harold's situation was cleared up, Jimmy would throw everything he had behind the New York senator.

* * *

Harold's first ten days with the Eighty-second Airborne included a ten-mile forced march, a jump from a Hercules transport, two inspections, and rigorous physical conditioning. He enjoyed every minute of it.

On the eleventh day, the company first sergeant sent for him. "Captain Lawrenson wants to see you."

Harold wondered what he'd done to be noticed by the company commander. When the first sergeant told him to enter Lawrenson's office, he snapped to attention in front of the CO's desk, and saluted. "Sir, Private First Class Isaacson reporting."

Lawrenson returned the salute. "At ease. I'm afraid there's been some kind of foul-up in your orders, Isaacson. You didn't qualify for airborne status after all."

Harold's jaw dropped. "I beg your pardon, sir."

"You heard me. Your grades got mixed up with someone else's. You shouldn't be here and they should. Turn your gear in to supply, turn your weapon in to the arms room, and move your personal things to the transit billets. Orders are being cut to get you out of here. From now on, you're a straight leg."

"Sir . . . ?"

"That's all, Isaacson. You may leave." Lawrenson already had his hand up in anticipation of Harold's parting salute.

Stunned, Harold left the company commander's office. He didn't understand any of it. There couldn't have been a mix-up. He knew damned well that he'd done more than enough to earn his wings. He'd met and passed every criteria the army set for its airborne troops. The following morning, he received his new orders. He was to remain at Fort Bragg, reassigned to the training center. A personnel sergeant told Harold that he would be working in the center's public information office.

"PIO?" Harold gasped in disbelief. "What will I do there? Take away my airborne status and I'm still infantry. I don't know the first thing about PIO."

"Someone saw that your family owned newspapers and magazines so they figured you'd make a good PIO man. Your MOS has been changed. You're an information specialist

636

now. You'll be writing stories on the training center for *Paraglide.*"

"Outside of essays, I've never written anything in my life."

The sergeant shrugged. "Ours is not to reason why . . ."

Harold reported that afternoon to the training center's headquarters company. After checking in, he went to his new job. The information officer, a draftee lieutenant named Levins, put him to work filling out hometown news releases, forms which were sent to the local newspaper of any trainee who achieved anything remotely remarkable.

When he returned to the company that evening, Harold told the first sergeant that he wanted to see the inspector general. When asked why, he answered, "Yesterday I was an airborne soldier. Today I'm writing hometown news releases. I'm being given a royal screwing, and I'd like to know why."

The first sergeant relayed the request to the next level. A week later, Harold got the opportunity to air his complaints to the inspector general. Another week passed before he heard news, and then it was not what he wanted to hear. A memo from the inspector general's office stated that mistakes had indeed been made, and Harold had not rightfully qualified for airborne status. Harold asked for the name of the man whose passing grades he had taken only to be informed that it was not necessary for him to know. He had reached the classic military dead end.

When Harold called home with the news, Jimmy made all the proper compassionate noises. "It sounds like you've had a really raw deal, Harold. The inspector general's office wouldn't even let you know the name of the man you were mistaken for?"

"Told me it was none of my business."

"That's a shame. It must be specially galling for you now, to be so close to the Eighty-second and be stuck in some mundane desk job." Jimmy's sympathetic tone was not reflected in his smile. William Baron had paid back every favor he had ever owed the Isaacson family, paid them back in spades! Getting Harold switched to the public information office was a nice extra touch. Even if he received orders for Vietnam, his new military occupation specialty would serve him well. Public information office—he'd be stuck in some backwater helping to organize press conferences for a bunch of civilian journalists. It might even be good training for when he was discharged and came back where he belonged. Messenger Publications.

"Galling isn't the word. I feel sick every time I see an Eighty-second shoulder patch and know that I'm wearing this dumb Third Army insignia."

"Make the best of it. You've got two years left, then you can come back here and forget the whole lousy deal."

"Two years writing hometown news releases," Harold muttered before hanging up. "Life in Attica sounds more appealing."

Jimmy worked hard to lift his son's spirits. In January, on Harold's twentieth birthday, a man in civilian clothes entered the public information office and asked for PFC Isaacson. He handed over some documents and a couple of keys on a ring that bore a Union Jack.

"What's this?" Harold asked. The man pointed through the window to the street. Outside sat a brand-new Jaguar XKE, dark-green with a black soft top. Harold ran out to it. On the passenger seat he saw an envelope with his name. He ripped it open. Inside was a card signed by his parents with the message: "Happy birthday. Be comfortable in your misery."

Harold slipped into the driver's seat, started the engine, and drove the powerful sports car to the main PX. Heads swung in his direction, even the heads of men wearing silver wings and the Eighty-second Airborne patch. Grinning happily, Harold drove back to the training center. He'd bet he was the only guy writing hometown news releases who drove a brand-new Jaguar! And he'd parlay those winnings into another bet that no one else writing hometown news releases—no one else in the entire army—had the kind of loving father he did!

Jimmy contacted William Baron again to thank the senator for his help. During the conversation, Baron mentioned that he had reached a decision regarding the election later that year. Once more he was going to seek his party's nomination. Eager for an early line, Jimmy asked Baron for his campaign issues.

"Two major points. Vietnam and crime. I'm going to win both the nomination and the election by addressing both. An honorable end to that mess Kennedy and then Johnson got us into in Vietnam, and a crackdown on the criminals who are taking over our streets. Eight years of Democrats in the White House has left this country a sorry sight. The electorate is more than ready for a Republican administration."

Jimmy jotted down two short sentences on the notepad he kept by the telephone. Bring the boys home. Law and order. With those two promises, Baron could not fail to win.

"This coming Monday I'll be spreading the gospel in my old stomping grounds, talking to a group of political science majors at Syracuse University."

"Let me have a copy of your speech."

Baron chuckled. "Thought you'd never ask."

Baron's speech was hand-delivered to the *Messenger*. After instructing Richard Hartford to place it on the front page, Jimmy wrote an editorial praising Baron's clear thinking on the two subjects that were of deepest concern to every American. He ended with: "If this is Senator Baron's first riposte in the 1968 election campaign, it will be welcomed by those Americans victimized by the nation's increasing crime, and by those of us who have sons, brothers, or fathers of military age."

When the speech and the editorial appeared in the *Messenger*, Josephine telephoned her father's office. "Doesn't this strike you as hypocritical? Your previous editorials have had readers believing Vietnam was the best thing since sliced bread."

Jimmy was pained by his daughter's comment. "If that's what you thought, Josephine, then I'm afraid you misunderstood every single one of them."

"You waved the flag with every word."

"Nowhere did we claim war was beneficial. Our editorials support our men who are over there, and criticize those back here who do everything in their power to destroy morale."

"It's one and the same damned thing," Josephine said before hanging up.

Replacing his own telephone, Jimmy wondered if he would ever bridge the chasm with his only daughter. He saw less and less of her now. She kept in touch with Sonya, but it seemed to Jimmy that whenever she contacted him it was to complain. To protest. His twenty-six-year-old daughter's philosophies belonged firmly to the left. Jimmy had always considered such feelings to be the privilege of the young college kids flexing mental and political muscles. Harmless really. Josephine had never expressed such sentiments at Vassar. She'd been too busy studying, too busy preparing for life as a photographer. Political interest had bloomed only after she had finished college. Today she saw her father as a prime example of everything she opposed. He owned a newspaper. Instead of using it to state views with which Josephine sympathized, he went in the opposite direction. From being her friend, her father had become her enemy.

Jimmy questioned whether his bungled attempt to protect Josephine was the cause. He had tried to shield both his children, sheltering them from danger as much as he could. Wasn't that, after all a father's responsibility? His scheme had worked with Harold—getting him reassigned from an airborne combat unit to a soft job in the public information office—but it had backfired badly with Josephine. Josephine was angry because she had learned about the scheme. Harold hadn't. Jimmy crossed his fingers that he never would.

Sonya was the first to mention Zalman's deterioration.

At eighty-three, he continued to travel into the city a couple of times a week, always eager to involve himself in the business. On those days he remained in Rye, he worked in the grounds, enjoying his gardening hobby. His back was straight, his almost pure white hair thick and curly. He was as thin as ever, a sprightly old man who continued to look at the world with a cynical gleam in his dark-brown eyes.

It wasn't Zalman's physical condition that concerned Sonya, though. She worried about his mental state. She shared those anxieties with Jimmy one evening after Zalman had retired to his apartment.

"Has anything struck you odd about your father lately?"

Jimmy considered the question. "Only one thing. I still

can't get over his statement that 'at Harold's age I knew what I had it for.' That was completely out of character for him. He was always tough—he could stand up for himself in any crowd—but he was never anything other than a gentleman. He never lowered himself to smut in mixed company."

Sonya thought back to the night eighteen months before when Harold had shared the secret of his girlfriend at Columbia. "That just about coincides with the start of it."

"Start of what?"

"Your father has been acting very strangely of late. He's becoming forgetful, his mind wanders. Sometimes he's as sharp as a tack, lucid. At other times, it's almost as though he's living in the past."

"Mr. Z.'s getting old, Sonya. The great majority of his life is behind him, and it was a damned remarkable life. Can you blame him for reminiscing?"

"It's not reminiscing, Jimmy. I've lost count of the times he's breezed into *American Miss* and called me Pauline."

"Haven't you ever called anyone by the wrong name?"

"Not repeatedly. And certainly not after being corrected. The first couple of times, I just let it go. I thought he'd made a genuine mistake, somehow still associating the magazine with Pauline Fulford, although she's been gone some fifteen years. When he called me Pauline again, I told him that she was the editor who refused to work in a sardine can. I was Sonya, the editor who tolerated such conditions because my husband owned the cannery. Mr. Z. laughed, and then a minute or two later, while we were still talking, he called me Pauline once more."

Jimmy wanted to challenge Sonya again, because he hated believing that any weakness could befall his father. Deep down, he knew she was right. Only a week ago, Jimmy had heard his father talking about *Messenger* editor Richard Hartford, and constantly referring to him as Ed Beecham. Were such moments of absentmindedness simply signs of old age? Or was there more to it? Like the outbursts Jimmy now recalled, tantrums in miniature when Zalman saw something he didn't like. One such incident from the previous month sprang to life in front of Jimmy's eyes. Zalman had spotted a typo in a front-page story. Livid, and in hearing of at least a dozen people, he had chewed out the editor responsible. "I didn't make the *Messenger* into a top-class newspaper just for you to make mistakes a fifth-grader would be ashamed of!" Zalman had shouted. "One more blunder like that and you'll find yourself on the street!"

"I think your father should see a doctor, Jimmy."

The prospect horrified Jimmy. All his life, he had worshipped his father, using his achievements as a yardstick for himself. How could such a man possibly need *that* kind of a doctor? "What do you expect me to say to him? 'Mr. Z., I think you're cracking up and I want you to see a shrink.' He'd tell me *I* was the one who needed help."

Sonya smiled. That was exactly what Zalman would do. "You can be more tactful."

Jimmy was. He consulted a psychiatrist, who visited the newspaper on the days that Zalman came in from Rye. Jimmy passed off the psychiatrist as a business consultant, studying where savings could be made. After a couple of weeks, the doctor had his findings ready.

"For a man of eighty-three, your father's really quite remarkable. His lapses of memory are common in older people. Nothing to worry about there."

"And the outbursts of temper?"

"Frustration. At growing old. At seeing what he built managed by other people, not always to his satisfaction. And perhaps at outliving his contemporaries. From what you've told me, all the people now at Messenger Publications are your appointments. Your father's people are all gone. His wife has gone. He feels he's outlived his time, and for a man of your father's drive, that's one hell of an admission to make."

Jimmy digested the information. One fear nagged at him. "Do you think he might consider—"

"Suicide?" The psychiatrist shook his head. "Your father's an achiever. Suicide's a way out, not an achievement."

Jimmy spoke to department heads, asking for their patience with his father. They understood, and they agreed. Jimmy appreciated their cooperation. He could think of no other company where management personnel included humoring an elderly gentleman in their job descriptions. But without this particular elderly gentleman, how many would have jobs to describe?

Unaware of his son's concerns, Zalman continued to visit the company he had created. He came into the city every Monday and Thursday, spending most of his time reading magazines published by the company. With the aid of a secretary from the steno pool, he compiled a report on each publication, stressing what he considered good and bad points. Jimmy always found time to glance at the reports; the old man might finally be showing signs of age, but he still knew the business.

In March, the 1968 primary season opened in New Hampshire. William Baron won the Republican primary. Jimmy's joy at the victory was offset by the knowledge that, barring a tremendous upset, President Johnson would once again lead the Democrats into the election. Should Baron win his party's nomination, he would be hard pressed to defeat an incumbent President. Two weeks later, at the end of March, the upset occurred. Johnson, stating that he would not accept his party's nomination again, quit the race; he would see out his term in office and retire. The burden of Vietnam had destroyed him. Jimmy's editorial in the *Messenger* maintained that Johnson's decision had thrown the Democrats into disarray, while the Republicans were united behind William Baron.

Johnson's bombshell signaled the beginning of an avalanche of activity for Jimmy, a turbulent mix of international news and personal events that left him with scarcely enough time to draw breath. April began with the murder of Martin Luther King, which triggered riots in major cities. A week after King's death, President Johnson signed the Civil Rights Act. The same month included a fresh breeze from Czechoslovakia, where rigid Communist rule showed signs of thawing. In May, Americans got the chance to see riots elsewhere—in Paris—but attention quickly reverted to the United States when, in June, the most popular of the Democratic contenders fell by the wayside—Bobby Kennedy, shot while celebrating victory in the California presidential primary.

Early in August, Jimmy attended the Republican party convention at Miami Beach, applauding as loudly as anyone when his friend William Baron, Republican senator for New York, was nominated on the first ballot as the party's candidate for the coming election. With the cheers of victory still ringing in his ears, Baron sought out Jimmy.

"You're a lock!" Jimmy yelled as Baron hugged him and slapped his back. "Better get used to being called Mr. President."

"And you'd better start thinking about a job in my cabinet."

"What on earth would I be? Your press spokesman?"

Baron laughed, gave Jimmy an extra squeeze, and moved on to the next well-wisher. Jimmy returned to New York to write the first of a series of articles endorsing Baron.

A few days later he was anxiously scanning news reports from Czechoslovakia as the Prague spring became the bloody oppression of summer. Street rallies were crushed by Russian tanks. Within days, more demonstrations were being smashed with equal ferocity. Not by tanks, but by police armed with clubs and tear gas. Not in Czechoslovakia, but in Chicago, where the Democratic convention became a bloodbath as Mayor Daley's police battered antiwar demonstrators, newsmen, and a candidate or two.

As appalled as anyone by the violence in Chicago, Jimmy nonetheless derived a certain satisfaction from the mayhem that would surely harm Democrat hopes for the November election. Republican conventions always seemed so orderly in comparison. His smugness disappeared the instant he learned that among those arrested was his daughter. Josephine claimed that she had been photographing the melee that occurred when baton-wielding police charged an antiwar march as it left Grant Park on its way to the convention. The police asserted that she had used her camera as a weapon, swinging it from the strap to strike at least two police officers. Irritation at his daughter's arrest was overshadowed by embarrassment. Josephine stated several times to both police and reporters that she was covering the convention for her father's newspaper, the New York *Messenger*. Jimmy instructed company lawyers to settle the case.

644

When Josephine returned to New York, he visited her apartment. "Are you happy now that you've held the *Messenger* up to public ridicule?"

"I didn't hold it up to ridicule. It does a good job all by itself, unflinchingly supporting the Republican party. They'll keep Vietnam boiling for as long as one munitions manufacturer somewhere in America can make a fast buck out of it."

"Pardon me. I never realized Johnson was a Republican. Nor, for that matter, Kennedy before him. How foolish of me." The ice in Jimmy's voice melted. "Josephine, I support William Baron because he's a friend. He's never given this family anything but the greatest respect. That's a lot more than I can say about many other people in high places."

"A newspaper owner should have a conscience. He should be doing everything in his power to stop the carnage over there. No one needs to hear politicians talk about an honorable end. How can a thoroughly dishonorable war have an honorable end? Only McGovern and McCarthy have the right idea—to begin making peace by putting an immediate end to the bombing of North Vietnam."

"And with that right idea they still lost to Humphrey."

"He supports our involvement in Vietnam. He might just as well be a Republican."

"No. He just has more common sense than your heroes. Their plan—their peace plank—would put our soldiers in even more jeopardy than they are already."

"You're even sounding like your editorials now. Just wait"—she struggled to conjure up the most frightening scenario for her father—"until Harold is sent to Vietnam. Then see how grandly you wave the flag."

Jimmy left his daughter's apartment no closer to healing the differences. And he took with him some guilt. Josephine's last comment had wounded him. If Harold were sent to Vietnam, it would be to a safe job, thanks to the man who now stood poised to become America's thirty-seventh President. Jimmy wondered if he could both support the war and have a son who benefited by favored treatment to avoid its dangers.

He hoped Harold was never assigned to Vietnam. That

way he would not have to concern himself with such a paradox.

Harold received orders two weeks later for Vietnam. Before he left, he visited his parents' home. His father and grandfather put on brave faces. His mother was not so adroit an actress. Tears brimmed in her eyes as she looked at her son, and she shook her head sadly. God had never intended mothers to watch their sons march off to war.

"Cheer up," Harold urged her. "I've been in the army twenty months. When I come back from thirteen months in Vietnam, I'll have three months left. I'll be a ninety-day loss, with not enough time remaining to be transferred anywhere else."

"You're talking about thirteen months in hell."

"He'll be sitting in some comfortable office," Jimmy assured Sonya. "Information specialists don't get sent to the fighting war. He'll be helping to set up press conferences. Before you know it, Harold will be Westmoreland's personal press officer."

"Just make sure you give preferential treatment to anyone representing the *Messenger,*" Zalman said, with a wink in his grandson's direction.

Harold was due to return to Fort Bragg on Sunday evening. Minutes before he left Rye, Josephine breezed into the house. "Couldn't let my little brother leave without wishing him well. Here"—she pushed an envelope and a small package at him—"a farewell present."

Watching, Jimmy remembered his farewell gift to Helen when she'd sailed to cover the Spanish Civil War—an enormous bouquet and a silver necklace in the shape of a horseshoe. He did not think Josephine's gift would be as tasteful.

Harold opened the envelope first. Inside was a card wishing him bon voyage and a one-way bus ticket from New York to Montreal. He undid the package to reveal a North Vietnamese flag. "If this is your idea of a joke, Josephine, you're not getting any laughs from me."

"Vietnam's nothing to joke about. You're half Canadian.

Go there and get out of this asylum before it costs you your life."

Harold tore the card and bus ticket to pieces, then dropped the flag onto the floor and walked on it. "You've got it all wrong, Josephine. That's the flag we should be burning." He kissed his parents and grandfather good-bye, then stood in front of his older sister. He gave her the slightest peck on the cheek. "I'll bring you a real North Vietnamese flag, Josephine. Full of bullet holes."

Harold mailed a letter as soon as he arrived at his new posting. He was at Tan Son Shut, the headquarters of the American presence in Vietnam, doing the same job he had performed at Fort Bragg. At least, he wrote to his parents, in Vietnam he had genuinely remarkable achievements to mention in hometown news releases.

Jimmy shoved the letter in front of Sonya's eyes. "See? He's working at a desk job in the safest place in all Southeast Asia. He'll be lucky if he even gets to eat a Chinese meal."

Sonya read the letter over and over again, as if searching for a flaw somewhere. She found none. It was all as Jimmy had said it would be. He had used outstanding favors to protect their son. She sat down to reply immediately.

The next high point of Jimmy's hectic year came in November, when more than twenty years of waiting culminated with the election of William Baron to the White House.

Three weeks after the election, toward the end of November, Baron visited Jimmy's home for the first time since assuming the title of President-elect. Unlike earlier visits, he did not come alone. This time he was part of an entourage that included advisers and secret service agents. William Baron was now a very public and well-protected figure.

Jimmy met with Baron in the study. He disconnected the wire; the country's next President was more important than any news that might break during the next half hour.

"Throughout my political life, I've been able to rely on you and your paper, Jimmy. You've been a great friend, a tremendous supporter. Now I want you to do me just one more good turn."

"If it's within my power, Mr. President, consider it done."

Baron acknowledged the title with a slight bow of the head. "I have a very difficult position to fill. It's a high-profile job that requires class, intelligence, and old-fashioned charm and courtesy, all attributes you possess. It also calls for an Anglophile. No bigger Anglophile exists than you. You've driven Rolls Royces or Bentleys for as long as I've known you. You bought your children English sports cars. You even get your clothes made in Savile Row."

Jimmy smiled. He'd first had suits made in London in 1953, when he had visited for the coronation. He had ordered many more since then, either on visits to London or when an agent for the tailoring firm visited the States. "What's the good turn?"

"Ambassador to the Court of St. James."

The enormity of the offer stunned Jimmy. Ambassador to the Court of St. James, the plum of diplomatic jobs, and Baron was offering it to him! He sat there, head moving slowly from side to side, mouth gaping open like a fish out of water.

"There's a lot of speculation about this appointment, Jimmy. Many people believe I owe them favors. They even remind me from time to time and hint that a proper payoff would be London. You've never done that. In fact, outside of one small favor regarding your son, you've been appalled each time I've mentioned doing anything for you."

"I supported you because I always thought you were the best man for the job. No other reason."

"Which is precisely why I want you to take London. Because no one—not even my biggest enemies—could point to favors being repaid." Baron got up to leave. "I need to have an answer within a couple of weeks."

As Baron held out his hand, Jimmy said, "I can't accept."

"Why not?"

"I'd be an embarrassment to you in any confirmation hearing."

"How?"

"Any enemy of yours worth his salt would bring up the fact that my father spent three years in prison for income tax evasion. He would bring up the fact that much of the Isaacson family's wealth is based on a highly successful newspaper

648

that goes to horse players. He would mention that some of our wealth stems from the racing wire. He would allude to a hundred connections that would hurt you."

"Did you, personally, ever do anything wrong?"

"No."

"Then what do we have to worry about? I want you, Jimmy, and I'll fight for you. It requires a certain kind of American to deal with the British, and I believe you're it."

Jimmy shook his head. "It took me nearly all my life to become a newspaperman. I'm sorry, William, but I don't think I have enough time left to learn how to become an ambassador."

Like Jimmy, Sonya was both amazed and flattered that William Baron should have made such an offer. "Imagine me at the Court of St. James," she said. "I'd be the envy of every Canadian conservative whose heart beats a little quicker when he hears 'God Save The Queen.' "

"We had that song first, only we called it 'My Country 'Tis Of Thee.' "

"I beg to differ! That piece of music was played in Canada long before it was played here."

Jimmy grinned and hugged Sonya. Despite twenty-nine years in the United States, despite coming so close to being an American diplomat's wife, she remained Canadian, as proud of her native country as Jimmy was of his. She would have made one hell of an ambassador's wife. And he sensed she was more than a little disappointed to have the opportunity removed. "Tell me you don't mind my not accepting William's offer?"

"If it's what you think is best, I don't mind. Besides, what would you have done about Mr. Z.?"

"I think he was at the back of my mind when I turned William down. We couldn't leave him here alone . . ."

"Why couldn't we have taken him with us?"

"You don't uproot a man in his eighties. My father has his routine. He goes into town a couple of days a week, he gardens, he keeps busy. What would he do in London? Prune bushes in Hyde Park? Tell Fleet Street editors what to do? That's if we could even persuade him to go there."

Sonya understood. No matter how big a prize tempted Jimmy, Zalman's welfare came first. She loved her husband for such consideration.

When they went on vacation, Jimmy always asked his father if he wanted to go with them. Sometimes he agreed; at other times he gave reasons why he wished to remain at home.

In the middle of December, when Jimmy and Sonya took a week off to go to the Breakers in Palm Beach, Zalman joined them. On the flight to Florida, Zalman asked Jimmy if he remembered when he had owned a winter home in Miami Beach.

"The one you charged off as renovations on some office building in New York?"

Zalman's lined face became even more wrinkled as he found some pleasure in past chicanery. Jimmy turned to Sonya. "He sold it at a loss because he didn't like his neighbor."

"Who was his neighbor?"

"Al Capone," Jimmy answered, laughing when Sonya gasped and held a hand to her mouth. "When you consider the characters my father ran around with, you realize what a miracle it is that I'm so civilized and cultured."

"Civilized and cultured enough to be offered the pick of all diplomatic jobs."

"And smart enough to turn it down," Jimmy said. Despite her denials, he could see Sonya still wished that he had acceded to William Baron's request. He felt torn. He would love to oblige her, take the job—if such a position could be referred to as a *job!*—and let her be the wife of the Ambassador to the Court of St. James, the hub of the entire American social scene in London. In all of Europe even.

They remained in Palm Beach for a week, sitting in the sun, shopping on Worth Avenue, and just relaxing. They needed to relax—1968 had been the most hectic year Jimmy and Sonya could remember. A couple of times, at Zalman's suggestion, they went racing. While Jimmy and Sonya watched from the clubhouse, Zalman wandered away. After twenty minutes, Jimmy became worried. He was just about

650

to get up and search for his father when he saw him returning. A huge smile covered his face.

"Did you hit a winner?"

"In a way. I counted forty-eight copies of *Form Guide* in
the hands of people lining up at the windows. That's not
bad."

"You're incorrigible, you know that?" Jimmy said.

Zalman looked at Sonya and shook his head sadly. "He
didn't learn a thing about newspapers, did he? After all these
years, you'd think he'd know better than to use a five-syllable
word when a two-syllable word will do just fine." He turned
back to Jimmy. "Don't use incorrigible when you can use
hopeless!"

They returned to New York two days before Christmas,
midway through a Monday afternoon. Jimmy had arranged
for his chauffeur to meet them at the airport. Instead, waiting
in the arrivals area was the tall figure of Richard Hartford.
The black coat wrapped tightly around his thin frame and the
black hat covering his gray hair set him apart from the
surrounding clamor.

Jimmy's stomach contracted. His legs lost their strength.
He remembered only too well Hartford's predecessor, Edward Beecham, bearing bad tidings about Helen. There could
be no other reason for the *Messenger* editor to be waiting at
the airport. Josephine! The last time she'd spoken with
Sonya, she had mentioned some assignment she'd been given.
Where was it now, and what danger could it have involved?

Clutching Sonya's arm with one hand and his father's arm
with the other, Jimmy forced himself toward Hartford. The
editor, face set in a grim expression, met them halfway.

"Josephine!" Jimmy burst out. "What's happened to Josephine?"

Hartford slowly shook his head. "Not Josephine, Mr. J.
Your son, Harold. I'm sorry to have to tell you he's dead."

Sonya's shriek of grief and horror eclipsed every other
noise in the arrivals area.

Harold's body came home on the last day of the year. Two
days later, an army honor guard escorted the flag-draped

651

casket to the cemetery where Harold's aunt and grandmother lay.

Holding his wife and father, Jimmy watched the funeral service with a sense of disbelief. Had he not gone to all the trouble of arranging his son's life just so this scene would never occur? He had removed as much jeopardy as possible, and still Harold had returned home, like so many other young men, covered by Old Glory. The tragic irony was that it need not have happened. Harold had not been in any danger so he'd gone out to seek some. Jimmy learned the story from a soldier who had brought back Harold's personal belongings. Bored of filling out hometown news releases, Harold had grabbed a camera and talked his way into a helicopter carrying troops into action.

"Seasoned photographers never rode on anything before the fourth or fifth wave," the soldier told Jimmy. "The chopper Harold rode was in the first wave. It took a rocket as it approached the landing zone, burst into flames, and crashed. The bodies were recovered after the LZ was secured."

The service finished. Never letting go of Sonya, Jimmy hugged his father and then his daughter, who had spent the entire service clinging with both hands to her mother's free arm. Josephine's eyes were red, her face tear-streaked. She tried to wrap her arms around everyone, as if to mold the remaining family members into a tight, inseparable unit.

"I cried all night long over that last time I saw Harold. I cried for him, I cried for all of you, and I cried for myself because I know I'll never be able to apologize to him for what I said. For what I did. For that stupid farewell present I gave him. What he must have thought of me right until the end . . ."

Jimmy let go of Sonya so he could have two free arms to hold Josephine. "Harold understood that you had every right to your own beliefs. He didn't think badly of you. How could he . . . you were his sister."

Sniffing back tears, Josephine broke from her father's embrace and turned to her mother. Jimmy brushed tears from his own eyes with a gloved hand. He looked at his father and saw Harold there. He turned to Sonya and Josephine, and saw Harold there as well. Wherever he looked, he would see his son, just as his father and mother had seen Helen in every corner of the townhouse on Fifth Avenue. He dreaded it.

A hand touched his arm. Jimmy swung around. "I can't even begin to express how sorry I am that my one favor to you worked out this way," William Baron said.

Thelma Baron held her husband's arm tightly in this place of death. "What kind of wicked fate twists a well-intentioned favor into a tragedy like this?" she asked.

"Thank you for coming," Jimmy murmured, looking past the President-elect and his wife. A dozen secret service agents and police officers stood out sharply against the background of genuine mourners. "I know how busy you must be now."

Baron rested a hand on his friend's shoulder. "Never too busy to comfort a friend in a time of need."

Jimmy watched the Barons offer condolences to Sonya, Zalman, and finally to Josephine. No antiestablishment fire remained in Josephine. She accepted the Barons' compassion quietly, as grateful as her father for the trouble they had taken to attend this bleak event.

Jimmy's eyes followed William and Thelma Baron as they walked to the limousine that had brought them to the cemetery. Secret service agents and policemen followed. Jimmy was even more certain now that he had been right to throw the *Messenger*'s weight behind William Baron. The President-elect was a good man. He had taken time out of a hectic preinaugural schedule to pay respects to a friend, showing genuine remorse over a favor that had gone horribly awry. It wasn't Baron's fault. He had tried to help Harold; he hadn't told him to cover himself with glory. Not only would Jimmy see his son's face in every corner of his home and in every action of his family, he would see Harold every time he picked up a newspaper or turned on a television and saw President Baron. Nowhere in America would there be escape from the grief.

"William . . . !"

Before he realized what he was doing, Jimmy started running after the Barons. They had reached the limousine. A tall, brawny man held open a door.

"William . . . !"

Baron turned around. Waving away the secret service

agent's urging to enter the limousine, he walked back toward his friend. "What is it, Jimmy?"

"Is it too late to change my mind about your offer?"

Baron shook his head and smiled gently. "Not at all, Mr. Ambassador."

Chapter Twenty-nine

Rachel marked her eightieth birthday in March 1966 with an afternoon party at her apartment in the Grosvenor House Hotel. Midway through the celebration, the telephone rang. Manny and Rita grabbed for it together. Manny reached it first, yelled "Hello!" and, beaming, passed the receiver to Rita. She listened, spoke a couple of words, then handed the receiver back to her husband. Threading her way between the party guests she approached the easy chair in which her mother-in-law sat.

"Congratulations," she said, kissing Rachel on the cheek. "Manny and I are grandparents, and you're a great-grandmother. Jonathan and Susan have a beautiful baby girl."

Rachel smiled and blinked back a tear. She could not have asked for a better birthday present.

Six weeks later, she was great-grandmother to two more children, when Andrea and her husband Robert Goldman—partner in the advertising agency where she had once worked—became the parents of a twin boy and girl. Rachel's joy was complete. She had truly fulfilled the promise made so many years before. With great-grandchildren she had left an enormous footprint to prove that the Isakharov family had once existed. And she had left a second footprint, proving that the Dekkers, too, had lived. The club in London's East End, opened two years earlier, thrived. Managed by Gerry Silver, who had given up driving a taxi to work full-time with youngsters, the Tobias and Hannah Dekker Youth Club catered to the entire East End. Ethnic background or religion had no bearing on membership; only an address mattered.

The club derived support from grants, private contributions, and one major fund-raising event each year. That took place on a Sunday in September at the Showcase Theater in Coventry Street, scene of Sidney's disastrous variety experiment. Sunday performances were rare, limited as a rule to charity shows. Sidney, who produced the show as a favor to his mother, chose that particular Sunday for an excellent reason. The following day he produced the annual Performing Artists' Gala at the London Playhouse. Most, if not all, of the big stars performing at the gala were only too happy to contribute their talents to the club fund-raiser the previous day.

That weekend in September was Rachel's busiest social period of the year. The first time she attended the double performance, in 1965, she complained it was too much. "At my age I should be getting selective about how I expend my energy," she told Manny. When he suggested she drop the gala, she was horrified. "Who would present the bouquet to the guest of honor?" she demanded. She returned for both shows in 1966 and 1967. It was only in 1968, halfway through her eighty-third year, that she failed to make both performances. Leaving the Showcase after the club fund-raiser, she felt pain spread across her chest. She clutched at the arm of the nearest person, Rita.

"I think . . . I think . . ." That was as much as she said before her knees buckled. Rita screamed for help. Rachel would have fallen to the floor had not Manny wrapped his arms around her and held her upright.

When the Performing Artists' Gala began the following night, Sidney was absent. It was the first show he had failed to present since assuming the responsibility from Gordon Prideaux. He and Manny were at the hospital where their mother struggled to recover from a heart attack far more serious than the first seizure fourteen years earlier.

Rachel hovered between life and death. White-faced and barely breathing, she neither moved nor spoke for two days. Sustenance dripped in through a tube. A machine with a moving line was the only indication that her heart continued to beat. On the third day in the hospital, she opened her eyes and said her first words since collapsing at the Showcase.

"My sons. Where are my sons?"

For five minutes, all the doctor would allow, Manny and Sidney sat on either side of their mother's bed. Her eyes moved from one to the other. Her voice was barely a whisper. "I am the luckiest person in the world. I've met queens and cabinet ministers. I've known great actors and musicians. I've lived a life every mother envies, and all because of you, my wonderful sons. If God says now that it's time for me to go, He won't get any argument from me. I would not have missed a thing." She raised her hands to touch each head as if in benediction. "My wonderful sons, a *leben* on your *kopele*, both of you."

Manny glanced across the bed at his brother. Tears shone in Sidney's eyes, mirroring those in Manny's. A minute later, when the doctor ushered them out of the private room, both brothers held handkerchiefs to their eyes. They stopped in a small waiting room and closed the door. Manny blew his nose loudly. Sidney leaned back against the door and let the tears flow.

"I can't believe it," Manny said. "I always thought she was indestructible. I wasn't even bothered by that attack back in '54. I knew she'd recover. But now this . . ."

Sidney rationalized. "She's eighty-two, Manny. No one lives forever. We knew that sooner or later something had to happen."

"You might have known. I never did."

Sidney reached out to hug his older brother. "I never did, either," he admitted as tears flowed down his cheeks.

On her fifth day in the hospital, Rachel showed signs of recovery. The indomitable spirit that had carried her through so many crises asserted itself. When her family visited that evening, they found her sitting up in bed. Color dotted her cheeks like heavily applied rouge. She smiled weakly when her sons and their wives entered the room, and said, "God decided he doesn't have an empty room for me just yet."

"How about the other fellow?" Naomi asked.

Manny answered before his mother could. "His quota for former agents was filled up years ago."

Sidney laughed at his brother's joke. They could relax now. They had been right after all—their mother was indestructible.

Rachel remained in the hospital for two weeks. When she was discharged, a limousine took her to a hotel in Bournemouth for a month's convalescence. She walked a little, but most of the time she sat and chatted with other elderly guests. She enjoyed being a celebrity and promised her newfound friends free tickets for everything from hit London shows to the Performing Artists' Gala. When Manny and Sidney visited on weekends, they had to dream up excuses for reneging on their mother's wild commitments.

Rachel returned to London at the start of November. Despite the objections of her family, she insisted on going back to her apartment on Park Lane. The Grosvenor House was her home; she had been there fourteen years and she was too old to start moving again. As a compromise, she allowed her sons to hire a nurse to be her full-time companion.

To her own surprise, Rachel found that she did not have a quarter of the energy she had before the heart attack. Even the shortest walk left her breathless. As autumn yielded to winter, and a cold wind whipped along Park Lane, Rachel felt less and less like walking. God had decided not to take her after all, but He had given her a warning to travel through the remainder of her life at a slower place. She would get where she was going soon enough.

On New Year's Eve she stayed at home, happy to watch the celebrations on the television. The rest of the family was at The Paddocks, enjoying the New Year's Eve party Manny and Rita customarily threw. At ten o'clock, before the old year died, she went to bed. At midnight, she was awakened by a gentle touch on the shoulder. The nurse stood over the bed, holding a bubbling glass in one hand, and the telephone in the other.

"It's your son, Mrs. Lesser. Manny."

Rachel took the receiver. "Happy New Year!" Manny roared.

"A Happy New Year to you, too, but the morning would have done just as well to give me your good wishes."

"Morning would have been too late. The entire country would have known by then."

"Known what?"

"You're supposed to have champagne. Do you have it?"

Rachel took the glass from the nurse, who stood beside the bed smiling. "What am I toasting?"

"I'm in the New Year's Honors List, Mama. Your little boy Emmanuel is going to be Sir Manny Lesser. How about that?"

"Mazel tov!" Rachel shrieked, and spilled champagne over the bedspread. "That's wonderful. It couldn't happen to a more deserving person." She tried to drink the little champagne remaining in the glass. "Why are you being knighted?"

"Because of White Hart Productions. Export, all the British television shows we've sold abroad."

"Not because you're such a good agent?"

"Who'd make an agent a knight? Hold on, here's Sidney."

"Happy New Year, Mama!"

"It is, isn't it? Isn't that wonderful news about Manny?"

"Manny? What about me? We're a two-man show!"

"You?"

"Me!"

"Two brothers together . . . has that ever happened before? And why didn't you tell me any of this earlier? Why did you keep it a secret until midnight?"

"I don't know is the answer to your first question. As for everything else, we're sworn to secrecy until the New Year. How do you think we felt, knowing about it all this time and not being able to share the news? We were bursting, the pair of us. I'd told Naomi, and Manny had let Rita know, but we weren't even aware of each other's knighthoods until a few minutes ago when Manny got all smug and said it was time to let you know you had a knight in the family."

Rachel could see what had happened. "So you asked him how he knew about your knighthood?"

"Naomi did. She couldn't understand how he could have known. And then we both burst out laughing and flipped a coin to see who told you first. Manny won."

"What is your knighthood for?"

659

"For my work in the theater . . . and for producing the galas."

Rachel looked up to see the nurse watching her closely. Her heart beat quickly. A little excitement was permissible. Too much was no good. "Go back to your party. And thank you for telling me." She handed the receiver and glass to the nurse and waited for the woman to change the damp bedspread.

Memory recalled the time she had spoken to her sons while she lay in the hospital bed. Had God decided to take her then, she'd said, she would have given him no argument. Not much! She'd have given Him the biggest battle He'd ever seen in all the years He'd been running the world!

The investitures took place at Buckingham Palace. The families of the two brothers remained in the Great Hall while Sidney and Manny, along with others named in the New Year's Honors List, waited their turn to be knighted by the Queen. After the ceremony, they answered questions from the press before rejoining their families.

"What happened?" Naomi, Rita, and Rachel asked together.

Sidney answered. "I knelt on a stool, Her Majesty placed a sword on my right shoulder . . ." He looked at his brother. "It was the right shoulder she tapped, wasn't it?"

Manny nodded. He thought so, too, but he could not swear to it; everything that had taken place was such a blur.

"And then?" Rita wanted to know.

"She spoke to me for a few seconds, maybe half a minute."

"About what?"

Once more Sidney turned for help to Manny; he could not recall a thing. Manny came to his rescue. "Her Majesty asked me if Mama had accompanied us to the investiture."

As they left the palace, Sidney whispered to Manny: "Is that really what the Queen said to you . . . you know, about Mama?"

Manny shrugged. "I'm like you—I couldn't remember a thing, either—but it made Mama's day, didn't it? Did you see her face brighten when I said it?"

Sidney laughed and slapped his brother on the shoulder. "You're such a good son, Sir Manny."

"And so are you, Sir Sidney."

Arms around each other, they walked toward their cars.

Congratulatory letters and telegrams poured into the offices of Lesser Brothers, White Hart Productions, and the Rialto Playhouse Partnership. Celebration parties were held. Sidney set pictures of the investiture in a scrapbook—he now had an even dozen such books—while Rachel gave pride of place in her living room to a large framed photograph of both families taken outside Buckingham Palace. She had an identical picture on the dressing table in her bedroom, as well as half a dozen small copies which she always carried in her purse. As far as she was concerned, this was the greatest thing that could happen to the Lesser family. A survivor of the Kishinev pogrom had sons who were British knights!

While Sidney soon grew accustomed to hearing himself referred to as Sir Sidney Less, Manny sometimes appeared startled by the title. When he heard Sir Manny Lesser mentioned on the radio or saw the name in a newspaper or trade magazine, he had to think twice before realizing it meant him. Often, he ignored greetings from people in the street because he did not realize they were addressing him. To friends and family he was still Manny; only people on a more formal footing used the title. The one exception was his long-serving secretary, Carol Jones. She took great delight in addressing him as Sir Manny, as if relishing the fact that she worked for a knight.

Envelopes addressed to Manny and Sidney always displayed the title, whether they contained notes from friends, business correspondence, or formal invitations to an affair of state. One such invitation arrived in the middle of April at both Lesser Brothers and the Rialto Playhouse Partnership. When Manny arrived at the office, Carol Jones set down his first mug of tea on the desk and handed him the morning's mail.

"You're a popular man this morning, Sir Manny. Half a dozen invitations including one from the American Embassy."

"Tell them I'll be out of town. I've had enough of embassy cultural affairs officers trying to promote second-rate dancers."

"This one's different." Carol removed the invitation from the pile of mail and showed it to Manny. "The ambassador himself wants the pleasure of Sir Manny Lesser's company at a reception on May the seventh to celebrate his new appointment."

Manny read the invitation. Below the beautiful copperplate were a few words written in a wide-nibbed script. "Look forward to seeing you there. Regards, Jimmy."

Leaning back in the chair, Manny grinned and waved the invitation in his hand. "You know who this is, don't you, Carol? It's Jimmy Isaacson. I didn't know he was the new ambassador. Come to think of it, I don't even know who the old one was. Did you see anything in the papers about it?"

Carol shook her head. "I don't concern myself with ambassadorial appointments."

"Neither do I. Get my brother on the phone, will you?"

Sidney was reading his own invitation, complete with the handwritten note, when Manny got through. He was as surprised as his brother. Like Manny, he read trade news rather than world news. "We thought we did well," Sidney said, "and all we got were knighthoods. This man's an ambassador, for God's sake."

"Are we going?"

"You bet! No American ambassador's reception is complete without a couple of genuine English knights!"

A hundred people attended the reception at the American Embassy, one of several Jimmy and Sonya hosted during their first weeks in London. Present were politicians, newspaper editors, bankers, and businessmen; anyone who might, at one time or another, be useful to the new ambassador. The moment Manny and Sidney arrived with Rita and Naomi, Jimmy and Sonya broke away from half a dozen Foreign Office people to greet them. "How delightful to see you again!" Jimmy declared, clasping the men by the hand and kissing the women on the cheek. "How good of you to come!"

"We wouldn't have missed this for the world," Manny

answered. "But why didn't you mention anything about your appointment?"

"It was all very sudden and hectic. There were confirmation hearings, and President Baron's enemies tried to make capital out of the fact that the Isaacsons have a few family skeletons."

"Who doesn't?" Naomi said.

"You remember meeting the President, don't you?" Sonya asked. Manny gazed blankly at her. "You had dinner with him at our home in Gramercy Park when you first came to New York in 1948. He was Congressman Baron then."

Manny's eyes widened. "Him? With the fortune-telling wife? He's President of the United States?"

Jimmy raised a finger to his lips. "She keeps quiet about the fortune-telling now. That would be a cartoonist's dream, having President Baron looking into his wife's crystal ball for some solution to a trick problem with the Soviets."

"She wasn't bad at telling fortunes," Sidney said. "Now that I remember that evening, she told Manny and me that we'd sit next to more than our fair share of national leaders. We saw the Queen earlier this year to be dubbed knights."

"I know. Imagine my surprise—and pleasure, I might add—when I included your names on the invitation list to this reception, and my administrative assistant asked if I meant *Sir* Manny Lesser and *Sir* Sidney Less. Congratulations." Seeing Manny shaking his head slowly, Jimmy asked what was wrong.

"I can't believe we had dinner with the man who's now President, and we didn't remember it."

"Do you find this much of a change," Naomi asked, "from running a publishing company?"

Jimmy's face turned somber. "Yes. And it's a very welcome change. Sonya and I had to get away from familiar surroundings. Our son Harold was killed in Vietnam last December. I had already turned down the President's request to be his ambassador here. On the day we buried Harold, I asked the President if I could change my mind. Good friend that he is, he agreed."

The Lessers and Lesses stared uncomfortably at each

663

other. The happy reunion and the pleasure in mutual accomplishments were dimmed by the closeness of death.

Manny was the first to find his voice. "I'm truly sorry. You and Sonya show tremendous strength in the admirable way you're continuing with life."

"We draw strength from having friends around us," Sonya answered. Jimmy nodded absently at her words. He was thinking of his father, wondering where Zalman was drawing his strength these days. The obstinate old fool!

Shock jarred Jimmy's mind. Never had he dreamed he would think of his father in such terms. But what else did you call a man who acted so irrationally? When Jimmy had broken the news that he was taking the ambassadorial position, Zalman had resisted every persuasion, every rationalization, and eventually every argument to join his son and daughter-in-law in London.

You go, he'd told Jimmy and Sonya. I'll stay here.

Who's going to look after you if we go? You're eighty-four years old, you can't take care of yourself!

Zalman had found an answer for that as well. The servants in the big house in Rye would care for him. Jimmy's chauffeur would drive him into town whenever he wanted to go. He'd be all right.

Jimmy was torn between the need to get away from surroundings haunted by Harold's spirit and concern for Zalman. Josephine came to his assistance. Harold's death had been a crossroads in her life. Her politics were no closer to her father's than they had been, but the animosity had disappeared. Instead of warring, they respected each other. She had even hinted that if Mo Blackman made the right kind of offer, she would return to the *Messenger*. When Jimmy was only moments away from placing anxiety for his father above his own welfare, Josephine said she would give up her Sullivan Street apartment and return to Rye.

Jimmy took up his new position a week later, living with Sonya in Winfield House, the London home Barbara Hutton had donated to the United States government. In a ceremony filled with pageantry, he presented his credentials to the Queen. Although familiar with London, he was totally unfamiliar with the work of diplomacy. He had to be coached at every turn by experienced civil servants, but like everything else in his life, he learned quickly. No matter how busy he was, he called New York daily. Sometimes he spoke to his father, at other times to Josephine. Just as frequently, calls crossed the Atlantic from the other direction as Richard Hartford kept Jimmy in touch with the *Messenger*. The magazines—even *American Miss,* now under the control of a new editor—could take care of themselves, but the *Messenger* was Jimmy's worry. He could never break from it completely. Zalman shared those feelings. Each time Jimmy spoke to Hartford, the editor commented that Zalman was spending more and more time there. Jimmy didn't know whether that was good or bad. Obstinate old devil!

"What was that?" Sonya asked.

Jimmy snapped alert. He'd been daydreaming. During a reception at the American Embassy, the ambassador had completely lost it. "What was that?"

"It sounded like 'obstinate old devil' to me," Manny said.

Jimmy recovered quickly. "My tailor. For the past fifteen years or so, I've had my clothes made in London. Once I let my tailor know that I'd be able to see him on a more regular basis, he confided that he was this year's chairman of appeals for some tailoring charity and he wanted me to be guest speaker at the society's annual dinner, which is next month. A stag dinner, no less," Jimmy added congratulating himself for the adept way he had handled being caught in his daydream. "And he wouldn't take no for an answer, the obstinate old devil."

"What does an ambassador say to a banquet hall full of tailors?" Rita asked.

"My assistant will find out something about the trade that I can base a talk on."

"Have him contact *Tailor and Cutter* magazine," Manny suggested. "It's in Gerrard Street, in the heart of Chinatown."

"Thank you. I'll do that."

"On the subject of charities," Sidney said, "I produce an annual show for one. The Performing Artists' Gala, in September. Would you and Sonya be my guests? We had Tony

Marino many years ago, but I can promise you he won't be there this year."

"Where does the show take place?"

"The London Playhouse." Seeing Jimmy's eyes narrow, Sidney nodded. "That's right, that's where the bomb landed that killed your sister and my brother. Over the past twenty-five years, the good memories have almost washed away the bad."

"Thank you," Sonya said. "Jimmy and I will be delighted."

"Provided I don't have to make any speeches," Jimmy added.

Sidney smiled. "I promise."

Jimmy passed the London summer in a whirl of lunches, dinners, and meetings. He shook hands with statesmen from five dozen countries, smiling as they praised the United States, or frowning as they criticized it. Jimmy understood that part of his job was to polish his country's somewhat tarnished foreign image, but he was not the man to do so at the expense of his own integrity. When students protested American policy in Vietnam outside the embassy, Jimmy refused to ignore the commotion. Disregarding the warnings of his own security people and the Marine commandant, he stood on the embassy steps and addressed the students in no uncertain terms. "It's too bad you young people don't put as much time and effort into studying as you put into whining and complaining. You might achieve something worthwhile with your lives then, instead of wasting them." The British popular press took issue with Jimmy, claiming he should look first at students in his own country before criticizing those in England. The shelling he took from the British press was more than offset by the congratulatory wire he received from President Baron.

Oddly enough, the event Jimmy enjoyed most that summer was the one he had initially scorned: the annual dinner of the tailoring trade charity. The event was held at the Europa Hotel, just off Grosvenor Square and a short walk from the embassy. For once, Jimmy did not have to worry about protocol or diplomacy. He drew applause by praising tailors as bastions of independence in an off-the-rack, conforming world, and he complimented British tailors in particular, whose clients came from all over the world. The tailors were not the only admirers Jimmy made that night. At the press table sat the editor of the magazine Jimmy's assistant had contacted. While listening to the speech, the editor took a short letter written in a wide-nibbed script from the pocket of his dinner jacket. He would never get over the fact that an American ambassador had gone to the trouble of sending a handwritten note of thanks for such a simple favor as offering a topic for a speech.

Toward the end of August, Jimmy returned to the United States for the first time since taking up the appointment in London. Two reasons existed for the short trip. The first was to meet with President Baron to discuss several matters of British-American interest. The second, and most important reason, was to do something about his father. Since the beginning of the month, he had been receiving disturbing messages from Richard Hartford. Zalman had suddenly started to act as though he still controlled the *Messenger,* throwing his weight around in editorial meetings, criticizing the way the paper was made up, and making a general nuisance of himself. If it were not his own father, and if it were not the *Messenger,* Jimmy might have found the idea of an old man creating such havoc funny. But it was his father, and it was his newspaper, and Jimmy was not in the least amused.

After spending a day in Washington, Jimmy flew to New York. He arrived in the early evening. Josephine met him at the airport with the chauffeured Rolls. Jimmy kissed her and asked where his father was.

"Where he always is these days. At the paper. He goes in every evening now, so he can see the first edition put to bed. He's had memos distributed that he wants to personally okay every page before it goes to press. He's even talking about launching some huge circulation drive to get us up there with the *Times.* "

"What kind of circulation drive?"

"Souvenir teaspoons." When she saw the shocked expression on her father's face, she added, "Richard Hartford didn't tell you the half of it. God only knows how many man hours are wasted each day keeping Grandpa happy."

Jimmy gritted his teeth. He had returned home just in time. He instructed the chauffeur to take him into the city; he was going to get to sort this mess out right now. The first stop was Richard Hartford's office. The editor appeared tired, his face lined, eyes sunk deep in their sockets. He shook Jimmy's hand, told him he was glad to see him, and then launched into a lament about Zalman.

"He must have been one hell of a newspaperman in his day, Mr. J., but he's a one-man wrecking crew right now. He's running us all off our feet. He's telling everyone how to do their jobs, from the newest reporter right up to me. We make special page proofs just to keep him happy, then the moment he leaves we push the real thing through. I wish I knew where he got his energy. I'd put it in a bottle and become a millionaire."

"Where is he now? In his office?"

Hartford looked at his watch. "Try composing. The business section's being wrapped up."

Jimmy found his father standing next to a compositor who was applying the final touches to one of the business pages. Zalman was scanning the page intently. Jimmy rested a hand on his father's shoulder. "Mr. Z., what are you doing down here?"

Zalman forgot about the page. He shook his son's hand and stared hard at him. "Diplomacy agrees with you. You look good. When did you get in?"

"An hour ago." He drew Zalman to one side, allowing the compositor to continue with his work. "What's this I hear about you coming in every evening to put the first edition to bed?"

"Someone's got to keep an eye on these people, otherwise they'd put out a terrible paper. Did you hear about my idea for updating the old souvenir-spoon campaign? It's perfect timing, especially when you consider we've got two more states than we had back then."

Jimmy understood what Hartford meant about his father's energy. The old man was almost eighty-five, and he brimmed with nervous vitality. His eyes darted all over the place, missing nothing. His hands trembled continually, itching to work. Even as Jimmy watched, Zalman spotted something that merited his attention. He called out to a young woman carrying a black-and-white photograph. "Let me see that!"

The woman gave him the print. It was of a fire that had destroyed a nursing home in Brooklyn that afternoon. "This is no damned good!" Zalman shouted. "Can't you get something more graphic? For crying out loud, six people died in that blaze! Where the hell are the bodies?"

Jimmy took the picture from his father's hand and returned it to the woman. "Let's go home, Mr. Z."

For the first fifteen minutes of the journey, Zalman kept up a running commentary on what was wrong with the *Messenger*. "Half of it's your own fault, Jimmy. You let people get away with too much when you were there. You didn't exert the control a publisher should have. Now the place is rife with anarchy."

The tirade brought home to Jimmy just how far his father had slipped. He knew where Zalman got the energy Hartford envied. Some deep-down craziness supplied him with it. "The only thing wrong with the paper, Mr. Z., is you. You're causing chaos because you don't belong there. When I return to England tomorrow, you're coming with me. I'm not leaving you here alone anymore, do you understand?"

"Listen to the bigshot talking! You're still wet behind the ears and you're trying to tell me what to do."

No longer did the time-worn phrases make Jimmy smile in a tolerant manner. "Not any more, Mr. Z. My ears dried a long time ago. You're going to England with me. I don't care if I have to strap you in a straitjacket and take you on a private plane, you're coming!"

His son's anger had a calming effect on Zalman. He spoke barely a word for the rest of the journey. When they reached Rye, he retired to his apartment immediately.

The next day, when Jimmy returned to London, there was no need for either a straitjacket or a private plane. Zalman slept through most of the first-class flight. He only opened his eyes as the aircraft circled over the Thames before touching down at Heathrow. It was Zalman's first visit to the city since he had collected Helen's body twenty-four years before. Perhaps it was time, after all, to put some ghosts to rest.

Jimmy did not press his father. He allowed him to settle down in Winfield House and become accustomed to the time change. It seemed odd to Jimmy that a man as dynamic as his father had really traveled so little. He had covered the United States, but he had rarely crossed a national border, even to Canada or Mexico. He owned a current passport, but he never used it. He had found America, liked it, and decided it was large enough to keep him happy for the remainder of his life.

On his third day in London, Zalman asked Jimmy if he would take him to Leicester Square. Lost in the lunchtime crush of office workers enjoying the summer weather, the two men stood together on the south side of the square.

"So this is where it happened," Zalman murmured.

"Right here. Apparently Helen was standing next to this theater, the London Playhouse. You can see it's new. The old one was destroyed." Jimmy watched his father closely. He could see the fight draining out of him like water flowing down a drain. The anger of twenty-five years was dying.

Zalman stepped into the shadow of the wall, placed his back against it, and looked up at the clear blue sky trying to see what Helen had seen that day so long ago. Had she spotted the flying bomb as it homed in on the very spot where she stood? Had she been given some presentiment of death? Or had she been taken completely by surprise, plucked from life in the blinking of an eye? Zalman hoped it was the latter. All these years later, the exact manner of his daughter's passing remained important to him.

"My friend, Sidney Less, manages the organization that owns this theater," Jimmy told his father. "Do you remember him, Mr. Z.?" Zalman nodded. "He's a knight now. Sir Sidney Less. His brother Manny, too."

"Their mother must be very proud. A lucky woman."

"No luckier than you." Jimmy did not even know if the mother was still alive; neither brother had mentioned her during their meeting at the embassy, and he had neglected to ask.

"You're right, no luckier than me. I might only have one

670

son, but he's a match for anyone else's two." Zalman's bony fingers gave the back of Jimmy's neck a fond squeeze. "You know, I feel better now that I've seen where it happened. I feel as though a part of Helen was waiting here for me all the time, just to say good-bye properly. Now she's at peace, and so am I."

"Shall we go?"

"No. Let's wait a little while longer." Zalman looked across the small expanse of greenery. People sat eating lunch. Hundreds of squawking birds filled the trees, flocking down to chase any scrap of bread thrown from a sandwich. "How many of these people, Jimmy, ever stop to think about the bomb that landed here and killed so many? How many of them, do you believe, even know? The war was so many years ago." He leaned back against the wall of the London Playhouse and sighed. "Even grief dies eventually, you know. It'll die for you as well, Jimmy. But if you have to go all the way to Vietnam to see where it happened, don't be a pigheaded fool like me. Do it, do what you have to do to straighten out your life."

Jimmy did not interrupt as his father rambled on. Zalman was unloading twenty-five years of pain and frustration. While he talked, Jimmy thought about his own dead child. Without the appointment to London, he did not know how he and Sonya would have coped. When London was all over, and they returned to America as two ordinary citizens, sorrow's sharp edge would be dulled. They would be able to live with the memories then.

Zalman clutched his son's arm. "I want to go back home, Jimmy. This isn't home. New York is. I want to go back there."

Jimmy's mind gave his father's words an odd translation. He wanted to go home because he had no wish to die in a strange land. "A couple of weeks, Mr. Z. Sonya and I will be taking a vacation in the middle of September. We'll take you back home."

And then, if Zalman were ready to die, the people who loved him most would be on hand. Helen had died alone. So had Harold. Jimmy would make sure the same sad fate did not befall his father.

Chapter Thirty

Summer was Sidney's least favorite season. While other people made plans to go away to the coast or take exotic vacations, Sidney eagerly awaited summer's end. All through July and August, he anticipated September, when his life shifted from neutral into high gear. Summer was the doldrums. Autumn meant the opening of new shows at theaters owned by the Rialto Playhouse Partnership. New triumphs, and sometimes failures. The two went hand in hand. In theater as in horse racing, there was no such thing as a sure thing. Each production was a risk, and the thrill was what Sidney loved most. He handicapped shows as racegoers handicap horses. Had it not been for theater, he believed he might have been an incorrigible gambler. Theater had saved him a fortune.

September also meant for Sidney two regular but very special shows: his own long-term favorite, the Performing Artists' Gala, and the newer but equally favored Showcase Theater production to raise money for his mother's pet project—the Tobias and Hannah Dekker Youth Club—named after his mother's honorary parents and managed by his own wife's first husband.

It was a very odd world, Sidney decided, as he walked in the warm September sun to his office. But then, only in a world brimming with peculiarities would he and his brother be knights of the realm. In their youth, they'd had absolutely nothing in common. Now, in later middle age, they seemed to have so much. Both were titled, both were quite content to carry on living where they'd lived for more than twenty years, and both stubbornly resisted change. Sidney continued to walk to his office from Marble Arch, and Manny still muttered and swore his way to work each morning, fighting the traffic into London. Sidney did not know how his brother did it. On the other hand, Manny never understood how his younger brother enjoyed walking, so they were even.

In the afternoon, Sidney dropped into the Showcase to see part of the rehearsal for the club fund-raiser that would take place in two days time. It might just as well be a rehearsal for Monday night's Performing Artists' Gala as well, as many of the same stars would be appearing in both. He watched three turns: the Easterners, who always seemed to have at least one hit record on both sides of the Atlantic; Matt Monro; and Louis Armstrong, who had arrived from the United States only the previous day. Satchmo sang "What A Wonderful World," and Sidney applauded loudly. If everyone had such warmth and goodness, it would indeed be a wonderful world.

On Sunday, though, the real star of the show was Rachel. Diminutive and frail, with carefully coiffed silvery hair, she understood that this was her special day, and she made the most of it. She greeted each star and thanked them for offering their services to help the club. She had a special word of thanks for the Easterners, who had never forgotten their own humble beginnings. Chart-toppers across half the world, they always returned to their roots, as if drawing strength from them. Feeling her own small hand enveloped in Louis Armstrong's hand, she looked up into his dark, smiling face.

"It's nice to meet someone every now and then, Mr. Armstrong, who has been in this business for as long as I have."

"I don't believe anyone as pretty as you," came the raspy reply, "could possibly be as old as an ugly dog like me."

A party followed the show. Rachel did not attend. She needed to rest in preparation for tomorrow night's Performing Artists' Gala. She would see many of the same stars, but they would not be shaking her hand. Instead, they would be presented to the Queen Mother. That was all right. The Queen Mother was entitled to have her day as well.

Rachel undressed and prepared for bed. The last thing she

did was empty the evening bag she had carried that night. It contained only four articles. A delicately scented lace handkerchief and the three items without which she never left home: red ribbon, a copper penny, and a watch fashioned to be worn around a woman's neck.

Sitting up in bed, she examined the articles. She took them all so much for granted that she hadn't looked at them closely for at least a year. Probably since she had been released from the hospital, the last time her talismans had been called upon to work their magic. The piece of ribbon was worn and twisted; its original vivid red had turned almost mauve from so much handling. She switched her attention to the penny, remembering Tobias giving it to her as she lay in the infirmary bed in Rotterdam. Sixty-six years ago, 1903. Good God! The penny had been bright and shiny then. Now it was dull and tarnished. Nonetheless, the head of King Edward the Seventh stood out in sharp relief, as did Britannia on the other side. Rachel smiled as she recalled asking what Britannia did. "Do?" Tobias had replied grandly. "She rules the waves." Rachel weighed the large coin in her hand. Soon, when the shift to decimal currency was complete, the penny would not even be legal tender. That thought saddened her. Britain's complicated currency system had been one of the barriers that kept out the rest of the world and its unwelcome influences.

Finally, she looked at the gold-and-turquoise enamel watch, the exquisitely crafted piece shaped and detailed like a large beetle. She opened the wings to reveal the face. The hands stood at seven minutes after twelve, the same time they had shown for sixty-six years, since the night she had thrown herself into the canal. She wondered if anyone searching through the charred rubble of the Klaas house in Rotterdam had ever found the other watch? If so, where was it now, and did its present owner have any idea of its significance? Often, when she wore the watch around her neck, people expressed their admiration for it. She told them it was a family heirloom. Who would she leave it to? There was no specific mention of the watch in her will, and neither of her sons had ever asked for it. She refused to worry. She'd let others worry about it when she was gone.

Setting the watch gently on the bedside table, she closed her eyes and fell asleep.

On Monday morning, Gordon Prideaux visited Sidney in his office. Prideaux was retiring at the end of the year, and tonight would be his final Performing Artists' Gala.

"If last night's Showcase production was anything to go by," remarked Prideaux, "tonight will be a fitting culmination to my time here."

"Hard to imagine the Partnership without a Prideaux at the helm. In my mind, the two names were synonymous." Sidney found it difficult to believe that Gordon was sixty-five, but then he also found it equally perplexing to understand how sixty years of his own life had flown by so quickly.

"Perhaps, but I have no desire to emulate my father by dying at my desk. There are things I haven't yet done, Sidney, places I haven't seen. And I intend to rectify those shortcomings. Have you given any thought to retiring?"

Sidney shook his head. "I love this business too much to ever want to think about quitting. To paraphrase you, there are stars I haven't booked yet, shows I haven't seen. I'm going to rectify those shortcomings as well."

"What do you believe to be the best thing you've done in your time with the Partnership, Sidney?"

Sidney examined several answers closely. Which play was his favorite? Which musical stood out above others? And what about London Lights, the nightspot that still gave the average man in the street the best value for his money? "It's hard to put my finger on any one thing, Gordon."

"I don't find it so hard to pinpoint my finest achievement."

"What was that?"

"Driving you out of business so I could persuade you to join the Partnership."

Sidney felt his face burn. "That's a fine compliment."

"It's the truth. Too much was expected of me because of my father, because of the family name. I didn't have his flair, I could never have lived up to his reputation—"

"He wasn't that good," Sidney broke in. "Don't forget that he let one hell of a fantastic act get away from him."

Gordon laughed. "Even God's entitled to a lapse of judgment now and again."

Sidney studied the former rival who had become his closest business associate. He'd often wondered how Gordon viewed his knighthood, but he'd never felt comfortable about asking. Until now. Gordon did not even have to think about an answer. "I was never the least bit jealous, Sidney. You deserved the honor because you've performed marvelous services for both the Partnership and British theatergoers. I could never have achieved half as much. Every time a decision was needed, I would have wasted time wondering what my father would have done, while you just went out and did what you thought was best. You deserved it, and you were also lucky."

"Lucky?"

"You weren't chained down by a ghost." Gordon stood up and reached across the desk to shake Sidney by the hand. "Good luck for tonight."

"Thank you." As Gordon walked stiffly from the office, the telephone rang. Sidney lifted the receiver. A slightly nasal American accent informed Sidney that Ambassador Isaacson wished to speak with him.

"Sidney, forgive me for leaving this so late, but I need to ask a favor of you concerning tonight's performance."

Sidney's first thought was that Jimmy and Sonya had to back out. A crisis had materialized. An ambassador had to put an emergency before entertainment. "What is it, Jimmy?"

"Could you find space for one more person? My father's been with us for a couple of weeks. We've had to leave him on his own almost every night while we've attended official engagements. I think he'd enjoy tonight's show."

"By all means bring him. You *are* coming to the party later on, aren't you?"

"Of course. We're all looking forward to it. All three of us." Jimmy replaced the receiver, grateful that he would not have to leave his father alone again tonight. Zalman was growing impatient to return to the United States, and his restlessness was accompanied by irascibility. He found fault with everything, with his accommodation, with the food, with the weather. Jimmy did his best to find diversions for his father. Sonya, in her free time, had given him a tour of London. An aide of Jimmy's, with an interest in horse racing, had taken the old man to Ascot for the day. Wherever he went, Zalman always returned to Winfield House with poor comparisons to America. London was not as exciting as New York, and Ascot wasn't half the racetrack Belmont was. Jimmy could have argued both points, but he chose not to. He wanted to placate his father, not irritate him further. Family rows at home were one thing. Arguments at the embassy became grist for the diplomatic service mill. Jimmy hoped he could keep his father happy for just a few more days, until he and Sonya were ready to go to the States.

The gala began at eight. At seven-fifteen, a limousine collected Rachel from the Grosvenor House. Wearing a long green dress with a mink stole around her shoulders, she sat in the back of the limousine and wondered how many such trips she had made. Limousines to take her to and from the Grosvenor House indeed! She'd come a long way from the rattle of the tram. Or before that, from the clip-clop and rumble of a horse and cart.

The instant the limousine stopped outside the Playhouse, Manny appeared to help his mother into the theater. Sidney was always too busy on gala night to think of anything but the show, Rachel understood that. Holding Manny's arm with one hand, Rachel entered the theater, smiling at people she recognized in the crowded lobby. The heart attack had caused her to miss the previous year's performance, and gala regulars welcomed her back. Rachel wondered if she would be on hand to celebrate next year's gala. It was a valid concern. At eighty-three, she did not expect to see acorns become oaks.

"Let's wait a few minutes before we go upstairs," she said.

Concern showed instantly on Manny's face. "Are you all right, Mama?"

"Of course I'm all right. I just want to catch my breath. Perhaps it's time for your brother to find me a seat downstairs instead of putting me in his personal box. It's a great honor, I know, but those half dozen stairs after you get out of the lift have no respect for my age."

Rachel remained in the lobby for five minutes, enjoying the bustle of activity that was so much a part of her life. The stars always turned out for gala night, and she spoke to half a dozen top-line entertainers who had come to watch and applaud their contemporaries. As she and Manny walked toward the elevator for the trip upstairs, a man called her son's name.

"Mama, you remember Ambassador Isaacson, don't you?" Manny asked as he drew his mother around to face the three people who approached. Between Jimmy and Sonya was a thin, elderly man with white hair and a wrinkled face. Sharp brown eyes gleamed behind gold-rimmed glasses.

"Belated congratulations on your appointment," Rachel told Jimmy. She shook hands with Jimmy and Sonya, and then regarded the elderly man questioningly.

"Allow me to introduce my father," Jimmy said. "You did meet once before, under very unfortunate circumstances. Mr. Z., this is the mother of my friends, Sir Manny Lesser and Sir Sidney Less. Do you remember—"

"Of course I remember meeting the lady before," Zalman retorted, and Jimmy swallowed hard. He hoped his father's short temper wasn't about to make an appearance. "My memory hasn't gone, you know. We met at that damned cemetery . . ."

"Willesden," Manny said.

"That's the place." Zalman offered Rachel his hand. It felt like sandpaper, rough and dry. "It happened right here, didn't it? I wouldn't come and see where it happened for all these years, but my son nagged me and nagged me, so finally I came. Do your sons nag you?"

"Sometimes. And usually for my own good."

"For your own good." Zalman shot Jimmy a scathing look before returning his attention to Rachel. "Ironic, isn't it? We start out by deciding what's good for our kids, and we finish up being told by our kids what's good for us."

"We should be glad our children care enough to tell us." Rachel tried to connect this testy old devil with the man she had met at Willesden. His hat had been pulled low over his face, but she remembered him as polite, as sensitive to her grief as he was to his own. That man bore no resemblance at all to this one.

"My son's idea of caring for his father was to hijack me from New York where I was happy to London where I'm not."

Rachel turned to Manny. "I think we should go upstairs now."

After expressing the hope that the Isaacsons enjoyed the show, Manny escorted his mother up to Sidney's box. "If I ever become like that," Rachel whispered, "promise that you'll take me out and shoot me."

"Jimmy and Sonya have had him for a couple of weeks. The old boy's probably bored to tears, and Jimmy has no time to spend with him." Manny smiled as an idea surfaced. "Why don't you take him off Jimmy and Sonya's hands for a few hours? Have him over for tea? The embassy residence is just around the corner from the Grosvenor House."

"I have too little time left to waste it on miserable people. I only want people who can make me smile. That's why I'm here."

They took their seats in Sidney's box, along with Rita, Gordon Prideaux and his wife, Jonathan and Susan, and Andrea and Robert. Rachel was glad that Sidney hadn't found room in his box for the Isaacsons. She would not have enjoyed the show at all sitting close to that sharp-tongued old misanthrope.

The gala proceeded like well-oiled machinery, twenty-two acts incorporated into two and a half hours of outstanding entertainment. The loudest applause of all came for the show's oldest performer, Louis Armstrong. Disregarding the rule of not playing to the royal box, Satchmo directed "Hello, Dolly" right to it. By the Queen Mother's smile, Rachel knew she was enjoying the gravelly-voiced serenade. In the same box, Sidney was also smiling, obviously forgiving Satchmo for his effrontery.

Following the show, Sidney presented the performers to the gala's royal guest of honor. Once the presentation was over, the catering staff from London Lights began serving a midnight dinner for a hundred guests. Rachel found herself sitting between Rita and her grandson, Jonathan. Directly across the wide table sat the Isaacsons. She wondered how they had enjoyed the gala. Jimmy and Sonya appeared happy enough—and who wouldn't be, after seeing so much talent on one stage—but the old man seemed just as sour as he'd been before the show. Rachel tried to recall what his son had called him. Mr. Z., that was it. What did the single initial stand for. Zacharias? Zachary? Zvi? What a thoroughly miserable man!

Seeing Rachel staring, Zalman shifted uncomfortably in the seat. Why did she look at him like that, this Mrs. Lesser? Did she think she was better than him, with her two knighted sons? Someone should put her in the picture about how valuable an ambassador was. An American ambassador had the President's ear. What did a couple of knights have? A pair of archaic, useless titles, that's what.

Despite herself, Rachel smiled across the table. Zalman looked away. He was in no mood for pleasantries. He had fidgeted throughout the show, and all he wanted to do now was get out of here. He had never enjoyed sitting for protracted periods of time. He was a man of action, not leisure. That was his problem now. He couldn't get accustomed to the restrictions of age. He had a young, aggressive mind trapped in a body that was no longer suited for it.

Glasses were filled with champagne. Waiters distributed hors d'oeuvres of smoked salmon. As Zalman lifted the outside fork, a knife rapped against glass. Jimmy rested a hand on his father's arm. "Wait a moment."

Zalman looked around. Everyone on the table had been served. "Wait for what?"

Jimmy angled his head toward another table. A tall, thin man with silvery hair stood up and gave a short nondenominational benediction.

Zalman's mouth dropped in disbelief. "Grace? I haven't eaten a meal over which grace was said since Roosevelt was President!"

Jimmy tugged at his father's arm and hissed at him to be quiet. Manny, sitting midway between Rachel and the Isaacsons, was more tolerant. "It's a tradition, that's all," he

680

explained quietly. "The saying of grace, and the lack of smoking until after the royal toast, are traditions here."

Rachel saw Zalman's eyes swing around the table, challenging anyone to support Manny. She decided to do so. "I happen to believe it's a lovely tradition. I have plenty to be thankful for, and I'm sure most of the people here feel the same way."

Zalman poured scorn on Rachel's ideas. "You really believe you should be thankful to God? You think a religious conviction has helped you in life? You believe some pious hypocrite in a dog collar can communicate with God, when no one's ever proved that God even exists? If you believe all that, then I've got some prime real estate in New Jersey to sell you!"

"I know nothing about land in New Jersey. What I do know is that God has been very good to me."

"You lost a son! How good is that?"

"Mr. Z.!" Jimmy hissed, still holding his father's arm. "Will you lower your voice! You're creating a disturbance!"

Zalman looked around. People at other tables stared at him. Waiters had stopped their work to watch. Zalman let the audience fuel his anger. "You all think God exists as well, do you? You all agree with this crazy old woman over here? Well, let me give you the whole story about God and the millstone around humanity's neck that's called religion!"

He shrugged off Jimmy's restraining hand and stood up, turning around as he spoke to give everyone the benefit of his opinions and his prejudices. "My father was a religious man. He believed it all, right down to the bit about God creating the whole world in just six days. We lived in a city in Russia called Kishinev. In 1903, Russia was in a state of upheaval. Revolution was rife. The government, in order to take the pressure off itself, stirred up the peasants against the Jews. Sound familiar?" He looked down at his son. Jimmy held a hand to his face to hide his embarrassment; his biggest nightmare was coming true. "My son never thinks about any of this. He never mentions it to anyone. He doesn't have to. He's safe, he's secure, he's part of the American establishment so he can afford to push such ugliness from his mind. But I can't, because I was there and I saw it all happen. I know exactly what faith in God is worth." He swung past Jimmy to Rachel, barely registering her wide-eyed amazement at hearing the name of her hometown, and then he moved on.

"My father had a drapery shop. It was broken into by drunken peasants. My father died, his head crushed by a peasant's club as he prayed to God for help. I didn't pray to God! I just took an axe and sliced that *muzhik*'s belly wide open!"

Rachel thrust a fist into her mouth to stop herself from crying out. In memory. In shock. In pain. She saw Manny's head swing toward her, face covered with incredulity, finger pointing. Sidney jumped to his feet, his white face a mixture of puzzlement and disbelief. Zalman saw none of it. He was too wrapped up in his tale, too intent on destroying every false hope these people had. "We fled from Kishinev the very next day, my sister and me. She was like my father, a believer. She sought salvation in prayer, while I sought salvation in strength. My sister died in a fire in Rotterdam the very night before we were due to leave for America. That was how . . ." Suddenly the strength left Zalman's body. He slumped down into his seat, head hanging. "That was how God answered my sister Rachel's prayers," he murmured. "With the flames of hell."

Ignoring the rapid beating of her heart, Rachel felt inside her evening bag. Past the lace handkerchief and red ribbon, past the copper penny. Her fingers closed around the watch. She tried to stand. Vitality fled from her legs. She could not move. She passed the watch to Jonathan on her right. "Be a good boy, darling. Take this watch and give it to that man."

Jonathan asked no questions. He got up and walked around the table to Zalman. Every eye was on him as he bent over, whispered something in the old man's ear, and set the watch down on the table. Slowly, Zalman raised his head. He picked up the watch and brought it toward his eyes. His thin, bony fingers caressed the head and short, stubby antennae, then opened the wings to reveal the face. He squinted at the minute letters engraved on the inside of the case. Zalman Ben Itzhak. His father's father. After whom he was named.

Zalman stared across the table at the old woman, trying to match up the lined and wrinkled face with the smooth skin of the seventeen-year-old sister he had left lying on the bed while he went out shopping for a farewell gift for the Klaases, the Dutch family who had shown such hospitality.

Rachel gazed back, superimposing her last memory of her brother's face on the features of the irascible old man sitting opposite. The hair, still thick, had changed from dark brown to pure white. The nose had lengthened; once-taut flesh now hung loosely. In his eyes she saw the truth. Dark and brooding, with the sharp, cynical gleam she remembered so well.

Closing the case, Zalman let the watch swing gently from his fist by the gold chain. "You kept your watch all these years."

"Didn't you?"

"I sold it to buy an engagement ring. My wife's family wanted their daughter to have a ring that would not embarrass them. I had no money, so I sold the watch."

"Papa would not have minded," Rachel said. She dabbed tears from her eyes with the lace handkerchief. After sixty-six years, they could find no more meaningful a topic of conversation than the watches their father had given them. And somehow Rachel knew that no other topic could carry such significance.

"No, Papa would not have minded at all."

JANELLE TAYLOR

ZEBRA'S BEST-SELLING AUTHOR

**DON'T MISS ANY OF HER
EXCEPTIONAL, EXHILARATING, EXCITING**

ECSTASY SERIES

SAVAGE ECSTASY	(3496-2, $4.95/$5.95)
DEFIANT ECSTASY	(3497-0, $4.95/$5.95)
FORBIDDEN ECSTASY	(3498-9, $4.95/$5.95)
BRAZEN ECSTASY	(3499-7, $4.99/$5.99)
TENDER ECSTASY	(3500-4, $4.99/$5.99)
STOLEN ECSTASY	(3501-2, $4.99/$5.99)

CATCH A RISING STAR!

ROBIN ST. THOMAS

FORTUNE'S SISTERS   (2616, $3.95)

It was Pia's destiny to be a Hollywood star. She had complete self-confidence, breathtaking beauty, and the help of her domineering mother. But her younger sister Jeanne began to steal the spotlight meant for Pia, diverting attention away from the ruthlessly ambitious star. When her mother Mathilde started to return the advances of dashing director Wes Guest, Pia's jealousy surfaced. Her passion for Guest and desire to be the brightest star in Hollywood pitted Pia against her own family — sister against sister, mother against daughter. Pia was determined to be the only survivor in the arenas of love and fame. But neither Mathilde nor Jeanne would surrender without a fight. . . .

LOVER'S MASQUERADE   (2886, $4.50)

New Orleans. A city of secrets, shrouded in mystery and magic. A city where dreams become obsessions and memories once again become reality. A city where even one trip, like a stop on Claudia Gage's book promotion tour, can lead to a perilous fall. For New Orleans is also the home of Armand Dantine, who knows the secrets that Claudia would conceal and the past she cannot remember. And he will stop at nothing to make her love him, and will not let her go again . . .

SENSATION   (3228, $4.95)

They'd dreamed of stardom, and their dreams came true. Now they had fame and the power that comes with it. In Hollywood, in New York, and around the world, the names of Aurora Styles, Rachel Allenby, and Pia Decameron commanded immediate attention — and lust and envy as well. They were stars, idols on pedestals. And there was always someone waiting in the wings to bring them crashing down . . .

Available wherever paperbacks are sold, or order direct from the Publisher. Send cover price plus 50¢ per copy for mailing and handling to Zebra Books, Dept. 3655, 475 Park Avenue South, New York, N.Y. 10016. Residents of New York and Tennessee must include sales tax. DO NOT SEND CASH. For a free Zebra/ Pinnacle catalog please write to the above address.